The Geste Novels
Part B

The Collected Novels of P. C. Wren
Volume 1B

Fiction Titles by P. C. Wren

Dew and Mildew. 1912
Father Gregory. 1913
The Snake and Sword. 1914.
Driftwood Spars. 1916
The Wages of Virtue. 1916
The Young Stagers. 1917
Stepsons of France. 1917
Cupid in Africa. 1920
Beau Geste. 1924
Beau Sabreur. 1926
Beau Ideal. 1928
Good Gestes. 1929
Soldiers of Misfortune. 1929
The Mammon of Righteousness. 1930 (U.S. title: Mammon)
Mysterious Waye. 1930
Sowing Glory. 1931
Valiant Dust. 1932
Flawed Blades. 1933
Action and Passion. 1933
Port o' Missing Men. 1934
Beggars' Horses. 1934 (U.S. title: The Dark Woman)
Sinbad the Soldier. 1935
Explosion. 1935
Spanish Maine. 1935 (U.S. title: The Desert Heritage)
Bubble Reputation. 1936 (U.S. title: The Cortenay Treasure)
Fort in the Jungle. 1936
The Man of a Ghost. 1937 (U.S. title: The Spur of Pride)
Worth Wile. 1937 (U.S. title: To the Hilt)
Cardboard Castle. 1938
Rough Shooting. 1938
Paper Prison. 1939 (U.S. Title: The Man the Devil Didn't Want)
The Disappearance of General Jason. 1940
Two Feet From Heaven. 1940
The Uniform of Glory. 1941
Odd—But Even So. 1941

The

Geste Novels

Part B

by

Percival Christopher Wren

BEAU IDEAL
SPANISH MAINE

Edited

by

John L. Espley

Riner Publishing Company
Riner Virginia
2015

ISBN
978-0-9850326-8-5

Contents

PREFACE

The Geste Novels Part A and *The Geste Novels Part B* by
Percival Christopher Wren are the first of a multi-volume series,
The Collected Novels of P. C. Wren. The purpose of publishing this
series is to make the novels written by P. C. Wren more available
to the reading public. His novel, *Beau Geste*, is usually recognized
by most of the book dealers I have met over the years, but his other
works are not so easily remembered.

I have been collecting P. C. Wren for over fifty years, and have
been working on a comprehensive bibliography for almost as long.
The text of the twenty-eight novels were easily obtained from
copies in my own collection. For that collection, I certainly need to
thank the hundreds of used book dealers I have purchased items
from, and I need to thank some by name; Steven Temple, David
Mason, Walt Barrie and, especially, the late Denis McDonnell for
the advice and help they have provided over the years.

Mr. John Venmore and Mr. Philip Fairweather, both descendants of the late Mr. Richard Alan Graham-Smith, Wren's stepson,
and the executor of Wren's estate, have both been very helpful in
providing information about Wren.

As it has been over seventy years since the death of P. C. Wren
(November 21, 1941), Wren's works have passed into the public
domain in the United Kingdom. In the United States fourteen of the
twenty-eight novels are still under copyright. Thanks to
information provided by Messrs. Venmore and Fairweather, the
heirs to Wren's literary estate, Mr. Danny Adekoya Campbell and
Mr. Christopher Oladipo Graham-Smith, were located and
permission has been granted to reprint Wren's works.

I also need to acknowledge the help and guidance of my family
members: my daughter and son-in-law, Dawn and Andrew; my son
and daughter-in-law, Jared and Claudia; and my long-suffering
wife, Cathy. Thank you.

In conclusion, I need to thank Percival Christopher Wren for
the many years of great enjoyment that his novels have provided. I
know that Wren is not a literary or critical success, but, for me, he
is one of the great storytellers of the early twentieth century.

John L. Espley

Riner, Virginia
May 28, 2015

INTRODUCTION

Percival Christopher Wren is best known as a novelist, publishing twenty-eight novels from 1912 to 1941, the most famous being *Beau Geste* (1924). Wren also published seven short story collections; *Stepsons of France* (1917), *The Young Stagers* (1917), *Good Gestes* (1929), *Flawed Blades* (1933), *Port o' Missing Men* (1934), *Rough Shooting* (1938), and *Odd—But Even So* (1941), containing a total of 116 stories. There were also two omnibus collections, *Stories of the Foreign Legion* (1947) and *Dead Men's Boots* (1949), containing stories taken from *Stepsons of France*, *Good Gestes*, *Flawed Blades*, and *Port o' Missing Men*. All 116 short stories can be found in the five volume collection, *The Collected Short Stories of Percival Christopher Wren.*[1]

Wren was a man of mystery in that the more popular biographical statements about him seemed to be more fiction than fact. A typical biography places his birth in Devon in 1885, educated at Oxford, and having a career of world traveler, hunter, journalist, tramp, British cavalry trooper, legionary in the French Foreign Legion, assistant director of education in Bombay, and a Justice of the Peace. Most of the above biography, however, has not been verified. Wren was born Percy Wren on November 1, 1875 in Deptford, a district of South London on the banks of the Thames. He did attend Oxford University, graduating in 1898 with a 3rd class honours in History leading to a Bachelor of Arts degree. He attained his "M.A." in 1901. In those days, a person acquired a "M.A." after a certain number of years (three in Wren's case) and purchasing it.

After leaving Oxford, he married Alice Lucie Shovelier in December 1899 with whom he had a daughter, Estelle Lenore Wren, born in February 1901, and a son, Percival Rupert Christopher Wren, born in February 1904. Percy worked as a teacher at various commercial schools until 1903 when he and his family left England for India. From 1903 to approximately 1919 Wren was employed as an educator by the Indian Educational

---

[1] For further information on *The Collected Short Stories of Percival Christopher Wren* see rinerpublishing.wordpress.com

Service (I.E.S.). During that time he published a number of educational textbooks, some of which are still in use in Indian schools today. It was during this period that he started using the name Percival C. and Percival Christopher on the textbooks. From 1905 to 1915, he also served in the Volunteer Corps (Sind and Poona) in India (see the novel *Driftwood Spars*, which has a description of a Volunteer Corps), and was appointed a Captain in the Indian Army Reserve of Officers, the 101st Grenadiers of the Indian Infantry, in November 1914. He probably saw action in the East African campaign of World War I (see the novel *Cupid in Africa*, which takes place in East Africa), and resigned from the Indian Army Reserve of Officers in November 1915.[2]

Wren's first novel, *Dew and Mildew*, was published by Longmans, Green in 1912. His first novel of the French Foreign Legion, *The Wages of Virtue*, was written in 1913 and published by John Murray in 1916. One of the many questions about Wren is whether he actually did serve in the French Foreign Legion. Given the chronology of his documented biography it is hard to see where he had time to actually serve in the Legion. Wren himself always maintained that he had served, and his stepson, Richard Alan Graham-Smith, who died in 2006, "strongly maintained that Wren had indeed served in the French Foreign Legion and was always quick to refute those who said otherwise."[3]

The series, *The Collected Novels of P. C. Wren*, is intended to include all twenty-eight novels in seven thematic, omnibus, volumes. The final number of physical volumes might be as many as fourteen, depending on how large (number of pages) the later volumes are. The individual volumes will not be in Wren's original publication order, but will instead have a connecting theme such as characters or locale. The seven volumes are:

> v. 1 - The Geste Novels
> Beau Geste
> Beau Sabreur
> Beau Ideal
> Spanish Maine

---

[2] Most of the biographical information about Wren has been obtained through certificates, documents, and original research at the British Library, Bodleian Library, and the India Office papers. Detailed documentation and sources will be cited in the biographical essay to be included in the forthcoming publication, *An Annotated Bibliography of Percival Christopher Wren*.

[3] http://en.wikipedia.org/wiki/P._C._Wren

*   *   *   *   *   *   *

Volume one of *The Novels of P. C. Wren, The Geste Novels,* is in two physical volumes and contains the four novels that feature the Geste brothers and their friends. These novels are the well-known *Beau Geste* (1924), and the lesser known direct sequels: *Beau Sabreur* (1926) and *Beau Ideal* (1927). The fourth novel, *Spanish Maine* (published in the United States as *The Desert Heritage*) was published in 1935, eight years and twelve books after *Beau Ideal*. Wren also wrote a number of short stories featuring the Geste brothers. The majority of those short stories were published in the book *Good Gestes* (1929), with one additional story in *Flawed Blades* (1933). All of the short stories can be found in volume two of *The Collected Short Stories of Percival Christopher Wren*.

*   *   *   *   *   *   *

The Geste Novels Part B

The first part of the third novel, *Beau Ideal*, starts with a group of forgotten prisoners at the bottom of an underground silo in the desert. One by one they are dying, and passing the time by relating their various experiences in the Legion. This part of the story will be familiar to anyone who has read Wren's Foreign Legion short stories, but the second, and major, part of the novel is difficult to comment upon. While it has its moments of typical Wren adventure and romance, its basic premise is a little hard to swallow. This part of *Beau Ideal* is the story of Otis Vanbrugh (brother of Mary, the heroine of *Beau Sabreur*), and his quest to rescue John Geste, who has gone back to the Sahara to find Hank and Buddy, his American friends. John Geste has been captured by the French authorities as a deserter from the Foreign Legion. Otis is in love with John's wife, Isabel, to whom he promises that he will rescue John. It is hard to maintain the suspension of belief, required in fiction, that Otis is such a romantic idiot who is so in love with Isabel that he would willingly enlist in the Foreign Legion and deliberately get sent to the convict battalion in the hope of rescuing John. Wren has presented such a theme over and over again in several short stories and novels, but it reaches an unbelievable height in *Beau Ideal*.

During the course of his adventures Otis meets a young, part Arab and European, woman, Zaza or the Angel of Death. This young woman falls in love with Otis and attempts to make Otis love her. Zaza, however, eventually proves to be Otis's half-sister, and she provides the heroine for the next novel, *Spanish Maine*.

Beau Ideal was first published in book form in July 1928. It was reprinted as a serial in the United States in *McClure's Magazine* (October 1928 to March 1929) and in the United Kingdom in *Nash's Magazine* (December 1928 to June 1929). There have been thirty-six different editions identified. In 1931 a motion picture (not silent) was released based on *Beau Ideal*, though it has several distinctly different plot points from the source material. It is available on YouTube[4] or for purchase as a DVD.

The final novel in *The Geste Novels* is that of *Spanish Maine* (U.S. title *The Desert Heritage*). In this story, Otis Vanbrugh is traveling with his half-sister, now known as Consuela Vanbrugh, on a cruise ship. During the voyage, Consuela and Sir Harry Vane, the Twelfth Baronet of Vane Court, have fallen in love. During a diversion to the Bahamas, one of the passengers that boards the ship is Señor Manöel Maine, also known as Spanish Maine. Maine knows Consuela from her past when she was known as Zaza, the Angel of Death, a courtesan from the Street of a Thousand Delights in the city of Bouzen, North Africa.

Maine attempts to blackmail Consuela and Otis by threatening to inform Sir Harry and his mother about Consuela's past; and thus, ruining their future in the "high society" of the English aristocracy. When Otis meets with Spanish Maine, Maine tries to justify his blackmail by relating his life story, which includes stints in the Foreign Legion and French prisons. The stories told by Maine are very typical of the Foreign Legion stories that Wren is famous for. This part of the story constitutes about one-third of the novel.

As part of Maine's life story, he recounts several tales that are also told, in slightly different form, as individual short stories: "McSnorrt's Love Affair", "Spanish Maine's Little Joke", and "Diamond Cut Glass". The fourth Spanish Maine short story, "The Statue and the—Bust!", is not related in the novel.[5] All four short stories were published before the novel.

One of the main themes of *Spanish Maine* is the question of how far can a person go when trying to redeem themselves from their past. Wren touches on the double standard between the sexes during the first part of the twentieth century, and on how a woman's standing in society could easily be placed in jeopardy. This theme of blackmail in English society is also featured in another novel of Wren's, *Cardboard Castle*, published three years later in 1938. In *Cardboard Castle*, the blackmailer is a former husband who has come back to England, presumably having died in the "colonies". A similar problem is what led to Merlin Montague joining the Foreign Legion in *The Wages of Virtue* (1916).

Spanish Maine was published (and likely written) during the

---

[4] https://www.youtube.com/watch?v=8FaRz-Gi0po and
https://www.youtube.com/watch?v=E8wRPtzJSUM
[5] All four stories were published in the book *Port o' Missing Men*, and are also included in *The Collected Short Stories of Percival Christopher Wren*, volumes three and four.

British monarchy crisis of Edward VIII and Wallis Simpson. The questions that Wren asks through the characters of Otis Vanbrugh, John Geste, and Consuela were probably questions that were being asked during the monarchy crisis. Or at least, should have been asked. Wren makes an explicit reference to this problem during a discussion between John Geste and Otis:

> "But, as I say, that's neither here nor there. Damnably unfair I admit, that the man should demand absolute innocence and purity of the woman, while the woman scarcely expects it of the man. It's vile. But the fact remains. And it's not as though Sir Harry Vane, twelfth Baronet, a figure in London Society, and in that of this County, were just a mere nobody."
>
> "By Hell! You make me . . ." exploded Vanbrugh.
>
> "Not a bit as though he were an ordinary nobody," continued John Geste. "And I'm not, as you think, talking mere snobbism. It's a big position that he has got to fill, with big duties and responsibilities; and he's got to marry the right woman. Just as, to compare small things with great, a king has got to marry the right woman."
>
> "To Hell with kings," growled Vanbrugh.
>
> "Now, answer the question honestly, truthfully, and with detachment, if you can. Is a girl born out of wedlock—and the English law unfortunately is cast-iron and cruel on that subject—brought up in a brothel by a courtesan, a girl who practised the profession of courtesan for years . . ."
>
> "It was no fault of hers!" burst out Otis Vanbrugh. "She was . . ."
>
> "I know; I know; Otis. But the facts remain. Now then—I hate saying it, as

much as you hate hearing it—is that girl
a fit and proper wife for a man in Vane's
prominent position; a fit and proper
daughter-in-law for Lord and Lady
Athelney, future Viceroy and Vicereine
of India?"[6]

That this type of problem is still of interest in today's society can
be seen in the success of the television series, *Downton Abbey*.

Spanish Maine was first published October 1935 and there
have been, at least, ten different editions identified. It was also
published in serial form in early 1936 in *The Australian Women's
Weekly*, and probably in other newspapers around the world. Of all
of the four novels, *Spanish Maine* has the most inconsistent copy
editing. The same words, usually names, are spelled differently in
different places. A particularly annoying problem is that Vanbrugh
was sometimes spelled Vanburgh.

*   *   *   *   *   *   *

The original spelling, punctuation, and grammar, except for
obvious errors, have been preserved as found in the latest
editions/printings of the stories during Wren's lifetime (1875-
1941). The footnotes, in the novels, are also found in the original
source material.

---

[6] *The Geste Novels Part B*. page 459-460

BEAU IDEAL

"Judge not the Play, before the Play is done Her plot hath many changes: every day Speaks a new scene; the last act crowns the Play."

Hank: All a matter of what's your own private 'Bo Ideal', as they call it.
—Beau Sabreur.

DEDICATED TO

WILLIAM FARQUHARSON

THE

GOD-FATHER

OF

BEAU GESTE

CONTENTS:

PROLOGUE

The heat in the *silo* was terrific, and the atmosphere terrible.

A whimsical remark from the man they called Jacob the Jew, to the effect that he wondered whether this were heat made black, or blackness made hot, remained unanswered for some minutes, until a quiet voice observed in good French, but with an English accent:

"It is the new heat Jacob. Red hot and white hot, we know. We are now black hot . . . And when I have to leave this quiet retreat I shall take a chunk of the, atmosphere . . . a souvenir . . . keep it in my haversack."

The man spoke as one who talks against time—the time when sanity or strength shall have departed.

"Good idea," mused another voice with a similar accent. "Send a bit to one's National Museum, too. . . . You an Englishman?"

"Yes," replied the other. "Are you?"

"No—American," was the reply.

Silence.

The clank of irons and a deep groan.

"Oh, God," moaned the wounded Spaniard, "do not let me die in the grave. . . . Oh, Mother of God, intercede for me. Let me die above ground."

"You are not going to die, Ramon," said the Englishman.

"No indeed," observed Jacob the Jew. "Certainly not, good Ramon. No gentleman would die here and now. . . . You would incommode us enormously, Ramon. . . . I go the length of stating that I absolutely do prefer you alive—and that's the first time you've heard *that*, Ramon. . . . Worth being put in a *silo* for."

"That's enough, Jacob," said the Englishman; "hold your tongue."

The irons clanked again, as though the sick man turned in the direction of the last speaker.

"You'll keep your promise, Señor Caballero?" moaned the dying man. "You *have* forgiven me? . . . Truly? . . . You'll keep your promise? . . . And the Mother of God will come Herself and tend your death-bed. . . . If you don't, my dying curse shall blast . . ."

5

"I'll see to it, Ramon," said the Englishman quietly. "Don't bother about cursing and blasting. . . ."

"You'll see that I die kneeling! . . . You won't let me die until I kneel up? . . . You'll hold my hands together in prayer . . . my head low bowed upon my breast? . . . And then you'll lay me flat and cross my hands and make the Sign of the Cross upon my forehead . . ."

"As I promised, Ramon."

"You'll let God *see* that I fear Him. . . . *He wouldn't mistake me for my brother*? . . . He wouldn't visit my brother's sins on *me*?"

"God is just," said the Englishman.

"Yes, my poor Ramon," observed Jacob the Jew, "I greatly fear that you'll find God just. . . . But don't say that you have a brother, Ramon?"

"*Nombre de Dios*, but I have, *hombre*! . . ." gabbled the Spaniard. "And he is in Hell . . . *Seguramente*. . . . He was an enemy of God. . . . He hated God. . . . He defied God. . . . And God took him and broke him. . . . *Caramba!* It is not fair the way God . . . *Yes*. . . . *Yes*. . . . *Yes*. . . . It *is* fair, and God is good, kind, loving and—er—just."

"Yes. *Just*—Ramon," said Jacob.

"If I could find your nose, my friend," said the American, turning in the direction of the last speaker, "I would certainly pull it."

"I will strike a match for you later," replied Jacob, a man famous among the brave for his courage; brilliantly clever, bitterly cynical, and endowed with a twofold portion of the mental, moral and physical endurance of his enduring race.

"God will not punish me for my brother's sins, will He, Señor Smith?" continued the Spaniard.

"No," replied the Englishman, "nor him for his own."

"Meaning him, or Him?" inquired Jacob softly.

"We punish ourselves, I think," continued the Englishman, "*quite* sufficiently."

"*Mon Dieu!*" said a cultured French voice, "but you are only partly right, *mon ami*. Woman punishes Man, or we punish ourselves—through Woman."

"Bless ourselves, you mean," said the Englishman and the American immediately and simultaneously.

"The same thing," replied the Frenchman. And the utter stillness that followed was broken by a little gasping sigh that seemed to shape a name—"Véronique."

"*Basta! . . . My brother! . . . My brother! . . .*" babbled the Spaniard and sobbed, "God will distinguish between us. . . . *Gracias a nuestra Madre en el cielo! Gracias a la Virgen Inmaculada. . . . Un millón de gracias. . . .*"

"And what of this accursed brother? Surely no brother of yours committed an interesting sin?" inquired Jacob.

"*Cá!* It was the priest's fault," continued the Spaniard, unheeding. "We were good enough boys. . . . Only mischievous. . . . Fonder perhaps of the girls and the sunshine and the wine-skin and the bull-ring than of religion and work. . . . My brother *was* a good boy, none better from Pampeluna to Malaga—if a little quick with his knife and over-well acquainted with the smuggler track—until that accursed and hell-doomed priest . . . No! No! No! . . . I mean that good and holy man of God—cast his eye upon Dolores. . . .

"Oh, Mother of God! *He killed a priest.* . . . And he defied and challenged God. . . . And I am his twin brother! . . . God may mistake me for him."

"God makes no mistakes, Ramon," said the Englishman. "Excuse my playing the oracle and Heavy Father, but—er—you can be quite sure of that, my lad."

"Yes, yes, yes—you're right. Of course you are right! How should God make mistakes? . . . Besides, God knows my brother, *well.* He followed him. . . . He warned him. . . . When he swore he would never enter a church again, God flung him into one. . . . When he swore he would never kneel again, God struck him to his knees and held him there. . . . Because he swore that he would never make the Sign of the Cross, God made a Sign of the Cross, *of* him."

"Quite noticed the little man, in fact," observed Jacob the Jew. "Tell us."

"My brother caught the priest and Dolores. . . . In the priest's own church. . . . My brother married them before the altar . . . and their married life was brief! . . . But of course, God knew he was mad. . . . As he left that desecrated church, he cried, '*Never will I enter the House of God again! . . .*'

"And that very night the big earthquake came and shattered our village with a dozen others. As we dashed through the door—the old mother in my brother's arms, my crippled sister on my back—the roof caved in and the very road fell from before our little *posada*, down the hillside. My brother was in front and fell, my

7

mother still in his arms. . . . And where did he recover consciousness? Tell me that! . . . *Before the altar*, upon the dead body of his victim, the murdered priest—who thus saved my brother's life, for he had fallen thirty feet from the half-destroyed church-roof, through which he had crashed. . . . Yes, he had entered the House of God once more! . . .

"It was to South America that he fled from the police—to that El Dorado where so many of us go in search of what we never find. And there he went from worse to worse than worst, defying God and slaying man . . . and woman! For he shot his own woman merely because she knelt—just went on her knees to God. . . . And one terrible night of awful storm, when fleeing alone by mountain paths from the soldiers or *guardias civiles*, a flash of lightning showed him a ruined building, and into it he dashed and hid.

"It may have been the rolling thunder, the streaming rain, or an avalanche of stones dislodged by the horses of the police who passed along the path above—I do not know—but there was a terrible crash, a heavy blow, a blinding, suffocating dust—and he was pinned, trapped, held as in a giant fist, unable to move hand or foot, or head. . . .

"And, when daylight came, he saw that he was in a ruined chapel of the old *conquistadores*, kneeling before the altar—a beam across his bowed shoulders and neck; a beam across his legs behind his knees; a mass of stone and rubble as high as his waist. . . . And there my brother *knelt*—before the altar of God—in that attitude of prayer which he had sworn never to assume—and thought his thoughts. . . . For a night and a day and a night, he knelt, his stiff neck bent, but his brave heart unsoftened. . . . And thus the soldiers found him and took him to the *calabozo*. . . .

"The annual revolution occurred on the eve of his garroting, and he was saved. Having to flee the country, he returned to Spain, and sought me out. . . . Owing to a little smuggling trouble, in which a *guardia civil* lost his life, we crossed into France, and, in order to get to Africa and start afresh, we joined the Legion. . . .

"*Válgame Dios!* In the Legion we made quite a little name for ourselves—not so easy a thing to do in the Legion, as some of you may know. There they fear nothing. They fear no thing, but God is not a thing, my friends. *Diantre!* They fear neither man nor devil, neither death nor danger—but they fear God. . . . Most of them. . . . When they come to die, anyhow.

"But my brother did not fear God. . . . And his *escouade* of devils realized that he was braver than they . . . braver by that

much. . . . And always he blasphemed. Always he defied, insulted, challenged God. He had a terrible fight with Luniowski the Atheist, and Luniowski lost an eye in the defence of his No-God. My brother fought with awful ferocity in defence of his God—the God he *must* have, that he might hate and revile Him—the God Who had sat calmly in His Heaven and watched Dolores and the priest.
. . .

"In Africa there was little fear of his finding himself flung into a church, or pinned on his knees before a chapel altar! We aren't much troubled with chaplains and church-parades in the Legion!

"But one day my brother saw a lad, a boy from Provence, a chubby-faced child, make the Sign of the Cross upon his breast, as we were preparing to die of thirst, lost in desert sand-storm. . . . My brother, with all his remaining strength, struck him upon the mouth.

" '*Sangre de Cristo!* If I see you make that Sign again,' he croaked, I'll do it on you with a bayonet.' . . .

" 'If we come through this, I *will* make the Sign of the Cross on you with a bayonet,' gasped the boy hoarsely, and my brother laughed.

" 'Try,' said he. 'Try when I'm asleep. Try when I'm dying. . . . Try when I'm dead. . . . Do you not know that I am a *devil*? Why, your bayonet would melt. . . . *Me!* The Sign of the Cross! . . . *God Himself could not do it!*'

"And next day my brother was lost in that sand-storm, and the Touareg band who found him, took him to the Sultan of Zeggat. . . . And the Sultan of Zeggat *crucified* him in the market-place, 'as the appropriate death for a good Christian!' . . . Wasn't that humorous! . . ."

Silence.

"Yes, God made a Sign *of* my brother," said Ramon the Spaniard, and added, "Help me to my knees, Señor Smith, and keep each word of your promise, for I think I am dying."

Silence. . . .

And then a cry of "*Dios aparece*" from the dying man.

Jacob the Jew, great adept at concealment, produced matches and struck one.

The flare of the match illumined a deep-dug pit, its floor hard-beaten, its walls sloping to a small aperture, through which a star was visible. It had been dug and shaped, for the storing of grain, by Arabs following a custom and a pattern which were old in the days when Carthage was young.

It was now stored, not with grain, but with men[7] sentenced to punishment beyond punishment, men of the Disciplinary Battalions, the *Compagnies de Discipline*, the *"Joyeux,"* the *"Zephyrs,"* the *Bataillon d'Infanterie Légère d'Afrique*—convicted criminals.

The light from the burning match revealed a picture worthy of the pencil of the illustrator of Dante's *Inferno*—a small group of filthy, unshorn, emaciated men, clad in ragged brown canvas uniforms which, with the grime upon their flesh, gave them the appearance of being already part of the earth to which they were about to return, portions of the living grave in which they were entombed.

Some lay motionless as though already dead. One or two sat huddled, their heads upon their clasped knees, the inward-sloping sides of the *silo* denying them even the poor comfort of a wall against which to lean.

Beside a large jug which held a little water, a man lay upon his face, his tongue thrust into the still-damp earth where a few drops of water had been spilt. He had drunk his allowance on the previous day.

Another looked up from his blind search, with sensitive finger-tips, for grains of corn among the dirt.

As Jacob held the match aloft, the Englishman and the American gently raised the body of Ramon the Spaniard from the ground. It was but a body, for the soul had fled.

"Too late," said Jacob softly. "But perhaps *le bon Dieu* will let him off with eight days' *salle de police* in Hell, as it wasn't his fault that he did not assume the correct drill-position for dying respectfully. . . .

"No use heaving him up now," he added, as the head rolled loosely forward.

Without reply, the Englishman and American lifted the dead man to his knees, and reverently did all that had been promised.

And when the body was disposed as Ramon had desired, Jacob spoke again.

"There are but five matches," he said, "but Ramon shall have

---

[7] A prohibited and illegal form of punishment.

two, as candles at his head and feet. It would please the poor Ramon."

"You're a good fellow, Jacob," said the Englishman, ". . . if you'll excuse the insult."

Jacob struck two matches, and the Englishman and the American each taking one, held it, the one at the head, the other at the feet, of the dead man.

All eyes were turned to behold this strange and brief lying-in-state of the Spanish smuggler, court-martialled from the Legion to the Zephyrs.

"Pray for the soul of Ramon Gonzales, who died in the fear of God—or, at any rate, in the fear of what God might do to him," said Jacob the Jew.

The Frenchman who had observed that Man's punishment was Woman, painfully dragged himself into a sitting posture and crawled toward the body.

"I have conducted military funerals," said he, "and remember something of the drill and book-of-the-words."

But what he remembered was not available, for, after the recital of a few lines of the burial-service, he fainted and collapsed.

"This is a very nice funeral," said Jacob the Jew, "but what about the burial?"

§2

Suddenly a man leapt to his feet and, screaming insanely, beat the wall with his manacled hands.

"Come! Come! Smolensky," soothed the huge grey-haired Russian who had been Prince Berchinsky. "We mustn't lose our heads; comrade. . . . I nearly lost mine once. . . . Sit down. . . . I'll tell you about it. . . . Hush now! . . . Hush! And listen. . . . Yes . . . I nearly lost my head once. It was offered as a prize! Think of that! There's an honour for you!

"It was like this—I was with Dodds' lot at Dahomey, you know. He was almost a nigger himself, but he was a soldier all-right, believe me. Faraux was our Battalion-Commander and General Dodds thought a lot of him—and of us. It quite upset Dodds when Faraux was killed at the battle of G'bede, but he kept the Legion in front all the same. . . . So much in front that he lost me, *le Légionnaire* Badineff. . . .

"I was with a small advance-guard and we were literally pushing our way through that awful jungle when the Amazons ambushed us. . . . Wonderful women those Amazons—far better fighters than the men—braver, stronger, cleverer, more soldierly. . . . Armed with short American carbines and *coupe-coupes*, they're no joke!

"I don't want to fight any better troops. . . . Not what you'd call good shots, but as they never make the range more than about twenty yards, they don't miss much! . . .

"Well, it wasn't many minutes before I was the only man of the advance-guard who was on his feet, and I wasn't on those long. . . . For these she-devils were absolutely all round us, and as three or four rushed me with their *machetes*, one of them smashed me on the head, from behind, with the butt of her carbine. . . . Quite a useful bump too, *mes amis* . . . for it put me to sleep for quite a while. . . ."

"Lost your head, in fact," put in Jacob the Jew.

"No, no," continued the old Russian, "not yet . . . but I nearly lost my wits when I recovered my senses . . . if you understand me . . . For the ladies had divided my property among them to the last rag of my shirt, and were now evidently turning to pleasure after business.

"Dahomeyan is not one of the languages which I speak. . . . I only know fourteen really well . . . so I could not follow the discussion closely. . . . But it was quite clear that some were for fire and some for steel. . . . I think a small minority-party were for cord. . . . And I was under the impression that one merry lass capped the others' laughing suggestions with the proposal for all three! . . .

"Do you know, it was for all the world like a lot of nice little girls sitting on the lawn under the trees with their kitten, joyously discussing how they should dress him up, and which ribbons they should put round his neck. . . .

"You know how they laugh and chatter and pull the kitten about, and each one shouts a fresh idea about the dressing-up and the ribbons, and the fun generally. . . . Well, those nice little girls discussed dressing me—for the table—though it wasn't a ribbon they proposed putting round my neck. . . . And undeniably they pulled me about! . . .

"I could not but admire the way they had tied me up. . . . I was more like a chrysalis in a cocoon than a bound man. . . . They *were* playful. . . . Good actresses too—as I realized afterwards—When they saw that I had come round, one of them, eyeing me archly, drew her finger across her throat, and the others all nodded their approval.

"The young thing got up, took a bright sharp knife from her waist-belt, and came over to where I lay against the bole of a tree.

"Grabbing my throat with her left hand, she pulled up the loose skin and began to cut, just as the Leading Lady called out some fresh stage-directions—whereupon she grabbed my beard, pulled my head over to one side, and put the point of the knife in, just below my ear. . . . I closed my eyes and tried to think of a prayer. . . .

"When it comes to it, having your throat cut is the nastiest death there is. . . .

"And just as I was either going to pray or yell, there was a loud burst of laughter, and the girl went back to her place in the jolly group. . . . The Leading Lady then, as far as I could make out, said:

" 'Now we must really get to business or the shops will be shut' . . . and told another lassie, who possessed a good useful iron-hafted spear, to put the butt-end of it in the fire, explaining why, with appropriate gesture. . . .

"It was evidently quite a good idea, for the girls all laughed and clapped their hands, and said what a nice party it was. . . .

"While the spear was getting hot, they propounded all sorts of other lovely ideas, and, over the specially choice ones, they simply rocked with merriment. . . . It *did* seem a pity that one couldn't follow all the jokes. . . . When the pointed haft of the spear was glowing nicely, its owner picked it up, and stepping daintily across to me, held the point a few inches from my eyes. . . .

"Not unnaturally, I turned my head away, but, saying that that wasn't fair, the Leading Lady and the Soubrette made one jump for me and grabbed my head. . . .

"Fine strong hands and arms those ladies had. . . . I couldn't move my face a fraction of an inch. . . .

"And slowly . . . slowly . . . slowly . . . that red-hot point came nearer and nearer to my right eye. . . . It seemed to approach for hours, and it seemed to be in the centre of my brain in a second. . . .

"When it comes to it, *mes amis*, having your eyes burnt out with a red-hot spear-haft is the nastiest death there is. . . .

"But when my right eye seemed to sizzle and boil behind its closed lid, and to be about to burst, my young friend changed her mind, and began upon the left . . . and when the iron was just about to touch it she remarked, in choice Dahomeyan, I believe:

" 'Dammit! The blooming iron's cold!' and, with a joyous whoop, bounded back to the fire, and thrust it in again. . . .

"Shrieks of laughter followed, and loud applause from the

cheap seats.

"Meanwhile the ladies hanged me. . . ."

"*Hanged* you?" inquired Jacob the Jew. "Don't you mean they cut your head off? . . . You said you lost your head, you remember."

"No, my friend," replied Badineff, "I said I *nearly* lost it. . . . Not completely—as you have lost your manners. . . . What I am telling you is true. . . . And if you don't like it, pray go elsewhere. . . ."

"There's nowhere to go but Heaven, I'm afraid," was the reply, "being in Hell—and Earth being denied to us. . . . But pray finish your story, as it is unlikely we shall meet in Heaven. . . ."

"Yes. . . . They hanged me as neatly and as expeditiously as if they had had the advantage of an education in Christian customs. . . . They simply jerked me to my feet, made a noose in a palm-fibre cord, threw the end over the limb of a vast tree, hauled upon it and danced around me as I hung and twisted. . . .

"They say a coward dies many times. . . .That was undoubtedly one of the occasions upon which I have died. . . .

"When it comes to it, *mes amis*, being hanged by strangulation—and not by mere neck-break—is one of the nastiest deaths there is. . . .

"But evidently they let me down in time and loosened the rope from about my neck, for bye-and-bye I was staring up at the stars and in full enjoyment of all my faculties. . . . Particularly the sense of smell. . . .

"The intimate smell of Negro, in bulk, is like no other smell in the world. . . . There is nothing else like it, and there is nothing to which one can compare it—and here is a curious fact which should interest the psychophysiologist. . . . Whenever I wake, as we of the Zephyrs do, dumbly sweating or wildly shrieking, from a ghastly nightmare, I can always *smell* Negro, most distinctly. . . . Very disgusting. . . .

"Curiously enough, these fearless savage fiends, who will charge a machine-gun with the utmost bravery and with a spear, are arrant cowards at night . . . in mortal fear and trembling horror of ten thousand different devils, ghosts, djinns, ghouls, goblins and evil spirits. . . . And when I came to, they were huddled around me for protection. I was almost crushed and buried beneath the mass of them as they lay pressed round and across me. . . .

"As I was still most painfully bound, I can only suppose that I was, in myself, a talisman, a *juju*, a mascot, or shall I say, an *ikon*.

14

"And they had gathered around me in the spirit in which simple peasants might gather round a Calvary, and were using me as some might use a Cross, a holy relic or a charm. . . .

"Yes, to this day I smell that dreadful odour—dreadful because of its associations, rather than of itself—in my worst nightmares and delirium of fever or of wounds. . . .

"I can smell it at this moment. . . .

"I have passed some bad nights—one, impaled on bamboo stakes at Nha-Nam in Tonkin—but this was the worst night of my life . . . almost. . . .

"And in the morning the ladies awoke, made no toilette, and gave me no food. . . .

"But they had given me a faint hope, for I could not but realize that, so far, they had only tortured me by not torturing me at all—and it seemed that they might be keeping me, not only alive and whole, but without spot or blemish, for some excellent purpose. . . .

"They were! . . .

"And when I discovered it, I was inclined to wish that they had killed me with fire or steel or cord—as they did all of our men whom they took prisoner. . . .

"For some reason, possibly on account of my unusual size—I was a fine specimen in those days, six foot six, and with golden hair and beard—they were taking me to good King Behanzin at Kana, as an acceptable gift for a burnt-offering and a bloody sacrifice unto his gods and idols. . . .

"There was a story afterwards, that Behanzin had been told by his sooth-sayers and medicine-men, that he would undoubtedly beat the French if a strong *juju* were made with the blood of a white cock that had a golden comb. . . . One of our officers, Captain Battreau, said I probably owed my life to my golden comb. . . . I have a very white skin where I am not sunburnt. . . .

"Anyhow, the ladies took me along—by the inducement of *machete*-points and rhinoceros-hide whips chiefly—to Kana. . . .

"I don't know whether we marched for a day or for a week. . . . Yes. . . . I was strong in those days . . . for I believe I ate nothing but raw carrion, and my arms were bound to my body the whole time, as though with wire. . . .

"Kana stands on a hill and is built of earth, clay, and sun-baked bricks, inside a great high wall, yards in thickness. . . .

"We entered through a gate like a tunnel, and, by way of filthy narrow red-earth streets, came to a second, inner wall, which surrounded the royal palaces, *hareems*, temples, and the House of

Sacrifice. . . .

"The yelling mob that had accompanied us from the outer gate, crowding and jeering and throwing muck at me—though they kept well out of reach of the weapons of the Amazons—evidently feared to enter this inner city, for that is what it amounted to. . . .

"And I was handed over to a guard of long-speared ruffians and filthy priests who slung me into a big building and slammed the huge double gates. . . . As I staggered forward in the darkness, I slipped on the slimy, rounded cobble-stones, sprawled full-length and collapsed. . . .

"There was a loud roaring in my ears—not the conventional roaring in the ears of a fainting man, but the buzzing of millions of billions of trillions of huge flies, that soon so completely covered me that you could not have stuck a pin into my body without killing one. Their blue-grey metallic bodies made me look as though I were clad in a complete suit of chain-mail. . . . And I could not move a finger even to clear my eyes. . . . I could only blink them.

"And as my eyes grew accustomed to the gloom, I saw that the whitish gleaming cobble-stones were the skulls of men, sunk in the red earth. . . . And I realized why I was being nauseated by a terrible slaughter-house stench. . . .

"It *was* a slaughter-house. . . . The House of Sacrifice, of Kana, the Sacred City of King Behanzin of Dahomey. . . .

"That was another unpleasant night, *mes amis*. . . . Oh, quite unpleasant. . . . We are in clover here—pigs in clover. . . . But, mercifully, I was at the end of my tether, and I had now so little capacity for suffering, that I was not clear in my mind as to whether certain things that happened that night were real or imaginary, fact or nightmare. . . .

"They were real enough. . . . And in the morning I found I was, even as I had either dreamed or realized—actually inside a great wicker bottle or basket, from the top of which my head protruded. . . .

"I could not move a single muscle of my body save those of my face. . . .

"The priests and executioners had been busy during the night, and I was now like a mummy in its bandages, neatly encased in the Sacrificial Basket, all ready to play my helpless part in the bloody ritual of their unspeakable religion. . . .

"Half-dead as I already was, my one hope was that the Service would be short and early—the sacrifice soon and quick. . . . It is most uncomfortable to lie in a bottle with nothing to support your head. . . .

"I could see nothing, and hear little, by reason of the huge flies . . . but I was aware of tom-toming and shouting without, and hoped that it concerned me. . . . It did. . . . The gates of the House of Sacrifice were thrown open and a number of guards, priests, and executioners heaved me up from that terrible floor and carried me outside.

"Oh, the sweetness of that morning air—even in an African town. . . . It almost made me want to live. . . . And oh, the relief to have one's head freed from an inch-thick covering of flies. . . .

"The great Square of the inner town—a Square of which the sides were formed by, shall we say, the Palaces, Cathedrals, Convents, Monasteries and Municipal Buildings of King Behanzin —was thronged by hundreds and hundreds of warriors, both men and women. As my guards carried me across to the biggest of the buildings, all these people fell back to the sides of the Square, leaving the centre empty, save for me and my guards.

"In front of the palace, an ugly clumsy building of red earth and baked clay bricks, sat Behanzin, King of Dahomey, on the Royal Stool. Around him were grouped his courtiers. . . . I think that His Majesty and they formed one of the least pleasing groups of human beings I have ever encountered—and I have known quite a lot of kings and their ministers. . . .

"As I have already observed, I do not speak Dahomeyan, and at that moment I deeply regretted the fact, and equally so, that none of them understood Russian or even French. . . . However, French I spoke, in the vain hope that a word or two, here and there, might be understood.

"A few were, as I will tell you. . . .

"My speech was brief and blunt. . . . I told Behanzin that he was the nastiest thing I knew . . . the ugliest . . . the foulest . . . the filthiest . . . the most abandoned and degraded. . . . And I should be much obliged if someone would remove me from a world which he contaminated. . . .

"I had not finished even these few and well-chosen words before I was again seized by my porters and carried to the very centre of the Square, and there abandoned.

"Immediately the Public, obviously well accustomed to these out-door sports and pastimes, fell into perfectly straight lines on each of the sides of the Square, and assumed the position of sprinters at the starting-point of a race—but each with a coupe-

coupe, knife, axe or spear in his right hand—and looked to His Majesty for the signal.

"The King rose from his royal stool, raised his spear aloft and gazed around. . . .

"I also gazed around, having just grasped the underlying idea of the National Sport, a game in which I had never hitherto taken part, nor even seen. . . .

"Of course—how stupid of me—it was a race-game, a go-as-you-please, run-walk-hop-or-jump. . . . And my head was the prize!

"I wondered whether His Majesty had gathered that my brief address was not couched in diplomatic language. . . . He certainly now prolonged what was, to me, a painful moment. . . . He stood like an ebon statue, his white ostrich feathers nodding in the breeze, his handsome cloak hanging gracefully from his great shoulders, his spear uplifted, motionless. . . .

"When that spear fell, I knew that every competitor of those hundreds surrounding me, would bound forward like a greyhound unleashed. For a few seconds I should see them race toward me, their bloodthirsty faces alight with the lust of slaughter, their gleaming weapons raised aloft. . . . And I should go down, the centre of a maelstrom of clutching hands and hacking blades. . . .

"I wondered what would be the reward of the proud winner of the King's Trophy—the head of the white cock with a golden comb . . . the essential ingredient for the making of the strong *juju* that was to defeat the French. . . .

"That black devil, Behanzin, stood steady as a rock, and there was absolute silence in that great Square, as all awaited the fall of the flag, or rather the shining spear-head. . . .

"A woman, standing in a doorway, giggled nervously, and a crouching sprinter, presumably her lord, looked back over his shoulder—only to receive her sharp rebuke for taking his eye off the ball. . . .

"Another woman dashed forward and handed her husband a *machete*, taking his spear back into the hut. . . . I imagined his saying to her, just before he left the house, 'Tatiana, my dear, run upstairs and find that new *machete* I ordered last week. . . . I think it's on the top of the wardrobe in my dressing-room, unless that wretched girl has put it somewhere.' . . .

"And then I glanced again at the King. . . . Even as I did so, the raised spear-head, which probably had only been uplifted for five seconds after all, began to travel slowly backward. . . . And there was an audible intaking of breath. . . . Evidently the giving of the signal had begun, and in the fraction of a second, the broad, bright spear-head would come flashing downward. . . .

"I closed my eyes. . . .

"*Boom—BANG!*

"I nearly jumped out of my bottle. . . .

"*Boom—BANG!*

"Two shells had burst in Kana, one just above the inner wall, the other in the corner of the Square itself. . . .

"Our guns! . . . Our guns! . . .

"The runners were running indeed—for their *own* heads. . . . King Behanzin also 'ran' . . . if indeed he did not get a win or a place. . . .

"I was forgotten . . . before ever the third and fourth shells arrived. . . . Oh, God! I was *not* forgotten! . . . There was *one* competitor left! . . . I supposed he felt attracted by the walk-over. . . . As he dashed toward me, straight as an arrow, yelling madly, a great spear in his hand, I saw that he was one of the group of courtiers . . . the man indeed who had stood nearest to the King. . . .

"I admit, *mes amis*, that it seemed to me a little hard, more than a little hard, that with the flight of all those hundreds and hundreds of murderous slayers, this solitary one should prefer my life to his own . . . should not realize that the match was abandoned . . . the race scratched . . . the proceedings postponed. . . .

"A fellow of one idea. . . . A case of the *idée fixe*. . . . No sportsman, anyhow. . . . The sort of man that steals the Gold Cup. . . .

"I had been through so much, *mes amis*, from the time that that Amazon had hit me on the head, that I really rebelled a little at this last cruelty of a mocking Fate.

"Saved by the bursting of the shells at the fifty-ninth second of the fifty-ninth minute of the eleventh hour, and then this one solitary, implacable madman to fail to realize that I had been saved! . . .

"Nearer . . . nearer . . . he came—and by the time that he was a few yards from me, he and I were alone in that great Square. . . .

"Would he drive that huge spear through my body, and then clumsily hack my head off with the edge of its broad blade?

"How I hoped that the next shell would blow his limbs from his body, though it killed me too. . . . Another bound and he would be on me. . . . I closed my eyes—and the Nightmare Slayer flung his arm round me, and, in execrable French, panted:

"You tell Frenchies I be verra good man, massa. . . . I belong

Coast . . . belong French shippy. . . . I good friend loving Frenchies. . . . I interpreter. . . . I show Frenchies where old Behanzin bury gin, rum, brandy, ivory. . . .'

"Another shell burst. . . . And the Nightmare Slayer tipped my basket over, and, flat upon the ground, the lion and the lamb lay down together. . . .

"That, *mes amis*, was how I nearly lost my head. . . .

"We must not lose ours here, for, as you perceive, there are far worse places than this one. . . . I rather like it. . . ."

§3

A long heavy silence was broken by Jacob the Jew.

"The lad we want here is the bold bright Rastignac . . . Rastignac, the Mutineer. . . ."

"Oh, did you know him?" said the Englishman.

"What about him?" asked the Frenchman.

"What *about* him? Ho, ho! . . . He gave the Government some trouble, one way and another. . . . They stuck him in the Zephyrs, but they didn't keep him long. What do you think he did? . . .

"He used to carry a flexible saw-file round his upper gums from one cheek to the other, and they say he carried some little tool that he used to swallow—on the end of a string, with the other end tied round a back tooth—on search days.

"Well, he filed his manacles and got out. . . . And he killed two sentries, absolutely silently, by stabbing them in the back of the neck with a long darning-needle, to which he had fitted a tiny wooden handle. . . . There is a spot, you know, at the base of the brain, just where the skull rests on the backbone. . . . The point of a needle in *there* . . . just in the right spot . . . and *pouf!* . . .

"Rastignac knew the spot, all-right. And when he was clear, and dressed in a dead sentry's uniform, did he run off like any other escaping prisoner? . . . Not he. . . . He broke into a Public Works Department shed . . . took a pot of black paint, and a pot of white, and some brushes, and marched off at daybreak, as bold as brass. . . ."

"Where to?" inquired the American.

"To the nearest milestone," chuckled Jacob the Jew, ". . . and neatly touched up the black *kilometre* figures and their white border. . . . And then to the next. . . . And the next. . . .

"When patrols passed, he gave them good-day and exchanged jokes and the latest news, for cigarettes and a drink. . . . They say he visited several camps and made himself useful, with his paint, to one or two officers, and reported some rascal who had smeared one of his nice black figures because he wouldn't give him tobacco! . . .

"And so he painted his way, milestone by milestone, to Oran, where he reported himself, produced the dead sentry's *livret* and leave-papers, and was wafted comfortably, by *Messageries Maritimes*, to France. . . ."

"Well, and what would he do if he were here?" asked a querulous voice. "We may suppose that your Rastignac had neither the wings nor feet of a fly. . . . And if he were here and got us out, where could we go? . . . More likely to have caused the death of us all. . . . Like those two devils Dubitsch and Barre nearly did to their gang. . . ."

"What was that?" asked Badineff.

"Why, these two unutterable swine were with a working-party in the *zone dissidente*, and at night were in a little perimeter-camp made with dry cactus and thick heavy thorn. . . . Their beautiful scheme—and they nearly brought it off—was to creep out on a windy night and to set fire to these great thorn-walls of the zareba! This stuff burns like paper, and they'd got hold of some matches. . . . It mattered nothing to them that the remaining ninety-eight of their fellow-convicts would inevitably be roasted to death in the process. . . . Those two would easily escape in the confusion, while the men of the escort were vainly doing their best to save the rest of the wretched prisoners. . . . *Their* position, as you may imagine, would be just that of a bundle of mice tied together by their tails and packed round with cotton-wool soaked in kerosene. . . .

"As luck would have it—the luck of the other ninety-eight, anyhow—the first match was blown out, and a sentry had seen the glare of it. . . . He fired and challenged after, wounding Dubitsch and so flustering Barre, who had the matches, that he dropped the lot and was unable to strike another before the sentry was upon him. . . ."

"What happened then?" asked the Englishman.

"The Sergeant-Major in charge of the escort simply returned them to their place in the gang—but took care that the gang should know exactly what had happened. . . ."

"And then? . . ." prompted the Englishman, when the man stopped, as one who had said enough. . . .

"Oh—they died . . . they died. . . . They died that same night, of something or other. . . . Judging from their faces, they had not died happily. . . ."

"Sounds as though you saw them," observed Jacob the Jew.

"Quite," observed the narrator laconically.

"Not like poor dear little Tou-tou Boil-the-Cat," observed Jacob.

"What happened to him?" asked the Querulous Voice.

"Oh, he died . . . he died. . . . He died suddenly, one night, of something or other. . . . But no-one was able to judge from his face whether he died happily or not. . . ."

"Tell us about him," suggested the American.

"About Tou-tou Boil-the-Cat? . . . He wasn't a nice man. . . . Made quite a name for himself, Montmartre way, before he went to the Legion. . . . There was some talk about a Lovely Lady, the Queen of his Band. . . . Wonderful golden hair. . . . Known to all kind friends as *Casque d'Or*. . . . They say he cut it off. . . . Her head, I mean. . . . Got into bad trouble in the Legion too. . . . Life sentence in the Zephyrs. . . .

"A brave little man, but he hadn't the other virtue that one rather demands. . . . No. . . . Something of a stool-pigeon. . . . There were thirteen convicts in a tent . . . a most unlucky number . . . but it was soon reduced to twelve, through M'sieu Tou-tou Boil-the-Cat giving information that affected the career—indeed, abbreviated, it—of one of his comrades. . . .

"Yes . . . thirteen went forth from that tent to labour in the interests of France's colonial expansion that sunny morning, and only twelve returned to it, to sleep the sleep of the unjust, that dewy eve. . . . A round dozen. . . .

"But they did not sleep through the stilly night, though the night remained quite stilly. . . . And behold, when another bright day broke, those twelve were now eleven. . . .

"The guard, who was but a simple peasant man, could not make the count come to more than eleven. . . . The corporal—possibly a shade more intelligent, could not by any means make the count a dozen. . . . The Sergeant, a man who could count quite well, swore there were but ten and one. . . . Not the Commandant himself could make us twelve! . . .

"With the help of a bottle of absinthe he might make us twenty-two—but even then he realized that he should have seen twenty-four. . . .

"No. . . . Tou-tou Boil-the-Cat was gone. . . . Gone like a beautiful dream . . . or like the foul brutish nightmare that he was. . . .

"And that, you know, puzzled our kind superiors. . . .

22

"For, as it happened, it was quite impossible for anyone to have escaped from the camp that night—full moon, double sentries, constant patrols, and all-night wakefulness and uneasiness on account of expected Arab attack. . . .

"But gone he had. . . .

"We were interrogated severally, and collectively, and painfully . . . until they must have admired our staunchness and the wonderful cleverness of the missing man. . . .

"We eleven slept in the tent for a month . . . and the country round was scoured until not one grain of sand was left upon another, and there was not a locust, a scorpion, a serpent nor a vulture, whose *dossier* was not known. . . .

"And at the end of a month the whole camp moved on. . . ."

"Did they ever find him?" asked Badineff.

"No . . . *they* didn't," was the reply. "The jackals found him. . . ."

"Where?" asked the Englishman.

"Under the sand that had formed the floor of the tent of the eleven . . ." was the answer.

"Sounds as though you were there . . ." said the Querulous Voice.

"Quite . . ." replied Jacob the Jew, and yawned.

§4

The sun had risen and set once more, causing a spot of light to travel slowly across a portion of the interior of the *silo*, with the search-light effect of illuminating brilliantly the tiny area upon which it rested, while leaving the rest of the place in darkness darker than that of night.

There was curiously little movement, and less sound, in the *silo* —the uneasy stirring of a nightmare-ridden sleeper, a heavy sigh, a faint groan, the clank of a chain. Talk had ceased, and scarcely a sentence had been uttered for hours.

The last subject of general conversation had been that of the cause of their abandonment to a lingering and terrible death in that dreadful tomb. Speculation had wandered from sudden Arab attack and the annihilation of the Company, to the familiar theory of wanton malice and deliberate devilish punishment. Men, condemned from the Legion for military "crimes," had advanced the former theory; civilian prison criminals, the latter.

The Frenchman who had attempted to recite the Burial Service had accepted neither of these views.

"We are *forgotten*," he had said. . . . "We are the Forgotten of Man, as distinguished from our friends the Touareg, the Forgotten of God. It is perfectly simple, and I can tell you exactly how it happened.

"As you may be aware, *mes amis*, a list of *les hommes punis* is made out, by the clerk of the *Adjudant*, every morning, before the guard is changed. The form on which he writes the names is divided into columns showing the class of punishment and the number of days each man has still to do. . . . And the clerk of the *Adjudant*, God forgive him, has written the number of our days under the heading *salle de police*, or *cellules*, or *consigne*, and has left the column 'prison,' blank. So, each day, our sentences are being reduced by one day, in those places where we are not, and the Sergeant of the Guard for each day, observes that there are no men in '*prison*,' for the column so headed is blank. . . . We are *not* in 'prison' because we are not recorded as being in 'prison'—and therefore we cannot be released from 'prison.' . . ."

And Jacob the Jew had observed:

"Convincing and very cheering—Monsieur must have been a lawyer before he left the world."

And the man had replied:

"No. . . . An officer. . . . Captain of Spahis and in the Secret Service—about to die, and unashamed. . . . *No!*—I should say *Légionnaire* Rien of the Seventh Company of the Third Battalion of the First Regiment of the Foreign Legion. . . . I was wandering in my mind. . . ."

§5

"Tell me," said Jacob the Jew (or Jacopi Judescu, the Roumanian gypsy). "What was really your reason for that sloppy feeble 'kindness' to Ramon Gonzales. . . . I am a philosopher and a student of that lowest of the animals, called Man. . . . Was it to please your Christian God and to acquire merit? . . . Or to uphold your insolent British assumption of an inevitable and natural superiority? . . . You and your God—the Great Forgivers! . . . 'Injure me—and I'll forgive you and make you feel so damned uncomfortable that you'll be more injured than I am.' . . . Aren't you *capable* of a good decent hate or . . ."

"Yes. I hate your filthy voice, dear Jacob," replied the Englishman.

"No. Tell me," persisted Jacob. "I loathe being puzzled. . . . Besides, don't you see I'm going mad. . . . Talk, man. . . . These corpses. . . . Why did you behave like that to Ramon Gonzales? . . . He betrayed you, didn't he? . . . I would have strangled him. . . . I would have had his eyes. . . . Didn't he betray and denounce you after you had found him in the desert and saved his life? . . . To Sergeant Lebaudy?"

"Yes. He recognized me—and did his, ah—duty," was the reply.

"For twenty-five pieces of silver! . . . Recognized you as one of the Zinderneuf men he knew at Sidi, and promptly sold you? . . .

"Consigned you to sudden death—or a lingering death—for twenty-five francs and a Sergeant's favour! . . . And here the Judas was—wondrously delivered into your hand—and you 'forgave' him and comforted him! . . . Now *why*? . . . What was the game, the motive, the reason, the object? Why should a sane man act like that? . . . What *was* the game?"

"No game, no motive, no reason," answered the Englishman. "He acted according to his lights—I to mine."

"And where do you get your 'lights'? What flame lit them?"

"Oh—I don't know. . . . Home. . . . Family. . . . One's women-folk. . . . School. . . . Upbringing. . . . Traditions. . . . One unconsciously imbibes ideas of doing the decent thing. . . . I've been extraordinarily lucky in life. . . . Poor old Ramon wasn't. . . . One does the decent thing if one is—decent."

"You don't go about, then, consciously and definitely forgiving your enemies and heaping coals of fire on them because you're a Christian."

"No, of course not. . . . Don't talk rot. . . ."

"Nor with a view to securing a firm option on a highly eligible and desirable mansion in the sky—suitable for English gentleman of position—one of the most favourable residential sites on the Golden Street. . . ."

"Not in the least. . . . Don't be an ass. . . ."

"You disappoint me. I was hoping to find, before I died, one of those rare animals, a Christian gentleman—who does all these funny things *because* he is a Christian—and this was positively my last chance. . . . I shall die in here."

"I expect Christianity *was* the flame that lit those little 'lights,' Jacob. . . . Our home and school and social customs, institutions and ideas are based on the Christian ideal, anyhow. . . . And we owe what's good in them to that, I believe. . . . We get our *beau idéal* quite unconsciously, I think, and we follow it quite unconsciously—if we follow it at all. . . ."

"Well, and what *is* it, my noble Christian martyr?"

"Oh, just to be—decent, and to do the decent thing, y'know."

"So, indirectly, at any rate, you returned good for evil to Judas Ramon Gonzales because you were a Christian, you think?"

"Yes. . . . Indirectly . . . I suppose. . . . We aren't good at hating and vengeance and all that. . . . It's not done. . . . It isn't—decent. . . ."

"But you puzzle me. What of Ramon the Judas . . . Ramon who sold you? He was a *great* Christian, you know. . . . A staunch patron of your Christian God. . . . Always praying and invoking your Holy Family."

"There are good and bad in all religions, Jacob. . . . I have the highest admiration for your great people—but I have met rotten specimens. . . . Bad as some of my own. . . ."

Silence.

"Look here, Christian," began Jacob the Jew again. "If I summoned up enough strength, and swung this chain with all my might against your right cheek, would you turn the other also?"

"No. I should punch you on the nose," said the Englishman simply.

Silence.

"Tell me. Do you kneel down night and morning and pray to your kind Christian God, Englishman? The forgiving God of Love, Who has landed you *here?*" asked Jacob the Jew.

"I landed myself here," was the reply. "And—er—no. . . . I don't pray—in words—much. . . . You won't mind asking questions for fear of being thought inquisitive, will you, gentle Jacob?"

"Oh, no. . . . Let's see now. . . . You forgive the very worst of injuries because you are a Christian, but not *because* you're a Christian. . . . You do as you would be done by, and not as you've been 'done' by. . . . You don't pray in words, and hold daily communion with your kind Christian God—you regard Him as a gentleman—an English gentleman of course—who quite understands, and merely desires that you be—decent, which of course, you naturally would be, whether He wished it or not. . . .

And you'll punch me on the nose if I smite you on the cheek—but you don't even do that much to anyone who betrays you to a dreadful death. . . . And really, in your nice little mind, you loathe talking about your religion, and you are terrified lest you give the impression that you think it is better than other people's, for fear of hurting their feelings. . . ."

"Oh, shut up, Jacob. You'd talk the hind leg off a dog."

"What else is there to do but talk? . . . And so you are perfectly certain that you are a most superior person, but you strive your very utmost to conceal the awful fact. . . . You're a puzzling creature. . . . What is your motivating force? What is your philosophy? What are you *up* to? . . ."

"Well, at the moment, I'm going to issue the water-ration. . . . Last but one. . . ." said the Englishman.

"I can't understand you English. . . ." grumbled Jacob.

"A common complaint, I believe," said the Englishman. The quiet American laughed.

§6

"Should any gentleman here survive, I wonder if he would be so extremely obliging as to write to my Mother," said the French ex-officer later. "She is an old lady—quite alone—and she foolishly cherishes a fondness for a most unworthy son. . . . Darling Mother! . . ."

The Englishman and the American memorized an address in Paris, and each declared that he would not only write to Madame de Lannec, but would visit her, give her her son's last message, and assure her of his gentle happy death from honourable wounds received in the service of France, and describe his grand military funeral.

Neither of these two men would admit that he also was already in his grave.

"Been in lots of tighter places than this," said the Englishman.

"I've been nearer death too," observed the American. "Been dead really. . . . In this same Zaguig. . . ."

"Ah—an unpleasant place, Zaguig," said the Frenchman, "I know it well," and added, "I, too, have occasionally been in danger. . . . But I finish here. . . ."

"Never say die," urged the American. "Personally, I refuse to die. . . . I've got a job to do, and I intend to live until it's done. . . ."

"Same here," agreed the Englishman. "I must be getting home

to tea shortly. . . . My wife. . . ." He coughed.

"Ah, *mes amis*, you wish to live. . . . I, on the contrary, wish to die," whispered the Frenchman, and shortly after became delirious and raved—of "Véronique," of a terrible painter and his devilish picture, of a Colonel of Chasseurs d'Afrique, of a Moor of the Zarhoun whom the speaker had apparently killed with his bare hands, and of his mother. . . . But chiefly of "Véronique"—until he sank into a state of coma.

In the morning, the spot of light fell on his face and he awoke and, from time to time, spoke rationally, though he did not appear to realize where he was.

He desired the services of a priest, that he might "make his soul." On either side of him, the Englishman and the American did what they could to soothe his passing, and Jacob the Jew produced his last scrap of biscuit for the nourishment of the sick man. . . . . He offered to chew it for him if he were unable to masticate. . . .

"It's a privilege to die in your society, *mes amis*," said the Frenchman suddenly, in a stronger voice. "To die with men of one's own sort. . . . Officers once, doubtless, and gentlemen still. . . . I am going to add to the burden of debt I owe you. . . . But I am going to give you something in return. . . . My dying assurance that you are going to live. . . . I most clearly see you walking in the sunshine, free and happy. . . . Walking towards a woman—a truly beautiful woman. . . . She loves you both—but one far more than the other. . . . You fight on her account . . . your weapons are generosity, unselfishness, sacrifice, self-abnegation, the love of a man for his friend. . . ."

Silence.

"Poor chap," murmured the Englishman, staring across at the almost indistinguishable form of the American. "Wandering again. . . . He seemed better. . . ."

No reply came from the darkness where the other crouched beside the dying man.

"And this is the further request I have to make of you. . . . Will one of you go to the little cemetery and stand by her grave and say:

" '*As he died he spoke of you. . . . He spoke only words of kindness and love. . . . He did not breathe one word of reproach. . . . Only kindness, love and gratitude.*'

"She will be able to understand—now. . . .

"And will you take violets—a few violets, from me. . . . Always they were her flower. . . . A few of the beautiful big violets that welcome one home from Africa. . . . Once I kissed an old grandmother who was selling them on the *quai* at Marseilles, and gave her a gold piece. . . . They were not violets she sold to me. . . . They were *France* . . . they were *Home* . . . they were *Véronique.* . . . Their odour was the distilled soul of the sweetness of all that is in those three wonderful words. . . . France, Home and Beauty. . . .

"Oh, God . . . I can smell violets. . . .

"Véronique, did ever you see violets again without thinking of me? Did I ever see them again without trembling from head to foot, without wondering how my frozen brain could function . . . how my burning heart could beat. . . .

"Forgive me, gentlemen. . . . But you never saw her. . . . She was God's triumph. . . . Yes, often I called her, 'You Evidence of God'—for such beauty and wonder and untellable glory of woman-hood was final proof to me of the existence of a great good God of Beauty.

"And Beauty is Truth—and Goodness."

Silence.

Jacob the Jew crawled painfully toward the spot of light.

"You can give him my water-ration," he croaked.

"*Stout fella!*" said the Englishman, in his mother-tongue.

The American started, as a slight jingle of iron indicated.

"*Say that again, will you?*" he said in English.

"I said, '*Stout fella*'," replied the Englishman.

"*Merciful God!*" whispered the American; and the dying Frenchman raised himself on his right elbow, and endeavoured to point with his left hand.

"*Véronique!*" he cried. "I did my best. . . . I *did* save you from Dummarcq—the great César Dummarcq—the world-famous painter, the idol of Paris, the huge vile pig, the half-mad cruel devil. . . . No—*he is there!* . . . Do not move! . . . Do not stir hand or foot . . . a hair's-breadth—or he will shoot. . . . He will shoot *you*, not me, the fiend!"

He sank back upon the ground.

"Dearest Mother! . . . I nearly broke your heart when I told you I would marry her. . . . And you nearly broke mine when you said that I should not. . . . An artists' model. . . . True. . . . César Dummarcq's model. . . . But a model of beauty and grace. . . .

Lovely in all her ways and thoughts and movements. . . . César Dummarcq's model. . . . But a model for all women to copy. . . . Every fascination and charm of mind as well—witty and clever and of the sweetest disposition. . . . With her, one laughed. . . . One laughed the whole day through. . . .

"Oh, but she was *dear*—dear and sweet and a living charm. . . . Was it her fault that she had no heart? No fairy, mermaid, elf, sprite, no magic princess from the golden castle on the crystal hill, ever *has* a heart! . . . So I gave her mine—to break. . . .

"Oh, that terrible picture! . . . Véronique, how was I to know that he had painted us, all save the last few touches? . . . The jealous devil! . . . He did not even love you. . . . You were merely his model, his chattel, his property. . . . No one must take you from him—not even to marry you. . . .

"Behind that sinister black curtain. . . . A pistol in his hand. . . . My arms about you as I implored you to be my wife. . . . Your terrible shriek as you saw him appear . . . smiling . . . smiling . . ."

Silence.

The Frenchman's voice changed completely. It was as though an entirely different personality possessed his body.

"No—don't move, my young cub! . . . Move hand or foot, and our fair and frail young friend will have her beauty marred! . . . Oh, a *great* picture! . . . '*FEAR!*' *by César Dummarcq* . . . the greatest portrayer of human emotions, of all time. . . . Yes . . . '*FEAR!*' . . . Do you *fear*, little cockerel? . . . Do you fear you have brought death to your mistress? . . . I *am* Death! . . . Death the great Artist! . . . Oh, ho! his macabre compositions! . . . His lovely colours of corruption and decay! . . . The great César Dummarcq's greatest picture—'*FEAR!*' . . . Now keep still. . . . See, I lay the pistol on this table beside the easel. . . . Ah! *would* you! . . . You'd rise from that rug, would you? . . . *Down*, dog! . . . Would you murder this woman whom you love so much? . . . That's better. . . .

"No, my dear Véronique, do not faint. . . . Just a minute. . . . Your glazing eyes staring from the white mask of your face. . . . '*FEAR!*' Aha! . . . Wonderful models! . . . One has to go to some trouble to find them, of course. . . . That's right, popinjay—excellent! . . . Moisten your lips with your tongue again. . . . See, little pimp, I think I will shoot her, after all—as I have finished her face. . . . Yes—you a little later. . . . Another marvellous picture! . . . She lies on the divan—same attitude—blood on her breast, a

30

thin stream trickling down her white arm, a stain on the white bear-skin—lovely colours! . . . And you? . . . One arm and your head and shoulders across her body. . . . The rest of you on the rug—much the same position as now. . . . A bullet-hole beneath your ear. . . . I am not too near, here, I think. . . . No. . . . What shall we call the second picture? . . . *'REVENGE!'* . . . No, a little banal. . . . What about *'FINIS!'* . . . No. . . . No name at all, I think—*a 'problem' picture. . . .*

"Oh? . . . You think *I'll* make a fine picture on the guillotine, do you? . . . That's where you're wrong, puppy. . . . This is going to be a *crime passionel.* . . . Glorious advertisement for the great César Dummarcq. . . . Anyhow, the present picture is going marvelously. . . .

" *'FEAR!'* . . . Never was *FEAR* so portrayed before. . . . Hi! *Down*, dog! There . . . That bullet stirred her hair. . . . Stirred your heart too by the look of you, you little hound. . . ."

Silence.

"*Ce bon Monsieur César Dummarcq* would seem to have been a gentleman with a sense of humour," murmured Jacob. "I would we had him here."

"To jest with us?" inquired the Englishman.

"No, for us to jest with *him*, I think," replied Jacob.

Silence.

"Water!" gasped the Frenchman.

"Mine," said Jacob.

"We'll all contribute," said the American.

The Englishman took the jug to the ray of light and carefully measured water into an iron mug.

"A good spoonful each, left," he said, stepping gingerly between two corpses.

The Frenchman drank avidly. Upon this little stream of life-giving water his conscious mind seemed to be borne to the surface.

"Thank you! . . . Thank you, gentlemen!" he said. "I do hope I have not drunk more than my share. . . . I was not noticing. . . . One of you will see to that for me, will you not? . . . Get them on the *quai* at Marseilles, and put them on her grave in the little cemetery. . . ."

"Why certainly, of course," said the American. "Where is it?"

". . . And tell her that my last thoughts were of her. . . . She will understand now. . . . She understood nothing when she died. . . . She was like that when I saved her from the Beni Zarkesh. . . . God is very good and He had taken away her understanding. . . ."

Silence.

". . . That roof. . . . In the starlight. . . . He was twice as big and strong as I, that Moor. . . . But I killed him with my bare hands, as I had killed the watchman dozing at the foot of the stair. . . . Oh, that lovely silent struggle, with my hands at his throat. . . .

"And she thought I was de Chaumont, her Colonel of Chasseurs d'Afrique. . . . His name was Charles. . . . She called me '*Charles*' as I carried her to the horses. . . . She called me '*Charles*' through the brief remainder of her life. . . . She died calling me '*Charles*.' . . . A little hard for me to bear. . . . Yes, I suffered a little. . . . I had thought bitterly of Charles de Chaumont and I had written him a rather terrible letter when, on the strength of his rank and seniority, he declined my challenge to a duel. . . . But I am grateful to him for his kindness to her, and for making her so happy all those years. . . . He must have loved her truly. . . . Who could help it? . . . And how she loved him! . . . She must have been happy as the day is long, for she had changed but little. . . . A girl when I lost her. . . . A woman when I found her. . . . Even more beautiful, if that were possible. . . . The mad are often very lovely. . . . An unearthly beauty. . . . Very terrible. . . . But I firmly believe her last days were happy. . . . She had forgotten that *hareem*. . . . And I was her adored *Charles de Chaumont!* . . . Yes. . . . Unconscious fingers can play a fearful threnody upon our heart-strings. . . . Can break them one by one. . . . *Véronique—Véronique*. . . ."

Silence.

"Is he dead?" asked Jacob, later.
"Yes," said the Englishman, and coughed slightly.
"Well, do you know," said Jacob, "I think I shall join him. I have always been deeply interested in the Hereafter, and I confess to being a little weary of the Here. . . . Yes, I think it's time to go."
"Are you talking about committing suicide?" asked the American.
"Not at all," replied Jacob. "I am talking about being murdered and taking it upon me to shorten the process. I have no strong

views on the subject of man murdering his fellow-man on the scaffold, or against the wall at dawn. But this slow murder is quite indefensible, and I feel justified in expediting my end."

"You'll look a most awful ass if they remember us and a release-party comes, after all," said the Englishman.

"I shall look very nasty, anyhow, by the time a release-party comes," was the reply. "So will you, my friends. And you will have suffered a few hours or a few days longer than I. . . . Either the Company has moved on, and there are a few more miles of the Zaguig-Great Oasis Road, marked, or else there was a sudden raid and the Company is obliterated. . . . Anyhow—I've had enough."

"Don't give up, Jacob. Don't be a coward," said the Englishman.

"No, I will not give up—my right to dispose of myself; the only right left to me," was the answer. "No, I will not be a coward who dare not step uninvited into the next world. . . . What do you do, my friend if you sit on a tin-tack? You promptly remove yourself. I am going to remove myself. I have already sat too long upon this particular—ah—tin-tack."

"Rot," said the Englishman.

"You're beat," said the American.

"You can't commit suicide," said the Englishman.

"It isn't—'decent,' I suppose," smiled Jacob.

"That's it," said the Englishman. "It's a rotten thing to do. One doesn't commit suicide! It's not done. It isn't—er—decent."

"A matter of opinion," said the Jew. "Is it better and wiser to suffer indescribable agonies of the mind, and ghastly tortures of the body, for days, hours, or seconds? It seems to me to be more logical to let it be a matter of seconds."

"Well, logic isn't everything," said the Englishman. "Most of our best impulses and ideas are illogical. . . . Damn logic. . . . Love is illogical."

"Surely," said the American.

"Yes. Life is illogical and death is illogical, and God is illogical," said Jacob. "And it is also perfectly illogical to lie here and die of thirst, starvation, heat, suffocation and insects for another twenty-four hours when you can do it in twenty-four seconds. . . . Good-bye, my friends! May we meet again and discuss our discoveries concerning God, Jehovah, Allah, Christ, Mahomet, Buddha and the other manifestations of man's incurable anthropomorphism. . . . *Adieu!* Or *au revoir*—whichever it may prove to be."

"Hi! Here! Hold on!" cried the Englishman.

"You! Jacob!" called the American.

"Well?" chuckled the Jew.

"Look here," said the Englishman, "be decent, Jacob. You objected to Ramon dying at all."

"Ah—he was the first," replied Jacob, "and there was some hope then. . . . There are only we three now, and one more corpse will not further discommode you. I beg you to believe me that I would not have done this were all the others still alive—not even though I knew there would be no release. . . .

"To have done that would not have been—'decent,' " he added with a chuckle.

"Look here, Jacob, will you do me a favour?" asked the Englishman.

"I shall be most delighted," was the reply. "It will be my last opportunity. And it will have to be soon," he added, his weak voice growing perceptibly weaker.

"Well, I want you to promise to wait another day," said the Englishman. "Only another twenty-four hours. Just till the spot of light falls on the Frenchman's body again. . . ."

"Come on, Jacob," urged the American. "Stick it till then. Please yourself after that. But I believe we'll be saved to-morrow."

"Too late," was the whispered reply. "I have opened a vein. . . . When you want it, you'll find the piece of steel in my right hand . . . razor-edge one side, saw-edge the other . . . Pluck up your courage and come along with me, both of you. . . ."

Silence.

A deep sigh.

The Englishman and the American found it was indeed too late.

§7

"*Now*, my friend," said the American, "we can attend to our own little affairs! . . . Do you know that our meeting in here is one of the most astounding things that have *ever* happened? . . . Do you know you are *the one man in all the world I have been looking for*! . . . And *this* is where I find you! . . . I did my damnedest—and then Providence took a hand. . . . Heaven helps those, etc. . . . ."

"I am afraid I don't quite understand," began the Englishman.

"You certainly don't. . . . I don't myself. . . . We're dreaming, of course. It's delirium. We aren't in any *silo*. . . . *You aren't John Geste*."

"But I *am* John Geste!" gasped the Englishman.

"You aren't John Geste and I didn't spot you directly you said '*Stout fella*,' in English. And I didn't hear you call your wife 'Stout fella' at Brandon Abbas when you were kids and . . . Oh, my God!

"Where's your hand, man. . . . Oh, *John Geste! John Geste!*. . . We'll be out of here to-morrow, boy. . . . We *can't* die here. God doesn't mean us to die and rot in this hole that was ordained to be our meeting-place. . . . Ordained from the beginning of Time as the place where I should find you, after all. . . . And Isobel's well and only waiting to be happy as soon as she hears you're corning home to—er—tea, John Geste! . . . And I was to tell you Michael didn't take the 'Blue Water' from under the cover. It wasn't he who stole it. . . . And I'm going mad, John Geste—mad with joy—and starvation, and weakness, and happiness. . . ."

"Hadn't noticed the happiness much," said the Englishman. "What are you gibbering about, my dear chap? Who *are* you? How do you know my name—and about Isobel?"

He coughed slightly. "I'm delirious, I suppose. . . . Both delirious. . . . Both dreaming. . . ."

"We're both dreaming the same dream then, John Geste. . . . I want to tell you. . . ."

An ominous clink of metal and a sigh were audible above the feeble croaking of his voice.

"Here, what's up? . . . You listening? . . . Here, *wake up*."

The Englishman had collapsed and lay inert, unresponsive, either in a faint or the last sleep of all.

§8

The arrival of the spot of sunlight found the American moistening the lips of the dying Englishman with the remaining drops of water.

"Worn out," he murmured later. "God! I feel as strong as a horse now! . . . He had given up hope before I recognized him. . . . Oh, Isobel . . . I've found him and he's dying. . . . No, God can't mean that. . . . I'm talking out loud. I must catch hold of myself. . . . Help me, God, for I am going to help myself—to help them."

The American crawled across to where lay the body of the strange man known to his fellows as Jacob the Jew.

Feeling over the corpse he found the right hand and in it a piece of wonderfully-tempered steel, which, together with a few matches, the man had somehow hidden from those whose duty it had been to search him. Securing it, he returned to the side of the Englishman, and once again endeavoured to revive him.

Panic seized him as he realized his efforts were unavailing. Putting his lips to the ear of the unconscious man, he whispered urgently, and his whisper quickly grew to a hoarse shout.

"*John Geste! John Geste! Come back, John Geste!* Come *back*, man! You *can't* die! You can't die, *now*, John Geste! I've *found* you. . . . *Hi! John Geste!* Think of Isobel. . . . Isobel! . . . Isobel!! *Isobel!!!* Do you hear me? . . . Do you hear me, John? Fight, man! Fight for your life! . . . Think how Beau would have fought! . . . Beau Geste. . . . Think how Digby would have fought. . . . Digby Geste. . . . Fight, John! . . . Fight for Isobel. . . . Come back. . . . Isobel! . . . Isobel!! *Isobel!!!*"

As though the name had reached his semi-conscious mind, the dying man stirred. The other crowed inarticulately, and suddenly fell quiet.

"Wish I knew something more about that blood-transfusion stunt," he murmured in his normal voice, as he deeply incised the side of his wrist, forced open his companion's mouth, and pressed the bleeding wrist firmly against it.

"Excuse me, son," he said, and laughed hysterically.

THE STORY OF OTIS VANBURGH

"A lean man, silent, behind triple bars
  Of pride, fastidiousness and secret life.
  His thought an austere commune with the stars,
  His speech a probing with a surgeon's knife.

His style a chastity whose acid burns
  All slack, false, formlessness in man or thing;
  His face a record of the truth man learns
  Fighting bare-knuckled Nature in the ring."
                         —John Masefield.

A man's place in the scale of civilization is shown by his attitude to women. There are men who regard a woman as something to live with. There are others who regard her as someone to live for.

CHAPTER I

I shall never forget my first sight of Isobel Rivers—a somewhat foolish remark, in view of the fact that I have never forgotten any glimpse I have ever had of her. I don't think I have even forgotten any word that she has ever said to me. Nay, more, I do not believe I have forgotten any word that I have ever said to her.

It was, as was most fitting, one of those truly glorious English spring mornings when one is consciously glad to be alive, and unconsciously aware that God's in His Heaven and all's well with the world.

I was on a visit to the home of my maternal grandmother at Brandon Regis and had that morning walked out from the big old house which was half farm and half manor, where my yeoman ancestors had lived since Domesday Book, or before.

I suppose it was the utter glory of that lovely morning, and not a premonition that this was to be an epochal day in my life, that made me feel so joyously exalted.

I had walked a mile or so, in the direction of Brandon Abbas, and was seated on a gate that opened into one of those neat and tidy English fields that always look to me as though they were tended rather by parlour-maids than by agricultural labourers. I was whistling merrily, and probably quite tunelessly, when a dog-cart, its small body perched high on big spidery wheels, came smartly round a bend in the high-hedged narrow lane to which my face was turned.

On the front seat were two boys, extraordinarily alike, as I saw when the horse was brought to an extremely sudden stand-still at my gate. Back to back with these obvious twins, sat a boy and a girl, the boy an unmistakable younger brother of the twins, and the girl younger still.

They were an astoundingly handsome quartette, and the girl's face was the loveliest I had ever seen.

It is still the loveliest I have ever seen.

I will not attempt to describe her, as it is foolish to attempt the impossible. I can only say that the face was typically Anglo-Saxon in its fair loveliness of pale golden hair, large, long-lashed eyes of corn-flower blue, perfect complexion and tender mouth, faultless and sweet.

The boy who was driving the restless and spirited horse, addressed me in a form of words, archaic and unusual.

"Prythee, gentle stranger, seated pensive on thy gate, and making day hideous with shrill cacophony. . . ."

"Doesn't look coffiny to me," interrupted his twin.

"Nor too blooming gentle," said the boy behind him.

"And I am *sure* he was making day delightful and wasn't a bit s'rill, and he isn't a stranger now we've talked to him," said the girl.

"Good-morning Madam, and gentlemen," said I, stepping down and raising my cap to the lovely little maiden who had spoken in my defence.

"Have it your own way, pups," cried the first speaker, as the three boys gravely and gracefully returned my salute. "He's not a stranger within our gate, nor on it, now; he is making day beautiful with uninstrumental and unearthly music. . . ."

"Do you mean an unearthly row?" asked his twin.

"No, vulgarian; I meant heavenly music. Music such as ne'er was heard on earth before—let's hope! . . . But what's all this got to do with the dog? The dog may be dying while we trifle thus—dying of a broken heart."

"Oh, don't say such dreadful things, Beau," begged the little girl.

"Nothing dreadful about that," replied the boy called Beau, manfully checking the horse's obvious desire to bolt. "Compliment to the dog. D'you mean to suggest that the callous brute is not by now dying of a broken heart?"

"Spare a father's feelings," requested his twin, and wiped away a tear. "It's *my* dog. . . . And what we want to know, Sir, if you could be quiet for one second, is—er—have you seen a dog?"

"Often," I replied, trying to enter into the light inconsequent spirit of this joyous charming band.

"Where?" they inquired simultaneously.

"Oh, Wyoming, Texas, Oregon, Nevada. . . ."

"Nirvana?" inquired the owner of the dog. "Then dogs do go there. Good."

"California," I continued. "Boston, New York, Paris, London, Brandon Regis. . . ."

"He's getting 'warm,' " said Beau.

"Brandon Abbas?" prompted his twin.

"I'm not certain," I replied. "I rather think I did, though. . . ."

And here the little girl broke in.

"Oh, do stop talking nonsense, Beau and Digby and John. . . ."

"Not talking at all," said John, through whose arm the girl's hand was tucked.

"Well *do*, then, and say something sensible," was the feminine reply, and she turned to me.

"We've lost our dog, and he can't have been in *all* those funny places you said. Have you seen her here? Will you help me find her —for I do love him so?"

"Why, *of course* I will," I said, and added impulsively, "I'd do anything you asked me. *I'll* find him if he or she is alive."

And the twins on the front seat, promptly assisted by John, thereupon simultaneously chanted what appeared to be a family *cliché*.

"*Oh—isn't—he—a—nice—boy. . . . He—must—come—and— play—with—us. . . . Won't—Auntie—be—pleased. . . .*"

"What's the dog like?" I inquired of the one whom they called Digby. "What breed, if any? And what sex?" as there seemed to be a variety of opinions on this point.

"Sex? Oh—er—she's a bitchelor—feminine of bachelor, you know," replied Digby. . . . "As to what she's *like*," he continued, "that's a difficult question to answer. She's rather like. . . . No, she isn't. . . . She isn't a bit like a giraffe, really. . . . No. . . . She's rather like—a dog. Yes. . . . She is. . . . And she is one of these new Andorran Oyster-Hounds. . . ."

"Oh, good! That's helpful," I said appreciatively, while four pairs of bright young eyes summed me up. I was being weighed, and most earnestly I hoped I should not be found wanting.

"An idea," I exclaimed. "What name does she answer to?"

"She never answered *me*," replied Digby, and turning to his twin inquired, "Did she ever back-answer you, Beau?"

"Never a cheep out of her," was the reply. "Not a word. Sulky beggar."

"Not at all," contradicted John, "merely respectful. . . . Reserved, taciturn chap. . . . Strong silent dog."

"Well, she always answers *me*, anyhow," asserted the little girl warmly. "She always *smiles*. . . . He has a most lovely smile," she added, turning to me.

"Now we're getting on," I declared. "I'm to search for a dog that is very like a dog and answers with a smile. . . . Now what is the likeliest way to win her smile? What shall I call her when I see her?"

"Call her home," said Digby.

"I don't know *what* you'll call her when you see her," said Beau. "Have you a kind nature and a gentle tongue? . . . You must tell us later what you *did* call her when you saw her. . . . Especially if you called her it in American."

"Darned gosh-dinged gol-durned dod-gasted smell-hound?" suggested Digby.

"I've never heard the expressions," I replied, "but I'll try to remember them if you think them appropriate. . . . But to get back to the dog."

"It's what we want to do," replied Digby, "or to get her back to us. You don't know the state I'm in. Am I out in a rash?"

"No. In a dog-cart," said Beau, "and you won't be in that long, when we start playing chariots. . . . Well, goodbye, old chap. Thanks awfully. I hope you haven't bored us—I mean we haven't. . . ."

"Stop, stop, Beau," cried the little girl, turning round and thumping the boy's broad back. "He's going to be a search-party and we haven't told him what he wants to know, yet. . . . I think he's most awfully kind and nice. . . . And we ought to help him to . . ."

"Oh, *yes*, Beau," said Digby in a tone of deep reproach, "when he's in such trouble about a dog. . . . Of course we must help him. Now let's see," he continued. "It's got four canine teeth."

"I should think all a dog's teeth are canine," observed John judicially.

"And five toes on his fore-feet."

"That makes twenty," remarked Beau.

"And four on each hind one. . . . He wags his tail from left to right; not right to left. . . . You get the idea, don't you? Like a pendulum. Or an Aberdonian his head, when asked to subscribe."

"But hasn't she a *name?*" I interrupted.

"A *name?*" replied Digby. "Now that's an idea. That's really helpful. Oh, yes, I know she's got a name because I was at the christening—but I've clean forgotten most of it. . . . What's her name, Beau?"

"Well—I always call him Jasper Jocelyn Jelkes, but I think of her as Mrs. Denbigh-Hobbes of The Acacias, Lower Puffleworth."

"Oh, do stop rotting," begged John, and turning to me assured me that the dog's name was Simply-Jones, though generally addressed as Mr. Featherstonehaugh—whereat the little girl was moved to climb down on to the step at the back of the cart, and jump to the ground. Coming round to where I stood, she seized my arm and proceeded to lead me down the lane.

"Come away from those sillies, American Boy," she said, "and I'll just tell you all about it, and you *will* find her for me, won't you? She is Digby's dog, but it's me she loves, and I know she's grieving and sorrowing like anything, for she has such a nice loving nature and a good heart. Her name is Joss and she's middle-sized and middle-aged and sort of middleish altogether—not exactly a spaniel nor a terrier nor a hound, but just a dog, and if you call '*Joss, Joss, Joss, Joss, Jossie!*' in a kind sweet voice, rather high, she'll run to you and smile like anything. You'll know her by her smile. You *will* find her, won't you? Our home's at Brandon Abbas —Auntie is Lady Brandon."

"If she's alive on this earth, I'll find her," I said.

"Isobel! *Hi!* Isobel!! *Isobel!!* Come on, if you want to be Boadicea," came borne on the breezes, and with a "*Thank* you, nice American Boy," and a smile that went straight to my heart—and also to my head—Isobel turned and scampered back.

Later, while searching the world for Joss, I had another glimpse of this party.

The dog-cart driven at a reckless gallop across a great lawn-like field, contained a boy and a girl, both wearing fencing-masks, the girl, armed with a bow and arrow, returning the fire of two presumed Roman soldiers who, with javelin and arrow, assailed the chariot, skilfully driven and controlled by a charioteer.

I was relieved to observe that the horse was apparently accustomed to these martial exercises, and that the chariot came round in a graceful curve before reaching the ditch-and-hedge at the end of the field.

§2

Being a strictly truthful person, I cannot say that I found Jasper Jocelyn Jelkes, *alias* Joss, for it was really she who found me. What her business may have been, I do not know, but she was visiting at High Gables, my grandmother's house, when I returned for lunch.

As I emerged from the shadows of the avenue, I beheld a very nondescript dog sunning herself on the lowest of the white steps of the porch, and smiling, most positively smiling, with extreme fatuity and foolishness, at my Grandmother's tiny Pekinese, a microscopic by-product of the dog-industry, which found no favour in my sight. Lifting up my voice to the level of the hope that rose in my heart, I invoked the smiling caller, in the very tones and accent in which I had been instructed, and in the most mellifluous and wooing way at my command. The excellent Joss, for such, beyond peradventure of a doubt, her conduct proved her to be, lolloped straightway to my feet and sitting on end, smiled and smiled and was not a villain, I felt sure.

"Joss!" I cried, patting that smiling head. "*Dulce ridentem Lalagem amabo*; grinning idiot; Minnehaha, Laughing Water; I'm *very* pleased to meet you. . . . You shall lead me, gentle Jossie, like a blind man's dog, straight to Brandon Abbas, to the house of Aunty, to those delightful boys and to—Isobel. Are you a bit of a card, Jossie? For my visiting-card you shall be. . . ."

Oh, to be seventeen again! Seventeen, on a most glorious English spring day, the day on which you have first encountered the very loveliest thing in all the world—that is to remain, for ever, the very loveliest thing in all your world.

CHAPTER II

After lunch, on that day of days, with Hail Smiling Joss as my sponsor, excuse, and loud note of introduction, I "proceeded," as they say in the British Navy, to the great house of Brandon Abbas, after so feasting the excellent dog that it seemed highly probable she would again lose herself in the direction of High Gables.

Up a few miles of avenue of Norman oaks I tramped, from the Lodge at the gates guarded by heraldic beasts well known to students of Unnatural History—the Returning Wanderer straining at the leash and obviously striving to compose her features to a mask of becoming gravity, tempered by gladness while chastened by shame.

Arrived at a large square of mossy gravel surrounded by a dense shrubbery, I beheld a great porch and an open door through which I had, in passing, a glimpse of a panelled hall, gleaming floor, and suits of armour. A passing glimpse, because it was clearly obvious that Joss intended me to pass, and my will was not brought into conflict with hers, as I heard shouts and peals of laughter from the band of whom I was in search.

Guided by the now excited dog, I crossed a rose-garden and, by a path through some great old elms and beeches, reached an open space of turf which was a view-point overlooking half the county.

As we burst from the gloom of the wood into the sunshine, a hubbub arose; the four, now augmented by several others, converged upon me, and, with a shriek of joy, as she sped forward ahead of the rest, the little girl literally flung herself upon me, threw her arms about my neck, and kissed me warmly. Truth compels me to add that she promptly did precisely the same to the errant Joss, who instantly abandoning her expression, pose, and air of a Misunderstood-but-Hopeful-Dog, stood upon her hind legs, her paws against her mistress, wagged her tail and her tongue, and smiled and smiled to the point of laughter.

"Oh, Stout Fella!" cried Beau. "Splendid! Good scout!"

"Put it right there, Mr. Daniel Boone—or are you Kit Carson? Or Buffalo Bill? Or the Pathfinder? . . . Anyhow, you're the Dogfinder," said Digby, extending his hand, and wringing mine powerfully. . . . "A father's thanks . . . The Prodigal Dog . . . Good mind to *kill* the fat-headed calf!" and seizing the dog in his arms, he rolled upon the ground in apparently terrific combat with the savage beast, who, with horrid growls and furious barks, worried the throat of her fiercely-stabbing antagonist, and bloodlessly bit him with all her canine teeth.

"In the end, I die, having saved all your lives from a mad dog, and so find a hero's grave," announced Digby. . . . "The dog was born mad," he added, and lay motionless, while the Andorran Oyster-Hound surveyed her tooth-work, wagged her tail joyously, and seated herself upon the chest of her victim.

The youngest brother, meanwhile, having slipped his hand inside my arm, while he critically watched the progress of the fight, stood by my side as I waited—holding the grubby little paw which Isobel had thrust into my hand—and feeling unreasoningly and unreasonably happy.

"I say," said the boy, "you ought to join the Band. Will you? Would you like to?"

"Oh *yes*," chimed in Isobel. "*Do*, American Boy. . . . Have you ever been tortured by Indians, or been the Victim of a Cruel Fate, like Mazeppa? Do you think we might roast you at the stake? . . . We've all got mustangs, and Joss is quite a good wolf or coyote. She's being a wolf now, and she's not mad at all—not even half-witted."

"Not nearly half," agreed Digby, arising. "Er—this is—er—the Captain—Michael Geste, Captain of the Band. I am Digby Geste, Lieutenant of the Band. The object on your right hand is John Geste, or Very Small Geste, or Not-Much-of the Band. The female prisoner is Isobel Rivers, the Music of the Band. The beautiful woman enthroned yonder is Claudia, Queen of the Band; and the gentleman at present struck dumb by toffee-on-the-jaw, is Augustus Brandon, and can't be helped. I may add that, as you doubtless suppose, he is not such a fool as he looks. How could he be? . . . The small fat boy and girl on the pony are twins, Marmaduke and—er—Marmaduchess. Marmaduke's step-mother, who eats vinegar with a fishhook three times a day, says he is Wholly Bad. We call him the Wholly of Whollies. Marmaduchess is of course the Roly of Polies. . . . These camp followers—scamp-followers—er—no, that won't do, as they follow the Captain, are Honorary Members of the Band. In view of your great services, I have the pleasure . . ."

"You'll have the pleasure of bread-and-water and six of the best, if you don't take a holiday," interrupted the Captain of the Band, and proceeded most warmly to invite me to become an

Honorary Member of "Beau Geste's Band," and to take part in all its doings, for so long as the country was enriched by my presence, and whenever my inclinations prompted me so to do.

Gratefully accepting the Band's hospitality, I was initiated and enrolled, and quickly appointed stage-manager of its activities in its Western American manifestations, and became its authority upon the dark ways of Red Indians, Bad Men, Buffalo Bills, Cow-boys, Deadwood Dicks, and other desperadoes.

I won my spurs (but did not wear them) by finding myself able to catch, mount, and ride a horse that was loose in the paddock. A horse that had never been ridden before and apparently intended never to be ridden again. . . .

After a most delightful tea with these extraordinarily charming young people, I walked back to High Gables feeling happier, I think, than I had ever felt in my life. It was a rather wonderful thing to me, a lonely stranger in a strange land—for there was nobody but my Grandmother and her servants at High Gables—suddenly to find myself a member of so attractive a society, a family so friendly, so welcoming, so uncritically hospitable that, almost on sight, they had admitted me to membership of their Band, with all the privileges attaching thereto. . . .

But as I lay awake in bed that night, the picture most vividly before me was the beautiful face of the darling child who had given me that sweet spontaneous kiss of gratitude and innocence.

It surely was the nicest thing that had ever happened to me.

§2

I shall be believed when I state that I missed few opportunities of accepting the warm invitation to "come again soon" which invariably accompanied the farewells at the end of each of my visits to Brandon Abbas. The more I saw of the three Gestes, the better I liked them, and I knew that I could never see too much, nor indeed enough, of Isobel Rivers—that lovely little fairy; charming and delightful child; ineffably sweet, and absorbingly interesting, little friend. . . .

Of the boys, I liked John best; for, in addition to all the attributes which he possessed in common with his brilliant brothers, he was, to me, slightly pathetic in his dog-like devotion to the twins, who ruled him with a rod of iron, chastened and chastised him for the good of his soul, kept him in subjection, and loved him utterly. In return for their unwavering and undemonstrated love, he gave them worship. They would have died for him, and he would have died under torture for them.

Yet, at the same time, I like Beau enormously; for his splendour—and it was nothing less—of mind, body and soul; his unselfish sweetness and gentleness, and his extraordinary "niceness" to everybody, including myself. Even when he had occasion to punish a member of his Band, it appeared to me that the victim of his arbitrary justice rather enjoyed the honour of being singled out, even for admonition and the laying on of hands. . . .

But then, again, I liked Digby as much; for his unfailing mirth and happiness. He was a walking chuckle, and those who walked through life with him chuckled too. He was merriment personified; his day was a smile; and if he fell on his head from the top of a tree, the first use he made of his recovered breath was to laugh at the extraordinarily amusing funniness of Digby Geste's falling thirty feet and nearly breaking his neck. . . . He was the most genuinely and spontaneously cheerful person I ever met, and somehow one always laughed when Digby began to laugh, without waiting for the joke.

Isobel was their pet, their fairy, their mascot, their dear perfect play-mate; and Claudia was their Queen—"Queen Claudia, of Beau Geste's Band"—held in the highest honour and esteem. They loved and obeyed Claudia; but they petted and adored Isobel.

I suppose Claudia was of an immaculately flawless beauty, charm, and grace of form and face, even as a young girl—but personally I never liked her. There was a slight hardness, a self-consciousness and an element of selfishness in her character, that were evident—to me at any rate, though not, I think, to the others. Certainly not to Michael Geste, for she was obviously his *beau idéal* of girlhood, and he, her self-constituted paladin and knight-errant. When they played "tournaments" she was always the Queen of Beauty, and he her Champion, ready, willing and able, to dispose of all who disputed his (or her) claim that she was the loveliest damsel in all the world. . . .

Nor could I like Lady Brandon, fascinating as she was to most. She was kind, gracious and hospitable to me, and I was grateful—but *like* her I could not. She was an absolute re-incarnation of "Good" Queen Bess, and I do not think any living woman could have better impersonated Queen Elizabeth than she, whether on the stage or off. Although beautiful in her way, she was astoundingly like the portraits of that great unscrupulous Queen, and, in my belief, she resembled her in character. She was imperious, clever, hard, "managing" and capable. She was very queenly in appearance and style, given to the cherishing of favourites—Michael and Claudia especially—and extremely jealous. She was a woman of strong character and could be both ruthless and unscrupulous. At least, that is the impression I formed of Lady Brandon—and I am very intuitive, as well as being a student of physiognomy, and possessed of a distinct gift for reading character.

No, I disliked Lady Brandon and I distrusted her—and I thought that she and Claudia were not unlike in character. . . . I was very intrigued when my Grandmother dryly remarked, "Henry VIII is, I believe the '*Rex*' of Brandon '*Regis*,' " when, in reply to a question of hers anent Lady Brandon, I had observed, "She reminds me of Queen Elizabeth—"

She resembled the Queen, too, in her power of inspiring great love in men, a noble love, worthy of a nobler object. . . .

On one of my visits to the Band, I was scolded for my absence of several days—I had been to London, on business of my Father's—and told that I had missed the chance of a lifetime, a chance of seeing and hearing a veritable Hero of Romance, a French officer of Spahis, son of a senior school friend of Lady Brandon's, who had been week-ending at Brandon Abbas, and who had for ever endeared himself to the children, by his realistic and true tales of Desert warfare, and of adventures in mysterious and romantic Morocco.

Promptly we ceased to be Red Indians, Knights of the Round Table, Crusaders, Ancient Britons, Big Game Hunters, or anything else but Spahis and Arabs, and the three Gestes and I spent a portion of our lives in charging—mounted on two ponies, a donkey and a carriage-horse—a *douar* of gorse-bushes stoutly defended by a garrison of Arabs clad in towels, sheets and night-shirts and armed with pea-shooters, bows and arrows, lances, swords and spears, toy rifles and pistols which made more sound than sorrow.
. . .

The Band certainly "lived dangerously," but accidents were few and slight, and the absolute freedom permitted to the children, as soon as morning lessons with the Chaplain were finished, was really not abused. Being trusted, they were trustworthy, and the Captain led the Band not into temptation irresistible, nor into more than right and reasonable danger.

This chaplain was a puzzle to me. I felt certain he was essentially good, honourable and well-meaning; but he struck me, in my youthful intolerance, as being too weak and feeble in character to be worthy of the name of man. Certainly he was well-placed in the skirted cassock that he wore; and that, together with his sweet and gentle face and manner, seemed to put him in a class apart—neither man nor woman, just sexless priest. He loved the children devotedly—and was more like a mother than a father to them. Lady Brandon, he obviously adored. He too, was one of this queenly and imperious woman's favourites, and her handsome face would soften to a great gentleness when she walked and talked with him upon the terrace.

It was an extraordinarily interesting household, and when the time came for me to return home and prepare to go to Harvard, I was extremely sorry.

It was with a slight lump in my throat that I spent my last afternoon with the Band, and with a miserable turmoil in my heart that I said good-bye to them. They, too, seemed genuinely sorry that I was going, and seriously considered John's proposal that they should accompany me *en masse*, at least as far as Wyoming, where they might remain and adopt the profession of cow-puncher.

I think I walked back to High Gables that afternoon as quickly as I had ever walked in my life, for I was trying to walk away from myself, from my misery, from the sense of utter loss and desolation.

I was astounded at myself. . . . Why was I feeling this way? What had happened to me? I had not felt so wretched, so bereaved, so filled with a sense of loss and loneliness, since my Mother died. . . . I was like a man who, stricken with some sudden mortal pain, strives to account for it, and cannot do so. . . .

Isobel had put her arms round my neck and kissed me good-bye.

"You *will* come back soon, nice American Boy?" she had said. And I had positively been unable to answer anything at all. I could only laugh and nod my head in assent.

That night, being absolutely unable to sleep, I rose from my bed, dressed, and, creeping quietly from the house, walked to Brandon Abbas to see, as I told myself, how that ancient pile looked by the light of the full moon. . . .

Next day I began my journey, suffering horribly from home-sickness—sickness for the home of my heart—Brandon Abbas. Each mile that I was carried, by train and ship and train again, from that lovely place, increased my misery, and when at length I reached my Father's ranch, I had hard work to hide it from my sister Mary, that dear determined and forceful young woman. My Father—my hard, overbearing, autocratic Father—was not given to noticing whether others were wretched or not, and my kid sister, Janey, was too young. Noel, the eldest of our family, was still "missing," and my Father professed neither to know nor to care where he was. . . .

However, I soon began to enjoy my sweet unhappiness, and I lived on horseback until the day came when I must go East to college, and leave this free and glorious open-air life behind me.

As a matter of fact, I went willingly enough, for I loved books, and desired above all things to become a fine scholar. . . . I considered "My mind to me a kingdom is," to be a grand saying if one could say it (to oneself only, of course) with real truth. . . . I could never understand Noel's flat refusal to study anything but horses, Nature, and the lore of the Indian and the Plainsman; nor his oft-expressed view that education is not of books but of life. Nothing, according to Noel, could educate one for life except life itself; and books and schooling could but educate one for more schooling and books, the examination-hall, and the realms of false values. And yet he read the books that he liked, my wonderful brother Noel—but to school and college he would not go, and thither not even my dynamic and violent Father could drive him.

"Honour thy father and thy mother" . . . We could not do otherwise than honour Mother, as well as love her almost to the point of adoration.

What shall I say of my terrible Father? We did honour him. We respected him and most certainly we obeyed him—all of us but Noel, that is. Noel ceased to obey him as soon as he was big and old enough to stand up for Mother.

His refusal to go to school and college was, I believe, due to his wish, that he might be near her and take her part. Nor did he leave home until the day when he found that in his wrath he had pulled his gun on Dad, and realized that he had to choose between that sort of thing—and departure.

He departed, and returned after a quarter of a century in such wise as I shall relate.

My Father was not a bad man. He was a very "good" one. He was not cruel, vicious, nor vindictive; but he was a terror and a tyrant. He crushed his wife and broke her spirit, and he turned his children into rebels, or terrified "suggestibles."

Noel and Mary were rebels. Janey and I were cowed and terrified.

Of all the marvellous deeds for which, as a child, I worshipped Noel, his defiance of my Father, was to me by far the most wonderful.

At different times, my Father in his austerity and tenacity reminded me of Abraham Lincoln; in his rugged and ferocious "piety," of the prophet Elijah, John Wesley, Brigham Young, and John Knox. There was something in him, too, of Mr. Gladstone, of Theodore Roosevelt, and a good deal of William Jennings Bryan at his most oratorical, most narrow, and most dogmatic.

And there was undoubtedly something in him of King David of Jerusalem. Yes, most undoubtedly there were many points of strong resemblance between my Father and that brave, strong, wily man, that pious and passionate king.

And a king, in his own wide realm, my father was, brooking scarcely a suggestion, much less a contradiction, from any man—a king terribly and unhappily aware of the state of sin in which lived all his subjects, especially those of his own household.

He believed that the Bible had been dictated—in English of course—by God, and that to take it other than literally was damnation and death. He almost flogged Noel to death when, at the age of sixteen or so, the latter impiously dared to wonder how Noah gathered in both the polar bears *and* the kangaroos, for his menagerie, and how he built the fifty-thousand-ton liner necessary for the accommodation of all the animals and their food.

This was after Father's return from a trip to Europe to buy a twenty-thousand-dollar pedigree prize Hereford bull, and the finest pure-bred Arab stallion that money could purchase.

During his absence, Noel had caught out the overseer, a pious-seeming hypocritical rascal, in whom Father firmly believed; had thrashed him, and run him off the Ranch.

Undoubtedly Noel had saved Father a great deal of money and unmasked an unmitigated rascal, and for this, I verily believe, Father hated him the more, and never forgave him.

Yes, Father certainly spoilt Noel's life and made him the wanderer that he became.

To this day, when I have a nightmare, and I have a good many, it is generally of a terrible conflict with my Father, and I awake sweating and trembling with indignation, rage and horror.

For, in the dream, he always rushes at me, bawling invective, his face inflamed with rage, and, seizing me by the throat he raises his cutting-whip to thrash the wickedness out of me, as he so often did in reality. And, to my horror, I find myself clenching my fist to smash that mask of mad ferocity, and then I realize that I am about to strike my own Father, in my indignation that I, a grown man, should be treated thus.

It sounds nothing, but it is a *dreadful* dream.

"Honour thy father" . . . I believe that Mother worshipped him and feared him, and I believe that I, subconsciously, hated him most bitterly, while I consciously respected and feared him.

To the world, our little western world, he was a great man—a man of his word, a strong man, a dangerous man to cross, a good friend and a bad enemy.

One of Mary's *obiter dicta* on the subject of Father sheds a great light on his strong and complex character.

"Father has never done wrong in his life," said she, "for whatever Father does is right—in the sight of Father."

Mary inherited much of Father's strength and force of will, as well as much of Mother's attractiveness.

She was a girl of character, and what she set her heart on, she got. If Father's strength were that of granite, iron and adamant, hers was the strength of tempered steel, for she was pliant and knew when to bend that she might not break. She managed Father and refused to be crushed. Where Noel openly defied and fought him, she secretly defied and out-manœuvred him.

Father certainly loved her—as men do their daughters—and I think Mary loved him, up to a point.

§3

Much as I enjoyed everything, from books to base-ball, at glorious Harvard, I found myself obsessed with the desire to visit England again. Nor was it wholly due to a yearning to see the fine face of my kindly-caustic Grandmother Hankinson once more. Greatly I yearned to revisit Brandon Regis at the earliest opportunity—for Brandon Regis is but a pleasant walk from Brandon Abbas.

I wanted to see the Geste boys again—and I wanted to see Isobel. . . . That's the plain fact of the matter—I wanted to see Isobel. Every single separate day of my life I wanted to see her.

I do not say that, during my Harvard years, I mooned about in a hopeless state of calf-love, a ridiculous young sentimentalist, nor that her lovely little face came ever and ever between me and the printed page, and was always in my mind, sleeping and waking, playing and working—but I certainly admit that I thought of her regularly. . . .

It was my practice nightly, on laying my head on the pillow, to project my mind to the Park of Brandon Abbas, and to enter into a lovely secret kingdom of my own, and there to dwell, happy, remote, and in lovely peace, until I fell asleep.

This kingdom was shared by Isobel, and we two—devoted friends—did delightful things together; had wonderful talks; explored a world of utter beauty; and walked hand-in-hand in a fairyland of joy and fun and laughter. . . .

I am not sure but that this was my real life, at that time; this and the dreams that followed almost invariably, when I fell asleep. Certainly, it was so real that I looked forward to it each day, and if not consciously doing so, was always half-aware and semi-conscious of something delightful that was in store for me, something good and sweet and precious, something "nice" that was coming to me. And when I analysed this feeling of joyous promise I found that it was my soul's anticipation of its visit to the Kingdom of Enchantment where Isobel would meet me and we would walk and talk and laugh together in our Paradise Unlost.

When a sleep-dream followed the consciously induced day-dream, I always awoke from it to minutes of ineffable happiness, a happiness experienced at no other time and in no other way. . . . I felt *good*. . . . And I realized how singularly blessed was Otis H. Vanbrugh, above other men. Nor did the corollary escape me—how incumbent it was upon me to keep myself fit to enter our lovely secret kingdom, and worthy to meet Isobel there.

I do not think that what are supposed to be the inevitable and terrible temptations of wealthy young men at College, existed for me at all. Late hours would have been hours that made me late for the Secret Garden; the odour of wine was not one that would mingle favourably with that of the dewy roses there; nor could one who was daily privileged to commune with Isobel, find the faintest possible charm or attraction in the halls of the Paphian dames. . . . So I filled my days with work, read hard and played hard, lived dangerously when living in the West, pursued with ardour there the study of International Law and of the ways of the mountain lion and of the grizzly bear, and earned the warm approval of my brave and hardy sister, Mary. . . .

And imagine if you can, the frame of mind in which, at the end of my College days, I sailed for Europe—on a visit to a life-long friend of my Father's, who was then our Ambassador to France—and incidentally to visit my Grandmother at Brandon Regis. . . .

As I stepped from the Southampton-London boat-train at Waterloo Terminus, another train was in the act of departure from the opposite side of the same platform, and gliding forward with slowly increasing speed. At a window, waving a handkerchief to three young men, was a girl, and, with a queer constriction of the heart, a rush of blood to the head, and a slight trembling of the whole body, I realized that the girl was Isobel Rivers—the child Isobel, grown up to most lovely girlhood . . . wonderfully the same and yet different. . . . She had put her hair up. . . .

In the baggage-car of my own train were my cabin-trunks and portmanteaux. In the hands of a porter were already my suit-case and grip. Without ceremony, I rushed across that broad platform, threading my way through the crowd like a football-forward in a hurry. As I reached the now quickly-moving train, seized a door-handle and ran swiftly while I turned it, an official of some sort made a grab at me and shouted, "Stand back! You can't get in there, sir," in fiercely indignant remonstrance, not so much at my daring to break my neck as at my daring to break a railway bye-law.

"Hi! You can't get in there," he roared again.

"Watch me," I replied, eluding him, and swung myself on to the foot-board as the door came open. "I won't hurt your train," I shouted back, as he was left gesticulating in sorrow and in anger, at the end of the platform.

In the compartment that I then entered, were three Englishmen and an Englishwoman. Not one of them looked up as I took my seat, nor spoke to me nor to each other during the long hours of non-stop run that ensued. . . .

Wonderful people, the English! . . .

And there I sat in that antediluvian non-corridor car through those long hours, my baggage abandoned, my hotel reservation unclaimed, my destination unknown; but with the knowledge that Isobel Rivers and I were in the same train and that I should speak to her just as soon as that prehistoric Flying Dutchman, or Roaring Rocket, reached its destination or first stopping-place.

In spite of cold, hunger, disorientation, and a certain slight anxiety as to the ultimate fate of my baggage, those were, I verily believe, among the happiest hours of my life; and when the train slowed down—it must have slowed down, I suppose, though no change of speed was to me perceptible—to decant its phlegmatic inhabitants at Exeter, I, the last man into that train, was certainly the first man out.

§4

Isobel, I am most perfectly sure, was really unfeignedly glad to see me, and Lady Brandon very kindly pretended to be. I knew that Isobel was glad because, as she recognized me, that wonderful sparkle—a kind of dancing light, that indescribable lighting-up, as though with an internal illumination, that always signalized and beautified her joy—came into her eyes. One reads of people dancing with pleasure and jumping for joy. Isobel did not do these things, but her eyes did, and one could always tell when a gift or a jest or any happening had given her real pleasure, by watching her eyes.

I had often heard John Geste say "*That*'ll make Isobel's eyes shine" when there was something amusing to tell her, or some piece of good news; and I thought to myself that surely no-one could conceive a more glorious and wonderful way of spending his life than in bringing this beautiful light to Isobel's eyes.

Imagine, if you can, the joy that it gave me to realize that I had been able to do it now.

"Why," she said as I approached and raised my hat, "the nice American boy! . . . Oh, how lovely! . . . The boys *will* be sorry," and she gave me both her hands in the most delightful and friendly manner.

Lady Brandon gave me both fingers in a less spontaneous and friendly manner that was nevertheless quite pleasant, and—God bless her—invited me to share their compartment in the train to Brandon Abbas and their carriage which would meet them there. She displayed none of the surprise that she must certainly have felt on learning that there was no luggage problem, as I had no luggage. Beneath her half-kindly, half-satirical gaze, I did my best to conceal the fact that, on catching sight of Isobel, I had abandoned everything but hope, and dashed from one train to the other.

I do not know whether selected prophets, such as Elijah, ever found ecstatic joy in their rides in fiery chariots and similar celestial vehicles, but I do know that my short ride by train and carriage with Isobel, was to me the highest summit of ecstatic joy —a pure happiness utterly indescribable and incommunicable—the higher, the greater, and the lovelier for its purity. And it was not until I was deposited at High Gables after leaving Isobel and Lady Brandon at Brandon Abbas, that my soaring spirit came down to earth, and, it having come to earth, I was faced with the problem of explaining my unheralded arrival and the absence of further provision than a walking-stick and one glove. Also, alas, with the realization that I should not see Isobel again, as she and Lady Brandon were going to Wales on the morrow, and, later on, to Scotland on a round of visits. They had been staying in London with the boys, who were now setting off for a walking-tour in Normandy.

However, *I had seen Isobel* and received confirmation—if confirmation were needed—of the fact that not only was she the most marvellous thing in all the world, but that everything else in the world would be as nothing in the balance against her.

I have mentioned this trivial and foolish little incident—which ended next day with my return to London and the pursuit of my baggage—because it was on this night, as I lay awake, that there came to me the great, the very greatest, idea of my life—the idea that I might conceivably, with the help of God and every nerve and fibre of my being, some day, somehow, contrive to make myself worthy to love Isobel and then—incredibly—to be loved by Isobel, and actually to devote my life to doing that of which I had thought when her eyes sparkled and shone at seeing me.

It is curious and true that the idea had never occurred to me before, and I had never envisaged the possibility of such a thing as not only loving her, but being loved by her in return, and of actually walking hand in hand along the path of life in the spirit of sweet and lovely companionship, as we did nightly in our Dream Garden. . . . And there, I remember, a little chill fell upon my heart and checked my fond imaginings, as it occurred to me for the first time that the Dream Garden was a creation of my dreams alone, and not of Isobel's as well. There we met and talked and walked and were dear friends, with a reality as great as that of anything in my real and waking life—but of course, it was only *my* dream, and the real Isobel knew nothing of the Dream Garden.

But did she know nothing? Why should I assume that?

Suppose—only suppose—that she dreamed it, too! Suppose Isobel had this curious and wonderful double life, as I had, and met me in her dreams precisely as I met her, night by night! Absurd, of course, but much too lovely an idea to discard with even pretended contempt. I would ask her the very next time I saw her. How unutterably wonderful if she could tell me that it was so! . . . Moreover, if it *were* so, it would mean *that she loved me*—and, at this, even I laughed at my own folly. Still I would ask her the very next time we met. . . .

But the next time we met, I asked her something else.

CHAPTER III

I suppose that among the very happiest days of my whole life were those I spent on my next journey from New York to Southampton and Brandon Regis. I must have seemed insufferably joyous and pleased with myself. When not actually whistling or singing with my mouth, I was doing it in my heart. I loved everybody. What is less certain is whether everybody loved me. I loved the glorious sunshine, the perfect sea, the splendid ship, the jolly food, the passengers, every one of them, the young, the old, the merry, the grumpy, the active, the lazy, the selfish, the unselfish. . . . If all the world loves a lover, surely a lover loves all the world . . . the great grand glorious world that lies at his exalted feet. . . . The world that contains, and exists to contain, the one and only woman in the world. . . .

I loved the stars, the moon, the marvellous night-sky, the floor of Heaven pierced with millions of little holes through which shone rays of the celestial light—and I sat late and alone, gazing, thinking, dreaming, longing.

I loved the dawn, and late as I may have sat upon the boat-deck at night, I was there again to see the East grow grey and pink and golden, there to welcome and to greet the sun that ushered in one more milestone day upon the brief and lovely road that led to Brandon Abbas and to Isobel.

Brandon Abbas and Isobel! . . . One day, when a poor rich youth whom I comprehended in my universal love—in spite of his pimples, poor jokes, unpleasing ways and unacceptable views— asked me if I were going to Paris, and I replied, "No—to Brandon Abbas," and he, astonished, inquired where that might be, and I answered:

"Next door to Paradise," he rightly concluded that I was out of my mind or else drunk. Doubly right was he, for I was beside myself with joy and drunk with happiness.

Yes; I loved all things; I loved all men; and greatly I loved God.

At Southampton I let the boat-train go upon its foolish way to London, and at the terminus hotel of the South Western Railway I awaited the far far better one that meanders across the green and pleasant land of England to the little junction where one may get one better still, one that proceeds thence to Exeter where waits the best of all—the final and finest train in the wide world—that carries its blest occupants to Brandon Abbas.

I was not sitting in a train made with mortal hands, but in a chariot of fire that was carrying me, ecstatic and uplifted, to the heaven of my dreams, my night-and-day dreams of many years.

From the station I drove, in what to the dull eye of the ordinary beholder was a musty, mouldy carriage, drawn by a moth-eaten and dilapidated parody of a horse, to High Gables, and was welcomed with the apparently caustic kindness and grim friendliness with which my wonderful old Grandmother Hankinson hid her really tender and loving nature.

And next day I walked over to Brandon Abbas.

I remember trying, on the way, to recollect some lines I fancied I had read. Were they written by the Marquis of Montrose or had Queen Elizabeth scratched them with a diamond on a window-pane for the encouragement of some young adorer? Was it, "*He either fears his fate too much, Or his deserts are small, Who dares not put it to the touch, To win or lose it all.*". . . ? Something like that anyhow, and probably written by Montrose.

Well, my deserts were small enough, and at times I feared my fate, but I was certainly going to put it to the touch before I went away, if I stayed for a year or a life-time.

I was going to tell Isobel that I loved her—had loved her unceasingly and increasingly, from the moment that I had seen her, a lovely child sitting in a dog-cart, and much concerned about a dog.

True—I was utterly and wholly unworthy of her, but so was everybody else. I had nothing to recommend me but an absolutely perfect and unquenchable love—but I was not ineligible from the point of view of such a person as Lady Brandon, for example. I was a foreigner, an American, but I had roots in this very soil, through my Mother. I was obscure and unknown, but that could very quickly be put right if I became Isobel's husband. That alone would be a great distinction, but I would undertake to add to it, and to promise that Isobel's husband should one day be the American Ambassador to St. James's, to Paris, to St. Petersburg—any old where she liked. . . . President of the United States of America, if she set her heart on his being that. . . . I was very far from being poor, and should not be far from being very rich, someday.

Thirty-cent things of that sort would be quite germane and

material in the eyes of Queen Elizabethan Lady Brandon. To my mind, the only really relevant thing was that I loved Isobel to the point of worship and adoration, and that this love of mine had not only stood the test of time, but had gained from Time himself—for the wine of love had mellowed and matured, grown better, richer, sweeter, nobler, year by year. . . .

Poor boy! . . .

I turned in at the Lodge gates, and walked up the long drive of which I knew every Norman tree.

Good old Burdon, the perfect butler, fine flower of English retainerhood, was in the hall as I appeared in the porch, and greeted me in the perfect manner of the perfect servant, friendly, welcoming, respectful.

But Her Ladyship was Not at Home. . . .

Miss Claudia was Not at Home. . . .

Miss Isobel was Not at Home. . . .

Mr. Michael, Mr. Digby, and Mr. John were Away from Home. . . .

Nothing for it but to leave my cards and depart, more than a little dashed and damped.

I walked down the drive less buoyantly than I had walked up it. It actually had not entered my silly head that one could go to Brandon Abbas and not find Isobel there. . . . The sunshine was not so bright nor the sky so blue, and what had been the sweet singing of the birds, was just a noise. . . .

And as I rounded a turn in the drive, my heart rounded and turned and drove, for a girl was riding toward me, a little girl on a big horse. The loveliest, dearest, kindest girl in all the wide world. . . .

My heart turned right-side-up, pulled itself together, and let me get my breath again. . . . *Isobel.* . . .

The sun shone gloriously bright and warm, the sky was a deep Italian blue, the English song-birds were birds from Paradise—and Isobel held out a gloved hand which I took and pressed to my lips as she smiled sweetly and kindly and said:

"Why! It's our nice American Boy come back! I *am* so glad . . . Otis . . ." and then I knew that something was wrong. Her voice was different; older. Her face was different; older. She was unhappy. . . .

"What is the matter, Isobel?" I asked, still holding her little hand as she bent toward me from her big horse.

"Oh . . . Otis. . . . How did you know? . . . *John has gone.* . . . The boys have gone away. . . ."

Her lip trembled and there was a suspicion of moisture in her eyes.

"Can I help? . . . *Let* me help you, Isobel," I begged.

"There's nothing you can do—thank you so much," she said. "It's nice of you. . . . I am so glad to see you again, Otis. . . . I have been so wretched. There is no-one I can talk to, about it. . . ."

"There is," I said. "There's me," and I think that moment marked the absolute top-most pinnacle of happiness that I have ever known, for Isobel pressed my hand hard.

"I'll tell you a great secret," she said, and smiled so sweetly through the unshed tears that I could scarcely forbear to reach up and lift her from her horse, lift her into my arms, my heart, and my life.

"I'll tell *you*, Otis. . . . Keep it a secret though," she added. And then Isobel said the words that in that second cut my life into two distinct halves. . . .

"*John and I are engaged to be married.* . . ."

No—she couldn't have said that. I assured myself that she had not said *that*. These queer hallucinations and strange waking dreams! . . . She had not said that. . . . I was not standing staring and open-mouthed, and watching, watching, watching for years and life-times and ages and æons, while two great tears slowly formed and gathered and grew and rolled from her eyes. . . . One did not splash upon my hand as she said:

"And he has had to go away. . . . And I am so miserable, Otis. . . . We were engaged one evening and he was gone the next morning! . . . And I have no-one to talk to, about him. . . . I am so *glad* you have come. . . ."

But a tear *did* splash on my hand. She *did* say it.

"You and John Geste are engaged to be married, Isobel?" I asked, gently and carefully, very very gently and very very carefully, to keep my voice level and steady, to keep myself well under control. . . .

I heard myself say the words, and I watched her face to see whether I had said them normally. . . . Or had I not said them at all? . . . I had uttered some words certainly. . . .

Her face did not change. . . .

"Yes, Otis," she said. "And I had to tell somebody! . . . I am glad it was *you*. You are the only person, now, who knows. You'll be the first to congratulate me. . . ."

Yes. *I* should be *the* first person to congratulate her!

"I congratulate John—and you—Isobel," I said, "and from the bottom of my heart I hope that every hour of your life will be a happy one."

"Thank you, Otis," she said. "That is nice and dear of you. . . . Oh, I shall be almost too happy to breathe . . . when John comes back. . . .

"You'll come and see us again, won't you? Aunt Patricia will be delighted to see you. . . . And we'll go for some rides, you and I. . . . I do so want to talk to you—*about John*."

Words of excuse rose to my lips. I must go to London to-morrow. I must hurry over to Paris. Some business for my Father. After that I must go quickly back to America, and so forth. . . . But before I had spoken, I had a swift vision of a face I knew well, though I had only seen it in dreams. A hard clean-cut cruel face, grim, stern and stoical, the face of that Indian Chief who was the father of my father's grandmother—the face of a man from whom no sign of anguish was ever wrung, a man to whom pain was as a friend, proven and proving.

"Thank you very much indeed, Isobel," I said. "I shall love to ride with you—and—talk about John." . . .

(Thank *you*, also, great-great-grandfather.)

Yes, it would give her pleasure. I would ride with her—and *talk about John*!

During the next month I saw Isobel almost daily, Lady Brandon occasionally, the Chaplain once or twice, and the girl, Claudia, from time to time.

Isobel and I talked unceasingly of John. I thought of things that would please her—dug up what had been fragrant joyous memories.

She did not tell me where he was, being, I supposed, pledged to secrecy, and I asked her no questions as I realized that there was some secret which she was hiding. It occurred to me though, that it must be a mighty strong inducement, an irresistible compulsion, that took John Geste from Brandon Abbas on the day after the declaration of his love for Isobel!

And then, thank God, she went away to stay with friends, and I fled to Paris, plunged into the wildest dreariest round of dissipation (Good God! is there *anything* so devastatingly dreary as pleasure pursued?) and quickly collapsed as reaction set in, reaction from the dreadful strain of those days with Isobel—Isobel and the ever-present absent John.

I was very ill indeed for some weeks, and, when able to do so, crawled home—dropped back again, the burnt charred stick of that joyous rocket that had rushed with such brilliant soaring gaiety into the bright sky of happiness. . . .

Finished and down—like a dead rocket. . . .

§2

Things were, on the whole, rather worse than usual at home. My Father was becoming more and more tyrannical and unreasonable, and my sisters were reacting accordingly. Strong Mary, the rebel, home from College, was fast approaching both the snapping-point of her temper and the frame of mind in which Noel had cast off the dust of the ranch from his feet and the shackles of his Father from his soul, mind, and body.

Weak Janey, the "suggestible," was fast approaching the end of her existence as an individual, a separate identity, and was rapidly becoming a reed, bending in the blast of her Father's every opinion, idea and wish; a straw upon the mighty rushing waters of his life; thistle-down floating upon the windy current of his mental and physical commotions.

While firmly believing that she loved him, she dreaded the very sound of his footsteps, and conducted the domestic side of his affairs in that fear and trembling of a Roman slave for the master whose smile was sole reward and whose frown portended death.

Filial love is a beautiful thing, but the slow destruction of a character, a soul, a personality, an individuality, is not.

Poor Janey did not think. She quoted Father's thoughts. She did not need or desire anything; she lived to forestall and satisfy Father's needs and wishes. She did not live any life of her own, she lived Father's life and existed to that end.

Janey was abject to Father, and propitiatory to Mary. Mary was defiant and rebellious to Father; and sympathetic but slightly contemptuous, to Janey.

Father was protective, overbearing, loving, violently autocratic and unbearably irritating toward both of them. Apparently he simply could *not* forbear to interfere, even in things in which he had not the faintest right to interfere, and in which a different type of man would have been ashamed to do so.

Of me, he was frankly contemptuous, and what made me boil with anger was not that, nor the way in which he treated me, but the fact that *I was afraid of him*. Time after time, I screwed up my courage to face him and out-face him, and time after time I failed. I could not do it. His fierce eye, his Jovian front, quelled me, and being quelled, I quailed.

It was reserved for my Father to make me a coward, so poor a creature that I could not even stand up for my sisters against him.

But the enemy was, of course, as always, within. Deep down in my unconscious mind were the seeds sown in babyhood, in childhood, in boyhood—the seeds of Fear—and they had taken such root, and grown so strong a weed-crop that I could not pluck them out. When I conceived the idea of refusing to obey some unreasonable order, of asserting my right to an opinion, of remonstrating on behalf of one of the girls, I was physically as well as mentally affected.

I stammered and stuttered—a thing I never did at any other time. I flushed and paled, I perceptibly shook and trembled, and I burst into a cold perspiration. My mind became a blank; I looked and felt and was, a fool; I was not sufficiently effective even to irritate my Father, and with one frowning piercing stare of his hard eyes, one contemptuous curl of his expressive lips, I was defeated, silenced, quelled, brought to heel.

Do not think that our Father was deliberately and intentionally cruel to any of his children. Cruelty is a Vice, and Vice was the abhorrent thing, the very seal and mark of the Devil—footprint of the cloven hoof. Did he not spend his life in the denunciation of Vice in every form and manifestation—though with particular abhorrence and detestation of, peculiar rage and fulminations against, *Sex*—its, to him, most especially shocking and loathsome form?

He was not cruel, but his effect upon us was, and it drove Mary and me to the decision that home was no place for us. . . . We had decided independently—I, that I could not work for, nor with, my Father on the ranch, nor live with him in the house: she, that any place in the wide world would be preferable to the house in which her Father intended that she should live and move and have her being, wholly and solely and exactly as he in his wisdom directed.

We discovered our decisions to each other and agreed to act together when the time came; and, as soon as possible thereafter, to rescue Janey from the loving thraldom and oppression that would turn her into a weak, will-less and witless old maid, an ageing servant in her father's house, before she had been a girl.

It was the "old maid" aspect of affairs that particularly enraged Mary on behalf of both Janey and herself. For on the subject of "young whelps loafing round the place," our Father grew more and more unreasonable and absurd. A presentable man was a suspect, a potential "scoundrel," a thinker of evil who would become a doer of evil if given the slightest opportunity. To such we always alluded as "Means"—by reason of Father's constant quotation of the Shakespearian platitude:

"The sight of *means* to do ill deeds, makes ill deeds done."

Any sort or kind of non-business communication between a man and a woman was, unless they were married according to the (Protestant) Christian Dispensation, undesirable, wrong, improper; and avowed friendship between them was little better than Sin, Vice—nay, was almost certainly but a cloak for Sin.

Strong Mary, the rebel, suffered most perhaps; weak Janey and I suffered much, certainly. But we stuck on somehow, for some reason—"the inertia of matter," apathy, custom, loyalty to Father, and the feeling that our defection would hurt him more even than his interfering, regulating tyranny hurt us. Most of all perhaps, because we knew that Janey would never have the courage nor the "unkindness" to leave him.

It was a very wretched time indeed for me, apart from the fact that I was so spiritually bruised and sore and smashed. My dreams of Isobel came no more, and my day-dreams of her were poignant suffering. I tried to fight the lethargy, the hopelessness, the selfish sorrow of my soul, and to throw myself into the work of the ranch, to live on horseback a life of constant activity, and to find an anodyne in labour.

But I was selfish. . . . I nursed my sorrow. . . . I thought, young fool that I was, that my life was permanently darkened and that none had plumbed such depths of suffering as I.

And I worked on, hopelessly, sunk in a deep and dark Byronic gloom. . . .

§3

It was a dead hand that released Mary and me from the irksome dependence of our captivity. I do not know whether the hand provided "the means to do ill deeds" in providing us with the opportunity to leave our Father and our home, but it certainly gave us the power to choose our paths in life, and we promptly chose the one that led straightest out into the world of men.

The said hand was that of a Bad Old Man, a meretricious ornament of the city of San Francisco, a gay dog, a buck, a lover of Life, who was, alas, my Father's cousin, once his partner, and known to us from our earliest days as Uncle Joe. He had all our Father's strength of will and character; his ability, grit and forcefulness; his uncanny business skill and his marked individuality. But he had none of his fervid piety; none of his Old Testamental patriarchal self-importance; none of his self-righteous domineering violence; and, I fear, but little of his moral integrity, virtue, and highly-conscious rectitude.

In spite of this latter lamentable truth, we children loved him, as our Mother had loved him—and as Father hated him. He corrupted us with treats, gifts, sympathy, and support; he took our part when, as so frequently happened, we were in disgrace; and he endeavoured to sow in our young breasts the seeds of revolt and rebellion against what he considered harshness and oppression.

For some reason I was his favourite. I amused him intensely, and he apparently saw in me merits and virtues which were hidden from other eyes. And the misspelling of a word in a letter that I wrote to him, changed my life and Mary's life, the lives of my Father and of Janey, and indeed of very many other people—for it was the cause of his leaving me a very large sum of money indeed, the money that was my ransom from bondage—and Mary's ransom too.

It had been my innocent and disinterested custom to write a letter to Uncle Joe, upon the occasion of his birthday. On one of these anniversaries, I, being some seven or eight years of age—and having just discovered the expression "hoary old age"—wrote my annual letter and concluded by wishing him eventual safe arrival at such penultimate years. But having acquired the phrase by ear and not by eye, I misspelt a word.

The hoary sinner was delighted beyond measure, roared with laughter, shouted with joyous amusement, and swore then and there that he would make me his heir and leave me every last red cent of which he died possessed. He then rushed forth brandishing the letter, in search of all to whom he might impart the jest, and for days and weeks the bars of San Francisco's clubs, restaurants, saloons and hostelries echoed with laughter and my Uncle's shame.

Such conduct gives the measure of the wickedness of the man

who had been a thorn in the side of my Father—until the day on which the latter felt that he could prosper without him, that Mammon of Unrighteousness, and cast him forth; the man who had been our dear, dear friend; the man to whom Mary and I owed our salvation.

And at this critical moment he died—and he left me all his money.

Of course, what was mine was Mary's, and at the earliest moment we fared forth together, "to seek our fortunes"—though not in the material sense, and to see the World.

A drop of regret in the cup of our joy was the fact that we found it utterly and completely impossible to induce Janey to come with us. She would not "leave Father"—the simple truth being that she lacked the courage to tell him that she was going with us, the courage to let us tell him that she was going with us, the courage even to slip away with us, or to run away and join us after our departure.

There was nothing for it but to leave her at home, though with the most urgent entreaties to join us at any time that she could induce Father to permit her to come, or pluck up sufficient courage to come unpermitted. . . .

Our idea was, of course, to make straight for Paris—the name of which place, Mary declared, was but an abbreviation of the word "Paradise"—and after sating ourselves with its wonders, make the grand tour of Europe. After that we were going to settle down in Paris, and I was going to obtain employment at our Embassy, for I had no liking for the profession of rich-man's-son and idler. Mary was going to keep house for me—but I doubted that it would be my house that she would keep for very long, and so I think did she. . . . Anyhow, that was roughly our programme, and, after what seemed an age of delay, we set forth, without the paternal blessing, to see how far we should carry out the scheme.

CHAPTER IV

Life in Paris was, to Mary, wholly delightful, and to me was at least as good and as bad as life in Wyoming. In point of fact it was wholly lacking in savour wheresoever I might endure it—but in Paris the heavy cloud, that was our Father, was on the far western horizon and no longer obscured the sun—a further exemplification of the ancient truth that they who flee across the sea change nothing but their sky.

Our friends at the Embassy were more than kind to us, and before we departed for London, Rome, Venice, Naples, Athens and finally Algiers, we had a large and delightful circle of acquaintance, French, American and English.

Mary is one of those girls who are "very easy to look at," and the young men of our circle looked. They also danced, dined, drove and flirted with her to her heart's content, if not to theirs.

As I spent my money very freely, she was soon reputed to be the usual fabulously wealthy American heiress, and the report did not lessen her popularity.

Prominent among her admirers was a much-decorated and be-medalled Colonel of Zouaves, a man who might have sat for a portrait of a typical Sergeant of the Old Guard of Napoleon Buonaparte. He was a middle-aged self-made fighting soldier—a man of the kind that one rather admires for excellences of character than likes for graces of mind and person—and I fear he amused Mary almost as much as he loved her. For he was obviously and hopelessly in love, and I do not think that the dollars in any way gilded the refined gold of *La belle Americaine* in the eyes of the tough and grizzled Colonel Levasseur. . . . Poor fellow! . . . Bravely playing his part in the ballroom, or at the garden-party, he reminded me, when dancing attendance on my sister, of a large bear heavily cavorting around a young deer—though I realized that the Colonel would remind me still more of a large bear if I saw him engaged upon his real business, which was fighting.

Here again was coincidence or the hand of Fate—or as some, including myself, would prefer to say—the hand of God. For when, after our European travels, we reached Algeria to bask in winter sunshine, Colonel Levasseur was preparing to set forth, as the point of a lancet of "peaceful penetration," to the fanatical city of Zaguig, a distant hotbed of sedition and centre of disaffection, a desert Cave of Adullam wherein the leaders of every anti-French faction, from eastern Senussi to western Riffian, plotted together and tried to stem the flow of the tide of civilization.

They stood for savagery; for blind adherence to the dead letter of a creed outworn; for ferocious hatred of all that was not sealed of Islam; and for the administration of rapine, fire, and slaughter impartially to those who brought, and those who accepted, northern civilization and its roads, railways, telegraphs, peace, order and cultivation of the soil. . . .

While Zaguig remained secret, veiled, inviolate and aloof, there could be no safety, and, as Colonel Levasseur put it, Zaguig was a boil that the French must lance—that there might be health in the body-politic of a great and growing colony, a future granary and garden and farm for the sons of civilization.

Colonel Levasseur showed better in Algiers than in Paris, and he showed best of all in Zaguig at the head of his men, in his element and on his native heath—or his adopted heath.

For, later on, as I shall tell, I yielded to Mary's impulsive yearnings to go and see a "really unspoilt" desert town, and I accepted Colonel Levasseur's invitation to visit him there, an invitation that coincided with her disillusionment at Bouzen, a spoilt and vulgarized place at the end of the railway, a plague-spot where alleged "desert" Arabs spoke broken French and English to the trippers, and richly earned broken necks every day of their ignoble touting lives.

And to Bouzen from Zaguig came Colonel Levasseur—ostensibly to confer with the Commandant of the big garrison there—fairly quickly after learning that Mary was shedding the light of her countenance on that already well-lighted spot.

He took Mary riding on horse and camel, turning a withering Colonel-glare upon the gay and gorgeous subalterns who had hitherto danced attendance upon her. . . . He amused her and he had the inevitable appeal of the strong man who has done things, who has a fine and big job and holds it down.

And he played up to her growing love of the desert, for she had succumbed to its lure and its loveliness of sunrise, sunset, space, colour, cleanness and enduring mystery. Also he told her that *this* was not the desert—that she had not yet seen the real desert, nor set eyes on a genuine inhabitant thereof, Bedouin, Senussi, Touareg, nor any other. . . . Also, that now was her chance, her chance to cross a tract of the genuine desert-Sahara and see a genuine desert-city, a lion's den whereof he had effectually cowed and tamed the lions. . . .

I asked Mary if the acceptance of his very kind and attractive invitation might not be construed as portending her acceptance of the inevitable proposal of marriage which would most surely ensue, if we entered the said lions' den—whereof Colonel Levasseur was now the lion-tamer—but only to receive the enigmatical reply that sufficient unto the day is the proposal thereof, and that if I did not take her to Zaguig, Colonel Levasseur would.

The which there was no gainsaying—and Mary is a witch whom there is no gainsaying.

The delighted Colonel Levasseur, for some reason, inferred that I had had a helpful hand in Mary's decision to accept his invitation. And he expressed his gratitude to me in various ways, in spite of my denial of deserts.

One took the curious form of insisting upon showing me "life" in Bouzen, by night—*recherché* "life" not seen of the tripper, but solely of the elect—such as highly placed executive officials, for example, only by whose grace and favour, or ignorance and blindness, such "life" could exist.

Most men accept an invitation of this sort, and offer a variety of reasons for so doing. Some allege that "life" is, and must be, interesting to any intelligent person, and murmur "*nihil humanum . . . a me alienum puto,*" adding that none but the fool misses any rare, genuine "local colour" that may be seen; and that, in any case, one would not like to hurt the feelings of the good fellow who had gone to the trouble of providing the opportunity.

As these were precisely my authentic reasons for accepting the invitation, I went with the worthy Colonel—and mine eyes beheld strange things.

We set forth after Mary had said her good-nights, she imagining that we were also about to seek our respective chaste couches.

Nothing was said to her on the subject of our expedition lest she insist upon joining us, and we be put to the shame of telling the truth or of abandoning the tour of the select improprieties. Incidentally I noted, in my mental *dossier* of the Colonel, that he was unselfish enough to devote to me time that might have been spent with Mary had he chosen to announce some different form of nocturnal entertainment, and also that he was of the type that could go straight, from looking upon the face of the beloved lady, to where every prospect pleases only a man who is vile. . . .

Let us, however, concede that it takes all sorts to make a universe, and humbly thank Allah for the diversity of his creatures.

As I had anticipated, I found, once more, that the deadliest, dreariest and dullest pursuit upon which the mind and body of man can embark is the deliberate pursuit of pleasure—that butterfly that flies indeed if chased, but will often settle if ignored—settle and delight the soul of the beholder.

I suppressed all yawns, endeavoured to simulate a polite if not keen interest, and failed to give the worthy Colonel the impression that I was enjoying myself.

So when he asked me if I were doing so, I said:

"Yes, indeed, Colonel" . . . and added, "It is the only thing I *am* enjoying" . . . whereat he laughed, commended my bluntness which matched his own, and promised that I should find the next place stimulating, for I should there encounter the Angel of Death.

I assured him that I was unready, unfit, unworthy; that I did not desire to encounter the Death Angel with all my imperfections on my head; unshriven, unassoiled and unannealed. . . . So young. . . . So promising. . . .

"Wait till you have seen her," replied the Colonel, and I withdrew my objections and listened, as we drove through the silent streets, to his account of the lady whose disturbing and deterrent title was "the Angel of Death," a title well-earned, I gathered, and well-given in return for disservices rendered. . . .

Well, it would be something to make the acquaintance of an incarnate Death Angel, especially if one might then plead fear of anti-climax as an excuse for abandoning the pursuit of pleasure, going straight home, and prosaically to bed.

As the car stopped at a gate in the high wall surrounding a native house and garden, on the outskirts of the town, I, in Hunnish vandal mood, murmured certain lines learned in childhood from Uncle Joe:

> "The Death Angel smote Alexander McCloo
> And gave him protracted repose;
> He had a check shirt and a number nine shoe
> And a very pink wart on his nose."

Well, the Death Angel smote me also, that night, but did not give me protracted repose (nor any protracted lack of repose—at the time).

The brightly-lit scene of our entertainment was the typical compound of the typical house of the wealthy town-Arab, the soft-living degenerate *hadri*, for whom the son of the desert has so great a contempt.

Our host, one Abu Sheikh Ahmed, a rotund well-nourished person with a bad squint, a bad pock-pitted face, and an oily ingratiating manner, received us with every evidence of joy, pride and respectful affection. He seemed grateful to us for existing; declared that all in his house was ours; that we were, each of us, his father and his mother both; and that Allah had this night been merciful and gracious unto him in that He had caused the light of our countenances to shine upon him and illuminate and glorify his humble gathering of guests.

Colonel Levasseur received these transports with dignity and restraint—particularly restraint—and informed me in English that Abu Sheikh Ahmed was a carpet-dealer and had the distinction of being the wickedest, most untrustworthy and most plausible old scoundrel that he had ever met.

"He'd be the first to fly to the Commandant with completest revelations of any plot that could not succeed; and the first to shoot him in the back, or cut his throat, in the event of one that did succeed," said he. "So we take him at his true value and use him for what he is worth. . . . He'll give us an amusing show anyhow. . . ."

He did; a show of which there were two items that, as far as I am concerned, proved quite unforgettable; the one for its hideousness, the other for its beauty—and its sequel.

The former was a "turn" by a troupe of Aissa dervishes, and consisted of maddeningly monotonous music and dancing—the twirling and spinning dancers quickly and obviously falling into a state of hypnosis; of a disgusting exhibition of self-mutilation by means of knives and skewers, driven into the arms, chest and legs and in some cases through the cheeks and even the tongue; of the eating of burning tow; and of the genuine chewing and actual swallowing of quantities of broken glass.

It is not given to the Sons of the Prophet to know the joys of a "next morning" head, as teetotalism is a primary essential of Muhammedanism, but I was moved to ponder the sensations of a "next morning" stomach, after an indiscreetly copious feast of broken glass.

Colonel Levasseur had seen this sort of thing before, and

regarded it with the cold eye of familiarity, if not boredom.

"Enjoying yourself?" he asked me, when the din and devilry were at their climax.

"Not even myself, this time," I replied, and was very glad when these holy men completed their exhibition of piety, and departed. The odour of sanctity was as unpleasing as the saints from whom it emanated.

I do not know whether Mr. Abu Sheikh Ahmed was an amateur of entertainment sufficiently skilful to appreciate the value of contrast, and deliberately to preface the beauty of the next item by the bestial ugliness of this one. Probably not—but certainly the vision of loveliness, that now enthralled the gathering, lost nothing by the juxtaposition.

In the centre of one side of a square, three sides of which were rows of Arab notables, and the fourth, the high white house, the Colonel and I occupied plush-upholstered European arm-chairs of astounding ugliness, while our host and his young son sat cross-legged upon the sofa of the same afflicted and afflicting family, the six pertaining small chairs being allotted to his chief friends, or enemies, who awkwardly sat upon them in dignity and discomfort.

In the guest-surrounded square, servants spread a large thick carpet, a carpet whereof the sheer beauty made me blush—for the European furniture that affronted it and the perfect night and the austere grace of the snowy draperies of the assembly. . . .

A current of awakened interest now ran through the hitter, a movement that announced the arrival of an awaited moment. There was an atmosphere of pleased anticipation that indicated both the *pièce de résistance* and the certainty of high entertainment therefrom.

Brilliant teeth flashed white, as bearded lips parted in joyous smiles. Almost I fancied that pink tongues licked, beast-like, anticipatory, appreciative.

Our host beamed upon us, a pleased and pleasing smile of promise and of pride.

"Behold the Angel of Death," murmured Colonel Levasseur, and a woman appeared at the entrance to the house, walked disdainfully to the carpet, threw off a gauze veil and gazed calmly around.

There was a murmur of admiration, wonder, praise—and appraisal; and I heard Colonel Levasseur sigh and gasp with a little catch of the breath. There was something very simple and elemental about poor Levasseur.

And there was something indescribably arresting, fascinating, wonderful about the real and remarkable beauty of the girl. . . . She was at once pretty, lovely, beautiful and handsome . . . quite indescribable. . . . Yes. . . . She was astounding. . . .

To begin with, she was so fair that you thought her European until you realized her blue-black hair, unbelievable black eyelashes and eyebrows and the Oriental moulding of the cheek-bones and lips—so brunette and Oriental that you thought her the true Arab Princess of a dream of an Arabian Nights' tale, until you realized her white skin, her rose-pink cheeks, her obviously northern complexion and European blood.

Of her figure I can but say it was worthy of her face. It was perfect, and what was to be seen of her neck and limbs was as white as flesh can be. . . .

She was a human flower. . . . An orchid—a white orchid marked with scarlet and with black. And as these flowers always do, she looked wicked—an incarnate, though very lovely, potentiality for evil.

Catching sight, I suppose, of Colonel Levasseur's gay uniform, she came straight to us, or rather floated toward us on her toes, her graceful arms and hands also appearing to float upon the air, quietly waving around her head and body like thistle-down and like gracefulness personified. One forgot the crudeness of the music, for she subordinated it to her purposes, and, becoming part of her and her movement, it was beautiful.

Straight to us she came, and at me she looked, giving no glance of recognition to the chagrined Levasseur. With a deep, deep curtsy of mocking homage and genuine challenge, that broke her slow revolving dance at my very feet, she sank to the ground, and, rising like a swift-growing flower from the earth—like Aphrodite herself from the wine-dark sea—she gazed straight into my eyes, smiled with the allure of all the sirens, Delilahs, Sapphos, Aspasias, Jezebels and Cleopatras that ever lived, and whispered—to me—as if she and I were alone in all Africa . . . alone in the gracious night, beneath the serene moon and throbbing stars . . . alone together, she and I, at the door of our silken tent under the graceful palms of our secret oasis . . . she and I, alone together upon the silken cushions and the silken carpet spread upon the warm honey-coloured sands. . . .

Good God in Heaven—what was this? I struggled like a drowning man . . . I *was* a drowning man, sinking down . . . down . . . hypnotized . . .

"*No! No!*" I shouted. "*No! . . .*" The only flower for me was an English rose. . . . What had I to do with orchids of Africa? Had I really shouted? . . . What was she whispering? . . . French? . . .

"*Beaux yeux bleus! . . . J'aime les yeux bleus! . . . Baisez-moi! . . . Aimez-moi! . . . Venez avec moi . . . après!* . . . I lov' you so. . . . *Je t'aime! . . . Je t'adore!* . . . Kees me, sweetheart. . . . Crrrush me in your arms, darling. . . . *J'ai attendu. . . . Et tu es arrivé . . . J'ai attendu . . . depuis longtemps . . . il y a longtemps . . . J'ai attendu. . . . Et tu es arrivé. . . . Maintenant. . . . Baisez-moi! . . . Embrassez-moi, mon amant Anglais* . . . ah . . .*"

She was talking French. . . . Was she speaking at all? . . . Was she talking faulty French and broken English, with the accent of the educated French-and English-speaking Arab? . . . No. Her lips were not moving—but her eyes were holding mine; burning into mine. . . . Her eyes were great irresistible magnets drawing my soul through my eyes into hers and through them, down into her soul where it would be lost for ever, engulfed, held, drowned, destroyed.

"*No!*" I shouted, and burst into a profuse perspiration as I clung with the strength of despair to—to—sanity, to self-respect, to honour . . . to Isobel. . . .

And then I shook off the shackles of this absurd folly—or this devilish, hellish danger—and was an ordinary tourist from the north smiling at this ordinary dancing-girl of the south. . . .

But . . . and I shivered slightly . . . she was not ordinary . . . Neither in her evil loveliness, nor in her evil, conscious, or unconscious, hypnotic power, was she ordinary.

Had she actually spoken?

Had I actually cried aloud!

With a real effort, I wrenched my eyes from hers, and glanced around. The Arabs were watching her as a circle of dogs a luscious piece of meat—which is what she was to them.

Levasseur was smiling cynically and without amusement.

"You are favoured, my friend," he growled, as she floated away on her toes—her hands and her arms floating about her as she did so.

"Did she speak to me?" I asked.

"Not that I heard," he answered in surprise. "She certainly intends to do so, though. . . . Beware, St. Anthony. . . . They don't call her the Angel of Death for nothing. . . ."

I decided that neither she nor I had uttered a sound, that she had paused before me for but a moment—and yet I *knew* that, if ever she spoke to me, she would speak in faulty French and broken English, with the accent of those Arabs who have learnt a little French and English—as many of the town-dwelling Arabs do, for purposes of business.

This was interesting, a little too interesting perhaps. It was also absurd, utterly ridiculous, perfectly impossible. I could have sworn that I had shouted *"No!"* at the top of my voice, and had recoiled violently.

Obviously I had uttered no sound and had not moved in my arm-chair. . . . But why was I trembling from head to foot, and wet with a cold perspiration that had no relation to the pleasant temperature of the night? Why did I recover my normal serenity and self-control in inverse proportion to her proximity?

While she swayed mockingly before an Arab who sat in the most distant corner of the square, her back toward me, I took my eyes from her and turned again to Levasseur, as the Arab, his face transfigured, his burning eyes riveted on her face, his clutching hands extended, rose slowly to his feet.

"Who *is* she?" I said, controlling my voice as best I might.

"Who *is* she, M'sieu' St. Anthony?" mocked the Colonel, evidently still a little piqued. "She is the Angel of Death, as I think I have already told you."

"Well; tell me a little more about her," I said, shortly.

"Well; she is what you see she is—and a good deal more. . . . Among other things she is the daughter of a very famous Ouled-Naïl dancing-girl. . . . Eh, *mon ami*, but a dancing-girl of a beauty. . . . Of a beauty . . . of a fascination . . . of an allure . . . *ravissante!*" and the Colonel kissed his stubby fingers and waved them at the stars, his somewhat heavy, bovine gaze momentarily aflame.

"Ah! the marvellous . . . the incredible . . . the untellable 'Zara Blanchfleur,' as we called her. . . . But *that* was a woman . . . a houri from Paradise. . . ."

"And the father?" I broke in upon the rhapsody. "A Frenchman I suppose?"

"Said to be an Englishman," replied the Colonel.

"Certainly European," I observed.

"Oh, but yes, it leaps to the eye, that; does it not, *mon ami*? That white skin, those unpainted cheeks. . . . Yes, they say he was an Englishman. . . . The Death Angel believes so, anyhow . . . and her great desire in life is to meet him."

"Filial affection is a wonderful thing," I observed.

"It'll prove so, in this case," said the Colonel. "For if the little angel gets near enough, she'll cut his throat till his head falls back-ward—*boump!*—so. . . . Yes; she loves all Europeans—especially the English—for her father's sake!"

"What! Ill-treated her, I suppose?" I said, my eyes again turning to where the girl beguiled the Arab, and was now bending over backward towards him, that he might place a coin of gold on her forehead among the gold coins of the *sokhab* tiara that adorned it.

"No, no," murmured the Colonel lazily, as he gazed at the smoke that was curling from his cigarette. "She never knew him, I believe. It's her mother she wishes to avenge."

"Ill-treated the mother?" I asked.

"Well; I wouldn't say *that*. . . . He merely did—er—what one does. . . . One tires, of course . . . of the loveliest of them. . . . One gathers that *ce bon Monsieur Anglais* took her from the Street of a Thousand Delights away out into the—er—Desert of One Delight. . . . An individualist, one perceives. . . . Installed his *chère amie* in the desert-equivalent of a flat or a *maisonnette*—probably a green canvas tent from London. . . . A desert idyll. . . .

"A great lover, one would say, this Englishman . . ." mused the Colonel. "Of a certainty he captured the heart of our Zaza—and broke it. . . . No . . . nothing cruel. . . . He just dropped it—and it just broke . . . like any other fragile thing that one drops. . . . He left her. . . .

"She was never the same again, our little one. . . . She became positively nun-like. . . . And then, a little strange . . . *distraite*. . . . Other-world and other-where, one would say . . . even in moments of love. . . . And, in time, a little mad. . . . And then more than a little mad. . . . And then quite mad. . . . Oh, mad as Ophelia. . . . And through these years, the years of hoping . . . the heart-sick years of hope deferred . . . the heart-broken years of realization . . . the years of growing insanity . . . the years of madness, she talked of him. . . . Always she talked of him and his return. . . .

"Yes, of a truth, he broke her heart."

"One does not somehow imagine the heart of a Zaza Blanchfleur to be very fragile," I observed.

"That is why I say this Englishman was a great lover," said Levasseur. "For certainly the little one's heart had been taken up—and dropped—before. . . . By General and by Subaltern . . . by civilian and by sheikh . . . by aristocrat and by plutocrat . . . by the richest and by the handsomest. . . . Had been dropped—and had gracefully rebounded to be caught by the next. . . .

"But when the Englishman dropped it, it was shattered—and Zaza Blanchfleur lived with a broken heart until she died of a broken heart. . . .

"And the Angel of Death desires earnestly . . . oh, but *earnestly* —to meet her papa. . . . And, meanwhile, any white man serves her purpose—her purpose of revenge . . . serves to glut her hate, to fill her coffers and to slake her passion to avenge her mother."

"She must have adored her mother," I observed.

"Everybody adored her mother," said the Colonel sententiously, and heaved a deep sigh, a sigh that, one felt, claimed one's sympathy and the tribute of a tear. . . .

The Angel of Death—and certainly she moved with the lightness and grace of a being endowed with wings—came circling, gliding, floating toward me again.

Row upon row of enigmatic dark faces. . . . Hundreds of hard watching eyes. . . .

The fierce-looking hawk-faced young Arab, with whom she had coquetted, arose from his place, and came round the outside of the square of intently-staring onlookers, until he was behind the chairs occupied by the Colonel and myself.

"Have you a gold coin?" asked Levasseur. "She is going to favour you again. The correct thing is to lay a twenty-franc piece, or a sovereign, on her forehead, when she bends over backward with her face turned up to you."

Should I avoid her gaze this time—refuse to look her in the face? Absurd—a half-caste dancing-girl of the bazaars of Bouzen. . . .

She was before me again, and I was a captive fly about which a lovely and bejewelled spider was weaving the bonds from which there is no escape but death. . . . Her arms were weaving . . . weaving . . . weaving . . . mesmeric . . . hypnotic . . . compelling. . . .

She approached yet closer.

With a great mental and moral effort I wrenched my mind or soul violently from hers, and thrust my hand into my pocket for a coin. I would simply follow the "custom of the country"—signify my approval of her skill in the usual manner, tip this perfectly ordinary dancing-girl—and then tell Levasseur I was more than ready to return to the hotel. . . .

The Angel of Death saw my movement in search of money, but instead of turning her back to me and bending over until her face looked up into mine, she threw herself at my feet, knelt with arms out-stretched, and bringing her wonderful face closer and closer to mine, whispered:

"*Chèri! . . . Beaux yeux bleus!* . . . Lov' me! . . . I lov' you! . . . Kiss me, Beau'ful blue-eyes. . . . Kiss me! . . . Quick! . . ."

Now, Heaven knows, I am no saint, and I know I am no priggish pompous fool. . . . There could be no earthly harm in my kissing this girl. No more harm than there is in any snatched under-the-mistletoe kiss. But the last kiss that I had ever exchanged, had been with a dear little child at Brandon Abbas—ah, how dear!—a sweet and lovely little angel; an Angel of Life, if this was the Angel of Death. . . .

I did not want to hurt this dancing-girl's feelings, but neither did I want to kiss her. In fact, I wasn't going to kiss her, whatever happened.

"*Kiss* her, man," snapped Colonel Levasseur, disgusted, I suppose, at the stupid, graceless and cold-blooded Anglo-Saxon.

"Thanks—but I never kiss," I said, both to the girl and to him.

The Colonel snorted; the girl's eyes blazed; and I felt an uncomfortable fool.

Simultaneously the young Arab made some movement behind my chair, Colonel Levasseur shouted something at him in Arabic, and the girl thrust her angry face almost against mine.

"*Kiss me!*" she whispered tensely, and the eyes, that had seemed to blaze, narrowed, and looked as deadly cold as those of a snake.

I shook my head.

"I never kiss people," I said, and before my lips had well closed, her right hand went to her sash, flashed upward and fell with a sharp and heavy blow on my shirt-front, exactly over my heart. . . .

I felt no pain. . . . That would come. . . . Numbed. . . .

Levasseur sprang to his feet, hurled the young Arab back, and seized the girl's wrist as though to snap her arm.

"You she-devil!" he growled and, as she laughed mockingly, glanced from the knife that gleamed in her hand, to my breast.

I laughed also—a somewhat nervous laugh of relief. She had not stabbed me as I had supposed. She had struck with all her strength, but in the moment of impact she had turned the point of the knife inward, and had merely struck me with the clenched fist that held the knife.

It was over in a second, and she was whirling away again upon the tips of her toes. But few had seen what actually happened—and they had merely seen a girl offer a kiss, receive a refusal, and give a blow.

Turning swiftly from the girl to the jealous Arab, Colonel Levasseur showed something of the tiger that undoubtedly lurked beneath the heavy and somewhat dull exterior of the man.

What he said, I did not catch; but the Arab recoiled from the ferocious glare of the French officer's baleful eye, the gleam of his bared teeth. I thought the big clenched fist was about to crash into the Arab's face, but it shot out with pointed finger, as the Colonel concluded with an order, shouted as at a dog.

"*Imshi!*" he roared. "Get out of it, you black hound! . . ." and the Arab slunk off toward the compound gate.

Impassive faces seemed to harden . . . hundreds of watching eyes to narrow. . . .

Our host, apparently petrified with terror and amazement, now pulled himself together, rolled off his sofa, and prostrated himself before his guest.

When he had finished his protestations of grief, horror, outrage and alarm—perfervid declarations that he was shamed for life, his face blackened for ever, his salt betrayed, his roof dishonoured, his fame besmirched, his self-respect destroyed, his life laid in ruins—by the action of the vile criminal whom the Colonel had so rightly driven forth into outer darkness—Levasseur quietly remarked:

"*Bien!* I hold you responsible then, that every movement of that seditious, insolent dog, Selim ben Yussuf, is reported to the *Bureau.* . . . And look you, Abu Sheikh Ahmed, if he sets foot in Zaguig without my knowing it, on your head be it. . . ."

"On my head and my life, Excellency," replied Abu Sheikh Ahmed, touching his forehead and breast, as he bowed humbly before the angry Colonel.

Levasseur then thanked him for the entertainment, bade him continue the music and the dance until we were well away; and then, with a brief, "Come along, Monsieur Vanbrugh," marched off to the door, our host trotting beside us, voluble to the last.

"What was wrong with the good What's-his-name—Selim?" I asked as we seated ourselves in the waiting car.

"A cursed great knife, my friend," replied the Colonel, "broad and sharp and curly. . . . That's what was wrong. . . . His hand was on it as I happened to glance over my shoulder. . . . I believe that both he and the girl each thought the other was going to stab you, and so neither did. . . ."

"Oh, nonsense, Colonel," I laughed, "she was only giving me a little fright because I refused her kiss, and he was just being dramatic—to please her. . . ."

"Ah, well, my friend," replied Levasseur, "doubtless *you* know the Arab best—and particularly Mademoiselle the Angel of Death and Monsieur Selim ben Yussuf, who is literally mad for her."

"Who is he?" I asked.

"The son of the Sheikh of an extremely powerful and important tribe," was the reply. "An old man whose friendship is worth a very great deal to us. . . . Make all the difference at Zaguig. . . . Worth a whole brigade. . . . He's very loyal, friendly and peaceable, but things will be different when his mantle descends to Master Selim —if our fool politicians let it. . . . I'd shoot the dog on sight, if I had *my* way. . . . Let's stop the car and walk a bit, shall we? I've been sitting down all day."

I was quite agreeable. We got out, and the Colonel bade the soldier-chauffeur return to his quarters.

"Are these streets at all dangerous at night?" I asked my companion, as we strolled along through the silent moonlit dream-city of whitest light and blackest shadow.

"*That* is, very—in more ways than one," he replied, pointing up a somewhat narrower lane, the entrance to which we were just passing. "There are a good few murders, up there, in the course of the year. . . . We can go that way. . . . It's rather interesting."

"Murders?" I observed, as we turned into the street. "Robbery?"

"Yes. Robbery . . . Jealousy . . . Hate. . . . Sometimes the spider kills the fly. Sometimes the fly is a wasp and kills the spider."

It was a strange street. Silent as Death; wide awake and watchful as Life: furtive and secret as Night: open and obvious as Day.

There was no movement, no sound, no invitation; but there were eyes, there were open doors that looked like the mouths of tombs, there were mystery and evil and danger in the black shadows, in the very moonlight, the air. . . .

As we passed the first open door, I saw that it framed a curious picture. Back in the darkness, with which a small native lamp struggled feebly, sat a perfectly motionless figure, bedizened, bejewelled, posed, suggesting an idol dressed up for a barbarous religious ceremony, or the priest of such an idol, watching through the night before its shrine. No movement of the body of this priest or idol caused the slightest change in the reflections from bright jewels, shining gold, or gleaming cloth of silver, the slightest sound from heavy armlets, chains, anklets, girdle or bracelets—but, as we passed, the eyes followed us, gleaming. . . .

And so in the next house . . . and the next . . . and the next; so in every house in the silent listening street, the waiting, watchful, motionless street, which the bold and hardy man beside me had declared to be very dangerous. in more ways than one.

"Interesting people, those Ouled-Naïl dancing-girls," observed Levasseur. "They've danced, and they've sat in this street, for a couple of thousand years or so. They danced for Julius Caesar and Scipio Africanus—and for Jugurtha too—as they danced for you and me, and for old Abu Sheikh Ahmed. . . . Roman generals took them to Rome and French generals take them to Paris. . . . There isn't much they don't know about the art of charming. . . . A hundred generations of hereditary lore. . . . Most intriguing and attractive. . . ."

"A matter of taste," I observed. "Personally I'd pay handsomely—to be excused. I don't see how a bedizened, painted, probably unwashed, half-savage Jezebel is going to 'interest, intrigue, and attract,' a person of any taste and refinement."

I spoke a little warmly and wondered whether I did protest too much, as I thought of the Angel of Death.

The Colonel was faintly annoyed, methought. Perhaps he, a person of taste and refinement, had been interested, intrigued and attracted.

"One of them attracted the Englishman to some purpose," he growled. "He took her from this very street. . . . I could show you the house. . . . Zaza Blanchfleur. . . . He treated her like a bride. . . . Regular honeymoon. . . . Fitted out a splendid caravan, and went off a long way into the desert. . . . Oh, yes, she interested *him* all right, and for quite a while too. . . . And what about her daughter, the Angel of Death. She has interested a few people of taste and refinement, I can tell you! . . . Some names that would surprise you. . . ."

"And did she sit in this street too?" I asked.

"Of course she did, at first. . . . But she has walked in a few other streets since . . . Bond Street: Rue de la Paix: Unter den Linden: Nevsky Prospect: the Ringstrasse: Corso: Prado: Avenido: visited nearly all the capitals of Europe, she says."

"What's to become of a girl like that?" I asked.

"Oh—marry a big Sheikh and go out into the desert for good— or a rich Moor and go into a *hareem* in Fez—stay here and amass wealth—go to Paris, Marseilles or Algiers—she may die a princess on a silken bed in a Sultan's palace, or on the floor of a foul den in Port Said. . . ."

The Colonel sighed, and the subject dropped.

CHAPTER V

At Zaguig, Colonel Levasseur was in his element, monarch of all he surveyed, and greatly he loved playing the monarch before the amused eyes of Mary, who enormously enjoyed the opportunity of "getting nearer to life" as she called it, and "seeing the Oriental on his native heath," unoccidentalized and undefiled—or unpurified and unregenerate.

Zaguig contained nothing European, and it intended to contain nothing European if it could help it. Unfortunately, its representatives had not even that moderate degree of straight speech and fair dealing which prevails in European diplomacy, and hid the bitterest hate and most evil intentions behind the most loving protestations, honeyed words and outward signs of friendship.

I am not a politician nor a world-reformer, neither a publicist nor a sociologist, and I have no views to offer on the subject of the ethics of the "peaceful penetration" of an uncivilized country by a civilized one. But nobody could travel southward from Bouzen, contrasting the Desert with the Sown, without perceiving that the penetration was for the greatest good of the greatest number, and ultimately for the whole world's good, inasmuch as cultivation and production succeeded fallow waste; order and peace succeeded lawlessness and war; and the blessings of civilization succeeded the curses of savagery.

Not always are the "blessings" immediately recognized for what they are, by their unconsulted recipients.

Certainly, in this case, there could be no two opinions on the subject of whether the penetrated approved the process. They were not altruists and they were fanatical Mussulmans with an unfathomable contempt for all Christians and all other God-forgotten Infidels. . . . Particularly was this true of the Zaguigan dervishes, marabouts, mullahs, priests, preachers, and teachers, for Zaguig was what is known as a "Holy" City, and it was wont to make a most unholy mess of any unauthorized intruder. . . .

Probably Mecca and Medina themselves were not more hopelessly reactionary and murderously fanatical than Zaguig, and certainly they could not have approximated more closely to the state of Sodom and Gomorrah than did this Holy Spot. . . .

However, the tide of civilization was encroaching upon the hitherto undefiled sands that surrounded it; waves of progress were lapping against its very walls; and the first wavelets of that irresistible ocean were the men of Colonel Levasseur's Military Mission.

It was in this peculiarly unholy Holy City that Mary met the man who instantly awoke her keenest interest, admiration and approval; who later won her devoted love; and ultimately became her husband.

Mary was—wholly unconsciously, I believe—becoming very interested in the subject of love and matrimony, and had, I feel sure, been wondering whether her twin soul might not be right there, when she sojourned in New York, London, Paris, Monte Carlo, Algiers, Biskra, and Bouzen respectively, where charming eligibles abounded.

To think that he should be in Zaguig where nothing abounded but unwashed Zaguigans, heat, dirt, smells and an almost unadulterated orientalism . . . !

I liked the handsome, hard, clean-cut Major Henri de Beaujolais from the first; and he attracted me enormously. To the simplicity and directness of the soldier he added the cleverness and knowledge of the trained specialist; the charm, urbanity and grace of the experienced man of the world; and the inevitable attractiveness of a lovable and modest character.

He combined the best of two nations, with his English public-school upbringing, and his English home-life of gentle breeding, on the one hand, and his aristocratic French birth, breeding and traditions on the other. . . . I heard that he was as brave as a lion, extremely able, and likely to go very far in his profession—quite apart from the fact that he was the nephew of a most distinguished general and related by marriage (through his uncle's wife) to an extremely powerful and prominent politician.

We first met him at dinner at Colonel Levasseur's table, and I was surprised to note that Mary's attitude to him was anything but encouraging and kind. In fact she rather annoyed me by apparently endeavouring to annoy him. I taxed her with this after he had gone, and asked if she disliked him.

"*Dear* old Otis!" she smiled, and added later. . . ."Why—no—why should I? . . . I altogether like him . . . and *then* some . . ."

"You certainly hid it," I observed, and,

"Did I? . . . Did I?" she asked.

Whereupon I also waxed wily, and remarked:

"He reminded me of d'Artagnan. . . . Just that swaggering self-confidence and assurance . . . a faint touch of the somewhat gasconading swash-buckler . . ." and got no further.

"What!" interrupted Mary, "*Are* you as blind as a mole with a monocle *and* as stupid as a fish with a headache? . . . Why I never met a more modest unassuming man in my life! . . . You couldn't prise a word out of him—about what he has done. . . . Not with a crow-bar. . . ."

"Ah!" I observed profoundly, and chuckled, whereupon Mary marched off to bed.

I love Mary, and I love to watch her at work. What she wants, she goes for; and what she goes for, she gets. Our Red Indian streak is, at times, fairly strong in her, and shows particularly when she is in danger. . . . Then she is the coolest thing invented, and apparently at her happiest. . . . It shows also in a certain relentless tenacity, a determination to achieve her purpose—and, I may add, a certain recklessness—not to say unscrupulousness—with which she handles obstacles and opposition.

The idea that entered my mind that memorable evening remained, and it turned to a certainty. As the days went by, and Mary saw more and more of Henri de Beaujolais, she grew more and more interested in him, and he in her. . . . All his spare time was devoted to "making her visit agreeable," and to satisfying her insatiable thirst for knowledge of North Africa and the Africans.

Poor Colonel Levasseur could but acquiesce, and show a delight that he did not feel, when she assured him of how enormously she was enjoying her stay in Zaguig—thanks to Major de Beaujolais' wonderful knowledge of the place and people, and his extraordinarily interesting way of imparting it.

"Yes," thought I to myself in the vernacular, "Mary has fallen for Major Henri de Beaujolais, and Major Henri de Beaujolais has fallen for Mary—though possibly he doesn't yet know it. . . . But he is certainly going to know it—if the first part of my surmise is correct."

I was filled with hope and joy, for he was just the man I would have chosen for my sister to marry, and I longed to see her married and with a home of her own. . . . A woman needs a home more than a man does—almost more than she needs anything—and our own home in Wyoming was no "home" at all. . . .

It did not greatly surprise me, when, entering the spacious tiled breakfast-room, with its great pillared verandah, one morning, to hear de Beaujolais remark, as he turned to go:

"Well, I have warned you, sir, and done all I can. . . . We're sitting on a powder-magazine and there are quite a lot of lads inside it—*striking matches*. . . . And one of them is our friend Selim ben Yussuf too! . . . There's going to be a big explosion—and a conflagration as well—and pretty soon. . . ."

"Won't you stop and have some coffee . . . before it happens! . . ." smiled Colonel Levasseur in a particularly irritating manner; and, with a haughty salute, de Beaujolais strode from the room, his face set and scowling.

"Wonderful noses for a mare's-nest, these Intelligence people," smiled the Colonel. "Have you seen Mademoiselle this morning? . . . Been out riding? . . . Wish I could find all the spare time these Intelligence fellers can. . . . *I* can't go riding with her every morning. . . . Yes, nothing but mare's-nest after mare's-nest, full of addled eggs—like the Intelligence feller's brains. . . . Yes, addled. . . . Another mare's-nest now—revolt, rebellion, mutiny, murder, massacre and I don't know what all! . . . I suppose the Secret Service must justify its existence and earn its pay somehow. . . . *Intelligence*, eh? . . . Pity some of them haven't *got* a little. . . . Ah! Here's Mademoiselle. . . . Bring the coffee at once, Alphonse. . . . *Bon jour, ma chère Mademoiselle Vanbrugh*, you look like the morning itself—only cool . . . cool . . . always cool. . . ."

One afternoon within a week of the delivery of these *obiter dicta* by the wise Colonel Levasseur, I received a message, at the Residency, from de Beaujolais, bidding me hurry to his quarters. The messenger, a fine Spahi, named Achmet, de Beaujolais' orderly, calmly informed me that my sister, the Sitt Miriam Vanbrugh, was in great danger and that I was to go instantly, on the horse that he had ridden. It appeared that de Beaujolais himself had come to the Residency to find me, and had taken my sister's maid away with him. . . .

. . . At least this was what I gathered from Achmet's curious mixture of French, *sabir* and Arabic.

I rushed down to the street, guided by Achmet, who ran swiftly before me; rode to the house near the Babel-Sûq where de Beaujolais lived, fearing I knew not what, and noting the strange emptiness of the bazaars, lanes, squares and streets, due, I supposed, to the fact that there was a big parade and review in the great Square of the Minaret. . . .

Arrived at de Beaujolais' quarters, I dismounted in the courtyard at the back of the house, gave the horse a smack that sent him trotting to the stable, and dashed up the wooden stairs. I either kicked down or opened the first door to which I came, and found two Arabs in the room. One of them announced himself to be Major de Beaujolais—I recognized the voice after I had heard the name—and said that Mary was in his bedroom with her maid, dressing up as an Arab female. . . . The massacre was to be for that evening, and not a foreigner would survive it, save those who successfully hid themselves. . . . He had sent for me to look after the girls and to share their chance of escape by hiding, in disguise, until a punitive expedition arrived. . . .

So it had come! . . . De Beaujolais had been right and Levasseur wrong, criminally wrong. . . . And Mary was in the heart of one of the most dangerously fanatical towns in the world, at the moment of a *jehad*, a Holy War upon infidels, their slaughter and complete massacre. . . . Mary and her excellent English maid, Maud Atkinson. . . . And I was to disguise myself as an Arab and hide in a bedroom with them—hide cowering, trembling, sickening, starving, until the arrival of a relief-force from Ain-Zuggout or somewhere! . . .

One thing was fairly certain, Mary wouldn't consent to do anything of this sort—and I said so. . . .

"What about the troops?" I asked.

"Not a chance," replied de Beaujolais. "They are hopelessly inadequate in number, and they couldn't be worse placed than they are. . . . Scattered about the city. . . . If you hide here, you'll be the only white people alive by midnight. . . . It's absolutely your one and only chance. . . ."

"Mary won't stay hidden here for days," I said. "And I don't like the idea much for myself, either. . . . Let's hear what she's got to say about it," and we went into the next room, followed by the other "Arab"—a Captain in the French Secret Service, named Redon.

Mary, calm and cool as ever, appeared more interested in the Arab clothes than in the prospect of death and destruction.

"Look here, Mary," I said. "What about it? Will you lie low here and keep the place all silent and shut up, and wear those clothes in case anybody gets a glimpse of you—and wait until the relief-force comes?"

"Answer's in the negative," she replied, observing the effect of her head-dress in a shaving-mirror. "These what-is-its over the face

don't give a girl much chance, do they? . . . The just and the unjust.
. . . the fair and the unfair . . . all start from scratch, so to speak. . . .
Er—no—Otis, I am not paying a long visit. . . . What's Major de
Beaujolais going to do in the massacre? Show great Intelligence
and offer us sure, but Secret, Service—or which?"

And then de Beaujolais made the devastating announcement
that he was going to clear out, cut and run—before the show
started, if he could. . . . He had at that moment got his orders from
the dirty, ruffianly-looking "Arab" who was Captain de Redon. . . .

And I, at that moment, got something too—the idea of a
lifetime! *He should take Mary with him,* wherever he was going!
. . . It would save her from the massacre, and it would, moreover,
throw her and de Beaujolais together in the protracted intimacy of a
desert journey.

And that would surely lead to the lasting happiness of both of
them! . . . In the imminence of battle, murder and sudden death, I
thought of orange-blossoms, bridal veils, and the Voice that
breathed o'er Eden. . . . I suppose it was because I knew that it was
hopeless and useless for me to think of such things in connection
with myself, that I so often thought of them for other people. . . .

And it promptly appeared that my bright idea had not occurred
to me alone, for Mary observed that since Major de Beaujolais was
escaping, she and her maid might as well escape with him. She said
it as one might say: "If you're going to Town too, we might as well
catch the same train."

But de Beaujolais apparently had other views.

He declared that it was utterly impossible. He was going on a
secret mission of the greatest delicacy, danger and importance. . . .
He simply could not take women with him. He repeated his
suggestion that I and the two girls should lie hidden in that house,
and take our chance of surviving till a French column arrived.

I was glad that Mary did not for one moment suppose that I
should do anything of the sort—do anything, in fact, but join my
host and his men and throw in my lot with theirs.

For herself, she merely brushed de Beaujolais' refusals and
explanations aside, and made it clear that no masculine trivialities
and puerilities of politics, Secret Service, or Special Missions, were
of sufficient importance to be talked about—much less considered
as obstacles in the path of Miss Mary Vanbrugh.

When he waxed urgently explanatory and emphatically
discouraging, finishing by an absolute and uncompromising
refusal, she merely did not listen, but bade the departing Achmet to

take along the portmanteau that Maudie had brought—to wherever he was going. . . .

And so extremely vehement and final was de Beaujolais' negative, so absolutely convincing his reasons for refusing to take her, that I was certain he longed to do it, and was but fighting what he believed to be his own weakness. I conceived him to be in the horrible position of having to leave a girl, with whom he had fallen in love, to the mercies of the men of Zaguig—or else take her with him, to the greater danger to herself and the greatest danger to the success of his mission. . . .

To my mind, the second alternative was wholly preferable, and I set about doing what I could to bring it to pass—for it gave Mary not only a chance of life, but a chance of happiness. . . . Also, I am bound to confess, because it transferred to the broader shoulders of de Beaujolais the terrible responsibility of saving her. . . .

"Take her, for God's sake," I said, "it is her only chance. . . . She will never hide here. . . . She'll come back to the Residency with me, and use a rifle. . . . She is as good as a man. . . . You say there is no shadow of hope. . . . Think of the end then. . . . I can't shoot her. . . . There is at least a chance for her with you. . . ."

"Against my instructions and orders," he said, his face a study of conflicting feelings. "I have to travel as light as possible; as swiftly as possible—and with the irreducible minimum of followers. . . . More people means more kit and camels . . . more delay . . . less speed. . . . And she'd never stand the journey. . . . Wholly against my instructions and almost certain death for her. . . ."

"And this is absolutely certain death for her," I said.

I wished I could see Mary's face, but it was hidden beneath the out-door garment that covers the purdah Mussulman woman from the crown of her head to the soles of her feet. Not even her eyes were visible through the strip of muslin that covered the aperture left in the thick material, to permit the wearer to see.

Captain de Redon added his voice to mine—evidently sympathizing to the depths of his gallant Gallic soul with his unfortunately-situated friend; with a girl in terrible danger; and with the girl's brother, pleading for her life. Probably he saw, as clearly as I did, that the one thing de Beaujolais longed to do, was to give way. . . .

And give way he did, with every appearance of reluctance and ill grace.

"Very well," he said. "On Miss Vanbrugh's head be it. She and her maid can leave with me—provided she understands that my business is not to save her, but to serve my country. . . . I shan't let her safety or life stand in the way of duty, for a second. . . ."

I wrung his hand and I knew that Mary was safe. . . . He'd do his duty, all-right, but he'd make it square with the safety of the woman he loved. . . . Yes, he certainly loved her, whether he knew it or not—and a terrific load was lifted from my mind.

A few minutes later, they were all in the street—still empty and silent, I was glad to see—and on their way to the house of the wealthy and friendly Arab, Sidi Ibrahim Maghruf—a party of entirely ordinary and convincing natives; de Beaujolais, a Sergeant-Major Dufour, Captain de Redon, Mary, and Maud Atkinson—the last-named, in her invincible ignorance and cheerful cockney courage, thoroughly enjoying the whole business.

De Beaujolais refused to let me come with them to the house of his friend Ibrahim Maghruf, where the caravan was waiting, as I was not in Arab dress, and begged me (since I refused to quit the town with him, and then take my chance in the desert), to hurry back to the Residency. I was to tell Colonel Levasseur of the arrival of Captain de Redon with orders for de Beaujolais' instant departure, and to try to get the fact into the good Colonel's thick skull that the revolt would break out that very night. . . .

I gave Mary a warm and loving embrace, kissed the place where I imagined her mouth to be, and murmured in the neighbourhood of her ear:

"God bless you, darling girl . . ." and added a *cliché* of our childhood anent "a buggy-ride with a nice young man."

That Mary heard and understood my allusion was indicated by the fact that I received an entirely perceptible jab in the sub-central region of my waistcoat, as I took my arms from about her neck.

Crushing down my feelings of loneliness, apprehension and anxiety, I told myself that Mary was in splendid hands, and, hurrying out from that boding and oppressive house, I quickly lost myself, completely and hopelessly, in the maze-like tangle of alleys, bazaars, winding lanes, and crooked streets, that lay between it and the Residency.

The atmosphere of the place was inexpressibly sinister—sly, minatory and enigmatic. There was no-one to be seen, but I felt that I was seen by a thousand watching eyes. . . . What lurked behind those iron-barred window-spaces, those lattices, gratings, slightly opened doors; behind those high blind walls, and upon those screened balconies? . . . Frequently the lane through which I hurried was roofed completely over, and was a mere tunnel beneath the upper rooms of the houses that formed its sides.

As I emerged from one of these and turned a corner into a narrow bazaar of tiny shops, each but a shuttered hole in the wall, I heard a heavy murmur such as one may suddenly hear when approaching the sea-shore and emerging into the open. . . .

It was indescribably menacing and disturbing, this growing noise as of a hive of infuriated bees, and it quickly grew into the most terrible sound there is—the blended roar and howl and shout and scream of a vast infuriated mob of maddened men, yelling and blood-lusting for rapine, fire and slaughter. . . . The man who can hear it unmoved is a man of iron nerve, a superman indeed—for a mob is infinitely worse and wickeder, more destructive and dangerous, than any single member of it. It is the most wild and savage of all wild and savage beasts; and is infinitely powerful, with its innumerable hands to rend and slay and burn, its innumerable brains to think of evil things for those hands to do.

I was certainly frightened.

The appalling noise increased in volume and came nearer.

I was lost—and knew not which way to turn to avoid the mob nor to rejoin my friends, those splendid soldiers—many of them Africans—who would die to a man, without thought of parley or surrender.

To die fighting with them would be nothing—an exhilaration, a fierce joy—but to be torn to pieces in these stinking gutters, handled and struck by these foul bestial brutes, trampled to a jelly of blood and mud and mess . . . there could be no more dreadful death. . . . The loathsome indignity of it—a white man struggling impotent in the hands of blacks—his clothes torn from his body . . .!

That was what frightened me, not Death—for he was a fellow I was quite willing to meet whenever he came along. . . .

§2

As the noise made by the mob—the noise varying from the roaring of ten thousand lions to that of a mighty sea breaking on an iron-bound coast in a terrific storm—rose and fell, advanced and withdrew, when I turned corners, entered narrow gullies or crossed open squares, I prayed that Mary was out of the city and safely on her way.

I fervently blessed de Beaujolais and his thought for her; his fetching her maid and me; his final decision to take her with him. I could not refrain from contrasting him with Levasseur—who had invited her to Zaguig that he might impress her and that she might see him in the most favourable conditions.

Well—he had invited her to Zaguig for his own ends and had so been instrumental in bringing de Beaujolais into her life. Long might de Beaujolais remain there!

And suddenly I turned another corner and found, with utter dismay, that I had walked round in a circle; for in the open space where several lanes met, lay a dead horse that I had seen an hour or two earlier, and, not very far from it, lay the corpse of an Arab.

The sight—an unpleasant one—of the man's body, gave me an idea. My object was to rejoin Levasseur and to be of use; but it was absolutely certain that I should never reach him in European clothes. I should be torn to pieces by the mob, killed by the first gang I ran into. Dressed as I was, my one chance of life was to creep into some hole and hide. Dressed as an Arab, I might make my way to the Residency, and get into it—if I were not shot by its defenders.

Disguised as an Arab, I might be able to approach and shout, in French, that I was one of them. Dressed as a European, I couldn't shout to the mob that I was really an Arab in disguise—and get away with it. There wouldn't be time to shout, for one thing.

The dead man's clothes were filthy, and they were soaked in blood. He had certainly been in bad trouble. . . . Could he be another Secret Service man, like de Redon? One who had fallen by the way? I should somehow feel less compunction about putting on his foul *burnous*, if he were. . . . Should I put his things on over my own, or discard European clothing entirely? . . . I should have to look "right" about the head and feet, anyway. There wouldn't be much point in going about with European boots and trousers sticking out at one end of a *burnous* and a European sun-helmet at the other.

But what should I look like, if a gang came round the corner, and saw me sitting in the gutter, swapping clothes with a corpse?

These thoughts flashed through my mind in the moment that I reached the body. Apparently the man had been stabbed, or run through, with a sword.

He had bled very copiously, and I glanced at the trail which connected him with the gate of a compound. . . . No, I couldn't squat down in the open street, pull off my boots and trousers—fancy being caught without one's boots and trousers—and change clothes with a corpse! . . . Or could I? . . .

And right here the corpse fetched a deep groan and settled the question. I could not pull the clothes off a dying man. . . . If I could do nothing to help him, I could at least leave him to die in peace.

I turned and hurried away, wondering which of the five streets that entered the square was the one by which I had followed Achmet from the Residency to de Beaujolais' quarters. They all looked alike to me, and I had been too anxious about Mary to take any note of the winding route by which we had come. . . . I found that I was following the trail left by the wounded Arab, and saw that it led into the compound of an apparently unoccupied building, and to the foot of an outside staircase that went up to the flat roof.

As I halted, there was a sudden burst of nearer noise, the sound of men running as well as shouting; and, glancing over my shoulder, I saw that, two or three hundred yards from where I stood, a mob was streaming across the end of the alley down which I was looking. Any one of the running men might at any moment glance in my direction—and in a very few minutes it would be, "Good evening, St. Peter," for mine.

I dashed into the compound, up the stairs to the roof, and found myself in the presence of some half-dozen Arabs—all dead. . . .

"Dirty work at the cross-roads!"

The place was like a butcher's yard, a slaughter-house—also a perfectly private dressing-room provided with an assortment of that kind of fancy-dress of which I was in such desperate need. The garments were all filthy, more or less torn, and plentifully bloodstained; but I realized that this was all to the good, since my object was to make my way through streets swarming with the scum of the city, similarly apparelled, and many of them similarly gore-bespattered. In point of fact it was amazing good luck that I had happened upon this sinister and revolting shambles.

Promptly I divested myself of my outer clothing and boots, and got to work.

It was the nastiest job I have ever undertaken, and there were moments when I was tempted to resume my own clothes, take one of the Arab swords that lay about, and run amok. Still more was I tempted to scurry back to de Beaujolais' quarters and hide. . . . I could find the place by returning to where the dead horse lay. . . .

I suppose that if I were a strong silent man with a big chin (and a thick ear or two), I should have proceeded coolly and swiftly with my task, and should have swaggered forth from that house "every inch an Arab," correct to the last detail.

In point of fact I felt ill and shaken; I was very frightened and nervous; and I could scarcely control my trembling sweating fingers.

Possibly most other ordinary people would have felt nearly as bad as I did?

It was growing dark. . . . The sky was lurid with the glare of great conflagrations. . . . There was a ceaseless nerve-shattering mob-roar, a roar punctuated by hideous howls, rifle shots, and the crashes of volley-firing. . . . I was in the midst of a select assembly of corpses, and their hideous faces seemed to grimace in the waning and flickering light. . . . I had to pull them about, to get their clothes from them—their beastly blood-sodden clothes . . . and they resented this, and clung to their rags with devilish ingenuity. . . . And there was viscous slimy blood upon my hands. . . . There were knotted strings—and the knots would not come undone—and this made the owner of the garment grin and grin and grin at me, and shake his horrible head as I tugged and tugged, the perspiration streaming from me. . . . And once stepping back, I slipped and stumbled and, in saving myself from falling, I trod upon the chest of a man lying behind me, and my weight drove the air from his lungs through his throat, and the dead uttered what seemed a loud cry—the ghastliest, the most loathsome, the most terrifying sound that I have ever heard: the dead voice of a dead man raised in loud protest against the indignity, the defilement of my treading foot. . . .

I hear that sound in nightmares to this day. . . .

From that man I took nothing, though I coveted his *burnous* and great curved dagger. . . . I dared not touch him, lest his dreadful glazed eyes turn to mine, his horrible snarling mouth shout at me again, his dead hands seize me by the throat. . . .

Yes, I was certainly frightened by the time I had wrested a complete Arab outfit from those reluctant corpses, and I was certainly sick by the time I had rubbed a mud of blood and dust and dirt upon my hands and arms, my feet and legs and—it makes me shudder to think of it even now—upon my face. . . .

Having dressed, I wound a filthy cotton thing about my neck, chin, mouth, nose and ears, almost to my eyes, beneath the head-cloth I had transferred complete from its late owner's head and shoulders to my own; picked up a knife and a sword; and fled from the horrible scene of my unspeakable labours.

As I emerged from the compound, a man dashed from a side-turning into the alley in front of me, and came running swiftly in my direction.

I raised my sword and waited, realizing that my ghastly work up above must, at any rate, have made a terrible spectacle of me, and that standing there, bloody, grim, silent, well-armed, I was scarcely likely to be attacked by one man—nor by any number, until I had to speak, or my disguise was penetrated. . . .

The running man drew near, and I saw that he was a filthy ragged creature, gaunt and wild, carrying a great staff in one hand and a rosary in the other. Flecks of foam lay in white spots on his mangy beard. . . . One of those bestial "holy" beggars, so full of divinity that there is no room for humanity. . . .

As he rushed by, a few yards from me, he glanced in my direction, took me for a fellow tough, and yelled something or other, in Arabic—a profession of faith or an incitement to slay and spare not—and I got a clear glimpse of his face.

It was Captain de Redon.

Dashing after him, I laid my hand on his arm, raised my sword and emitted a meaningless howl. He swung about, cursing me vehemently, and up went his long staff. He looked as pleasant and easy to tackle as a hungry grizzly bear. . . . And he did not know me—nor dream that I was anything but the Arab thing I was trying to appear.

"This one's on you, Captain," I remarked.

His staff and his jaw both dropped as he stared.

"*Mon Dieu!*" he said. "Who are you? . . . I thought I was the only . . ."

"Otis H. Vanbrugh," I told him. "Major de Beaujolais introduced us an hour ago."

"*Mon Dieu!*" he said again . . . "But you have made good use of your time, Monsieur! You took me in completely. . . . What happened? . . . I am going back to de Beaujolais' quarters to see that everything is all-right. . . . No papers undestroyed. . . . He had to leave rather hurriedly. . . . And I want another bite of Christian food, for I'm starving. . . . Also a scrap of soap if I can find some. . . . Very useful for pious foaming at the mouth. . . ."

As we hurried along, I told him how I had lost my way in trying to get from de Beaujolais' quarters to the Residency, and of my finding the dead men on the roof.

"A queer business," he said. "But corpses will be sufficiently common before to-morrow. . . . And your idea is to rejoin

Levasseur and take a hand? . . . You'll have to be careful. It would be bad luck to get through the mob safely and be shot by the Zouaves. . . .

"Your sister is safely away," he continued, and went on to tell me how he had accompanied de Beaujolais' party to one of the gates, and had been able to divert a mob from that quarter, lead them running to imaginary loot, and, by dashing round a corner and over a wall and through a house and garden that he knew, to get into one of the tunnel-like bazaars and shake them off.

"Perhaps you'd better stick to me for a while," he concluded, as we entered de Beaujolais' place. "If anybody speaks to you, howl and hit him. . . . Sure sign that your heart's in the right place and that you're feeling good to-day—nice and fanatical and anti-French. . . . We'll get as near to the Residency as we can without being shot, and I may be able to get you in. . . . If not, you'll have to manage it, somehow, to-night. . . . Call out in French and say that you want to speak to Levasseur. . . . It'll be a risky business for you, though, between the Arabs and the Zouaves. . . ."

"But aren't you going to join your comrades too?" I asked. "The one of us that got in first could warn them to look out for the other—if we failed to get in together."

"No," replied de Redon. "My job is outside. I'm going to play around with the lads-of-the-village, and speak that which is not true. . . . Just when they are going to start something, I yell that a French army is round the corner. . . . Or I accidentally drop this club on top of the head of the most prominent citizen, at the moment of his maximum usefulness to the community he adorns. . . . Dupe and mislead the poor fellows as effectually as if I were a professional labour-agitator, in fact. . . ."

I liked this Captain de Redon, a cool, competent and most courageous person. As he ate the leg of a fowl, and swiftly searched the two rooms that de Beaujolais had occupied—presumably for papers or other traces of its late occupant—he chatted as though we were not both in imminent danger of a beastly death, and about to go out and look for it.

It was a most interesting and amusing thing to hear a cultured and very delightful voice, speaking excellent English, issue from that dirty ragged scarecrow, skinny, mean and repulsive-looking.

Gazing at him in some amazement, I had an idea, and went to a small framed mirror, a cheap bazaar article, that hung on the wall of the back room.

I was positively startled. Sick and sorry as I had been at the time, I had done my work well—and had so smeared the handful of blood, mud, dust and dirt into my face and eyes that there was not a vestige of my white (or red) skin exposed. The said face was a most revolting, bestial, and disgusting spectacle—barely human in its foul filthiness. . . . No wonder that de Redon had not recognized me nor dreamed that I was a Christian. . . . As I stared at myself, I was glad that Isobel could not see me.

"Ready?" said de Redon, in the doorway. . . . "Excuse my rushing you. . . . We'll get as near the Residency as we can. . . . When we're among the simple villagers, you just follow me and do more or less what I do. . . . If anybody seems offensive or gets inquisitive, hit him—or else spin round and round, and howl. . . . And, look here—if we get in front of the troops, throw yourself on the ground and be a wounded man. . . . If you go running towards them dressed like that, you'll be shot or bayoneted. . . . Wait for a chance to crawl near enough to shout, in French, to Levasseur or an officer, as I said. . . ."

I thanked him and forbore to remark that I had played Red Indians before—and with tame Indians who had themselves trodden the war-path in their time.

We went down into the street and hurried in the direction of the big square, not far from which was the Residency.

De Redon evidently knew every inch of the route, each twist and turn, and he went so fast that I could only just keep him in sight as he kept vanishing round corners and into dark tunnels.

Every moment the horrible noise grew louder and louder as we came nearer to the scene of the fighting.

As we turned from a foul gully into a broader street, a gang of looters came running round a corner a few yards from us.

Waving his staff and rosary of black wooden beads, de Redon howled like a wild beast, and spun round and round, shouted something I could not understand, and dashed on—I at his heels, in the middle of the yelling and excited Arabs. They had evidently come into the city from the outside, being differently dressed from the townsmen, darker and hardier-looking toughs.

Some had long guns and some carried perfectly good rifles.

The street down which we ran, debouched into the big market-square, the Square of the Minaret, and this great place was packed almost solid with people, all moving in the direction of the Residency. Certainly "the heathen raged furiously together," and when we got fairly into the middle of them, I began to feel that it was as safe a place as any, so far as risk of discovery went, and I yelled and waved my sword with the best.

De Redon wriggled, thrust, and fought his way through the crowd aggressively, and with the air of an important person who has very urgent business in hand. In an exceedingly violent and truculent assembly of fanatical ruffians, he seemed the most violent, truculent and fanatical of the lot. I followed him as best I could, and endeavoured to behave as he did.

Suddenly the shouting crowd gave back, just as crowds do when shepherded by mounted police, and, in a few moments, de Redon and I found ourselves in the foremost ranks, and then in front, and ahead of the mob. Turning to face the swaying crowd, de Redon twirled his staff above his head and bawled in Arabic at the top of his voice:

"Back! Back! . . . Run! Run! . . . The *Roumi* dogs . . . the *Franzawi* are coming . . ." and pointed to where from a side-street, a detachment of Zouaves came charging at the double—stoned and shot-at from the roofs, and followed by a howling mob, only kept at bay by the rear-guard-action tactics of a Sergeant, who, every now and then, halted the end squad of the little column, turned them about, fired a volley, and rushed back to the main body, who slowed up during the operation.

Occasionally a soldier fell and was instantly the centre of a surging mob that slashed and tore and clubbed him almost out of semblance to the human form.

As the little column, evidently fighting its way to the Residency, debouched into the square, the officer in command, a young Lieutenant, charging at their head, threw up his sword-hand and shouted:

"*Halte! . . . Cessez le feu! . . . Formez le carré!*"

And, in an instant, the company was a square, bristling with bayonets, steady as a rock, front ranks kneeling, rear ranks standing close behind them, awaiting the next order as if at drill.

"Run! Run! My brothers!" yelled de Redon, in the comparative quiet that followed this manœuvre, a slight lull before the storm.

"Run! Run! . . . The *Franzawi*! . . . We shall be slain!" and he dashed at the wavering crowd that hung uncertain whether to charge in holy triumph or flee in holy terror.

Following his voice came that of the French officer, full, clear and strong.

"*Attention! Pour les feux de salve! . . . Enjoue! . . .*"

"Quick! Quick! . . . Run! Run . . ." yelled de Redon.

A huge man, wearing the green turban of a *haji*, and bearing aloft a green banner, thrust through the crowd, sprang forward, sent de Redon sprawling and yelled:

"*Allah! Allah! Allah Akbar! . . . Fissa! Fissa! . . .* Follow me and die for the Faith. . . ."

The crowd howled in response and moved forward,

De Redon, apparently representing a different brand of holiness, and full of the *odium theologicum*, returned the violent assault of the *haji*. He returned it with his club. The *haji* dropped, and the subsequent proceedings interested him no more.

The crowd rushed forward.

"*Feu!*" shouted the Zouave officer, and either instinctively or because de Redon did so, I flung myself to the ground.

Crash! . . . rang out the volley of the Zouaves.

"*En joue! Feu!*" cried the officer.

Crash! came the second volley from all sides of the now surrounded square of troops.

The crowd about me scattered like leaves before the wind, and de Redon and I were two of dozens of motion-less figures upon the ground.

"*Garde â vous!*" cried the officer. . . . "*Par files ae quatre! . . . Pas gymnastique! . . . En avant! . . .*"

Before he could give the order, "*Marche!*" a great voice boomed forth from above our heads, as though from Heaven.

On a little balcony at the top of a needle-like minaret, appeared the *muezzin*, and, on a clarion note, fairly trumpeted forth the words:

"*Kill! Kill! . . . In the name of Allah! . . . Gazi Gazi! . . . There is no god but God and Mahomet is His Prophet! . . . Slay! Slay! . . . Charge together, in the Name of Allah! . . . Burn! . . . Destroy! . . . Kill! . . .*"

The mob rallied and from every street, alley, courtyard and doorway poured forth again in hundreds.

"*Charge!*" boomed forth again the great voice of the mullah.

Bang! went a rifle and, as I glanced from the figure of the Iman toward the sound, I saw the Sergeant lower his rifle.

"*Marche!* " continued the officer, even as the body of the *muezzin* struck the parapet of his eyrie, reeled over it and crashed into the courtyard below.

A terrific yell went up from the vast crowd, and many rushed to the spot, while others turned to pursue the Zouaves, now retreating at the double.

In front of the following crowd, a recumbent figure sprang to its feet, and with extended hand and every appearance of tremendous excitement, pointed away to the opposite corner of the square.

"Beware! Beware!" he shouted. "A trap! A trap . . . Danger! . . . Big guns! Cannon! *Boom! Boom!* . . . Run! Run! . . ."

Bewildered and excited eyes turned in the direction to which de Redon pointed.

"Follow me!" he shouted, and ran toward the nearest street.

I sprang up and dashed after him, waving my sword and yelling, "*La illah ill allah ill Allah!*"

It seemed to me as good a noise as any, and quite fashionable at the moment—in fact, literally *le dernier cri.*

As always happens when a mob is given a lead, a large number followed, and, though de Redon's heroic effort did not prevent pursuit of the soldiers, it delayed it, as our section of the crowd streamed across the front of those who were dashing forward to avenge the death of the holy man who, with his last breath, had incited them to rapine and slaughter.

Keeping as near de Redon as I could, I galloped along behind him, waving my sword and emitting appropriate noises.

Into a side alley dashed de Redon still yelling:

"Big guns! Cannon! Machine-guns! . . . The French army! The French army! . . . Fly! Fly!" and in a minute it was filled from end to end with the surging rushing river of our followers, each man running because everybody else did.

Out into another street we turned, and into yet another and another, and along them kept the uneven tenor of our way, until before us appeared a city gate, leading out into the desert.

Toward this we streamed, some of us yelling, "*Kill!*" others, "*Fly!*" . . . others, "*Franzawi! Franzawi!*" . . . some in search of secular salvation, others the salvation of their souls and life-everlasting, through the slaughter of the Infidel.

Through the gate thundered the yelling mob and, as the inevitable moment approached when those who run begin to ask, "What precisely are we running for?" de Redon began to slacken his pace, drop back into the crowd, and to edge toward the side.

Snatching at my wrist as he did so, he turned about, dropped into a walk, and, a moment later, limped lamely and blindly into a yard-wide opening between two high native houses.

Excited and hurried out of my normal poise and dignified deportment of a perfect little gentleman, I was moved, for no particular reason, to smite him with the flat of my sword where the seat of his trousers should have been, and to hound him along with such opprobrious epithets as I had learned.

"Quicker! Quicker! Misbegotten son of a dog!" I howled; and belaboured the poor half-blind tottering creature in the best Oriental manner.

We rounded a corner, and de Redon laughing heartily, straightened up.

"Splendid!" he said. "But I'll borrow the sword and drive *you*, next time. . . . Splendid!" he gasped. . . .

"Now we'll cut in ahead of Bouchard and his Zouaves and try to get you into the Residency with them. . . . Come on. . . ." and he started running again.

We turned a corner and ran into a gang of looters.

Some were yelling, wrangling, squabbling, in front of a house, while others appeared to be literally turning the house inside out.

As a bed, fittings and occupant complete, came flying over a balcony, de Redon executed a number of those dance-steps which had already won my admiration, while defying emulation so far as I was concerned.

Scarcely slackening his pace, he spun round and round like a top, whooping fiendishly. This interested the looters not at all, and we passed on unmolested—my immediate wonder being whether the occupant of the deciduous bed were an invalid, and my immediate decision being that at any rate he soon would be. . . .

Turning again and dashing through a narrow stinking close, we heard a dreadful scream, that pierced the more distant din of the shouting and fighting.

In a dark and deeply-recessed porch, the back of which was an open door, a man stood with one foot on the breast of a child—a little girl, whose skinny arm he appeared to be turning and twisting from her body in his effort to secure the wide thick armlet of silver, which was apparently too small to pass the elbow.

I have to testify that de Redon was into that doorway before I was.

Turning with a fierce snarl the brute snatched a great knife from his sash, as de Redon, unable to swing his staff up, used it like a spear. The end of the staff went home with a pleasant thud, and drove the man sprawling back against the wall.

Raising the knife, he sprang at de Redon, seizing the staff in his left hand as he did so; and I simultaneously swiped the brute with my heavy sword.

It was the first time in my life that I had struck a man in anger, and I did it unskilfully . . . so unskilfully that, though he had every cause for complaint, he had no opportunity. The sword was so sharp and heavy, and wrath and indignation had so nerved my arm, that I had split his skull and killed him dead as a door-nail.

"*Mon Dieu!*" observed de Redon, as the man went down, taking the sword with him. "Don't you hit me with that sword any more."

Picking up the sobbing child, I lifted her inside the heavy door, and shut her in the house.

"Papa and the men-servants all gone to the fair, I suppose," observed de Redon, as we ran on down the alley. . . .

This same alley became a tunnel which led into a small square. As we came out into this, the noise became terrific, and, looking down a narrow bazaar which joined it to a main street, we saw that this latter was packed with a dense crowd of armed men all streaming along past the end of it.

"Bouchard will never do it," said de Redon, slowing up. "He should have stayed where he was posted. . . . Perhaps they burnt him out, though. . . .

"Look here," he continued, "if you turn to the right at the end of this bazaar, I expect you'll know where you are. It leads straight to the Residency. . . . Suppose you try to get in, and let Levasseur know what's happening. . . . Tell him Bouchard is fighting his way from the market-square to the Residency, and that I say he'll need help. Then Levasseur can use his own discretion as to whether to make a sortie. . . . I'll go along with the crowd and try the 'French-Army-with-cannon-behind-you' game again. . . . Good luck, *mon ami*. . . . If anyone interferes with you, give him one like you gave our late friend in the doorway. . . . Good-bye. . . ."

And those were the last words spoken to me by Captain Raoul d'Auray de Redon of the French Secret Service.

"Good-bye, old chap, and good luck," I said, and, a minute later, we were into the crowd, de Redon attracting all the attention he could by whooping, twirling his staff, spinning round and round, and howling like the demented dervish he was impersonating.

I, on the contrary, hugging the wall, made my way along in the opposite direction as unobtrusively as possible, and attracted no attention. It struck me as I dodged, elbowed, pushed and evaded the impulsive pedestrian traffic, that, in a way, a fugitive is a good deal safer in time of tremendous public uproar and disturbance than during profound peace, inasmuch as everybody is far too excited to be observant.

Anyhow, not a soul molested me as I went along muttering, gesticulating and foaming at the mouth. It is a curious fact that I did not taste the fragment of soap which I had placed beneath my tongue.

§3

In a few minutes, the throng thinned and slackened and I found that this crowd had detached itself from the outskirts of the vaster one that surrounded the Residency.

Here I made quicker progress, and eventually came, at a run, into a dense mob that filled the street and faced in the direction in which I was going.

Backward and forward they moved, as the front ranks advanced and retired, and into these front ranks I could only make my way by clinging tight to posts, throwing myself down against walls, or diving into doorways, whenever the mob was driven back.

At last I was where I wanted to be, and looked upon a stirring scene of battle, murder and sudden death.

A regular siege of the Residency was in progress, a siege enlivened by constant assault.

From every window, balcony, roof-top, wall, minaret, tower, doorway and street corner, a steady fusillade concentrated upon the building, while, every now and then, a great company of wild death-seeking fanatics rushed at the low wall that surrounded its compound, only to break and wither beneath the blast of the steady rifle-fire of the defenders, and to find the death they sought.

Crisp and timely, crash upon crash, came the volleys from the treble tier of fire of the troopers at the wall, the windows and the roof. Wave after wave swept forward and broke upon that steady rock, throwing up a white spray, as survivors of the ordeal-by-fire sprang on the low wall, and the bayonets of the French soldiers.

And, the whole time, a ceaseless rain of bullets struck the house, so that it was in a nimbus of its own dust—a kind of halo of its own glory and suffering, as each bullet registered its impact with a puff of whitewash, dust and powdered brick. . . .

How to get in there? . . .

From the surrounding wall, from every window and balcony, and from the parapet of the flat roof, the rifles of the defenders cracked unceasingly. It would be plain and simple suicide to advance openly, dressed as I was, and it would be suicide of a more unpleasant kind to strip off my Arab head-dress and *burnous*, and so proclaim myself a Christian.

Edging along the walls of houses, crawling on all fours, dashing from doorway to doorway and shelter to shelter, I gradually made my way from among those who played a comparatively safe and waiting rôle—onlookers who would turn to looting murderers as soon as the wall was cleared, and the doors beaten in—until I was among the fighting fanatics who made the frequent hand-to-hand attacks upon the low wall, the wall that must be captured before the house could be set on fire or taken by assault.

There was a hellish din from the hundreds of guns and rifles banging in all directions, and the continuous animal howling of the mob.

It would have been impossible in this inferno to hear what anybody said, and the wild rushes that broke upon the wall were the outcome of herd instinct and mob-intuition rather than of any definite organization, orders and leading.

Suddenly everybody would dash forward, the mouth of every street vomit hundreds and hundreds of men, and a great sword-waving mob would surge across the open, hack and hew and slash as it reached the wall, waver and fall back—and then turn and run for dear life to the lanes, alleys, buildings and compounds from which it came.

And, each time, the litter of dead and wounded increased and lay ever thicker along the wall. Soon the besiegers would be able to charge straight over the wall on a ramp of bodies. . . .

From where I crouched in a deep gutter, my head and shoulders behind a stone post or mounting-block, I could see two sides of the Residency, and did not doubt that it was under heavy fire on its two garden sides.

As I watched and cast about in my mind for a plan, the strange psychology of mobs decreed another sudden simultaneous assault, and I found myself running and yelling with the best—or the worst—in a desperate charge upon the desperately defended wall.

Let it not be supposed that I displayed heroism or strove to find a hero's grave. Far from it. I displayed such prudence as was possible, to avoid getting into the front rank of the rush, and rather strove to keep a hero's body between me and the rifles as we ran. And when at last I reluctantly found myself bounding over the prostrate forms of those behind whom I had hitherto been sheltered, I promptly joined them in their biting of the dust, until a living wall of humanity was once more between me and the wall of stone.

Leaping to my feet again, I made another rush at the spot where the fighting-line was thickest and cast myself at the feet of the brave.

Of the feet of the brave I soon had more than sufficient, for they were planted heavily on every portion of my person, as the un-led unorganized hordes again retreated.

Left high and dry by this ebbing tide of horny-hoofed humanity, I found myself within a few feet of the wall, and one of hundreds of motionless, or writhing and twitching bodies.

Of the defenders of the wall I could see nothing save their gleaming bayonet-tips, the occasional *képi* of someone who ran crouching along, and the heads of watchful sentries placed at intervals.

A moving cap halted, rose slowly upward and a man looked over the wall.

Now was my chance.

Raising myself on my hands, I shouted:

"*Hi! Monsieur! Je suis Americain!* . . . *Je suis un ami!* . . . *Aidez-moi!* . . . *Je viens.* . . ."

And down I flopped with the utmost alacrity as the worthy man, with a swift neatness, theoretically quite admirable, drew and fired an automatic pistol.

Though he had drawn and fired practically in one movement, his aim was extraordinarily good, for the bullet hit the ground within an inch of my head.

I believe I gave an excellent rendering of the rôle of a dead Arab.

And I decided to play this easy part until there were again some braver men than I, between myself and that wall. Nor did I have long to wait.

With a howl that seemed to achieve the impossible by drowning all other sounds, the mob charged again, materializing with astonishing swiftness, and in astounding numbers.

A shout, a whistle, a sharp order . . . the wall was lined with heads and rifles . . . and I fairly burrowed into the filthy dust with my nose, as a volley crashed out . . . again . . . again . . . and I felt as though I should be blown away upon the blast. . . .

With my hands protecting my head, I endured the rush and trample for a few seconds; and then, with a bound and the record sprint of my life, I flung myself at the base of the wall, as a rifle seemed to blow my head off, and a bayonet tore my filthy *kafieh* just beside my neck.

As I fell and snuggled into the friendly base of that lovely wall, I thought I was blind and deaf and probably dumb, or "alternatively," as the lawyers say, quite completely dead.

Quickly, however, I decided that none of these things was so, as I could see filthy feet and brawny brown legs scuffling around me, and hear the sounds of combat, and shout a curse when a charging, bounding *ghazi* landed fairly on my stomach, and, for a few minutes, that seemed like a few hours, I was kicked, trampled, trodden and struck until I was almost driven to spring up and take my chance at the wall . . .

And suddenly I was free, and the feet that had trampled me, were either once more in headlong flight, or else stilled in death.

Free also I was to make all the row I wished, in French, and to tear off my Arab head-dress and reveal myself to whomsoever would lend me his ears. . . .

But I remembered the shoot-first-and-ask-afterward gentleman with the automatic, and restrained my inclination to poke my head over the wall.

Something had to go over the wall, however, so I lifted up my voice and started, more or less tunefully, to bawl in French, a version of a song which I had very often heard on the lips of Colonel Levasseur, and the tune of which I had often heard soldiers singing and whistling on the march. In point of fact, Major de Beaujolais had picked it out on the piano and sung it at Mary's request after dinner only last night—the Marching-Song of the Legion . . .

> "Tiens voilà du boudin! voilà du boudin! voilà du boudin!
>   Pour les Alsaciens, les Suisses et les Lorraines;
>   Pour les Belges il n'y en a point,
>   Pour les Belges il n'y en a point,
>   Car ce sont des tireurs au flanc.
>   Pour les Belges il n'y en a point,
>   Pour les Belges il n'y en a point,
>   Car ce sont des tireurs au flanc.

I sang, or rather shouted, and I was heard.

A head suddenly appeared over the wall. . . . Hell! It was my friend of the automatic, and most markedly I did not move.

"*Tiens!*" I cried. "*Voyez!* and also *Regardez!* and *Ecoutez!* and all that, *et ne tirez pas.* Don't shoot the singer, he's doing his best, and have you seen the pen of my aunt, *parceque je suis Americain et Anglais, et Français, et bon garçon et votre ami. Oui! Oui! Je vous aime, Monsieur le Sergent. Comment allez-vous ce matin, et Madame votre femme et tous les petits sergents?* . . . 'Kiss me Hardy,' said Nelson, and 'War is Hell' replied Sherman."

The man's head and shoulders came up over the wall, and, placing both hands upon it, he leant right over and stared at me, his mouth open and his eyes starting from his head.

"Que le diable emportez-vous?" the Zouave growled. "Who the devil are you and what the hell are you doing there?"

And with a watchful eye upon his empty right hand, I raised myself from the ground, swiftly gabbling that I was a friend and guest of Colonel Levasseur, that I brought most urgent and important information, and that he must either call the Colonel instantly, or let me come over the wall.

The wary man's right hand disappeared from sight, and I flopped back into the dust as it returned holding that beastly automatic.

Damn the thick-headed fool I had torn off my head-dress exposing my fair neck, ears and hair, and the mob would charge again at any minute.

"When I shout '*Come*,' jump over the wall and throw yourself on the ground," bawled the quick-witted clever man whom I had so miscalled. "And lie down quick on this side, or I'll blow your head off," he concluded and disappeared.

"Come!" he shouted a second later, and I fairly threw myself over the wall and at the feet of the Sergeant, while he and several of his officious braves covered me with their rifles.

"Colonel Levasseur will be round here in a minute. You stay like that till he comes," said the Zouave Sergeant, and, as he turned away, bade two of his men to shoot me if I moved, or if they felt like it.

I proceeded to play at Living Statuary and tried not to twitch a muscle even when flies endeavoured to explore my brain by way of my eyes, ears and nose.

Among the men who crouched lining the wall were many others who lay at full length upon the ground, dead or too badly wounded to make further effort. The garrison had suffered heavily, both from rifle-fire and from the constant hand-to-hand *mêlées*, when the swords of the Arabs had met the bayonets of the soldiers.

As I watched, a military surgeon, followed by four hospital-orderlies, or stretcher-bearers, came round the corner of the house, and, in spite of the continual heavy fire, had the severely wounded carried away, and the dead laid in a row where they would not cause the feet of the fighting-men to stumble. The less-severely wounded were bandaged where they sat with their backs to the wall.

"What's this?" asked the Surgeon-Major, whom I knew well, as he passed me. "An Arab prisoner. What do you want *prisoners* for?"

"True," I answered, to his great astonishment, "especially when they are not only civilians but neutrals."

"*Mon Dieu!*" ejaculated the Major. "But you look a pretty bloody neutral and a fairly war-like civilian . . ." and he bent over the still form of a Zouave. . . .

Colonel Levasseur came round the same corner, cool as on parade, followed by his *officier d'ordonnance.*

" 'Evening, Colonel," I called, rising to my feet. "Excuse a certain disorder of dress. . . ."

"Good God It *is* you, Vanbrugh!" he said, seizing my hand and leading me into the house. "*Where's your sister?*"

"De Beaujolais has taken her away with him," I replied, "and Captain de Redon says they have got clear of the town. . . . And I am to tell you that a detachment of Zouaves, under Bouchard, is fighting its way here, and is held up in the Street of the Silversmiths . . . a huge mob between them and you. . . ."

"And you fought your way in here to bring them relief?" cried the good Colonel, and for one dreadful moment I thought he was going to embrace and kiss me. "You shall get the Cross of the Legion of Honour for that, my brave friend. . . . You have offered your life for Frenchmen and for France. . . ."

"Fought nothing, Colonel," I assured him. . . . "Offered nothing. . . . I snooped around in a great funk, pinched these rags from dead men's backs, and crawled in here on my tummy. . . . But if you'll give me a rifle and a quiet corner, I can hit a running Arab at twenty yards, especially if he is running at *me.*"

Levasseur smiled.

"Up on the roof then," he said, "and snipe their snipers. There are some swine with Lebel rifles on neighbouring high buildings, who are doing a lot of damage. . . . Take care of yourself. . . . Better put on a *képi* and tunic before you go up—you look like the President of all the Dervishes and you might get a bayonet in you before you could explain. . . . Excuse me, I must get Bouchard's lot in. . . . Down the Street of the Silversmiths, you said? . . ."

Outside the room which the Surgeon-Major had turned into an operating theatre, there was a pile of blood-stained clothing and accoutrements. From among these I took a *képi*, regimental jacket, pouch-belt and rifle, and made my way up through the well-known interior—so familiar and yet so utterly different—to the roof, the parapet of which was lined with sharp-shooters who kept up a continual independent fire at surrounding minarets, watch-towers, and roofs of higher houses, which overlooked and commanded this one.

"Hi! Who are you?" cried a bearded officer crouching against the wall opposite the little stone porch, built over the top of the steps that led to the roof.

I knew him by sight but couldn't remember his name.

"Colonel Levasseur's guest, Vanbrugh," I shouted. "He told me to come up here."

"Run across and lie down here," he called back, and I noticed that he drew his revolver as I did so.

"Excuse me," he said, "I didn't recognize you—I don't think that *Madame votre mère* would do so, either. . . . Now, if you can get the sportsman who is ensconced in the corner of that roof *there*, you'll have earned your corn for the day. . . . He's shot four of my men already, in spite of the bad light. . . ."

So, for a brief space, I was an unenlisted man, fighting for France and my own skin. It was extremely exciting and thrilling, and one was too busy to be nervous. Snap-shooting by flickering firelight, mingled with bright moonlight, is very interesting.

The sniper and I fought our little duel out. . . . I got quite fond of him. . . . R.I.P. . . . Perhaps my rifle was better than his, though I had no fault to find with the latter when it took my *képi* from my head, nor when it spoilt the perfectly good collar of my unbuttoned jacket. . . . The light was good enough for him, anyhow. . . .

I was aware of the increasing sounds of approaching volley-firing. Evidently Bouchard's detachment were overcoming resistance and fighting their way in.

The officer in command of the roof was sending more and more men over to the side that commanded the square, so I went across to that side too, chiefly with the object of getting a good view of the show when the Zouaves burst into the open, and charged through.

Cautiously I peeped over the parapet.

Another assault was impending, and down the Street of the Silversmiths came the swiftest of those who were fleeing before the

Zouaves.

At their head was a figure that I recognized—an almost naked scarecrow that spun round occasionally as he ran, and twirled a great staff above his head.

I rushed to my officer and indicated de Redon to him, and then with a brief "Excuse me," cast military propriety to the winds, dashed across to the stairs, and down them in search of Levasseur. . . . I could not run round to every officer, non-commissioned officer, and soldier in the building, and point out de Redon to him individually—but I had some sort of idea that Levasseur might sound the "Cease fire!" while de Redon did his work and then rushed off elsewhere. . . .

I made a swift tour of the upper floor, of which each window and balcony was crowded with soldiers, behind whom lay the bodies of those who would fight no more.

I had expected to find the Colonel on the big wide verandah that ran the length of the front of the house, on either side of the vast roof of the colonnaded porch. This verandah had a low wall or parapet and, like the compound-wall below, was lined with soldiers.

Levasseur was not here, and, as I glanced below, I saw great masses of men gathering to surge across the square in a mighty overwhelming wave once more. I saw a mob come rushing down the Street of the Silversmiths, and de Redon—far ahead of them—bounding, leaping, twirling and yelling in front of the main attack opposite the front of the Residency.

"*Back! Back!*" he howled. "*Beware! Beware! . . . The big guns are coming. . . . Run! . . . Run! . . .*"

I also ran, down the stairs that led to the entrance-hall, and out into the compound, where the soldiers—whose fire-control was admirable—crouched along the wall like statues with levelled rifles, awaiting the volley-signal.

As I rushed past the bearers of a pitiful blinded Zouave, and down the steps under the porch, I saw Colonel Levasseur, standing between his second-in-command and his aide-de-camp, pointing with raised arm, and, as I saw him, I received a tremendous blow that knocked me down. I thought someone had hit me, looked round, and got to my feet, feeling very queer. . . .

What was it that I had been about to do? . . . Something very urgent and important. . . . De Redon!

As I reeled forward, trying to shout, Levasseur's voice rang out with tremendous volume and authority. . . . He was still pointing.

. . . He himself was ordering a volley! . . . I staggered towards him mouthing silently. . . .

With a great crash, every rifle along that side of the compound was fired. . . . The earth rose up and hit me or else I fell to the ground. . . .

Another great shout from Levasseur. . . . Another volley. . . .

I tore myself from what seemed the powerful grip of Mother Earth, steadied myself, and saw de Redon doing exactly what I was doing, standing, swaying, tottering, his hands pressed to his breast. . . . Why was he imitating me? . . . Why could I not shout to Levasseur? . . .

De Redon fell heavily, head foremost. . . . So did I. . . . Why was I imitating him? . . . A great faintness. . . . A grim fierce face before my closing eyes. . . . An Arab about to slay me? . . . No, a feathered head-dress—a face more powerful than that of any Arab. . . . Thank you, Chief. . . . Dogged does it. . . . Grit . . . and grit . . . and iron guts. . . .

I was on my feet again; breathing more easily too; pulling myself together again; coming round; blood running down my chest and arm. . . .

I reached Levasseur's side somehow—and found I could not speak!

"*Vous êtes bien touché, mon pauvre ami!*" he said, in his great rough kindly voice.

I could not make a sound in answer, and he turned from me and bawled another order. The aide-de-camp shouted something about going inside and finding the doctor.

I tried to pull my jacket off and he gave me a hand, thinking I was trying to get at my wound.

Dropping my *képi* on the ground by the jacket, I made for the wall, wearing only an Arab garment like a long shirt, and very baggy Arab trousers—both garments filthy and covered in blood, mine and that of their late owner.

I managed to get over the low wall without being grabbed by one of the defenders, and a stumbling, tottering run brought me to where de Redon lay in his blood.

Stooping to give him a hand, I found that it would only be a hand, for my right arm had ceased to function. It merely swung numb and useless, as I bent down.

De Redon did not move. I seized him and began to drag him in the direction of the wall. . . . His rotten rags tore away, and I fell. . . . The pain, for which I had been subconsciously waiting, began then, and I think it stimulated me.

I got up again and turned de Redon over. I wanted to get a grip on something he was wearing. Lift him I could not, with only one arm and scarcely the strength to keep myself erect. It seemed beastly to pull him by the arm or leg or hair. . . . He was most obviously dead. . . . Horribly riddled. . . .

None the less, I must get him. . . . I would *not* go back without him, and, with a word of apology I seized his wrist and began to drag. . . .

I was astonished to find myself alive.

Why was I not shot by one side—or both?

I concluded that the very few on either side who had time to notice me, took me for a friend. The French soldiers were not firing independently but were awaiting the order for the next volley, and they had seen me run out from the compound. The Arabs saw a blood-stained Arab, escaping presumably from the French; but they would begin to shoot at me as soon as they saw me dragging a body to the compound. . . . Or would they think me mad? . . . Anyhow I was going on the return journey, making good time, and in another minute I should be at the wall. . . .

Was it *possible* that not three minutes ago I had been up on the roof exchanging pot-shots in a friendly and sporting spirit with a very competent sniper? . . .

A few more yards and . . .

There was a sudden deafening crescendo of the infernal din, a hellish roar from ten thousand throats . . . a crashing volley . . . another . . . and I was hurled headlong, trampled flat, smashed and ground and crushed, a living agony—until a smashing blow upon the head was a crowning mercy that brought oblivion.

§4

I must have been unconscious for a very long time—or, what is more probable, I must have been unconscious and semi-conscious, off and on, for hours—as I have a recollection of terrible battle-dreams, of receiving further injuries, and of being partly buried beneath a heavy weight.

When I awoke, or regained full consciousness, the sun was setting and the battle was over. . . . Gradually I realized that I must have been where I was, for nearly a day. . . . Absolute silence reigned where the very spirit of devilish din had so long rioted. . . . I was lying where I had fallen. . . . The body of a big Arab lay across my legs. . . . The head of another was on my stomach, face downwards. . . . More were sprawled and huddled close against me. All very intimate and cosy together.

With great effort and greater pain, I slowly turned my head in the direction of the Residency, and beheld its charred and blackened ruins affronting the rising sun. The compound wall appeared to be hidden by the piles of dead.

I hoped that the garrison had died in the compound and not in the burning building I thought of the wounded laid out in rows in the corridor outside the operating-room.

My next effort was in the direction of self-help, and was fruitless. What I earnestly desired to do was to remove the head of the dead Arab from the pit of my stomach, where it seemed to have the weight and size of a mile-stone.

I soon discovered that it would be all I could do to remove a fly from the end of my nose, and that by the time I did it the fly would be gone. I don't suppose I could have moved if those two bodies had not been lying upon me. I had lost a great deal of blood, from two bullet wounds in the neck and shoulder, and a bad sword-cut on the head. . . .

It is a truth as well as a truism that we don't know our blessings when we receive them. In fact it is impossible to tell a blessing from a curse. But for those wounds, I should have got back into the Residency and died with the rest. When that enthusiast with the sword did his good deed for the day, he saved my life (and a life worth a thousand of mine, as well) and I never even saw his bright countenance.

That night was just endurable, but to this hour I do not greatly care to dwell upon the day that followed. How much was delirium, nightmare-dream, subjective horror, and how much was real, I do not know. But there were unutterable agonies of thirst and terrible pain, and the unbearable burning of the sun upon one's exposed unmoving flesh; there were vultures, kites and pariah dogs; prowling ghouls who robbed the pitiful dead; times when I gained full control of my faculties and lost them again in paroxysms of screaming terror, pain and fear—silent screams that did not issue from cracked black lips.

And always there were flies in thousands of millions.

At times I was mad and delirious; at times I must have been mercifully unconscious; and at times I was quite clear-headed, and perhaps those were the worst.

I distinctly remember concluding that my father was right and that I was wrong. There was a Great Good God of Love and Mercy who let us be born filled with Original Sin and who had created an Eternal Hell for all that sinned. I had sinned—and here I was, nailed down and being slowly roasted, in unspeakable pain, for ever and for ever. Yes, Father was right, and Noel and I had been wrong in agreeing that such would not be the nature of a God of Love, but rather of a Devil of Hate.

I believe that I slept when kind beneficent Night succeeded hellish torturing Day. At any rate, I was unconscious for most of the time, and remember nothing but occasional glimpses of the stars, and then, with shrinking abject terror, seeing the sun rise.

That was the last of conscious suffering, for I remember no more, and I afterwards learned that I had a very narrow escape of being buried alive when the French relief-force arrived and began clearing up the mess.

It was my white skin that saved me. The men of the burial-fatigue party who were removing my body with those of hundreds of others, noticed that I was some kind of a European, and drew the attention of their Sergeant to the fact. This man informed an officer, and the officer discovered that I was alive as well as white —in parts.

In the military hospital I was most kindly and competently nursed, and, when fit to be moved, I was transferred to Algiers that I might have the benefit of sea-breezes, ice, fresh fruit, better food, and the creature comforts unprocurable in the desert city of Zaguig.

And here I told my tale to the authorities, or rather to the very charming representative of the authorities who visited me in hospital.

Having given all the information that I could, concerning the fate of the garrison of Zaguig, I sought for news of de Beaujolais, but I forbore to mention that my sister was with him. . . . He had seemed so very averse from taking her, and had made the military impropriety of such a thing so clear, that I thought it best to say nothing on the subject—particularly when I found that they knew absolutely nothing as to his fate, and did not expect to do so for weeks or months. My informant professed absolute ignorance of de Beaujolais' destination even.

I decided that, whether the doctors released me from hospital or not, I would remain in Algiers until there was definite news of de Beaujolais. I would then fit out a caravan and go in search of him and of my sister. . . .

After a certain point, I did not progress very favourably. My wounds healed well, but I suffered most appalling headaches—whether from the sword-cut or from sunstroke did not seem clear. At times I thought a splinter of bone must be pressing on my brain, but the admirable surgeon assured me that the bone was not splintered at all, and that the headaches would grow less frequent and less painful.

They did neither, and I decided that I would go to London and see Sir Herbert Menken, then considered the greatest consulting-surgeon in the world.

And while I was slowly gathering energy and still putting of the evil day of travel, Mary arrived, well, smiling, radiantly happy, and engaged to marry Major de Beaujolais.

She had accompanied him to his destination and returned with him to Zaguig, fearing the worst so far as I was concerned. Here they had heard of my escape, and a black cloud had been lifted from Mary's mind—for the joy and happiness of her engagement to the man whom she had "loved at first sight" had been darkened and damaged by her fear—fear amounting almost to a certainty—of my death.

However, she had hoped against hope, and had moreover been conscious of an illogical but persistent belief that I was not dead.

She assured me that one corner of her mind had not been in the least surprised when they got the astounding news that I had survived and was, in fact, the sole survivor of the massacre. . . .

Mary and I took up our temporary abode at the Hotel Splendide at Mustapha Supérieur, and she nursed me while de Beaujolais reported himself and his doings to the military authorities, and obtained furlough for his marriage and honeymoon.

I went with them to Paris after the wedding, where de Beaujolais shopped assiduously with Mary and showed himself not only brave but *foulard*-y, and thence, alone and very lonely, ill and miserable, I went on to London in the desperate hope that Sir Herbert Menken could do something to relieve my almost unbearable headache, insomnia, neurasthenia and general feeling of hopeless illness.

I was quickly coming to the point where either something must be done to me, or I must do something to myself—something quite final, with a pistol.

CHAPTER VI

How shall hasty and impatient Man know his blessings from his curses, his good from his evil?

Good came upon me at this time in most terrible form, and in my ignorance I prayed to be delivered from my good, from the blessing that brought me my life's usefulness and joy. . . .

I arose on this particular morning, in London, feeling ill and apprehensive, afraid of I knew not what, but none the less afraid. I was in the grip of Hell's chief devil—Fear—the fear of something wholly unspecified.

Having dressed, with trembling fingers, I avoided the hotel dining-room and, as early as was reasonable, I set forth, bathed in perspiration, to keep my appointment with Sir Herbert Menken.

"Taxi, sir?" inquired the Jovian hall-porter, as I passed the counter behind which he lurked, all-seeing and omniscient—and it was borne in upon me that his query was absurd. *Of course* I could not enter a taxi! What a horrible idea! . . . I would as soon have cut my throat as get into a taxi—or any other vehicle.

"Good Heavens, no!" I replied shuddering, and passed out into the street, much perturbed at the man's horrible suggestion.

Dreading and hating the throng, the noise, the traffic, I made my way along the street, feeling as I had never felt before, and as I pray God I may never feel again.

I would have given anything to have been back in Zaguig with all its murderous dangers, provided I could have felt as I did there.

I was not in pain . . . I did not feel definitely ill in any definite part of my body . . . I was not afraid of anything to which I could give a name . . . And yet I felt terrible. Every nerve in my body shrieked to God for mercy, and I knew that unless I did *something* (but what, in the name of Pity?) and did it quickly, I should go mad or fling myself under a street-car or truck. . . .

I fought my way on. . . .

Merciful Christ have pity! This was suffering such as the Zaguigans could never have caused me with knives or red-hot irons. . . . Where was I? . . . *What* was I? . . .

Suddenly I knew what I was. . . .

Of course! I was a shell-fish deprived of its shell, and wholly at the mercy of its environing universe. Yes, I was a creature of the crustacean kind, a sort of crab or lobster, without its armour. Every wave of ether could strike me a cruel blow; the least thing touching me would cause me agony unspeakable—even rays of light impinging upon my exposed nerve-surfaces would be,—nay, *were* —as barbed arrows, spears and javelins. . . .

If a passer-by brushed against me, I should shriek—a flayed man rubbed with sand-paper. . . . Yes—I was a naked crustacean, and I must find a hole into which to creep. . . . A nice hole beneath a great rock; a hole just big enough to contain, without touching, me. . . . There I should be saved from the eyes and hands, the mouths and antennae of the million-headed . . .

But I could see no hole into which to creep. . . .

I took a grip upon my courage, and passed on, in search of one —a beautiful dark cave, just big enough . . .

I reached the end of the block and was about to step off the side-walk when I realized my new danger. If I stepped into the road, the flood of traffic that streamed along it would bear me away irresistibly; away, on and on, into some wild and whirling Charybdis, wherein I should for ever go round and round with accelerating velocity for all eternity, never, never to find the beautiful dark cave that was my great necessity. . . .

I had had a narrow escape from a terrible danger, and I drew back from the gutter, and crouched against some railings. These seemed friendly. At any rate, they did not hurry along, nor whirl round. I clung to them, conscious of the stares of the curious as they hurried past, immersed in their own affairs, but with a glance to spare for mine.

Two errand-boys passed, one in a many-buttoned uniform.

"Blimey! *'E*'s 'ad a 'appy evenin' somewheres," observed one of them. " 'E sang '*Won't be 'ome till mornin*'—and 'e ain't."

"Yus," agreed the other, eyeing me with a large toleration, "some people 'as all the luck."

I tried to give them money, to get them to go away and cease to look at me, but my hand so shook that I could not get at my pocket.

I turned my face to the railings and, peering through them, saw that they guarded an "area" or small paved yard on to which looked the basement-windows of the house. And into this yard, some twenty feet below me, opened the door of a coal-cellar, or some such place—a dark, quiet, beautiful cave into which one could crawl and be safe from mocking eyes and jeering voices, from touching hands and feeling antennae, from *everything* that could, by the slightest contact, agonize one's utterly exposed and unprotected surfaces.

If only I could get to that dark beautiful cave! . . . But if I loosened my grip of the railings I might fall, or be carried along until I was thrust into the dark river of the roadway and whirled to destruction never-ending.

I moved along the railings, not releasing one hand-grip until I had secured the next, and the perspiration streamed down me as I concentrated every faculty upon this difficult progress to the gate that I could see at the head of a flight of stone steps, leading down to my cave of safety. . . .

And then a Voice smote me, and I looked over my shoulder, my heart in my mouth.

"What's the game, Sir?" said the Voice.

It was a vast and splendid London policeman, one of those strong quiet men, wise, calm, unarmed, dressed in a long authority, the very embodiment of law, order and security, the wonder and admiration of Europe.

Terrible as it was to be addressed and scrutinized, I felt I could bear the agony of it, because these men are universal friends and helpers to all but evil-doers.

"I am an unshelled crustacean . . . I want to get down to that cave," I said, pointing.

"Crushed *what*? . . . Want to get home, you mean, I think, Sir," was the reply. "Where's that?"

"In America," I said.

"Longish way," observed the policeman. "Where did you sleep last night, if it isn't asking?"

"At my hotel," I replied.

"Ah—that's better, Sir," said the good fellow. "Which one? . . . We might get back there perhaps, eh?"

"No, no—I couldn't . . . I simply could *not*," I assured him. "I would sooner die . . . I *should* die—a dreadful death. . . ."

"*Pass along, please!*" said the policeman suddenly and sharply, to the small crowd that had collected. " 'Ere, you—'*op* it—quick," he added to a blue-nosed loafer, who stood gazing bovine and unobedient. . . .

I can remember every word and incident of that truly terrible time, for myself stood apart and watched the suffering wretch that was me, and could give no help, could do nothing but look on—and suffer unutterably.

"Now then, Sir," said the policeman, "if you can't go 'ome, an' you won't go to your 'otel, where *can* you go? . . . We all got to go somewheres, y' know. . . .

"You don't want to come along o' me, do yer?" he added as I pondered his dark saying that we must all go somewhere, shook my head in despair, and clung to the railings.

"With *you*? Where to?" I asked, with a new hope.

"Station," he replied. "Sit down in a nice quiet little—er—room—while we find out something about yer."

"I should love it," I told him. "Could you put me in a cell and lock the door?"

"You'd have to *do* somethink first," the kindly man assured me.

This seemed a splendid chance! Fancy being concealed in a beautiful dark cell until my shell grew again and there was something between my exposed nerves, my bare raw flesh, my ultimate innermost self, and the rough-shod rasping world!

"If I gave you a sovereign and thumped you on the chest, would you arrest me for assault and lock me up?" I asked. "Do—for Mercy's sake . . . I'll give you anything you like—all I have."

"*Come*, come now, sir," expostulated the officer, "you let me put you in a taxi, and you go back to your 'otel an' go to bed an' 'ave a good sleep. . . . If you don't feel better then, you tell 'em to send for a doctor. . . .

"You a teetotaller?" he added, as I stared hopelessly at his impassive face.

"Practically," I said. "Not in theory, you know, but . . ."

"Any'ow you ain't drunk *now*," he admitted, sniffing, and added briskly, "Come along, now, sir! This ain't no way for a gent to be'ave at ten o'clock of a Monday morning," and, turning to the lingering passers-by, suddenly boomed, "*Will* you pass along, please," in a manner that swiftly relieved me of the painful stare of many gazing eyes.

One man did not pass along, however, nor go by on the other side. . . . No Levite, he. . . .

He was a small neat man, very well dressed in a quiet way.

"You are like a moth," I said. "For God's sake spread your wings over me. . . . My shell has come off. . . ."

Of course he was like a moth. He had great black eyebrows and deep luminous eyes . . . sphinx-like, he was . . . the sphinx-moth. . . .

I had seen moths with just such eyebrows, and eyes shining in the lamp-light. . . .

"Ill?" he asked, and took my wrist between finger and thumb.

"What's your name and address?"

"I don't know," I replied. "Do help me . . . I'm in Hell—body and soul . . . and I shall shriek in a minute. . . . For the love of God help me to find a cave or a hole . . ."

"Come along with me," he said promptly, "I've got a beauty. . . ."

He stared hard into my eyes, and in his I saw goodness and friendship, and I believed and trusted him implicitly. . . .

I had fallen into the hands of the greatest alienist and nerve-specialist in England. . . . Coincidence? . . .

Tucking his arm through mine, he detached me from the railings, led me to the house, close by, in Harley Street, where he had his consulting-rooms, gave me a draught of the veritable Waters of Lethe, and put me to bed on a sofa in a back room.

Without troubling to discover whether I was a pauper, a criminal, an escaped lunatic, or a prince in disguise, he took me that night to his far-famed nursing-home in Kent.

And here, my salvation, in guise incredible, most wonderfully awaited me.

§2

At Shillingford House, a great old mansion of warm red Tudor brick, Dr. Hanley-Blythe kept me in bed for a week or so, visiting me upon alternate days and submitting me to an extraordinarily searching cross-examination, many of the questions of which, I was at first inclined to resent. I soon realized, however, that there was absolutely nothing in the specialist's mind but the promotion of my welfare, and I answered every question truthfully and to the best of my ability.

One day, after carefully and patiently extracting from me every detail of a ghastly dream that I had had the previous night—a dream in which I dreamt that I murdered my father—he asked:

"Did you love your father when you were a boy?"

"Yes," I replied.

"Certain?" he queried.

"Er—yes—I think so. . . ." I said.

"*I* don't. In fact I know you didn't," he countered.

I thought a while, and realized that the doctor was right. Of course I had never loved my father. I had respected, feared, obeyed and *hated* him. . . . He had been the Terror that walked by day and the Fear that stalked me by night. . . .

"Face the facts, my dear chap," said the doctor. "What is, is—and your salvation depends on freeing your mind from repressions, and making a new adjustment to life. . . . The truth will make you free—and whole. . . . Get it up, and get it out. . . ."

I pondered deeply and delved into the past.

"I am sorry to say that I have always hated my father," I confessed. "Feared and hated him terribly. . . ."

"Yes—and you made your God in your father's image," said the doctor. . . .

"I have 'feared God' but not hated Him," I replied.

"Nonsense!" exploded Dr. Hanley-Blythe. "Don't we hate *everything* and everyone that we fear? . . . Fear is a curse, a disease, a deadly microbe . . . the seed of death and damnation. . . . Since we are speaking of God—get rid of that foul idea of 'fear God.' . . .

"*Love* God. . . . What decent God would rather be feared than loved? . . . Let's have a God that is a *little* more divine than a damned savage Ju-Ju! . . . That cursed injunction to *fear* God! . . . Killed more souls and bodies than anything else. . . . Love God and fear nothing! . . . Some sense in that. . . .

"Now look here—get your father in perspective. He's a poor human sinner like yourself and me. A man of like passions with us. . . . Probably always meant for the best—and did his best—by you. . . . Nothing to *fear*—a frail sinner like the rest of us. . . . No power over you now, anyhow. . . .

"When you go to sleep to-night, say out loud:

" 'Poor old Dad! I feared and hated you—but now I do neither. . . . I never understood you—but I do now.' Then say, also out loud, 'God means Good, and Good means God. . . . God is Love and Love is God.' . . . See?"

And another time.

"You are a bachelor? . . . Well, you shouldn't be. . . . No healthy man has a right to be a bachelor at your age. . . . And you have always lived the celibate life in absolute chastity? . . . Hm! . . . We shall have to find you a wife, my boy! . . . I prescribe sunshine and fresh air, occupation and plenty of it, a trip to see your father—whom you will smite on the back and address as 'Dear old Dad—you heavy-father old fraud'—*and a wife*. . . . Yes, a wife, *and*, in due course, about three sons and two daughters. . . .

"What do I think caused your breakdown? . . . I don't 'think'—I *know*. . . . Your father, of whom you had too much, and your wife whom you never had at all. . . . Caused a neurosis, and when you got physically knocked out at Zaguig, it sprang up and choked you. . . . And now get up and dress and go out in the grounds and sit in the sun and realize what a harmless old chap your father is, and what a kind friendly fatherly jolly old God made the beautiful jolly old world that we muck-up so much. . . . And think over all the girls you know, and decide which one you will ask to marry you. . . . *Marriage will be your sure salvation.* . . . I prescribe it. . . ."

A couple of nurses—kind devoted souls—helped me into an invalid chair and wheeled me out into the grounds. They found me a beautiful hidden spot among great rhododendron bushes where I should be safely concealed, protected from the rear and on either hand, and have a glorious view of the rolling Kentish park-land before me. They assured me that the path by which we had come was very rarely used, and left me in my wheeled chair to wonder whether I should ever be a man again. . . .

. . . "Think over all the nice girls you know, and decide which one you will ask to marry you. . . . *Marriage will be your sure salvation.*"

There was only one woman in all the world, and she was already married. . . .

I hope no-one in this world suffers as I suffered in mind and body during those days.

§3

I believe that there really are people to whom "experiences" of the psychic and super-normal order are vouchsafed.

I have both read and heard of well-attested cases of dreams and appearances, inexplicable voices, and waking visions whereby information was imparted, or help sought.

Nothing of that sort has ever occurred to me.

I have not, on looking into my mirror at night, beheld the agonized and beseeching face of the woman who needed my help beyond all things, the woman whom I was to love and to marry.

I have not dreamed dreams and seen visions in which such a woman has implored my instant aid and told me exactly what to do, and how, and when and where to do it.

I have not heard a mysterious voice, clear and solemn as a bell, speak in my astounded ear and say, "Come. I need you. Hasten quickly to such-and-such a place and you will find. . . ."

I have seen no ghost nor apparition that has given me a message.

Nothing of the sort.

But the following fact is interesting.

I sat in my retreat, one day, thinking of Isobel, wondering where she was and what she was doing, whether she were happy every minute of the day, and whether it would be my fate ever to see her again. . . . Long, long thoughts between waking and sleeping. . . . And then with shaking hand and fumbling trembling fingers I opened a book that one of the nurses had left with me, "in case I felt like reading for a little while." . . .

And, opening at random in the middle of the book, I read:

". . . his vision of her was to be his Faith and Hope and was to be all his future. She was to be his life and his life was to be hers. . . . For he was a Worshipper, a Worshipper of Beauty, as were they who lived 'or ever the knightly years had gone with the old world to the grave,'—they to whom the Face was not the face upon a coin, the pale and common drudge 'twixt man and man, but the face of a beautiful woman, the Supreme Reality, the Focus of Desire—that desire which is not of the body, not of the earth, not of the Self, but pure and noble Love—God's manifestation to the world that something of God is in man and something of man is in God . . . .This knight thus worshipped God through the woman, with a love that was spiritual of the spirit, with no taint of Self. . . . And his motto and desire was Service. . . . Her service without reward; the service that is its own reward. . . . For he felt that there must come for the World's salvation from materialism and soul's death, a Renaissance, a Reformation—of Love. . . . .

"Love that was once the road to all perfection; man's cry to God, to Beauty, to the Beauty of God and the God of Beauty. . . . Love that once leapt free from flesh and cried aloud, not, 'Love me that I may be blessed and comforted and rendered happy,' but 'Let me serve thee with my love, that I may help and bless and comfort thee and render thee happy. . . .' Love that was Service, the highest service of God through the service of His noblest expression— Woman. . . . Love, that divine selfless thing, Man's great and true salvation, the World's one need, the World's last hope. . . .

"He would dedicate his life to the service of this woman, asking of her nothing more than that he might dedicate his life to her service in the name of Selfless Love, the Love that is its own *reward, its exceeding rich reward. . . ."*

and at the sound of a footstep, I here looked up—and beheld Isobel.

§4

Isobel, actual and alive . . . looking older and looking ill and pale and too ethereal, and lovelier if possible.

Our eyes met. . . . For a second we stared incredulous.

"Isobel!" I cried, still dreaming.

"The dear nice American boy!" she whispered.

Tears came into her beautiful eyes, her sweet and lovely face grew yet paler, and she swayed as though about to faint.

With a strength that I certainly had not possessed a minute before, I sprang to my feet, caught her in my arms and lifted her into the chair. Her need and weakness gave me strength, and I was ashamed—ashamed that I had sat trembling and shaking there—envying any healthy hobo that tramped the road—longing for death and thinking upon ways of finding it. . . .

Isobel! . . . Here! . . .

She must be a patient of Dr. Hanley-Blythe . . . ill. . . . in great sorrow, judging by the look upon her lovely face. . . .

I was shamefully conscious of noting that, by her dress, she was not a widow. . . . And then I rose above my lowest, and strove to put myself aside entirely. . . . *Isobel* was here—and ill. . . . Surely I could serve her in some way, if only by wheeling her about in a bath-chair . . . reading to her. . . .

"I can't believe it. . . . I must be dreaming . . ." she said as these thoughts flashed through my mind.

"Oh, dear American boy—will you help me. . . . I am in such trouble. . . ."

Help her! Would I *help* her!

My illness fell from me, and I stood erect, and strong—I who had recently been assisted to crawl to that invalid's chair, a wretched trembling neurotic. . . .

"John . . . my husband. . . . They have taken him. . . . Oh! . . ." Her eyes brimmed over and her trembling lips refused their service. . . . She covered her face and gave way to tears. . . .

Her husband! . . .

I knelt beside the chair. . . . By the time my knee had touched the grass, I had crushed back the thoughts, "Her husband. . . . 'They' have taken him. . . . Dead by now, probably. . . . *'Think of all the girls you know. . . . Marriage will be your sure salvation.'* . . ."—and I was unselfish and pure in heart—purified by the clear flame that burnt within me, before this woman's altar that was my heart.

"Tell me," I said. . . . "And then believe! Believe with all your soul that I can help you somehow. . . . Be sure of it. . . . *Know* it. . . . Why—surely I was created for that purpose. . . ."

I was a little unbalanced, a little beside myself, and more than a little inspired. . . .

And I inspired Isobel—with hope. . . . And with faith and with belief—belief in me, her servant.

Under the influence of my assurance and re-assurance, she told me her pitiful tale from beginning to end. . . .

I sat on the ground beside her chair, and she forgot herself and me as she poured out her woe and trouble—poured them out until she was empty of them, and their place was filled by the hope which I gave her, the faith that I had—for the time, even the *certainty* that I felt.

When she had finished, I took her little hand in both mine, and looked into her eyes.

"I *know* he is alive," I said. "I am as certain of it as I am that we are here together. He is alive and I will find him. I will not only find him but I will rescue him and bring him back. *Alive and well, I will bring him back to you. . . .*"

And at that moment I believed what I said. There is no such thing as "chance"; and God had not brought me to that place for nothing—nor to make a mock of us for His sport. . . .

What Isobel told me on that golden English summer afternoon—as I sat beside her chair, in a short-seen Seventh Heaven of bitter happiness and sad joy, listening to her voice with its soft accompaniment of the murmuring of innumerable bees in immemorial elms—is indelibly written on the tablets of my memory, and I can tell it exactly as she told it to me.

CHAPTER VII

"I shall tell you absolutely everything—right from the beginning," whispered Isobel. "That is the least I can do—after what you have just offered . . . and promised. . . . Everything, right from the beginning. . . . What it was that caused them to disappear . . . and caused their deaths. . . . Oh, those splendid boys. . . . And John, my own darling, John . . ." and she wept anew.

"John is alive," I said. "And he's coming back to you. . . . Believe me. . . . Trust in me. . . ."

"I do," she answered. "Oh, I do. . . . You have given me new life. . . . I always felt that you could and would do anything that you promised. . . . I have always liked you so much. . . . Otis. . . .

"I'll tell you *everything*. . . . You would hardly believe it. . . . You remember Claudia, of course? . . . The loveliest girl. . . ."

"Yes," I said. " 'Queen Claudia of the Band.' . . . Michael loved her very much, I think. . . ."

"Michael worshipped her," agreed Isobel. "He would have died for her. . . . He did die for her—in a way. . . . Poor wonderful noble Beau. . . . It nearly broke John's heart. He came back so different . . . poor John. Michael and Digby both. . . . Yes, John returned different in every way, except in his love for me. . . . Oh, John! . . ."

"Michael and Digby *dead*?" I exclaimed. "*Beau Geste* dead? . . ." This was horrible. What had happened?

"Yes, and Claudia is dead too," replied Isobel. "She was Lady Frunkse. I expect you read that she married Sir Otto Frunkse, 'the richest man in England.' . . . A motor-smash. . . . You must have seen it in the papers? . . . She lived—or rather died—for three days. . . . Poor Claudia—she was blinded and terribly disfigured by broken glass, and her back was broken. . . . Her husband went out of his mind for some time. He loved her passionately—and he had bought her . . . and he was driving the car . . . and was not quite sober. . . .

"She asked for me on the last day. I was in the room at the time. . . . She knew she was dying. . . . Her mind was absolutely clear, and she did not want to die until she had made a confession. . . . She asked me to tell everybody—after her death. You are the only person I have told. . . . I want you to know everything that concerns John. . . . It was very dreadful. . . . Only her mouth was exposed. . . . In that vast golden room and colossal Chinese bed, poor lovely Claudia was merely a mouth. I knelt beside her and held her poor groping hand and she whispered on and on . . . and on. . . .

"I'll try to tell you.

" *'Is that you, Isobel?'* she said. *'There is no-one else here, is there? . . . Listen . . . Tell this to my Mother—Aunt Patricia is my Mother—and to John and Otto and George Lawrence, everybody—after I am dead. . . . I cannot tell my Mother myself . . . Digby knows, now . . . And poor little Augustus . . . My Father knows too. I think he knew at the time. The mad know things that the sane do not. . . . Poor darling "Chaplain,"—we all loved him, didn't we, Isobel?*

" *'Didn't you love Beau too, Isobel?* Really *love him, I mean. . . . I worshipped the ground he trod on. . . . But I was only a girl— and bad. . . . I was* bad. . . . *Rotten. . . . I loved money and myself. Yes, myself and money, more than I loved Beau or anything else . . .* anyone else. . . .

" *'And Otto had caught me. . . . Trapped me nicely. . . . It served me right. . . . How I loathed him, and feared him too—and I actually believed he would let me be disgraced—let me go to prison—if I did not either pay him or marry him! . . . It was more than two thousand pounds. . . . It seemed like all the money in the world to me, a girl of eighteen. . . .*

" *'And if I married him I should be saved—and I should be the richest woman in England. . . . I thought it was a choice between that and prison. . . . Otto made me think it. I couldn't doubt it after he had sent his tame solicitor to see me. . . . The awful publicity and disgrace and shame. . . .*

" *'But Michael saved me—for a time. . . . He saved me from everything and everyone—except from myself. . . . He couldn't save me from myself. . . . And when he was gone, and Otto was tempting me and pestering me again, I gave way and married him—or his money. . . .*

" *'Isobel, it was I who stole the "Blue Water"—the mad fool and vile thief that I was. . . . I thought I could sell it and pay what I owed Otto—and a dozen others—dressmakers and people; shops in London. I must have been mad—mad—with fear and worry. . . .*

" *'Michael knew—before the lights came on again. . . .'* "

Isobel broke off here and wiped tears from her cheeks.

"I must tell you about that, Otis," she said. "You heard about the great sapphire, 'Blue Water,' when you were at Brandon Regis, I expect? It was kept in a casket in a safe that stood in the Priests' Hole—and the Priests' Hole is really undiscoverable. Its secret is never known to more than three people, though scores of people are taken to see the chamber. It is said that nobody has ever discovered the trick of it, in four hundred years.

"Aunt Patricia used to show the 'Blue Water' to favoured visitors, and sometimes she would have it out and let us handle it and gloat over it. It lived on a white velvet cushion under a thick glass dome in the steel casket.

"One night—it was not long before I last saw you—we were sitting in the drawing-room, after dinner, and Claudia asked Aunt Patricia if we might have it down and look at it again. We hadn't seen it for ages. The Chaplain—who was one of the three who knew the secret of the Priests' Hole—went and got it, and we all handled it and loved it. Then the Chaplain put it back on its cushion and put the glass cover over it—and suddenly the electric light failed, as it often used to do, in those days.

"When the lights came on again—the 'Blue Water' had disappeared. . . . Everyone denied having touched it—and next day, Beau ran away from home. . . . Then Digby disappeared. . . . Then John—and I was the most miserable girl in England. He told me, quite unnecessarily, that he had not stolen the wretched thing, and of course we also knew that neither Beau nor Digby was capable of theft.

"They joined the French Foreign Legion . . . and . . . and . . . Michael was killed . . . and Digby was killed . . . but John came back safe and sound—but *oh*, so changed . . . and now . . . *they have got him again*," and the poor girl broke down and wept unrestrainedly.

"I'll bring him back," I said, keeping a powerful grip upon myself, lest I put my arms about her, in my yearning ache to comfort her. "I *know* I shall find him and bring him back. . . ."

"Why—so do I," she smiled. "I believe it. . . . I feel it's *true*. . . . God bless you. . . . I . . . I can't . . . I. . . ."

My eyes tingled.

"I'll finish telling you about Claudia," she said. . . . "Poor Claudia went on:

" 'Yes, Michael knew. . . . *He came to my bedroom that night. . . . I was in bed, wide awake, and in a dreadful state of mind. . . . I felt awful. . . . Filthy from head to foot. . . . I was a thief, and I had robbed my Aunt, my greatest benefactress. . . . I did not then know that she was my Mother—she only told me when the Chaplain died and she was broken-hearted and distraught. . . .*

" '*Michael crept in like a ghost.*

" ' "CLAUDIA," he whispered, "GIVE ME THE 'BLUE WATER.' I AM GOING TO PUT IT BACK. THE KEY IS IN THE BRASS BOX ABOVE THE FIREPLACE IN THE HALL AS AUNT SAID."

" '*I pretended to be indignant—and talked like the hypocrite and liar that I am. I ordered him out of the room, and said I'd ring the bell and scream if he did not go at once.*

" ' "CLAUDIA," he said, "GIVE IT TO ME, DEAR . . . IT WAS ONLY A JOKE, OF COURSE. . . . LET ME PUT IT BACK, CLAUDIA. . . . NO-ONE WILL DREAM THAT IT WAS YOU WHO TOOK IT . . . ."

" ' "*No-one but you, you horrible cad,*" I said. "*How dare you. . . . How could you. . . .* "

" ' "DON'T, DEAR," he begged. . . . "DON'T. . . . I KNOW! . . . YOU BRUSHED CLOSE TO ME AS YOU MOVED TO THE TABLE AND AS YOU RETURNED TO WHERE YOU WERE STANDING. . . . YOUR HAIR ALMOST TOUCHED MY FACE. . . . DON'T I KNOW THE FRAGRANCE OF YOUR HAIR, CLAUDIA? . . . *COULD* I BE MISTAKEN. . . . SHOULDN'T I KNOW YOU IF I WERE BLIND AND DEAF—AND YOU CAME WITHIN A MILE OF ME? . . . HAVE I WORSHIPPED YOU ALL THESE YEARS, CLAUDIA, WITHOUT BEING ABLE TO READ YOUR THOUGHTS? . . . I KNEW IT WAS YOU, AND I WENT AND STOOD WITH MY HAND ON THE GLASS SO THAT IT WOULD LOOK AS THOUGH I WAS IN THE JOKE TOO, IF ISOBEL TURNED THE LIGHTS ON WHILE YOU WERE PUTTING IT BACK. . . . GIVE IT TO ME QUICKLY, DEAR— AND THE JOKE IS FINISHED. . . . OH, CLAUDIA DARLING, I DO LOVE YOU SO—AND I HAD NOT MEANT TO TELL YOU UNTIL YOU WERE OLDER. . . . GIVE IT ME, DEAREST CLAUDIA. . . ."

" '*His voice came to me out of the darkness, like that—and I was racked, Isobel. . . . I loved him, you see. . . . And I loathed Otto, and I had to have two thousand pounds or marry him—or go to prison—I verily believed.*

" '*And I stood out against Michael, and lied, and lied, and lied, and pretended to be indignant—hurt—enraged—wounded . . . and I called him horrible names, and all we said was in dreadful tense whispers.*'

" ' "CLAUDIA! CLAUDIA!" he said. "YOU CAN'T POSSIBLY DO IT. . . . I KNOW IT'S ONLY A JOKE—BUT DON'T PLAY IT ANY FURTHER. . . . IF IT DOESN'T BRING HORRIBLE DISGRACE AND HURT UPON YOU, IT WILL BRING DISGRACE AND HURT UPON SOMEBODY ELSE—ISOBEL, DIGBY, JOHN, GUSSIE. . . .AND EVEN IF YOU WENT

MAD AND DID SUCH A THING, YOU COULDN'T GET AWAY WITH IT. . . . NOBODY WOULD BUY IT FROM YOU. . . . GIVE IT ME, DEAR. IT IS SUCH A DANGEROUS PRACTICAL JOKE TO PLAY ON A PERSON LIKE AUNT PATRICIA. . . ."

" '*And he begged and begged of me to give it to him—and the more certain he was that I had got it, the angrier I grew. . . . Isn't it incredible—and isn't it exactly what a guilty person does? . . .*

" '*At last he said:*

" ' "LOOK HERE, THEN, CLAUDIA. I AM GOING AWAY TO MY ROOM FOR AN HOUR. . . . DURING THAT TIME THE 'BLUE WATER' IS GOING ITS WAY BACK. *SOMEONE* IS GOING TO PUT IT IN THE DRAWING-ROOM BEFORE—SAY ONE O'CLOCK—AND AUNT WILL FIND IT IN THE MORNING. . . . AND NOBODY WILL EVER KNOW WHO PLAYED THE SILLY TRICK. . . . I SHALL GO DOWN MYSELF, LATER ON, AND SEE THAT IT IS THERE. . . . SPLENDID! . . . GOOD-NIGHT, DARLING CLAUDIA . . ." *and he faded away like a ghost.*

" '*I lay awake and lived through the worst night of my life. . . . I could not go down and put it back—tacitly confessing to Michael that I was a thief—I loved him so, and I valued his good opinion of me more than anything—except my beastly self. . . . If he had come back then, I should have given the horrible stone to him. . . . I should . . . And later I grew more and more angry with him for suspecting me—and I got up and looked my door and bolted it. At about four o'clock in the morning I weakened and grew afraid of what I had done. . . . I saw myself arrested by policemen. . . . Taken to prison . . . in the dock . . . tried and sentenced to penal servitude.*

" '*I added cowardice to wickedness, and at last, overcome by fear, I jumped out of bed, took the "Blue Water" from the toe of a riding-boot where I had hidden it, slipped on a dressing-gown and mules, and crept downstairs. Every board seemed to creak, and my heart was in my mouth. I dared not carry a candle nor switch on any lights.*

" '*Every stair and board, I trod on, creaked and groaned, and I felt that every soul in the house must know what I was doing. . . . And suddenly I knew I was being followed, and I think that perhaps that was the most dreadful moment of my life.*

" ' "AUNT PATRICIA," *I thought, and I nearly shrieked. I felt that if she turned on the lights and caught me there, with the "Blue Water" in my hand, I should scream myself insane. . . . And then a cold hand touched me, and I did scream—or thought I did—before I realized it was the hand of a man in armour. . . .*

" '*And then my one need was to get rid of that awful jewel. I rushed to the fireplace and fumbled at the high mantel for the brass box in which Aunt Patricia had put the key. I found it, and hurried on, to the drawing-room door. The noise that I made in opening it sounded like thunder, but by that time, all that I cared about was to be rid of the sapphire, and back in my room before I was caught. It didn't matter to me who was suspected of having taken it. . . .*

" *'And as I reached the table on which the glass cover stood, someone entered the room.*

" *'Do you know, I believe my heart really stopped beating as I waited for Aunt Patricia to switch the lights on. . . .*

" *'And then a voice said,* "Oh, thank God, Darling. . . . I knew you would . . . ."

" *'It was Michael.*

" *'And in the sudden and utter revulsion of feeling, I could have cursed him. . . . I had been so absolutely certain that it was Aunt Patricia, that I was utterly enraged at the fright he had given me. . . .*

" *'And can you believe that I turned about and marched out of that room, to bed, without a word, still clutching the "Blue Water" in my hand? . . . Later he came and tapped softly and turned the handle. He stayed there for over an hour, tapping gently with his finger-nails and turning the handle. . . . And I lay there trying not to scream . . . trying to get up and give him the sapphire . . . trying not to get up and give him the sapphire. . . . And as the time wore on, I got more and more frightened at what I had done. . . . In the morning, I got up and went out into the rose-garden and he came to me there.*

" ' "LAST CHANCE, CLAUDIA DEAR," *he said.* "GIVE ME THE 'BLUE WATER' NOW, AND THERE SHAN'T BE A BREATH OF SUSPICION ON YOU. . . . IF YOU DON'T, IT IS ABSOLUTELY CERTAIN THAT YOU'LL GET INTO THE GHASTLIEST TROUBLE. AUNT IS BOUND TO GET TO THE BOTTOM OF IT. . . . HOW COULD SHE IGNORE SUCH A BUSINESS—EIGHT OF US THERE. . . ? AND SUSPICION WILL BE ON POOR LITTLE GUS—AT FIRST. . . . YOU CAN'T *POSSIBLY* SELL IT . . . GIVE IT TO ME AND I'LL GIVE YOU MY WORD NOBODY WILL EVER *DREAM* THAT YOU. . . ."

" *'I burst into tears. . . . I had had such an awful night, and I was so filled with anger and fear and* hatred—*hatred of Michael and Otto and of all the men in the world—that I broke down. . . . I nearly gave it to him. . . . And after breakfast I did give it to him, too late, and I told him I loathed him utterly, and that I hoped that I should never set eyes on him again! . . . I never did, Isobel, as you know. . . . And I have never had a happy hour since. . . .'*"

Isobel paused and wiped tears from her eyes. I would have left her but that I felt it was good for her to talk and get it all out.

"Poor, poor Claudia," she went on. "She died that night. Sir Otto Frunkse went insane for a time. I thought Aunt Patricia would die too. Claudia was all she had, after the Chaplain died and Michael was killed. . . . She blamed herself for the boys' deaths. . . . And now, John! . . . Oh, John! . . . John! . . ."

"Why did she blame herself?" I asked. "Surely it was Claudia's —er—act, that led to Michael's and Digby's going away . . . ?"

"I will tell you everything, as I said," replied Isobel. "It's wonderful to have a Father Confessor and friend . . . and you are going to find John for me. . . . I *know* you are. . . . I feel as though I were coming out of a tomb. . . . You have lifted the cover a little already. . . . I shall tell you everything. . . .

"Michael knew that Aunt Patricia had sold the real 'Blue Water'—sold it to the descendant of the Rajah from whom it had been—acquired—by her husband's ancestor, in India. . . . She had a right to sell it, I believe, as her husband gave it to her as a wedding-present. . . . This man, Sir Hector Brandon, used to leave her for years at a time. He was a very bad man—a bad husband and a bad landlord. . . . I know that she put almost every penny of the money into the estate. . . . She had had a model of the 'Blue Water' made before she parted with the original. . . . Michael ran away with this model. He thought it would be a splendid way of covering up what Claudia had done, and of what Aunt Patricia had done, too —and Sir Hector was about to return to England. . . . Poor darling Michael—it was just what he *would* do! . . . It must have seemed such a simple solution, to him, and the end of terrible and dangerous trouble for the two women he loved. . . . It saved Claudia from shame and disgrace and from Aunt Patricia's anger, and it saved Aunt Patricia from her husband's. . . . Sir Hector Brandon would simply think that Michael had stolen the 'Blue Water,' and Aunt Patricia would think that he had stolen the dummy—in ignorance of its worthlessness."

§2

This Beau Geste! . . . It was an honour and a boast to have known him! . . . And those two women—that mother and her daughter! . . . My God! . . .

§3

"Uncle Hector never came home after all," continued Isobel. "Nor Beau either. . . . Nor Digby. . . . And now, *John*—my John! . . . Oh, Claudia, the trouble and misery and tragedy you caused that night! . . ."

"Tell me about John," I said.

That would do her more good than anything. . . . I had learnt from Dr. Hanley-Blythe, and from my own experience, what repression can do to one!

"When Michael ran away, taking the suspicion and the blame, and Digby followed him to share it, John felt that he must go too. You see the three boys had always done *everything* together, all their lives. And John felt that they were shielding him because nobody would dream of suspecting Claudia or me—and there was a reason why Gussie should not be suspected. As a matter of fact, I was in a position to prove his innocence—as well as my own—for I had hold of his arm the whole time that the room was in darkness. . . . So it was *John or Claudia*—and John went. . . . Then it *must* be one of the Geste boys. . . .

"John felt certain that Michael had gone to the French Foreign Legion because the very name of it had fascinated him, ever since a French officer had stayed at Brandon Abbas and told us about military life in Africa. . . . . Why—you may have met him there! . . . De Beaujolais is his name. He was the son of an old school-friend of Aunt Patricia's and, at Eton, was the fag of George Lawrence, her second husband. . . ."

"No, I didn't see him at Brandon Abbas," I said. "But I saw him in Africa, in a place called Zaguig. . . . He saved my sister. . . . It's a queer little world. . . !"

"It *is* a queer world . . ." mused Isobel. "Think of that! . . . You know Major de Beaujolais! . . ."

"Related to him," I smiled. "My sister married him. . . . I mean he married my sister. . . ."

"*What* a coincidence!" said Isobel.

"Not it!" I ventured to contradict. "There are no such things! . . . It was no coincidence that Jasper Jocelyn Jelkes ran away from Brandon Abbas and came to my Grandmother's place . . . nor that a Colonel Levasseur became enamoured of my sister and invited us to Zaguig, with the result that I got all broken up . . . nor that Dr. Hanley-Blythe chanced upon me when I was just enjoying the nervous reaction from it! . . . Go on about John. . . ."

"He went to the French Foreign Legion, and there he found Beau and Digby as he had felt certain he would. . . . At the siege, by Arabs, of a fort at a place called Zinderneuf, Beau was killed, and John stabbed the Commandant of the fort, in self-defence. . . . The man had heard that Beau and Digby and John were jewel-thieves and had a huge diamond! . . . Digby wasn't at Zinderneuf. He came with the relief-party and was sent into the empty fort. He saw Beau's body reverently laid out, beside that of the Commandant—who had John's bayonet through his heart. He went half mad and set the place on fire and escaped to look for John, because John wasn't among the dead. . . . He soon found him, because John had done just the same thing—dropped from the wall furthest from the entrance, and had run to the nearest sand-dunes. . . . Then two friends of theirs, scouting or patrolling on camels, found them, and the four of them got away together. . . .

"Then Digby was killed by a raiding party. . . ."

Her voice broke again and there was silence.

"Poor darling Digby. . . . He was such a kind, happy, *dear* boy. . . . And after awful hardships and dangers, just when escape seemed sure, the other three were stranded in the desert without camels. . . . And they only had about a quart of water. . . . And one of the two friends, one they called 'Hank,' went off in the night . . . to give John and the other man a chance . . . the water. . . .

"Then John and the other—'Buddy,' John called him—got to a desert village and they stayed there a long time, hoping to find the third man or to hear something of him. . . . He had given his life for them. . . . And at last they gave up hope, and found a caravan going south to Kano. . . . There they got into touch with George Lawrence, who was a Commissioner or something, in Nigeria. . . .

"And as soon as they were there, John's companion turned round and went back to look for the lost man—Hank. . . . They were a sort of David and Jonathan pair, and the man said he was going to search until either he found his friend or died. . . .

"John was too ill to go back with this man, Buddy. . . . I have no doubt he would have done so, otherwise, as soon as they had got camels and supplies. . . . Men do such foolish things. . . . But John went down with enteric, and nearly died. As soon as it was safe to move him, George Lawrence brought him home. . . . Oh, I nearly died of joy, although I cried and cried when I heard about Michael and Digby. . . .

"And we were married. . . . And I was the happiest woman in

the whole world . . . for a time. I was *too* happy, of course. . . . We aren't meant to be as happy as I was, or we shouldn't want to go to Heaven. . . ."

"Oh, yes, we are," I interrupted, "and you are going to be just as happy as that again. And it's *going to last*, this time. . . ."

Isobel sighed and pressed my hand as she smiled gratefully at me.

"Yes—I was too happy," she resumed, "but it did not last very long. . . . John did not recover properly. He simply did not get fit again. . . . He had had a most terrible time. . . . The deaths of Beau and Digby before his eyes, and the awful hardships he had suffered, ending up with this enteric or typhus, when he was so weak. . . . George Lawrence said he looked like a dying skeleton when he first saw him in Nigeria. . . . And even then of course, he couldn't get proper nursing or invalid food. . . . It was a marvel that he lived.

"Well—we hadn't been married long, before I saw there was something very wrong with John. . . . He hardly ate anything at all, and he scarcely slept. . . . I don't think he ever got any sleep at all, at night. I used to hear him walking up and down, up and down, in the corridor. He would go out there so that he should not wake me, and then he would sit in his dressing-room and smoke for a while and read. He used to be able to doze a little in the afternoons, and I would make him sit in a long chair under the trees in the Bower—you know—where we used to play. . . . I couldn't get him to go to bed in the daytime, as he ought to have done.

"And if he fell asleep in the chair, he had horrible dreams and woke with a dreadful start, or else he would talk all the time. . . . That was how I found out what was really at the root of the trouble. He felt he had left his friend in the lurch—had deserted the man who would never have deserted him, abandoned the David who had gone back into the desert to look for his Jonathan instead of escaping when he had the chance. . . .

"I was so worried and frightened that I got Dr. Hanley-Blythe to come to Brandon Abbas. He wanted John to come here and be under observation, but John wouldn't hear of it. . . .

"Then one night, John was walking up and down in his dressing-room, and, as I was going to him, I heard him say, groaning, '*I shall go mad if I don't go back!*' . . . I made up my mind immediately, and as I pushed the door wider open, I said:

" '*John, darling, I know what is the matter with you,*' just as though I had had a sudden brain-wave. He stared at me. My heart seemed to turn right over—he looked so ill and so unlike himself, too—and I felt absolutely dreadful at the thought of what I was going to do. . . .

" 'You must go back, darling,' I said . . . 'and find them. . . . I shall come with you—as far as Kano anyhow.' . . . I meant to stay with him and never let him out of my sight, of course. . . . He stared and stared as though he could not believe his ears—and then his poor sad face lit up with joy, and I thought my heart would break.

" 'ISOBEL!' he said, and took me in his arms as though he loved me more than ever, for what I had done. 'You see they may be alive . . . they may be slaves . . . they may be in some ghastly native prison . . . they may be in some place where they'll have to stay for the rest of their lives, for want of camels. . . . Isobel—they offered their lives for Digby and me when they helped us away from Zinderneuf. . . . Hank gave his life for Buddy and me when he went off in the night, and left us the drop of water. . . . Buddy saw me safe to Kano before he went back to look for Hank. . . . And I left them there, and am living in safety and luxury! . . . They may be alive. . . . There may be time to save them even yet. . . . I can't sleep for thinking of them . . . in Arab hands. . . .'

" 'We'll start as soon as you like, John,' I said—and I felt myself going dead, as it were—dead and cold at the very heart of myself. . . ."

There was silence for a while, a silence broken only by a little sob, and I looked away over the beautiful Kentish scene. Should I let her go on? Was it too painful to be beneficial, or was it her salvation?

"You are distressing yourself," I said, moved almost unbearably by her tears. "Tell me the rest tomorrow."

"Oh, no, no! Let me tell you now. . . . If you are not—tired. . . . Oh, if you knew the relief it is . . . and the hope that you have given me . . . my friend-in-need . . ." she answered at once.

"George Lawrence was wonderful," she went on, "and Aunt Patricia did not raise a word of protest when he said he would come with us. . . . Of course, his help would be absolutely invaluable. He was in Nigeria for about twenty years, himself, and could pull all sorts of strings, give us the soundest advice and assist us in numberless ways. . . . I think that Aunt Patricia realized it was a life-and-death matter for John, especially after what Dr. Hanley-Blythe had said to her. . . . What I did not then realize, was that

George Lawrence's real object was to take charge of *me*, if anything happened to John when he went off into the real desert, right away from civilization and help. . . . He never expected that John would, return alive, and he did not expect that John would ever get better if he did not go. . . .

"Do you know, John began to improve from that night—from the very moment that I had suggested his going back. . . . He went to bed and slept, and I heard him singing in his bath, the next morning! . . . Several times during that day he actually whistled as he went about his preparations for the journey. He was a changed man, and I got some idea of what he had suffered by sitting idle while his friends whom he had 'deserted' might be dying in the desert, or be living in captivity worse than death. . . .

"On the voyage from Liverpool to Lagos, he put on weight daily, and was almost himself again by the time we got there. . . . And then he revealed the plot hatched by George Lawrence!

"We were to go to friends of his, and I was to stay with them while John and he went on to Kano. After he had seen John off, with a proper caravan—to go to the village where he and his friend had lived while they had been searching for the third man—George was to return to me and take me home again! . . . These two precious lunatics thought I was going to agree to *that*—and sit down quietly with George's friends for weeks and weeks, and then go quietly home without John.

" 'Oh, yes,' they said, 'George's friends are most delightful people; have a charming house in quite the best part of Nigeria; really very good climate at this time of year; plenty going on, at the Club; tennis, racing, polo, bridge and dancing; I should have a lovely time. . . .'

"I didn't argue. I merely smiled and shook my head.

"When they realized, at last, that I was going with John, and that nothing on earth would stop my going with John, there was frightful consternation and alarm! They even talked of abandoning the whole scheme and returning by the next boat. . . . I wouldn't hear of that, and they wouldn't hear of my attempting to make the caravan-journey into that part of the Sahara, one of the most waterless, hot and dangerous of deserts. . . . We compromised eventually. . . . I was to come with them to Kano, and John was to go on with the best guides, camels, camel-men, outfit and provisions that money could buy. He was to take special men, as messengers, too. He was to send a man back with a message, as soon as he reached the village, and send messages at regular intervals afterwards. . . . The men were to report to an English official at Kano, a Mr. Mordaunt—an old friend of George Lawrence, and he would cable news to us. . . . John promised that he would not go further north than Zanout, himself. . . . His idea was to promise a big reward to anybody who brought him genuine news, and he hoped to get into touch with one or two big men, Arab or Touareg chiefs, who are famous and influential in that part of the Sahara. . . . And to tell the great Bilma salt-caravan— thousands of people—about it. . . .

"John thought that the 'desert telegraph'—that mysterious spreading of news which turns even the desert into a whispering-gallery—would soon make it known, far and wide, that a great sum was being offered by a rich European for news of two friends of his. . . . All sorts of *canards* would soon be flying about, and hundreds of false clues would be discovered. . . . And among tons and tons of chaff there might, one day, be found a grain of truth. . . .

"Poor John! . . . Oh, my darling John! . . . He was so hopeful. . . . He was so happy again, now that he was, at any rate, *trying* to do something for his friends—if only they were still alive. . . . There was hope that the second one was, and just a bare chance that the first one had been found and saved."

"You are tiring yourself," I said again, as Isobel fell silent.

"No, no! Let me finish—unless you are tired yourself," she replied. "It does me good to tell you . . . and the sooner you know everything, the sooner you may be able to do something. . . ."

"John got to the place, where he had lived with his companion, in about three weeks, and sent back the first messenger. Nothing was known there, apparently, but he had hardly expected to get news so soon, and was still full of hope. Two more messages came, the second from Zanout, where he thought he had found a trace of the man he called 'Buddy.' . . . It seems the Touareg of those parts know the appearance and brand-marks of every camel, and the full history of every raid in which camels are stolen. John thought that Buddy and his caravan had been captured by Touareg or Tebu robbers, and the next thing was to find somebody who could give details as to the band and where they came from, and whether there had been any survivors of the caravan. . . .

And then . . . And then . . . We got a cable from George Lawrence's Kano friend, *saying that John himself had been captured!* . . . Not by raiders. . . . He had been recognized by a French patrol and had been arrested. . . . Oh John, John, dear! . . . I let you go back there—but you would have died if you had stayed here. . . ."

I could do nothing to comfort her—except reiterate my promise to find him and bring him back.

"George Lawrence was splendid again," she continued. "He took me back to Africa. . . . I would have gone alone if necessary. . . . Before going, he moved heaven and earth. . . . He went to the Foreign Office and the Colonial Office and to see several Members of Parliament and visited the offices of the London newspapers. Then he got into touch with his friend, Major de Beaujolais—who was at our wedding and knew all about John. . . . We went to Paris, and he saw various influential people there, and thence to Algiers to see the Commander-in-Chief. . . . Everybody was most kind and sympathetic and helpless—especially helpless in France and Africa. . . . *'Nothing could be done. . . . The law must take its course. . . . We civilian officials cannot interfere with the military authorities. . . . We military officials cannot interfere with the civilian authorities. . . . Fair trial, of course. . . . Court martial. . . . Death penalty generally inflicted*—very properly—in cases of desertion in the face of the enemy. . . . Some very peculiar features about this case moreover' . . . and so-on.

"It was unspeakably dreadful to feel so powerless, baffled and ineffectual. . . . I felt I must get as near as I possibly could to the place—in Africa. . . . I must have every scrap of news. . . . I lasted out—as far as Kano.

"Mr. Mordaunt was so kind and helpful. He had kept the man who had brought the last information—a Touareg camel-driver, hired in Kano. . . . This man had told the whole story to George Lawrence, over and over again. . . . They had found a soldier of the French camel-corps, who had strayed or deserted from a patrol—apparently what they call a *peloton méhariste*, out on a *tournée d'apprivoisement* through the Touareg country. . . . John had befriended the man, of course—given him food, water and a camel, and the man had gone straight off and brought the patrol down on his benefactor. . . .

"From what this camel-man said, George Lawrence and Mr. Mordaunt concluded that the soldier had recognized John and had denounced him, for reward and promotion, or else—having had enough of desertion in the desert—to ingratiate himself with the leader of the patrol and palliate his offence. . . .

"Anyhow, what was perfectly clear, was that John had been captured and arrested in French Territory by the 'competent military authority'—as a deserter from the Legion. . . .

"*Oh John, John, my darling! . . . Shall I ever see you again! . . .*

"And when I had learned everything there was to learn at Kano, I collapsed altogether, and only just didn't die. . . . I think it was the belief that I might, somehow, be able to help John, that kept me alive. . . . It must have been a dreadful time for poor George Lawrence. . . . I remember very little about it, but I get fleeting glimpses now and again. . . .

"And here I am, Otis . . . and can do *nothing*. Everything possible has been done—and all we know, through the kindness of Major de Beaujolais, is that he is alive—or was—and is a convict in the Penal Battalions in Africa! . . . Eight years! . . . And then to return to the Legion to finish his five years there! . . . *Eight years!* He couldn't survive eight months of that life. . . . And here am I—and I can do *nothing . . . nothing. . . .*"

"*I* can, though," I said, and arose to begin doing it.

§4

A week later, I was in Sidi bel Abbès—an earnest and indefatigable student of Arabic and of all matters pertaining to the French Foreign Legion and to the French Penal Battalions of convicts, as well—the "Zephyrs" or "Joyeux."

A fortnight later, I was an enlisted *légionnaire* of the French Foreign Legion, and, secretly, a candidate for membership of the Zephyrs.

It was my intention to see the inside of Biribi,[8] the famous or infamous convict depot of the Penal Battalions, and only by way of the Legion could I do so. Thence, and only thence, could I possibly find John Geste, and until I found him, neither I nor anybody else could rescue him.

---

[8] Recently disestablished and abolished.

CHAPTER VIII

I have very rarely found anything as good as I expected it to be, and almost never as bad. If the joys of anticipation are generally greater than those of experience, the terrors are almost always so, and the man who said, "We suffer far more from the calamities that never happen to us, than from those that do," talked sense.

I had expected life in the French Foreign Legion to be so rough, so hard, so wholly distasteful from every point of view, that I had anticipated something much worse than the reality.

It was hard, very hard; it was rough, wearisome, monotonous and wholly unpleasant; but it was bearable.

I don't think I could have faced the prospect of five years of it —unless, of course, it were for Isobel—but as things were, I contrived to carry on from day to day.

What made things worse for me than for some people, was the fact that I had no military leaning whatsoever, and that the soldier's trade is the very last one that I should voluntarily adopt.

Of course, if one's country is at war, and there is need of more men than the standing army provides, one is fully prepared to learn the soldiering trade, to the end that one may be as useful as possible as quickly as possible. But this was different, and to me, at any rate, the whole business seemed puerile, stupid, and an entirely unsuitable occupation for an intelligent man.

There was not one solitary aspect of life that was enjoyable, and I do not think that I was ever faintly interested in anything but the *salle d'honneur*.

This wonderful museum of military trophies and of concrete evidence of superhuman courage, devotion and endurance, did more than interest me. It thrilled me to the marrow of my bones, and I took every opportunity of gazing at the battle pictures, portraits of distinguished heroes, scenes from the Legion's stirring history—all of them, without exception, painted by legionaries who were survivors of the scenes depicted—or comrades of the men whose portraits adorned the walls.

Every captured standard, weapon, and other trophy, illustrated some astounding story, a story as true as Life and Death, and far, far stranger than any fiction that ever was conceived.

The single exhibit that thrilled me most was, I think, the hand

143

of Captain Danjou in its glass case beneath the picture that told the story of the historic fight of sixty-five against two thousand two hundred better-provided troops; a fight that lasted a whole day, and ended in the capture, by assault, of five wounded survivors— wounded to death, but fighting while strength remained to load a gun and pull a trigger.

What I suffered from, most of all, was a lack of companionship. There wasn't a comrade to whom I could talk English, and none to whom I cared to talk French, or what passed for French, in the Legion.

Stout fellows all, no doubt, and good soldiers, but there was not one with whom I had an idea in common, or who appeared to have a thought beyond wine, woman and song, unless it were food, money and the wickedness of noncommissioned officers.

One of my room-mates, a poor creature named Schnell, who appeared to me to be not only the butt and fool of the *escouade*, but also of Fate, attached himself to me and made himself extremely useful.

For some inexplicable reason, he developed a great admiration for me. He put himself under my protection, and in return for that, and some base coin of the realm, he begged to remain my obedient servant, and was permitted to do so.

I was to meet the good Schnell again—in different circumstances.

Things improved somewhat when, after some weeks, I completed my recruit's course, took my place in my Company and came under the more immediate notice of Sergeant Frederic.

§2

I did not look upon it as a piece of great good luck when I found that my Sergeant was an Englishman, and one of the best of good fellows. I regarded it rather as a Sign.

I never knew his real name, but he was a Public School man, had been through Sandhurst, and had served in a Dragoon regiment. How he had fallen from the Officers' Mess of a British Cavalry regiment to the ranks of the Legion, was a mystery, for he was one of those people in whom one cannot detect a weak spot, and with whom one cannot associate any form of vice or crime.

I often wondered.

It may have been debt, a love affair, or sheer boredom with

peace-time soldiering, and I often hoped that he would one day be moved to tell me his story. Naturally I never asked him a question on the subject of his past. It can't be done in the Legion. . . . Not twice, anyhow.

Of course, a Sergeant cannot hob-nob with a *légionnaire*, walk out with him or drink with him, but Sergeant Frederic, as he called himself, gave me many a friendly word and kindly encouragement when we were alone; and later, when we were away down in the desert, he would march beside me and talk, or come and chat in the darkness of bivouacs. On one occasion, when he and I were in the same mule-*peloton*, he and I were out on a patrol, or a *reconnaissance*, by ourselves, for a whole day, and he laid aside his rank and we talked freely, as equals, and man to man. It did us both good to talk English once again, and to converse with a man of our own level of education, social experience and breeding.

It made all the difference in the world, to me, that my Sergeant was a man of this type, and regarded me with the eye of friendship and favour. Moreover it was not unnoticed by the Corporals that I was a compatriot (as they supposed), and something of a protégé of the Sergeant.

Had I, at that time, proved a slack and inefficient soldier however, I am pretty sure there would have been a prompt end to the favour of Sergeant Frederic and his myrmidons.

Thanks to this position of affairs, I did not in the early days, have too bad a time in the Legion. It was hard, terribly hard, and I was only just equal to the life, physically speaking, when real marching began in earnest, and I took part in some of those performances that have earned the Legion the honourable title of "The Foot-Cavalry" in the XIXth (African) Army Corps.

At first I used to be obsessed with the awful fear that I should fail and fall out, and share the terrible fate of so many who have fallen by the wayside in Algeria and Morocco. But it is wonderful how the spirit rules the body, and for how long the latter will not give in, if the former does not. . . .

Time after time, in the early days, I was reduced to a queer condition wherein I was dead, not "from the neck, up," as we say, but from the neck, down. My head was alive, my eyes could see, my ears hear; but I had no body. My head floated along on a Pain. No, I had no body and I was not conscious of individual parts that had been causing me agony for hours—blistered feet, aching calves, burning thighs, cruelly lame back, cut shoulders. These were amalgamated into the one great amorphous and intangible

Pain that floated along in the white-hot cloud of dust, and bore my bursting head upon it.

I used to think that I could be shot, when in that condition, without knowing it and without falling, provided that no vital part were hit, and that I should go on marching, marching, marching. . . .

For, once I had reached this condition, I was almost immune and immortal, indestructible and unstoppable—while the spirit held, high and unfaltering. But when the last "*Halte!*" was cried, and the voice of an officer rang out:

"*Campez*," and the Company Commanders bawled:

"*Formez les faisceaux*," and "*Sac à terre*," and the unfaltering spirit went off duty, its task accomplished, then the poor body had its way. . . . It trembled . . . it sagged . . . it collapsed . . . and it lay where it was, until kindly and more seasoned comrades dragged it aside and disposed its unconscious head in safety if not in comfort.

I fully and freely admit that this marching was the worst thing that I encountered in the Legion, thanks to my good luck in being in Sergeant Frederic's *peloton*. The next worst things were the lack of acceptable companionship and society, the deadly wearisome monotony, and the impossibility of natural self-expression for one's ego. I am no militarist, no "born soldier," and I wished at times that I had never been born at all.

It was on the occasion to which I have referred, the day when Sergeant Frederic and I were alone together, from before dawn to after midnight, that I asked him the question which probably surprised him more than any other that he had ever been asked. . . . We were riding at ease—so far as one can ride at ease on a mule. . . .

"How can a man who wishes to do so, make certain of getting sent to the Zephyrs?" I inquired suddenly. "Just that and nothing worse—nor better . . . the happy medium between a death-sentence from a General Court-martial, and thirty days' solitary confinement from the Colonel." . . .

Sergeant Frederic laughed.

"The *happy* medium!" he said. . . . "Well—they're called the '*Joyeux*'! You're a queer chap, Hankinson. . . . D'you mean you want to join the honourable *Compagnies de discipline?* Don't you get enough discipline here?" and he laughed again. . . . "Well—I dunno—I suppose you'd find yourself in the Zephyrs all-right if you gave me a smack in the eye, on parade, one morning. . . . "

That was a thing I most certainly should not do—and I little thought, at the time, that it would actually be through this most excellent chap that I should come to wear the military-convict uniform of the African Penal Battalions. . . .

"Better not risk it, though," he continued, smiling. "It is much more likely that you'd be shot, out of hand. . . . It is the law, even in peace time, that the death-penalty be awarded for the striking of any *supérieur*, no matter what the provocation—and no matter what the rank of the striker or the stricken. . . . And you know the awkward rule of the French Army, *'No man can appeal against a punishment until he has served the whole of it.'* "

"Yes. . . . Plenty of fellows do get sent from the Legion to the Zephyrs, though," I said. "What's the trouble usually?"

"You've got Zephyrs on the brain," was the reply. "Are you afraid you'll get sent there? . . . Not the slightest fear of that, unless you wilfully get into serious trouble. . . . What do men get sent there for? Oh, insubordination, desertion, damage to Government property, sedition—or just continued slackness and indiscipline. . . . The Colonel can give six months for that, and the General Court-martial can give you penal servitude, to any extent, for a serious 'crime' or continued bad record. . . . Those who get themselves a term in the Zephyrs earn it all-right, and thoroughly deserve it, as a rule. . . . Almost always. . . . As far as I can remember the wording in Army Regulations, it is, *'The Minister of War has full power to send to the Compagnies de Discipline any soldier who has committed one of several faults, the gravity of which makes any other mode of repression inadequate. . . .* I like that word 'repression'! . . . They *repress* them all-right, in the Penal Battalions! . . . Of course, 'Minister of War,' in this case, means the General Court-martial that sits at Oran, and the General Court-martial knows that when the Colonel sends a man before it, something has got to be done with the sin-merchant.

"So they either shoot him, or plant him in the Zephyrs for a few years, and the Colonel is rid of him. . . .

"Naturally the Colonel doesn't want to lose any man who is a ha'porth of good—so you may take it a *légionnaire's* a pretty hard case and a Republic's Hard Bargain before he gets as far as the General Court-martial."

"Yes," I agreed. . . . "But one hears stories of innocent, harmless and well-meaning fellows who fall foul of a Corporal or a Sergeant, and are so constantly run in, by the non-com., that the Company Officer has to take notice of it, and begins doubling the dose that he finds put down in the *livre de punitions* against the man's name. . . . By the time the Captain has begun to give the maximum that his powers allow, the Colonel has got his eye on the poor devil, and starts doubling the Captain's dose, and, before long, the man has got the Colonel's maximum of solitary confinement and an ultimatum—reform, or six months deportation to the Zephyrs. . . . And he can't 'reform,' for the Sergeant won't let him —and it's the Sergeant's word against his. . . ."

"One *does* hear such stories . . ." said Sergeant Frederic, and changed the conversation.

§3

The days passed swiftly—swiftly as only days of continuous hard work can do, and I began to find myself becoming a routine-dulled *légionnaire*, with so much to do in the present that I could scarcely think of the future.

This would not do, and I must get action. I had not come to the Legion to settle down, serve my time, and take my discharge! It appeared unlikely that there was anything more about John Geste, for me to learn, and it was high time that I decided on the course which I should pursue to achieve my safe transfer from the honourable ranks of the Foreign Legion to the dishonourable ranks of the working-gangs of the Zephyrs.

The great question was—should I embark on a course of slackness, insubordination, petty "crime" and general unsatisfactoriness, so that by the thorny path of more and more punishment, and increasingly long and heavy sentences of imprisonment, I should sound to their depths the Colonel's powers of "repression," until I touched the very bottom and was repressed from the regiment altogether for the space of six months—or should I conceive, and then commit, some crime for which no punishment was adequate, save such as could only be awarded by a General Court-martial—to wit, penal servitude or Death.

On the one hand, it would be a long and painful—a most distasteful and degrading—business, to play the bad soldier so sedulously that I went through the whole gamut of regimental punishment until the Colonel sent me to the Zephyrs for six months —a disgrace to my Corps, my country, and myself.

On the other hand, it would be unspeakably tragic, if, in attempting to qualify for penal servitude in the Zephyrs, I overdid it, and earned the death-penalty—thus failing in my task of finding

John Geste; depriving Isobel of her last chance of happiness; ending in a felon's grave all the high hopes that I had held out to her; and breaking the fine promises that I had made.

In favour of the first course was its comparative safety.

Against it, was its protracted misery and moral abasement, and also the fact that the six months which the Colonel could and would give me, might prove all too short for my purpose—indeed would almost certainly prove too short. Twenty years would probably not be long enough.

In favour of the second course, was its comparative decency and brevity. A serious military "crime," a Court-martial, a sentence.

Against it, was the possibility of the sentence being a death-sentence.

Which to choose? . . . I wondered whether, ever before, in the long and astounding history of the French Foreign Legion, a man had deliberately endeavoured to earn a sentence in the Penal Battalions, and had solemnly weighed the respective merits and conveniences of a Colonel's short-term sentence, and a Court-martial's penal servitude decree.

§4

I hate to look back upon the period of my life that now began. It was, in a way, almost a worse time than that which I spent in the actual Penal Battalion—as much worse as mental suffering is than physical suffering—for the misery of the constant punishment and imprisonment that I deliberately brought upon myself, was nothing in comparison with what I suffered in *earning* that punishment.

I loathed myself; I loathed the thing that I had to make myself appear to be—insubordinate, dirty, untrustworthy, lazy, incompetent and wholly detestable to the normal military mind. What hurt me most, was Sergeant Frederic's disappointment in me, a hurt and bewildered disappointment that quickly turned to scorn and the bitterest contempt.

When I first began to lapse from grace—which was as soon as I had decided that I would lapse by slow degrees and a gradual slipping down Avernus, rather than by the commission of a General Court-martial crime—the good fellow did his best, by light punishment, by appeal to my better nature, and then by sharp punishment—to stay my downward course. He would send for me when I had completed eight days *salle de police* or some other punishment, and talk to me for my good.

"Look here, Hankinson," he would say, "what's the game? . . . You're in the Legion and you've got to stay in the Legion for five years, so why not make the best of it, and of yourself? Why not go for promotion? You could rise to Sergeant-Major and re-enlist for a commission. . . . And—other things apart—you might play the game, since you *have* come here! . . . And I thought you were such a decent chap . . .

"It's bad enough when some of these ignorant unintelligent clods are bad, dirty, and drunken soldiers. For a man like you, it isn't decent. . . . I can't make you out, Hankinson. . . . One of the weaklings with a screw loose somewhere, I suppose. . . . Come man, pull yourself together . . . for the credit of the Anglo-Saxon name, if for nothing else. . . . Dismiss!"

And I would salute, and go, without a word, but with a bursting heart.

Yes, what I was doing now *was*, undoubtedly, by far the hardest of the things I was privileged to do for Isobel.

§5

But, one day, a ray of light and warmth shone into the dark cheerlessness of my life at this period.

Sergeant Frederic had an idea.

He wasn't a brilliant man, but he was one of those sound solid, sensible Britishers who are richly endowed with that uncommon thing, common sense.

He sent for me, and said, as soon as we were alone, "I've come to the conclusion, Hankinson, that for some reason, best known to yourself, you are deliberately trying to get into the Zephyrs! . . . If so, you're a damned fool—a mad fool. . . . But I can understand a mad fool, if there's a woman in it. . . .

"What I want to say is, I shall punish you exactly according to your deserts—without mercy. . . . But if you are trying to get into the Zephyrs, perhaps you'd better give me a smack in the eye, on parade, and get it over. . . ."

"And now get to Hell out of this," he concluded, with an eloquent handshake.

*　　　*　　　*　　　*　　　*　　　*　　　*

Fate was in a slightly ironical mood when all my painful efforts to deserve and attain a Court-martial, were rendered superfluous.

A sand-storm—aided by a brief failure of the commissariat, over-fatigue, and frayed nerves—provided me, without effort on my part, with that for which I had schemed and suffered for months.

The battalion formed part of a very large force engaged on some extensive manœuvres, which were, I believe, partly a training-exercise for field-officers, partly a demonstration for the benefit of certain tribes, and partly a reconnaissance in force.

My Company was broken up into a chain of tiny outpost groups, widely scattered in a line parallel to the course of a dry river-bed which was believed by the more ignorant legionaries to form a rough boundary between Algeria and Morocco.

Small patrols kept up communication between the river-bed frontier line and these groups, and one day I found myself a member of such a patrol.

As it happened, the rest of the *escouade* consisted entirely of Russians, with the exception of my friend Rien, a Frenchman, and a couple of Spaniards and a Jew. All the Russians were in a clique, except Badineff, who hated the others.

This man, Badineff, a huge, powerful fellow, was a gentleman, and was commonly supposed to have commanded a regiment of Cossacks. After his third bottle of wine, he would talk of his "children," and say there were no cavalry in the world to compare with them. "My regiment would ride round a whole brigade of Spahis, while it galloped, and then ride through it and back." . . . After his fourth bottle he would lapse into Russian, and further revelations were lost to his interested audience.

Badineff had re-enlisted in the Legion twice, was now serving his fifteenth year in the ranks, and must have been about sixty years of age.

He spoke perfect English, French and German, and had certainly seen a great deal of life—and of death too.

The other Russians were "intellectuals," political plotters and refugees—a loathsome gang, foul as hyenas and cowardly as village pariah-dogs.

Our patrol started from bivouac, after a sleepless night, long before the red dawn of a very terrible day—one of those days when a most terrific thunderstorm is always just about to break, and never does so.

By one of those unfortunate concatenations of untoward circumstance that render the operations of warfare an uncertain and much over-rated pastime, we had to start with almost nothing in our water-bottles, less in our haversacks, and least in our stomachs.

Sergeant Frederic, however, comforted us with the information that our march was to be but a short one—about ten *kilomètres*—and that the outpost to which we were going was actually holding a well, water-hole or oasis, and was properly provisioned.

All we had to do, was to step out smartly, arrive promptly, eat, drink and be merry, and then lie like warriors taking our rest with our martial cloaks around us.

It was Sergeant Frederic who lied.

The post was quite thirty kilometres away, and we had marched about twenty of them, through the most terrible heat I have ever known, when the sand-storm came on, and we were lost.

It began with a wind that seemed to have come straight from the opened mouth of Hell. It was so hot that it hurt, and one laid one's hand over one's face as though to save it from being burnt from the bones behind it. Dust clouds arose in such density as to obscure the mid-day sun. As the wind increased to hurricane force, the dust was mingled with sand and small stones that cut the flesh, and, before long, gloom became darkness.

We staggered on, Sergeant Frederic leading, and in every mind was the thought, "How can he know where he is going? . . . We shall be lost in the desert and die of thirst."

Darkness by day is very different from the darkness of night, for at night a man can take a bearing from the stars and keep his direction.

It is difficult to give an adequate idea of the conditions that prevailed. We were deafened, blinded and suffocated.

To open one's mouth and gaspingly inhale sufficient air to rid oneself of the terrible feeling of imminent asphyxiation, was to fill one's lungs with sand; to open one's eyes to see where one was going, was to be blinded with sand; to stagger on, buffeted and bedevilled through that black night-by-day, choking and drowning in a raging ocean whose great breakers were waves of sand, was to be overwhelmed and utterly lost; to give up hope and effort and to lie prone, with face to earth, in the hope of escaping the worst of the torture, was to be buried alive.

Perhaps this was what Sergeant Frederic feared, for he kept us moving—in single file, each man holding to the end of the bayonet-scabbard of the man in front of him, and with strict orders to give the alarm if the man behind him lost touch.

Frederic put Badineff, Rien and myself last. . . .

How long we struggled on, bent double against the wind, I do not know, but I was very near the end of my tether, and feeling as though I were drowning in a boiling sea, when I was jerked to a standstill by the halting of the man in front of me.

A Russian *légionnaire*, one Smolensky, appeared to have gone mad, and with his clenched fists forced into his eyes, and face upraised as though to lift his mouth above the flying sand, screamed that he would go no further; that Frederic was a murderer maliciously leading us to our deaths, an incompetent fool who did not know in the least where he was going nor what he was doing, and a scoundrel who merited instant death. . . .

A man threw himself on the ground. . . . Another. . . . Another. . . .

As Rien, Badineff and I pushed forward, Sergeant Frederic loomed up through the murk of this fantastic Hell.

"What's this?" he yelled, leaning against the wind.

Another man threw himself on the ground, and the mad Russian began loading his rifle, shrieking curses at Frederic as he did so.

"Let's *die* like gentlemen, at least," cried Rien, as Badineff sprang on the madman, wrenched his rifle from him and knocked him down.

Another man, a friend of the madman, swung up his rifle to club Badineff, and I seized it as it came back over the man's shoulder.

Rien shouted something that was carried away by the wind, and I received a heavy blow on the head.

I saw Sergeant Frederic draw his automatic, as I stumbled and fell.

Like a prairie fire leaping from tuft to tuft, madness was spreading from man to man, and the unauthorized halt was becoming a free fight. The single-file column had become a crowd —a maddened crowd ripe for revolt and murder.

Sergeant Frederic acted with wisdom and his usual coolness. As I staggered to my feet he roared the blessed words:

"Halte! Campez!"

He was instantly obeyed, and everyone sank to the ground. Going from man to man he pushed, pulled, shouted, and exhorted, until he had got all but the weariest and most despairing, crouched on knees and elbows, soles of the feet to the wind, heads tucked in, chin upon chest, and the face in the little space protected by the body.

In this posture, such as the Arab assumes in the lee of his
kneeling camel, when caught in a sandstorm, one might hope to
breathe, and by frequent movement to avoid burial.

In a few minutes the patrol was almost obliterated and, to any
eye that could have beheld it when that awful storm was at its
height, it must have suggested an orderly arrangement of sand-
covered boulders, rather than a company of men.

How long the sand-storm lasted I do not know, but it was only
by dint of frequent change of position that we were not buried
alive. Nor do I know how long it had been day when the sun's rays
again penetrated the dusty gloom. Whether Sergeant Frederic really
had the least idea as to where he was, or where he was going, I do
not know, but he bravely strove to give the impression that all was
well—that we were not lost, and that a brief march would bring us
to water and to food. Encouraging, praising, shaming, exhorting,
promising, he got the escouade on its feet and together, and after a
brief brave speech, gave the order to march, and as some of us
turned to step off, a Russian, Smernoff—a typical sample of "the
brittle intellectuals who crack beneath the strain," a loathsome
creature, mean as a jackal, and bloodthirsty as a wolf, suddenly
yelled:

"*March?* My God, yes, and where to? . . . You have lost us;
you have killed us, you swine! . . ."

And as Sergeant Frederic strode toward him, the beast threw up
his rifle and shot him through the chest. Evidently he had slipped a
cartridge in, during the storm.

Frederic fell, rolled over, gasping and coughing blood, drew his
automatic, and, with what must have been a tremendous
concentration of will-power, shot Smernoff just as Badineff swung
up his rifle to club him.

"Hankinson," gasped Frederic as I sprang to his assistance.
"Take command. . . . Shoot any man who disobeys you. . . . March
straight into the wind—due south. . . ."

Hubbub arose behind me. A rifle was fired, and, looking round,
I saw that Dalgaroff had fired at Badineff and apparently missed
him, for Badineff sprang upon him and bore him to the ground, his
hands at his throat.

In a moment the *escouade* was in two fighting factions,
Smernoff's Russian gang against Badineff, Rien, myself, the
Roumanian and the Spaniards. I rose to my feet, and, as I threw
open the breech of my rifle, shouted words of command which I
hoped might be automatically obeyed. The result was a clicking of

breech-bolts as rifles were loaded.

"Rally here, the loyal men," I shouted. "Come on, Badineff," and to my side sprang Rien, Jacob the Roumanian, Badineff and the two Spaniards, and stood shoulder to shoulder with me, between Frederic and the Smernoff faction.

"Now, you fools," I bawled. "Aren't we in danger enough? Follow me, and I will get you out of it. . . . I know the way."

There was a groan and a movement behind us.

"Stand aside," said the brave Frederic, who had struggled to a kneeling position, one hand pressed to his chest, the other holding his automatic steadily.

"Mirsky," he croaked, "return to your duty. Fall in here instantly."

Mirsky laughed, and Frederic shot him dead.

"Andrieff, return to your duty," continued Frederic. "Fall in here instantly."

Andrieff flung his rifle forward and they both fired. Frederic fell back. There was a thunder of hoofs, and a troop of Spahis came down upon us at the charge—their officer riding some fifty yards ahead.

"*Surrender!*" he roared, as he pulled his horse on to its haunches. "*Ground arms.*" . . . And as his troop came to a halt at the signal of his up-flung hand, he bade his Troop-Sergeant arrest the lot of us. Leaping from his horse he strode to where Frederic lay, bleeding to death, and knelt beside him.

"Tell me, *mon enfant*," he said, and put his ear to Frederic's feebly-moving lips.

"Mutiny," he whispered. "Not their fault. . . . *Cafard.* . . . No water. . . . Lost. . . ."

And with a last effort raised his hand, and, pointing to me, said: "This man is . . ." And died.

"Ho, this man is the ring-leader, I suppose," snapped the officer, rising and glaring at me. "Tie his hands. Tie the hands of the lot of them," and, drawing an officer's field pocket-book from beneath his Spahi cloak, he entered his observations—quite erroneous, as, at the Court-martial, they proved to be. Having noted that the dead sergeant had shot three of the mutineers in self-defence after being twice wounded by them, and that I was apparently the ringleader, he made a list of the names and *matricule* numbers of the prisoners, snapped the elastic band upon his book, and returned it to his breast-pocket with a certain grim satisfaction. He then had the prisoners released and set them to work to dig two graves, one for the Sergeant and one for his murderers, while his troop off-saddled and took a mid-day rest. . . .

That evening, we found ourselves strictly guarded and segregated prisoners in the camp, and, after a brief field Court-martial next day, at which our Spahi officer testified that he had caught the lot of us murdering our Sergeant, we were despatched to Oran for the General Court-martial to decide our fate. Out of the mass of perjury, false witness, contradictory statements and simple truth—the latter told by Rien, Badineff, Jacob the Gypsy, and myself—emerged the fact that the *escouade* had murdered its Sergeant, losing three of its number in the process. . . . Further it was decided that if those three, as might be assumed, were the actual murderers, the remainder were certainly accessories, even if they did not include the actual slayers.

It was a near thing, and I believe that only one vote stood between the death-sentence, and that of eight years' penal servitude, *travaux forcés*, in the Disciplinary Battalions of France.

The President of the Oran General Court-martial was a Major de Beaujolais. . . .

CHAPTER IX

It will perhaps be quite comprehensible that I do not care to dwell over-much upon the time I spent in the Penal Battalions of Madame la République.

I certainly am not going to complain of the treatment I received, inasmuch as I was there by my own desire, and had been at some considerable pains to arrive there.

Each country has its own penal system, and each country can criticize that of the other, if it has nothing better to do. Our own system is not without spot or blemish, and one has heard unpleasant things of the treatment of convict-workers in our coal-mines.

Charles Reade had considerable fault to find with the English convict system, and those exiled to penal servitude in Siberia have a poor opinion of Russian methods of punishment.

And I am the less disposed to assail the French convict-system because Biribi is now abolished (and also, perhaps, the Devil's Island, where Captain Dreyfus suffered, and the Guiana penal settlement), and the worst punishments that we endured were inflicted upon us illegally and in defiance of the law. These latter, generally the outcome of the vicious spite of some local petty tyrant, struck me as rather unnecessary, for the prescribed and lawful punishments were wholly adequate—apart from the fact that life itself was one long punishment.

For example, I personally needed nothing more in the way of correctional attentions than twenty-four hours of *la planche*. This ingenious device was, as its name implies, merely a plank. To the observer's eye, a simple plank, but to the sentenced man it was something more.

In the first place, the plank was some twelve feet above the ground. In the second place, it was neither sufficiently long, nor sufficiently wide, to enable a man to lie down upon it in anything but acute discomfort and danger of falling. He could merely sit upon it—and he could not do that for long, without changing his position in the hope of finding one less racking and tormenting. In the third place the heat and glare of that white-washed, white-hot prison-yard was a cruel and dangerous torture in itself.

The punishment of *la planche* sounds mild and moderate. So did some of those of the Holy Inquisition of old—particularly the worst of all, that of water dripping on the head.

Let anyone who thinks it mild and moderate, try it for an hour. Let him not try it for twenty-four hours, however, lest he do not regain his sanity.

But could not one throw oneself off this hellish perch of the devil? One could. One did. But not twice. He was ready, willing, nay positively anxious, to return to that now attractive plank, by the time he had discovered what happened to those who voluntarily or involuntarily quitted the post of dishonour.

Nor indeed was there any real necessity to exceed the simple and lawful punishment of deprivation of water; of standing facing the sun in a white-washed corner from sunrise to sunset without food or drink; or of being chained to a wall with the hands above the head.

In fact one would have thought that "hard labour"—harder perhaps than that known to any other convict in the world—by day, and lying chained to an iron bar and to one's neighbour on the stone floor of a shed, by night, might, with the absence of all that makes life supportable, and the presence of everything calculated to make life insupportable, have rendered even "lawful" punishment unnecessary.

But no. Punishment beyond punishment had to be inflicted, and then illegal and indefensible torture added.

Chief of these were the *silo* and the *crapaudine*, both once permitted by law, and both absolutely prohibited and "abolished" by General de Negrier. I saw both these tortures inflicted, and I suffered one of them myself. But I wish to repeat, and to make it clear, that this villainous brutality was wholly contrary to law and in flat defiance of most definite military regulations.

Also, I wish to repeat that, in any case, I am not complaining. What I got, I asked for.

Further, if the system was severe to the point of savage and brutal cruelty, it is to be remembered that the bulk of the convicts were desperate and dangerous criminals, many of them barely human in their horrible depravity, and far more dangerous to those in authority over them, than any cageful of lions, tigers and panthers to the wild-beast-tamer who ventures among them.

While there was a sprinkling of soldiers whose horrible "crimes" were those of dirty buttons, slackness, drunkenness, earning the enmity of an N.C.O., and being generally and congenitally non-military, there was also a certain number of ordinary criminals who had been, perhaps, more unfortunate than wicked. But there was, as I have said, undoubtedly a very large proportion of the worst and beastliest criminals in the world, prominent among whom was the typical Parisian *apache*, who has no faintest shadow of any solitary virtue, save occasionally the savage courage of the cornered rat.

As is natural and very right and proper, the officers and non-commissioned officers—and more particularly the latter—are chosen with an eye to their suitability for the work they have to do.

Stern disciplinarians are required and stern disciplinarians are selected. Not only did the success of the system depend upon the iron discipline of these men, fierce, unbending, remorseless—but their own lives as well. Many have been killed in the execution of their duty, either by the sudden action of a maddened and despairing individual, or as the result of a cunning plot, planned and executed with fiendish ingenuity and ferocity.

They carry loaded revolvers in unfastened holsters, and their hands are never far from them. In time, they come inevitably to regard the convicts not only as enemies of the State and of Society, but also as personal enemies, and behave toward them accordingly. This is more particularly true of the non-commissioned officers, and in the conditions prevalent in far-distant desert places, where the great French military roads are in course of construction by convict labour.

And to one of these road-making gangs it was my fate to be drafted—the fate "written on my forehead," as the Arabs say—to which I had been destined, as I believed, from the beginning of time, that I might fulfil myself.

The latest road—a Road of Destiny indeed for me—was to run from the city of Zaguig, of horrible memory, to a place called the Great Oasis, a spot now of the greatest strategic importance to France. On this road were working a large proportion of the military convicts.

So, once again, to Zaguig I came, and from Zaguig marched out along the uncompleted high-way that was miraculously to lead me to my goal.

§2

Of that spell of road-work I remember but little.

Each day was exactly like its terrible predecessor. Each night a blessed escape from Hell, if not to Heaven, at any rate to a Nirvana of nothingness.

Often I wondered how men of education and refinement, such as Badineff and Rien, delicately nurtured, were able to bear the horror that was life, inasmuch as it was all that I, with my great sustaining inspiration and need to live, could do, to force my body to obey my will and keep my will from willing death.

In point of fact, it was patent to me that Rien was failing and that both the temper and the body of the giant Badineff were wearing thin.

And then a spell of bad weather, with terrific heat and sand-laden winds, that seemed to have been forced through gigantic furnaces, precipitated, as so often happens, one of those catastrophes of madness, mutiny, murder and heavy retaliatory and repressive punishment.

I am sorry to say that I was the innocent cause of this particular example of these tragedies that are all too common, and indeed inevitable, in such circumstances.

Small beginnings! . . .

As is so often the case, the beginnings of this affair which was to cost the lives of so many men, were small enough, God knows.

A Sergeant, one of those "hard cases" that are naturally selected for their aggressive harshness, merciless severity, and all the qualities that go to make the ferocious disciplinarian and martinet, stood watching me as I swung my pick; with blistered hands, aching arms, eyes blinded with sweat, a terrible pain at the back of my neck, and the feeling that if I bent my body once again, my back would surely break. . . .

As I painfully straightened myself, he stepped towards me, and, with his stick, struck my cap from my head. To be quite just, I think he was only making a sudden raid upon that place of concealment, in search of tobacco, food, paper, pencil, a piece of steel, or a sharp-edged stone.

However, the stick struck my head as well as my cap, and I was still sufficiently near, in memory, to civilization, to find his act discourteous. I must have given expression to this wrong mental attitude, and looked upon him with the eye of mild reproach.

Now, in the ranks of *les Joyeux*, looking can be an offence. A cat may look at a king, but a convict may not look at a corporal—save with the glance of the most respectful, humble and obedient reverence. Any other kind of look may be mutinous; a mutinous look may precede a mutinous act; and a mutinous act precedes death. The red blossoms of wrath must be nipped in the bud, and the Sergeant promptly nipped mine.

In a second I was sent sprawling with a blow that partly stunned and wholly confused me—and it was with a sense of confusion worse confounded that I saw Badineff raise his spade and fell the Sergeant from behind, while Rien snatched the automatic that the man was in the act of drawing.

Ludicrously enough, Rien shouted at the stunned Sergeant, "You insolent dog! How dare you strike a gentleman!" and was himself struck to the ground by a convict, a Spaniard named Ramon Gonzales, a poor mean soul who hoped to curry favour for his virtue, and gain remission for his sins.

At the same moment, a Corporal dashed into the mêlée, kicked me in the face, fired his automatic at Badineff, and was promptly felled by a man belonging to another *escouade*—and, even in that moment, I noticed the splendid straight left with which he took the Corporal on the point of the jaw, and the fact (which should have astounded me) that he ejaculated in excellent English, "Dam' swine!" as he did so.

As to exactly what happened then, I am not perfectly clear, save that there was a rush of guards and convicts, as Badineff picked up the automatic dropped by Rien, shot the Spaniard who had felled the latter, shot the Sergeant who rose to his feet and pluckily tackled him with his stick, and then shot a guard who charged him with fixed bayonet.

There was a terrific hubbub, some more indiscriminate shooting, and within a few minutes of my original impious glance at the Sergeant, a number of bodies was lying prone upon the sand, whistles were blowing, voices barking orders, convicts shouting insanely, and chaos reigning in the very home of the world's most rigid discipline.

But not for long.

As always, discipline prevailed, and within another minute or two, order was restored. All the bodies but two or three, promptly came to life and were found to be those of wise men who had flung themselves down until the shooting was over, with the double view of dissociating themselves from the evil doings of wicked men, and of having a little nap.

Apart, very much under arrest, stood the villains of the piece, myself, Badineff, Rien; the Roumanian gypsy known as Jacob the Jew; the Spaniard, Ramon Gonzales; the man with the useful left who had knocked the Corporal out, and three or four more.

Well! We'd done it now, all-right! And it was a drum-head

Court-martial for ours that evening, and our backs to a wall and our faces to a firing-party at dawn next morning. Except that there wouldn't be any wall.

There would be a grave though, and we should dig it. We should also stand by it and topple neatly into it when the volley was fired. I hoped I should be dead before they shovelled the sand in.

I also thought of a wily convict who was said to have toppled before he was shot, and to have crawled out before he was buried, and I pondered the possibility of contriving these duplicities.

It did not come to this, however, and I am still in doubt on the subject.

Chained together, and surrounded by guards with loaded rifles and fixed bayonets, we were marched from the scene of our sins—a long and miserable march, to the temporary depôt of the slow-progressing, ever-moving Company.

This depôt proved to be a deserted Arab village, and for want of better or worse accommodation, we were hastily consigned to its large underground grain-pit, or *silo*.

Confinement in these *silos* had been expressly forbidden because men had gone mad in them, died in them, been forgotten in them, had murdered each other in them for the last drops of water. But many forbidden things are done in those distant places where subordinates rule, where public opinion is not, where the secrets of the prison-house remain secrets, where the grave is very silent, and where necessity not only knows no law, but is apt to be the mother of diabolical invention.

Into this grain-pit we were dropped, one by one; those who preferred to do so, being allowed to climb down a rope by means of which a large pail of water and a sack of bread were lowered for our sustenance until such time as a field Court-martial could be assembled.

That might be upon the morrow, or, again, it might not.

I do not think that there was any intention of actually imprisoning us in this *silo* as a punishment—our offence was too desperate for that.

I think that the officer commanding the Company—if he knew anything about it at all—merely gave the order to put us there as the simplest and easiest means of keeping us secure for the brief space that remained to us—probably only a day, or, at most, a couple of days—before we were tried and shot for murderous revolt against authority.

What then happened, above ground, we did not know—and only two of us ever did know—but by piecing together information which, as I shall tell, I obtained later, I came to the conclusion that a whirlwind attack by Touareg or Bedouin tribesmen, upon the Company, drew every man from the depôt to the scene of the fight, where they shared the fate of escort and convicts alike, there being not a single survivor.

What happened below ground may be quickly told, for the worst hours of my life, hours which seemed certain to be my last, hours during which I was compelled to abandon hope of helping Isobel, ended in the greatest moment of my life, *the moment in which I found John Geste*, the moment in which I knew that I had, against all probability, succeeded.

During those dreadful days, we died, man by man, according to our kind; some in fear, some in wrath; some in despair, some in faith and hope; and one by his own hand.

The two Anglo-Saxons survived, whether by tenacity, strength, the will to live, or the Will of God; and on the fifth day there remained alive only myself and the bearded man who had struck and damned the Corporal—*and who was John Geste.*

And then I should never have known him, but that he used an expression that I heard nowhere else but at Brandon Abbas.

Stout fella!

I really cannot, even now, give the faintest idea of my feelings in that hour. As nothing I can say would be adequate, I will say nothing.

I had found John Geste!

Think of it. . . .

CHAPTER X

Alive we were, but only just alive. Thirst, starvation, suffocation, corpses, flies and other attendant horrors had almost done their work on men not over-nourished, nor in too good condition, at the start—and when we were discovered it was none too soon.

We actually owed our salvation, I believe, to the predatory, or at any rate, the acquisitive, instincts of an aged party who, knowing of the existence of the *silo*, came to see whether it contained anything worth acquiring.

It did. And he acquired us.

I was lying beside the inanimate body of John Geste, and doing my utmost to persuade him not to die, when the light from the small man-hole in the roof was obscured suddenly, and I knew that we were either remembered or discovered.

I called out in French, and then in Arabic, seeing what I thought to be the silhouette of the head of a native.

And, in the same tongue, a thin piping voice called in wonder upon Allah, and then in question, upon us. I hastily assured the owner of the silhouette and the voice, that he was indeed the favoured of Allah in that he had discovered us, powerful and wealthy *Roumis* who would, in return for help, reward him with riches beyond the dreams of avarice.

Apparently my feeble croakings reached not only the man but his intelligence, for the head was withdrawn from the top of the short shaft which connected the *silo* with the ground above, and, a few minutes later, a rope came dangling down into our dreadful prison.

I promptly decided that it would be better for me to attempt the ascent first, for if I could get up I could certainly get down again, and I wanted to see who and what was up above, before fastening the rope to John Geste.

I did not like the idea, for example, of his being hauled up to the roof and then dropped. I accordingly passed the rope round my body beneath my arms, tied it on my chest, and shouted to whomsoever was above, to pull.

For several minutes nothing happened—minutes that seemed

like hours, and then suddenly with a swift but steady lift, I rose the fifteen or twenty feet to the opening.

I thrust, fending, with my hands and knees, and was ignominiously dragged out into the blessed light and sweet air of day, at the heels of a camel to whose saddle-tree the end of the rope —the identical rope with which we had been lowered—was fastened.

The man leading the camel halted. I untied the rope, and perceived myself to be in the company of three extremely decrepit-looking old men, and three remarkably fine riding-camels.

It was soon quite evident to me that the leader, at any rate, of this aged trio was anything but decrepit mentally, and he quickly grasped the idea that I was to be lowered again into the pit, that I might bring up another man who was alive but too weak to help himself.

Not only did he grasp my idea, but produced a better one of his own—and I had only just understood it and ejaculated, "God bless you, Grandpa," when my knees gave way, my head spun round, and with infinite regret and annoyance, I collapsed completely.

When I again opened my eyes upon the glorious and wonderful world from which I had been absent for five days in Hell, I was lying in the shade of a mud wall, and John Geste was lying beside me.

Grandpa warmly welcomed my return to consciousness, and explained that he and his young brother had been down quick into the pit, while his youngest brother—a lad who looked about eighty to me—had operated the camel. Also that he had only brought up this one, albeit a doubtful case, as the others were all dead, very dead indeed.

I commended Grandpa most warmly, and promised to set him up for life, whether in a store, a saloon, or a houri-stocked Garden of Eden, and to see both his young brothers well launched in life.

Not only had the excellent old man had the sense to bring up our own pail, and fill it with water, but he had concocted a millet-porridge abomination, which, with some filthy and man-handled milk curd, formed the noblest and most welcome feast which had ever been set before me.

More, and what gave me infinite joy on John Geste's account, he had sent one of the boys for the milk.

While I was wondering where the dairy might be, Grandpa mentioned that there was a Bedouin encampment "just over there", and any amount of fresh camel's-milk was to be had for the asking, and still more for the giving of a cartridge or two.

When I began to question the ancient as to who he was and whence he came, the light of intelligence faded from his eye, all expression from the mask-like mass of wrinkles which was his face, and he announced he was a very poor man—a *miskeen* of the lowest type, and that I was his father and his mother.

What he did tell us, and what was of the very deepest interest, was that, five days ago, there had been a sudden Touareg raid upon the road-gangs, a brief fight and a relentless slaughter. Apparently this had taken place a few miles from the deserted village where we lay, and the Touareg *harka* had swept through it, slaying every living soul they encountered.

As Grandpapa pointed out, it was lucky for us that they had not chanced upon the *silo*. Modestly he contrasted our present fortunate position with the fate that might have been ours.

Excellent as were the ministrations, however, of these three wise men of Gotham, or elsewhere, I doubt whether either John Geste or I would have recovered in their hands. We might have done, for we were both pretty tough and imbued with the most intense yearning to live; but John, I learned, had recently been most desperately ill, and needed something more than curds and soaked millet-seed. That he lived at all, was due, in the first place, to the fact that we had a plentiful supply of fresh camel's-milk, and, in the second plate, that we were promptly captured by semi-nomadic Bedouin, and, in a sense, fattened for the killing.

§2

On the second day after our rescue from the *silo*, as John Geste and I lay in a deserted mud-hut, a tall Arab, followed by our deliverer—volubly explaining that he had just found us—stooped into the hut and favoured us with a long, hard, searching stare, slightly amused, slightly sardonic and wholly unfriendly.

And the Arab was Selim ben Yussuf, that handsome human hawk.

There was no mistaking the high-bridged aristocratic nose, the keen flashing eyes beneath the perfectly arched eyebrows, the thin cruel lips between the canonically clipped moustache and the small double tuft of beard.

In the extremely dirty, dishevelled, unshorn and emaciated creature before him, Selim utterly failed to recognize the "wealthy tourist" whom jealousy had nearly prompted him to stab in the garden of Abu Sheikh Ahmed at Bouzen.

What he did see in me and John Geste, was a pair of French convicts, delivered into his hand—an extremely welcome capture, valuable whether for purposes of ransom, hostage, torture, or mere humiliating slavery.

"*Salaam aleikoum, Sheikh*," I croaked. "I claim your hospitality for myself and my comrade. . . . And listen. . . . He is a great man in his own country, and his father would pay a ransom of a thousand camels, for he is a very wealthy man and loves his son. . . ."

But ere I could embroider the theme further, Selim ben Yussuf laughed unpleasantly, and with a contemptuous:

"Filthy convict dogs!" turned to our ancient rescuer and bade him deliver us alive at the *douar*, whence he had been obtaining the milk for us.

With profound obeisances and assurances of the promptest and most willing obedience, the ancient backed from the hut, vanished into thin air and was seen no more.

When, a little later, a band of ruffians came to fetch us, my strength and temper were both sorely tried. For when I tried to carry John Geste to the miserable baggage-camel provided for our transport, I was tripped up, kicked, struck, reviled and spat upon, by these well-armed braves; bitter haters, every one, of the Infidel, the *Roumi*, the invader of the sacred soil of Islam.

Luckily we were not bound, and I was able to hold John more or less comfortably on the camel. What I feared was that his illness was typhoid fever, and that rough movement would cause perforation and death. Luckily again, it was only a short ride to the encampment of the semi-nomadic tribe of which Selim ben Yussuf's father was the ruling Sheikh.

From what I saw and heard of the old man, I got the impression that he was a gentleman—a real courteous, chivalrous, Arab gentleman of the old school, a desert knight of the type of which one often reads, and which one rarely meets.

Unfortunately, like so many Oriental fathers, he was so besottedly devoted to his son that he could see no wrong in him, and would deny him nothing. Further, although the aged Sheikh had by no means abdicated, the reins were slipping from his feeble hand, and were daily more firmly grasped in the strong clutch of his son.

Selim, though not yet ruler, was the power behind the throne—

but there was another and a stronger power behind him.

It was before these three, as they sat at the door of a big white and brown striped tent, that we were driven, I staggering along with the unconscious John—who otherwise would have been dragged along the ground by one foot—on our arrival at the *douar*. And, in a moment, it was manifest that the old Sheikh spoke the final word, that the young Sheikh's thought was expressed by that word, while the third person's brain inspired the thought.

And the third person was the Angel of Death.

There, between the father and son, evidently beloved of both, sat the indescribably beautiful half-caste of Bouzen, the daughter of the Ouled-Naïl dancing-girl and the Englishman who had loved her and left her.

She knew me instantly, even as our glances met, and I was apprised of the fact by her long cool stare, and mocking smile, though she spoke no word and gave no sign of recognition.

Remembering the effect produced upon Selim by her previous recognition of my personal attractions, I welcomed her present reticence.

And now what? . . . Here was a bewildering and astonishing turn of affairs!

I had fallen into the hands of a bitter enemy of France, who was also a bitter and jealous enemy of myself. Behind him, and swaying him as a reed is swayed by the wind, was a girl notorious for her destructive evil-doing—a girl who loathed Christians in general, for her hated father's sake, and me in particular for my lack of response to her overtures at the house of Abu Sheikh Ahmed.

If she had been ready to kill me then, when I was a person of some importance, and actually in the company of the all-powerful Colonel Levasseur, what would she do to me now that I was completely in her power—helpless and harmless—a miserable piece of desert flotsam, an escaped convict, whose killing the authorities would be more disposed to approve than to punish.

I addressed myself to the old Sheikh, throwing myself upon his mercy and appealing to his chivalry and honour—in the name of Allah and the Koranic Law and his own desert custom—for at least the three days' hospitality due to the "guest of Allah," the traveller who is in need.

"Traveller!" sneered Selim. "Convict, you mean. . . . A pariah dog that is condemned even by its fellow dogs. . . ."

Evidently the gentle Selim knew our brown canvas uniform for what it was.

But the old gentleman rebuked him.

"Peace, my son," he gently chided, "the prayers of the unfortunate are acceptable to Allah, the Merciful, the Compassionate, for they are His children. . . . And he who is merciful to the children of Allah is pleasing in the sight of Allah, before Whom all True Believers must one day stand. . . . Let these two men be guests of the tribe for three days, and let them want for nothing. . . . Thereafter let them go in peace, praising God. . . ."

"So be it, my father," smiled Selim. And so it would be, I decided—but I doubted that we should go far "in peace."

"And if they be the condemned prisoners of the *Roumis*," he continued, "are they not then the enemies of the *Roumis*? And are not the enemies of the *Roumis* thy friends?"

"No dog of an Infidel is my friend," growled Selim, eyeing us savagely, and I felt truly glad that the old Sheikh was still master in his own house.

For the next three days we were regarded as honoured guests, and had we been the Sheikh's own sons, we could not have been more kindly and generously treated.

Our food was of the best, we were given complete and clean outfits of Arab clothing, and we shared a tent plentifully provided with rugs and cushions. We were favoured with the services of the Sheikh's own *hakim*, a learned doctor who did us no harm—as I did not give him the opportunity—and who did us much good by decreeing that we be immersed in hot water and then be clipped and shorn by the Sheikh's own barber. It was fairly easy to get the good doctor to prescribe this and whatsoever else I wanted him to prescribe, by pretending to assume that he would prescribe it. And I had only to say:

"I am sure that my sick friend will benefit *enormously* by hot broth of goats' flesh, provided you will add to it your learned and pious incantations . . ." to procure abundance of both.

That three days of perfect rest, with unlimited fresh milk, broth, cheese, curds, *cous-cous*, bread, sweet-meats, butter, eggs, lemons, and occasional vegetables, did marvels for both of us, and led me to the blessed conclusion that John Geste was not, after all, suffering from malignant disease so much as from general debility and weakness.

I had only been just in time.

But—Merciful, Gracious, Benignant God—I *had* found him.
. . . I *had* found him. . . . *I had found John Geste and I had saved
Isobel.*

And I was curiously content and unafraid—strangely happy
and unanxious, in spite of our position, our almost hopeless
position between the upper French and the nether Arab mill-stones
—for I knew, I *knew*, I had not been allowed to go so far that I
might go no farther. . . . I had not found John Geste to lose him
again—by the hand of man or the hand of Death.

Curiously enough, John Geste and I talked but little during this
time.

For the first couple of days he was so weak that I discouraged
conversation; and when, by the third day, he had turned the corner,
and, thanks to his splendid constitution and great natural strength of
mind and body, he was making a swift recovery, conversation was
difficult.

There was so much to say that we could not say it, and our talk
consisted quite largely of those foolish but inevitable repetitions of
expressions of incredulity and wonder.

I think it was some time before he really grasped what had
happened, and realized who I was; and when he did, he could only
lie and gaze at me in bewildered amazement.

And when I had slowly and carefully told him my story from
the moment when I had met Isobel at Dr. Hanley-Blythe's nursing-
home, to the moment when he felled the Corporal who kicked me
in the face, he could only take my hand and endeavour to press it.

As became good Anglo-Saxons, we were ashamed to express
our feelings, and were, for the most part, gruffly inarticulate where
these were concerned.

Obviously John was worried at his inability to thank me, and,
every now and then, he would break our understanding silence with
a slow:

"Do you really mean that you actually enlisted in the Legion in
order to get sent to the Zephyrs on the off-chance of finding *me*?
. . . What can one say?. . . .How can I begin to try to express . . .?
Isobel shouldn't have let you do that. . . ."

"Isobel had no say in the matter,". I replied. . . . "Entirely my
own affair. . . . Gave me something to do in life. . . ."

"It's incredible . . ." said John.

170

"Yes. . . . A wonderful bit of luck. . . . No, not luck. . . ."

"I mean it's incredible that there should be a man like you, who . . ."

"Well, you yourself came back to Africa to look for a friend," I reminded him.

"Yes . . . but he had a claim on me. . . . I owed him my life. . . ."

"Well . . ." I fumbled, "a claim. . . . If you're going to speak of *claims* . . ." and I stopped.

"God! How Isobel must have *loved* you—to let you come." I said.

And:

"God! How you must *love* Isobel—to have come," said John Geste, and from the great hollow eyes the very soul of this true brother of Beau Geste probed into mine.

I looked away in pain and confusion.

His hot and shaking hand seized my wrist.

"Vanbrugh," he said, "you have done for Isobel what few men have ever done for any woman in this world—will you now do something for me?"

"I will, John Geste," said I, and looked into his face. "What is it?"

"It is this. . . . Will you answer me a question with the most absolute, perfect and complete truth—the truth, the whole truth, and nothing but the truth—without one faintest shadow of prevarication or limitation."

"I will, John Geste," said I.

"Tell me then," he begged, "does Isobel love you?"

Let those who can, be they psychologists, physiologists, psychotherapists, physicians, lovers, or plain men and women whose souls have plumbed the depths of emotion—let them, I say, explain why, in that moment I was stricken dumb.

I could not speak.

I could see the lovely face of a girl bending down to me from the back of a horse . . . I could see the boy, who but those few years ago was myself . . . I saw her smile . . . I heard her voice . . . I felt again the marvellous and mighty uprushing of my soul to the zenith of such joy as is known to human kind, when the declaration of my love had trembled on my lips—and now, *I could not speak*. I was stricken dumb—dumb as I was stricken on that morning of my highest hope and happiness, that morning of my deepest despair and pain.

John coughed slightly.

I fought for words. . . . For a word. . . . I wrestled as with Death itself for the power to shout, "*No! No! No! A thousand times, no!*" And I was dumb—sitting smitten, aghast, horrified, staring into the tortured eyes of poor John Geste.

His pale pinched face turned impossibly paler and yet more pinched, and from the white lips in that frozen mask came hollowly the words that seared me so.

"Then what I ask of you, Vanbrugh, is this. Get you back safely to England. For the love of God, take care of yourself and get back quickly. . . . And with this message. . . . That I died in Africa—for die I shall—and that the very last words I said were . . . that my one wish was that you and she would be happier together than ever man and woman had been before."

And then I found my voice, a poor and ineffectual thing, hampered by a great lump in my throat, and after a cracked and miserable laugh, I contrived to say:

"Why now . . . that's certainly the funniest thing you would hear in a lifetime. . . . Isobel love *me*! . . . Why she loves any pair of your old boots that you left at home, better than she loves the whole of the human race, myself included . . ." and I contrived another laugh. "Why, my dear chap, Isobel would rather be on the ground floor of Hell with you, than on the roof-garden of the Seventh Heaven with the greatest and finest man that ever lived, much less with *me*. . . ."

His eyes still burned into mine.

"You're speaking the truth, Vanbrugh? . . . Yes . . . you *are* speaking the truth. . . . Isobel could only love once. . . . How could I doubt her. . . ."

"You're a very sick man," said I.

"I must be," he said, and coughed slightly, again. "But oh, Vanbrugh, you . . . you . . . you . . . *stout fella!* . . . hero. . . . What can I say to you but that I understand, Vanbrugh . . . I understand . . ." and being at the highest pitch of emotion, his English hatred of showing what he felt, came to his rescue, and with an embarrassed grin upon his ravaged face, he squeezed my arm.

"Stout fella! You're a stouter man than I am, Gunga Din," he said, and fell back upon his mattress.

Yes, the Gestes could *accept* generously, as well as give generously—which is a thing not all generous people can do.

§3

During the three days' hospitality and grace, we had received no visits save those of the doctor, the barber, and the servants who waited on us with food, clothing and hot water; and though I had no doubt that our tent was pretty strictly guarded, we had been treated as guests rather than prisoners, in accordance with the order given by the old Sheikh.

On the fourth evening there came a change.

Instead of servants bearing a brass tray laden with excellent food, Selim himself, followed by some half-dozen of his familiars —young, haughty, truculent Sons of the Prophet—swaggered into our guest-tent.

The change which came over his face as he did so, would have been ludicrous had it been less ominous.

Expecting to see two foul and filthy ruffians, shaggy, unshorn —garbed in the tattered remnants of brown canvas uniforms, he beheld two clean and shaven gentlemen of leisure, clad much as he was himself.

And then he recognized me.

"*Allah Kerim!*" he ejaculated. "Our blue-eyed tourist of Bouzen! The contemptuous, haughty *Nazarani* dog, who had not the good breeding to accept the kiss with which the Angel of Death would have honoured him! . . . She shall be the Angel of Death for you indeed, this time. . . . A kiss? . . . You shall kiss a glowing coal. . . . An embrace? . . . You shall embrace a burning brazier. . . . Perhaps that will put some warmth into your cold heart, you dog. . . . And who is this other escaped convict, masquerading in that dress like a jackal in a lion's skin? . . . Have you slept warm, you *Roumi* curs? . . . You shall sleep warm to-night—on a bed of red-hot stones. . . ."

And he gave an order that I could not hear, to one of his followers. John Geste yawned.

"Chatty lad," he said. "What's biting him?"

"He doesn't like you much and he doesn't like me a little," I replied, "and I am a bit worried. I don't know exactly how far what he says goes, in this outfit. . . . He's the lad I was telling you about —the lover of the lady who was sitting in papa's pocket."

"And the lady?" asked John Geste. "I dimly remember that there was one."

I stole a glance at Selim. His back was turned—he had gone to the door of the tent and was looking out, seemingly in reflection.

"I am not sure that she isn't the *deus ex machina*—or shall we say the little 'dear' *ex machina*," I replied.

"Or *cherchez la femme*, since we're talking learned," smiled John. "You think she may be our fate, eh? Beware of a dark woman, what? . . . You know her?

"I have met her twice, and I am not looking forward to the third time," I replied.

"What sort of a person is she?"

"Well, the gentleman at the front door has been calling as dogs quite freely—shall we say something of a lady-dog?"

"What poor old Digby used to call a bitchelor," grinned John. "Poor dear old Dig . . . God! I wish he and Beau were with us now. . . ."

"Amen," said I, and was moved to add, "I'll bet they're watching, mighty interested," and, at that moment, Selim's order bore fruit in the shape of some husky negroes.

"Get up, you dogs," he snarled.

"Why certainly, most noble and courteous Arab," said John Geste, as he rose painfully to his feet. "I have eaten of your salt, and I thank you."

"You have eaten of my father's salt and you may thank him—that three days have been added to your miserable life," was the uncompromising reply.

"The arm of the French is very long, Selim ben Yussuf," I said.

"Yes, convict," he replied, "it will reach you, I think, or rather your body. . . . The terms of the reward are 'dead or alive' I believe."

"Selim ben Yussuf!" mused John, aloud. "Son of a famed and noble Sheikh, and seller of dead men's flesh! . . . Does he eat it too?" he added, turning to me.

"Why no," I said. "He's far too good a merchant . . . he can get money for it. . . . He sells those who eat his salt too. . . ."

It was a dangerous line, but it *was* a line—on Selim's pride and self-respect. Torture me he might, but I did not think he would sell me alive or dead, much less John Geste, against whom he had no grudge save that of his nationality and religion.

My last remark had certainly got him on the raw, for he strode up to me, his hand upon the big curved knife stuck in the front of his sash.

"Lying Christian dog, you have *not* eaten of my salt," he shouted. "It was my father's. . . . 'Three days,' he said . . . and he is no longer in the camp."

"A great gentleman," I observed. "The old order changes . . ." and I shrugged my shoulders.

I had an idea that the old Sheikh had not gone very far, nor for very long—or our shrift would have been shorter.

"Throw the dogs out," he snarled, turning to his slaves, and we were unceremoniously hustled from the tent, and with sundry kicks, blows and prods with spear-butt and *matrack*-sticks, we were personally conducted to some low mean goat-skin tents, situated at a distance from the main camp and much too near an enclosure obviously tenanted by goats.

Into one of the tents we were thrown, and for the moment, left —but around a camp-fire that burned in front of it, certain unmusical loud fellows of the baser sort rendered night hideous and escape impossible.

A glance round the filthy and dilapidated tent showed it to be entirely unfurnished, nor was anything added unto us save a huge and disgusting negro, who entered and made himself one with us, who were evidently his sacred charge.

John Geste, courteous ever, gave him welcome.

"Take a chair, Archibald, and make yourself at home," said he. "Take three, if you can. . . ."

Archibald, or rather Koko, as we later discovered his name to be, made no reply.

He merely sat him down and stared unwinkingly and unwaveringly.

If he had been told to watch us, he certainly did it. And after his eyes had bored into us like gimlets for a few hours, we were constrained, with many apologies, to turn our backs on him.

For more hours we sat and talked of plans of escape, and could only conclude that, in our weak state, our one hope was the good-will of the old Sheikh.

Nor was this hope a strong one, for however kindly the old man might treat us while we were in his power, it was too much to hope that he would do anything but hand us back, safe and sound, to the French authorities.

Any Bedouin tribe grazing its flocks in the neighbourhood of the Zaguig-Great Oasis Road, would act wisely in giving every possible proof of its innocence, virtue and correct attitude towards the French, in view of the recent attack upon the road-gangs.

CHAPTER XI

That night I was taken horribly ill; so ill that, after thinking it must be cholera, thought departed altogether, and I knew nothing more for several days.

When I did return to a realization of my surroundings, I found that I was back in the guest-tent, and that I was alone.

Where was John Geste?

My last memory was of his helping me in that foul goat-skin hole, while that beastly nigger, callous as an animal, sat and stared.

A horrible panic fear gripped my heart, and feebly I called John's name. And even as my heart almost stopped, I was reassured by the thought, the conviction, the certainty, that this wonderful thing, this finding of John Geste, against all probability, was no chance, no piece of luck—much less a colossal mockery. We are *not* the sport of mocking Fates.

But I called his name again, with what little strength I had.

Quite possibly the old Sheikh had returned, and, finding that we had been evilly entreated, had had us brought back, not only to the guest-tent, but had given us a tent each. The better sort of Arab is capable of much fineness in the matter of hospitality—a hospitality enjoined by his religion and by countless centuries of desert custom, the outcome of desert need.

At my second feeble call, a man stepped into the tent, in the shade of which he had probably been sleeping. He was one of the servants who had previously waited on us in this same tent.

"Where is my brother?" said I.

"Gone, *Sidi*," replied the man, and promptly departed, returning in a few minutes, accompanied by the *hakim*.

From this gentleman's delight in finding me conscious, I gathered that he had been strictly charged to effect my recovery, the credit for which he promptly awarded himself. To this he was very welcome, as was, to me, the broth which he prescribed—together with pills, potions and Koranic extracts. These last he painfully wrote on scraps of rag wherewith he enriched the mutton broth.

The pills I pushed into the sand beneath my rug. With the potions I watered their burial-place. The rags, in my gratitude and generosity, I bestowed upon the deserving waiter, by way of a tip.

For the broth I found a good home, and felt the better for it.

But when, after thanking and congratulating the eminent physician I asked:

"And where is my brother, *Sidi Hakim?*" I got the same unsatisfactory reply.

"*Gone!*" and a gesture of the thin hands and delicate fingers, to indicate a complete evanishment as of smoke into thin air.

In spite of my continued reassurement of myself, I was anxious, worried, frightened, and filled with a horrible and apprehensive sense of impotence.

However, there was nothing to be done, save to recover strength as quickly as might be possible.

"Now let me think—clearly and calmly," said I—and promptly fell asleep.

When I awoke, the Angel of Death was sitting beside me, chin on hand, and regarding me with a look which was anything but inimical.

Staring, startled from my sleep, I read her thoughts.

I am quite certain that at that moment, all that was European in her was uppermost. She was her father's daughter, civilized, white, kind.

She smiled, and while the smile was on her face she was utterly and truly beautiful, more beautiful than any woman I have ever seen, save one.

Extending a gentle—and very beautifully manicured—hand, she wiped my brow with a small and scented handkerchief, product of Paris.

"Ze poor boy," she said softly. "But he has been so ver' ver' ill," and kissed me in the manner and the spirit in which a mother kisses a sick child.

"Thank you—er—Mam'zelle," I said. "Where is my friend?"

"*Gone,*" she replied.

For the third time I had received that sinister reply to my question.

"Gone—*pouff!* Like zat," she continued, and this time the gesture was that of one who blows away a feather.

"I play a trick on Selim, wiz him. . . . Zat Selim think himself too clever. . . . *Oui . . . Sacré Dieu. . . .*"

"What trick? Tell me quickly. . . . Where is he!" I begged

"Zat Selim?" she asked.

"No, no, no! My friend, my brother! Quick! Where is he?"

She laughed mischievously, obviously quite pleased with herself.

"*Oh, la, la!* He does not matter. . . . He serve his purpose. . . . He serve my purpose too. . . . Oh! zat great fool, Selim! . . . But now you go sleep again. . . ."

"Yes, yes, but tell me first, where is my friend? What have you done with him?" I begged.

"What is he to you?" she asked, and her pleased smile faded a trifle.

"My friend! My brother!" I replied.

Her expression changed. A look of doubt succeeded the smile.

"Oh, well!" she shrugged, as she rose to her feet, ". . . he is only a man! . . . But *I* am a *woman!* . . ."

And her smile, as she left the tent, was not in the least motherly.

§2

My state of mind may be imagined.

Against all probability, against possibility almost, I had found John Geste, had thanked God for that miracle—and John Geste had vanished. . . . The cup dashed from my lips. The fruit of my sufferings and labour—dust and ashes.

I groaned in spirit, and I was near despair. But, if I can be understood, I lost hope without losing faith—and did the one thing I could do. I strove to regain my physical strength, while I walked delicately in the path of friendship with the Angel.

That evening she visited me again, all smiles and honey, honey that grew a little over-sweet and cloying.

I learned that Selim ben Yussuf was away, with most of the fighting-men of the tribe, and that the old Sheikh was at Zaguig, presumably by pressing request of the Authorities, who would probably be making life a little difficult for every tribal leader within a hundred miles.

On this and other topics of local interest, she chatted freely, and seemed quite willing to tell me truthfully everything but the one fact I wanted to know.

The moment I spoke of John Geste she became evasive, laughed mischievously, and as I pressed for an answer, seemed first embarrassed and then impatient and annoyed.

After she left the tent, I thought I would see what happened if I attempted to leave it too.

Koko happened.

He made it quite clear to me, though without violence or even truculence of manner, that the guest-tent was my home and that from home I should not stray. As I returned and dejectedly dropped upon my mattress, the *hakim* entered and I had a bright idea.

I asked him whether he had any personal interest in my recovery.

He replied that my life was dearer to him than that of his oldest son. I said that that was very nice, but ventured to point out that one would scarcely have thought it, when I lay practically dying, down by the goat-farm.

Ah, that was quite a different matter. Selim ben Yussuf had left no doubt, in reasonable minds, that the news of my early demise would be received with equanimity. Hence something in my *couscous*, which had nearly done the trick.

But the news of my approaching demise had not been received by the Sid Jebrail, the Angel of Death, with any equanimity at all.

On the contrary.

She had left no possibility of doubt in any reasonable mind that my death would only precede that of the good *hakim* by a very few minutes—and hence the fact that my life was dearer to him than that of his oldest son, and that I, being possessed of the feelings of a gentleman would undoubtedly consider the feelings of another gentleman, and live for all I was worth.

This was most excellent, and I returned to my original point.

"So you *do* want me to live, *Sidi Hakim*?"

"I desire nothing more fervently, *Sidi Roumi*."

"Well, I can and shall live, on one condition, and on one only. . . . That I am at once told what has become of my brother, and that I am thereafter at once restored to his society. . . . Get that right plumb in the centre of your intelligent and most noble mind, *Sidi Hakim*."

The good doctor's face fell.

"*Allahu Akbar!*" he murmured in astonishment. "I have heard of these things. . . . People pining for each other. . . . Men for women. . . . Women for men. . . . Even the lower animals. . . . But a man for a man! . . . Is it possible? . . ."

"It is here under your nose, *Sidi Hakim*," I said earnestly. "I'm going to die right here, to your great inconvenience, I fear. . . . Where is my brother?"

"He is gone, *Sidi* . . . but do not grieve. . . . He is alive and well

—in the best of health, and full of happiness. . . . And he is being *well* looked after . . . Oh yes. . . . On my head and my life. . . . And on my son's head and on my son's life. . . . I swear he is being most carefully looked after. . . . Yes. . . . By the Ninety and Nine Names of Allah. . . . By the Beard of the Prophet. . . ."

I shut my eyes and fetched a fearful groan.

"Tell me everything quickly, for I am on the point of Death," I whispered as deathfully as I could contrive.

"*Sidi! Sidi!*" he wailed, "I dare not say a word. . . . *She* would have my feet set in the fire. . . ."

"All-right. . . . Good-bye," I replied, and, like King Hezekiah, I turned my face unto the wall, continuing this death-bedlamite comedy, in the hope of getting some scrap of information from this gibbering pantaloon.

"*Stop! Stop! Sidi,*" squeaked my medical attendant. "Will you swear not to betray me to her, if I tell you what I know . . . I know nothing really."

"I will not betray you, *Sidi Hakim,*" I said. "And I will not die if you tell me the truth."

"Your brother has gone back to—er—his—er—friends," announced the *hakim*, diffidently.

His information certainly brought me back to life, all right. I shot up in bed and seized him, almost by the beard.

"Do you mean to say that the *French* have got him again?" I shouted.

"Yes . . . Yes . . ." admitted the *hakim*. "He is perfectly safe now. . . ."

I fell back upon my pillows feeling like dying in good earnest. "He was perfectly safe now! . . ."

John Geste was back in the hands of the French and all my work was to do again. . . .

CHAPTER XII

I don't think I gave way to despair. Although my heart sank into the very depths, there was, as it were, a life-line to the surface —a line of faith and hope. I had found John Geste once. . . . What man has done once, man can do again. Evidently this girl knew something, and apparently had some hand in whatever had happened; and almost certainly Selim ben Yussuf had played a part. I imagined myself with my hands at Selim's throat, squeezing and squeezing until either the eyes came out of his head, or the truth out of his mouth.

What had the girl said?

"I played a trick on Selim with him"—and I half-wished it was recognized good form, and quite permissible if not praiseworthy, to serve her as, in imagination, I had just served Selim.

What I must find out was whether the *hakim* had spoken the truth—which was quite problematical—and, if so, whether John had been taken to Bouzen, Zaguig, or one of the construction-camps on the Road. Of course it was quite possible that he was even now within a few yards of me—either above ground or below it.

What in the name of God could be the trick that she had played on Selim ben Yussuf *with John.*

Followed by a fine-looking Arab, whom later I knew to be Abd'allah ibn Moussa, she again entered the tent.

"Tie his feet firmly, but without hurting him, and his hands in such a way that he is not uncomfortable," she ordered. "He will get strong very quickly now, and I don't want him to run away."

"Will you kindly tell me what has become of my brother, Mademoiselle?" I asked politely. "There can be no harm in my knowing, can there, especially now that you have tied me up so securely?"

"*Eh bien*, how he chatter about zis friend of his! I tell you he has *gone*—gone where you nevaire see him any more. . . .But you see *me*, isn't it? . . . Don't I look nicer than that friend of yours, *hein*?"

"You'd look a lot nicer than you do, if you told me everything, Mademoiselle," I replied. "You are a European—you are a woman

—we are Europeans—we have done you no harm. Why behave like one of these uncivilized Arabs?"

"*Ah, oui,* zat's so," agreed the Death Angel. "You are both Europeans. I wish all Europeans have only one heart, and I can stab it. I wish all Europeans have only one throat, and I can cut it."

She looked like a tiger-cat, and while I watched, her face changed utterly, and, with a sweet and gentle smile, she dropped to her knees and leant over me.

"All Europeans except you, I mean, Blue-Eyes. You are nice and good and *gentil.* You would nevaire *desert anybody*, isn't it? *Nevaire would you do that*, I know in my heart." And she kissed me on the lips.

"You kiss me," she said. "You kiss me quick, and say you nevaire run away, and I untie your hands and feet, and take your *parole*, isn't it? Kiss me, *kiss me*, I tell you."

I closed my eyes, set my lips firmly—and received a stinging blow on the face.

§2

What shall I say about this astounding woman, known as "The Angel" among the Arabs, and as "The Angel of Death" to those Europeans who had the privilege of her acquaintance.

She was the most extraordinary and remarkable human being whom I have ever met, yet at the same time there was really no reason that she should astonish and astound, for she was the perfectly logical outcome of her heredity and her environment.

What should the daughter of a hundred generations of savage courtesans—unscrupulous, avaricious and unbridled—sometimes be, but an evil unscrupulous savage? What should the daughter of a blue-eyed Nordic sometimes be, but balanced, self-respecting and amenable to ideas of civilization.

We are assured that in every Jekyll there is some Hyde, and in every Hyde there is some Jekyll; and the best and the worst of us are well aware that the materials of which our characters are woven are not of even quality. But with this "Angel," it was not only a case of a mixed nature reflecting mixed descent, but a case of a complete and undisputed occupation of her body at different times, by two utterly distinct and different personalities.

For part of the time—for the greater part of the time—she was just herself, the Anglo-African, the half-caste, with all the expected attributes of the mulatto. But for the rest, she was either "The

Death-Angel," the savage, the African, the lawless and evil native courtesan; or else Mlle. Blanchfleur, the European, the normal white woman, calculable, and, within her sphere, conventional. . . .

Be that as it may, she most certainly astonished and astounded me—this most pathetic, most terrible, nightmare woman. . . . Nightmare indeed—for, thinking of her frequently, as I do—I often dream of her, and though these dreams are not nightmares in the sense that dreams about my father are, their warp is horror and their woof is pity; and the dream is sad, melancholy and depressing beyond belief.

If I could but put the Angel from my mind!

I cannot and I never shall. . . . I think of her, to this day, as frequently as I think of Isobel herself, and infinitely more unhappily. (That is a foolish thing to say, for there is nothing whatsoever of unhappiness in my thoughts of Isobel. What did Isobel ever bring to any living soul but happiness?)

Some of the truth of what I have said of the Angel of Death can be grasped by realizing that her actions ranged from the decreeing and superintending of torture, to the performance of acts of trusting and noble generosity; from venal bestiality, to a high idealism; from a bitter savage vengefulness, to a noble and generous forgiveness.

In short from the worst of her Arab mother to the best of her Christian father.

§3

Whenever Koko, the negroid slave, whose precious charge I was, took his yellow-whited eyes from me, yawned, scratched himself, and stared vacantly out into the wonderful desert night, I gnawed at the palm-fibre cords which bound my wrists. Should I succeed in freeing my hands, it was my unamiable intention to free my feet, and then to do my utmost to incapacitate this gentleman.

He had a long sharp knife, and a heavy stick, short and thick. I had a hard and useful fist. With one of these three weapons something might be done. I did not at all like the knife idea. My own fancy ran in the direction of a swift and knock-out presentation of the fist, followed by a more leisured confirmatory application of the heavy stick. This seemed to me a reasonable compromise between the slaughter of a citizen, who after all was but doing his duty, and my continuation in a position of extreme peril.

"*Eh bien! On dîne donc, n'est-ce pas?*" murmured a silky voice, as I sat with down-bent head, my teeth fixed in the unpleasant-tasting hairy cord.

" 'Ow you like it, *hein?* . . . Eat a bit more then, M'sieur Blue-eyes. P'raps that the las' food you get, what?"

"*Bon soir, Mademoiselle,*" I replied, with an attempt at a debonair smile and an air of gay bonhomie that I was very far from feeling. "Won't you join me? . . . Have a bite . . ." and I raised my bound wrists toward her.

"Ah, so you say, is it, Blue-eye . . . Yellow-hair. . . . Laughing face . . ." replied the Angel, and kneeling beside me, seized my wrists and deliberately bit my hand with the ferocity and strength of a wild beast.

"Laike what you call savage dog, *hein?*" she said, thrusting her face against mine.

"Or a dog of a savage," I observed.

"*Sacré Dieu!* How I *hate* you . . . *hate* you . . . hate you!" she cursed, and, even as I was thinking, "Better than loving me, anyhow," she seized my head and crushed her lips violently against mine. . . .

"*Baisez-moi! . . . Baisez-moi! . . . Baisez-moi! . . .*" she cried.

"Soh! You will not kees me, noh? . . . Naow, leetle Blue-eyes, you kees me, or see what come," and she took me by the throat.

I was revived from the faintness of strangulation by the pain of her setting her sharp teeth in my lip.

. . . Darkness, and a roaring in my ears. . . .

. . . A voice speaking from very far away. . . . Had I been clubbed on the head. . . . What was that? . . . Oh yes, the gentle Angel.

"Oah, you *won't* kees me, *hein?* You won't lov' me, *hein?* You won't 'ave me any price, noa? S'pose I say you never kees any other girl, *hein?*" she panted. "S'pose I cut your lips off, yes?" and she seized my ears and shook my head violently to and fro. . . .

Most painful, undignified and humiliating.

"Uh! You say nothing on that, is it! You don't grin some more, *hein?* . . . What s'pose I say you never *look* any other girl? . . . What s'pose I have those blue eyes for myself. . . . 'Ave them out your silly 'ead, yes? . . ." and as she spoke, she thrust her thumbs violently and most painfully beneath my eyes. I suffered most horribly in the next few minutes, but I can truthfully say that the idea of surrender to this tempestuous petticoat absolutely never entered my head. I don't know why, but the idea simply never occurred to me. Nor do I think that the reason for this lay in any Joseph-like virtue inherent in my character, nor in any definite feeling that when I did fall from grace, it would not be with the Angel of Death as a companion.

I think my resistance was simply and solely due to the fact that I am one of those stubborn creatures whom you can lead on a hair, but cannot drag with a cable. Also I have Red Indian blood, and my "No" means "*No.*"

Every fibre of my being rebelled against this coercion, and the Angel was beating her head not only upon mine but against a stone wall—compounded of the dogged, unyielding rock of Anglo-Saxon stubbornness, and the cement of Red Indian stoicism, tenacious and prideful.

Not unto me, but unto mine ancestors the credit, if I bore well the sufferings and the temptation—the temptation to escape torture —that were put upon me. . . .

But always I had to remember that a dead, maimed, or blinded Otis Vanbrugh would be of but little service to John Geste . . . to Isobel. . . .

Springing to her feet, the Angel of Death (by means of a violent kick upon his latter end, tactfully turned towards us) attracted the attention of our chaperon, who squatted in the doorway of the tent, pondering perchance, Infinity, Life and the Vast Forever—or indeed, his latter end.

With a nasty oath and a stream of guttural orders, in Arabic, she drove him from the tent.

During his absence, the Angel gave me what she termed my last chance, and made it clear to me, beyond the peradventure of a doubt, the terms upon which I might retain my right to life, liberty and the pursuit of happiness.

By the time I had made it equally clear to the Angel that, since I was not a person to be led along the primrose paths of pleasant dalliance, still less was I one to be scourged adown their alluring ways, the good Koko had returned and entered with seven devils worse than himself.

By the Angel's clear and explicit direction, I was roughly jerked to my feet, dragged from the tent, and thrown down at the root of the nearest tree.

With promptitude and dispatch, a young palm was cut through, some six feet from the ground.

Impalement! Surely not? It could not be possible that this girl, who had European blood in her veins, who had consorted with Europeans, who knew something of Christian teaching, and who was, after all, a woman—was going to have me stripped and stuck upon the sharpened end of this tapering stump, to die miserably . . . to die a lingering death of unspeakable agony, while a crowd watched, jeered and gloated.

A woman! . . . But Hell hath no fury like a woman scorned. . . . If Hell had a fury such as this Angel at that moment, the Devil himself must have felt unsafe. . . .

No, they were not sharpening the top of the stump.

I was again jerked to my feet, held in position and tightly bound to it.

It was to be a stake and not a spear.

Surely she was not going to have me burnt alive. . . . Burnt before her eyes. . . .

A woman! . . . But a woman scorned. . . .

What should I do as the flames mounted, and death was imminent. . . . Plead to the woman? . . . Agree? . . .

Dead, I could not serve Isobel. . . . A hard choice. . . .

No. I saw no preparation for a fire.

Their immediate task completed, the black soldiers stood about —incurious, stupid, animal. The Angel gave them a curt order and they went, with scarce a further glance at me—and I and that she-devil were alone.

§4

"Now, my friend," she said when we were alone, "we just see 'ow long you defy ze Angel of Death! . . . *Sans doute* you t'ink yourself ver' fine man and bear pain like Aissa dervish, *hein*? But I tell you somesing. . . . Don't you leave it too late, so that when you say '*All right, Mademoiselle; I finish—I give in—I do what you laike*,' you are not already too spoilt, see? . . . No good saying zat after you gone blind for always, or after your tongue cut out for always, or you are too burnt ever to walk about any more, see?"

I saw.

"Tell me, Blue-Eyes," this well-named young woman continued, "you rather be deaf and dumb both, or blind only—if I be kind and give you choice? . . . Perhaps you anger me, and you get all three! . . . Perhaps I get ver' angry and you 'ave no 'ands and no feets. . . . *Oh, la, la,* zis poor lil' Blue-Eyes! . . . He ver' proud man until one day he got no eyes, no tongue, no ears, no hands, no feet. . . . Oh, ver' proud man—ver' 'andsome man—till someone cut off his lips and his nose and his eye-lids—-not so pretty then. . . . What you t'ink?"

I remembered John Geste's cold iron courage, and yawned. The Death Angel was certainly taken aback.

It then occurred to me to use my lips, while I had them, to whistle a little air. And the first that came to my mind was the one I had sung, or howled, to the Zouave Sergeant as I lay under the wall in Zaguig.

"Mon Dieu," whispered the girl. "Is it you are ze bravest man ever I have met—*or is it perhaps you t'ink I am making ze bluff and will not torture you?"*

A little bit of both, I thought. I am playing at being a brave man —and surely no human girl could cut a man's eyes out, stab his ear-drums, hammer a wedge into his mouth and cut his tongue out. . . . Not even an "Angel of Death."

"Because if it is zat, I soon show you," continued this she-devil. And drawing her knife she ripped my *jubba* and *kaftan* downward from the throat, exposing my chest.

"Kees me," she said softly, rising on her toes, and placing her lips on mine.

"No?" . . .

And on the right side of my chest she made a horizontal gash.

I started and quivered with the sudden pain, and was thankful that she had not, as I had expected, driven the knife into my throat or heart.

She stepped back a pace.

" 'Ow you like *zat*—for start?" she asked, and, again placing her lips on mine, whispered "Kees me."

"No?"

And again she slashed my breast with a horizontal gash an inch below the other.

"*Now* kees me," she said, and put her lips to mine.

"No?"

And with a sloping cut she joined the ends of the two gashes with a third.

"See?" she asked. "Ze letter Z! . . . I write my name on you— ZAZA. . . . Always you remember Zaza then. . . . For ze little time you live, I mean. . . . Twelve cuts, it is. I do it ver' neatly now."

Evidently a case of practice making perfect, I thought.

"You kees me now, *hein?*"

I tried to think coolly. If I let this fiend kill, or utterly incapacitate, me, there was the end of my search for John Geste— the end of my service to Isobel. I must give way, for their sakes. But, I told myself, were John Geste safe in England, this young woman should not defeat me. Pride is a poor thing to be proud of, and so is stubbornness, but I freely confess to being proud of both.

Well, the dozen cuts would not put me out of action, so she could carry on. . . . But if it really came to blinding, she would win —and, as she felt my unresponsive lips, she changed from cold anger to red-hot rage—which was probably ray salvation.

"*Kees me! Kees me! Kees me!*" she screamed, hammering my face and body with her clenched fists.

"You *won't, hein?* . . . Then I'll waste no more time! . . . Now you kees me and say you love me—or you die . . . and you die slow —and blind," and she pressed the point of her knife sharply in under my right eye.

I saw the grim face of the Sioux Chief, my ancestor, but even to be worthy of him, I must not hold out longer. She was going to blind me—and no blind man could help John and Isobel.

I gave in.

"*Zaza,*" I began—and the word was drowned in a scream, as the girl flung down the knife, threw her arms about my neck, and kissed me passionately and repeatedly.

"Oh, forgive, forgive!" she cried. "I was mad. . . . A devil comes into me and I must be cruel—cruellest to what I love best. Forgive me, dear Blue-Eyes, and see—promise me you will come back to me, and I will let you go after your friend—I will do anything for you if you will promise to come back to me. . . . I cannot live any more without you. . . . Look—I will do *any*sing— *every*sing if you promise to come back," and, with a slight return of her former manner:

"And I swear to God, on this piece of the True Cross"—and she touched her book-shaped locket—"and to Allah, by this Hair of the Beard of the Prophet, and by my mother's soul, that, if you do not promise, I will stab you to the heart, and then stab myself to the heart also, and we will die together here."

"I promise," I said, only too thankfully—"that I will come back to you as soon as I have seen my friend leave Africa in safety—if you will tell me the truth and give me every help you can."

"Yes, and suppose zat is not in many years—in ten years and

twenty years, when I am ugly old woman?

"I give you one year," she added. "You come back to me in one year, or directly you save your friend," and picking up her knife she placed its point above my heart, and I knew with perfect certainty that, if I refused, I should die.

"I will return to you in a year," I said, "or before, if I have found my friend within that time, provided you tell me the truth, and help me in every way."

"And you will marry me?" she asked.

"Of course," I replied.

"And you will take me from this vile country where I am a wicked woman, and neither Arab nor European?"

"I will," I said, "but get this clear—the sooner my friend is found and saved, and sent out of Africa, the sooner will you get what you want. . . . Now tell me. . . . What was this trick you played on Selim ben Yussuf?"

As she cut at the cords that bound me, she told me how Selim ben Yussuf, in jealous rage, had decided to torture me to death, as soon as his father went safely away to Zaguig.

At that moment, a French patrol, a *peloton méhariste*, had ridden into the camp, and Zaza had pointed out to Selim ben Yussuf that a far finer vengeance than mere death by torture, would be to hand me back to the ghastly slavery from which I had escaped! . . . Moreover, he would be killing two birds with one stone, for, by giving up an escaped convict, he would be doing a good deal to sweeten the somewhat unsavoury reputation that he bore with the French.

Selim ben Yussuf had agreed that the idea was a splendid one, and had given orders for the *Roumi* prisoner, in the white burnous, to be brought and handed over to the *goumiers* of the patrol.

Anticipating this, she had instructed Abd'allah ibn Moussa to take away John's blue burnous and give him my white one. . . .

So the *hakim* had told the truth! . . .

After chafing my limbs, and lavishing upon me the loving tender care and kindnesses of a mother or a wife, Zaza helped me back to my tent—did everything for my comfort, and suggested that, since our bargain was made, I should now relax my foolish and insulting behaviour, and show myself as fond and loving toward her as she was more than willing to be toward me.

The position was a delicate one.

The last thing in the world, that I wanted to do, was to offend her, to bring back her spirit of savagery, to make her anything but my most earnest helper. And the last thing but one, that I wanted to do, was to make love to her.

"Zaza," I said. "Listen. We've made a bargain. Are you going to keep your side of it?"

"Most pairfectly," she replied, "but, oh, most truly."

"And so am I," I said. "When I come back I will be your husband. I will be kind, and gentle, and everything you want me to be to you, but now it is business, work, planning and thinking—not love-making. Do you understand?

"I onderstand," said Zaza. "You *will* come back to me. Yes, yes, I trust you. . . . I *know* you will come back—my dear. . . . You would never desert a woman. . . ."

CHAPTER XIII

I suppose that it is a perfectly vain imagining when I wonder whether the Angel's last fiendish outbreak—that so nearly cost me my sight, if not my life—*was* her last. It would give me very great peace of mind to think that the mood that followed, the mood of remorse and utter repentance, could be thenceforth her normal condition, and that her vehemently expressed hatred of savagery, violence and vice, would last.

Vain imaginings and foolish hopes, I fear. For a temperament is a temperament and she was as much the daughter of her Arab mother as she was of her Christian father.

But the girl that sat the night through, beside my couch, was lovable, gentle, a civilized white woman and rather the ministering angel, "when pain and anguish wring the brow," than the sinister Death Angel of so short a time before. She was, moreover, pathetic and pitiful, and it touched my heart to hear her aspirations to that way of life, way of thought, and way of conduct, that befitted the daughter of her father.

"We will never come near this accursed country ever again, my dear one, when you are my 'usban'. . . . We will go to Paris, and Wien, and Londres, an' I will be so good an' r-r-respectable. . . . An' everyone will call me Madame and Missis, an' not silly evil names like Angel of Death. . . . An' we will have a fine 'ouse an' everysing *comme il faut*. . . . An' all my clo'es shall be make in Paris. . . . An' we will go to the Opera. . . . An' we will ride in ze Bois. . . . An' I will not be Moslem at all, but all Christian. . . . An' scorn all zem *demi-mondaine* like 'ell. . . .

"You *will* come back to me. . . . You will start to come back to me ze day your frien' go on board his ship? . . . Or else you give up ze search for 'im, an' start back to me, one year from zis day, *hein*? . . . You *promise*? . . .

"Yes . . . Yes . . . I know you speak truth. . . . I know men. . . . I know ze true voice an' ze false voice. . . . Ze true eyes from ze false eyes. . . . From us of ze Ouled-Naïl no man can hide behind his face. . . . No, no. . . . I am *not* of ze Ouled-Naïl. . . . *A bas les Ouled-Naïls*. . . . I am English. . . . I am daughter of Omar ze Englishman. . . . Yes . . . Yes . . . I know you speak truth. . . . Your blue eyes are true eyes. . . . Your kind voice is true voice. . . . I *know* you will come back to me. . . .

"Look, dear one, . . . will you not swear it for me on Bible and Koran both? Swear it before your God and my Allah. . . . Will you not swear it on zis leetle gold book I wear roun' my neck. . . . Nevaire I take it off . . . it is a great talisman an' great amulet. . . . One side is my Father and a piece of True Cross. . . . That is God side. . . . On other side is my Mother an' one hair of ze Beard of ze Prophet. . . . Zat is Allah side . . . Ze Sultan himself gave it to her mother. . . . No harm can come to me while I have such a thing as zis, can it? . . . I would put it roun' your neck, dear one, an' give it to you, but I dare not let it go from me. . . . All would be good for you, an' that I would laike. . . . But it might not be bringing you back to me. . . . If I keep it, all will be good for *me*, an' then it will be bringing *you* back to me. . . . But when you come back to me, you shall have it an' wear it always, night an' day, an' then no harm can ever come to you. . . . I will show you ze pictures of my Father an' my Mother to-morrow. . . .

"Always I am afraid to open it at night-time, lest I lose ze piece of ze True Cross which is only a tiny splinter; or ze hair of ze Beard of ze Prophet. . . . Zat would be too ter-r-rible. . . . I should die. . . .

"Oh, it will be bringing *you* safe back to me. . . . Yes . . . Even though I wear it you will be safe, because unless it kept you safe and brought you back to me, it would not be bringing good to me, an' making me happy, isn't it? . . . Yes . . . it will keep you safe for me. . . . An' your truth, honour and goodness will make you come. . . .

"Oh! an' I know. . . . Such fun. . . . Old Haroun el Rafiq shall do a sand-reading and tell us. . . . Now I have nevaire spoke your name an' you have nevaire seen him, so he cannot know. . . . We shall see. . . ."

Calling to Koko, she bade him fetch Haroun el Rafiq, and, half an hour or so later, a strange hairless creature of indeterminate age and with the deadest features and the livest eyes I have ever beheld, followed Koko into the tent, salaamed humbly to the Angel, fixed his burning eyes on mine, and squatted cross-legged on the ground. From a small sack he tipped out a pile of sand before him, smoothed it flat with the palm of his hand, made a geometrical pattern upon the surface with white pebbles, and studied his handiwork with rapt attention.

After a minute or so of this contemplation, he wiped out the pattern, smiled as to himself and at his own thoughts, shook his head, rose to his feet and made to leave the tent.

"Stop! Stop!" cried the Angel. "You've told us nothing. . . ."

"What does the Sitt desire to know?" inquired the soothsayer.

"First of all, whether this Sidi will return?"

"Return where?" asked the man. "To this place?"

"Will return to me, I mean," said the girl frankly.

"He will," promptly replied the man, and the enigmatic smile again disturbed the frozen calm of his dead features. "I saw him riding at the head of a goodly company. . . . Riding from the north, straight to you. . . . I saw the *kafilah* arrive amid scenes of joy and welcome. . . . I saw him stride to your tent and I saw you rush forth and embrace him as a lover. . . . I saw you feasting with him, alone, in a bridal tent. . . ."

The Angel sat with parted lips and shining eyes.

"Did you see more? . . . More . . ." she urged.

"No," answered the man, and I knew he was lying. "It is enough. . . ."

"Yes, it is enough," murmured the Angel.

"More than enough," I thought.

The sand-diviner's prophecy elated my companion as unreasonably as it depressed me.

"Yes . . . You will come back. . . . *C'est vrai.* . . . I feel it *here* . . ." she said, laying her hand upon her heart.

"Yes, I shall come back, as I have promised," I said, "if I live. . . . But the more immediate question is when shall I *start?*"

"Oh, my dear one . . . my dear one . . . my love. . . . *Must* you leave me at all? . . . Why must you go? . . . He is only a convict . . . a *scélerat.* . . . A what-you-call dam' rascal. . . ."

"He is an innocent man, and the finest man that ever lived," I remarked, "and he is my friend. I only came to this country to find him. . . . And through you I lost him. . . . The sooner I go to look for him, the sooner I shall be able to return to you."

"Oh, my dear one, my dear one, if I had only known! . . . What a *fool.* . . . What a *devil*, I was. . . . Oh, cannot I come wiz you? . . . Yes, *why* cannot I come wiz you? . . . It is not zat I do not trust you, but I cannot bear zat you should leave me. . . ."

"You cannot come with me," I said. "In the first place, Selim ben Yussuf would be on our track with half the tribe, the moment he returned to find you gone. . . . In the second place, you cannot live like a hunted wild beast, as I may have to do. Besides, I may give myself up to the French again, if I can get news of him in no other way."

And I pondered the fact that there would be no record nor witness of the mutiny that had led to our incarceration in the *silo*, if, as our deliverer had told us, the whole unit had been surrounded and wiped out, to a man. John Geste and I, if I returned, would merely be two of the convicts who had somehow escaped the massacre.

"No, I cannot come wiz you," sighed the Angel "I should be 'indrance an' not ze 'elp, an', as you say, Selim ben Yussuf would capture us and keel you. . . . But I can help you. . . . Yes, I can send you off wiz ze best of everysing. . . . You shall have my own camels an' men—when you mus' go. . . ."

"You cannot go until you are stronger," she added.

"I must go before Selim ben Yussuf returns," I reminded her.

"Yes . . ." she agreed. "But you need not go far until you are strong. You could go a day's ride and camp. . . . An' I will tell Selim zat you, zat is to say *your frien'*, as he thinks, died. . . . The *hakim* will swear it. . . . He fears me greatly. . . ."

"He certainly does," I agreed.

"Yes . . . I have one or two spells . . ." she smiled. "Spells an' magics zat you buy in ze chemist's shop in Algiers. . . . An' potions. . . . Ah, *oui*! . . . potions. . . . One drop of which makes ze hard stone or ze steel, bubble an' smoke. . . . An' I will send Abd'allah ibn Moussa wiz you. . . . My own faithful servant. . . . He is faithful as ze horse of ze Arab, an' ze dog of ze Englishman. . . . He is as brave as ze lion, an' as true as Life an' Death. . . .

"He was ze devoted servant an' frien' of my Mother, an' he nurse me when I am a baby. . . . An' now he lof me laike he lof my Mother. . . . If I say to 'im, '*Go you, Abd'allah ibn Moussa, wiz zis man. He is my lover . . . die for him, or die wiz him*,' he will not come back wizzout you, an' I will feel comfor'ble in my 'eart. . . . Nevaire, nevaire will he leave you. . . ."

I felt that such fidelity might prove embarrassing.

"He'll be a useful guide, anyhow," I agreed. . . . "But I'll send him back as soon as I am well on my way, and feeling fairly strong."

"I shall tell him not to leave you," said the girl.

"Well, I may have to leave him," I replied. "But anyhow, the sooner you give him instructions to get your camels and people together, the better."

I knew something of Arab dilatoriness and the utter meaninglessness of time, in the desert.

Without further remark, she rose to her feet, drew her veil about her face, and left the tent.

I followed her to the entrance, with some vague idea of escape from the terrible silken meshes of the dreadful web that this jewelled spider was spinning about me.

"Salaam, *Sidi*," grinned the unutterable Koko.

"Hell!" I replied, and again flung myself down upon my cushions.

§2

A few minutes later, the Angel returned, followed by an Arab, whose fine and noble face was that of a man of middle age, great intelligence, philosophic calm, high courage, and great determination and tenacity.

I speak without exaggeration. The man's face was noble and he proved to be a noble man, if fidelity, endurance, unswerving loyalty and courage, connote nobility.

"Zis is Abd'allah ibn Moussa," said the Angel, and the man salaamed respectfully. "Zis is a *Roumi* lord," she continued, turning to Abd'allah.

"Also he is my Lord and my Master, and your Lord and your Master. . . . He is my lover and he will raise me up to be his wife. . . . Go with him, Abd'allah. . . . Follow where he leads. . . . Sleep where he sleeps. . . . Live where he lives. . . . And die where he dies. . . . But he will not die, Abd'allah . . . for you will guard his life with yours, and you will bring him back to me. . . ."

"On my head and on my life be it," replied the man.

"Go and make ready," said his mistress, and he went away.

There was a commotion of hails, shouting, and men running—alarums and excursions without, in fact.

Abd'allah ibn Moussa turned back into the tent.

"A *kafilah* comes," he said, and went about his business.

The Angel's eyes met mine and her face paled.

"Zat Selim!" she said, as with a bitter laugh, I ejaculated:

"Selim ben Yussuf!"

"I will keel heem, zat so-clever Selim," whispered the Angel, and the European side of her character seemed to fade somewhat.

"I must hide you. . . . I must hide you. . . . He must not see your face. . . . See! You must go back to the goat-herds' tents as soon as it is safe. . . . I will keep Selim in his tents. . . . I will send Abd'allah to take you back. . . . I will tell zis Selim zat ze frien' of

ze blue-eye Nazarani is dead, an' Abd'allah shall disguise you. . . .
Yes, like a poor blind *miskeen*. . . ."

Well, things seemed to be going wrong indeed.

What would I not have given for a few hours of normal health
and strength.

I must leave it to the wit and the wiles of the Angel to keep me
hidden until I could get away.

The estimable Koko stooped into the tent, very full of himself.

"His Highness, the Sidi Emir, the Sidi Sheikh el Hamel el
Kebir, Shadow of the Prophet, and Commander of the Faithful, has
arrived with his great Wazir, noble sheikhs, captains, and many
soldiers," he announced pompously.

"He calls for the high Sheikh Yussuf ben Amir, and for Selim
ben Yussuf his son, and for the Sheikh's captains and *ekhwan* of
the tribe."

The Angel's face relaxed and she heaved a sigh of relief.

"Ze good God be praised! It is not zat Selim!"

"But who is it?" I asked.

"*Oh, la, la!* He is ze gr-r-reat big man! He is ze chief of ze
chiefs. . . . He mak' treaty wiz ze French. . . . He is ver' civilized
an' important! He marry English girl—laike me. . . . He is frien' to
French an' treats well all *Roumis*. . . . Oh, he is *ver'* big man. . . .
An' often, before, I have want to see him. . . . But now I have you,
dear one, I care not at all. . . ."

A pity!

And now, what? How was this going to affect me and my
fortunes?

If this Emir were a staunch ally of the French and "kind to all
Roumis," presumably he would be kind to me—until he handed me
back to his allies.

How long would he stay here? What exactly was the extent of
his power over this tribe?

Would the *hakim*, or one of the servants, attempt to curry
favour with him by informing him that there was a captive *Roumi*
in the camp—or would they fear the Angel more than they feared
him?

An idea occurred to me.

If this Emir were truly great, as the Angel implied, might he
not be touched by a truthful "David and Jonathan" story?

Suppose I told him everything, threw myself upon his mercy,
and begged him to help us. . . . Might he not accede, and,

moreover, be a very tower of strength, if his heart were touched and his imagination fired? I would speak of John Geste figuratively as my brother, and quote the Arab proverb:

> "The love of a man for a woman, waxes and
> wanes as doth the moon:
> But the love of brother for brother is constant
> as the stars,
> And endureth like the word of the Prophet."

And if I failed, and if he were inimical, or merely disposed to do his duty to his allies, the French, should I be in any worse position?

If he handed me over to the nearest "competent military authority," I should be promptly sent to Zaguig, and thence to the nearest road-gang, where, in all probability, John Geste had already been sent.

That would be something, but now that I knew of his whereabouts, I could probably help him better from without than from within.

It was almost impossible—it was certainly too much to hope—that another such series of events as had set us free together, could ever happen again, even if he and I were in the same *escouade*.

What to do?

As these thoughts passed through my mind, I watched the face of the Angel, who also was pondering deeply, pinching her lower lip the while. . . .

"I sink I will go an' see zis Emir," she said at last. "Perhaps I will make him do somesing, *hein*?"

Doubtless she had excellent reason for putting faith in her powers of persuasion where Arabs were concerned. It was wholly hateful, but I brought myself to say:

"You know best. . . . If this Emir can and will help us. . . ."

"*Enfin*: If he get your brother for you, *he get you for me*, isn't it? . . . *Oui!* . . . I mus' quickly see zis Emir. . . . He will camp close by. . . . I will send Abd'allah to say zat I will pay heem a leetle visit. . . . I sink he has heard of me. . . . Oh, yes. . . . Zen he will make feast, an' I will see which way ze cat jump. . . . If he get *ver'* friendly, I will tell heem he must help you and your brother. . . . Ze good God grant zat zat Selim does not return before I get you away. . . . Ah, but if I mak' *great* frien's wiz ze Emir, I could mak' him keep Selim in his camp as hostage for ze good be'aviour of zis tribe. . . . I will *tell* him sings about zat Selim. . . .

"Now do not let anybody see your face until I come back, dear one. . . . And you go to sleep and get strong while I am gone. . . . I will send some more of ze beef-tea of muttons. . . ."

§3

And sleep I did, long and heavily, possibly by reason of some unusual ingredient in the beef-tea of mutton.

When I awoke, it was as a giant refreshed, and I was filled with an unwonted sensation of hope and confidence.

My first visitor was the *hakim*, followed by a servant bearing hot stew in a jar, and most welcome coffee in a brass bowl.

So much better was I feeling, that I wondered whether my excellent medical attendant, having poisoned me at Selim's request, had administered an antidote when ordered by the Angel to save my life if he wished to save his own.

In point of fact, the creature did not strike me as being of sufficient intelligence and medical knowledge to deal with a cut finger or a blistered heel, but undoubtedly some of these rascally quacks are familiar with poisons unknown to the European pharmacopœia.

Anyhow, I felt unexpectedly stronger and fitter and, having finished the stew and enjoyed the coffee, I demanded more.

Having fed, washed and been shaved, I peeped from the door of the tent to see what was doing in the great world.

The first object that met my interested gaze was the indefatigable Koko, leaning against the stump of a tree, just in front of the entrance to my tent, and gazing at it—gazing and gazing.

I wondered whether the creature ever shut his eyes at all: Certainly the Angel knew the secret of inspiring obedience and fidelity in her servants.

About a quarter of a mile away, a couple of remarkably fine tents, marquees almost—before which flags and pennons fluttered from the hafts of spears stuck in the ground—marked the temporary residence of the Emir.

Near to these big tents was the extremely orderly and well-aligned camp of his followers or body-guard, a camp much more like that of European troops than of a band of Arab irregulars. . . .

Once more I wondered what had taken place in those pavilions —whether the Angel had visited the Emir, and if so, with what success her power of intrigue, allurement and diplomacy had been brought to bear upon the incalculable mentality and character of this powerful lord of the desert.

I was soon to know.

A little later, she entered my tent, threw back her *haik*, and seated herself upon the cushions.

Obviously she had succeeded beyond her wildest hopes.

Seizing my hands in hers she laughed gleefully.

"Oh, my dearest dear one. . . . It goes well. . . . I am so happy. . . . Ze Emir is *gentilhomme*. . . . Oh, he is gr-r-reat man . . . civilized and good and kind. . . . And oh, zat Wazir of his. . . . *Oh, la, la!* Oh, he is one naughty little man. . . . Oh, *mais c'est un grand amoureux*, zat one. . . . He mak' lof to me . . . oh, laike 'ell. But listen. . . . What you sink? Zis Emir, he know all about everysing. . . . He know there is a *razzia* on the French. . . . He know zat some of you are hiding down in a pit, an' all die excep' two. . . ."

"But how on earth does he know that?" I exclaimed.

"Oh, I don' know. . . . He know everysing zat happen in ze desert. . . . Everysing. . . . They say ze vultures tell him. . . . He know two of you are in zis camp. . . . So when I find zat he know everysing, I tell him ze truth. . . . Oh, he was ver' angry wiz zat Selim. . . . I tell him old papa Yussuf ben Amir go to Zaguig before ze French come to *him*. . . . An' I tell him Selim give back one prisoner to ze French patrol. . . . An' now he want to see you. . . . Do not be afraid. . . . It is good zat you go to his camp, then Selim cannot do anysing at all. . . . An' ze Emir promise me he will not give you up to ze French. . . . Now I tell papa Yussuf ben Amir, an' zat Selim, an' everybody, zat you are *died*. . . ."

CHAPTER XIV

Accompanied by Abd'allah ibn Moussa, Koko, the *hakim*, and the Angel's servants who had waited upon me, and knew me to be a *Roumi*, I set forth, my *haik* well across my face, to visit the Emir el Hamel el Kebir, Chief of the Confederation of Bedouin tribes that inhabited the desert country which extended from Zaguig to the Senussi sphere of influence, and had its capital or centre in the Great Oasis.

His name, titles and position I had learned, as far as possible, from the Angel; from Abd'allah ibn Moussa, who appeared to have for him an admiration almost amounting to veneration; and from the *hakim*, the tribal gossip, scandal-monger, and news-agent.

Seated on a rug-strewn carpet in front of the largest tent, were two richly dressed Arabs. They were alone, but within hail was a small group of sheikhs, *ekhwan*, and leaders of the soldiery.

Sentries, fine up-standing Soudanese, stood at their posts, or walked their beat in a smart and soldier-like manner.

I got an impression of discipline and efficiency not usually to be found about an Arab encampment.

From the little group of officers and officials, a broad squat figure detached itself and came to meet us—a deformed but very sturdy dwarf, whom I knew later as Marbruk ben Hassan, the Lame. He saluted me politely while my following salaamed profoundly.

"His High Excellency the Sidi Emir bids you welcome and gives you leave to approach," he said, and bidding the others remain where they were, he led me to the carpet, whereon sat the man who so mysteriously "knew all things" that happened in the desert.

With a wave of his hand, the big man dismissed the dwarf, and beckoned me to draw near.

The huge Emir, and his small companion, presumably the "naughty Wazir," eyed me with a long and searching stare.

I decided to stand upon what dignity I had, to hold my peace, and let the Emir speak first.

He did.

"Mawnin', Oats," he said casually. "How's things? . . . Meet my friend El Wazir el Habibka, known to the police and other friends, as Buddy. . . ."

What was this? . . . Sun, fever, lunacy, hallucination? . . . Most annoying, anyhow. . . . How could one carry on, if one's senses played one such tricks as this? . . . One expects to be able to believe one's own eyes and ears. And yet here were my eyes apparently beholding the face of my brother Noel—bronzed, lined, wrinkled and bearded—and my ears apparently hearing his voice. His absolutely unaltered voice. With regard to the face I might have been deceived; as to the voice, never—much less the two in conjunction. Besides, the man had called me "Oats," Noel's own special nickname for me since earliest childhood.

"Pleased to meet any friend of Hank's," said the smaller man, his grey eyes smiling from an unsmiling face.

"He's my young brother," said the Emir.

"Oh?" observed the other slowly. "Still—that ain't his fault, is it, Hank Sheikh? Why couldn't you say nothing, an' give the man a fair chance?

"Don't you brood on it, friend," he added, waving his hand, "and anyway I don't believe it."

Fever, sun, hallucination? Only in dreams and in the delirium of fever do typical Arab potentates talk colloquial English. These men *were* most obvious Arabs; Arab to the last item of dress and accoutrement; Arab of Arabs in every detail of appearance and deportment.

But could my eyes be normal while my ears deluded me?

No. This *was* real enough. This *was* my brother. This man with him *was* talking English.

"*Noel!*" I said, beginning to recover and accept and believe.

Noel winked heavily, and laughed derisively in a manner most familiar This was real enough anyhow.

"*Noel!*" I said again—helpless but beginning to be hopeful.

"*Know-all!*" ejaculated the little man. "It's what he thinks he is, anyhow. . . . But that ain't his name. . . . B'jiminy-gees, yes it is, though." . . .

And turning to Noel he said:

"You *said* your name was Know-all Hankinson Vanbrugh . . . after Miss Mary come to the Oasis. . . . Gee! I believe you had an accident and spoke the truth, Hank Sheikh. . . . Ain't it some world we live in! . . ."

"*Noel!*" I said again for the third time. "*Hell!* Am I mad, or drunk, or dreaming or what?"

"Say, sport, if you're drunk, tell us where you got it, quick," interrupted the little man urgently.

"*Oats!*" mocked my brother, my obvious, undeniable indubitable brother, Noel.

"Say, did Mary send you? . . . I've been wearing mourning for you, Son. . . . Mary said you were all shot up, in Zaguig. . . . In a regular bad way about you she was—only she was in a worse way about her Beau. . . ."

"Sure—Beau Jolly," put in the incredible nightmare Wazir. "Ol' friend o' mine, only he don't know it. . . ."

"Mary been *here*? . . . Excuse me if I sit down. . . . Will it be in order? . . ."

"No, most certainly not," said my brother. "Common people like you don't sit down in the presence of royalty . . . don't you know *that* much? . . . We'll go into the parlour. . . ."

And the two rose and led the way into the tent, the Wazir dropping the felt curtain behind us as we entered.

And then my brother fell upon me, and there was no illusion about the thump and hand-grip with which the proceedings opened.

And Buddy was real. Quite as real as anybody I have ever met, by the time he finished welcoming me as the accepted and undeniable brother of "Hank Sheikh."

And at the tenth or perhaps twentieth attempt, sane and coherent conversation took the place of ejaculation, marvellings, and the callings upon various deities to bear witness that this was indeed a staggerer.

"I am still dreaming, or wandering in my mind, Noel," I found myself saying. "But *did* you say that Mary had been here?"

"Not right here, but down this way. . . . In our home town. . . ."

It was his turn to marvel.

"And she never said a word! . . . Gee! And they say women can't keep a secret. . . ."

"It was to *you* then, that de Beaujolais was coming on his secret mission from Zaguig. . . . And of course brought Mary with him . . ." I said.

"It certainly was, Boy. . . . But he didn't know it then. . . . And he don't know it now. . . . And as far as you was concerned you wasn't going to know it either, it seems. . . . Gee! What do you know about that, Son?. . . . Good for lil' Mary!"

"She always loved you very dearly, Noel," I said.

My brother smiled.

"Yes, sure," he mused. "And now she loves de Beaujolais a whole heap more very dearly. . . . It's for him, and from him, she's keeping the State Secret."

"What? . . . Doesn't de Beaujolais know who you are?"

"Not a know to him," replied my brother. "He thinks I am the Emir el Hamel el Kebir, Shadow of the Prophet, Commander of the Faithful, Protector of the Poor . . . Mahdi, Shereef and Khalifa . . . Overlord, Ruler, Spiritual Head and War-Lord of the great Bedouin Confederation of the North South Western Sahara . . . Friend and ally of France. . . . So I am too. . . . Three loud cheers."

"Don't foam at the ears, Son," observed the Wazir gravely. "Mustn't let no loud cheers in the hearing of the Injuns."

And then I sprang from my cushions and certainly there could have been no sign of weakness about that uprising . . . and probably my hair stood as erect as I did.

"*Hank!*" I shouted, pointing in Noel's face.

"*Buddy!*" I yelped, pointing in the face of the little man. They regarded me tolerantly.

"*Hank and Buddy!*" I cried. "*The men that John Geste came back to look for!* . . . Hank went off and left them the water. . . . Buddy stayed by sick John Geste and took him to Kano. . . . Buddy went back to look for Hank. . . . John Geste came back to look for Buddy. . . ."

"*What?*" the two shouted as one man.

"*Yes!*" I shouted in reply. "And *I* came out to look for John Geste and I *found him!* . . . And Selim ben Yussuf has just sold him back to the French, thinking it was I. . . ."

Both were staring.

"*Hell!*" growled my brother. "I'll take that Selim ben Yussuf on the ball of my thumb and smear him on a wall . . . the damned dog's-dinner!"

And:

"I'll so take him to pieces that no-one won't ever be able to put him together again," promised the little man. "I'll sure disestablish him."

"God!" breathed my brother, "*John Geste?*"

"Say!" whispered Buddy. "John Geste come back to find *me*?

"What! Didn't his gel marry him then? . . ." he added.

"She did," I replied. "He went home nearly dead, and they were married—and he could hardly eat, sleep or breathe for thinking of you two in the hands of the Arabs. . . . When he did get a sleep he'd start yelling, '*Hank gave his life for me*,' or, '*Buddy *went back and I slunk home,'* until his wife said what he'd been praying God for her to say, and told him to come back and look for you. . . ."

"She must be a fine woman," said Noel.

"She's the finest and noblest woman in the world—the truest, the sweetest and the loveliest. . . ." I said.

Noel gave me a long and searching look.

"Gee! I wisht I were an orayter!" said Buddy. "Sure ain't it the biggest tale you ever heard tell! . . . And ain't he the White Man? . . . My God, he's like his brothers! . . . Come back to look for *me*! . . ."

And we three sat and stared at each other in silence, each thinking his own thoughts, realizing fresh aspects of this astounding business and trying to grasp the stunning fact that, approaching from opposite directions, and in ignorance of each other's movements, we had met at the heart and centre of this wonderful maze of circumstance.

"And how in the name of the Almighty Marvellous, did *you* come to know John Geste?" asked Noel suddenly.

"I knew all three of them," I said, ". . . when they were kids. . . . Their home is at a place called Brandon Abbas, a regular castle . . . only a mile or two from Granny's place at Brandon Regis. . . ."

"If anyone rises to remark that it is a small world we live in, I'll hand him one," observed Buddy. "Gee! Ain't it some world!"

We pondered the smallness of the world and the marvels packed into its limited space.

There literally was so much to be said that there was nothing to say.

"And why on earth did those three boys from the Stately Homes of England come to the Legion?" asked Noel. "The three of them combined couldn't put up half a dirty trick, if they gave their whole time to it."

"Beau Geste ran away and enlisted to shield a girl—she's dead now—and the other two followed him to share the blame."

"Something about a dam' great di'mond, weren't it?" said Buddy.

"Something of the sort," I agreed.

"And how did you come to know that?" continued Noel.

"I met his wife in a Nursing-Home after I had been shot up, in Zaguig," I said. "She was a kid at Brandon Abbas too."

"And she told you that John Geste had come back to look for *us*, she not knowing we were *your* Brother and Co.?" said Noel.

"He come back to look fer *me*, I tell you," put in Buddy. "He didn't give a curse for you, Hank Sheikh."

"And you offered to come and look for him?" continued Noel, contemplating me thoughtfully. "And you joined the Legion to get sent to the Zephyrs on the chance of getting in touch with him. . . .?

"Good Scout. . . ." he murmured, and sat pondering, stroking and fingering his beard in true Arab fashion.

"Well, Son, the good God Almighty meant you to find John Geste," he observed at length. "Fancy your getting sent to the same Battalion, and then being stuck down in the same *silo* together, and then the Touareg swiping every living Frenchman between there and Zaguig."

"Yes," I agreed. ". . . And this is what I want to know. . . . How in the name of the Almighty Marvellous once again, do *you* come to know all about *that*? Who told *you* that there were two French convicts in Sheikh Yussuf ben Amir's hands, and that they were saved from a *silo* after a massacre?"

"Who saved you, Son?" smiled Noel.

"Three aged scarecrows—village beggars, loafers. . . . United ages about three centuries . . ." I said.

"Meet Yacoub-who-goes-without-water and his two young brothers. . . ."

"Alf and Ed," murmured Buddy.

". . . the Chiefs of my Desert Intelligence Department. You were hardly above ground before I knew that there had been a raid on the road-gangs, and you were hardly in the power of Selim ben Yussuf, before I knew that a couple of French prisoners had been found down a *silo*. I learnt that much while I was on the way here. . . . I'm Keeper of the Peace in these parts. . . ."

"And the pieces . . ." murmured the Wazir.

". . . And I rushed my Camel Corps straight for here when Yacoub sent me word that the Touareg had got busy in my country. . . . I surely will learn Mr. Selim ben Yussuf a lesson he'll remember, and let him know who's Emir of this Confederation— when there are any deals to be done with the French. . . . It was his business to treat you properly and to notify me that he'd got you. . . .

"Yes, damn him," he went on. "It would have been you he'd have handed over, but for that Death Angel girl. . . . And as it is, it's *John Geste*. . . ."

"And now we got to go get John Geste. . . ." put in Buddy. "And that's a game what'll want some playing. . . . Blast Selim ben

Yussuf. . . . I'll hang him on his own innards. . . .

"One thing," he added, "I kissed his gel for him, an' that surely doth get the Arab goat *sur*-prising. . . ."

Silence.

"Bud," said my brother to the Wazir, "we've built up a big business here. . . . We've put the Injuns wise to a lot of things. . . . We've made the old man's seat safe for the boy. . . . We've taught 'em how to handle the Touareg, and we've got 'em in right with the French. . . . It's a fine, sound, going concern, with me President, you Vice-President, and the Board of Directors hand-picked, and a million francs invested under the old apple tree. . . . We're made for life. . . .We pay our own salaries and we fix our own pensions . . . also age of retirement. . . ."

"Sure, Hank Sheikh," said his Wazir. "We sure are the deserving rich. . . ."

". . . On velvet," continued my brother. "Just made good and got all the lovely things that was coming to us. . . . Why, we're Near-Emperors. . . . Sure enough Presidents of a Republic, anyhow. . . . And now here this John Geste comes along, gets into the Zephyrs, Our Own Representative gets him out, and he gets in again. . . . Are we to lose everything to save him again? . . . *Let's leave him where he is.* . . ."

"Let's don't, Hank Sheikh," replied the Wazir.

"Are we to undo our life's work?"

"Sure," said the Wazir promptly.

"Are we to lose everything we've worked and toiled and suffered and risked our lives for?"

"Every last thing," agreed the Wazir.

"Are we to break our Treaty with the French? . . . Break our word to the Tribes? . . . Break the hearts of the men who love and trust us? . . ."

"Break everything," assented the Wazir.

"Are we to start life afresh at our age? . . . Take the road again? . . ."

"Sure. . . . Take the road and everything else we can get. . . . What's bitin' you, you ol' fool?"

"You mean you'll throw away *everything*—chuck up the grandest golden success two hungry hoboes ever made. . . . Go back from wealthy prince to tramping beggar?" . . .

"Ain't our friend in trouble, Hank?" replied Buddy. "What you talkin' about?"

"Shake, Son," said my brother. And the two men shook hands.

"Some folk'd say our duty to the French and these Arabs came first," said Noel.

"Let 'em say," answered Buddy.

"Some folk'd say a man ought not to go back on his word," continued Noel.

"*Word!*" spat Buddy. "Ain't our friend in trouble! What's the word you've spoke, against the word you *haven't* spoke? . . . That you stand by your pard through thick and thin. . . . You remember what you said to me, Hank Sheikh? . . . '*It's all accordin' to what they call your "Bo Ideel."* ' "

"Goo' Boy," observed my brother, taking the small man by the scruff of the neck and shaking him affectionately. "When your friend's in need, he's your friend indeed."

"Sure thing, Hank Sheikh. . . . For a minute I wondered if you'd gone batty in the belfry or woozy in the works."

"I was only trying you out, Son. . . . I apologize. . . ."

"So you oughter, Hank Sheikh," snorted Buddy.

"Don't think I doubted you, Son, but I thought I'd remind you that it's a hard row to hoe, and ruin at the end of it."

"Harder for you, Old Hoss," grinned Buddy. "You got a wife, an' I ain't. . . . Me! . . . I got more sense. . . ."

"Married, Noel? . . . My congratulations. . . . An Arab lady?" I said. "Why, no, of course, I remember . . . the Death Angel said you'd married an English girl like herself. . . ."

"An English girl—very unlike herself," replied Noel, and eyed me queerly.

"I shall look forward to meeting her and paying my respects as a brother-in-law," I said, wondering what sort of extraordinary person my brother could have picked up in this part of the world.

"You have met her, Oats," replied Noel, and I stared astounded, beginning to wonder again whether this were not, after all, an extraordinary dream.

No, it was not a dream. It was more like a good dream wasted.

"Met her?" I said. "Where?"

"She was a Miss Maud Atkinson," said my brother with excellent nonchalance, and both he and Buddy watched me expectant, and, I thought, a little on the defensive.

I don't think my jaw dropped, nor my face expressed anything other than what I wished them to see.

"Congratulations again, Noel," I cried. "When I congratulated you before, it was the usual form of words. . . . I can now congratulate you on having married one of the bravest and best little women that ever lived. She went *literally* through fire to help a friend—in a burning house in England. . . . She's pure gold."

"Thank you, Oats," said my brother, extending his hand.

"Nearly married her meself," observed Buddy glumly. "He butted in, the day before. . . . Stuck his great hoof in our love affair before I . . ."

Spreading a useful hand across his Wazir's face, the Emir thrust his Minister out of the conversation.

"And Mary never told you *that* . . ." continued Noel.

"No. . . . She just mentioned that Maudie was married," said I. "Doesn't she rather complicate the situation?"

"Like Hell she does," pondered Noel. "She'd be the first to chase me off to get John Geste. . . . She'd never forgive us if she knew we'd left a friend in trouble. . . ."

"Where is she now?" I asked.

"At my headquarters at the Great Oasis," replied my brother. "In the charge of my Council and a great old bird who is Regent of my chief tribe. . . . At least they think she is in their charge. . . . As a matter of fact she is the best man of the lot."

"Did she marry you as an Arab?" I asked.

"She married me as a Lovely Sheikh, out of a book," was the reply. "Going to marry me again as a common man, out of a job, when we go home. . . . I'm still a bit of a mystery to her. . . . Girls like mysteries. . . . She always wanted a Sheikh and now she's got one. . . . And she's a *houri*. . . ."

"Wicked shame," muttered the Wazir. "Married the gel under false pretences. . . . Tole her he'd bought a book an' learned English so as he could talk to her—the rambunctious ole goat. . . . Spoilt the one and only love affair of my life. . . ."

"Never mind, Son," soothed the Emir. "You started another last night."

"I certainly did," agreed Buddy with prideful mien. "I'll tell the world she fell for me, right there. . . . And she cert'nly is the Tough Baby. . . . I'm going over to call on her, bye-and-bye."

"You certainly made an impression on her," I said. "She spoke of you when she returned from the visit."

"And that brings us to the point," said Noel. "She tells me that Selim ben Yussuf handed a convict over to a *peloton méhariste* some days ago; and that means that he was taken straight to Zaguig, examined on the subject of the Arab raid, and sent back to a road-gang. . . . Now by the mercy of God, old Yacoub-who-goes-without-water knows his face—and I back him to pick him out from ten thousand. . . . I'll have him and his gang off within the hour, and as soon as John Geste is working on the road again, I shall know it. . . .

"What will Yacoub do?" I asked.

"Everybody," grunted the Wazir.

"Beg mostly," replied my brother. "Loaf about . . . cadge . . . steal rusty cans and run for his life . . . look silly . . . do a bit of water-carrying . . . pick up a job . . . hold a horse . . . lead a camel. . . . They're the three finest old actors that never went on the stage. . . . Believe me, Henry Irving never had anything on Yacoub-who-goes-without-water. . . ."

"And when he locates him?" I asked.

"Them *un*corrigible Touaregs again . . ." suggested the Wazir. "There'll be another raid and John Geste will be took captive by them. . . . Even the Zephyrs will pity the pore feller. . . ."

"That's the scheme," said Noel. "It'll want some planning. . . . I don't want to hurt anybody, and I don't want to get my people shot up, either; but John Geste's coming right out of that road-gang. . . ."

"I get the idea," I mused. "In the meantime what becomes of me?"

"You're dead and buried, Son. Your ghost turns Injun and stays with us, keeping its face hidden. . . . We'll brown it up a bit. . . ."

"But there are half a dozen people who know I'm alive," I said. "The lot out there who brought me over. . . ."

"That's Miss Death Angel's trouble. . . ." replied my brother. "They're her people. . . . It's up to her to see they don't squeal about her little games, to Selim ben Yussuf, or anybody else. . . .

"I don't think they'll talk much, when I've had a word with them," he added, and the Wazir chuckled grimly.

"I'm dead of course, as far as the French are concerned," I remarked.

"You perished in the massacre, Son. . . . Poor old John will be in a bad way," he continued. "He can't very well tell the French you're alive and ought to be rescued from the wild Bedouin, and he can't very well leave you to be tortured by Selim ben Yussuf, as he thinks. . . ."

"I suppose Selim ben Yussuf couldn't do any good, if you were to put the screw on him?" I asked.

"No," replied my brother. "*He* can't do anything. . . . Once he's handed an escaped prisoner back, there's an end of it. . . . I myself couldn't do a thing, although I'm Emir of the Confederated tribes of the Great Oasis, and ally of France.

". . . No, Selim can only tell me all about the patrol and then take what's coming to him. . . . The fool! . . . The damned impudent presumptuous *fool!* . . . Why, I could prevent him succeeding his father as Sheikh of his Tribe. . . . If I were staying on, that is . . ." and he smiled wryly. "I'll get him, as it is . . . if he comes back in time. . . ."

"He's bound to come back soon, I should think," said I. "The girl expected him to roll up at any minute. In fact, when we heard the commotion of your arrival, we thought he had come. . . ."

"What's the position there exactly . . . d'you know?" asked Noel.

"Yes," I replied. "I do. . . . It's the hell of a position. . . . Selim is madly infatuated with the girl, which you can quite understand. . . . And the girl is apparently madly infatuated with me . . . which you probably cannot understand. . . .

"I met them both in Bouzen a long time ago, and the trouble began as far back as that. . . . Selim was after her then, and wanted to stab me because she singled me out at a dancing-show. . . .

"I gather that, being heartily tired of Town, she came for 'a day in the country' . . . Giving Selim a trial trip before marrying him, perhaps. . . . Just as likely to become his step-mama I should say. . . ."

"And then you came on the scene and the scene was changed. . . ." suggested my brother. "Friend Selim did himself some good when he brought you home, didn't he?"

"Yes. . . . And me too . . ." I sighed. "I paid her rather a high price for my freedom to go off again in search of John Geste. . . . Noel, old chap, *couldn't* you have come a day sooner?"

"No, Son . . . nor an hour. . . . Why?"

"Because I made a fair and square bargain with the Death Angel that I'd come back to her as soon as I had seen John Geste out of the country, or else at the end of a year. . . ."

"Come back to her? . . . What for? . . ." asked my brother.

"To marry her," I said.

My brother stared incredulous, and then laughed harshly.

"Marry her? . . . Well, that's an engagement that'll be broken off," smiled he.

"Not by me, Noel," I told him "It's a 'gentleman's agreement.' . . . I gave her my word and my hand on it. . . . She has done her part and I'll have to do mine. Just as soon as we've got John Geste out of the country . . ."

"You'll come too, Son—if you have to come in a sack," affirmed my brother.

"Noel," I said, "listen. . . . Before you came, this girl made a bargain with me. On her side she was to help me get John Geste out of the country. . . . In return for that help, I gave her my solemn promise that I would come back. And I shall do so. . . ."

"I get you, Son," he answered thoughtfully.

Silence fell, and we sat, each thinking his own thoughts—if gazing in wonderment upon incredible but undeniable facts, can be called thought.

The Wazir was the first to break the silence, and the trend of his cogitations was apparent.

"Do I understand that you are reg'larly engaged to this young woman then?" he asked purposefully.

"Yes," I said.

"You *would* be . . ." he observed glumly, and in reply to the inquiry of my raised eyebrow, added:

"I was going to propose to her meself, to-day. . . ."

"Then I sincerely hope you'll do it, and be entirely successful," I replied.

"Well, you cut in first, Bo. . . . We'll leave it at that. . . . I ain't bad at heart. . . ."

"No. It's your head that's bad," observed my brother. "Brains went bad long ago. . . . Now stop jabbering and put Marbruk ben Hassan wise. . . . I want Yacoub here quicker than Marbruk can get him. . . ."

The Wazir left the tent.

"Who *is* he, Noel?" I asked.

"The biggest little man that ever lived. . . . And my friend," replied my brother. "I took up with him when I ran away from home, and we've been together ever since. . . . He's the bravest man I ever saw and there never lived a stauncher. . . . He's true, Son. . . . And when you want him, he's *there*. . . ."

"What's that language he talks?" I asked.

"Well, he was born in the Bowery, New York, and that's his mother tongue. . . . And he got his schooling in South State Street and Cottage Grove Avenue, Chicago, and the slums thereabout, and he talks the dialect. . . . He graduated on the water-front at San Francisco, and learnt some good language there. . . . He was a barkeep in Seattle, and went to the gold-diggings. . . . He was a cow-puncher in Texas and Arizona, and he's used the roads of the U.S.A. a lot—and the railways more so, but I don't think he ever bought a ticket. . . ."

"And why do you talk like him when you are talking to him?" I inquired.

"Because I've got good manners," replied Noel. "And what's good enough for Bud is good enough for me. . . .

"Now you stay where you are for a bit, Son," he continued. "I'm going to hold a *mejliss* and get busy. . . ."

A few minutes later, the Emir and his Wazir were seated on the carpet and cushions of State outside the big tent in which I was concealed.

The Oriental Potentate was seated in judgment; if not "in the city gate" as of old, then in the door of his tent and shadow of the palm, as in days far older.

The dwarf, Marbruk ben Hassan, brought to the judgment-seat the party who had escorted me.

"And so there were two *Roumi* prisoners . . ." said the deep voice of the Emir, ". . . and one of them was given up to the French, and the other died. . . . Is it not so? . . ."

"It is so; O, Emir," said the voice of the good *hakim*.

"It is so indeed; O, Emir," said Abd'allah ibn Moussa.

And the voices of the servants chorused the refrain.

"And his body was buried in the sand," continued the Emir. "You were all present I think?"

"All; O, Emir . . ." was the unanimous reply.

"There could be no mistake about it?" suggested the Emir. "I should be sorry for one who made a mistake about it. . . . Sorry for him, and his son, his son's son, and his wives and his children, his camels, his goats, and all that he had."

All appeared perfectly certain that there could be no mistake on the subject.

"Was it a deep grave or a shallow grave, in which you buried this unfortunate prisoner?" pursued the Emir.

And it was the voice of Abd'allah that answered promptly:

"Oh, a very shallow grave; O, Emir. . . . It might be found that jackals had removed the body . . . should any search be now made for it. . . ."

And the voice of the *hakim* chimed in with:

"And it was a much-trodden spot, O, Emir, near the camel-enclosure. . . . A very difficult spot to find . . . even had the jackals not rifled the grave. . . ."

"It is well," concluded the Emir. "Go in peace, making no mistake . . . for my arm is long—long as the Tail of the Horse of the Prophet."

CHAPTER XV

I spent the following days in a curious condition of mind, and much comfort of body. I had complete and much-needed rest, and freedom from all personal anxiety and fear; and my hope concerning John Geste was rising high. . . . I had had him in my hands and I should have him again. . . .

This brother of mine was a strong man—a strong man armed—influential and powerful, unless he came into deliberate conflict with the French, whose friend and ally he was.

With him I was absolutely safe, and, though idly quiescent myself, I felt that everything possible was being done to further my affairs—which were now equally those of my brother and his friend.

I could lie upon my cushions, resting and relaxed, yet happy in the knowledge that more was being done to further John Geste's rescue than at any time since Isobel had told me of his capture.

I could not talk with these two without becoming imbued with a feeling of completest confidence. They were so sure that their Desert Intelligence—which had never yet failed them—would speedily discover John's whereabouts, and that their brave and faithful fighting-men would effect his rescue.

Naturally I had my moments of fear, gloom, anxiety and doubt, but I had my hours of hope and joy, and certitude that all would be well, and that I should live to see John Geste step upon the deck of a British or American ship.

And at that point I always awakened myself from my day-dream and refused to envisage the future.

Life—with the Angel of Death as my wife!

Well, I must make the best of it, and the best of her. There is good in everyone, and, probably, in her way—and given a fair chance—she was quite as "good" as I was. . . . And in any case I should be a happy man, if only I succeeded in saving John. . . .

I grew very near to my brother again, during this brief period of waiting, this tiny oasis in the desert of strenuous life, and got to know him very well.

The more I learned, the more was I filled with admiration at his astounding feat—his rising by sheer unaided ability, from being a practically dead man, possessed of the remains of one ragged garment and nothing else, to his present position—as a man of wealth, power and importance.

His was indeed a wonderful story, and in my private mind I ranked him with such men as that Burton who became an Arab and made the pilgrimage to Mecca, earning the title of *Haji*, a Mussulman of Mussulmans.

Little wonder that Major de Beaujolais, with all his Secret Service training, had found no grounds for suspicion, since the Arabs themselves believed him to be an Arab.

His years of wandering in the desert with John and Digby Geste must have been a hard apprenticeship, but the only possible one for such success as this.

And the same applied to my brother's *fidus Achates*, Buddy.

Neither of them was a man of book-education, but both were men of brains, ability, determination and character.

Noel was his father's son there, but oh, how different a man—with his wise broad tolerance.

When I endeavoured to discover Noel's mental attitude to our Father, I was somewhat baffled, but came to the conclusion that if he did not still actually hate him, he thought of him with some bitterness, and promised himself the pleasure of, some day, returning home, and "having it out" with him, "mastering him" as he expressed it. . . .

Not in a spirit of bitterness and revenge, or with the least idea of humiliating him, but rather as a sop to his own self-respect and to meet him on an equality, on his own level, and as man to man; and particularly, I think, Noel wished to demonstrate to him that a son of Homer H. Vanbrugh could, unaided, amount to something, without dwelling for ever in Homer H. Vanbrugh's pocket, or in the shadow of his crushing and overwhelming bulk.

Not only did my affection for my brother increase, as we talked together, but my respect also. And I envied him. . . . He was the Happy Warrior. He had deliberately chosen the way of life that suited him, and for which he was suited, rejecting the job of rich man's son, offered him by circumstance, and going out into the high-ways and by-ways of the world, the open roads that called to him.

He had climbed a steep and rugged path, and he had enjoyed the effort and the danger. He had made contact with realities, looked life in the face, and acknowledged the great God of Things As They Are.

And of all the interesting things about him, what interested me most was the fact that, having literally and actually been crowned with success, he was, without an instant's hesitation, prepared to cast that crown away at a word—a word of a friend in danger.

A crown was not his *beau idéal*.

A man who thought like Don Quixote though he chose to talk like Sancho Panza.

And, too, the more I saw of his friend, the more I liked and respected him, for my brother's standards and values were his in equal measure.

To what extent this was due to the uninfluenced nature of the man, and how much to the fact that my brother was his untarnishable hero, and impeccable model, I do not know—and if the latter, the more credit to him that such a man could be his ideal.

Yes—I liked Buddy. And I wrote him down a bold, unconquerable spirit, sterling and faithful and fine.

§2

"Lie low, Son," whispered my brother, entering my comfortable tent wherein I lay restfully at peace—in the peace of the great desert.

"French patrol coming. . . . You're all right behind that face-stain—your own father wouldn't know you. . . . No need to chuck your weight about though. . . . If you like to put an eye to one crack and an ear to another, you may have some fun. . . ."

It wasn't exactly fun, but it was very interesting, to hear the officers of the Patrol talking with the Emir el Hamel el Kebir and the Sheikh el Habibka el Wazir, over their three rounds of ceremonial and complimentary mint tea.

Marvellous was the impassive Arab dignity with which the Emir, his Wazir, Sheikhs and chief men met and greeted the French *sous-officier* and his European subordinates, and with which they conducted them to the rug-and-cushion-strewn carpet before the Emir's tent.

When all customary and proper formalities had been observed, the French *sous-officier* got down to business.

It appeared that the French authorities at Zaguig appreciated the Emir's prompt action in hurrying to the scene of the massacre, and hoped that, by now, he had some information on the subject of the raiders. . . .

Of course the Touareg at once came under suspicion—but it

was easy to cry, "*Touareg*"—and there were certain features of the raid that might or might not indicate Touareg. . . . The said features might have been covered by the Touareg face-veil, so to speak. . . .

But, and here was a point to consider, might not those veils have been borrowed, and might they not have veiled features that were not those of Touareg faces at all?

There were reasons for thinking so, and if the slaughter had been Touareg handiwork, why was the life of at least one of the road-gang spared? . . . And how had this man come to be in the hands of Selim ben Yussuf?

The convict himself would say nothing . . . absolutely nothing . . . though he had undoubtedly received every encouragement to speak. (My fists clenched as I listened and thought of poor John. . . . I cursed the Angel of Death.) . . . Of course he may have been knocked on the head and really remember nothing, as he said. . . . But *how* did Selim ben Yussuf get him? . . .

And what exactly was Selim ben Yussuf doing within a few miles of where the massacre took place?

Old Sheikh Yussuf ben Amir, his father, was all-right, no doubt, but Selim ben Yussuf was quite another coconut. . . .

His record was a bad one, or rather it was a record of strong continual suspicions. . . . It was firmly believed that he had been prominent in the Zaguig massacre, though as there was no survivor of that, except an American tourist, no evidence could be got against him. (Here I was indeed interested.) . . . Still, Major de Beaujolais had reported that he had seen Selim in Zaguig just before the massacre—and pray where was the gentleman at this very minute? . . .

The Emir stroked and fingered his beard, gravely nodding as the Frenchman talked. . . . And the Emir's Wazir stroked and fingered his beard, gravely and wisely nodding as his master did so.

It appeared that the Emir had himself entertained suspicions concerning Selim ben Yussuf, and had his eye upon him . . . and in fact, the sole reason why he remained encamped at this spot, with his Camel-Corps, was to see whether Selim returned to the Tribe and, meanwhile, to make wide inquiry as to his whereabouts and movements.

And had the Emir heard the rumour which *l'Adjudant* Lebaudy had picked up somewhere . . . that Selim ben Yussuf had had *two* French prisoners?

Here the Emir stroked his beard very thoughtfully.

"If he has another prisoner, he has taken him with him," he

said. "There is absolutely no question whatever of there being another French prisoner in their camp over there. . . ."

"That's certain, is it?" asked the officer.

"As absolutely certain as that Mahommed is the Prophet of Allah. . . . Have a tent-to-tent visitation if you like, but 'twill be but a waste of time . . ." said the Emir.

"It would be like the young fox," he added, thoughtfully frowning, "if he *did* have two, to give one up in token of good faith, and to keep the other as a hostage—or to torture, if he hates the *Roumi* as some say. . . ."

"H'm. . . . Give up one to show his love, and keep one upon whom to show his hate, eh?" said the Frenchman.

The Emir then inquired as to this curious rumour, and learned that an Arab *méhariste* with *l'Adjudant* Lebaudy's patrol had been told by a boy, a goat-herd, of whom he bought some dates, that there had been two *Roumi* prisoners, but one was said to have died. . . .

Probably nothing in it—except that one of the Secret Service spies had also brought in a story, admittedly somewhat fantastic, about a *Roumi* prisoner having been tortured to death by a woman. . . .

The Emir did not appear to be impressed.

"It'll be ten by the New Moon . . ." he smiled. "However, our young friend, Selim, shall enlighten us. . . . Oh, yes . . . Selim shall talk. . . ."

"Selim shall squeal, eh?" smiled the French officer grimly.

The Emir looked up.

"What does old Sheikh Yussuf ben Amir say?" he asked.

"He says he knows absolutely nothing about either Selim's movements or about Selim's prisoner or prisoners, and I think he is speaking the truth. . . ."

And the Emir bade the officer rest assured that he, El Hamel el Kebir, would know the truth, the whole truth, and nothing but the truth, as to there having been one or two French prisoners in the hands of Selim ben Yussuf, and as to the precise manner in which that suspect had acquired them.

One more thing—and the officer picked up his riding-switch and *képi*—orders were coming, for Sheikh Yussuf ben Amir's tribe, to migrate at once to the Oasis of Sidi Usman, near Bouzen, there to concentrate and remain until further notice.

Would the Emir facilitate their departure and keep a patrol in the neighbourhood, so long as it seemed likely that Selim ben

Yussuf, and the fighting-men with him, might return to where he
had left the tribe encamped. . . .

§3

And, next day, as we three sat in dignified isolation apart from
all men, a servant came running, spoke to the Soudanese sentry—
whose business it was to see that none unauthorized approached
within hearing—and drew near.

"Yacoub-who-goes-without-water sends a messenger; O,
Emir," the man said, making obeisance.

"Bring him instantly, el R'Orab," ordered the Emir, and, a
minute or two later, an aged and filthy beggar approached, a man
so old and decrepit that the flesh of his bent and trembling legs
seemed covered in dry grey scales rather than brown human skin.
His face expressed nothing but senile imbecility and, as his
shrivelled lips opened, exposing the toothless gums and a tongue
like that of a parrot, one expected to hear nothing but the shrill
piping voice of a pitiable dotard, well advanced in second
childhood.

Supporting his emaciated frame with the help of a staff, he
salaamed profoundly, glanced at me inquiringly, and, on receiving
the Emir's kind permission to speak freely, changed astonishingly.

Certainly he was still a dirty old man, but one whose face now
expressed shrewdness, alertness, and ripe wisdom. A hopeless,
helpless, doddering old pantaloon turned, before my eyes, into an
extremely knowing, spry and competent old gentleman.

"May the Sidi Emir live for ever!" quoth he, "and dwell in the
protection of Allah and the care of His Prophet. . . . Humblest
greetings from his meanest slave, Yacoub-who-goes-without-water,
and this message. . . .

" 'Know, O, Emir, that the *Roumi* prisoner sold by Sheikh
Selim ben Yussuf to the *Franzawi* was taken to the city of Zaguig
and there cast into prison. . . . At the gate of the prison have I sat, a
blind and naked beggar, asking "Alms for the love of Allah! Alms
for the love of Allah, the Merciful, the Compassionate. . . ." I have
not left this place by day nor by night, and all who have entered in
unto it, and all who have come out of it, have I seen. . . . Yea, every
one. . . . And behold, three times has the *Roumi* prisoner been taken
by soldiers from this old prison to the new barracks. . . . And three
times has he been brought back. . . . Each time did I follow afar off,
and what happened when he was taken to the barracks of the

Franzawi soldiers, I do not know, save that high officers assembled and questioned him . . . for I climbed on the back of a passing camel and saw through the iron bars of the "hole through which one looks out.[9]"

" '. . . And the fourth time he was taken from the prison, he marched with others like him, and with soldiers about them, down the Road that the *Franzawi* build from Zaguig to the Great Oasis. . . . And each night they halted for a night in an armed camp. . . . And now he, and those others with him, have come to the place of the deserted village, and they carry on the work of those that are dead. . . . With my own eyes I am watching this man and with my brother's voice am I speaking these words. . . . And may the peace of Allah abide with the Sidi Emir, and encompass him about. . . .'

"And that is the message of my brother, Yacoub-who-goes-without-water, O Lord. . . ."

And:

"It is well," replied the Emir. "Go and eat."

And as the intelligent old gentleman lapsed back into the idiot centenarian and tottered out of earshot:

"Good God above us!" said Noel. "*John Geste!* John Geste, himself, is not ten miles away from where we're sitting now, Otis!"

And I could answer nothing.

§4

We instantly became a Council of War.

My brother is a man of prompt action, but he is not of those who act first and think afterwards. I imagine his marvellous success among the Arabs was as much due to his wisdom in the Council-tent as to skill and courage on the battle-field.

In the strange rôle that my brother played at this period of his life, tactics and strategy counted for more than swashbuckling. It interested me greatly to see how he considered the views and opinions of Buddy and myself, and then of his most trusted Arab lieutenants, weighed them carefully, discussed them, and then produced his own, and his reasons for holding them.

Inasmuch as I had worked in the road-gang and knew, to the last detail, the method and routine of the daily and nightly procedure, my advice was asked, my suggestions invited, and I was flatteringly bidden to say precisely what I would do if I were the

---

[9] Window.

executive in charge of the work of rescue.

To me, it at once appeared that there were two methods open to us—that of force, and that of guile, and I promptly propounded this platitude.

"Take the force-idea first, Son," said Noel, "bearing in mind it's not to be a raid like this last one. I'll have John Geste if I kill every Arab and Frenchman in Africa, but I intend to get him without killing anybody."

"That rather cramps one's style for force, doesn't it?" I said. "Limits one's scope of action, a little. . . . What would happen if we swooped down upon the working-party in overwhelming strength, but unarmed. . . . Simply kidnapped John by main force. . . . We three seize him, while a hundred good men and true scatter everybody, all ends up, and we ride for it?"

"What would happen, Son? . . . We should leave about thirty dead . . . probably including John Geste and certainly ourselves. . . . As I say, I don't want anybody killed, especially my own men. . . ."

"What about a hand-picked party, to surround the spot in the dark, and shoot straight and fast—but high. . . . While they're carefully hitting nobody, we three, armed, say, with 'a foot of lead-pipe' each, dash in and get John. . . ."

"Dash in and don't get John," said my brother. "We get about seven bullets each, instead. . . ."

"Well . . . what about this idea? . . . Let your man, Yacoub, get a word of warning to John to be *ready* at sunset to-morrow . . . expecting something to happen. . . . Then let Selim ben Yussuf's tribe start their trek in the afternoon, and pass along the road just before the gang is due to stop work. . . . All your men might join in the procession, camels and all complete, and the more dust they raise the better. . . . We three, and a few chosen lads who can be trusted, can be in a bunch, and one of us carry a spare *haik* and *burnous*. . . . As we pass and jostle along the road, Yacoub gets beside John and says 'Now!' to him, and I shout 'Come on, John.' . . . He just steps into the midst of the crowd and we throw the spare burnous round him to hide his uniform, and he pulls it over his face. . . . Let Buddy be leading a spare camel, and we three push forward as quickly as we can, to the head of the column, and then ride for it. . . ."

My brother smiled.

"Bright idea, Oats," he said kindly. "But it would be 'Keep off the grass' as soon as the mob tried to use the Road. . . . '*At the stiffs in front, at five hundred metres, seven rounds rapid fire.'* . . . No, Son . . . especially after the recent raid, no clouds of dust are coming near any Zephyr party. Neither along the Road nor across it. . . ."

"Well, let's try guile," I said. "What about old Yacoub slipping John a file and hanging around until John makes a quiet get-away. . . . We're waiting near, with fast camels, and old Yacoub brings him to us. . . ."

"Waiting how long, Son? We might grow grey, or strike roots into the earth before John got his chance. . . . There won't be much slackness for a long time to come. . . . Suppose he's caught using the file? . . . Suppose he is shot, getting away? . . . You know about how many single-handed escape-attempts succeed. . . ."

"What about this?" I tried again.

"Supposing you, in your own proper person, as the Emir el Hamel el Kebir, in your whitest robes, heavy corded silk head-dress and scarlet and gold camel-hair ropes round your head, visited that particular section of the Road—with your Wazir, and high Sheikhs, chief executioner, cup-bearer, baker, butler, soothsayer, and holy panjandrum and all—and had an afternoon tea-party with the nice friendly White Men. . . . And while all goes merrier than a marriage-bell, there is a sudden raid by a few score of your best, unarmed . . . and, as they appear, some of us seize the rifles of our friends, and the rest of us seize the friends themselves. . . . While we hang on to them—grapple them to our hearts with hoops of steel, so to speak—the new-comers guided by Yacoub, simply cut out John from the herd and make their getaway. . . ."

"Leaving us in the soup, like . . ." murmured Buddy.

"Well . . . we'd have the rifles, and they'd simply have to 'hands up' while we backed away to our camels and cleared off. . . ."

"Gee! Hasn't he got a mind, Hank Sheikh," admired Buddy. "He sure is your brother. . . . Sim'lar kind o' train-hold-up nature. . . ."

"It's a scheme," mused Noel. "It's an idea, Bud. . . ."

"Or there's that *silo*," I suggested. "Suppose Yacoub provisioned it, and we three made a regular Red Indian swift-and-silent sort of raid, dressed in brown paint and coco-nut-oil. . . . We might get him and rush to that *silo* and lie low there . . ."

"Down among the dead men," murmured Buddy.

". . . until the first wild hurroosh is over. . . . That wouldn't lead a pursuit back to your own camp, either. Sneak away from the *silo* the following night to where Yacoub has the camels. . . ."

Noel shook his head.

"Too risky, Son," he mused. "That *silo* may have been discovered and be in use again. . . . And if it hasn't, it sure is an unhealthy spot. . . . What's your idea, Bud?" he continued, turning to his friend.

"Well, Hank Sheikh, I'd like a good up-and-down dawg-fight —a free-for-all, knock-down-an'-drag-out, go-as-you-please, bite-kick-or-gouge turn-up—an' run that boy, John Geste, outa gaol. . . . Life's gettin' a dam' sight too peaceful. . . . An' you're gettin' fat. . . .

"But since you've got so partic'lar an' no poor fightin'-man's to get hurt, what about dopin' the guard? . . . Have a party. . . . Have a supper-party an' hand oat the free drinks generous an' hearty *an'* doped. . . . You don't taste *hashish* in coffee, an' if we couldn't do anything else, we could work off three rounds of sweet coffee an' three rounds of mint-tea on 'em . . . not to mention something funny in the *cous-cous*. . . . Nothin' serious. . . . In the mawnin' twenty-five headaches *come*, an' one prisoner *gone*. . . . Hardly worth noticin'. . . ."

"Gee! Hasn't he got a mind, Oats?" admired the Emir. "Filled with treacly treachery, putrid poison, and mouldy mellow-drama. . . . But it cert'nly is an idea. . . ."

He turned to Buddy.

"Don't I seem to remember we already had one misfortunate igsperience with poison, Son?"

"Misfortunate Hell!" snorted Buddy. "It clinched the deal anyhow. . . . That's all the thanks *I* get. . . . That, and a broken heart. . . ." he added.

"It's an idea, Son. . . . It cert'nly is an idea. . . ." admitted Noel. "The fierce and treacherous Sheikh stuff, eh? Invite 'em to a hash party an' poison 'em . . ."

"Look here, Noel," I broke in, "excuse the question. . . . But where do you draw the line? . . . You want no bloodshed, and I can quite understand that, and I entirely agree. . . . But about the treachery part of it, since the word's been used. . . . If I know you, old chap, and I think I do, you'll hate that more than a fair and square fight—openly showing your hand as having suddenly become an enemy of the French. . . ."

"I needn't appear in the fair-and-square fight, Son," replied my brother.

"I could very easily turn a picked lot of my braves into

Touareg, and let there be another raid. . . . When the Guard was disposed of, Yacoub could identify John Geste, and they could bring him along . . . bring the whole lot along, if Yacoub got knocked out. . . . I should never be suspected. . . . It isn't that. . . . I simply don't want any killing, and I'll try everything else first.

". . . As to the treachery, that's the only alternative to fighting and that's why I'm considering it—"

"Suppose the French ever find you out?" I asked.

"They're going to find me out, Son. . . . Out of the country . . ." was the reply. "It's like this, Boy. . . . John Geste came back to save us. . . . I'm going to save John Geste. . . . I'm going to do it without hurting a man, if I can, and that means I've got to play false since I won't play rough. . . . Well . . . I've taken their money and I've given them good value and a fair deal. . . .

"Now here endeth the good value and the fair deal—so I take no more money. . . . I throw in my hand. . . . I'm a Bad Man all-right, Oats, but I've never double-crossed and I won't start now. . . . The day I break my side of the contract, the contract's broken, and I won't benefit by it any more. . . . I've kept the Treaty that I made with my young brother-in-law, good and proper, but it's got to lapse directly I start monkeying-about with French troops and actin' against French interests. . . . I'm sorry I've got to do it at all . . . *an' I wouldn't do it for any living soul*, except for John Geste an' you two. . . ."

"Thanks, Noel," I said. "I see. . . . Any trick to get John away . . . and it's your first and last 'treachery.' . . ."

"That's it, Son. . . . We don't bite the hand that feeds us, or rather we only bite it once—and that much against our will. . . ."

"And you two will give up everything to save John Geste?"

Noel looked at Buddy.

"Why, sure," said the little man, nodding at my brother.

And turning to me, he added:

"It's all a matter o' what he calls his Bo Ideel. . . ."

We talked "about it and about," until my brother said:

"Now we'll hear Marbruk ben Hassan and Yussuf Latif ibn Dawad Fetata on the subject."

The loud clapping of the Emir's big hands brought a slave running, and he was despatched for the two Arabs.

Marbruk ben Hassan, the deformed, but very powerful-looking, dwarf, heard, apparently without the very faintest shadow of surprise, that the Emir intended to seize a convict of one of the

French road-making parties. And, in reply to his master's inquiry as to how he would set about it, were he in charge of the business, replied:

"A swift rush, just before dawn, when sentries are sleeping and all men are at their weakest. . . . Crawl close. . . . Three volleys . . . and a swift charge pushed well home. . . ."

"And suppose no man on either side is to be killed, on peril of your life; O, Marbruk ben Hassan?" inquired the Emir.

"I am only a soldier, Lord," smiled Marbruk ben Hassan, and fingered his beard.

"A soldier who leads soldiers should have a brain and use it; O, Marbruk ben Hassan," replied the Emir.

Marbruk scratched his right calf with his left foot and reminded me of a discomfortable school-boy.

The other Arab eyed him with a look of affectionate tolerance.

"Taking a hundred men, I would make three parties," said the dwarf at length. "Two strong, and one weak. . . . The two strong parties, each making a détour, should, at sunset, as the men cease work and go to camp, suddenly charge each other, meeting at a spot quite near. . . . There should be much firing, shouting, falling from camels, a *lab el baroda*, a powder-play . . . but looking and sounding like a great fight. . . . There would be an alarm. . . . The guard would come running and form up in that direction, and while all was in confusion and nothing clear, the small third party should swoop down upon the prisoners and ride off with the man whose life the *Sidi* desires. . . . Word could be got to him of what was toward. . . ."

"Thou art not *wholly* a fool, O, Marbruk ben Hassan," smiled the Emir. And the Arab acknowledged the compliment with a low salaam.

"Yussuf Latif?" said the Emir, turning to the other, a lean large-eyed tragic-looking man.

"If guile is to be used and not the sword, I would try France's own pacific penetration," he said. "Open a little market . . . dates . . . *sharbet* . . . fruit . . . cooked meats. . . . Also a band of holy dervishes would arrive and rest. . . . There might be one or two slave women from the tribe yonder. . . .

"One day, at a given signal, a strong man springs on every soldier, while another snatches his rifle. . . . A small party at once liberates the prisoner and takes him to where two or three of the fleetest camels are waiting, and swiftly they ride hither. . . ."

"And—afterwards—what of those who have seized the guard?

. . ." asked the Emir.

"It will be their privilege to die, Emir. . . . All will volunteer . . . nay, quarrel, for that honour. . . ."

"None are to die, Yussuf Latif . . . neither in fight nor in willing surrender of their lives . . ." said the Emir.

"Speak again; O, Yussuf Latif. . . ."

"What of this then, Lord? When our peaceful and humble disposition has disarmed suspicion, and we have gradually been permitted to mingle with the soldiers of the escort, every one of these shall be allotted to two of our strong men. . . . Of every two men, one shall have two stout thin cords about his waist, or otherwise hidden. . . .

"At the given signal, every soldier shall be seized by the two appointed to him, and the moment that one has snatched his rifle, the other shall seize him round the arms and body. . . . The rifle-snatcher shall then bind the man's feet together and his arms to his sides. . . . The two shall then carry the man to an appointed place, where all the soldiers shall be laid together unhurt. . . . Except one. . . .

"This one shall be laid a mile away—his feet most strongly bound and one arm bound to his body tightly. . . . It shall be shown to him that there is a knife stuck in the sand, afar off. . . .

"When we have departed—taking with us the man whom you desire—this bound soldier will roll and wriggle toward the knife, and by the time he gets it and contrives to free himself and his comrades, we shall be very far away, and, making a détour, return hither. . . ."

"Leaving a track for all men to see?" asked the Emir.

The Arab smiled at the joke.

"Nay, Lord," he said, "the détour would take us up the stony Wadi el Tarish where a million camels would leave no trace. . . ."

"Do you like this plan; O, Yussuf?" inquired the Emir.

"Each man thinks his own fleas are gazelles," quoted Yussuf Latif ibn Fetata.

"And what do you think the prisoners will do, when the guards are bound and you are gone?" asked the Emir.

The Arab smiled and put his hand to his throat.

"They must be bound too," he said.

The Emir stroked his beard thoughtfully and pondered awhile.

"You have spoken well; O, Marbruk ben Hassan and Yussuf ibn Fetata. . . . I will reveal my mind later. . . . Meantime, each of you select two score of the best. . . . Yes, yes, I know that all are best—but select the coolest and steadiest. . . . Men who do not fire at shadows nor foam at the mouth as they fight. . . ."

The two withdrew, salaaming profoundly.

"A fine combination, those two," said Noel. "Cautious age and daring youth. . . . And both stauncher than steel and braver than lions. . . ."

"I surely am sorry for that Yussuf Latif boy," observed Buddy. "What's wrong with him is a broken heart. . . . I know the symptoms—none better. . . ."

"That's so, Bud," agreed Noel, and added:

"The wonder to me is that you ain't egsperienced the symptoms of a broken neck—or a stretched one anyhow. . . ."

The smile of the Wazir combined pity, superiority and contempt in exactly equal proportions.

"The point is, have you got a plan . . . chatterbox? he said.

"I have," said the Emir, and he detailed it to us.

"It ain't perfect," he mused, "but it's the best we can do. . . . It's funny without being vulgar. . . . It oughta succeed. . . . An' there won't be any killing. . . .

"The young woman would help us, all-right, Otis!" he asked, turning to me.

"She certainly would," I assured him "Only too glad to bring me a day's march nearer home. . . . Or right home in a day's march. . . ."

"That's the scheme, then," concluded Noel. ". . . And we'll bring it off to-morrow night. . . . I'll hate doing it—but I'd hate any other plan worse. . . . And the job's got to be done. . . ."

CHAPTER XVI

In all the changing scenes of life, one of the several that are indelibly printed on my mind, and which I shall never forget, is that of the feast and entertainment, given by the Emir el Hamel el Kebir, to the men of the advance-party of those who were the pioneers on the Road that was eventually to link the Great Oasis with Zaguig, the uttermost outpost of the African Empire of France.

Having a deep personal interest in this Road, the Emir el Hamel el Kebir had, with a considerable bodyguard, come from where he was encamped, to see with his own eyes something of the great Road's swift progress and to greet the fore-runners of its makers.

The feast was, of course, an Arab one.

Surrounded by cushion-strewn rugs, on a large palm-leaf mat, slaves placed a shallow metal dish so vast as to suggest a bath. In this, on a deep bed of rice, lay a mass of lumps of meat, the flesh of kids, lambs, and I feared, of a sucking camel-calf. A sea of rich thick gravy lapped upon the shores of surrounding rice, with wavelets of molten butter and oily yellow fat.

In the centre of the bath was a noble mound of heads crowned with livers, intact and entire. Among the mass of chops, cutlets, joints, scrags, legs, shoulders, saddles, and nameless lumps of meat, were portions of the animals not usually seen on Western dishes. These, however, could be avoided by the prejudiced.

I noticed that the genuine Arabs present, were not prejudiced. Around this dish we knelt, each upon one knee, his right arm bared to the elbow, and, with the aid of our good right hands, we filled our busy mouths, and ate . . . and ate . . . and ate . . .

And ate.

There were present, the Emir el Hamel el Kebir; his Minister el Habibka el Wazir; a gloomy taciturn Sheikh, dark of face and blue-black of hair and well-clipped beard, a man supposed to be under a curse and also suffering from the effects of a highly unwholesome love-potion administered to him by a jealous wife—a potion from which he would probably never recover, as the Emir, indicating my morose and surly self, explained to the French *Adjudant*; also Marbruk ben Hassan; Yussuf Latif ibn Fetata; and some half a dozen leading Sheikhs of the tribe to which the Emir belonged; and four or five Frenchmen.

From time to time, the Emir would fish out a succulent morsel and thrust it into the mouth of the guest of honour on his right, *l'Adjudant* Lebaudy, a man who interested me much. I had put him down as very true to type, a soldier and nothing more, but a fine soldier, rugged as a rock, hard as iron, and true as steel—a man of simple mind and single purpose, untroubled by thoughts of why and wherefore, of right and wrong, finding duty sufficient and the order of a superior more important than the order of the Universe. . . .

And by no means stupid—in fact watchful, wary, and fore-sighted, as we were to discover.

We ate in stark silence—as far as speech is concerned that is—lest light converse offend our host with indication that we were finding but light fare and entertainment. . . . When we had finished, and not a stomach could hold another grain of rice, we rose, indicated our profound satisfaction by profound hiccoughs, went to the door of the tent, wiped our greasy hands upon its flap, and then held them forth while servants poured streams of water upon them from long-necked vessels.

Meanwhile, other servants removed the depleted hip-bath, and so re-arranged rugs and cushions that, when two of the wall-curtains were rolled up to the tent roof, each man of the company reclined with his back to a tent-wall and his face to the star-lit night without.

The great guest-tent, in which we sat, was illumined by a hanging lamp within, and the flames of a great fire maintained at sufficient distance to cause no discomfort. A few yards from us, between the tent and the fire, servants laid palm-leaf mats, upon which they placed a rug.

Coffee was brought, glasses and clay cups upon a huge brass tray, and, to do them signal honour, the Emir himself, with his own hand, took glasses of coffee to his European guests.

But *l'Adjudant* Lebaudy excused himself, and I caught Buddy's eye as the *Adjudant's* deep voice, in very fair Arabic, rumbled words to the effect that so enlightened and understanding a man as the Emir would not wish him to drink coffee—which disagreed with him—merely for politeness' sake. . . .

The Emir was obviously greatly concerned and somewhat hurt. . . . Never in his two score years of desert experience had he met a man who did not enjoy coffee, or with whom coffee disagreed. . . .

Coffee! . . . One of the choicest of gifts that the Mercy and Munificence of Allah had placed at the disposal of man. . . .

Perhaps the *Sidi Adjudant* could not approve such poor stuff as the Emir had to offer? . . .

Not at all, not at all, explained the Frenchman. Doubtless there was none better than that of the Emir in all Algeria, nay in all the Sahara from Kufara to Timbuctu. . . . No, it was merely an affair of the digestion and strict injunction of the *Medécin-Majeur* against the drinking of coffee. . . .

The Emir expressed deep sympathy and great regret—the latter undeniably genuine.

However . . . the failure of hospitality could be rectified when the tea was brought. . . . That should be made entirely to the taste of the principal guest. . . . Either with or without *zatar*, which gives tea a scent and flavour so beautiful (to those who like it); thick with sugar . . . the first cup rich with amber; the second with lemon; and the third with mint. . . .

But, lo and behold!—an astounding thing—a shocking thing for any host to learn, the guest of the evening could not take *tea* either. . . . Tea had the same distressing effect upon his internal economy. . . .

This time the Emir was indeed concerned. . . . Scarcely could he believe his ears. . . . *Not take tea?* Tea of ceremony! . . . *Tea*, without which no host could honour a guest; no guest refuse without gravest discourtesy, nay, intentional insult! . . .

The Emir smiled tolerantly. His guest was of course jesting, as would be seen when the tea was brought. . . .

Meanwhile, at least five men in the tent could scarcely repress the sighs of relief they felt at the sight of the other Frenchmen who sipped and sipped, gave up their empty cups and twice accepted fresh ones. . . . Had they also refused, our plot had been frustrated.

The senior officer's refusal had filled those five with the fear that his continence had been pre-determined and enjoined upon the others. I decided that the incident was merely the outcome of his acquired or inborn mistrust of taking from an Arab host, food or drink so highly flavoured that the taste of a deleterious "foreign body" would be concealed. Also that he had no actual suspicions and had suggested none to his colleagues. . . .

Turkish cigarettes followed coffee. Turkish cigarettes, we learned, were also unacceptable to the digestion of *l'Adjudant* Lebaudy! . . .

In a quiet gentle voice, the Emir inquired whether a cigarette lighted and partly smoked by himself would be likely to disagree with the digestion of *l'Adjudant* Lebaudy.

"*Touché!*" smiled Lebaudy to himself, and hastened to assure the Emir that if there were a cigarette in this world that he could smoke and enjoy, it would be such a one—but alas, tobacco was not for him. . . .

Tea followed the cigarettes and, at last, the Emir was brought to understand that the guest of the evening actually *was* refusing ceremonial tea!

He swallowed the insult in a way which showed that he could not be insulted. Mannerless conduct hurt none but the person guilty of it. Gross discourtesy merely labels such a one as grossly discourteous. . . .

It was well acted, and the other Frenchmen hastened to show the excellence of their manners, and drained their cups—special white-ware cups for the European guests only—at each of the three ceremonial drinkings.

As the third was ended and the cups collected, strains of lively music burst from the adjoining tent, and out on to the carpet floated a cloaked, mysterious form. Her cloak being thrown aside, the lovely and enchanting figure of the Angel of Death was revealed, and *l'Adjudant* Lebaudy had evidently at length discovered a kind of hospitality prohibited neither by his doctor nor by his digestion.

That is the picture I shall never forget—the Death Angel dancing beneath the desert sky by the light of a great fire, to the insistent sensuous music, the soothing-maddening-monotonous strains of the tom-tom, the *raita*, the *derboukha* and the flute.

At a respectful distance, in staring silence, sat the soldiers of the Emir's Bodyguard, rapt, enthralled, stirred, excited.

Apart from them, French soldiers off duty—all indeed who were not actually on guard or sentry—also sat and stared, entranced, enchanted.

Only those who have not seen a woman of their own sort and kind, for years, can measure the meaning and appeal to these men of, not merely a woman, but a singularly lovely and bewitching woman, trained and experienced in every art of fascination and allure.

And undeniably the Angel moved more like a winged being from another sphere, than like a creature of flesh and blood.

As the music abruptly ceased, and her dance finished, there was a space of utter silence, followed by wild and tumultuous applause, as the Angel retired to her tent, wherein waited her negro women.

Before this tent sat Abd'allah ibn Moussa, guarding his mistress during her visit to the Emir's camp, but in a position from which he could watch me the while.

I fear that the next item on the programme, the singing of frank love-songs by an Arab youth with a beautiful voice and a remarkable repertoire, fell a little flat.

At its conclusion, the Emir gave orders for fresh coffee to be brought to us, and that yet more refreshment be served to the watching soldiers who had already been regaled with *cous-cous*, mutton-stew, sweetmeats and coffee.

Thereafter the Angel danced again, and her reappearance galvanized into fresh life and renewed interest, the now somewhat somnolent Europeans among the audience.

Again her performance was rapturously hailed and wildly applauded.

During the succeeding turn—some exceedingly clever juggling and conjuring—it was evident to a watchful eye that several of the French soldiers had lain back where they sat, as though overcome by sleep. . . .

For the third time the Angel emerged from her tent and danced, but, on this occasion, introduced a variation. From her dancing-carpet she moved across to that around which we sat cross-legged upon our cushions.

In this confined space she floated, whirling upon tip-toe.

Lebaudy's eyes shone and his lips parted. The Frenchman who sat on the Emir's other side, stared with a glazed and drunken gaze, though drunken he was not. His colleague, next but one upon his left, was frankly asleep. I watched the other *sous-officier*, and saw that he was struggling to keep awake—happy, drowsy, but desiring to see some more of this vision of loveliness before he went to sleep.

Next but one to him, the remaining *sous-officier* was making an effort to keep awake, while his head nodded abruptly at intervals, as his eyes closed and he relaxed for a second or two.

I admired the foresight of the Emir, who had so arranged his guests that they sat in a straight line to right and left of him, with Lebaudy between himself and the Wazir. Only by craning rudely forward, could Lebaudy see what was happening to his subordinates, who, so far, had not given way to snores as well as slumber. Furthermore, by no amount of craning, could he see the spot where his soldiers sat feasting eyes, ears, and stomachs.

Before *l'Adjudant* Lebaudy, the Angel paused, smiled seductively, and hovered, dancing divinely with her arms and body, while remaining stationary on the tiny spot covered by the tips of her bare toes. Anon she turned her back and bent right over until her face looked up into his. . . . French *sous-officiers* do not carry gold coins and place them upon the foreheads of appellant dancing-girls—but kisses are another matter, and, taking her face between his strong short-fingered square-nailed hands, he kissed her ardently, and again, with right good will.

With a ringing laugh, the Angel of Death swung her lithe body erect, and began to do her utmost to fulfil her name.

Before Lebaudy she danced, and with eyes for no-one else—not even for the great Emir; and we sat and watched a wonderful exhibition of purposeful seduction—seduction, fascination and captivation.

And, as was her wont, the Angel succeeded in her task. None watching the face of *l'Adjudant* Lebaudy could think of the simile of the fascination of the rabbit by the deadly serpent, but at least one watcher of this sinister drama thought of Samson and Delilah.

Before my eyes, this brave strong man weakened and deteriorated; ceased to be watchful, wary and alert; forgot his duty and his whereabouts—forgot everything but the woman before him, and succumbed.

Only two of the musicians had accompanied her to our tent, one with a two-ended little drum which he played with palm and finger-tips, the other with the *raita*, and between them and the girl was complete understanding.

I have heard the world's greatest musicians interpret the music of the world's greatest Masters, and I have been greatly moved. But never in my life has European music, rendered on European instruments, *affected* me, as did that Arab music, played upon the *raita* and the drum.

Well do the Bedouin call the *raita*, the Voice of the Devil, and I was but an onlooker, while Lebaudy was an actor in this drama of two.

I do not know for how long the girl postured, danced, beguiled, knelt beseechingly before him, sprang away ere his hands clasped her, teased, maddened, promised—all in gesture and dumb-show; but suddenly, after a quick look at four sleeping Frenchmen, she glanced at the Emir, flashing a message, 'I have done my best and can do no more,' and floated backward from us, turned, and disappeared into her tent.

As her intention of departing became obvious, Lebaudy, still but semi-conscious of his surroundings, involuntarily it seemed, rose on one knee as if to follow, remembered where he was, and sank back, "sighing like a furnace."

But only for a moment.

Distracted as was his mind from affairs mundane, he seemed suddenly to realize that he had seen something—and heard nothing.

He had seen a colleague most unbelievably asleep, and he had heard no applause.

Something was wrong. . . .

His trained military instinct of the approach of danger was awakened and, shaking off the last vestiges of the spell, he arose briskly to his feet, with a peremptory,

"Come along! Time we turned in!"—and realized that his four colleagues were all most soundly sleeping.

"*What's this?*" he shouted, half alarmed, half incredulous, and, striding across his left-hand neighbour, he nudged the nearest sleeper with his foot.

To speak more exactly, he fetched him a remarkably sound kick.

"Get up, you swine," he growled in French.

Receiving no response, he knelt swiftly, seized the man's collar, shook him so violently that his head rolled to and fro—and realized the state of affairs.

In that instant all alarm and bewilderment left him. He became as cold and hard as ice, and won my warm admiration.

Without haste or agitation, he coolly raised an eye-lid of the sleeping man, and gave a brief hard bark of disgust.

"*Drugged!* . . ." he growled in French, and glanced at the other sleepers, the only men now not upon their feet.

The raised tent-walls were lowered from without, and the *Adjudant* Lebaudy stood in a closed tent, and a circle of armed Arabs.

His hand went swiftly to a pocket, and ere he withdrew it with another short snort of disgust, I heard a voice whisper beside me. And the whisper was:

"It hath went before, Bo!"

As a guest, the *Adjudant* had worn no weapons, but he had certainly carried one, and the Wazir, his attentive host, had picked his pocket.

He was a brave man, this Lebaudy.

"Well, noble and honourable host," he said, with a bitter smile, and, with a swift change from sarcasm, added, "What's the game, you dog? You treacherous slinking jackal. . . . What now? . . . Do you hope for the pleasure of hearing me bawl for help—to my poisoned men? . . . What's the game, I say? . . ."

"One that I play with the utmost distaste, with the deepest regret, and with the profoundest apologies," replied the Emir. . . . "A game, I may add, in which you have made the wrong move . . . from my point of view, that is. . . ."

"Huh! . . . I was to be poisoned too, *hein*? . . . But I am too old a fox to be tricked by a mangy jackal. . . ."

"No, no, *Sidi Adjudant*. . . . Not poisoned! . . . No-one has been poisoned. . . . You were to have been our honoured guest—for the night—like these other gentlemen who sleep where they dine. . . ."

"And while I slept?" snapped Lebaudy. "All our throats cut? Rifles and property stolen? . . . More '*Touareg*' work, *hein*? . . ."

"No, no, again, *Sidi Adjudant*," the Emir declared "Not a throat. . . . Not a rifle. . . . Not a *mitka* worth of property. . . . It was something wholly worthless that I propose to take—a convict. . . ."

"Indeed! . . . You interest me . . ." sneered Lebaudy. "And might one venture to inquire which convict you kindly propose to liberate, and why? . . . He must have some very wealthy friends. . . .

"And the sentries . . . and the guard . . . ?" he continued. "To be stabbed in the back . . . treacherously rushed at dawn?"

"Not a stab . . . Not a shot . . ." the Emir assured him. "One or two of my Chiefs who speak French—sufficient for the purpose— were going to borrow, with many apologies, uniforms from a sleeping Sergeant and Corporal. . . . Half a dozen others, again with many apologies, uniforms from your excellent soldiers, now sleeping so soundly, as you rightly assume. . . . Everything would have been returned safe and sound and, in the morning, my dear *Adjudant*, we should all have awakened together, merry and bright, in the very places where we laid us down to sleep. . . . And by-and-bye you would have discovered that a prisoner was missing—and none so surprised as your simple Arab hosts, on learning the fact! . . . *Voilà tout.* . . ."

As the Emir spoke, the Adjudant nodded his head from time to time, a thin and tight-lipped smile distorting his face.

"And now?" he asked briefly.

"Ah . . . *now* . . . my dear *Adjudant* . . ." silkily replied the Emir, ". . . things are different. . . . You have been so wise . . . so cautious . . . so careful of your digestion . . . that you have changed my plans. . . . The 'game,' as you call it, will be a different one, and you will play the leading part in it. . . ."

"Again you interest me," sneered Lebaudy. "I might almost say you surprise me. . . . *I* shall play a leading part, *hein*? And pray what might that be? . . ."

"Listen, my dear *Adjudant*, and listen carefully—lest France have cause to mourn your loss. . . . You will lead a small party of *my* people dressed in the uniforms of *yours*. . . . You will—er— 'make the rounds,' do you call it?—reassuring each of your sentries with the countersign and the sight of your countenance, to which you will raise a hand-lamp.

"You will then proceed to the tents of the convicts, and will release the one indicated by the man who will go with you in the uniform of a Corporal, and who will hold a knife within an inch of your back the whole time. . . . That convict you will bring here. . . . I and my followers will at once depart with him . . . and we shall do ourselves the honour of inviting you to accompany us. . . ."

"And if I refuse?"

"You will accompany us all the same, my dear *Adjudant*. . . ."

"I mean if I refuse to have anything whatsoever to do with your infernal rascality? . . . To Hell with your sacred 'games.' . . . Are you a mad dog as well as a treacherous one? . . ."

"At least I am not mad, *mon Adjudant*," replied the Emir.

"But *you* are . . . if you refuse. . . . On the one hand, merely a convict the less—and *you* know how easily *they* can die, be shovelled into the sand, and struck off your roll. . . . On the other hand, the loss to France of a brave, resourceful, and, I am sure, valued officer. . . ."

"Murder, *hein*?" remarked Lebaudy.

"And worse I fear," confessed the Emir sadly.

"Torture?"

"Alas!" admitted the Emir.

"And what becomes of *you*, my friend?" sneered Lebaudy. "Are you not forgetting such trifles as the French Republic, the French army. . . . How long will you live, you treacherous rat, after this?"

"Mourn not for me, *Sidi Adjudant*," besought the Emir. "One thing at a time, and first things first. . . . Listen again, I beg—it is for the last time. . . . One of your prisoners is going to be liberated *now*, by me. . . . It will be done more quickly and more easily with your help and presence, but done it *will* be. . . . Give us that help, and I give you my word, a word I have never broken, that you shall be set free—unhurt. . . . And not only unhurt, my friend, but rewarded. . . . As you remarked, the convict has wealthy friends—and I am one of them. . . . What do you say to fifty thousand francs? . . . A fortune. . . . Would you care to leave the desert, to retire to your home in France? . . . Beautiful France. . . .And sit beneath the shadow of your own vine and your own fig-tree, a wealthy man. . . . And no harm done, mark you. . . . No betrayal. . . . No treachery. . . . No selling of the secrets of France. . . . Just an act of mercy to an innocent man. . . . What do you say, *Sidi Adjudant*? . . . What do you say to fifty thousand francs? . . ."

Profoundest silence in the tent.

Not one of the watchful circle of armed men made sound or movement. All seemed even to hold their breath as they awaited the Frenchman's answer.

"I say *nothing* to them," he shouted. "I spit on them. . . . And on you. . . . Now, you dog—lay a hand on me as I go to leave this tent, and you have assaulted a soldier of France—obstructed him in the execution of his duty. . . . Already you have bribed and threatened him. . . . *You*, calling yourself an ally of the Republic. . . . *You*, who have made a Treaty with France. . . . *You*, who have taken French gold and would use it to bribe a servant of France . . . and if I live, I will command the firing-party that shall shoot you like the dog you are. . . ."

"And if you die?" asked the Emir.

"Then with a French rope will you be hanged by another servant of France. . . ."

And upon my soul, I almost whooped "Hear, hear!"

The man was fine, as he stood there surrounded by his enemies, stood firm—wealth on the one hand, and torture on the other.

I felt sorry for Noel, for I knew how he must loathe the part he had to play, and I could not but admire the way in which he played it.

"Believe me, *Sidi Adjudant*, nothing but the sternest necessity could drive me to do this—to offer a bribe of gold or a threat of torture and death, to a soldier of France. . . ."

"Not to mention a guest, I suppose," observed the *Adjudant*. ". . . An invited guest. . . . The world famous Arab hospitality! . . ."

"Indeed if anything could further blacken my face and make more evil and distasteful my deed, it would be that fact . . ." admitted the Emir with sincerity. "By the Beard of the Prophet, and the Ninety and Nine Sacred Names of Allah, I loathe what I have to do. . . . Come, come! . . . It is but a little thing I ask. . . . Just the life of one of those wretched prisoners. . . . And let me whisper to you, a Frenchman, a man of sensibility. . . . *There is a lady in the case . . . a beautiful woman . . . a sweet and lovely lady whose heart is breaking. . . .*"

I thought for a moment that Lebaudy wavered then—but he yawned, tapped his mouth once or twice with his open hand, and with a formal:

"It grows late. . . . I thank you for your hospitality, Emir. . . . You must excuse me . . ." he turned to go.

Noel, Buddy and I seized him—and I for one, hated the job—and the others drew their knives.

"Ah! . . ." said Lebaudy.

And:

"Forgive me," said the Emir, and took him in a huge embrace as Marbruk ben Hassan, swiftly stooping, bound the Frenchman's feet together.

"*Sidi Adjudant*," said the Emir, "I detest doing this . . . more than I can say. . . . Is there any hope for a parole? . . . Give me your word to make no effort to escape, and I will not have you bound. . . . Nor shall you be gagged . . . Nor blindfolded when we shoot you—

"Help us to treat you well—To torture you, to make you aid me, would sadden me for a year—To kill you, to shut your mouth, would sadden me for a lifetime. . . ."

Noel released his grip.

The Frenchman drew back his clenched fist to strike, and his arms were instantly seized by Buddy, and pinioned behind him. "Carry him to the small tent," said the Emir, and the order was quickly obeyed.

Lebaudy made no resistance, but, the moment he was outside the large pavilion, he gave vent to the most tremendous shout I have ever heard from human lungs:

"*À moi! . . . À moi! . . .*" he bawled.

And the sound of his voice was enough to awaken the dead.

Marbruk ben Hassan and Yussuf Latif simultaneously drew their knives, and put the points of them to the Frenchman's throat and heart respectively.

"Another sound and you die," growled the Wazir.

"*Garde . . .*" roared Lebaudy instantly. And the hand of the Emir was clapped over his mouth.

"Into the tent with him, quick," he said. "The sentries may have heard him. . . ."

And in a moment, the brave Lebaudy was hustled into the tent.

"The uniforms! . . . Marbruk, Yussuf, and the rest of you . . . Quick. . . ." And all left the tent save my brother, Buddy and myself.

"Now then," he continued, addressing the *Adjudant*, and his voice and manner changed. "You saw that fire out there. . . . Suppose you were bound to a pole and fed into it, feet first? . . ."

"Then I should hardly be able to make the rounds with you, if I wanted to. . . . Even your intelligence might follow that. . . ." was the reply.

"Of course. . . . How foolish of me. . . . Thank you. . . ." replied the Emir. "We shall need your feet, as you say. . . . But we could lead a *blind* man, of course. . . . Or another idea. . . . We have ten minutes to spare while my men are dressing in the uniforms of yours. . . . Suppose we take off a finger a minute until you change your mind? . . ."

"A bright idea! . . . Guards and sentries are quite accustomed to seeing their commanding officer approach with both hands streaming blood! . . ." sneered Lebaudy.

"Well then, suppose we agree that you are incorruptible and immovable! Also that as you insist on spoiling our plans and thwarting our modest desire to take but one convict, we are going to give ourselves the satisfaction and compensation of torturing you to death as painfully as we know how. . . .

"That is as you please," replied Lebaudy, "but I shall only get for a few minutes what you will get for all Eternity, you foul dog."

"No, no, *Sidi Adjudant*! The removal of an Infidel is an act of merit on the part of a True Believer. . . ."

It occurred to me to feel glad that Lebaudy, whom my brother, of course, had no intention of injuring, much less of killing, had no suspicion that the Emir was other than he seemed. It would be a terrible blow to Mary should her husband's great drama be discovered to be farce.

"We shall know more about that later," growled the Frenchman. "What is not in doubt, is the question of your fate when my countrymen catch you. . . ."

"We shall know more about that later," smiled the Emir. "Meantime your fate takes precedence, *Sidi Adjudant*—and I will be generous. . . . For, in spite of your recalcitrance, and the trouble and annoyance you have given me, I will let you choose. . . . Shall it be the fire, feet first . . . Impalement on the sharpened trunk of a young palm . . . Or pegged out for the vultures? . . ."

The *Adjudant* shrugged his shoulders.

"It's a matter of complete indifference to me," he yawned.

And before my brother could reply, Yussuf pulled aside the curtain at the entrance to the tent.

"One came running," he said quickly, "a soldier. . . . He heard the cry of this officer. . . . We have bound him. . . . He is unhurt."

"He may have saved your life," remarked the Emir, turning to the *Adjudant*. "Perhaps he will help us in the little play-acting and give us the countersign, in return for his life."

"If he is one of my *légionnaires*, you will get nothing out of him," was the reply.

"Well, hope for the best, *Sidi Adjudant*. . . . If the man is amenable, I will not torture you. . . . Perhaps even I will not kill you. . . ."

The Emir then bade Yussuf bring four men and order them, on peril of their lives, to guard the French officer and see that none held communication with him.

He then led the way to my tent, where Marbruk ben Hassan awaited us with a bundle of French *képis*, coats, trousers, leggings, boots, side-arms and equipment.

In a surprisingly few minutes I was a French Sergeant, dark and bearded, it is true—but then the night was dark, and many of the soldiers were bearded—inspecting a guard consisting of a Corporal and eight men.

"Now then," said Noel, ". . . the captive. No need for him to see me, but he's got to see this guard. . . . You'll talk French to him, of course, Otis. . . . Also let him see, from not too near, the dead bodies of his slumbering comrades and of the *sous-officiers* in the pavilion. . . . Tell him his top-sergeant is elsewhere, tortured to death. . . . That was his dying yell he heard. . . . If he's only too glad to get his own back on the *Adjudant*, by helping, all's well. . . . If he's staunch, try fright, bribery and corruption."

"Suppose he double-crosses . . . gives us the wrong counter-sign, and lets a yell when we get into the convict camp. . . ." said Buddy.

"Well, we've got to take a chance," replied Noel. "It's up to you to be right in judging your man. . . . He may jump at the chance of gaining a few hundred francs and his liberty, especially if Lebaudy is as popular as he used to be. . . ."

"*Used to be?*" I said.

"Yes. . . . Used to be . . . when Buddy and I were in his *peloton*. . . ."

"He surely was some nigger-driver," confirmed Buddy.

"*What?* . . . When? . . ." I said. "What *are* you talking about?"

"When we were in the Legion, Son. . . . You've heard the great tale of the Relief of Zinderneuf, where Beau Geste was killed, and we started out with John Geste and his other brother, and tramped the desert for two years. . . . Well, old Lebaudy was Sergeant of our *peloton*, under our smart-Alec brother-in-law. . . . Lord, yes. . . . Lebaudy is a great old friend of ours!"

"Only he's another that don't know it . . ." said Buddy, and added:

"It surely hath been a pleasure to twist his tail this night. . . . He's give us many a unhappy night, an' I allow we've give *him* one, now. . . ."

I said nothing but thought much.

In the best Legion manner, I stepped back, rasped a "*Garde à vous! Par files de quatre. En avant! . . . Marche!*" and the drilled men of the body-guard, to whom none of this was new except their unaccustomed uniforms, moved smartly beneath the ferocious eye of the Corporal-Wazir.

We had not marched more than a few yards before I cried:

"*Halte!*"

I had had an idea, and turned back to the Emir's tent. Noel was reclining on his rugs, looking thoughtful and somewhat dejected.

"Son," he said, "I don't like it. . . . I can't sit here in safety and let you go into that camp. . . . If they pinch you, you'll never be seen again. . . . Nor Bud either. . . . The Legion wants him—just like the Zephyrs want you. . . ."

"I'm going anyhow, Noel," I said, "whether you go or not. . . . It's my privilege and my right. . . . I found him, old chap, and I'm going to save him. . . . It's you who are saving him really, but I mean—I must be there—and take the lead too. . . ."

"True, Son . . . but I don't like it. . . . For two pins I'd come along, as one of your men. . . . But I mustn't be caught and be found to be an American from the Legion—for Mary's sake. . . . And for the sake of my Arabs too. . . . I hate letting Bud go without me. . . . But I can't let you go alone with the men, and Bud insists because John came back to look for *him*! . . ."

"What did you return for?" he added.

"Why—I had an idea . . ."

"*No!*" said my brother, in feigned surprise.

"Yes, I've been thinking."

"You aren't here to think, Son. . . . You're here to obey orders, you know. . . . You go and collect the ideas of that man they've caught. . . ."

"What occurred to me," I continued unmoved, ". . . was this . . . I'm every inch a French Sergeant. . . . Suppose we put this disguised squad on their camels, and we make a little détour. . . . Then I ride in here again, at their head, and with some more of your body-guard behind us as *goumiers*. We ride in where this prisoner is, and he would at once see, with his own eyes, that we are a perfectly good French *peloton méhariste*. He'll shout for help, and you'll look guilty and confused. . . . I'll be haughty and truculent, and moreover I'll refuse to camp with you. . . . I'll have the man set flee, and tell him to lead us into the convict camp. I'll take command, in the inexplicable absence of Lebaudy and the *sous-officiers*, voice my suspicions that something is wrong, visit the sentries and tell them to be watchful. . . . Count the convicts—and bring one away with me to this camp. . . .With a good nerve and a little luck, that ought to work perfectly. . . ."

Noel smote his thigh.

"Oats," he declared, "you've said something. . . . Go and fetch Buddy. . . ."

I bade my squad—or *troupe*—"Stand easy!" and, in Arabic, told the Wazir that the Emir would fain have speech with him.

In the tent I repeated and elaborated my plan. It appealed to Buddy at once, and he preferred it to the other scheme on account of the human factor.

That was uncertain in both, but less so, perhaps, in my scheme. A bribed and intimidated man might well double-cross us—fearing the French authority more than us, and doubting whether he would ever get his thirty pieces of silver. He would probably agree to all that we suggested and then betray us—instead of his own people—as soon as we were well into their camp, and he in safety.

In a very few minutes my proposal was carried unanimously, the more readily in that none of us was at all enamoured of the debauching of a simple soldier from his duty, if it could be avoided.

"It looks water-tight to me," decided Noel. "So far, the prisoner has neither heard nor seen anything suspicious in this camp. All he knows is that they thought they heard Lebaudy shout. . . . The Corporal of the Guard, or someone, sent him down to see if anything was wanted, and he was seized and held as he came running into this camp. . . ."

"Quite right too," observed Corporal Buddy, with some indignation. ". . . Rushing into a respectable camp like this in the middle of the night. . . . Barging about like a steer at a rodeo. . . . *Course* he were arrested. . . ."

"Send a man for Marbruk ben Hassan," said Noel.

Buddy stepped out of the tent and, a few minutes later, Marbruk entered with him.

On being questioned by the Emir, it turned out that, as we hoped and supposed, the prisoner had been seized by the guard at the very entrance to the camp, had been put in the guard-tent, and could know absolutely nothing of what had occurred.

All seemed propitious for the success of my plan, and Marbruk was sent back with certain instructions to the guard—one of which was, to place the prisoner where he could see anyone who went by.

Marbruk was then to get my uniformed squad of hard-bitten dependable ruffians mounted, and to have them, with a dozen others in Arab dress, awaiting me at the opposite side of the camp.

Men and camels were of course drilled and experienced members of the Emir's body-guard, picked from his famous Camel-Corps.

"Good-bye, Son, and may God help you," said Noel, as I left the tent. "Keep cool, and act up to me and Bud, and we'll have John Geste here in an hour. . . . Now, don't forget. . . . You're an indignant and suspicious French Sergeant. . . . And you don't hold with Arabs as such. . . . You don't use language *too* frequent and free, to me, because I'm a Big Noise, and the French Government's very fond of me. . . . Still, you don't like having French soldiers arrested by Arabs, and you want to know all about it. . . . Play up, Son. . . . We'll get away with it. . . ."

His farewell to Buddy was less impressive, for, as that Corporal-Wazir turned on his heel without a word, the Emir's sandalled foot shot up and encountered ill-fitting French trousers.

Yussuf Latif ibn Fetata, in French uniform, stood at the head of my kneeling camel, his foot upon its doubled fore-leg to prevent its rising to its feet. He saluted as I approached and handed me the rein-cord.

I mounted, the camel rose, and I rode away from the camp, followed by my mixed *peloton méhariste.*

The night was dark and very still, and, at that hour—about three o'clock in the morning—*I* would willingly have been dark and very still, upon the comfortable rug and cushions of my tent. . . .

A quarter of an hour later, I approached the tents of the quarter-guard, and, as we drew near, the Soudanese sentry challenged and brought his rifle from the slope to the ready. I replied with a loud hail and the announcement that we were friends, come in peace.

The sentry turned and shouted, and from the guard-tent a powerful, mis-shapen dwarf came hurrying with a well-tended slush-lamp in his hand.

The guard turned out in fine style.

"*Franzawi!*" cried the dwarf, in great surprise. "Come in peace. . . . By Allah, is it well?"

"A *peloton méhariste Français!*" I cried. "What camp is this?

"The camp of His Highness the Emir, Sidi el Hamel el Kebir, Leader of the Confederation of the Tribes of the Great Oasis. . . ."

"Sir!" cried an indignant voice in French from the guard-tent. "I have been arrested by these Arabs. . . . Been taken prisoner, I have! . . ."

And a man in uniform struggled from the tent, closely followed by two Soudanese.

"Here! What's this?" I shouted, my voice hard with wrathful surprise. "A French soldier in uniform? By whose order was he arrested? Where's he from? . . . Send my compliments to the Emir. . . .

"Come here, you," I called to the man. "Tell me about it. . . . I'll look into this. . . ."

And with gentle taps of my camel-stick upon its neck, I brought my camel to its knees.

The light from the slush-lamp fell upon my face and upon that of the French prisoner.

"*Hankinson!*" he cried, using the name which had been mine in the Legion.

"*Sergeant* Hankinson, please!" I replied instantly, with stern reproof in my voice. "Have you gone blind, *Légionnaire* Schnell? . . ." And I brought into prominence the gold stripe on my cuff.

Yes. . . . I had been quick! . . . For once I had risen to the occasion with absolute promptitude and *aplomb*. And, by so doing, I had turned a ghastly contretemps into what might prove a piece of amazing good luck.

It was the miserable Schnell, the butt and buffoon of my barrack-room in the Legion, and, in another second, I should learn whether he had heard that I had been court-martialled and sent to the Zephyrs. It was extremely improbable, as he had gone from

Sidi-bel-Abbès to Senegal when I had gone to the Moroccan border.

"I—I—I beg your pardon, *Monsieur le Sergent*," gasped Schnell, saluting repeatedly. "I knew your voice and I recognized your face, and I called your name without stopping to look. . . . I am very sorry, *mon Sergent*."

All was well. The miserable Schnell had heard nothing.

"That's enough! Don't chatter like a demented parrot. . . . Tell me how you come to be here. . . . And where the end of the Road is. . . . That is what I was looking for. . . ."

"Oh, close here, *mon Sergent*," replied Schnell, standing stiffly to attention. "It's like this, sir. . . . The convict camp is just back there and this Arab—he's a big Chief, a 'friendly'—he gave a *fête*, a feast, and dancing-girls and all that, and invited the Commandant and *messieurs les sous-officiers*, and all men who were off duty. . . . I was on guard, and me and Schantz and Slinsky and Poggi were sitting outside the guard-tent, when suddenly Corporal Blanchard said, 'Silence, you! . . . Hark!'

"And we listened, but we heard nothing, and the Corporal said he thought he had heard the voice of *Monsieur l'Adjudant* Lebaudy. They say he has the biggest voice in the French Army. . . ."

"Oh, for God's sake," I growled, "cut it short. . . . And tell me what you are doing here. . . . You mean you assaulted some harmless Arab I suppose. . . . Or was it one of their women?"

"Oh, sir! No, no, no!" protested poor Schnell. "Corporal Blanchard said he thought he must be mistaken, but said I'd better come across and see whether everything was all-right. . . . And they arrested me. . . ."

"I suppose you came rushing into the camp like a Touareg . . . like a whole Touareg raid, a host in yourself . . ." I sneered.

"The Corporal said 'Run across,' sir, and I came *au pas gymnastique* and . . ."

"Silence!" I roared. "Don't you back-answer me, you jibbering jackass. . . . How long have you been here?"

"About half an hour, sir," admitted Schnell.

"Well, I'll have you put somewhere else, for about half a month," I bullied. "You blundering half-witted, half-baked, half-bred, half-addled, half-man you."

I was, I fear, beginning thoroughly to enjoy myself. Probably I was uplifted by excitement, hope, fear and tautened nerves. I then turned upon the dwarf.

"And you?" I stormed in Arabic. "How dare you arrest a French soldier on his way to speak with his commanding officer?"

The dwarf spread deprecating hands and shrugged tremendous shoulders.

"By Allah! A mistake . . . an accident. . . . Such fools as these Soudanese are. . . . But the *Roumi* soldier came running, and was violent. . . . His Highness the Emir will be distressed beyond words. . . . But the man was *very* violent. Some say he slew two with his bayonet . . . others say three. . . ."

"What!" I cried, "absurd! . . . Was the man drunk then?"

"Well, *Sidi*, this one was not very drunk," replied the dwarf.

"What do you mean?" I cried. "Let your speech be plain. . . . 'This one was not very drunk.' . . . Who *was* very drunk then?"

A quiet and orderly body of men, several carrying lamps, approached.

The dwarf was flustered.

"Our Lord, the Emir himself," he whispered.

And at the head of a body of Sheikhs, officers, officials, soldiers, and slaves, appeared the Emir el Hamel el Kebir.

"Please Allah! Well? . . . Come in peace! . . . The Peace of Allah be upon you!"

I saluted the Emir, military fashion.

"Health and the Peace of Allah upon you, O Emir! . . . *Le Sergent Hankinson, peloton méhariste, numero douze*, for Number One Construction Camp. . . . I saw your fire and came to ask. . . . In your camp I find a French soldier arrested and detained. . . . I have to request that you hand him over to me at once, with explanation. . . ."

"What is this, Marbruk ben Hassan?" inquired the Emir of the dwarf. His voice was harsh.

Marbruk, with low salaam, hastily repeated what he had said to me.

It appeared that the man had been very violent . . . some said five had been killed . . . or gravely injured. . . . The dwarf feared that the man had been under the influence of the strong *sharab* of the *Roumis*. . . . Fighting drunk, in fact. . . .

Indignantly Schnell denied that he had so much as seen liquor, for years.

"But how *could* he be drunk?" I interposed angrily. "Where would he get it? Do the wells then contain *sharab* in this part of the desert?"

The Emir smiled and stroked his beard.

"Nay, I never thought so," replied the Emir. "Until this day I had not thought it. . . . Strange indeed are the ways of the *Roumis*— but let us thank Allah for the diversity of His creatures. . . . Verily wine is a mocker . . . and well is it prohibited unto us. . . ."

"What is behind your speech, O Emir?" I asked. "Give me not twisted words from a crooked tongue, I beseech you. Let our speech be short and plain."

"Will the Commandant come with me a moment?" asked the Emir with quiet dignity. "And if perhaps he would bring this soldier who has seen no *sharab*. . . ."

"Corporal!" I shouted over my shoulder. "Let the men dismount and take an 'easy.' Each man to stand to his camel with rifle unslung."

And Corporal Buddy's salute and reply were the authentic thing. It would have taken a quicker brain than Schnell's to have found anything wrong with me and my *peloton*.

As I moved off with the Emir, followed by Schnell, the former remarked confidentially, but with care that Schnell should hear him:

"I did not wish to say too much in front of your men, Commandant. . . . And also I thought you would believe your own eyes more quickly than my voice. . . ."

Bidding his followers to halt and to await him where they stood, the Emir led me and Schnell to a tent.

"I regret this most deeply," he said, ". . . and I would fain have concealed it. . . . I gave a poor feast in my humble camp and invited all who cared to come. . . . It is not for me to make comment. . . . But my men are accused of arresting one who knows nothing of any drunkenness, any imbibing of *sharab* . . ." and he pulled aside the curtain of the tent.

By the light of the lamp in the tent, we beheld the distressing spectacle of three uniformed non-commissioned officers, deep sunk in drunken slumber.

I shrugged my shoulders and clucked my tongue in disgust.

"Tch! Tch! Tch! . . . And what of their men?" I asked, shame-faced and angry.

It was the turn of the Emir to shrug his shoulders.

I stirred one of the sleepers sharply with my foot, and shook the other by the shoulder (but not too violently).

"And the *Adjudant* Lebaudy?" I asked.

"Do not ask me, *Monsieur le Sergent*," said the Emir pityingly.

"Where is he? . . . I will see him. . . . I must satisfy myself. . . ."

I said sharply.

"*Légionnaire* Schnell," I added. "Remain in here until I return.
. . . Leave this tent at your peril."

The Emir led me away.

CHAPTER XVII

I returned and entered the tent, grave-faced, sad, indignant, but with the look, in my eye, of a good Sergeant who sees promotion in the near distance.

"Schnell," I said, "listen, and be careful. . . . A still tongue runs in a wise head. . . . Get you back at once to camp, and report to Corporal Blanchard that all's well here . . . *all's well*, d'you understand? . . . *Monsieur l'Adjudant* Lebaudy did not call for you. . . . He and the Sergeants are remaining longer. . . . *Remaining longer*, d'you understand? . . . Be very careful what you say. . . . I should be sorry for you if it were found that false reports—detrimental to *l'Adjudant* Lebaudy and your superior officers—were traced to you. . . ."

The good Schnell apparently understood very clearly.

"Very good. . . . Get along back then and . . . oh . . . report that a *peloton méhariste*—Sergeant, Corporal, eight soldiers and ten *goumiers*—is arriving at once. Tell Corporal Blanchard to warn the sentries. . . . I may as well have the countersign too. . . . What is it, '*Maroc*' still?"

"No, sir, '*Boulanger*,' " replied simple Simon Schnell.

"Well, be off then . . . and don't run like a mad bull into your own camp. . . . Get a bullet in your belly one of these days. . . ."

Schnell saluted and departed with speed, filled with the best intentions.

"Now for it!" I said, as we hurried forth to rejoin my circus of camels and performing Arabs.

"Great stuff! Son, you're The Goods!" whispered Noel, as he gripped my arm. . . .

I gave the order to mount, and, a minute later, I led the *peloton*, in column of files, at a swinging trot toward the convict camp.

Anxiously as I was awaiting it, the sentry's loud:

"*Halte! . . . Qui va là?*" brought my heart into my mouth.

I switched my mind from thoughts of John and Isobel—and became a French Sergeant again.

I answered, and gave the countersign in correct style—the style with which I was only too familiar—halted my *peloton*, and went forward.

"That you, Schantz?" I snapped.

"No, Sergeant," replied the man. "I am Broselli. . . ."

"Has Schnell just come into camp?" I asked.

"A few minutes ago, Sergeant," was the reply.

"Ah!" I said mysteriously, called my *peloton* to attention, and led them to the camp.

"*Halte!*" I cried at the top of my voice. "Dismount! . . . Stand easy!"

The guard turned out, the Corporal came hurrying, followed by a man bearing a lamp.

He saluted me smartly.

"Urgent and in haste," I said. "Take me to *l'Adjudant* Lebaudy, at once."

"He's over at the big Emir's camp, Sergeant," replied the Corporal. "A *fête* . . . a big show. . . . Everybody's there. . . ."

"So I gathered," I said grimly. "A little awkward if there was another raid, *hein*? However, that's the *Adjudant's* affair. . . . You in command here?"

"Yes, Sergeant. . . . I am senior Corporal," replied the man.

"Well, you'll do," I said. "They want that man back, in Zaguig. . . . The convict who says he was the only item not on the last Touareg butcher's-bill. . . . They seem to think, now, it wasn't a Touareg show at all. . . ."

"What! The convicts themselves?"

"No, fat-head. . . . They wouldn't all have killed themselves, would they?" . . . and I leant over and lowered my voice confidentially. "*Selim ben Yussuf!* . . . And his tribe one of the Allied Confederation and all! . . . Yes, that's the latest idea. . . . It was he handed the man back, y'know. . . . And there's about a dozen not accounted for. . . . Smart bit of bluff, what!"

"He hasn't a cold in the eyes, that one," opined the Corporal.

"No," I said. "Come on . . . I can't stop chattering here all night. . . . You know the man, I suppose?"

"Well . . . not to say *know* him, Sergeant. . . . I daresay I can . . ."

"All-right," I answered. "I know his ugly mug well enough. . . . I had charge of him at the Zaguig Court-martial. . . . We shall be old friends by the time they *do* make him squeal. . . ."

I turned to Buddy.

"Corporal," I snapped. "We shall be off again in a few minutes. . . . Where's that spare camel? You'll be in charge of it. . . . Tie the

man's hands behind him, and the end of the cord to your wrist. . . .
The men will mount again in five minutes. . . .

"Come on, Corporal Blanchard," I added. "That damned Court-
martial sits to-morrow."

And, preceded by the man with the hand-lamp, we marched
off, my heart beating like a trip-hammer.

Apparently this worthy soul was more observant than his
Corporal, for if he did not know the desperado by sight or by
number, he knew which tent he was in.

With a murmured, "*Tente numero B7*," he led us straight to one
of the tents.

"The bird's in here, Corporal," he said, as the sentry came to
attention.

"Fetch him out then," said Corporal Blanchard.

"And be quick about it," I snapped.

There were rustlings and growlings within, the kind of sound of
movement one might hear on stirring up a cageful of straw-couched
feral beasts, at night.

Two minutes later, the man with the lamp reappeared with the
sentry—and *John Geste . . . John Geste!* . . . ill, and broken and
worn, but still firm of lip and grim of jaw.

It was an anxious second. . . .

Just kicked from slumber and flung out into the night, face to
face with me, would he cry my name aloud in his incredulous
surprise? . . . If he did, I would take the same line that I had taken
with Schnell, but with greater sternness.

I might have known! . . . I need not have feared. . . . "*Bon chat
chasse de race.*" . . . Blood tells.

John gave me a quick look, and then stood with the surly hang-
dog convict slouch, his eyes on the ground.

"Here, you, put that lamp to his ugly mug. . . . I don't want to
take the wrong man," I snarled, giving him what cue I could, and
putting my hand beneath his chin, I rudely jerked his head up.

"That's the swine," I said. "Take him along and sling him on
the spare camel."

And we marched off.

Buddy's reception of the prisoner was not calculated to raise
suspicion in the slow mind of Corporal Blanchard.

With a business-like contemptuous roughness, he pinioned the
prisoner. And with a brief:

"*Voilà!* Undo that if you can!" he pointed with a jerk of his
thumb to the spare camel, now attached to his own.

"Get on, and enjoy your last ride in this world," he growled, "and if you so much as *look* crooked, I'll drag you behind it. . . ."

"Well, good-night, Corporal," I said to the excellent Blanchard, and mounted my camel, every second expecting that the man's detestable voice, with a tinge of respectful surprise, would utter the words for which I had been waiting from the first.

"What about the warrant, Sergeant? You haven't handed it over." Had he demanded it, as, of course, he should have done, it had been my intention to say:

"Ah, yes! Of course!"—to feel for it in my inner pocket, and—slowly, reluctantly, with growing horror, consternation, and alarm—to come to the conclusion that I had actually left it at Zaguig! I imagined Blanchard hastening to reassure his superior officer, and disclaim the slightest desire to embarrass him. . . . The warrant could be sent out with the next ration-party. . . .

In that case I would nod my agreement and offer to scribble him a receipt for the goods, as his authority meanwhile.

As I gave the order to march, another idea occurred to me, should he yet remember and yell for the warrant. I would say stuffily:

"Warrant! *You?* . . . How long have *you* been *l'Adjudant* Lebaudy I think I'll hand it to him, thank you . . ." (very sarcastically).

But the fool never thought of it at all, God bless him! *"Walk . . . march . . ."* I intoned.

The camels shuffled forward, the sentry saluted, and . . . *John Geste was free.*

§2

During the short ride between the two camps, I kept silence and stared straight ahead into the night.

I could not have spoken without disgracing myself. A choking held my throat, a smarting blinded my eyes, an acute pain stabbed my heart, and I trembled from head to foot.

Nor did I hear a word pass between Buddy and John Geste, close behind me.

I think that both, like me, had hearts too full for speech, and that John was being wary—riding, as it seemed to him, among French soldiers.

By our own guard-tent, I halted and dismissed the *peloton*, the admirable small-part characters of my caste, who hastened away to return their "properties" to their rightful owners. It would not be seemly that any good French soldier should awake to find his trousers missing.

One on each side of John, we marched to the Emir's tent, entered it, closed the opening and stood together—an Emir, a French Sergeant, a French Corporal and a convict!

Three Americans and an Englishman!

Shall I attempt to describe that meeting? . . . Tell of how John cleared his throat with a slight cough and remarked:

"Thanks awfully, you fellows. . . . These cords are very tight. . . . Anybody got a drink on him? . . ."—and collapsed in a dead faint.

. . . Of how we worked over him and brought him round, Buddy weeping freely and swearing fiercely . . . my brother, in grim silence, save when he blew his nose violently . . . I swallowing, and swallowing, and swallowing, while words of fire capered about my aching brain.

"*John Geste is free . . . John Geste is saved . . . Isobel . . . Isobel . . . Isobel . . .*"

Of how, in silence, John Geste put his left hand on my shoulder and with his right gripped mine with what strength he had left to him. . . .

Of how he did the same with Hank, saying nothing. . . .

Of how he did the same with Buddy, saying nothing. . . .

Of how we four men, stirred to our deepest depths, as perhaps never before in our lives, tried to behave as reticent white men should, with decent repression of emotion . . . though Buddy was once or twice shaken from head to foot by a spasm—followed by a torrent of shocking profanity . . . though Hank was constrained to blow his nose with a violence that shook the camp and caused Buddy to request him not to wake the Seven Blasted Sleepers . . . though John Geste, from time to time, uttered the slight cough with which he covered what would, in a woman, have been a sob . . . and I, I could not see properly. . . .

§3

There was a cry without.

The Emir sprang to the tent-door, and we heard the voice of Marbruk ben Hassan.

"Lord, *a raid on the French camp at dawn*! . . . Yacoub-who-goes-without-water hath sent in a rider. . . . Yacoub had news of a big *harka* encamped, and went thither. . . . He heard the talk around the camp-fires. . . . They are not Touareg. It is Selim ben Yussuf and his band—disguised as Touareg. . . . He knows his tribe moved north as ordered. . . . With an overwhelming rush they will stamp flat the convict camp, shouting Touareg war-cries lest any escape the slaughter and tell the tale. . . . Having slaughtered the guard and convicts, he will loot what he can of rifles, ammunition and stores. And having made another big détour will join the tribe near Bouzen. . . ."

"Man proposeth but Allah disposeth," said the Emir. "Bring me the messenger. . . ." and turned back into the tent where Buddy and I were swiftly resuming our Arab dress.

Noel quickly selected *jubba*, *kaftan*, *kaffieh*, *burnous* and head-cloth from his own stock of clothing, and John, tearing off his ragged convict dress, assumed them with speed and ease.

I remembered that he had worn Arab dress for a couple of years.

Had it ever been hidden from me, the secret of my brother's rise would now have been revealed. He thought of everything. . . . He ordered everything. . . . He foresaw everything. . . . He was cool, unhurried, supremely efficient, and the policy with which he handled the *Adjudant* Lebaudy was masterly. . . .

Yussuf Latif ibn Fetata came to the tent.

"The French soldiers are again arrayed in their uniforms, save two," and he glanced at the uniforms discarded by Buddy and myself.

"Go like the wind, good Yussuf," said the Emir, "and array those two also. . . . Take note that this bundle belongs to the man lying with three others in the big tent. . . ."

The messenger arrived in custody of Marbruk ben Hassan, and added but little to the latter's précis of his message.

We gathered, however, that Selim was counting on the Emir's being encamped ten miles off, or else on his way back to the Great Oasis, and not only unable to assist the French, but also unable to enhance their admiration and approval of his good-will and good ability in the matter of guaranteeing peace in the desert, and the policing of the new route.

To the Touareg the blame; to the Emir the discredit of inefficiency; to Selim ben Yussuf the loot, and revenge on the hated *Franzawi*. . . .

And as, with beneficent and approving smile, the Emir gave the messenger permission to retire, that ragged wisp of humanity smiled crookedly, displaying his tooth, and with profound obeisance added:

"Also Yacoub bade thy slave tell the Sidi Emir, that the attack will be made from the Zaguig side, as danger would be least expected thence. It will doubly fail because not only will the *Franzawi* be now expecting it, but Yacoub will himself ride behind the rear of Selim ben Yussuf's *harka*, and as they are about to charge, he will fire his rifle in the air."

"And be himself destroyed by the French volleys?" asked the Emir.

"Nay, Lord, he will be lying flat upon his back behind a sand-dune and his kneeling camel."

The Emir smiled and the messenger departed.

The Emir issued further orders.

"Marbruk ben Hassan," said he. "I need not give thee detailed instructions. A line of men behind a ridge across the Zaguig Road. . . . Camels twenty yards to the rear. . . . Orders to section leaders for ten rounds of rapid fire when Yacoub's rifle goes off, or your whistle blows. . . . Pickets far out, all round the camp. . . . Send out Yussuf Latif with a swift patrol, with Yacoub's messenger as guide. . . . Not a shot to be fired on peril of their lives. . . . We want to be 'surprised'—at fifty yards. . . ."

Marbruk ben Hassan, the happy light of battle on his soldierly face, departed, and the Emir turned back into the tent.

"Here's a pretty kettle of fish!" said he. "Bud, set R'Orab and all the servants to chucking water on that fire, and then on the drunks. . . . See there isn't a light in the camp. . . . You try and fetch the Sergeants round. . . . You come with me, Oats. . . . John, you lie low. . . . Go to bed, in fact, on those cushions. . . ."

John shook his head.

"Can't you find me a rifle?" he asked.

"Onto that bed with you, Boy. . . . I do most solemnly swear that I'll bind you hand and foot, if there's another word out of you . . ." and he strode from the tent.

As we hurried to the small one in which Lebaudy must have been having one of the worst hours of his life, Noel remarked:

"If I see Selim ben Yussuf over the sights of my rifle, doing the early bird, this morning, it'll be more worms than early bird for his. . . ."

The four men in charge of Lebaudy were ordered to report to Marbruk ben Hassan immediately.

"*Sidi Commandant,*" said the Emir, "no man can withstand his fate. . . . To some, good fortune; to some, bad. . . . What is written is written. . . . Your camp will be attacked at dawn. . . ."

"By *your* orders, you treacherous devil, of course. . . . I quite expected it," was the reply. "Huh! The faith of the Arab! . . . The noble untamed unsullied Son of the Desert, whose word is better than his bond! . . . you pariah cur! . . . Now we know who made the *last* raid! . . ."

"I think we do, *Sidi Commandant*—one Selim ben Yussuf. . . . It is he who will attack now. . . ."

"By *your* orders," sneered the *Adjudant.* "Do you take me for a fool—an Afflicted-of-Allah? . . . By your orders, of course. . . . I, in your power, bound hand and foot. . . . Three-quarters of my men decoyed here and poisoned . . . and my camp 'will be attacked at dawn.' . . . I've no doubt it will, you devil, you treacherous hound . . . you lousy, begging, lying oasis-thief. . . . Attacked at dawn, *hein*? . . . In other words, when you've cut the throats of everyone of us here, you and your foul gang of murderous ruffians will visit my camp with knives and pistols in your sleeves, and make a massacre—to avoid a fight . . . That'll be your 'attack.' . . . My soldiers shot in the back . . . stabbed in the back . . . butchered. . . . More '*Touareg*' work, *hein*? . . . Dead men tell no tales, *hein*? . . . And all that you may earn some gold for rescuing some rich criminal. . . .

"But you hear my last words, and remember them. . . . The arm of France is long. . . . You'll hang. . . . You'll hang—at the end of a rope, in Zaguig gaol. . . ."

"Are those the *Sidi Commandant's* last words? . . . Because, if so, I would fain lift up my own poor voice and utter one or two . . ." replied the Emir.

"Listen. . . . I have received information from my spies, that Selim ben Yussuf will attack your camp at dawn. . . . A sudden swift raid from the Zaguig side. . . . His object revenge—he does not greatly love the French, as you know—loot, rifles and sport. . . .

"As you have shown me, that would wipe out this night's work, for me, nicely. . . . I have but to saddle-up and go, with all my men —and the convict whom I wanted—and all record of my (shall I say?) impropriety of conduct, will vanish, even as will the aforesaid convict. . . ."

"*Lies!* . . . *Lies!* . . ." roared Lebaudy. "*Lies.* . . . You father of treachery and son of filth. . . . *Words*. . . ."

"Words *and* deeds, *Sidi Commandant* . . ." interrupted the Emir. "Time flies . . ." and he drew a great knife which, with its gold-inlaid hilt, worn upright in the middle of his sash, marked his rank.

"*Deeds!*" sneered the undaunted Lebaudy. "Worthy deeds! . . . Cut my throat, you Arab hero . . ." and throwing back his head, he closed his eyes.

My brother cut the cord that bound Lebaudy's feet, and set him free. Lebaudy stared incredulous.

"*Now* what's the game?" he growled.

"The game, *Sidi Commandant*, is this. . . . You jump on to a swift camel and ride with us—you to your camp to make those dispositions which will mark you as a second Napoleon—I to my men who are by now ambushed across the line of the Road from Zaguig to your camp, awaiting the attack which will come within the hour. . . .

"Meantime the very utmost will be done to revive your sleeping men, and to send them over, on camels, to your camp. . . ."

"Are you speaking the truth?" incredulously asked the astonished Lebaudy.

"Ride with me straight to where my men are protecting your camp," said the Emir.

"I will," replied the Frenchman grimly. "I shall be able to make my dispositions better when I have seen yours," he continued. "Not that I believe a word of it. . . . But I am in your power for the moment, and must play your game, I suppose. . . ."

"It would be wiser, *Sidi Commandant*," said my brother, helping the *Adjudant* to his feet.

"I will put my few men in, to stiffen your line . . . if there is a line," growled the latter.

"It will need no stiffening, *Sidi Adjudant*," smiled the Emir. "Might I respectfully suggest they be used as a mobile reserve under your command . . . reconnaissance . . . pickets . . . scouts . . . or even to cut off such retreat as will be left to friend Selim ben Yussuf. . . ."

"Seeing's believing . . ." growled the *Adjudant*. "I'll make my own arrangements, thank you. . . . And defend my own camp. . . ."

"Not with three men and a boy," smiled the Emir. "I'm going to fight Selim ben Yussuf when he attacks your camp, and you can help me as you like."

"Come on then," snapped the *Adjudant*, half-convinced. "If you are speaking the truth, they may come at any minute now. . . ."

"Arrangements have been made for their reception," said the Emir, and led the way to where the camels awaited us.

As we passed, I thrust my head into the Emir's tent, where John lay at rest upon the rugs.

He was awake.

"Look here, John—orders are that you don't leave this tent till we come back. . . . That'll be all-right, won't it? . . . Then I can push off with Noel and help save the French camp. . . . He's hopping mad that that young swine, Selim, should have gone on the war-path like this. . . . And on the one and only night when the French can't look after themselves—thanks to Noel himself!"

"Why, no, Vanbrugh, I'm not going to sit here, if Hank and Buddy are going out scrapping . . . I'm coming too. . . .

"Didn't I come out to Africa to save *those two*?" he laughed, "and now I've *saved* them, do you expect me to let them out of my sight—scrapping around in the dark and all?"

I grinned at this John Geste.

"Well, and didn't *I* come out to Africa to save *you*?" I asked. "And now I've saved you, do you expect me to let you out of my sight—scrapping around in the dark and all?"

"Better go together then," was the reply.

"Not a bit of it. . . . I must go and back my brother up, and you must have the decency to remember that it's cost us all no end of time and trouble to put you where you are—and you've got to stay put."

"Oh, well, of course," replied John Geste, "if you put it like that. . . . All I can say is—what I said before . . ." and here he laughed out-right, "we'll go together. . . ."

And we went together—a pair of perfectly good Arabs following their Emir.

§4

A short ride brought us to where we were challenged by one of Marbruk ben Hassan's vedettes, and, a few minutes later, we were being led by Marbruk himself, along the line of his ambush-defence.

If Yacoub's information were correct, and Selim and his raiders were going to attack in this direction, it would probably be Selim's last exploit, and the end of his career of treachery to the

French.

The wily and experienced Marbruk had proceeded sufficiently far from the camp to be at a spot where the raiders would still be riding in a crowd. A little nearer to the camp, and they would have spread out into a line—a line that would have outflanked Marbruk's, and soon become a circle completely enveloping the camp.

Already a scout, mounted on a fine Arab horse, had ridden in with information which entirely corroborated that of Yacoub—a *harka* some two to three hundred strong, had ridden toward the line of the Zaguig-Great Oasis Road, and, turning half-right, had swung on to it.

Having seen this, the scout had galloped back at once.

Adjudant Lebaudy grunted, and, with a guide, rode hard for his camp.

A quarter of an hour later, as I sat beside John, behind the ridge —possibly the most triumphantly happy person in the world—and wished the wretched Selim would hurry up, for I was very cold,—a rifle cracked.

I scrambled to the top of the ridge and looked over.

"Hullo!" said John. "What do you put that at—five hundred yards?"

"Or nearer," I said. "Now Noel will let them know that they don't surprise the camp, whatever else they do. . . . Nasty four-o'clock-in-the-morning shock for Selim. . . ."

A whistle blew near-by. A few minutes later a couple of short blasts were blown, and a crashing volley was fired from a distant section of the ridge.

Almost simultaneously, other volleys followed from other sections, and then the ceaseless banging of rapid independent fire from a hundred rifles.

A pandemonium of noise broke out from what had been the silent mysterious space in front of us . . . a noise to which wounded men and camels contributed, as well as every subordinate leader who had anything to shout—their cries varying in portent from charge to flight. Some I believe did one, and some the other, for I certainly saw vague blotches of white receding, while vague forms loomed up quite near.

A whistle blew loudly, a long strong blast, and all firing ceased. It blew again twice, and volley upon volley banged clean and crisp. The fire-control was astonishingly good.

The whistle blew again. From our front a few rifles cracked irregularly, and what other sounds could be heard indicated the retreat of our assailants.

"Got a bellyful, as well as a nasty shock!" observed John, as he jerked the empty shell out of his rifle.

"Hullo! There's a side-show," he added, as brisk firing broke out on our left-rear.

Evidently Noel had issued orders, for a section of men, running down the slope, mounted their camels and rode off, followed by myself and John.

Flashes were coming from distant sand-dunes on our left-front. The camel-section was halted in line, the men dismounted, and, a couple of minutes later, were enfilading the crest of the occupied sand-dune.

Undrilled, undisciplined and without any but mob-tactics, this body of raiders, who may have been an independent private effort, or a feint by Selim ben Yussuf, retired in a body to another sand-dune, offering an admirable target in the growing light, as they did so.

Commanded by Lebaudy in person, a small French party pursued in skirmishing order—there was always a number dashing forward and there was always a number firing—and drove them across our front.

As they retreated toward the main body, and in fact, finally fled in that direction, our line swung half-right, prolonging Lebaudy's line until both prolonged that of the Emir, and the whole advanced in skirmishing order from both flanks.

The Emir's aim and object was not, of course, slaughter, nor even the most severe and crushing defeat that could be inflicted upon Selim ben Yussuf. What he wanted to do was to defeat this attack, and in such a way that there would be no fear of its repetition until the French were in a position to deal with it themselves. Selim ben Yussuf's plan had most signally failed, thanks to the presence of the Emir's forces; the raiders were on the run, and the Emir's Camel Corps would keep them on the run. By the time the latter called a halt and returned to their camp, Lebaudy's force would be in a position—and a condition—to deal with any subsequent trouble.

As our line skirmished forward, a long low hill that lay at right-angles to the battle line, cut off Lebaudy's flank from our view. This long low hill, or high ridge, was about a mile in length and a half-section of our men advanced along it's narrow top. Suddenly one of these went running back to where his camel knelt, while another signalled "Enemy in sight," in spite of the fact that there was a retreating enemy in sight of all of us, in one direction or another. The signaller's meaning was made clear, however, when the messenger arrived at a lumbering gallop, and told his tale. Riding to where the Emir sat on his gigantic white camel, on top of a sand-dune, he told how there had been a sudden lightning raid, a veritable hawk-swoop, on the left flank of the line. A band of picked fighting-men mounted on the finest camels, and led by Selim ben Yussuf himself, had made a détour, and had approached unseen, by riding up a deep wadi and between high sand-dunes. They had approached sufficiently near the French flank to launch a charge and drive it home with terrific impact, before the flank-section could be swung back into line to meet them. The enemy, using shock-tactics, had broken and scattered Lebaudy's men, and, by the time Marbruk ben Hassan had got the flank-section of the Camel Corps in position to protect his flank and prevent the line from being rolled up, the raiders had wheeled about and fled.

"Fled?" said the Emir. "Then why all this chatter?"

"Yes, fled," said the messenger, and added deprecatingly and as though he were to blame—for every Oriental loathes to be the bearer of bad tidings—"They have taken the French officer with them."

Selim ben Yussuf had captured Lebaudy The Emir raised himself in the saddle and looked behind him.

"Horse," he shouted in a voice that would have done credit to Lebaudy himself, and waved a beckoning arm. Within a minute, his standard-bearer was beside him, and sprang from the back of the magnificent stallion that was the Emir's favourite.

"Oats," he said to me, as he sprang into the saddle, "find Buddy quick, and tell him I am chasing Selim, who's got Lebaudy. Tell him to follow with Yussuf Latif's section. He'll get his direction from the men on that ridge," and he bade the messenger ride back to the hill-top and watch. As he finished speaking, the Emir dashed off like a racing Centaur.

While I watched him go, I was struck by the disquieting thought that, riding at that pace in pursuit of camels, he would very soon overtake them. A camel will always beat a horse in the long-run, but not in the short. The speed is with the horse and endurance with the camel. To me it appeared inevitable that my brother would overtake Selim ben Yussuf and his cut-throats, long before he had the support of the section that was to follow him. . . .

I quickly found Buddy, in command of the right flank of our line, and following on his camel, with critical eye, the orderly and regular advance of his dismounted skirmishers. I shouted the news to him and, as he shook his camel into movement and wheeled off, he shouted:

"S'pose the old fool thinks he is going to hunt 'em about with a stick! . . . Chase after him, Son. . . . I'll be along in two minutes. . . . Wish we'd got some more horses. . . ."

CHAPTER XVIII

As I turned to go, I discovered that John had disappeared, and guessed that he was already trailing Noel. Urging my camel to its top speed—an undeniable canter—I took the straightest line for what I supposed to be the scene of the coming conflict. This took me across the ridge from which the messenger had come. From this eminence I could see, in the clear morning light, the fleeing band of camel-riders, a galloping horseman quickly overtaking them, and a solitary rider urging his camel in pursuit—Selim ben Yussuf and his raiders, my brother, and John Geste.

Careering in break-neck fashion down the slope of the ridge, I saw much of what then happened, and learned the remainder later from John and my brother.

§2

At the head of the fleeing raiders, rode Selim ben Yussuf on his famous horse. Its speed was restrained to that of the camels. By him, on a giant camel, also famous in that part of the desert, rode his cousin, one Haroun el Ghulam Mahommed behind whom the unfortunate *Adjudant* Lebaudy hung across the camel like a sack of potatoes, his arms bound to his sides and his feet tied together—a most undignified, painful, and dangerous situation, In a close group round this camel, rode the remaining dozen or so of Selim's selected ruffians, some of whom found time in the lightness of their hearts and the heaviness of their hatred, to award the unfortunate *Adjudant* a resounding blow with a *mish'ab* camel-stick, or a violent prod with the butt end of a spear. Suddenly, one of the raiders, hearing the drumming of a horse's hoofs behind him, looked over his shoulder and then shouted to his leader.

Selim ben Yussuf looked round, saw, and understood.

Wheeling out from his position in front of the camels, he shouted "*Ride on*," and, lowering his spear-point, charged head-long at the Emir.

Had the latter also carried a lance, the beholders would have seen a tournament like that of the knights of old—a combat belonging rather to the days of Saladin and Richard Cœur de Lion, the days of chivalry, when foemen met in single combat, man to man, horse to horse, and spear-point to spear-point. The Emir, however, carried only the Arab sword which he always wore, and an automatic pistol in a holster attached to the sword-belt which he wore round the sash beneath his *burnous*. . . .

Almost in the moment of impact, the Emir, a most perfect and powerful horseman, checked his horse, pulled it back on to its haunches and wheeled it from the line of attack—so deftly, so exactly, and so absolutely at the right second, that not only did the lance-point merely tear his wind-blown *burnous*, but the furious charge of his assailant missed him completely.

He drew his sword, but not his automatic, and spurred his horse at Selim as the latter was wheeling about, to return to the attack. It was too late for the Arab to attempt to charge, for the horse and man were upon him, and he could only lower his spear-point, that his charging opponent might impale himself upon it. The Emir's sword flashed down with tremendous force, and the deflected lance —either cut through or broken—was dashed from Selim's hand. Again checking and swerving his horse, the Emir wheeled away and gave Selim ben Yussuf time to draw his sword. Had he unslung the rifle from his back, the Emir would have shot him.

Selim spurred his horse and, rising in his stirrups, delivered a downward out at the Emir's head. The Emir parried, feinted like lightning, and, in his turn, aimed a downward stroke at the head of Selim. Selim parried, but a downward blow from the mighty arm of the huge Emir, delivered with all his strength as he stood in his stirrups, was a different thing from a stroke delivered by the slight but wiry Arab.

It was parried correctly enough, but Selim's sword was struck from his hand as though by a thunderbolt, and the Emir's weapon smote him a heavy glancing blow that caused him to reel in the saddle. Instantly the Emir, dropping his sword, grappled the Arab in his great hands, dragged him from his saddle, dropped him to the ground and fell heavily upon him. For the moment, Selim ben Yussuf was out of action and had ceased to interest himself in the phenomena of this world.

Rising, the Emir took the stunned man's rifle, slung it over his own back, and then took the reins of both horses. Mounting his own, and seeing John Geste and myself approaching, he again galloped off in pursuit of the retreating raiders. It was not long before his race-horse of a charger again brought him near to the band of camel riders. There was now no horseman to meet him on equal terms and charge him, lance in hand. As he drew near, two or three of those whose slower camels kept them in the rear, turned in their saddles and opened fire. But it takes a somewhat better marksman than the average Arab raider, to hit a man on a galloping horse, when shooting from the back of a trotting or cantering camel; nor did the plan of halting and dismounting appeal to any of these stragglers, in view of the fact that he would almost inevitably be cut down or shot, in the act of doing so.

With a wild whoop, and raised automatic, into and through the fleeing band, the Emir dashed. Men shouted, swung long lances round, un-slung long guns, drew swords, fired rifles, wheeled outward from the pursuing Vengeance—did anything but halt.

"*Ride on*" was their last order, and their very present inclination. At anyone who shot, cut or thrust at him, the Emir fired, and, in a tenth part of the time that it takes to tell, he was beside the leading camel—that of Haroun el Ghulam Mahommed. With a curse, the raider thrust his rifle sideways and downward and, without troubling to bring it to his shoulder, fired. Although the muzzle was not a yard from the Emir's body, the bullet missed him, thanks to the movements of both horse and camel. But an automatic pistol is different, and the robber Haroun el Ghulam Mahommed died, as he would have wished to die, weapon in hand and facing his man. With him died his camel which the Emir instantly, though reluctantly, shot through the head—and the band swept on, leaving behind it, its fallen leader, its best camel, and its prisoner, *l'Adjudant* Lebaudy.

The half-hearted attempt at a rally and a stand was quickly abandoned as the orderly line of the section of the Emir's famous Camel Corps, riding at top speed, came into sight.

§3

L'Adjudant Lebaudy interested me greatly that night, when he returned the Emir's hospitality.

He was not a man of breeding, culture and refinement, but he was a man of courage and tenacity; he was not what is called a gentleman, but he was a strong man. He may have been a petty tyrant, but he was not always and wholly petty. He somewhat pointedly assured the Emir that the latter could drink his coffee without fear, and that he could please himself as to whether he slept where he dined. He was grimly jocular, and his jokes were not always in the best taste, but when we rose to depart, he shook

hands with the Emir, stood to attention, honoured him with a
military salute, and said:

"You are a brave man, Sidi Emir. You should have the
Medaille Militaire for what you did this morning. Instead, you have
my complete forgetting of all that happened before dawn to-day.
. . . And if there should be a prisoner missing, I shall notify the
authorities that it is extraordinary that only one has been killed.
Goodbye, Emir el Hamel el Kebir."

Yes, an interesting man, our friend *l'Adjudant* Lebaudy, and
true to type, save that he was perhaps a little bigger than most of
his kind, and capable of a certain generosity and magnanimity.

My story grows long—and it might be very, very long indeed.

We set out, next day, for the Great Oasis. Here I did what I had
hardly expected ever to do—embraced and warmly kissed my
sister's maid, Maud Atkinson—now my sister-in-law and something of a desert princess.

I should love to have time and space to detail our conversations
and to describe our Maudie in her new rôle. She obviously
worshipped Noel, and confided to me that, much as she loved
Sheikhs, she was, on the whole, glad that her Sheikh-like lord had
proved (by slow degrees) to be a white man. Repeatedly she
assured me that he was a "one," and when, at length, the dear girl
realized that I was Noel's own brother, and her own brother-in-law,
she could only ejaculate a hundred times:

"Fancy that now! . . . Whoever would have thought it! . . . I
can't hardly believe it!"

*　　*　　*　　*　　*　　*　　*

I will not describe the solemn *mejliss* in which Noel took leave
of the assembled Sheikhs of his own and other tribes, after telling
them that he was going on a long journey to visit his allies the
Franzawi, nor of the really heartrending and pathetic farewells
between him and the men with, and for, whom he had striven and
worked and schemed and fought.

But, at length, a large well-equipped and well-armed caravan
set out from the Great Oasis, and with it went Marbruk ben Hassan
and Yussuf Latif ibn Fetata in command of the fighting men of the
escort; and, in time, by slow stages and by devious ways, the
caravan arrived and encamped not far from a town into whose fine

harbour came the ships of many nations—as they had done since the days of the Phœnician tramp and the Roman trireme.

On to a ship flying the French flag, my companions dared not go; and decided to voyage forth beneath either the American or the British flag, according to which entered the harbour first, for the sooner they were away the better.

To the delight of Noel and Buddy, it was an American ship that came—a huge vessel carrying a few hundred tourists and returning to New York from Japan, visiting the ports of the Southern Mediterranean, as she had visited those of the Northern shore, on her outward voyage. A cable to Isobel ensured that she would be awaiting John on the landing-stage at New York.

§4

I feel that I have not told all that I should have done, about John Geste. . . .

This dear wonderful John Geste. . . . This true brother of Beau Geste and of Digby Geste. . . . This man who could not settle down in happiness even with Isobel,—the wonderful and glorious woman who had given my life a purpose, my mind a lifelong dream, my soul a *beau idéal*—could not live even in that Paradise that her presence made for those she loved, while his friends were stranded where he had "deserted" them. . . . The man who loved Isobel so deeply and truly and nobly, as he most surely did—to *leave* her, after he had incredibly won back to her—to leave her, with little probability that he would see her face again! This is the greater love.

Poor John Geste. . . .

I was almost amused—grimly, sadly amused, when he again tried to thank me and to say good-bye, on that last night.

His repressed emotions, his repressed British soul, almost escaped. His British public-school reserve almost melted. . . .

He, Noel, Buddy and I, had eaten our last supper together, and in silence smoked the last pipe of peace. As the time drew near for us to seek our sleeping-rugs, John Geste rose to his feet, stretched himself and yawned most unconcernedly, and strode from the tent.

As he did so, he glanced at me, and with a jerk of his head, bade me accompany him. I rose and followed him as he strode out towards the cliff. Suddenly he wheeled about.

"Vanbrugh," he said, as he held out his hand. "I want to say

. . ." and his sudden spate of words ended in the little nervous cough that, in him, indicated strong feeling.

"What I want to try to tell you—" he began again, and got no further.

I would not help him. He was suffering an agony of emotional discomfort, and was utterly inarticulate. But I, too, was suffering an agony of pain, misery and grief.

He was going back to Isobel; and I—to the Angel of Death. . . .

I had grown to love him as much, I believe, as one man can love another. I had saved him. By God's grace and mercy and help, I had saved him, and kept my word to Isobel. . . . Yes, I loved him, but I would not help him.

And more than anything I wanted to see whether he would be able to "let himself go."

For myself, I somehow felt that had our positions been reversed, and had he been sending me back to Isobel, I should have embraced him. I should not have been able to refrain from hugging him. . . .

Not so John Geste.

"What I mean, Vanbrugh," he tried again, "is that. . . .

"Well. . . . You understand, don't you. . . . You know what I mean. . . ."

And I heard my knuckles crack, as his grip tightened, and he said it all in four words.

"My God! . . ." he ejaculated. . . . "Er. . . . Oh! . . .

"*Stout fella!*"

§5

For the sake of his followers, Noel decreed that the three were to remain Arabs until the ship sailed. Those of the passengers, if any, who saw three Arab Sheikhs and a heavily-veiled Arab woman arrive, must have been more than a little astonished to behold them, next day, in the ready-made reach-me-down garments of "civilization," previously purchased in the town.

To this day I hate to think of that parting.

In one way, it was wonderful as being the consummation of a life's work, or rather of the work for which I had been born; in another way it was terrible, tragic, unbearable.

I admit I was tempted—horribly tempted—and I thought it was fine of the other three to say nothing whatever to shake my resolution. They knew that I had given my word, and they would not ask me to break it, and when the Devil whispered in my ear, "A dancing girl—a half-caste, half-savage thing from the bazaars of Bouzen. . . . She doesn't expect it of you" . . . I clung grimly to my poor honesty, and replied, "It's not a question of what she is, but of what *I* am;—and I do expect it of me." But it was a hard struggle. Nor was my misery lightened by the sights and sounds around me, as the ship steamed out of the harbour.

On a cliff, a mile or two from the town, my brother's followers abandoned themselves to such transports of grief as I have never witnessed before nor since.

With Oriental lack of restraint, they wept—literally rent their clothing, and exhibited every symptom of unappeasable misery and heart-breaking grief. Brief—perhaps as brief as violent—but starkly genuine and very terrible.

It was long enough in the case of a man called el R'Orab, my brother's body-servant, and caused his death. From the moment that he took leave of his master, he neither ate nor drank nor spoke a word. He went about his duties until he collapsed from weakness, and in his weakness he died, refusing even water. Pitiful and absurd as such conduct may seem to the European, it was highly approved by the Arabs, not one of whom dreamed for a moment of urging the man to eat or drink.

Just before he died, he painfully raised himself from his prayer-rug and, seizing the hand of Yussuf Latif ibn Fetata, who, with the help of Marbruk ben Hassan and myself, was nursing him, said:

"We shall never look upon his face again."

Apparently this statement—regarded as inspired because spoken by a dying man—was the last straw upon the load of unhappiness borne by the fated Yussuf Latif.

That night, he left his sleeping-place beside Marbruk and myself, and was seen by a sentry to go forth and stand beneath the stars, his arms out-stretched towards the East. With a loud and anguished cry of "*Leila Nakhla! . . . Leila Nakhla! . . .*" he plunged his knife into his heart, and ended the tragic life that had now become insupportable. . . .

My own parting with Marbruk ben Hassan and the rest, near Bouzen, did nothing to cheer my depressed and miserable spirit, and it was in a most unenviable frame of mind that I rode away with Abd'allah ibn Moussa toward the camp of the old Sheikh Yussuf ben Amir at the Oasis of Sidi Usman.

Abd'allah ibn Moussa was to ride in and discover if the Death

Angel was still under the old Sheikh's protection, or whether she had returned to The Street, in Bouzen.

We camped, that night, beneath some palms, a far-outlying picket of the great host of trees of the Sidi Usman Oasis, and after a meal of dates, unleavened bread, and curded cheese as hard as stone, Abd'allah ibn Moussa rode off, bearing the message that I had seen my friend set sail, and that I was here to fulfil my promise; also that Selim ben Yussuf was a prisoner in the hands of the French at Zaguig.

At the close of one of the most miserable days that I have ever spent—somehow uncheered even by the realization that I had saved John Geste and sent him back to Isobel—Abd'allah returned. The Death Angel was in the tents of old Yussuf ben Amir. Apparently she went almost mad with joy at the news of my return, and Selim's capture. She was coming out on the morrow, with a small caravan of her own, to where Abd'allah and I now were. Her message to me was:

"Await me there. I send you my heart and my soul, and my life. I have given Sheikh Yussuf ben Amir that which has made him the happiest man in the Sahara, and my slave for ever—that Hair of the Beard of the Prophet that the Sultan brought from Mecca and gave to my Mother. I have done this to show you that I have given up Allah, and now belong to God altogether, and am a perfect Christian because you, my husband, are one."

It may be believed that I did not sleep that night. Perhaps I subconsciously feared somnambulism, and that I should arise and ride for my life, even while I slept.

§6

She arrived next day.

Certainly her own resources, and those of Sheikh Yussuf ben Amir, had been strained to their uttermost, judging by the pomp and state in which she travelled. Quite a small village of tents sprang up, as I saw when, at the invitation of her messenger, I rode over to the spot where she had pitched her camp. That the Sand Diviner's words might prove true in every detail, it had been her whim that I should come riding into her camp, and that she should run forth from her tent to welcome me.

In her present manifestation she was wonderful—gentle, sweet, submissive, and most obviously longing to be "good"—to play the rôle of civilized and Christian gentlewoman, and be wholly the white daughter of her white father.

It was piteous and pathetic.

Her plan was that we should go to Bouzen, where we should at once be married by a missionary, either Catholic or Protestant, or both if I liked. There she would get her jewels and instruct her Bank—as she was, I learned, quite wealthy. From Bouzen we were to go to Algiers and become European in every detail. From Algiers we were to take ship for Marseilles and become more fashionably European. From Marseilles we were to proceed to Paris and become the last word in European fashion.

We were then to live happy ever after, wheresoever I preferred, but the further we were from Africa, the happier she would be.

Poor little soul

A great feast was provided in the evening, and when we could eat no more, we sat together upon the wonderful cushioned rugs with which her tent was beautifully provided. And when I, unintentionally, evinced my unconquerable weariness, she bade me retire to the tent which she had provided for me, and sleep my last sleep as a lone and unloved man. As I rose to go, she held forth her tiny hands, and, as I took them, drew me down beside her.

From her neck she took the curious book-like amulet which was her most cherished possession and, putting its thin gold chain over my head, bade me wear it next my heart, for ever. That it would shield me from every danger was her deep certainty and sure conviction.

"My darling husband," she whispered, "I feel in my soul—yes, from the very depths of my soul—that this will save you. . . ."

It did. . . .

With her impassioned kisses warm upon my lips, I retired to my tent and threw myself down upon its sumptuous bed of cushions. The previous night I had not slept at all, and life had been a burden and a misery since I had said "good-bye" to John two weeks ago—two weeks that seemed like years.

I was too tired to sleep. The hours dragged by with leaden feet. Tossing and turning, groaning and cursing, I longed for daylight— and longed that it might never come.

Sitting up, I fingered the locket-amulet, now denuded of its greatest and most sacred of all Arab charms the (doubtless genuine) Hair of the Beard of the Prophet, but still enriched by its (doubtless equally genuine) Christian relic, the splinter of the wood of the True Cross.

Better not to open it now, by candlelight—as she herself had once said, the tiny splinter of wood might fall out and be lost—a loss that I could bear, but one which would probably trouble her beyond measure. . . .

But open it I did. Why, when I had just definitely decided not to do so? The psychologist can, of course, give the reason. I cannot. I know that my fingers opened the locket without any conscious instructions from my brain. I looked at the lovely face, beautifully painted on ivory—of "Zaza Blanchfleur," the Ouled-Naïl dancing girl, whom mighty Rulers had loved, and who had loved an ordinary Englishman, who had deserted her.

Almost in the same second I glanced at the other face, the face of that same man "Omar, the Englishman," the father of the Angel of Death.

I then closed the locket and sat awhile in thought. During that half-hour, my mind was as a leaf upon the sloping surface of a whirlpool; as a straw in an eddy of wind; nay, in a cave of all the winds, blowing in every direction at once.

Twice or thrice I rose to my feet, and then sank back upon my cushions.

Finally I rose, scribbled the Death Angel a message of four words, in French, on a scrap of paper, dressed myself fully, and crept forth like a thief in the night. This was not the camp of the Emir el Hamel el Kabir, or it would have been impossible for me to do what I then did. No wakeful sentries moved, watchful and alert upon their beat; none listened, stared, and challenged. Apparently not a soul was awake in the camp, except myself.

Creeping like a sneaking jackal to where the camels knelt, I thanked God that mine and Abd'allah ibn Moussa's were tethered in charge of our own camel-men, apart from the rest. With ungentle toe, I roused the man who had been in charge of my camel, ever since he became mine, and bade him saddle both it and Abd'allah ibn Moussa's beast. If I took this man with me, he could tell no tales in the morning.

A few minutes later, the camel-man and I were travelling at maximum speed in the direction of Bouzen.

CHAPTER XIX

Arrived at Bouzen, I gave the camel-man money and a letter for the Death Angel, and bade him await me for three days in the market-place, and, at the end of that time, to take the camels back to Abd'allah ibn Moussa and tell him that I had gone on a journey.

I went straight to the railway station and, squatting down, awaited the train for Algiers, as many other Arabs were doing. Arrived at Algiers, I walked warily, gradually accumulating a European outfit, and storing it in the second-rate, or perhaps twenty-second rate, hotel, in which I lived in the native quarter of the city.

It was a different Otis Vanbrugh, who now shuffled about Algiers in *burnous* and heel-less slippers, from that Otis Vanbrugh who, ages and æons agone, had descended from his Mustapha Supérieur hotel to escort his sister on her visits to the romantic Oriental bazaars.

In the crowd, hooded and bearded as I was, I was perfectly safe; and in restful peace and safety, I abode until the day when, having paid my bill, I went back to my room, shaved my face completely, dressed myself in my European clothes, seized my suit-case and grip, and marched straight out of the house, picked up a ramshackle carriage and drove to the quay where the good ship *Hoboken* awaited me and divers other items.

By way of Oran, Marseilles, Gibraltar and Tangier, she ploughed her uneventful way to New York, and, as in a dream, rather stunned and stupid and mechanical, I stepped once more upon my native soil.

My desire was to get home at the earliest moment and to hear, once and for all, that John had, at last, safe and sound, whole and hale and hearty, reached Isobel, and turned her life from a nightmare of suffering into a reality of happiness indescribable.

I endured the long, long train journey; I endured the apparently longer journey by stage; and the third and penultimate lap, by hired buggy, which brought me to where I was right welcome to a night's shelter and the loan of a good horse.

I started at dawn next morning, and a couple of hours' ride brought me on to my Father's land. By afternoon, I sighted the Ranch House, and, soon afterwards, drew rein by the great verandah on which the family spent the major part of what little time it lived indoors.

"Morning, Oats," drawled my brother, without rising from the rocking-chair in which he was seated.

"Hullo, Boy," spake the voice of Buddy, and, as my sun-dazzled eyes penetrated the shadow of the deep verandah, I saw that I had arrived in time to interrupt a family conclave.

There sat my Father, mighty, massive, domineering and terrible as of old, glaring at me with an expression which appeared to rebuke the presumption with which I dared present myself before him unheralded. Obviously he was in a towering rage.

Before him, miserable and shameful culprits, stood Buddy and my sister Janey, tightly clasping each the other's hand—Buddy white under the stress of some emotion, his eyes blazing, his mouth a lipless gash in his set face—Janey, of course, wilting and drooping, and dissolved in tears.

"*Otis*," cried Mary's voice, and she dashed forward from the side of a tall dark man arrayed in smart riding kit—the wide-cut tight-kneed style of which our Western horsemen are supposed to despise—and, without quite believing my eyes, I saw that it was her husband Major de Beaujolais. . . . (But of course it had been Mary's intention to bring him, sooner or later, to see her home, and something of the life that she had lived almost to the time that she had met him.) Dismounting and dropping my rein over the horse's head, I took Mary in my arms for a brief sound hug, and then followed her up the steps into the verandah.

"What's the row?" I whispered before turning the corner, to enter the grim presence of my irate parent.

"Janey wants to get engaged to Noel's friend Buddy," she whispered. "Says she'll die if she doesn't. Dad says she'll die if she does—and without his blessing—die of poverty, misery, shame, hunger, Father's curse, domestic slavery in a log cabin, disgrace, remorse, housemaid's knee. . . . Puritan Father . . . Scarlet Letter . . ."

"In fact, Dad says '*No*'—and there's an end of it, eh?" I asked.

"Of course," replied Mary. "Naturally he'd say '*No*,' and there'd naturally be an end of it! . . . Who's *Janey*—to dare to breathe, if Dad says she mustn't."

"And Buddy?" I asked.

"He's torn between a longing to pull his gun on the old man before doing a Young-Lochinvar-*into*-the-West with Janey, and his fear that Janey will never speak to him again if he dares be so impious and blasphemous as to thwart our so-religious Dad."

"So she'll either die of thwarting Buddy by obeying Dad, or else of thwarting Dad by obeying Buddy, eh?" I observed.

"That's the position," agreed. Mary, "and before Dad's much older, he's going to hear something."

"From whom?" I asked.

"*Me*," said Mary, with jutting chin, "and Noel. . . . Saintly old man! . . . While boundlessly hospitable to my husband, he is far from cordial, in fact barely courteous, and alludes to him—not in his hearing of course—as 'that Godless Frenchman,' or 'that foreign idolater.' He gets more holy-righteous, every day! . . . But come on, or he'll think we're conspiring, if you don't come and prostrate yourself before him."

I greeted my Father with a respectful warmth and cordiality that I did not feel, and received a grunt and a contemptuous stare in reply. The old man certainly was in a rage, and in one of his most violently autocratic and overbearing moods.

I kissed Janey, and also gave Maudie a warm fraternal embrace, wrung Noel's hand and that of Buddy, greeted de Beaujolais diffidently—and selfishly obtruded my own affairs immediately. The other matter could wait and I could settle it.

"John safe?" I asked.

"Oh, sure," was the reply.

"And with his wife?" I asked.

"Right there," was the reply from Noel.

"England, I suppose?"

"They wasn't, an hour ago," drawled Noel.

"Where are they?" I said, mastering a desire to hit him.

"Now be reasonable, Son. How should I know where they are?" replied Noel. "They went riding together about an hour ago, and at the present moment they may be here or there, or somewhere else. . . . She met us at New York," he continued, "and as there wasn't a suitable ship for a week, and John was ill, we just naturally brought them along here."

"Then I may see them at any moment?" I gasped.

"You certainly may, Son, at any moment or any other moment."

I sat down heavily on the nearest chair, for all my strength had suddenly gone, and my knees were trembling.

I might see Isobel at any moment! . . . And John Geste! . . . Should I mount my horse again, and ride . . . and ride . . . and ride . . .?

I could not ride away from myself, if I rode away from her.

No, I would see Isobel, *once* again. . . .

What was that booming, in my ears? Of course, the voice of my Father.

"And that's that," he was roaring, "and let me hear not another word about it, Janet. . . . And as for *you*, my friend, you can get out of this just as quick as the quickest horse will take you—and don't you come on to this ranch again until you are quite tired of life. Get me? Good afternoon." Buddy licked his lips, and stood firm.

"Now, Dad," said Noel, laying his hand on my Father's arm. "Remember Janey's a grown-up woman, and Buddy's my best friend, and I say. . . ."

"I'll tell you when I want your say," shouted my Father, "and Janey can sling off with him, and with my curse too, if she likes, and they'd better go while the going's good, and not come back either."

A wail and a fresh shower of tears from Janey, and an oath from Buddy.

"Coming, Janey?" he asked, as he turned to go.

Janey literally threw herself on her knees before her father. Noel rose from his chair, and Mary put her arm round Janey.

"*Go*, my dear," she said. "*Go*, you little fool, and be happy. . . . I'd be ashamed! . . . Don't you call your *soul* your own?"

But Janey had no soul to call her own. It was her father's, stamped and sealed. It was not filial love that was working, nor wholly filial fear, but rather the unbreakable habit of a lifetime, the inhibitions of a father-complex.

I conquered my selfishness and, for the moment, thrust self aside.

"Will everybody please go away—for exactly ten minutes," I said, and became indeed the cynosure of neighbouring eyes.

"Come on," I urged Buddy. "Get out, and take Janey with you—and come back in ten minutes. Off you go, Mary? Go on, Noel," and something in my voice and manner prevailed, and I was left alone with my Father, to face him and out-face him for the first time in my life. He gave a bitter ugly laugh.

"Are you graciously pleased to allow me to remain?" he sneered, "or do I also leave my house, to oblige you?"

From sarcasm he leapt to violent rage.

"Why, you insolent half-baked young hound," he roared, springing to his feet, and, meanwhile, I had produced and opened the Death Angel's locket.

As he advanced upon me, with blazing eyes and clenched fist, I held it toward him, and his eyes fell upon the two portraits. . . . It was dreadful.

I thought, for one awful moment, that I had killed my Father.

He staggered back, smote his face with his clenched fist, and dropped into a chair, white, shaking, and stricken. I felt dreadful, guilty, impious. . . .

"*Oh, God! . . . Where is she?*" he gasped, fearing, I suppose, that she was near.

"Dead," I replied.

He drew a deeper breath.

"*How did you get it?*" he asked, white-faced and frightened.

"From your *daughter*," I answered, ". . . from my *sister*."

"*My God . . . Where is she?*" he asked again, and I pitied him even more than I hated myself.

"In Bouzen," I said. "Where you bought the Arab stallion . . . and—other things. . . ."

"*Does she know?*" he groaned.

"No," I replied.

"*To how many have you shown that?*" he asked, and it seemed as though his whole life hung upon my answer.

"To no-one—yet," I replied, and added, as I pocketed the locket:

"By the way, Father, this chap Buddy is one of the very best, a real White Man. . . . He'd make a wonderful overseer for this ranch, and a wonderful husband for Janey. . . . And I might add that Major de Beaujolais is a most distinguished officer, whose visit to us is a great honour; and further, that Noel's wife, Maudie, is one of the best and bravest little women that ever lived. . . . You see, Father . . .?"

A long silence. . . .

"I see, Son," replied my Father, at last, "and you can give me that locket."

"Why, no, I can't do that, my dear Father;" I replied. . . . "When Janey's married, and Mary and de Beaujolais have gone, and Noel and Maudie have settled down here happily, and Buddy has an overseer's job, I must take it back to its owner. . . ."

"*Be careful of it*, meanwhile, Boy," said my Father.

"*Very* careful, Father," I replied, and shouted to the others to return.

They found Father wonderfully changed, and all went merry as a welling-bell.

§2

John and Isobel returned by moonlight.

John, clasped my hand, held it, stared me in the eyes—his fine level steady gaze—gave his little cough of deepest feeling and embarrassment, and went into the house without a word. Our silence was very eloquent.

I sat down on the verandah steps, and Isobel, who had stopped to give sugar to her horse, came toward me.

She did not know me until I removed my hat, and the moonlight fell full upon my face.

Like John, she said nothing, but, putting up her little hands, drew my head down and kissed me on the lips. She threw her arms tightly about my neck and kissed me again. The embraces and kisses were just those of the child Isobel who had walked and talked and played with me in our Dream Garden—as sweet and dear and beautiful and innocent as those. Her little hands then stroked my hair, and again we kissed, and then, still without a word, Isobel turned and ran into the house.

That is the moment in which I should have died.

Instead, I took a horse and rode away.

I rode further and harder than I had ever done in all my life, but I was not cruel to my horse. Who, that had been kissed by Isobel, should be cruel, or ever mean or base or bad?

Am I happy?

Dear God! Who that has been kissed by Isobel is not happy?

EPILOGUE

"He shall know a joy beyond all mortal joy, and stand, silent and rapt, beside the Gate. . . . There is but one Way to that Gate. . . . It is not Love Aflame with all Desire—but Love At Peace. . . ."

SPANISH MAINE

DEDICATED TO

THE HOUSE OF JOHN MURRAY

A SMALL TOKEN OF

GRATITUDE AND ESTEEM

COMMEMORATING TWENTY YEARS

OF

HAPPIEST ASSOCIATION

I

Captain Alexander Angus Browne of the *S.S. Amazon*, twenty thousand tons, latest and biggest vessel of the South America Royal Steam Navigation Company, received, without comment, instructions to deviate from his usual home route; and from Havana to proceed to Hamilton, Bermuda, there to pick up the personnel of the 84th Battery, Royal Field Artillery, it being due for Relief.

Incidentally, "For this Relief, no thanks," said the personnel of the 84th Battery, inasmuch as it regarded any change from Bermuda as a change for the worse.

But Miss Consuela Vanbrugh, tourist passenger by the *Amazon*, said, on the contrary, "For this relief very much thanks"; with rejoicings long and loud and joyful; with thanks to Heaven, to the War Office, and to Captain Alexander Angus Browne.

So far as she was concerned, this glorious voyage could not possibly last too long; and so it was with incoherent exclamations of delight that she heard from the Captain's own lips, of the extension of the number of these her days of bliss, the very happiest days of all her life.

For this was no mere common steamer ploughing the salt, plumbless, and estranging sea. It was a golden galleon, laden with jewels, wafted by the breath of Heavenly Cherubim over an ocean of lapis lazuli beneath a sky of sapphire.

"How glorious! How perfectly marvellous!" she cried, in the middle of lunch. "How hopelessly lovely! Dear Captain Browne, I could kiss you."

Hastily Captain Alexander Angus Browne wiped his lips with his napkin, as he turned a bright blue eye upon the lovely piquant face of this his most admired lady-passenger who, with clasped hands, seemed too delighted prosaically to proceed with lunch, too happy to sit still in her chair beside the Captain.

"*Hrrrrrmph!*" he observed, this being his favourite comment upon most topics, his usual contribution to conversation, and his common observation on things in general. Away from the dining-saloon and the havering passengers he said little else.

"Quite," agreed Consuela.

What glorious news that the *Amazon* was going to alter her course and go to the Bermudas on her way home! It would add days to the voyage. It would have been even better news that the ship was going back to Southampton by way of Japan and the North Pole. That would be farther—and the farther the better. The voyage couldn't be too long.

She told Captain Alexander Angus Browne as much. But Captain Alexander Angus Browne, dour silent man of long upper lip and longer experience of the foolish talk of flighty female passengers, patiently pointed out that the ship couldna proceed by way o' the North Pole.

"What a shame, Captain!" observed Consuela. "But never mind. It can by way of the Bermudas, can't it? And we'll anchor there for hours and hours and days and days, and we'll have the steam-pinnace and explore the Islands."

"And who said we'd anchor for days? And who gave ye permission to have ma steam pinnace?" asked Captain Browne.

"I took it for grunted," smiled Consuela.

Again Captain Browne eyed his favourite passenger; this time sharply.

"Ye took it for *what?*"

"Oh, you heard what I said, Captain."

"Aye, I did. . . . And are ye thinking about the lovely Bermudas or the lovely partners ye'll get when the Gunners come aboard. Ye'll want to dance all night."

"Whirled without end," observed Consuela.

"Ah! . . . Men," observed Captain Browne, and rose to his feet.

"Excuse me," he said, and bowing to the other members of the Captain's table, vanished through the doorway just behind his chair, and made his way to the bridge.

Chuckling inwardly, his face as set and solemn as a granite tombstone, he once again gave a few minutes to consideration of his most amusing, interesting, and unusual passenger.

An amazing lass, that, with a quaint and merry mind. God knew that most women passengers talked nonsense; but this lassie talked nonsense intentionally and intelligently. . . . Any fule can talk sense. . . . Not that they all did it. . . . Would anyone believe the things that had been said to him, the questions he had been asked, by the women who had sat on either side of him at the Captain's table?

"Captain, how do you put the brakes on when you want to stop the ship?"

"Good-evening, Captain Browne. I was afraid you weren't coming to dinner. Haven't seen you since last night. Have you been steering all day? How tired you must be!"

"Captain, do they never catch anything on the line they trail behind the ship?"

"Oh, Captain Browne, I'm going to the Fancy-Dress Ball as Britannia. . . . Do your engine-room firemen wear the same shape of brass-helmet as firemen ashore—and can I borrow one?"

"Captain, is *everything* off the ice? . . . Even this champagne is."

"Captain Browne, I particularly asked for a cabin with the window facing south. . . . To whom do I complain?"

"Captain, how often do you have the sweep? Do you ever get birds' nests in the chimneys? Or—funnel—is it?"

No, this Miss Consuela Vanbrugh had a brain; and, to anyone with half an eye, showed it best when she was talking silliest. Might have come from the right side of the Border instead of being a foreigner—Dago or French, or something. Only half, though. That would be where she got those eyes, the biggest and loveliest eyes the Captain had ever seen. And in his day he'd seen some eyes, too, among the *señoritas*. Aye, in his daft Apprentice days, when he was but young and a fule . . . in Rio, Havana, Buenos Ayres, Valparaiso.

Lovely girls! . . . There had been one at Shloimé Samuel's Joint . . . yes, at Slimy Sam's place—Carmelita Concepçion. . . . Eh, lovely! But not to be mentioned in the same breath as this girl. Not as beautiful; and not one tenth as clever.

Miss Consuela Vanbrugh. A puzzling young woman. Captain Browne had met all sorts, and could classify them almost at a glance; but this Miss Consuela Vanbrugh did not fit in. He hadn't a compartment for her at all.

Intriguing, fascinating, and yet—contradictory.

Whiles, you'd say she was a what-d'ye-call-it, an *ingènue*. Whiles, she looked as wise as Eve—and the serpent, too.

Whiles she'd talk like a school-girl, and ask ye questions of unbelievable innocence. Quite unbelievable. Whiles, she'd say something that made ye think that . . . well, that made ye think. Might have been the Queen of Sheba talking, or Cleopatra herself.

Not to say talking, though. Just a remark. She never held forth wise and experienced; but she'd say a word, a half-sentence, a brief observation—that would surprise ye. Ye'd wonder where she'd got her knowledge. But then, lasses read anything and everything nowadays.

Well, he wouldn't tell her so, but she was the first woman

passenger in whom he'd taken a real personal interest since he had commanded a ship. He'd like fine to know some more about her; what her history was. For it was an uncommon one—of that he felt sure. Aye, and fine he'd like to know if anything came of it between her and yon young laird—a good sound man that, for all he was a Mother's Idol, an ornament o' the Guards, and a Society Spoilt Darling.

Aye, Sir Harry Vane.

Where had he read,

'The Lord deliver me from Sir Harry Vane?'

Somewhere. Some time. Was it in Carlyle, about yon stiff-necked dour old Oliver Cromwell? Aye, that'd be it.

Cromwell was always saying, *'The Lord deliver me from Sir Harry Vane'*—the ancestor of this laddie, doubtless.

But if that had been Cromwell's prayer, it wasna this lassie's. Nay, 'the Lord deliver me to Sir Harry Vane,' 'twad be—though the laddie didna ken it.

And again the Captain chuckled internally as, with grim ferocity, he scowled at the Third Officer, who like a young pillar of sea salt, kept his Watch, staring steadily before him.

Yes, unless Lady Drusilla Vane put a spoke in its wheel, there wad be a wedding-coach on the road that these two young people were walking hand in hand. . . . Aye, he'd seen them hand in hand —on the boat-deck, one moonlicht nicht.

But there—that meant nothing, nowadays. It wasna that, so much as the way they looked at each other. Surely, young Sir Harry could hardly know what he ate, for at table his eyes were hardly ever off the girl's face.

Captain Alexander Angus Browne knew the signs. Yon was a good lad with a good face; and, although he looked all the time and with all his eyes, it wasna a stare. It was . . . homage, worship, love.

Aye, unless that fine aristocrat of a Lady Drusilla poured cold water on it, there was fire there that would burst into flame.

Well, the girl would make a fine ladyship—as good a Lady Vane as the mother; for she had courage and grace and dignity, as well as beauty. She'd look the part, and act the part, too; even if not so proudly and precisely as this Lady Vane.

Would it rest with Lady Drusilla? She had the boy quite in hand all right, or Captain Browne was the more mistaken.

And he loved her like she loved him. Yes, if her ladyship were against it, the lassie would be—well—up against it too.

Not but what the boy had a chin of his own. Still, even when heart and chin point in the same direction, a mother's little finger may be a finger-post pointing another way.

§2

That evening, Mr. Otis Vanbrugh, tourist passenger by the *Amazon*, strolled up and down the empty deck, in quiet converse with Consuela. It was his habit to dress in time for a stroll before dinner; and, this evening, Consuela, bursting with excitement and happiness, anxious for a glimpse of the Islands of the Blest, had also come up on deck some quarter of an hour before the dinner-bugle.

"But have you anything against him, Otis?" she was asking.

Silence.

"Isn't he a right guy?" she added mockingly, affecting an intonation and phraseology that did not fail to amuse her companion.

"Sure, he's a right guy," he replied, imitating her.

The boys had been pulling her leg, on the ranch, teaching her to talk as nobody really talked.

"No, I've nothing against him," he added. "Absolutely nothing. Not a thing. On the contrary, rather."

"*Alors?* What's the trouble, then?"

"No trouble, honey. . . . And I don't want there to be any."

"Why should there be, Otis?"

"There shouldn't."

"Darling, don't you want me to talk to him and go around with him? We'd planned to have such a lovely time at Bermuda. You go out in a boat with a glass bottom, and . . ."

"Hope it won't sit on a rock," commented Mr. Vanbrugh.

"And you look through it and see—all sorts of things," she assured him.

"Does he look through it, too? Or look into your eyes and see—all sorts of things?"

"Do you get that impression about him, Otis?"

"I do."

The news didn't seem to depress the young lady unduly.

"You don't dislike him, do you?"

"I like him very much indeed. I think he's one of the best. Straight. Solid."

"In fact, a right guy," observed Miss Vanbrugh. "What's the trouble then?"

How should he put it? It was difficult. Goddam difficult. How to say it without hurting her. And yet he ought to say something about it. . . . Warn her. Remind her . . . No. No. Not that . . .

"Say, how do you feel about him, Consuela?"

"I don't hate him a bit."

"Do you love your neighbour as yourself?"

"Getting along that way—and I'm very fond of me."

"H'm. Mustn't get too fond of him, you know."

"Couldn't."

"No, that's right. Just a good buddy, eh? Go around with him on board ship and in port, and say good-bye at Plymouth or Southampton, eh?"

" 'Say *au revoir* but not good-bye,' " hummed Consuela.

This wasn't getting him any for'arder. This didn't march.

He'd sooner bite his tongue through than hurt her, though. So happy and care-free—now. So different from what she had been.

God, she'd come a long way in the last two or three years. A different girl.

"How do you feel about him, really, honey?" he asked. "Excuse my butting in and asking questions, but . . ."

"How do I feel about him, Big Boy? Very much as I felt about you, when I first saw you at Bouzen—that night."

"Gee! You mustn't feel . . ."

"No, darling, and I mustn't breathe, nor eat, nor drink, nor look at the glorious sea, nor love you, nor . . ."

Lord, this was awful.

Consuela wasn't a girl who had fancies. Nor fancy boys. She hadn't had an affair all the time she'd been with him. Hardly looked at another man.

Not at one of those damned dancing Frenchmen.

Not at a heel-clicking monocled German officer.

Not at an ace of those wonderful Italian flying-boys.

Not at a Spanish *caballero*—from Madrid to Valparaiso.

Not at one of the smart Britishers that had given her such a wonderful time in Peshawur and taken her up the Khyber; danced with her at Simla; and given her a good time at half-a-dozen of the garrison places.

Not at one of the Navy boys at Malta and Gibraltar. Not even at a ship's officer by moonlight, on one of the scores of liners that had taken them to and fro, all over the world.

Why, she hadn't even seemed to cotton on to any of the splendid fellows she'd met on the ranch; at Palm Beach; at any of the resorts; at social functions in New York; at the country clubs—although he'd given her every chance of the best time a girl could have, with the nicest boys; and she'd had all the yachting, riding, dancing, camping and that sort of thing a girl could want or get.

Not one of them had seemed to interest her. Not a man. She'd seemed to find *him*, Otis Vanbrugh, enough.

And now, of all people on this earth, she must fall for a British baronet, very prominent in London and County society.

He had seen his name and photograph, dozens of times, in the magazines.

Hunt-balls, crack polo teams, point-to-point meets, famous race-courses; quite a figure—and not a word ever said against him.

"Catch of the season" sort of fellow. Several seasons. Scarcely a more eligible *parti* in the British Empire or America.

How could he put it without hurting her?

"Say, honey, I guess Sir Harry Vane gets around a lot and knows bunches and bunches of girls. . . . Pick of the British Isles."

"Who's the pick? He or the dames," yawned Consuela.

"I was alluding to Vane."

"Yes. I'll say he does," agreed Consuela.

"He hasn't been out of England much, but he certainly knows everybody on the Island," continued Otis Vanbrugh.

"All forty-five million of them, Otis?"

"Are there forty-five million girls there, Consuela?"

"What I meant was that he seems to know, obviously does know, all the people with Names."

"Yes, sure. That's what I was thinking, honey. . . . That's his job and his place."

"Yes. He has got a nice place, by all accounts."

"But that sort of thing doesn't cut any ice with us, does it, honey?"

"No-o-o-o-o," smiled Consuela ironically.

"We like him and Lady Drusilla and their crowd, but . . . well . . . we're good Americans, aren't we?" smiled Vanbrugh.

"Lovely," agreed Consuela. "Didn't your grandfather come from a place called Brandon Regis? And used you not to go there when you were a boy? And weren't you own-brothers-and-best-buddies with a mighty aristocratic family at Brandon Abbes? Lady Patricia Brandon and what-not and what-have-you; the people we are going to visit with, in England?"

"Sure. . . . But they call it paying a visit."

"Why not lend a visit, since you return it?"

"Don't know, honey."

"No, you don't know anything, Big Boy. And I'll tell you something else you don't know. Sir Harry Vane's place, Vane Court, is quite near Brandon Abbas."

"Oh, didn't I know that? Perhaps that's why it was I who told you."

"Oh, was it you who told me?"

"It was. And I've no doubt you've talked to Harry Vane and told him that you are going to Brandon Abbas, eh?"

"Hark, hark, the Lark! Playing the dinner-bugle," laughed Consuela. "Come on."

§3

Throughout a glorious day and a lovely night, the *Amazon* lay off the emerald islands of Bermuda, lay on the sapphire waters of the little gulf, round the corner of which dreams the happy town of Hamilton.

In boats and launches came the personnel of the 84th Battery Royal Field Artillery; and, in a beautiful little Bermuda-rigged yacht, one of the most graceful craft that sail the sea, came a civilian passenger taking advantage of the *Amazon's* call at Hamilton on her way to Southampton, a Spanish-looking *caballero*, one Señor Manöel Maine.

This gentleman aroused a certain amount of interest among the passengers of the *Amazon*, a fact to which testimony was borne by their endowing him with a nickname. Somebody, on the day after his arrival on board the *Amazon*, alluded to him as The Bright Bermuda Boy; and the name stuck.

For Señor Manöel Maine, albeit by no means a boy, was essentially bright. His hair, his teeth, his eyes—especially his eyes—were extremely bright; and bright were the sapphire buttons of the white waistcoat which he wore with his velvet dinner-jacket; bright the diamond that adorned his little finger; bright the patent leather of the shoes he wore with his flannel suit; bright, very bright, the smile with which he accompanied each remark; bright with gold even was the comb that he took from the breast-pocket of his dinner-jacket and passed through his curling hair after each dance that evening, and after each turn upon the windy deck.

For Señor Manöel Maine was essentially of tidy habit, and particularly disliked to feel his hair awry—a harmless if not actually laudable trait.

And yet insular Sir Harry Vane stared with wide-open eyes, if not wide-open mouth, when he saw the gentleman, at the close of a somewhat *allegro* and scrambling Paul Jones, relinquish his partner, and, with a gleaming smile, bow from the waist, turn away, take the comb from his pocket, pass it a few times through his ambrosial locks, regard it with interest, and return it whence it came.

"Good God!" quoth Sir Harry Vane. "Did you see that, Consuela?"

"Yes. I did see that," replied Consuela Vanbrugh.

"*And I have seen it before*," she added, in a whisper.

"Seen it done before?" asked Sir Harry Vane, incredulous.

"No, seen the man before."

"The Bright Bermuda Boy?"

"Yes. I have seen him before, somewhere."

Sir Harry was surprised.

"Think you have, you mean?"

"Yes. That—smile . . . I have seen him before. Somewhere."

"You really have seen The Bright Bermuda Boy before?"

"No. I am wrong. I have *never* seen him before."

"And don't want to see him again, I should think," observed the young man. "Combing his beastly hair in a ball-room!"

"He'll be making up his face next," he added.

"Right now," agreed the girl, with a curious change of accent and intonation. "You've said it."

And indeed, Sir Harry Vane had "said it," for the foreign-looking gentleman, having returned the comb to his breast-pocket, produced from a side-pocket a small object, also very bright.

From this compact he extracted a small powder-puff and proceeded to draw the line at brightness in the matter of his nose. This should not so shine before men (embracing women), however brightly shone his eyes, his hair, his teeth, his waistcoat-buttons, his studs, his links, his patent shoes.

"My God!" murmured Sir Harry Vane; again displaying that prejudice and insularity that mark the travelling Briton.

Turning to observe the effect of this upon Consuela, he saw that it was considerable; indeed extraordinary.

She was looking—queer . . . almost pale. No, hardly that, perhaps. It would be difficult for anything of such vitality, such vivacity, so glowing, so colourful, as Consuela's face, to turn pale —but somehow it was as though, quite suddenly, she looked a little tired, a little drawn. He was not good at expressing himself, but love made him almost eloquent, almost poetical. He thought of a lovely flower that drooped a little; of a woodland violet plucked by a hot hand; of a lovely rose-bud wilting for lack of water.

"It's hot in here," he said. "Let's go out on deck."

"Yes, it's hot in here. Let's go out on deck," repeated the girl mechanically.

And then for a couple of days The Bright Bermuda Boy disappeared from sight altogether. He was not sea-sick or otherwise ill; nor was he lonely, for he received numerous and, at night, lengthy, visits from a Spanish steward who gave him quite a lot of accurate information concerning the passengers, and did with him some very secret, extensive, remarkable, and mutually satisfactory business.

And during these days Sir Harry Vane and Consuela Vanbrugh also did with each other much mutually satisfactory business of a wholly different order, secret sweet traffic that made these hours the happiest of their lives.

On the third evening they descended from the boat-deck, to dance.

As they reached the ball-room door, they came face to face with the foreign-looking gentleman, The Bright Bermuda Boy, who, his hair arranged to his satisfaction, the light of his countenance agreeably shaded to the tint of his preference, his aristocratic nose guileless of gloss, smiled brightly upon all men, more brightly upon all women.

The Englishman, his stolid handsome face expressionless, regarded the foreigner without apparent interest.

Suddenly his usually impassive countenance frankly confessed and exhibited the real interest that he felt.

Not given to fancifulness, he was for a second—fanciful.

He fancied he saw a black panther; saw it offered meat.

A memory-picture sprang between him and the foreigner's face.

A zoological gardens, or perhaps a menagerie, circus, or fair; wild beasts in cages; savage dreadful beasts behind bars.

Most savage, most dreadful of all, a black panther, motionless, its terrible eyes half-closed; and yet, its eyes, its face, its attitude, its whole body expressive, horribly expressive—of danger, of threat, of menace, of incalculable ferocity, of colossal power of destruction; of a volcano—about to erupt most devastatingly; of a terrifically high explosive—about to explode.

Still as a statue; silent as Death; enigmatically expressionless as a skull; it was terrifying, nightmarish.

And suddenly—it came to life. Its great green glowing eyes opened wide; its lips retracted in a ghastly minatory smile, exposing fearful gleaming teeth; its awful mouth yawned cavernously; its claws, like sharp curved daggers, protruded from their sheaths, and it uttered a dreadful snarling sound. It had seen meat. Its keeper was bringing it raw meat.

Rubbish!

Sir Harry Vane frowned, pulled himself together, almost physically shook himself, as the memory-picture faded, and, through it, he saw the face, not of the black panther, but of the black-avised Spanish *caballero;* not the gleaming fangs of the feral beast, but the shining teeth of the Señor; not "the smile of the tiger" but that of Manöel Maine. And yet the change was not so very great as might have been expected.

Also Sir Harry Vane heard—not the dreadful snarling sound made by a hungry panther that sees its meat—but the voice of the Spaniard, saying,

"*So! . . . So-o-o-o-oh! . . .*"

And found himself almost pulled past the staring fellow by Consuela whose little hand was on his arm.

He glanced down at her.

Definitely, this time, she had turned pale.

Well! What an amazing experience for a matter-of-fact unimaginative young Englishman!

In the space of a couple of seconds he had seen all that. Seen that well-remembered black panther again; seen it come to life at sight of Consuela; seen the expression of its expressionless face change suddenly to vital interest, to hunger—predatory, fierce, determined.

"That's queer!" he said, as Consuela impelling him, they mutually, almost unconsciously, turned back into the quiet outer darkness of the promenade-deck.

"What is queer, Harry?"

"*Darling!*" he whispered, in answer to the pressure of her hand upon his arm, the little movement that she made of drawing closer to him, as for reassurance, protection.

"Why—that this feller, The Bright Bermuda Boy, seemed to recognize you! He seemed to know you."

"To recognize me, Harry? To *know* me?"

"Yes. As we came face to face with him, just now, by the ball-room door, he caught sight of you, and his whole face changed—sort of lit up. Well, naturally anybody's face would."

And he squeezed her arm.

"But it was more than that. It was a look of recognition. More than that too. Why—the fellow—what shall I say—licked his chops, if you'll excuse my putting it like that. Didn't you notice?"

"No, Harry. I didn't notice him. I didn't see him at all. Perhaps he was looking at somebody else."

"Not he. He was surprised—clean bowled over. I thought he was going to speak to you. He stared straight at you, opened his eyes wide, showed his teeth, and said, '*So-o-o!* . . .' Like that."

The girl laughed.

"You are making it all up, Harry."

"My dear, have you ever seen a sleepy cat suddenly catch sight of a mouse? It was like that. Have you ever fed a tame hawk? It was like a—like a black panther that suddenly sees meat. Sees—its prey."

"Oh, Harry! You are a funny boy. I must notice, next time I see The Bright Young Boy."

"Well, I hope he's not going to do that every time he sees you. He'd better not, anyhow. Queer that you should have *thought*, at first, the other night, that you knew him; and that when he caught sight of you tonight, he should be perfectly *certain* that he knew you!"

"Darling, he reminded me of somebody else. And he was just staring at me—like such men do, in South America. They are awful. He's just . . ."

But they had reached the solitude and friendly darkness of the portion of the deck outside the curtained windows of the forward music-saloon, and,

"What did you call me?" interrupted Sir Harry Vane.

"What *did* I call you—darling?" whispered the girl.

Instantly the young man halted in his stride, took his arm from beneath hers and put it about her, turning her towards him. With his right hand gently, tenderly, reverently, he raised her chin and gazed into her eyes.

"*Darling!* . . . *Darling!* . . ."

Consuela's sweet mouth smiled. Her eyes closed. Her lips trembled, as he bent over her and his face came down to hers. The trembling of her lips ceased as they met his in a long, long kiss, and her arms went about his neck, his about her body.

"Consuela! . . . Darling! . . . Then you *do* love me?"

"I do, Harry. . . . Oh! . . .

"Kiss me again. Do you love me, Harry?"

"I worship you."

"Oh, Harry! . . . Oh, we mustn't . . . I mustn't. . . ."

"You must, Consuela," replied Sir Harry Vane as he prevented further utterance on the subject.

§4

That night, Sir Harry Vane had a long and altogether pleasurable interview with his mother, in her cabin.

He had not only a great love but a deep respect for this wise and witty woman who was his best friend, whose mind was as broad as it was deep; who knew her world and was known by it; who was so understanding, and who had never, from his prep-school days until this day, let him down, as he phrased it, in any way whatsoever.

He asked her whether it were not time that he was married.

He gathered, among other things, that it was not; that Lady Drusilla Vane considered, in the first place, that there was no woman good enough to become the wife of her son; and that, in the second, if there were, it would not be one of the Bright Young Things—for they were never bright, had never been young, and were merely Things.

After some conversation, the name of Consuela was mentioned, *à propos* of Bright Young Things.

"Oh, but *she's* as bright as a flower and as young as the morning," smiled Lady Drusilla, "and one of the dearest things I ever met. Do you like her, Harry?"

"Er—yes—Mother. I do, rather," replied Sir Harry Vane. "Yes, I rather like young Consuela."

That night, Miss Consuela Vanbrugh had a long and wholly unpleasurable interview with Señor Manöel Maine—in her cabin.

She gathered that the *caballero*, in the first place, considered that there was no opportunity bad enough to be missed by a sensible *chevalier d'industrie;* and that, in the second, if there were, this was not it. It was, in fact, a literally golden opportunity, the opportunity of a lifetime.

That night, Mr. Otis Vanbrugh had a long and most painful interview with Consuela, in his cabin.

He gathered that, in the moment when the sun had risen on the life of his beloved Consuela, it had been eclipsed; that, in the very moment that the cup of joy had reached her lips, it had been dashed from them; that life had turned to dust and ashes at a touch—the touch of a man of whom he had never heard, and the fact of whose very existence she had, until that moment, utterly forgotten.

That night Señor Manöel Maine had a long and not wholly unpleasurable interview with Mr. Otis Vanbrugh, in the Señor's cabin.

As Consuela had done, Vanbrugh gathered that Señor Manöel Maine intended to make the utmost of the chance of a life-time; that Fate, having hitherto treated him scurvily, had obviously now relented; that his ship was coming home, and he was reaching port at last; that his ship was that *Amazon*, his port Southampton, or perhaps, Plymouth, as the Battery was being landed there; that his ship would not only come home, but he with her; and that he had no wish to be unpleasant, but had the fullest intention of making life pleasant (for Señor Manöel Maine) at any cost—to anybody.

II

Otis Vanbrugh eyed his man.

Yes, he had to admit that he was a man, and—saving a certain glossiness, not to say flashiness—was, in appearance, a gentleman.

Tall, straight, square-shouldered, well-built without heaviness; handsome in a hard, arrogant, and aggressive way; he had a good forehead, fine nose, strong cruel mouth; he had good hands, well-kept, powerful, sinewy; a typical adventurer; soldier of fortune; the type of Spaniard who followed Pizarro and stout Cortes, new worlds to conquer and incredible atrocities to commit.

A man to reckon with; to handle carefully. No petty criminal, poor sneak-thief, cheap pickpocket, this. No common gun-man tough, either.

No; definitely the predatory soldier-of-fortune type.

A gentleman gone wrong.

Of whom or what did he remind him? Lucifer, Son of the Morning, fallen angel?

And yet—*blackmail*. Blackmailing a woman.

Poor, poor little Consuela. On the very day that happiness had come to her—at last. The day on which the man she loved had declared himself. Her chance of happiness, her glimpse of such a future as she had so yearned.

"Sit down, Señor—er—Vanbrugh? What can I offer you? Cognac? Cigar?"

Quite a good voice. That of an educated man; a man of what is called culture, and what is termed refinement.

"No, thank you. All I want is a little talk with you. Yes—my name's Vanbrugh."

"Then pray sit down, Mr. Vanbrugh. For I want a *long* talk with you."

Otis Vanbrugh, without further remark, seated himself in one of the two small arm-chairs that the state-room boasted.

Coolly taking, cutting, and lighting a cigar, Spanish Maine eyed his visitor and took stock of him.

H'm! This complicated matters. Her "brother," eh? What a tale!

Of course the little bitch was lying. Her brother!

Why, he, Spanish Maine himself, looked more like her brother than did this tall, fair, blue-eyed Anglo-Saxon.

What would he be? Husband? Lover? *Souteneur?*

The last, most probably. He'd hardly be husband or lover as she was affiancing herself to the wealthy English Baronet.

The Baronet was the lover and the future husband.

This must be the current proprietor. And complaisant.

Or was she fooling this man Vanbrugh? Was she dropping the shadow for the substance—dropping this man for the rich nobleman, who was bigger game?

If so, there'd be trouble—for her—because this Vanbrugh was evidently a man. Not a tough guy, not a typical fighting-man; but a man who'd fight, nevertheless. He had a chin: and a look in his eye.

This fellow knew his onions. A man of the world who'd seen things and done things, and then some. Looked like an army officer —say a major in a crack cavalry regiment—British or American. Obviously an upper-class Englishman or American. And *her* brother!

Fancy thinking she could pull that bunk on Spanish Maine. Especially in view of what he knew about her. Did she think he was a fool?

Anyway, this fellow must be dealt with first, whoever or whatever he was, since she was travelling with him and using his name.

"Well?" said Spanish Maine, throwing his match out of the port-hole, blowing a long cloud of smoke and fixing Otis Vanbrugh with a hard and steady stare.

"I am Miss Consuela Vanbrugh's brother."

"*Oh, yeah?* . . . Yes?" murmured Spanish Maine with a smile that did not reach his eyes. "So? *Brother*, eh? Well! '*Á la mujer casta no le busques abolengo,*'[10] as we say in Spain."

"I am Miss Consuela Vanbrugh's brother. She has just been to my cabin to tell me that you came to hers. You forced your way in."

"No, no," deprecated Spanish Maine. "I knocked very gently on her door, and asked for an interview. She accorded it instantly! Isn't that surprising?"

"You forced your way in, by announcing yourself as an old friend who, some time ago, had known her *well;* and to whom she

---

[10] Don't worry about the ancestors of a virtuous woman.

would be wise to grant immediate admission."

"Which she immediately did! Isn't that curious?" smiled Spanish Maine.

"You then told her that you knew all about her. *Everything*. And that you proposed to use your knowledge to the utmost advantage to yourself. You gave her quite clearly to understand that, on penalty of 'exposure,' she must to-morrow recognize you publicly; remember you as an old friend; and introduce you to Sir Harry Vane, his mother, myself and her acquaintances on board as a gentleman . . ." Otis Vanbrugh paused and laughed . . .

"As a *gentleman*, of means and position; a *caballero*, of wealth, rank, and unblemished reputation; a *hidalgo*, in short, whom it would be an honour to know and with whom it would be a pleasure to associate. Am I right?"

"So far, pretty correct," smiled Spanish Maine. "Proceed, I beg; for that is but the overture."

"Yes. You then proposed to attach yourself to her . . ."

"In the discreetest manner," interrupted Spanish Maine with another smile that revealed bright teeth behind firm lips, but no humour behind hard eyes.

"In a parasitic capacity. To live upon her, in fact, until such time as she could produce a sum of money sufficiently large to purchase her freedom—from you. Blackmail, in short."

"An unpleasant word," observed Spanish Maine.

"For an unpleasant thing," continued Otis Vanbrugh. "A foul despicable thing; a poisonous dastardly thing; a cowardly devilish thing."

"Well, there are worse things, Mr. Vanbrugh. Worse things than blackmail."

"What—blackmailers?" inquired Otis Vanbrugh.

"Worse things than blackmail—and blackmailers," was the reply. "There are poverty—and the poor. As a man and a gentleman, I dislike blackmail. As a man and a gentleman, still more do I dislike poverty. And by God, I know what I'm talking about. Yes. I dislike blackmailers—but I dislike the poor even more."

"A matter of taste, Señor Maine. Mine differs from yours."

"I daresay. Have you ever been hungry—with no sign or hope of food? Really desperately, cravingly, starvingly hungry? So hungry that you'd have eaten a bellyful of orange-peel or saw-dust —and without the wherewithal, the hope, the chance, to get a crust of bread?"

"Of course not." Spanish Maine answered his own question. "Well I have, and to starvation I prefer what you are pleased to call blackmail. Incidentally, *I* call it the seizing of opportunity. Does not your poet, Dryden, bid us

> '*Take the good the gods provide thee*' when
> '*Lovely Thais sits beside thee*'?"

Otis Vanbrugh eyed Manöel Maine consideringly, speculatively.

What manner of man was this with whom he had to deal? What manner of man was this in whose hands lay Consuela's future life, her chance of happiness?

"Have you ever been ragged, Señor Vanbrugh—so ragged that you were indecent and ashamed? Have you been filthy, foul, lousy, stinking, a human scare-crow? . . . Of course not. . . . Well, I have. And I intend never to be in that condition again. I prefer what you call blackmail, and what I call seizing the opportunity of preventing it.

"Have you ever been utterly homeless, Señor Vanbrugh? Have you ever trodden the streets of a great city, soaking wet, chilled to the bone, weary to death, and with absolutely nowhere to lay your head? Utterly homeless, friendless, alone, without a coin in your pocket, fain to lie down to rest, to die, in the gutter, until kicked up by a policeman: and then thankful to be flung into a foul verminous cell with the criminal scum of the town? Not you. . . . Well, I have. And I don't intend to find myself in the gutter, in my old age, for want of seizing a golden opportunity.

"Oh yes, there are worse things than blackmail and the blackmailer, Señor Vanbrugh."

"Is a murderer worse?" asked Otis Vanbrugh.

"A murderer? Why?"

"I was only wondering," replied Vanbrugh. "Matter of taste again, I suppose. I think, on the whole, I'd sooner be a murderer than a blackmailer."

"Well, as you say, a matter of opinion. But isn't that rather beside the point."

"Not wholly, Señor Maine. Not entirely, perhaps. I was just thinking that if I—er—killed you, to prevent your blackmailing my sister, I should be a murderer."

"M'm! . . . Come now, Señor. Between *gentlemen*. What an ugly thing to say! Don't let's have any unpleasantness. So

300

unnecessary between gentlemen."

"*Unpleasantness? . . . Gentlemen? . . .*" murmured Otis Van-brugh, and laughed contemptuously.

"Yes. Let's settle this amicably and not use nasty words like blackmail—and murder—and so on. Let's lay our cards on the table. Let's come to an honourable understanding—a gentlemen's agreement—and live happy ever after . . . *I* intend to live happy ever after, anyhow."

"Do you?"

"Yes. And there's no reason why you and your—ah—'sister' should not do so. We don't want to wrangle like gutter-snipes, and talk about murder. An ugly word and an ugly thing. Difficult to do, too, in some cases. And such a drastic penalty for doing it. Oh, come now. Murder!"

And it was Spanish Maine's turn to laugh contemptuously.

As he did so, he gave a brilliant exhibition of amateur conjuring. A little *leger de main*; sleight of hand; juggling; skill and dexterity of which a professional might have been proud. For, before the interested eyes of Otis Vanbrugh, a fair-sized automatic pistol suddenly materialized in Spanish Maine's right hand, was tossed in the air, caught by the handle and, with a flash of blued steel, vanished.

One second it was there and, in the next, or in the same one, it was not. But in its place was a wicked-looking stiletto with a handle of gun-metal inlaid with gold, and a bright steel blade with blued ornamentation.

And this again turned in the air, was caught by the handle, and —vanished.

"Very neat. Very neat indeed," thought Otis Vanbrugh to himself. "The automatic under his left arm, the stiletto in his right hip pocket or something. Really an amazing little exhibition of deftness. The gentleman is prepared for emergencies."

"Yes. Murder's sometimes difficult," repeated Spanish Maine. "Sometimes. To some people. And not everybody can get away with it. Most murderers, you know, are despicable."

"Worse than blackmailers?" inquired Otis Vanbrugh.

"Despicable *as* murderers, I mean. Shocking bunglers. Ought not to be allowed to commit murders. Haven't the faintest idea, even where the murder is easy enough to commit. Any fool can murder some other fool—but no *fool* can do it and escape punishment. Without, for one moment being so discourteous, Señor Vanbrugh, as to suggest that you are a fool—even at murder—I do suggest that you would be up against a double obstacle. In the first place, you'd find it extraordinarily difficult to murder me. And in the second place, if you did succeed in doing it, you'd hang. Don't let us talk of such crude unpleasant things."

"Very well," agreed Otis Vanbrugh. "Let's talk of blackmail."

"Much better; since you insist on calling it that. As I was saying, I don't intend, ever again, to be hungry, to be ragged, to be homeless—in short, to be poor. Fortune knocks but once on a man's door, and only a fool neglects to open it when she does so. And '*Al hombre osado, la fortuna le da la mano,*' as we say— Fortune offers her hand to the brave. Well, I am not a fool, Señor; and I am brave."

"Against a woman? " observed Vanbrugh quietly.

"I do not wish to boast—but I venture to say I am brave even against a woman," smiled Spanish Maine. "Against men—of course. Well, now; what about a pleasant friendly understanding; a gentlemen's agreement; no hard feelings; all comfortable, clear and straightforward, and everybody satisfied. What do you propose, Señor Vanbrugh?"

"Why should I propose anything at all?"

"I understood that you had come for that purpose? Come from your—ah—'sister,' to give me the answer that she omitted to give."

"Answer to what?"

"To my plain simple question: whether she was prepared to buy my silence—at my price. My silence concerning her history. Shall we say her 'past'? Haven't you come for that purpose, Señor Vanbrugh?"

"Not exactly."

"Then?"

"Well, I wanted to find out what it was all about," replied Vanbrugh quietly, speaking slowly, carefully, as thoughtfully he considered Spanish Maine, "what sort of a creature you were; what you really knew about my sister; what you wanted. And to decide as to what would be the best way of handling you. Oh, to find out a lot of things."

"Well, now, Señor Vanbrugh, as to what I really know about your 'sister'; as to what I want; as to the sort of creature I am; and hence as to the best way of handling me—I'll enlighten you. Listen. . . ."

Settling himself comfortably in his arm-chair, Spanish Maine crossed his legs, leant back, gazed at the white-painted steel ceiling and listened, with gratification, to the sound of his own voice.

As follows:—

III

Would it surprise you to know Señor Vanbrugh., that I have the honour to claim some measure of, what shall we say—compatriotism, racial derivation, racial alliance—with your noble self? Oh, yes, I am partly Anglo-Saxon.

You have, of course, heard of Ladysmith in South Africa, rendered famous by its siege; and perhaps of the less famous Harrismith, in the same British Colony? Possibly you are also aware that those towns are named after Sir Harry Smith and his wife Lady Smith, and that Lieutenant Harry Smith of the 95th Regiment of Foot, was present at the capture and sack of Badajos. Here he rescued a Spanish girl, of fourteen years of age, from the drunken and licentious soldiery. He took her to his tent, married her next day, and she followed his fortunes, in war and in peace, for the rest of her life—until he became Sir Harry Smith, and Governor of Cape Colony.

You may wonder what all this has got to do with the matter. Nothing, except that his brother officer, Captain Charles Maine, did precisely the same thing—saved the life of a Spanish *señorita*, married her, and with her lived happy ever after.

Pues, a pretty romance that must appeal to you.

This Captain Charles Maine and his wife, Señora Maine, were blessed with a son, Alphonso Charles Maine. This son they made both English and Spanish, sending him to Eton School and to Oxford University to be educated, and bringing him back to Spain, to make a good *hidalgo* of him when his education was completed.

The young gentleman returned to his parents at Cadiz with an even wider education than they had expected or intended, for he brought back with him an English wife; and, in the famous old town of Cadiz where there was already a considerable English colony, this Alphonso Charles Maine, and Mary his wife, settled down. To them was born a son, Miguel Charles Maine who had at least one distinction. He was my father.

So you see I am the son of a man who was one-quarter Spanish and three-quarters English, and of a Spanish girl of the oldest and bluest blood of Spain. This *señorita* was a true daughter of Spain. Her father, a rich land-owner and noted breeder of bulls, had been, in his youth, at Court. Work it out for yourself and you will find (I am no mathematician) that I am what we might call three-eighths English. Yes, and well born—of English army stock and Spanish grandee stock.

My father, intensely Anglophile—in some ways more English than the English, although a Spaniard—had me taught English from the cradle. I grew up bi-lingual, reading as much English literature as Spanish.

Fortune frowned not on my noble birth, in one way; but in another it did, for my parents spoilt me. My troubles began in the nursery.

I was educated at the best school in Cadiz, my mother refusing to part with me, when my father wanted to send me to England. How different might my life have been, had he had his way; for, from school, I went to Cadiz University instead of to that of Oxford, and thus never left my home and the influence—or lack of influence—of my mother and her family.

I grew up an extremely dissipated young man.

I admit it.

Not that I was a loafer, a waster, mark you. Far from it. I had too much energy for that. I was indefatigable, both at work and at play: but, unfortunately, much of my energies in the latter direction was misplaced; for, although I read with avidity, and spent hours daily in the fencing-school, rode like a centaur, sculled like a water-beetle and swam like a fish, I also found time—far too much time—for the *señoritas*.

I am not sure that I had a hero, for I was something of a hero to myself, but had I consciously adopted one for emulation and worship, I think it would have been Don Juan.

He, or Casanova perhaps.

Yes, I was an elegant, spirited, scholarly, accomplished and dissipated young man; fencing and other sports my pastime; reading my relaxation; women my diversion—-or, shall we say, hobby?

As often happens with young *caballeros* such as I, I rode my hobby too hard—and got into serious and dangerous trouble with a girl who was, alas, of breeding and family equal to my own, and whose name was Dolores Floramar. Marriage being out of the question owing to my youth, her extreme youth, the fact that she was betrothed to a very wealthy vineyard-proprietor, and that my own parents had quite other views for me, the position was awkward.

Oh, very awkward.

And as though it were not sufficiently so, her silly brother had to go and get himself into trouble too. Trouble that kept him on his back in hospital, between life and death, for weeks; trouble that he found at the point of my duelling-rapier.

Yes, the presumptuous and foolish lad had the bad manners to strike me in the face with his open hand as I sat sipping a glass of sherry at the *Amontillado*, where we students of Cadiz University were wont to take our ease and our wine.

Well, he looked for trouble, and, as I say, he found it; for it was not my fault that I was a superb fencer, both in the French and the Italian styles.

Nor had the unbalanced ungentlemanly and selfish fellow considered the trouble that he was bringing on me. I had to disappear, *pronto;* and on my mother's advice and with her help and blessing, I sailed from Cadiz for England, left the ship at La Rochelle, took train for Paris, went to Berne, and from there to my real destination, Heidelberg.

At Heidelberg I became a foreign student, a young gentleman from Madrid desirous of pursuing his studies in "*alt Heidelberg*" at the feet of the German philosophers.

I had a good time at Heidelberg, though I confess it took me a good while to change my habit of savouring the world's finest Sherry to that of swilling vast quantities of Lager beer.

However, the spirit was willing and the flesh was strong.

And then, one day, misfortune overtook me again.

There was a girl, lovely in the German *madchen* way, Gretchen Kellner—whom I delighted to honour. There was also a Prussian corps-student whom I detested on sight, loathed on acquaintance, and abhorred on familiarity, who tried to supplant me in Gretchen's innocent heart.

He was everything that I was not—gross, coarse, colossal, ugly, hoggish, brutal—with his shaven head, his piggish little eyes, flapping ears, and bloated red face marked with a dozen of their silly duel-scars.

I suppose you know their absurd idiotic idea of fencing, their *schlager* play? You have a blunt-pointed razor-edged sword; you keep your right arm stiff above your head; you use only your wrist; you have your eyes protected with mask and goggles, and your cheeks, chin, and scalp exposed. There is no thrusting at all; no cutting at the body. Purely by means of wrist-play, you slash at your opponent's face and head.

The whole idea, of course, is to collect "honourable" scars on your cheeks, chin and skull. When you've got them, you keep them open as long as possible, with salt and beer, for fear they should ever fade away. When they are on your skull you keep your head practically shaven, so that they shall not be hidden. Childish in the extreme. Crude, clumsy, and truly Teutonic.

And if you are challenged to this travesty of a duel, you have to fight—to call it "fighting"—or be disgraced and kicked out of the *Studentenkorps*, your Student Club.

Well, one day as I sat at lunch in the *Red Hen, this* Prussian brute (I've forgotten his name—something incredible, ridiculous and unpronounceable) came past my table, followed by a couple of boar-hounds as big as elephants, or bigger. He was one of those *Blut und Eisen* bullies who copied Bismarck, even to the boar-hound touch, and thought that, to be a gentleman, you must be overbearing, boastful, and violent; and to be a patriot you must bawl *Deutchland über alles* and *Gott mit uns* all day long, swill beer all night, and swagger all the time. At my table he stopped, snatched up my plate, and threw its contents, some slices of excellent bolonia sausage, to his dogs, remarking as he did so,

"*Das ist zu gut für Sie.*"[11]

I sprang to my feet and did to him exactly what my foolish young Cadiz friend had done to me. I smacked his face.

So does bad example lead us astray; so do evil communications corrupt good manners.

I think the Prussian animal had never been so surprised in all his mis-spent life. Being flustered, he blustered, shouted, foamed at the mouth, shook his great fist under my nose, spat at me, and finally informed me that he would send me his seconds.

"I'll slash you to bits for that!" he growled. "I'll cut you in slices! . . . I'll kill you!"

I knew enough German by that time to retort in his own language.

"*Bellende Hunde beissen nicht,*"[12] laughed I contemptuously.

Of course I had to fight the *Schurke*, and to fight him in his own way; but, while doing it, I made up my mind that he should also fight me—in my way.

It was a maddening experience, trussed up like a fowl, with my hand above my head, and unable to do anything but slash, by a wrist-twisting flick of the sword, at his ugly head, of which I could only see the jowls and his eyes behind the iron mask and goggles.

---

[11] That is too good for you.
[12] Yelping curs don't bite.

Of course I had not a dog's chance. He was a past master at this idiotic game, and cut me across the top of the head within a few seconds of the word "go." Owing to the protective head-covering, which leaves only the scalp exposed, the duellists cannot receive a fatal wound, and only very rarely, a dangerous one. It is extremely painful, however, to have your head cut to the bone; and it's a very bloody business.

As soon as I had been mopped up, and the blood had ceased flowing into my eyes, we went to it again; and once more, within a few seconds of starting, I got a slash, this time across my cheek—as you see—a cut that laid the cheek-bone bare.

Though a bit sick from the sight of so much blood, as well as from the loss of it, I would not give in so long as my Prussian wished to go on; and there was always a chance that I might lay his ugly jowl open.

But not a hope. Our swords had hardly clanked for the third time, when I got another across the top of my head; and, at that, the referee, judges, seconds, or else the surgeon, decided that that would be enough.

The very next day, taking some friends of my Student-Corps with me, I went in search of the hero—oh, yes, Count Fritz von Rottendorff, that was his silly name, I knew it was something rotten—and found him, as I expected, drinking at the *Seppl.*

"Here, Count," said I, "you challenged me to fight according to your method of fighting, and I accepted. I now challenge you to fight according to mine; and, if you refuse, I say, before these gentlemen, my friends here and yours there, that you are a coward and a cur, a loud-mouthed swash-buckling bully, always willing to fight when he knows he'll win, never willing to fight when he thinks he might lose. I challenge you to fight me to-morrow, as *gentlemen* fight in my country."

"And how do they do it?" he growled, "With sticks? Broken bottles? Brick-bats?"

"No. I see you are as ignorant as you are cowardly and ugly—almost. In my country they fight with swords. I challenge you to fight with swords—German swords, too. What about it?"

"We have fought once," he growled.

I laughed aloud.

"Had enough, eh? And do you call that fighting? I am challenging you to *fight*. Take it or leave it. If you won't fight, get off the pavement in future whenever you see me coming. And an account of this conversation and challenge goes to the newspapers.

I'll see that it is known all over Germany."

And, of course, he had to fight.

I had spoken about German swords because, in the Student-Corps' fencing-rooms, on the upper floor of a huge old house called "The Royal Stables," I had seen a lovely pair of medieval rapiers hanging above the fire-place, splendid weapons of the Italian pattern, with Toledo blades, such swords as might have been worn by Wallenstein or Gustavus Adolphus; might have been worn by Alva in the Netherlands.

Of course the fellow could use an ordinary foil, after a fashion, but he was a child in my hands, especially with these rapiers of the cross-hilt-and-cup pattern. In point of fact, he didn't even know the proper grasp, and simply held that Italian-pattern rapier as he would have done a French one, with a simple grip above the cross-piece.

"Now," said I, when we crossed blades. "You went out of your way to insult me. You then challenged me to fight in a style of which I knew nothing, and of which you were a master. Good. Now we'll have some real fencing with real swords. Fight for your life. . . . *On guard!*"

The onlookers, his seconds and mine—and a few friends of both of us, who had been told of what was on, and invited to be present that summer morning, before dawn—were somewhat subdued, a bit out of their depth, a trifle anxious, perhaps. And well they might be. Student duelling was not forbidden. On the contrary, it was encouraged; but, as I have said, what they called "duelling" was merely a harmless, if painful and unpleasant, blood-letting. This was the real thing; and I could see those worthy Germans wondering exactly what was going to happen, and whether their own precious selves might not be in danger if anything serious occurred.

Suddenly, with a disengage, an under-hand feint, and a fairly quick return, the fellow lunged. Of course his own form of sword-play had given him a wrist of steel and whale-bone, and, for his great size, he was undeniably quick. I parried, and, as he recovered, riposted. With a heavy clumsy clashing guard, he saved himself.

Drawing back, I gave him "Invitation Number One" in the Italian style, my body completely exposed, my sword-hand out to the right, my point well away from his body. Blindly falling into the trap, he lunged with all his strength at my undefended breast. Instantly my blade flashed over, caught his, deflected it sufficiently —and my point came up, under his guard—and through his heart.

The bully was dead almost as soon as his body slumped to the floor.

Well, I had done it this time! And straight from the ancient Royal Stables I ran to the modern railway-station and took train for Belfort, where, in France, I should be, at any rate for the time, safe enough.

Unfortunately, owing to a certain spaciousness of habit, generosity, extravagance, what you will, I was almost penniless.

Also I was—I admit it—very frightened; for there was a tremendous hue-and-cry in the newspapers. Apparently this Count von Rottendorf was a somebody, his father being a distinguished General and a particular personal friend of the King of Bavaria. According to the account in the *Temps* and *Petit Parisien*, as well as the *Belfort Étoile*, the Count had been murdered—found stabbed to the heart, in the *Salle d'Armes* in which it was his habit to practise fencing; and the police were looking for a foreigner, said to be a Spaniard, who was known to have quarrelled with the Count and who was missing from his lodgings. Evidently the heroes who had been spectators of the duel had simply scattered and fled, gone to their lodgings, lain low, and not said a word when the "murder" was discovered.

Hungry, homeless, penniless, frightened, expecting the hand of a *gendarme* to fall heavily upon my shoulder at any moment, I sought refuge in the French Foreign Legion, enlisting at the *Bureau de Récrutement* in Belfort under the name of William Jackson, an Englishman, who of course, knew not a word of Spanish. I travelled at the expense of Madame la Republique, to Marseilles the next day; to Oran, three days later; and found myself in Sidi-bel-Abbès in Algeria, within a week of my Heidelberg misfortune.

How's that for bad luck?

On Monday morning—a gentleman of leisure, a student of literature and the arts, engaged in making metrical translations of our poets, Perez de Guzman, Lope de Vega, Yriarte, Ramon de Camporamor, Tirse de Molina, and Calderon, into English; enjoying life to the full, wanting for nothing, pursuing not only his studies and his sports, but the lovely blonde Gretchen Kellner by the hour; happy, light-hearted and an aristocrat.

On Saturday night—a private in the ranks of a foreign army, a *sou*-a-day soldier, a ha'penny hero, a sample of the cheap cannon-fodder of France, worked to death, bored to extinction, disciplined to madness, and paid threepence-halfpenny every Thursday to provide himself with such alleviations and distractions in the way of wine, women, and song, as he was left the strength to crave.

Living life in Heidelberg on Monday: a living death in Sidi-bel-Abbès on Saturday.

Talk of Fortune favouring the brave!

And bad luck dogged my footsteps there in Africa too.

Well, as you may have gathered, I was not a tender chicken when I entered the French Foreign Legion, and I can assure you I was a fairly tough bird by the time I had been there for a year or two. Very tough indeed, and if I had anything still to learn when I joined, I hadn't very much to learn by the time I left. Not very much—just a little—and that I learned later in the Penal Battalions, in prison, in Biribi; and in Maroni. Yes, bad luck dogged my footsteps still, again, all the while.

Do you know that twice—*twice*—I had a fortune—*a fortune*—in my hands, actually in my very hands, and lost it!

But not a third time. Not a third time. No! Not a third time will I lose a fortune—even if you do call it blackmail.

Pure bad luck.

Quite early it began.

Now, you read and hear all sorts of absurd stories about what happens to you in the French Foreign Legion.

All sorts of bosh, bilge, lies, rubbish.

Fellows write books saying that Legion Sergeants go about with heavy whips in their hands, and use them as readily and freely as an Arab donkey-boy uses his *matrack* on the rumps of the *burros* he drives. You'd think, to read some of the lies, that a Sergeant spent the whole of his working hours in striking *légionnaires* with all his might, and that he went to bed at night absolutely exhausted with the manual labour of flogging them.

Lies! Bosh! Rubbish!

Such a man wouldn't last a day. If the men didn't kill him, his officer would. Anyhow, he'd send him for *conseil-de-guerre*, court-martial.

In the Penal Battalions, away in the desert, where the N.C.O.'s have got it all to themselves—that's different. Things happen then, I grant you. But in the Legion? Bah! I never saw a Sergeant strike a man, the whole time I was there: except once. Only once: and I was the man who was struck.

It was a case of only once for the Sergeant, too, as well as for me.

He was a swine.

They're all tough, of course. They have to be. But, on the

whole they're all-right, especially when you take into account the fact that they are generally foreigners—always, in my case, for I never happened to be under a Spaniard—and, somehow, you take things from a man of your own blood that you don't from a foreigner. You resent it more when a foreigner bullies you, treats you unjustly, or insults you.

Well, this Sergeant, unfortunately for both of us, was not only a Prussian, but the living image of the Count von Rottendorf—but for whom I should still have been enjoying life in Heidelberg, if not at home in Cadiz among the *señoritas*. Amazingly like him, he was, in face and figure, voice and bearing, not to mention manners.

Well, this beer-swilling, *sauerkraut-snatching pickelhaub* had taken a dislike to me—right from the time I was a recruit when he was with the Depôt Company in Sidi-bel Abbès—and it was my bad luck to come under him again when I was drafted to a border station.

The more he saw of me, the more he disliked me, and I entirely reciprocated the sentiment. One red-hot thundery day of sandstorm and misery, he lost control—been drinking, perhaps, or got a touch of *cafard*—and struck me across the face with a little cane he was carrying.

I was for guard and he was inspecting us. His face was purple and there was a white fleck of saliva at the corner of his mouth when he stood in front of me and looked me over as though I were a dead and decaying mule.

Suddenly he tapped me smartly on the chest.

"That button's dirty," he snarled. "And so's your ugly face."

I stared straight past the dog's right ear and took no notice of him.

"D'ye hear what I say, *salaud?*" he bawled; and as I kept perfectly silent, knowing better than to speak, he boiled over.

"Answer me, you stinking camel!" he bawled; and as I never batted an eye-lid, he blew up, went mad, saw red—and hit me across the face with his cane and with all his might.

"Well! I am a gentleman, and I don't take blows, whatever German *canaille* may do, in their own army. I saw red too—and he was for it. Almost before he, or I, knew what had happened, I had knocked him down and was kicking him in the ribs, stomach, face, anywhere I could land one, with my heavy *brodequins*. By the time I was jumped on, grabbed, seized and held—and it took some doing—Sergeant Zampkin knew all about it.

And when I came to myself in the cells, I knew too. Knew what was in store for me. Or rather, I didn't know. For assaulting a superior officer—and they'd probably bring it in "on active service and in the face of the enemy," as there were a few Bedoui sniping around—I might very well get the death penalty. And if I didn't, I should get something worse; eight years *travaux forcés*, penal servitude with perpetual hard labour, under conditions unbelievably barbarous.

Much worse than death for a man like me, a person of quality, a scholar, a gentleman. So something had to be done about it.

I reflected—and I had plenty of time for reflection—that as Death or worse would be the result of remaining, I had better depart, since I could incur nothing worse by making the effort to do so.

I made up my mind to depart and to stand not upon the order of my going.

I was sorry for my comrade, poor Fritz Adler, but needs must when the Devil drives. Particularly when the Devil's a Frenchman. *Á grande mal, gran remedio.*[13] Yes, it was a case of *algo ó nada,*[14] for me then.

So, when Fritz Adler brought me my *gamelle* of tepid dirty water and my piece of hard dry bread, that night, I stood flat against the wall behind the cell door, and, as he entered, gave him of my best, just behind the ear.

I am afraid I overdid it.

However, to make assurance doubly sure, I gagged him, fastened his arms to his sides, and tied his boots together by their laces.

I'm afraid it was all unnecessary, though.

Then, in the role and guise of the late Fritz Adler, I sauntered out and away, unchallenged. Unfortunately—and here's luck again for you—I was not only out of the *cellule* prison-building, but past the quarter-guard and well away, when whom should I meet but the excellent Sergeant Zampkin, looking none the better for what I had given him the day before.

Saluting smartly, as is *de rigueur* between soldiers and Sergeants of the French army, I stared straight ahead and made to pass him by.

But, although it was night and we were in a narrow lane, there had to be a full moon, of course, and I had to meet him just under a lamp that stuck out from the caserne wall!

---

[13] Desperate ills need desperate remedies.
[14] Neck or nothing.

Instantly he knew me, just as I knew him.

"*Was zum Teufel!* It's *you*, is it? " he snarled, and his bayonet came out of its sheath as he sprang at me.

I hadn't time to draw mine, or rather Fritz Adler's. I had to parry the thrust. There was nothing he'd have enjoyed better than killing me himself with his own hands. That would have given him much more satisfaction than seeing me get a *conseil de guerre* sentence. And he knew he'd run no risk—self-defence: prisoner in the act of escaping: attempted murder—and so forth.

Well; there my superb fencing ability stood me in good stead, for I swivelled sideways so swiftly that his blade, instead of running through me, ran through my clothing, from right to left. And while the hilt was touching the right side of my tunic and the point was sticking out under my left arm—the blade lying flat across my breast—I swung right round, wrenching the bayonet from his hand.

As I completed the *volte face*, the spin, the twirl, the twist, I grabbed the handle of the bayonet, snatched it out, ducked low and lunged like a striking snake—or like the magnificent fencer I am.

Straight as an arrow, swift as a bullet, the point took him below the breast-bone and, slanting upward, pierced his body, coming inches out between his shoulder-blades.

And that was the end of Sergeant Hans Zampkin who struck Manöel Maine.

Well, now I *had* done it. There was no doubt now as to my fate if I were caught.

However, I had no intention of being caught and certainly none of being taken alive.

I have been up against it in the course of my life, had some bad breaks, and seen some hard times. This was one of them; not the first but almost the worst. What saved me on this occasion was the fact that I could speak Spanish.

When I was pretty well dead from exhaustion, starvation, and thirst, I was captured by a band of a tribe of Bedoui whose Sheik had been a prisoner of the Spanish at Ceuta or Melilla or somewhere, and who both understood and spoke Spanish.

While they were talking of taking me to the nearest French *poste* and handing me over for the twenty-five francs reward given for captured deserters, I told them in French, in broken Arabic, and then in Spanish, that I could give them ten times as much as the French would give them; and that, moreover, I was a bitter enemy of all *Roumis*, be they French, Spaniards, or any other.

I don't think I should have got away with it but for the Spanish version.

However, I did; and the Bedoui adopted me, partly because they are avaricious beasts, and partly because they hoped I should be useful to them for military training and when raiding.

Biding my time and watching my opportunity, I escaped from these people in turn, a simple enough matter when I had a good camel, Arab dress, and a reserve of dates, barley and water.

Eventually I got to the railway and to Algiers; and there I went straight to the house of the Spanish Consul, an old Cadiz acquaintance, still dressed as an Arab.

A risky thing to do, you think?

Yes; and it would have been, but for the fact that his wife had been one of my favourite *señoritas!* It was to her I went first—not to him.

Oho! The crop you get from sowing wild oats is not always a worthless one.

By no means.

In this case, I reaped a golden harvest, or rather a fat silver one —of *pesetas.* Luckily, we had not quarrelled and parted. We had separated with tears and kisses: tears, on my part, of thankfulness, for I had got tired of little Juanita.

"Had we never loved so kindly," I should not be here now. As it was, Juanita gave me the wherewithal to fit myself out as what I am, a Spanish gentleman of position; and, in that role, I called upon her husband at his office.

And what a tale he had to tell me!

My mother was dead. She had died quite recently. It must have been while I was with the Arabs. That meant that I should shortly be in funds, for I knew I was my mother's heir, and that, in addition to whatever she left me in her will, quite a considerable sum stood in my name at the Bank of Cadiz, to come to me on her decease.

My father, ever more English than the English, had been quite agreeable to this curious arrangement, the disposal, by a woman, of her own property.

So, after a good time with Juanita at Algiers—and who would ever dream of connecting the handsome and wealthy young Spanish nobleman, Manöel Maine, friend and *protégé* of the Spanish Consul, with the wretched runaway English *légionnaire,* William Jackson, who had deserted more than a year ago, and had doubtless died in the desert—I said farewell once more.

And tenderly again, this time, for who knew when Juanita

might be of service to me?

I took ship for Gibraltar; and, thence, train for Cadiz.

The return of the Prodigal Son.

What joy my father felt, he contrived to conceal fairly well; and though he received me quite kindly, he both advised and requested me to depart again just as quickly as was convenient, or even quicker, for the old matter of the girl and the duel with her brother still rankled in the bosoms of their family, and the father was a powerful, as well as vindictive and violent man.

Nothing loth, I assured my father that I would depart as soon as I had collected every *douro* that was due to me. And having done so, I went up to Vigo and there picked up the *Rey del Pacifico* of the South America Royal Mail Steam Navigation Company, for Rio de Janeiro, with every intention of seeing life.

Carramba! I saw life all-right in Rio, Monte Video, Buenos Ayres, Valparaiso, Santiago de Chile, Lima, Panama, Colon and Caracas; down to Buenos Ayres again—oh, the flesh-pots of Buenos Ayres!—up to Rosario by rail; on, over the Andes; down to Valparaiso once more, and back by ship to Rio.

Yes, I saw life all-right.

And I very nearly saw death too, at Paracaibo, when I went on to that lovely spot.

There I took part in a glorious rough-house, with some golden lads with whom I had come out on the *Rey del Pacifico*, in the Café del Oro in the Puerto del Sol; and it developed into a serious business with the Police.

I woke up in the famous, or rather, infamous, La Guaira Gaol of Paracaibo.

Madre de Dios! That's a marvellous institution. Unique, I should say. Weirdest prison ever *I* was in. They sling you through the gates, shut them, and there you are—absolutely free . . . inside the gaol.

It was a cross between a gaol for long-term convicts and a lunatic asylum for homicidal maniacs, and looked like a fortress. Everybody roamed about as he pleased, did what he liked, ate what he could, and slept where he fancied—inside the walls.

There were no rules and regulations, except that you couldn't go out.

No cells, no tasks, no meals, no punishments, no restrictions— within the walls.

The place was in charge of a Sergeant and ten soldiers, and their sole job was to see that nobody escaped. No-one was given food, clothing, or anything else. The wretched prisoners subsisted on the alms of the charitable, the bequests of the pious, and on what they could earn or steal from each other. You could buy anything you wanted, by giving twice its cost to a guard, who would purchase it outside and bring it in for you.

Paradoxically, that gaol was the freest place on earth; for, within its walls, there was perfect freedom to do anything you liked.

You could do any mortal thing there, except go outside.

As I had got an automatic, a long knife, a fat money belt and a way with me, I was all right; and, for a time, I quite enjoyed the amenities of La Guaira Gaol at Paracaibo; including as they did, the pleasure of the society of some of the most shocking criminals on earth; of some enlightened cultured charming men, perfectly innocent of any crime except that of having money, or political views opposed to those of the party in power at the moment; of some amazing and delightful crooks, who'd had bad luck in their profession, which might have been anything from selling salted gold-mines to picking pockets; of some unlucky Colonels, Generals, Admirals, Ministers of State and so forth, of the last Government; and of men of almost every breed and cross-breed, profession and lack of profession, on the face of the earth.

But, after a time, it wasn't so funny.

Life was a bit too hectic altogether; and I was quite ready for my case to come before the *Jefe de politico* and to buy my way out of trouble, when suddenly, over-night, there was a revolution, a general blow-up and conflagration; which latter literally included police-stations, police-courts, and law-courts—I won't say Courts of Justice—and their records. Not only their records but those who made them.

By the time the new Government of the State of Paracaibo came into existence, I, as an individual, had ceased to exist. On paper, at any rate. There was no charge on which I could be tried, so I remained untried. No-one left alive to accuse me, so I remained unaccused. Equally, no-one had any authority to release me from prison, so I remained in prison.

There I was, in the famous La Guaira Gaol of Paracaibo, for life; unless I bestirred myself and got out.

And that was easier said than done.

Escaping from the French Foreign Legion would be child's play compared with escaping from that place, which had only one gate, that gate never opened, and the iron wicket in it guarded, night and day, by a sentry who'd sooner shoot you than not.

However, I managed it all right. I gradually accumulated a Paracaibo Savile Row suit of clothes, piece by piece, by paying different guards twice the value of each article. And when the annual parody of a gaol-visitation was made, I simply walked out with the visitors. Had I been a dirty ragged bearded convict, I should have got a bang on the head from a rifle-butt, or worse; but being clean-shaven and arrayed in the local variant of purple and fine linen, I simply walked out behind the gang of Visitors—Judges of the High Court; the Bench and Bar; Sheriffs; Marshals; Mace-bearers; the Recorder of Paracaibo, and all the rest of the rascals. Just walked out, went to the railway-station, and took the first train to the most distant place.

Incidentally, I may mention that in my trousers' pocket was a damn great glass bottle-stopper which a half-witted old Abbé had sold me—as a colossal diamond of the first water! The poor old dear was much too gaga for one to call it a gold-brick confidence-trick. It was too farcically and patently absurd a swindle to be called that. I bought it from him as one buys things from a child playing at "keeping shop." To me, it was a joke. You couldn't call it a trick, much less a swindle.

However, on my way from South America—and I'd had quite enough of South America by then—I used it to play a trick myself. And on no less a person than the famous, or again, infamous, La Bella Lola, the dancer and *demi-mondaine* of international reputation, the professional Kings'-Mistress; known throughout the civilized world for her amours, her jewellery, her beauty and her wickedness.

Yes, I used the old half-wit's glass bottle-stopper to buy her "love," spinning her a marvellous yarn about how it had been given to my ancestor, Sir Marmaduke Maine, by Catherine the Great of Russia, to whose Court he was British Ambassador; how it had been in our family until my grandfather, a personal friend of the Emperor Maximilian of Mexico, had given it to that unfortunate monarch for the replenishment of his empty treasury and war-chest; and of how, after Maximilian's defeat and death, my father had bought it back again!

She fell for it, swallowed it whole, almost swallowed the diamond, and me too.

Naturally I knew that, at the earliest moment, she'd get it valued, with the view either to selling it or having it mounted, according to its worth; and that that would be the time for me to stand from under. La Bella Lola, for all that she was Queen of the Demi-monde, and had ousted real Queens of real countries, was gutter-born and bred, as fierce as a wild-cat, violent as a fish-wife, and dangerous as a snake.

Yes, when Lola found that the "Maximilian Diamond" was glass, I should have to take care that she found me—missing.

We disembarked together at Coruña and went straight on to Madrid. Laughing consumedly, I spent my last night with La Bella Lola, knowing that first thing in the morning she'd be off to da Guzman's in the Plaza Mayor, with the jewel; and that I'd be off to the railway-station.

Yes. . . .

In the morning I kissed her fondly, and went out and got my train; and La Bella Lola went out and got—twenty-five thousand pounds!

The old mad Abbé's yarn had been absolutely true; and the bottle-stopper was the biggest and most perfect diamond that ever came out of Brazil!

How's that for luck?

There was I, fleeing from La Bella Lola as fast as I could; while, as I afterwards learned, La Bella Lola was fleeing as fast as she could from me with a cheque for twenty-five thousand pounds in her pocket—a fortune that belonged to me—over half a million *pesetas* of my good money! Why, I could have lived happy ever after on the proceeds of that half a million. Or if I couldn't, I could have had a hell of a fine time for a hell of a long while.

And there was I, in fashionable San Sebastian, coming rapidly within sight of my last *douro*, and that bitch queening it on the Riviera on my twenty-five thousand pounds; filling the newspapers and magazines of half a dozen countries with accounts of her doings, and with portraits of her lovely self—dressed chiefly in jewellery and on my diamond, or the proceeds thereof.

Well, I am not cheated easily or often.

As soon as I read in the newspapers that the famous beauty and dancer—"actress," she had the impudence to call herself—had sold the famous long-lost Maximilian diamond to Señor da Guzman, the great Madrid diamond-merchant, I realized, as I say, that it was Lola who was fleeing from me, instead of me from Lola.

It also dawned on me that the she-devil must have been fooling me from the start, and had recognized that the sprat I was throwing to catch a mackerel, was a whale; a whale containing half a million *pesetas'* worth of ambergris; had realized that, while pulling her leg, I was giving her a chance to pull off a colossal deal; that while I was billing and cooing she could make a *coup* and I could foot the bill.

Carramba! I almost ground my teeth to powder. I'd teach La Bella Lola to swindle *me*. The Jezebel! The filthy shameless gutter-snipe!

I couldn't get my diamond back, but I'd get my money, if I had to choke it out of her. And choke her I would. I'd throttle her, but what I'd have my rights. I'd strangle her. I'd teach her a lesson. And I'd spend my last coin on my fare from San Sebastian to Monte Carlo where, according to the newspapers, the bitch was flaunting her flesh and her jewels and her money at the Casino, under the "protection" of a Russian Prince.

To Monte Carlo I went. Into La Bella Lola's hotel I made my way, at four in the morning. And learned something of the treachery, the perfidy, the wickedness, of women. Yes, even I, Manöel Maine, had something to learn of *that!*

Do you know what she did when she woke up and found me in her room?

Pretended not to recognize me!

Pretended not to know me at all.

Trumped up a case against me, swore she'd never set eyes on me, and that I was a jewel-thief whom she'd caught red-handed!

Covering me with the pistol she always kept under her pillow, she shrieked and screamed and rang the bell that dangled above her bed; handed me over to the hotel people, charging me with burglarious entry, assault and theft. And, backed by the liar with whom she was then living, Prince Vladamir Nicholai Marapoff, who had come in from the communicating bedroom, handed me over to the police, to the police on the wrong side of the road unluckily, the French police, not the funny little Monte Carlo gendarmes.

Yes, the good Lola meant to get me safely put away, all-right.

Well, you can believe me when I tell you that I had something to say on the subject. Oh, quite a lot, and I rather fancy La Bella Lola began to wonder whether she hadn't started trouble that might go a long way. Right back to Madrid for example, and to the recovery of a diamond that she had had no right to sell. All sorts of unpleasantness.

Now I don't want to say that the French Police are, as a body, corrupt. They are not. Nor that the average French magistrate is corrupt. He is not. But I do say that, the same night, I received a domiciliary visit in my cell, and was offered the choice of standing my trial as a hotel-thief—and I had to admit that I had been caught in extremely compromising circumstances when I was definitely trying to decorate myself with as much of Lola's property (or, rather, my own property) as I could lay hands on—or of making a voluntary enlistment in the French Foreign Legion! How's that for luck!

I had the choice between the certainty of a heavy prison-sentence and the probability of a death sentence.

For, if I joined the French Foreign Legion and were recognized as *ex-légionnaire* William Jackson, the deserter who had killed Sergeant Zampkin, I should be shot, as sure as Fate.

But that was hardly likely. I had grown a beard. I should not be recognized. It was years since William Jackson had disappeared. And I could prove, if necessary, that I was a genuine Spaniard, Señor Manöel Maine of Cadiz, and not an Englishman at all.

Better five years in the Legion than ten in a French prison. I would choose the lesser of two evils.

Moreover, if I decided to stand my trial for burglary, assault, rape, and whatever else Lola might make of it, I should run a very good chance of being recognized as the deserter I was. I should be in the dock, in the lime-light, and my portrait would be in the papers, the *Police Gazette*, the Rogues' Gallery.

I should run a ghastly risk; and the penalty would be death, inevitably. It's one thing to creep quietly, furtively, silently, into the Legion, to be disguised in the uniform, and lost in the crowd— but it's quite a different thing to be publicly tried in open court.

I decided to risk it.

Back to the Legion again, Sergeant!

I have often wondered if I did wisely, but no doubt I did. Prince Vladamir Nicholai Marakoff had a big pull and La Bella Lola a big push—of influential followers. That woman was a real power, at the height of her fame and beauty; and I hadn't much doubt that, had I stuck out, pleaded not guilty, and put up a defence, I should have been put away in a much more unpleasant place than the Foreign Legion, on the hotel burglary count—to say nothing of my being recognized as a deserter and the murderer of Sergeant Zampkin.

So, as though no charge whatsoever hung over me, and as though I were just a penniless drunk who, after a night in the cells, had nowhere to go, I asked to be allowed to enlist in the French Foreign Legion—exactly as I had been advised to do; and, within a few hours, I found myself in Marseilles, taken to the *Bureau de Récrutement*, and handed over to the Depôt Sergeant at Fort St. Jean.

It was rather amusing. When I joined before, I was an Englishman, and the one thing I did not know was a word of Spanish. Now I was a Spaniard, and had never so much as heard a word of English! How could anyone ever dream that I could be William Jackson?

And when, at Sidi-bel-Abbès, it became evident that I was "back to the Army again," a trained soldier, I let it be understood, with obvious reluctance and a little shame, that this was so, and that I had been a Spanish officer.

Yes, a sad case. A promising young subaltern who had lost his commission entirely through fault of his own. Nothing criminal of course; just wine, women, and song, and the usual high-piled top-heavy edifice of debt that eventually topples over and crushes its builder.

Well, in some ways I fared better in the Legion the second time; for I knew the ropes and was a much tougher customer, a much harder and more seasoned character, than I had been when, as a boy, I fled from Heidelberg.

In other ways I did not fare so well, for, this time, I had no money and no promise or hope of any.

However, I managed to get along after a fashion, for the experienced *légionnaire* generally knows how to get hold of a sufficiency of wine—if there be such a thing.

I cannot boast that I was particularly beloved of my officers, but I fancy I was fairly popular with my *escouade*, and was voted *bon camarade* and *bon légionnaire*, the one by no means always connoting the other.

Yes, I'm afraid that, by the time I had done three or four years of the second jolt, I was pretty much *bon légionnaire*, which is apt to mean pretty much of a Bad Man.

Then came my second big fortune, gained and lost. And through a woman again, the sly little devil.

Estella Margarita.

It was at a place called Maraknez, where she was a cabaret dancer. She was quite young and looked it, as she had worn remarkably well; for, probably, her perpetual pose of *ingénue* helped to keep her young-looking. I think we rather tend to grow into that which we profess to be, or pose as being.

She almost took me in, for a time; but I soon discovered that the sweet young thing had got a shadowy husband, or a *souteneur*, who looked her up, from time to time, and collected whatever he thought was due to him.

I also found that she was carrying on with a comrade of mine, and fooling him to the top of his bent—another Anglo-Saxon. Or no, he'd be a Celt, of course. He was a Scot, a great burly powerful, red-headed, red-bearded Highlander, MacSomething-or-other.

Estella Margarita and I laughed about him a good deal. I was not jealous, of course; for the girl had got to live, and it was damned little she got out of me, on a ha'penny a day.

However, I did give her a little necklace that cost me nothing—as I pinched it from another *fille de joie* who had annoyed me—and that necklace played its little part in what came to pass.

One day I got a note from her, telling me to come to her on Sunday evening at five sharp, and not to fail her on any account. She'd got something for me, and we'd have a great time.

I went. She was lying on the bed, as usual. But what was unusual, was that she'd been strangled with one of her own silk stockings. Her hands were bound together behind her back with the other one. Between her lips was a piece of paper on which was written :

"*Welcome, beloved. You will stay with me—again—to-night?*"

"H'm!" thinks I. "Let sleeping cats lie. This is where I fade away. *Monsieur le Mari complaisant* or *Monsieur le Souteneur* is not so complaisant as I thought. He has given the girl hers, for some reason—jealousy, or because she couldn't pay him enough—and he intends me to swing for it."

I turned about, closed the door behind me, and departed.

Now, as I learned long afterwards, the dirty dog who'd bumped her off, had sent a similar note to poor old Mac-What's-his-name, telling him to come at six. I suppose the man had tricked or frightened or tortured her into writing the notes, because undoubtedly it was she who had written them.

MacWhat's-his-name fell into the trap too, and found her exactly as I had done. He took it rather hard though. Went all to pieces. A regular old-fashioned sentimentalist. As though there weren't plenty more Easy Ethels in Maraknez!

How I came to know about it was through his getting drunk, one night, months later, and hundreds of miles from Maraknez, when we were out with a *groupe mobile* on very active service.

Maudlin and maundering, he started telling us the terrible tale of the one love of his life, a dancing-girl strangled by a jealous husband in Maraknez.

Without thinking, I took him up and said,

"You mean Estella Margarita? What? Were you her lover, too?"

"*What?* Were you her husband—who murdered her?" cried he, and came for me with his bayonet, like a raving lunatic, a homicidal maniac. He was mad.

We had a hell of a fight, and nearly killed each other.

Then, months later, again back in Maraknez, poor old MacWhat's-his-name and I were walking out together, strolling along, and thinking-up plans for getting hold of a bottle of wine.

One of our ideas was to relieve a wicked money-lender, pawn-broker, jeweller fellow, of some of his superfluous stuff; and when we came to his shop, we stopped and looked in the window.

And what do you think was one of the first things that caught my eye? The identical necklace that I had given to Estella Margarita. And just as I saw it, Mac gave one of his inarticulate growls, like a wild beast. He was staring at the necklace too. He'd seen it about Estella Margarita's neck; and, moreover, a little bangle, lying beside it, was one which he had given her!

Well, that settled Señor Mendoza's fate, and raised us from the plane of bad men who proposed to lighten his load of valuables, to that of righteous avengers: two Just Men with an ambition to punish him for the murder of Estella Margarita.

We decided, then and there, that he must be the murderer; and we entertained no such foolish theories as the possibility of the bangle and necklace having been pawned with him by somebody else, who was the murderer.

As we rightly argued, no common thief would have had letters written to me and Mac, and then have stuck an impudent message in the dead girl's mouth. Of course not. This must be the man.

We laid our plans, and did the thing systematically, thoroughly and properly. The rascal had all sorts of bolts and bars and burglar alarms, so we got in through a sky-light in the roof. We ransacked the shop and took the cream of the stuff—all that we could carry— and then attended to Señor Mendoza who lived alone over the shop. He was in bed and asleep, and snoring like a hippopotamus.

He woke up to find us, one each side of him; and obviously he recognized us. He must have seen us about with Estella Margarita, or coming and going to and from her room.

Moreover, I had the necklace in my left hand and Mac had the bangle.

Anyway he squealed, gave himself away, and proved how right we were.

"*I didn't do it!. . . I didn't do it!*" he shrieked. "*Didn't do what?*" we asked.

And then we got down to it.

If Estella Margarita were watching from her place in Heaven—and one gathers that all nice Magdalens go to Heaven—she must have been quite satisfied with the mess we made of Mendoza. If not, she was hard to please.

And when we'd finished, we went, taking with us, at a very conservative estimate, some thirty thousand pounds' worth of really magnificent jewels, gold coin, and high-denomination paper money.

Madre de Dios! It was a haul. A regular killing. And so portable; so saleable; once we'd got it to the right market.

Mendoza had been a very rich man, like so many of those money-lenders who are also pawnbrokers and jewel-merchants. There was the biggest and finest emerald I have ever seen, absolutely flawless; a necklace of perfectly-matched colossal pearls; diamonds, emeralds, rubies, sapphires; wonderful stuff that the old devil had taken in pledge for loans. It was said that he dealt with the Sultan of Morocco himself. Anyhow, there we were with the stuff in our haversacks and money in our pockets; and for the second time in my life, I had got hold of a big fortune.

For I meant to have the lot. Naturally. So did Mac, of course; and it was a case of let the best man win and the Devil take the hindmost.

So I deserted for the second time—but how differently. After the first few days, when the going was a bit rough, we travelled in comparative comfort; buying donkeys, horses, camels, as we wanted them; food, water, *burnouses*, disguise, anything we fancied.

The only draw-back was that we had to go precisely where we should not be expected to go—for, naturally, there was a hue-and-cry about us, as the suspicious-minded police connected our disappearance with the robbery and murder of Mendoza.

Madre de Dios! It was up to us not to get caught this time.

And the worst of it was that, by taking devious and roundabout desert tracks or no track at all, we were dependent, for very life, upon oases and water-holes.

With all the money in the world, we couldn't buy water where there was none; and sometimes a week's journey between oases was only possible if one discovered intervening water-holes at the right time and place, and in the right condition.

Well, we discovered one in the wrong condition. Dry. And we had reached it on very thirsty camels, and in an almost dying condition ourselves.

However, it was obviously a most ancient well, and the probability therefore was that, even if it were dry, there would be water not far beneath the surface of the wet sand at the bottom of the well.

And I determined that, after a night's rest, I'd slide down the well-rope and make sure.

Now, old Mac had insisted, the whole time, on carrying the loot himself; and in the side-pockets of his coat there was several thousand pounds' worth of big emerald, matchless pearl necklace, assorted jewellery, and thousand-franc notes—and those were the days, mark you, when a thousand-franc note was the equivalent of forty English sovereigns—not to mention a haversack stuffed with gold coin necklaces, jewellery and other good paper money.

Yes, Mac, who was about twice my size, or bulk, rather, insisted on taking care of the lot; which of course meant that he intended to take care of it for life. But though the excellent Mac had twice my brawn, he had about half my brain.

Well, we laid ourselves down to sleep, and our camels laid themselves down to grumble, beside the well mouth. And, as soon as Mac was sleeping the sleep of the unjust and snoring like a hog, I took over the responsibility of guarding the Treasury. Having picked his pockets and taken his haversack—cleaned him out absolutely—I went down the rope into the well to dig with my hands and my bayonet, for water, in the wet sand at the bottom, one hundred feet below. I had no intention of letting the excellent Mac wake up, find me down the well, and clear off with the loot.

But that is exactly what the idiot did do—or rather thought he was going to do.

And he did a thing I hadn't counted on. Instead of hauling up the rope and then calling down to me

"Good-bye, Spanish; I'm off wi' the siller!", he cut the rope with his bayonet, and chucked it down on to me.

There was luck for you!

If Mac had pulled the rope up, as I had expected, I should simply have called out,

"All right. Good-bye, old chap, if you *must* go. But the loot's down here with me." And promptly he'd have dropped the rope back and pulled me up again.

But as it was, the fool had thrown the rope down, and the loot was no good to either of us.

I couldn't get up with it, and he couldn't get down to fetch it.

It looked to me as though that was the end of Manöel Maine. For there I was, a hundred feet or so below the surface of the Sahara, and no possible means of getting up.

And there was poor old Mac, with thirty thousand pounds' worth of stuff just out of his grasp, and no earthly means of getting at it.

If he'd tied together everything we'd got in the way of camel-reins, girths, braces and boot-laces, it would not have been half long enough. Not if he'd plaited his whiskers into rope as well. Not half long enough to reach to the bottom; and if it would, not half strong enough to bear my weight and haul me up.

Stale-mate! Frightfully stale.

How I did laugh at poor old Mac!

And how poor old Mac did curse at me—as though I'd done it! If I objected to his having cut the rope, he objected quite as strongly, or more so, to my having taken the loot down the well.

All our trouble for nothing. And a very unpleasant death as the sole reward of our labours.

It was a moot point as to which of us was the better off. I, imprisoned down below had got plenty of water. Mac, waterless, up above, had got plenty of freedom.

A lovely situation. Laugh! I was never so amused in my life.

But the next two or three days weren't really amusing, and I didn't know whether they were worse for Mac or for me. Probably for him, I thought; as I at least had plenty to drink; whereas he must be dying of thirst.

And I was rather surprised to hear no more of him after I had called out that I had got the loot.

But Mac had a soft streak, a weak spot. Very sloppy and sentimental, really.

Before cutting the rope, he had hauled up our water-bottles two or three times, as I filled them; and he gave most of it to the better of the two camels, in the hope of getting it on to its feet again.

He succeeded.

And what do you think he did?

Rode straight to a French *poste*, the isolated out-lying Fort Bugeaud that we were carefully avoiding, and gave himself up—telling the Commandant of the place that he had left his *copain* alive and unhurt, at the bottom of the dried-up well, on the road to the oasis of Aïn Mendit. He did!

Of course you will say that the idea was that this would give him a chance of getting the loot. But—no. He must have known that he was landing us both in gaol with the certainty of a *conseil de guerre* sentence for desertion, even if they couldn't prove any connection between us and the murder of Mendoza.

He had no hope whatever of getting the loot. He had repented and was simply saving my life—or giving me a chance of life—at the risk of his own.

Promptly the Commandant at Fort Bugeaud clapped Mac in cells and sent off a Sergeant and a patrol of *goumiers* to the dry well, of the existence and location of which he was, of course, well aware.

I tell you I was glad to hear the voice of that Sergeant when he bawled,

"Hullo, below there! Is *Monsieur le légionnaire* Maine at home?"

"Yes, Sergeant," croaked I. "Won't you come in?"

"No," quoth he. "You're coming out."

And they got to work and lowered the palm-fibre rope which they'd brought for the purpose.

Naturally, long before they'd fixed up the new well-rope as the old one had been, I had buried the loot in the sand, right in the very middle—in the hole I had made, digging for water—thinking that, if I lived, I'd come back for it some day. I didn't keep so much as a five-franc note. Nothing that could in any way possibly connect me with the robbery and murder.

Well, they got me up, and, on the following day, I was in the next cell to Mac, in Fort Bugeaud.

On the long journey back to Maraknez I got several opportunities of a quiet word with Mac; and, speaking in English, reassured him on the subject of the loot. I told him it was "behind a loose stone five feet from the ground on the opposite side of the well from that on which the rope came down over the grooved palm-trunk edge"

The information reassured him a good deal. There was nothing now to connect us with the *affaire* Mendoza; and the loot was where he'd be able to find it if he survived to go and look.

I smiled to myself at the picture of Mac going down that well and digging out stones until the floor of the well was buried under them. The more he worked, the more deeply he'd bury the treasure

—under the stones and rock he tore out from the wall of the well!

More likely he'd find the well half full of water again, by the time he was free to visit it.

Anyway, whatever he found, he would not find the money. If anyone found that thirty thousand pounds of Buried Treasure, it would be I.

Yes, I or nobody. Nobody in the world but I knew where it was hidden. Nobody but I: and if the *conseil de guerre* decided that I was a murderer and gave me the death sentence, it would be—nobody.

However, as is quite evident, they did not shoot me. They gave me what some people consider worse, eight years' *travaux forcés*—eight years' penal servitude—undoubtedly, with one exception, the harshest and most brutal penal servitude on the face of the earth.

But I was in a rather different position from the average *détenu*, the ordinary miserable military *pénitencier*. I had something to live for—three-quarters of a million *pesetas* safely cached. And no other living soul on this earth knew where it was, except my *copain* Mac; and although he knew it was in the well, he did not know where; and if he got there first and dug out stones "five feet from the bottom on the opposite side from the well-lip," he'd find nothing at all; and would promptly conclude that I, or somebody else, had been there before him.

But in any case it didn't matter, for I'd beat him to it. I'd be there first, because I had brains; and it would not take me long to get hold of enough money to fit out a properly-equipped caravan, and do everything in style. I'd have camels, food, water, tents, a proper outfit; and tell the camel-men I was an officer of the Survey Department, mapping routes and reporting on wells and water-holes. I'd have myself lowered down and I'd come up with the stuff—concealed in a sack, of course. And once I'd got it, there'd be no more Bella Lola business. I'd settle down and enjoy life on my thirty thousand pounds.

But "man proposes . . ."

My bad luck still held; and I hadn't really quite grasped what Biribi meant.

I had heard it was tough; but—you know what people are.

Some people call life in the Legion tough. Those who've served in the *Zephyrs*, the *Joyeux*, the *Bataillon d'Infanterie légère d'Afrique*, call life there tough.

So when I had heard that *les pègres*,[15] *les pègriots*, got a rough time of it, I imagined that it was only comparative, about as much tougher than the *Bat d'Af* as the *Bat d'Af* is tougher than the Legion.

No. I hadn't quite realized what Biribi, the military convict system of France, meant.

I might mention that the *Bat d'Af*, the *Bataillon Chasseurs légère d'Afrique*, consists of young Frenchmen, conscripts, who have been convicted of some crime before the time comes for them to do their military service. Instead of being sent into the ordinary line regiments of the French Army, they are sent to these special African Light Infantry Regiments, and given special discipline, particularly strict and harsh.

So these battalions consist entirely of convicted criminals who committed their crimes before they became soldiers.

But the military criminals, condemned by the *conseils de guerre*, the Biribi victims, are those who have committed a military offence—such as insubordination, persistent slovenliness and drunkenness, striking a superior, loss or destruction of kit, *bris d'armes* or desertion—while serving their time as soldiers.

There are famous, or again let me say, infamous, prisons for these military convicts; Orleansville, Douera, Bossuet, Aïn Beida, Bougie, in Algeria; Térboursouk in Tunisia; Dar-bel-Hamrit in Morocco—some worse than others, but none better—and, of course, from these parent bee-hives, bands or rather gangs of workers *(Madre de Dios!* but they are workers) are sent out into distant camps on road-making and other construction work.

And if the Legion were Hell, which it is not; and the *Bataillons d'Afrique* were a far worse Hell, which they aren't really; and if the Biribi parent-establishments were genuine Hell, which they are; what about life in the road-gang camps?

There is hardly a name for that.

There is only one thing worse on this earth.

I will tell you about that later.

Of course, officially, these military-convict prisons are fine. Officially they are not golden cages for singing canaries, but they are everything that military prisons should be. Isn't there a special Book of the Words, a complete Code of Rules and Regulations, compiled, amended, revised, laid down, and promulgated, by the Ministry of War, signed by the Minister of War; and issued to all Generals and Commanding Officers?

---

[15] Military criminals.

Of course there is.

An admirable book of excellent rules, well known to all the (prison) world of Northern Africa, *le Livre Cinquante-sept*—Book 57.

It really is a fine Compendium of Laws concerning the Conduct and Maintenance of Military Prisons.

The only drawback is that no-one takes the slightest notice of it. No-one who has the enforcement of the rules, that is to say.

The Minister of War looks upon it, and finds it good. Each General reads it, and considers it admirable. Every *Chef de Bataillon* studies it, and declares it excellent. All Captains in the Prison Service have a look at it, and consider it wonderful. There is no *Adjudant* into whose hands it does not come, and who does not immediately pass it to the Sergeant-Major, observing that it is splendid.

Every Sergeant-Major examines it and finds it—bunk, bosh, bilge!

Still, Book 57 has its uses. It makes the Sergeant-Major laugh; and, as we know, humour is the salt of life, laughter its bubbling wine.

It is perhaps a little unfortunate—for the military convict—that Book 57 is produced at the Ministry of War, received at Headquarters in Algeria, Morocco and Tunisia; distributed to orderly-room in *maisons-mères*, central prisons, but finally hon-oured—in the breach—at all the lone, lost, isolated, out-of-the-way prison-camps, each of which is commanded by a Sergeant-Major.

And it was not long before I found myself in one of these lone, lost, isolated, out-of-the-way prison-camps, commanded by a Sergeant-Major.

This Sergeant-Major, a Corsican named Sartene—they are all Corsicans—had been too long at his job. He'd got nerves; and there is no tyrant so cruel, so dangerous, as the frightened tyrant.

I don't mean to say that Sergeant-Major Sartene was really frightened; but he'd got the jumps. He knew that some of his flock were pretty tired of life, that he was making them more and more tired of it, and that when one of them decided to quit it, he'd certainly take Sergeant-Major Sartene with him. The man lived with his hand on the butt of his revolver, and he seemed to spin like one of those Japanese waltzing mice. I believe the brain of these poor little beasts is diseased or deliberately damaged, and their only idea of motion is going round in circles.

Sergeant-Major Sartene's soul was diseased or damaged, and

he went round in circles. He never dared to turn his back to anyone or anything. And it is difficult to avoid turning your back to someone or to something.

Whichever way he was facing, he must spin round to see who was behind him, who was going to stab him in the back, brain him with a shovel, transfix him with a pick, knock him down with a great stone.

And the moment that he had sprung round to see who was behind him, he must spring back again to see who was—behind him.

He wasn't sane; and not merely our comfort—for we had none—but our lives, were in the hands of this distraught sadist.

And not only was this wretched man, with his few subordinates, in charge of a hundred dangerous criminals, any one of whom would have killed him as readily as he would a bug, but he was responsible for the making of a road through a *zone dissidente*, and at any time there might be a sudden swift attack.

Yes, he was a badly worried man, what with the heat, the dust-storms, the wicked *travaux publics* criminals, and the Chleuhs who might start sniping or, worse still, swoop down, at any moment.

Now, curiously enough, in spite of what I have said, this Sergeant-Major Sartene did regard Book 57.

It was his boast that, as a good and faithful servant of Madame la Republique, a scrupulously obedient subordinate to those set in authority over him, he prided himself on breaking none of the famous Code of Rules and Regulations of Book 57.

For example, he was forbidden to strike, to beat, and to whip, any of the convicts committed to his charge; and so he never did it. If he considered that a man was shirking and had not done, I won't say a good day's work, but the very utmost he possibly could do, he merely had him stripped and laid on the *éribas;* and, when he was stripped and laid upon the *éribas*, he merely walked about upon him. If he were so incredibly foolish, misguided, and wicked as to show a resentful, insolent, or insubordinate spirit, he would also lay *éribas* on top of the naked one who lay upon *éribas*, and himself tramp about on the top layer.

What are *éribas?* They are the branches of the *jujubier*, a desert tree provided with great sharp thorns. The *jujubier* is so prickly that the interlaced branches are used to make *bomas*, *zaribas*, enclosures, walls of thorn, that will keep wild beasts out, and wild men in.

Yes, they make hedges of them to enclose the prison-camps of the road-gangs. They are a real defence; and a force ensconced behind a wall of *éribas* is behind fortifications, so to speak. They won't stop bullets, of course, but they will stop a rush. In fact, they are a kind of natural barbed-wire, and quite as effective.

Now search Book 57 as you may, you will find it nowhere laid down that an obstreperous convict may not be laid down on a bed of *éribas* branches; nor that a coverlet of *éribas* branches may not be placed upon him when he is on his bed of *éribas* branches. Nor does any rule or regulation prohibit a Sergeant from walking about on a convict, whether he be on a bed of thorns or of roses.

Nevertheless, it is a very nasty punishment; and it was Sergeant Sartene's speciality.

His particular henchman, Sergeant Bonifaccio, taking his cue from his superior, as invariably happens, also regarded Book 57, and respected every one of its Rules and Regulations. He too noted that he was forbidden to strike, to beat, and to whip, any convict; and never on any account did he do such a thing.

Never on any provocation whatsoever.

If he felt he had occasion to punish a man, he would bid him lie on his side, on the ground; and he could lie on either side he liked. It didn't matter to Sergeant Bonifaccio in the least, on which side he lay.

And then, with all his strength, he kicked him in the pit of the stomach.

Nowhere in the whole of Book 57, though you search from cover to cover, will you find any prohibition of kicking, whether in the stomach or elsewhere.

It was his favourite cure for sickness of every kind; for he was of the advanced school of medical thought that does not believe in drugs and has little faith in surgery, but believes rather in manipulation, massage, osteopathy, the laying-on of hands—and feet.

He also believed that prevention is better than cure. Especially prevention of malingering.

So if a sick man voluntarily lay down because he could stand up no longer—or thought so—that was how Sergeant Bonifaccio showed him he was wrong. He'd soon have him up.

But he never struck a man, because that is forbidden. He merely ordered him to lie quiet until he had finished kicking him in the stomach.

Or, if he found him lying down, too ill to work, he got him up at once, by the same method.

Even so, there were rascals who defeated him; men who chopped off their left hands by repeated blows with their sharp shovels.

There was even one determined shirker who, working all night, hacked off the thumb and two first fingers of his right hand with no other weapon than a spoon.

What can you do with people like that? People who deliberately render themselves unfit for soldiering and the use of pick and shovel. You can only send them before the *conseil de guerre*, on a charge of destroying Government property.

And that would be just what they wanted. A change. A trip to Town. A rest from the eternal hard labour of the road-gang. And, moreover, a chance to say their piece. An opportunity to tell the *conseil de guerre* all about it. A chance, if they felt that way, to tell the Officers what they thought of them.

And if it meant a death-sentence—well, a good job too. So much the better. Death is the end. Death is peace. And those of them who were religious (and many of them were, like myself, extremely religious) took the view that, whatever happened after death, God must be better than a Biribi Sergeant-Major, and the Devil could be no worse—and, anyhow, they'd had their Hell already.

Oh yes, quite a number of the *pégriots*—and there were between three and four thousand of them—used deliberately to commit offences which they knew would bring them before a *conseil de guerre*.

Of course, it was bad luck if the Sergeant-Major did not take a sufficiently serious view of the matter, and dealt with it himself; but a man could always be sure of a through-ticket to the General Court Martial for the crime of self-mutilation or killing an N.C.O.

The latter was, of course, final and drastic, as nothing less than a death-sentence could possibly follow.

You had to be sure you brought it off, though.

I remember one chap, a Frenchman as it happened, called Dupont, a real *mauvais sujet*, a very tough guy—(he had tattooed on his forehead "*Victim. Prison Martyr*")—who, having felt that he'd had enough, decided to kill poor Sergeant Sargoni.

Now Sergeant Sargoni had done his very best to reclaim this scoundrel, by means of wise deterrent discipline, a complete and prolonged course of reformatory treatment that ought to have made him a wiser and better man. He had taken the greatest pains with him. Nothing was too much trouble.

He had hung him up by his hands with his toes just touching the ground. Oh, for hours at a time.

He had, at the end of a red-hot day of heavy dusty labour, served him out his water ration—super-saturated with salt.

He had kept him thereafter without water for forty-eight hours, and had then given him his water ration—super-saturated with salt.

He had tied his feet together and fastened the end of the cord to the saddle of a pack-mule and given him a ride—on the ground.

He had treated a nasty sore on the man's shoulder—a sore caused by carrying huge heavy stones resting on the bare flesh—with quick-lime.

None of the above punishments is prohibited by the Rules and Regulations set forth in Book 57.

But Sergeant Sargoni had inflicted upon him one of the punishments that *are* prescribed—detention for a given period, by means of being fastened to a post. Sergeant Sargoni had bound Dupont to a post, and had then sprinkled sugar on his bare head, face, and shoulders. Wasps, hornets, flies and all manner of insects like sugar.

But Dupont survived.

Sergeant Sargoni had given him the *crapaudine* punishment, tied him up with his hands and feet fastened together in the small of his back, in a bunch, from morning till night, until the man had screamed himself insensible. But he did not die.

Sargoni had, as I say, done everything to reform the fellow, to improve him, to deter him from further wrong-doing, but without success. Indeed, with such lamentable failure that he got worse, got so wicked that he determined to kill the Sergeant.

But Providence is always on the side of the good. I have often had occasion to note the phenomenon.

Sargoni's skull was so thick that even Dupont failed to crack it when he hit it with his shovel. And instead of going to the Better Land and taking Sargoni with him, Dupont went to an even worse one—Maroni.

Personally, I resisted all temptation to give expression to my feelings.

I had not the slightest desire to go to the Better Land, either with or without Sergeant-Major Sartene, or anybody else. This one was good enough for me, so long as I'd got thirty thousand pounds' worth of treasure hidden away in it.

But there again, "Man proposes . . ."

The chain-gang took Dupont's bad luck rather to heart, and

took Sergeant Sargoni's good luck rather badly. Fancy anybody working himself up to the point of giving Sargoni a bat on the head with a shovel, and not doing the job thoroughly! Merely making him more brutal, more vindictive, more savage; making things worse all round for everybody.

And it was just when the pot was nearly boiling over, that the chain-gang, still under command of Sergeant-Major Sartene and Sergeants Sargoni and Bonifaccio, went to Dar-bel-Hassin to carry out a piece of contract-work.

The contractor and the Sergeant-Major understood each other. If the work were completed by a certain time, it would be good for the contractor, and also good for the Sergeant-Major. Therefore, it would be bad for the gang. They'd have to work even harder and longer than ever, in order that the contractor might make his profit and the Sergeant-Major his rake-off.

Although one would scarcely have thought it possible, things went from bad to worse. The strain on the road-gang became so great that, at last, the limit was reached. The toughest material has its breaking-point, even the endurance of a chain-gang of military convicts.

Several men, whose most earnest desire in the world was to keep on their feet, fell down, collapsed from exhaustion, sickness, illness, weakness, and were promptly treated for their trouble by Sergeant Bonifaccio who specialized in this kind of cure.

At length, one night, the leader of the gang—and every gang has a leader whom it faithfully obeys, not only because he is the strongest, most determined, most desperate, and cleverest, but because he has a gang of toadies to back him up, in whatever he does—the leader, an *apache* who, amusingly enough, was named Falot,[16] decided that something had got to be done about it.

He passed round orders that, on the morrow, when tools were issued, spades, shovels, crow-bars, wheel-barrows, no man was to touch one.

It was to be a strike; passive resistance. Simply, we were to refuse to work.

That ought to give the worthy Sergeant-Major Sartene something to think about. You can take a horse to the water but you cannot make him drunk. You can punish a man for not working, but, if he is stout enough to stand up to it and hold on, you cannot make him work.

---

[16] Slang term for court-martial.

No; you can punish a man, you can forcibly feed him, you can kill him, but you cannot make him work if he won't do it.

Those were the orders; and what the leader said, went. It is one of the most amazing phenomena of the incredible Biribi system, this power of the convict leaders.

In a way, it is greater and stronger than that of the Sergeants, inasmuch as a Sergeant is occasionally defied and disobeyed; the convict leader, never. I suppose this is partly due to prison *esprit de corps*, convict loyalty; and partly to the knowledge that the wrath of the gang is more dangerous and more dreadful, its enmity more deadly, its vengeance more certain, than those of the Sergeant.

A Sergeant won't actually kill you, then and there, in cold blood—but the gang will. Nastily, too. Better defy the Sergeant than the gang-leader.

Wretched as I was, underfed and undernourished (for we got nothing whatever but *fevettes* twice a day and every day—dried vegetables, mostly grass) overworked, driven harder and more mercilessly than the Arab drives his wretched *burro*, brutally treated in every way, I was nevertheless extremely annoyed by this order of Falot's.

Bad luck again!

Between the devil and the deep sea.

If I disobeyed Falot's orders, I should certainly be killed; done to death in some horrible way; be written off as having "died"; and shovelled into a hole in the sand.

If, on the other hand, I disobeyed the Sergeant's orders and refused to work, Heaven alone knew what might happen. I might get my eight-year sentence turned into a twenty-year one by the *conseil de guerre*; for it would undoubtedly become a Court Martial matter if the road-gang refused to work, and an almighty serious matter too—quite possibly a death-sentence for the ring-leaders—and Falot and his band would be the last to figure in that role before the Court Martial.

More probably it would transpire that *Falot et Cie* were the only innocent ones; harmless pacific creatures who had been terrorized into doing as they had done; men more to be pitied than blamed for fearing the desperate ring-leaders of the conspiracy more than they feared the Law and the Authorities.

A very awkward position, and one in which I was left no choice save that of the lesser of two evils. And undoubtedly it would be a lesser evil to defy the Sergeant than to defy Falot; for, to disobey Falot and take up a shovel at dawn would mean to die at sunset, or soon after.

I could not even make my virtuous and law-abiding inclination and intention known to an N.C.O., and warn the Authorities as to what was about to take place, ranging myself on the side of the angels (the devils!) before the *émeute* took place. The mere attempt would have been my death-warrant.

Well, what I had feared and expected happened. The passive resistance turned into a fight. Blows were struck by the Sergeants —"self-defence" of course—and returned by the convicts. Picks and shovels were seized after all; but it was as weapons, not as tools, that they were taken up. The *garde auxiliare* came running, and opened fire as soon as they could do so without danger of hitting an N.C.O.—and of course, the affair ended in the only way in which it could end.

The survivors were overwhelmed, seized, thrown down, battered insensible, secured; and, next day, sent under heavy guard to the nearest *maison mère* prison, to go before the *conseil de guerre*.

They were a desperate crew. Very tough guys indeed. I couldn't be sure whether some of them were really mad or shamming mad; wanted to get the death sentence and be done with it all; or wanted to be transported for life, if only for the sake of change, a railway-journey, a sea-trip to France, a railway-journey again, French food in a French prison, and then a long sea voyage. That sort of thing.

I suppose some had one object, some another; and I verily believe that some had no object at all. They simply did not care.

There was Calendot, called on first, by the Colonel-President of the *Conseil de guerre*.

"Your name?" asked the Colonel, in his cold quiet voice.

"Carbuncle de Red-nose, the Man in the Iron Trousers," replied Calendot solemnly.

"Ah!" observed the Colonel, his face expressionless. "Have you anything to say?"

"*Oui, mon enfant*," replied Calendot. "I have to say—that you are a jelly-bellied, addle-pated old baboon, born in a Zoo; and that as your mama's cage had a red light over the door, she never knew, within a continent, which of the other animals was your papa. That's all I have to say. You may go."

He flung his *képi* at the Colonel's head—a very good shot too —and then sat down.

Pichon was next.

"Your name?" asked the Colonel-President.

"Bertrand Bulrush, by Moses out of Pharaoh's daughter. You may remember, *mon Colonel?* It was a *cause célèbre.*"

"Ah! . . ." observed the Colonel, his face expressionless. "Have you anything to say?"

"*Oui, mon Colonel.* I have to say that, like yourself, I am mad . . . mad . . . mad."

And at the top of his voice he kept screaming,

"*J'en at marre! J'en ai marre! J'en ai marre!*"

Whereupon the whole gang took up the cry, bawling together at the tops of their voices,

"*Nous en avons marre. Nous en avons marre. Nous en avons marre!*"

The Colonel eyed them patiently, his face still expressionless. He could afford to be patient. The last word would be with him.

Schwartz was next.

"Your name?"

"The same as yours, *mon frère*, naturally. Don't you recognize me? I am your twin."

"Ah! . . . Have you anything to say?"

"Only that it is not my fault."

"Not your fault that you refused to work?"

"No. Not my fault that I am your twin."

"Ah . . . !"

Then came Vlamislavski.

"Your name?"

"Call me Petit Po-po," begged Vlamislavski, a man about seven feet high.

"Have you anything to say?"

"No, something to do. Sit still."

And with great skill, accuracy, and force, he spat at the Colonel-President.

When Falot's turn came, it was as I expected. He was the injured innocent. He threw himself on the mercy of the Court. With tears in his eyes and with eloquent outstretched hands, he begged for justice, asked the Colonel and the members of the *Conseil* to try to put themselves in his place, and then to tell him how each of them would have acted in such a terrible situation; death on the one hand, *conseil de guerre* sentence on the other.

And the rest of his band followed his lead, until it certainly looked as though they had been an innocent and unwilling minority, terrified and coerced by the ring-leaders and the majority.

When my turn came, I was respectful, humble and truthful. I told the truth, the whole truth, and nothing but the truth.

And the result?

Condemned with the rest to twenty years' penal servitude and transportation for life!

Yes, the dry guillotine—Maroni. . . .

Next day, we were marched to the *maison d'arrêt* pending arrangements for our being taken to Oran, Marseilles, and the island prison of Saint Martin de Ré, four kilometres from the harbour of La Rochelle.

It is from the roadstead of La Rochelle that the convict-ship sails annually for Maroni; and it was for this ship that we and the rest of the inhabitants of the prison of Saint Martin de Ré waited.

Imagine what my feelings were in this harbour prison; in a cell, damp, cold, gloomy and terrible beyond description; far, far worse than anything we had known in Africa. Imagine my feelings as I sat in that cell and thought of my buried treasure, the fortune that awaited me in the well near the oasis of Aïn Mendit; the fortune from which I was about to be separated, in space by a hemisphere, in time by the remaining years of my life . . . by Eternity.

And through no fault of my own.

I had wished for nothing better than to behave myself; to be left alone to labour obediently; to work out my sentence, and, at the end of my eight years, to go and reap my reward, gather the fruits of my patience and endurance, collect the noble spoils, the riches that would enable me to live in comfort, in luxury, for the rest of my life.

And how I should enjoy all the comfort, not to mention luxury, after eight years of suffering, eight years of Hell. Eight years that seemed like eighty.

Can you imagine how I felt? No. Nobody could. I wonder I did not go mad.

A second fortune snatched from me, when it was almost within my grasp. Nay, actually was within my grasp; for was it not hidden where I alone knew where to find it?

Can you imagine how I cursed that swine Falot; those Sergeants who had driven him almost insane; that fool Mac who had cut the rope and thrown it down the well instead of pulling it up; and that bitch Estella Margarita who had been the cause of the whole trouble.

But for her I should not be here in this cold and dripping *tombeau*, on my way to a Penal Settlement—for life.

And how I cursed that girl in Cadiz, Dolores Floramar, who had been the *fons et origo mali*, the first cause of my downfall and ruin. But for her, I should never have fought the duel with her brother, the duel on account of which I had to flee: never have gone to Heidelberg to fight the second one, the one that was the reason of my first joining the French Foreign Legion.

And how I cursed that fat insipid lump of blond stupidity Gretchen Kellner, but for whom the ruffianly Count Fritz von Rottendorf would not have challenged me to fight.

And, again, *how* I cursed La Bella Lola who had robbed me of a quarter of a million *pesetas*—and but for whom I should never have joined the French Foreign Legion a second time, never have been in this dreadful situation.

Yes. Clearly, all too clearly, I saw how women had been my downfall, and how to four of them in particular—no; to three of them at that time—I owed my ruin; Dolores Floramar in Cadiz; Gretchen Kellner in Heidelberg; and La Bella Lola in Monte Carlo.

The fourth—and worst—came later.

Yes, I cursed all women, for the sake of those who had wrecked my life; and swore to be revenged on them as a sex; swore that I would never spare one.

And I never will. No—not though you do call it blackmail!

There were times in that cell in the cold Hell they call the Prison of St. Martin de Ré, when I nearly broke down and contemplated suicide.

It was too much.

Fate had treated me too badly; piled upon my shoulders a burden too great to be borne. But I am brave.

I have the blood of a hidalgo of Spain and of a gentleman of England, and am endowed with the natural virtues of both those great countries. While there is life there is hope.

Where there is a will there is a way.

Buen corazón quebranta mala Ventura.[17]

What the ingenuity of man can do, the ingenuity of man can un-do.

Stone walls do not a prison make, nor iron bars a cage—that a clever resolute and courageous man cannot escape from.

If, of my two heroes, Don Juan had hitherto held first place, I would now make Casanova my *beau idéal*, my exemplar; and I would escape from the prison of Maroni even as he incredibly did

---

[17] A stout heart overcomes bad fortune.

from the prison at Venice. I would be a second Casanova, and great as he in the role of prison-breaker, even as I had been great and successful as he in the role of lover.

I threw off despair. I took heart, plucked up courage, and bade myself be of good cheer and hope; for I would even now still have a purpose in life, an object to live for—escape.

Even from infamous Maroni in South America. Escape, and the recovery of my buried treasure, the thought of which was becoming a veritable *idée fixe*.

I cannot say how long I was in this horrible prison; but had it been much longer I should never have left it alive, unless I had done so as a lunatic, permanently insane.

I don't know whether the damp cold or the solitary confinement was the worse torture. I never spoke to anyone the whole time; scarcely saw anyone, in fact; for my food—stew, bread, and water—was thrust through a hatch in the door; and when I was taken out for exercise for half an hour on alternate days, it was to walk up and down, alone, between high walls.

Nevertheless, the change to the convict ship *Loire* was a doubtful blessing.

If I had then suffered unspeakably from cold and solitude, I now suffered unutterably from heat and multitude; for I spent the whole voyage in a cage with sixty other men, most of them criminals of the lowest type, bestial creatures of the most revolting habits. It was an absolute crime to herd a gentleman with such sub-human scum, such degraded animals.

My comrades in the Legion had not been entirely of the *haute noblesse*; in the Penal Battalion they had not been of the highest type; in the La Guaira gaol of Paracaibo I had lived cheek by jowl with some pretty awful specimens of humanity; but beside these sweepings of the gaols of France, *apaches*, sewer-rats, *nervis*, murderers, dope-fiends, perverts, those others were white-robed innocents, angels of light.

A great many of the convicts were foreigners, including Negroes and Arabs, and in a cage full of these creatures, like a cage full of monkeys, wild beasts, I spent the weeks of the voyage.

There were no complaints as to cold, in the hold of that convict ship; none as to solitude in that crowded cage, that pandemonium, which was only a little more noisy by day than by night, when filthy canvas hammocks were slung to the roof of the cage and we lay packed like sardines, and tried to sleep in a babel of moans, groans, cries, the noise of violent quarrelling, shouting, oaths; the raucous bawling of obscene songs.

Many never went to "bed" at all, but spent the night in card-playing, wrangling, quarrelling, fighting; and, by day, lay about the floor of the cage snoring. Many, unaccustomed to the sea, were sick. Many were ill in other ways; and the condition of those cages in those stifling holds may be imagined. No, I doubt if it can be imagined.

And in case the heat should not be sufficient, a perforated steam pipe ran into each cage. In the event of fighting, insubordination, mutiny, high-pressure steam could be turned on, and those who were scalded to death would be held to have deserved their fate.

This was the reverse of the repressive measure adopted in the prison of Saint Martin de Ré. There, in similar circumstances, a jet of water, so cold as to be almost freezing, was turned upon the prisoners; and if, left for the night in their sodden clothing, they died of cold, they too were held to have deserved their fate.

I confess that I have always preferred a knave to a fool; that I have usually found what is called a bad man more interesting than a good one; and that I have no rooted objection to a sinner *qua* sinner. But these habitual criminals were for the most part beasts, brutes, swine, ruffianly degraded *canaille;* and I had to live not only with them but actually touching them, from morning till night, from night till morning. I was always in actual personal contact with them. I was one of them, one with them, and dressed like them.

We had been given two coarse shirts, two pairs of cotton trousers, a blouse, an apron, and a brown peaked cap; and, later, a big straw hat, a sort of rough panama, for protection against the sun when we landed.

I had not objected to military-convict dress, similar to undress uniform, and a proper military *képi* with *liséré;* nor had I objected to my comrades, for they were soldiers, and their "crimes" were military. But to be dressed in this foul garb, this shapeless travesty of clothing, making me identical with these bestial criminals, revolted me, sickened my very soul. And to have these brainless, uncouth, ruffianly dregs as my companions was greater punishment than I, or any man of my birth, breeding, and calibre, could possibly deserve.

And I had to walk warily.

One convict, a wretched Polish murderer, managed to give offence to the cage-leader and his clique.

Rightly or wrongly, he was supposed to have complained of them to a guard, an unforgivable offence. The ruffians court-martialled him, held a mock *conseil de guerre*, more deadly than any real one, found him guilty and sentenced him to—he knew not what. That, as a refinement of cruelty, they kept secret among themselves, holding his head in a bucket of water while sentence was promulgated by the leader, who was president of the "court-martial."

The terrified man died a hundred deaths before, at length overcome by weariness, he dared to lie down and sleep.

As he lay sweating, racked by nightmare, a shirt was stuffed into his mouth, great powerful hands were pressed down upon his face, and half a dozen knives driven up through the hammock into his body.

In the morning the guards saw a pool of blood on the floor of the cage, found a dead man in the hammock above it—and no trace of blood on the person or clothing of any one of the remaining fifty-nine beasts in the cage.

There was no sign of a knife. Nobody had a knife, of course, for had not everyone been searched before coming on board the ship?

The body of the Pole was thrown overboard, and that was that.

Yes, one had to be careful.

Shall I ever forget that voyage—though really it is a wonder that what I suffered in Maroni has not wiped even that from my mind?

Shall I ever forgive the women who brought me to it?

Maroni! An incredible place. An indescribable life. It is unbelievable that a civilized people should allow their Government to maintain it.

As the *Loire* entered the broad deep River Maroni, and drew in to the landing-stage of St. Laurent de Maroni, the steaming, reeking jungle seemed to seize hold upon us, to grasp us, to growl beneath its foetid breath,

"*I have you! I have you now! I have you—for ever.*"

For the heat was terrific, the humidity appalling. It was like entering the hot room of a Turkish bath. It was like breathing pure steam while the lungs gasped for air.

When we were brought up from our cages on to the deck, I gazed around and realized that between me and my treasure was an ocean, a continent, an impassable swamp, an impenetrable jungle, a wide swift-running river.

What need had they to build a prison here? The whole place was a prison.

In my haste I had said that stone walls do not a prison make nor iron bars a cage; but what of jungle, swamp, river and sea? And if I had no respect for human guards—prison warders, Senegalese *askaris* and soldiers of the *Infanterie Marine*—what of those other guardians of the place, the man-eating sharks with which the waters swarmed; the snakes, the wild beasts, and the savages infesting the surrounding jungle?

As I learned later, the Indians obtained a rich reward for every escaping convict they captured and brought back, alive or dead.

With our ugly straw hats upon our heads; clad in cotton vests and shapeless trousers we, five hundred strong, filed down the gang-way; and, once again, I trod the soil of South America.

How curious, thought I, that twice I should visit this vast sub-continent, only to enter a gaol!

On the quay was a crowd of white soldiers in the French Colonial uniform, Senegalese, Indians, negroes, half-breeds, convicts, warders. There were also pyjama-clad *libèrés*, wretched people who, having served their prison sentence, had been set "free"—to starve in the *Commune Pénitentiare de Maroni*.

For how could they get away? Which of them could find the fare back to France, generous France?

Ashore, we were drawn up in long lines and passed, one by one, before the Commandant of Maroni, a dapper officer in white uniform, who sat at a table in front of a tent, on either side of which an armed guard of soldiers stood at attention.

As the convicts filed past, their names were read out and, occasionally, a man was stopped and questioned, those thus honoured being, for the most part, notorious malefactors whose crimes and trial had been a *cause celèbre*, made a public sensation, and been a nine-days' wonder.

According to some system which I did not understand, and for reasons which I could not follow, groups of convicts were sent to different places in the Penal Settlement, some to Kourou, some to Île Royale, others to St. Joseph, the rest remaining at Maroni.

And then began a strange and truly terrible life in that fever-haunted disease-stricken Hell-upon-Earth, with its worst of all possible climates, hot, damp, enervating, pestilential, almost asphyxiating.

From the quay we were marched to our prison quarters, stone sheds with corrugated iron roofs set in a jungle-clearing surrounded by high spike-topped walls.

In these human cattle-pens was nothing but rope-and-frame beds and the wretched men who lay upon them. In my shed were— besides Frenchmen, who preponderated—two negroes and three Arabs, probably quite innocent of anything that, by their standards, was wrong-doing; four Germans, two Italians, a Dutchman, an American and two Belgians.

There was also another Spaniard, an ex-bull-fighter, not a man of my own class, of course, but a veritable God-send, in that I could talk with him in Spanish; talk of Spain and of mutually-remembered joys in our happy lovely land; of the *señoritas*, the theatre, music-hall, bull-ring; of the Spanish songs and dances, Spanish food and wine; of Spanish places and of Spain . . . Spain . . . Spain. . . .

Happily, he knew Cadiz well; and I, Seville, Malaga, Barcelona, every town where there was a bull-ring of repute, and Madrid itself.

And it was equally a joy to him to talk of Home, of lovely glorious Spain. And of his own home in Barcelona and of his family. His son, Carlos, had been a great grief to him. When a bright and promising young *monosabio*,[18] already distinguished at the *novillados*,[19] already noted by the cognoscenti, the *aficionados*, he was gored by a *novillo*. Gored in the thigh and lamed for life. Only a very slight limp—but it finished him for the bull-ring. Never would he join his father's *quadrilla* now; never become second *espada* to Miguel the Matador, Miguel Braganza el Torero. Never become Carlos the Matador himself, hero of Barcelona, hero of all Spain, like his father.

No, instead of that he had to become—a waiter. And so great was his shame, grief, and disappointment that he went away. Went to London. Went and joined his uncle, head waiter in a Soho restaurant.

Yes. I almost came to know that family by sight, so well did I know them all by hearing about them. Carlos the unfortunate son . . . Ramon the head-waiter in London . . . Dolores the lovely daughter affianced to a serious man of position—in the retail wine business . . . Juanita, Miguel's adored wife, compendium of the domestic and conjugal virtues.

Dear Miguel Braganza!

---

[18] Apprentice.
[19] Fights with young bulls.

Little cause as I had to thank God, I thanked him for Miguel Braganza, the stout-hearted honest fellow, courageous, loyal, enduring and indomitable. It made just the difference between despair and hope; between the nethermost depths of misery and the stage above it—yes, between life and death itself—to have a *copain* again, and he a man who spoke my own language, knew my own country, knew the very places in which I had lived, laughed and loved.

Who but the French would have sentenced such a man as Miguel Braganza to such a fate as this—twenty years of penal servitude and transportation for life—just because he had acted like a man, struck in self-defence, defended his honour, and killed a man who was about to kill him.

Poor Miguel, needing a holiday, rest, and change of scene, had crossed from Barcelona to Marseilles. There he had taken up with a girl of the *Vieux Port;* and, one night, in the *Coq d'Or*, her jealous husband or lover had suddenly come upon them, made a scene, and struck Miguel.

Little did the fool think he was insulting and assaulting a matador, and that he would be treated as the mad bull that he was; until it was too late. For, as he rushed, Miguel, in one graceful movement, stepped aside, drew his knife, and, as the clumsy oaf passed him, struck, severing his spinal cord at the neck, as he had done a hundred times with his *spada* to other bulls.

Had Miguel been a Frenchman they would doubtless have called it a *crime passionel* and acquitted him. Being a foreigner he'd have "kissed Madame la Guillotine" had not the defending counsel made great play with the fact that the husband was in the act of attacking Miguel when he received the fatal blow.

Poor Miguel Braganza! God rest his soul; for, but for him I should not be here. And, apart from the fact that without his help I should never have escaped, I doubt whether I should have survived the horrors and dangers of the nights in that prison-house, to say nothing of those of the days in the plantations, the forests, the jungle and the swamp where we laboured, almost dead with the heat and suffocation, almost eaten alive by mosquitoes, ticks, flies and leeches.

Of the two, I am not sure which was the worse, the night or the day, "rest" in the burning stifling den, or labour in the sun-smitten jungle; danger from the human beasts in the one, or from the poisonous snakes and insects in the other.

No—without Miguel Braganza, I should not have survived;

without his abnormal strength and courage, his amazing gentleness and kindness, I should have succumbed.

For even the convict-captain, the room-leader, a sub-human creature known as The Gorilla, and who had won his position of acknowledged chief by his strength, ferocity, and brutality, was not anxious to tackle Miguel Braganza. It was known that Miguel was a murderer; and in that inverted society, the murderers are the aristocracy, entitled to respect as such. It was also known that Miguel had been a matador; and matadors are people of a special skill in killing.

Moreover, Miguel had a knife, and although it was only a home-made one, manufactured with patient skill and labour from an iron soup-spoon, it was, in Miguel's hands, a weapon of offence or defence, that would do anybody's business, *pronto*.

So that when my manners offended the lack of manners of The Gorilla, and that son of Sodom, that pillar of the pot-houses of Gomorrah, that lump of scum of the slime-pits of Siddim decreed that I should be taught a lesson one night, it needed only Miguel's quiet,

"I'll disembowel you if you lay a finger on him," to make me safe from open attack.

But for him I should have been put to death or driven to suicide, for the old hands in that shed were men, to call them men, who stuck at nothing—nothing whatever—and they had taken a violent dislike to me from the first.

Nor, when I was so ill with dysentery and malaria, should I have recovered but for Miguel's care, help, protection and nursing. He gave me his own *soupe*, when I could eat, and bribed guards to get him milk and wine for me. Yes, even there, a prisoner can get such things, if he has the money.

For some reason he loved me as much as The Gorilla and his band hated me. Loved me as a brother. With a love passing the love of woman.

Pues—why do I say that? The love of woman! *Ca!* What is it, after all?

It is an amazing thing, but, looking back, I can scarcely remember what I did during those years. I suppose the monotony was so terrible, so unbroken, that no impression is left on my mind; the suffering at the time was so great that one almost became immune to suffering; one's sensibilities so dulled that they ceased to function, and one ceased to feel.

What I remember chiefly is the ghastly oppressive heat, so

infinitely more enervating than that of the Sahara; the society of the lowest type of civilian criminals, the garbage and sweepings of great cities; insufficiency of horrible food; brutal treatment by mean, morose and evilly-disposed warders, and "trusties"; and the constant and increasing ill-health resultant on these conditions of life—to call it life.

I hardly remember the daily routine, what I did, all through those dreadful years.

At first, I was a prison sweeper, my work the cleaning out of the sheds in which we were herded at night.

Later, I was sent to a forest camp and put to the labour of felling trees and clearing jungle, terrible work in stifling steam-heat atmosphere; up to the knees in mud; the victim of constant attack by malarial mosquitoes and other poisonous insects; constantly in danger of death from the bite of the poisonous snakes with which the swamps and jungle swarmed.

From there I was sent to road-construction work, a pastime with which I was already over-familiar; but how different a labour in that dreadful climate and in that all-pervading stinking mud.

There was no question here of working against time in order that a Sergeant might share a contractor's profits; but, in a way, it made one even more resentful when the constant driving was simply and solely a matter of pure malice on the part of the warders.

What did it matter to them how much or how little was accomplished, how fast or how slowly a piece of work went on? They had no private and personal interest whatsoever in results; and, far more often than not, the work was entirely useless, simply something to keep the wretched prisoners employed. And yet there were warders who would hound the convicts on as though their lives depended upon getting a certain quantity completed in a given time.

As a matter of fact, everybody connected with that foul place, from the Governor to the lowest convict, was rendered morose, irritable, liverish and bad-tempered by the terrible climate and appalling conditions of life there. And the ill-health, ill-temper and discontent of the warders were visited on the wretched convicts.

Because they hated life there, they hated the convicts who were the cause of their being there.

And, of course, whatever the theory may have been, in practice they had plenary powers; and the convict who protested against the warders' treatment received worse treatment in consequence. The crime of striking a warder was punishable by death, and inevitably the convict who struck a warder received the death-sentence and was guillotined.

Nevertheless, occasionally, a man, goaded beyond endurance, did fell the warder whose injustice and brutality had driven him mad; and thus he ended his unbearable sufferings.

I myself should undoubtedly have found this way out— apparently the only way out—but for two deterrent and restraining causes; the watchful help and advice of Miguel Braganza, who did all he could to stand between me and trouble; and the thought of my buried treasure.

Should I allow one of these swine to rob me of it; to make me exchange it for the pleasure of smashing his brainless skull? No, I would bear everything, suffer everything, survive everything, and escape, to recover my treasure, to retrieve my fortune, literally to retrieve my fortune.

It was difficult, at times, to keep from boiling over.

At a whim, for amusement, with a word, these brutes could give a prisoner the *cachot* punishment; and they handed these sentences out, right and left, all day long. At his good pleasure and as the fancy moved him, he could give a man anything from a day to a month in the *cachot,* an absolutely pitch-dark cell; and there, in perfect blackness, utterly unrelieved by a ray of light; in completest silence, utterly unbroken by the faintest sound; the wretched prisoner could sit and go mad.

No wonder that many of the poor wretches did go mad.

Another punishment that lay in the hands of the warders, and was freely used, was that of despatching a prisoner, with or without reason, to the House of Correction or the Camp of Incorrigibles.

It is enough to say that in these places, incredible as it may seem, conditions of life were twice as terrible as in the rest of the penal settlement—work being twice as heavy, food twice as bad, housing-conditions twice as awful, and corporal punishments of inhuman severity.

In these Houses and Camp-sheds prisoners were at night chained, by means of iron anklets, to their beds, for fear they might even sleep in peace.

For such crimes as not having dug a ditch sufficiently deep; not having felled a tree sufficiently quickly; for having said I was too ill to work when I was almost too ill to stand; for not having looked sufficiently servile, humble, and broken-spirited, I have been sent to both these places; but I really do not think I suffered very much more in the House of Correction or the Camp of the Incorrigibles than I did normally.

The worst thing about them was separation, for weeks at a time, from my useful *copain*, Miguel Braganza and his watchful care, his humble love, attention, and gifts. He was in regular receipt of money, from his wife and friends in Barcelona—paper money, of course, ingeniously concealed in book-bindings and between the gummed-together leaves of magazines, things which certain good-conduct prisoners were allowed periodically to receive along with letters—and he would use this money for my benefit.

No, I don't really remember very much; the routine was so regular, the monotony so great.

At five in the morning we were aroused by the *tambourinage* of drums; whereupon we rose from our wretched beds; the door of the shed was unlocked; the pails of dirty water, faintly flavoured with coffee, were brought in by the "trusties" who were working as cook-house orderlies. Wretched as this stuff was, we got but a gill of it—a half tumbler. Frequently, for a merry jest, the warder in charge of the kitchen department would order the cook to use sea-water.

Half an hour later, another roll of drums ordered us to parade outside the shed. The warder for the week would note with a glance that our number was correct, and then tell off groups to march to various huts where tools were issued according to the work to which the group was allotted. For five hours, without a break, this work would go on—digging, hauling, tree-felling, sawing, loading, hoeing, pick-and-shovel work, wood-cutting, picket-fencing, carrying—whatever it might be.

At eleven o'clock work ceased. We were marched back, and searched by the trusties lest we had picked up anything edible or were attempting to smuggle forbidden tobacco or other contraband articles into the shed. We were then locked up while four of us went to the kitchen to fetch the two huge swill-tubs containing our dinner of thin watery soup, in which the only solids were grains of rice or pieces of bean.

On alternate days, a tiny ration of unattractive meat was issued, with the accompaniment of a crust of bad black bread, the chief constituents of which were dust, husks and straw. It needed not the microbes in the water to cause epidemics of dysentery, for the food was sufficient for that.

As soon as our starvation allowance of this starvation diet was swallowed, the drums again beat us out into the crashing glare of the sun; and again we paraded, were counted, and marched off to resume our axes, shovels, picks, wheel-barrows, machetes, spades, or other tools of our work.

Four more hours of hard labour in that smiting heat, that suffocating steamy atmosphere, and again back to barracks for the evening meal, precisely similar to that of the morning in quality and quantity—or lack of them.

The tubs having been removed, the iron door of the stone shed was fastened; and we were left to ourselves, with nothing to do, no sort or kind of interest, amusement, occupation, hobby, or diversion whatsoever, until five o'clock the following morning.

One small oil lamp, high up in a hole in the wall, gave the only light. And although the day had been spent in heavy manual labour under the most wearying and enervating conditions, the evening and night were not passed in peace, rest and quiet.

On the contrary, as a rule, throughout by far the greater part of every night, pandemonium reigned; different men bawling different songs; others insanely howling for the sake of making a noise; others violently quarrelling and frequently fighting. In corners, wretched creatures would sit weeping, shaken from head to foot by the violence of their sobbing; here and there parties would be playing games of chance and skill with filthy greasy home-made packs of cards; here and there, a sick man, shivering with fever or racked with pain, would groan unheeded, writhe in agony, or lie limp, contorted, still as though in death.

Where there is nothing to do and long hours in which to do it, Satan will find mischief for idle hands, and especially for those of men whose minds are evil, distorted, perverted and depraved. A favourite and common form of such mischief was the brutal baiting of some weakling, some poor boot-licking favour-currying would-be *protégé* of a warder, rightly or wrongly accused of bringing charges, giving evidence, lodging information, against his fellow prisoners.

Where such a man could not clear himself of the charge, had not the means to purchase immunity, had omitted to propitiate The Gorilla or had not been able to do so, his punishment was severe, frequently terrible, usually horrible and disgusting.

What nicer little Hell-upon-Earth can the mind of a fiend conceive or desire, than a mob of selected criminals, hardened and habitual, depraved and dreadful, shut up together and left to their own devices with none to oversee, none to interfere? As I have already said, I owed my very life to Miguel Braganza when I incurred their enmity.

And it was in keeping with the system that the warders, from whose all-seeing ever-watchful eyes no man was free for a second of the day, should be entirely absent at night when their presence might save the life of a tortured man, their orders procure quiet, peace, and rest for those whose life was one long torture.

But no, be the hellish din what it might, no interference was to be expected from without. At sunset we were shut in, at sunrise we were turned out, and what might occur between those hours was of interest to no-one else.

Nor, as at first I hoped, was this system in any way favourable to chances of escape. The stone walls were too thick, the heavy iron door too strong, the surrounding walls of the enclosure too high and unscaleable, the precincts of the prison too well patrolled.

I believe that no man in the whole history of the penal settlement ever escaped by night from one of these prison sheds.

The one or two heroes who had escaped and got clean away, surviving all the dangers and difficulties, the deadly perils and all-but-insurmountable obstacles of swamp and jungle, river and ocean, had made their get-away when working outside in the forest, the jungle or the swamp.

Of the many who tried, the majority were killed, whether shot down by warders as they fled; drowned in the Maroni river as they attempted to swim across it; devoured by sharks as they put out to sea on logs or home-made rafts; murdered by Indians who captured them in the jungle; or destroyed by disease, wild beasts and poisonous reptiles.

Of those who were not thus killed, nearly all the remainder died of starvation, sun-stroke and exposure in swamp and jungle.

Of the very few who got safely out of French territory, the majority were caught in Dutch territory, arrested by the Dutch police, discovered for what they were, and returned to the French authorities.

The case of these unfortunates was pitiable indeed, as punishment for attempted escape was extremely severe, the least part of it being the doubling of the offender's prison-term and the addition of a transportation-for-life sentence if he had not already received one.

He was, moreover, a marked man. Guards and warders could do to him whatsoever they pleased; he spent his indoor life in manacles; and his outdoor life with a fourteen-pound iron ball chained to the heavy anklet on his right foot.

Even so, cases were not unknown of men, who had attempted to escape and failed, attempting again and again, and finally succeeding.

What can one say of the determination, courage, endurance, perseverance; the heroism, of such indomitable souls? Words fail one.

I don't suppose that one in a hundred of those who tried to escape succeeded. Nevertheless, I was determined, not only to make the attempt, but to succeed. One or two others had done it. Why not I, who had brains far above the average; strength, skill and courage equal to those of the best of them; and a far greater incentive?

They were merely trying to get away from that Hell-upon-Earth to regain their freedom, get back to civilization, and begin life afresh. In addition to this I had a great fortune awaiting me. While they were going back, if they escaped, to begin at the bottom of the ladder, going back to poverty, to the gutter, I was going back to comfort, luxury, wealth. Yes, I had all their inducement to escape and the lure of buried treasure in addition.

And escape I would.

All I needed was the opportunity. Given that, I would find the rest—the resource, cleverness, determination, courage and ability.

Whenever I could do so, without drawing attention to myself as an intending escaper—for one never knew when one might be talking to a stool-pigeon, a traitor, a spy—I turned the conversation with my fellow-convicts to the subject of escape, in order to learn all I could, both about the failures and the successes of those who had made the attempt.

I wanted to learn exactly how and why the former had been recaptured; and, more particularly, the methods adopted by the few who had got away.

One advantage I should have over most of those who had tried and failed, an absolutely faithful and reliable companion—and his money.

The uses of the latter would be manifold, possibly before, and certainly after, the actual evasion. If it were impossible to bribe a warder—whether by reason of his honesty, his fear of discovery, or the inadequacy of the sum—it might be feasible as well as necessary to bribe a "trusty." And, once away from Maroni, the money might make all the difference between failure and success, by providing us with food and clothing, enabling us to hire a boat, to buy a ticket, to bribe minor Dutch officials or to out-bid the

French Government's reward of a hundred francs for our return, should we fall into the hands of Indians.

My friend Miguel, on land as strong as a bull, and in water as untiring as a fish, was all for the comparatively easy matter of hiding in the jungle and swimming the Maroni river, one dark night. To this I had two major objections and several minor ones. In the first place, I doubted whether, in my weakened condition, I was equal to the feat. In the second place, I had no intention of risking drowning, or seizure by sharks or alligators, for the pleasure of being arrested by Dutch guards on the other side, if I ever reached it.

Not only is it the custom of the Dutch police to arrest and return escaped convicts, but there is actually a treaty between France and Holland whereby the Dutch Government undertakes always to hand over to the Commandant of Maroni any such arrested suspects.

Could we have crossed in a boat; dressed as ordinary, or extraordinary, travellers; with something in the way of arms, provisions, boatmen and so forth; and a plausible story, we might have got away with it, might have escaped arrest and got to the port of Paramaribo, whence we could have taken ship for Europe.

But to come out of the river on the Dutch side, like a pair of drowned rats, with nothing but the rags we stood in, was merely to make our lot far worse than it already was.

It seemed to me that we should have a better chance if we could get out to sea in a boat, and sail, row, paddle or drift along the coast till we were clear of Dutch territory, and then land and take our chance. But, as Miguel observed, first find your boat; and secondly find out when you are clear of French and Dutch territory, the one extending a couple of hundred kilometres to the south-east, the other to the north-west.

Moreover, should we succeed in passing the coast of Dutch Guiana, we should reach that of British Guiana. And should we land at New Amsterdam or Georgetown and be suspected of being what we were, would the British officials return us to the French? Most probably.

Should we, on the other hand, sailing south-east, succeed in clearing the coast of French Guiana, we should reach that of Brazil. There we should be safe—safe to die of starvation and exposure before ever we reached anything approaching civilization.

It also seemed to me that we should have a better chance if, instead of swimming the Maroni from St. Laurent, we struck inland, followed the course of the river until we were far to the south of where the Dutch bank would be watched and guarded, made our way across Dutch Guiana to the Surinam river (only a distance of some thirty kilometres) and, obtaining an Indian canoe, made our way down it to the port of Paramaribo. There we should be obvious travellers from the Surinam hinterland, explorers from British Guiana; I, the leader, speaking perfect English; Miguel, my servant, a worthy half-breed from Venezuela, speaking nothing but his native Spanish.

Either of these two schemes—putting out to sea in a boat, or marching into the interior and approaching Paramaribo by way of the Surinam river—seemed to me to offer more chance of success than swimming across the Maroni straight to the watchful Dutch sentries; though, God knew, the chance in either case was slight enough.

Of the two, the boat journey would be quicker and probably entail less suffering; but as Miguel had said, first find your boat. And I had no intention whatsoever of being pulled off a log by a shark, nor of falling into the jaws of these monsters through the sinking of some frail canoe, canvas boat, or water-logged raft of sticks and string.

Fortunately Miguel was only too willing to be guided by me, and to make the attempt in whichever way I decided. In addition to his great love for me, he had a profound respect for my knowledge, wisdom, and cleverness; and willingly and unreservedly placed his strength, his money, and indeed his life, at my disposal.

After long, wide, and cautious inquiry, I came to the conclusion that I might as well abandon the idea of procuring any sort of reasonably safe and navigable craft, wherein to essay the voyage from the mouth of the Maroni river to distant British Guiana or Brazil. In the first place, the sum of money suggested was far beyond our means, or rather Miguel's means; and, in the second place, if we had had the money, we had no guarantee whatsoever that the rascally half-breed who owned the fishing-boat would not put it in his pocket, take us sufficiently far out to sea to call it an attempt to escape, and then collect an additional two hundred francs for "capturing" us.

Luckily for us, Miguel, talking with one of the convict rowers with whom he had been sent to serve in the Commandant's boat, heard the details of how this very trick had been played on a plucky and desperate Italian named Vittolini. The *capitaz*, having got his money, had taken him out to sea, returned, and then handed him over to the Commandant himself, in that very boat, swearing that, while out fishing, he had seen Vittolini drifting on a log, captured him, and brought him back.

No; the only possible chance of using a scoundrel like that, would be if one had a friend with money at some port in Brazil, who, promising a big reward, would give the *capitaz* something on account, and the remainder on one's safe arrival at the Brazilian port—which is precisely how the famous Zigzig Guilmés, *alias* Pierre Boncœur escaped.

I toyed with the idea of putting myself in the hands of such a creature and then, when well out to sea, knocking him on the head, throwing him overboard, and continuing the journey without him; but discovered that, as one might have expected, there would be a whole crew of the ruffians to be dealt with. Moreover, neither Miguel nor I knew the first thing about navigation; nor about tides, winds, currents, and the geography of the coast of the Guianas.

I decided on the overland journey—dangerous, difficult, well-nigh hopeless as it was.

That decided and settled, the next thing was to make such preparations as we could, in the way of secreting and hoarding food and anything else that might be useful; and then to wait until we were together on some work that took us well out into the jungle. Then, the first time we found ourselves out of sight of the guard, we would make a dash for freedom. With any luck at all, we could quickly penetrate so far into the dense and tangled forest as to exchange the danger of being shot by pursuers, for that of death by starvation, fever, poisonous reptiles and insects, jaguars, alligators or the arrows of wild and savage Indians.

It was not long after we had accumulated a small store of *xarque*,[20] dried fish, and biscuits, secretly purchased here and there by Miguel, when on scavenger-gang work in St. Laurent, that we were sent into the forest to search for *balata*. This is a tree-bark, strong, tough and supple, extensively used as a substitute for such fabric as leather. The convicts' shoes are soled with it, for example.

This was our chance, a god-send; for, in the first place, the nature of our work would necessitate the scattering of the group, and the penetration of individuals deep into the forest to look for the balata-bearing trees; and it would be very bad luck if Miguel and I, while keeping in touch with each other, could not get well out of sight and hearing of the warder in charge of the group.

---

[20] Salt sun-dried meat.

In the second place, axes were issued to us for the work, and no tool could have been more useful for our purpose, save a *machete*. In that almost impenetrable jungle, an axe would be at once an essential tool and an invaluable weapon.

At the end of our five-hour morning labour, during which we kept well within sight of our guard and worked in an exemplary manner, we were marched back to our quarters, were searched as usual, and then fed.

When we fell in, for the four-hour afternoon spell, Miguel and I had concealed about us our store of provisions, some bags of beans, one each of meat, some biscuits, tobacco, matches, string, fish-hooks, a knife each—one made from a file, the other from an iron cooking-spoon—and a few other such things, laboriously and furtively acquired, as occasion offered, from fellow-convicts, trusties, *libérés* and towns-people with whom we had been able to make contact when weeding gardens, when lent on domestic service, or when otherwise working in or about the houses and streets of St. Laurent. In a manner that I will not mention—but the description of which would astound you if you credited it at all—Miguel had concealed his money in hundred franc notes, each of which was then worth about four pounds.

Had it been the custom to search the convicts as they went out to work, we should have been undone.

As it was the custom to do this only on our return from work, our one anxiety was as to whether our appearance should arouse suspicion; for undoubtedly we bulged, here and there, and were definitely somewhat bulkier than usual.

However, thanks to the fact of our guards being, at that hour of the day, somewhat somnolent, what with the heat, their meal, and their glass of *pinard*, we passed unnoticed and were marched safely back to the scene of our labours.

Before long, gradually, quietly, imperceptibly, but each keeping an eye on the movements of the other, we drew away from the spot where our warder, his back to us, seated on a log, his loaded rifle between his knees, nodded, yawned and lit a cigarette to keep himself awake. In a few minutes we were out of sight, completely hidden, dense jungle between him and us, our only immediate danger that of discovery and betrayal by some treacherous devil of a fellow-convict who might hope to win favour and reward by denouncing us.

But we had chosen our direction well.

A los osados ayuda. la fortuna.[21]

We were free—until we were re-captured; unseen, unheard, unimpeded, we were making our way, according to my calculation, pretty well due south, and parallel with the Maroni river.

So long as I kept the sun on my right shoulder, I knew I should be going roughly in the right direction, and that by bearing west as the sun set, we could, at any time, come to the river bank.

There again I have forgotten most of the details of that appalling time, that living death, that incredible nightmare journey.

Crossing the Sahara had been child's play compared with it. There the sand might be soft and deep, water non-existent, the sky a fiery furnace, the earth too hot to touch, sand-storms a living burial—but you could move forward unimpeded.

Here, for much of the time, we had to hack our way; literally make a way for ourselves where there was no way. At others, when we were clear of hitherto unpenetrated and almost impenetrable virgin jungle, we came to vast swamps, shallow lakes and great expanses of mud; water-logged sodden tracts that were neither land nor water; and through these we had to wade, to plough, to swim, to splash our way as best we could, arriving at the more-or-less dry land on the other side, black, literally black, with foul and filthy slime, from head to foot.

Within a fortnight or so of leaving Maroni, we looked scarcely human. With hair and beards matted with mud; clad in tattered rags, the remnants of the clothes that had been almost torn from our bodies by the thorns; we fought our way through the jungle; filthy beyond description; haggard, emaciated, starving, fever-ridden wrecks; covered in suppurating sores where thorn-scratches had festered; our feet a mass of septic blisters; to say nothing of ulcers, boils, and a horrible rash induced by insect-bites, prickly-heat, or poisonous condition of the blood due to the food we ate and the stagnant water that we drank.

We had devoured all our provisions, and were subsisting on tropical fruit and such horrible things as lizards, grubs, mushroom-like fungi, leaves and roots.

It was a marvel we did not poison ourselves.

We had several narrow escapes from snakes, and some bad frights at night when, in spots too wet for the lighting of a fire, jaguars prowled, growled and sniffed around where we lay at the foot of a tree that we were too weak and weary to climb.

Nombre de Dios, but Miguel was strong! When, weakened by

---

[21] Fortune favours the brave.

dysentery and a bout of malaria, I could not stand, much less march, he carried me on his back, staggering along for miles.

At length I could bear it no longer, and decided that, whether far enough inland or not, we would now make for the Maroni, swim it, and, turning due west, cross the strip of Dutch Guiana that lies between that river and the Surinam. There we must buy or steal a canoe, float down to Paramaribo, make good our tale, and take ship for—anywhere. We would go by the very first ship that was leaving the port, no matter what its destination, provided it was not France or a French Colony.

But that was counting our chickens prematurely, reckoning without our host, as the English call it, and *qui compte sans son hôte compte deux fois.*

That day, I do remember, because we had an extraordinary piece of good luck. We found a priceless treasure;—nothing more nor less than a dead pig. Dead but scarcely cold. Of what this little peccary had died, whether of a broken heart, poisonous berries, fast living, or snake-bite, we neither knew nor cared; but that day we feasted on roast pork, reckless as to consequences.

Consequences there were none, save renewed strength and vigour. Bearing such mortal remains as we had been unable to eat at one sitting, we pushed on, and before nightfall we reached the river.

Here we camped, finished the pig, slept, and in the morning, tied our precious matches on our heads, and swam across.

And once again Miguel's great strength saved my life. Unable to swim another stroke, I clung to his shoulder; and, with redoubled vigour, he struck out and brought me safely ashore at a spot where, fortunately, the bank shelved to a little sand-spit. On this we decided to camp for a day or two, catch fish, eat all we could, and attempt to dry some in the sun; thus providing ourselves with food for the journey thence to the Surinam.

The march across from the Maroni to the Surinam was but a renewal of the nightmare.

How long it took, I do not know. Looking back, it is like a dreadful dream wherein I was delirious, as, doubtless, for much of the time I was. What I do remember clearly is our coming one evening upon the Surinam, and my being suddenly grabbed by Miguel and dragged down into the undergrowth.

There, in full sight, quite near to us, was a canoe, full of Indians.

We could scarcely believe our eyes, hardly dare to breathe.

Within a few yards of where we crouched, was the means of getting easily, quickly, safely to Paramaribo; of arriving there in the convincing role of intrepid but unfortunate explorers; the means of escape from this accursed land; of attaining liberty and happiness; of saving our skins. To me that frail canoe represented wealth, joy, salvation, life itself.

What would be the best thing to do?

Hail them and offer money for a passage down the river?

Quite probably—if they were sufficiently civilized to understand and value paper money—they would take it and cut our throats. If money were of no interest to them, could we make them understand that if they would take us down to Paramaribo we would reward them with whatever did interest them—guns, knives, tools, coloured cloth, beads, mirrors, bottles of *taffia*, and such things as appeal to savages? Probably not.

Might the Dutch perhaps have made themselves so feared by the Indians that they would not dare to kill white men who fell into their hands? Probably not.

We were far, very far, from civilization and if these Indians knew anything about Europeans at all, it would be nothing in their favour, nothing to give them pause, nothing to deter them from killing us—with, or without torture.

What would be the best thing to do?

In a whisper, I put the question to Miguel.

His advice was to wait and to watch; see what they were doing; follow them, so far as possible, along the river bank; and refrain from action until it was a case of hailing them or losing them altogether.

In the event this proved good counsel, the best we could have followed, for, even as we watched, they ceased paddling, conferred awhile, and then turned the nose of the canoe in toward the bank—the opposite bank, alas.

They were going to land . . . to camp for the night perhaps . . . to lie down on the warm sand and sleep . . . possibly to leave the canoe unguarded.

And that is precisely what they did.

Doubtless they were travelling far, to or from their tribal country, paddling by day and resting by night in places that they knew to be distant from villages whose inhabitants would inevitably be hostile.

They lit a fire, cooked food, sat about talking and, one by one, lay down to sleep. After waiting until there was perfect silence and stillness on the sand-spit, Miguel removed what was left of his boots and clothing, gave me his matches and money, put his knife in his mouth, slipped quietly into the water, and swam across the river, his head beneath the surface almost the whole time.

His plan was to reach the stern of the canoe, look into it, stab its occupant, if it had one—and nobody more competent to deliver a sure and silent death-stroke than Miguel—then softly, gently, and gradually, draw the nose of the canoe from off the sand, and return, either swimming and pushing the boat before him, or climbing into it and paddling, if that were feasible.

Once away, all would be well, as the Indians, if they awoke and saw what was happening, would have no means of following.

His plan succeeded. The canoe proved to be unoccupied and unguarded, the sand-spit shelving and the water shallow. It was the work of a moment for Miguel to push the canoe off, step into it, take a paddle and re-cross the Surinam.

And here Miguel's convict-experience of river-work came in useful, for he was as much at home in a boat as he was in the water.

By striking two or three of our precious matches, I guided him to where I was waiting. A few minutes later we were out in the middle of the Surinam river, being borne along upon its gentle current toward our goal.

After what we had gone through during those last terrible weeks, this was comfort, almost luxury. Scarcely need we paddle unless we wished to do so, as, happily, we were going downstream. However, the mighty Miguel in the bows paddled hard; I, in the stern, giving an occasional touch with my paddle to keep us straight and in the middle of the current.

Nor was this the first time that I had managed a canoe, having been devoted to aquatic sports both at the yacht club in the bay of Cadiz, and on the more placid inland waters of Germany. In fact, our one problem was food; and, inasmuch as we had our fish-hooks and string, it was not insoluble.

Occasionally we went ashore, preferably on little peninsulas or islands of sand, to stretch our legs, sleep in comfort, cook our fish, and search for fruit and other vegetable food.

For a while, it was wonderful; and I began to feel that I really was on the first stage of the long journey that should end at the dry well on the road to Aïn Mendit where my treasure lay.

And then misfortune overtook us.

Having landed one evening for rest and relaxation and the cooking of our fish, Miguel, going into the bush in search of fruit and the fungus which we had found edible, satisfying, and harmless, climbed a tree to get its fruit, a large green somewhat kidney-shaped thing, having a pleasant sweetish thirst-quenching juice, of which I did not know the name. In descending the tree, he foolishly seized with both hands a rope-like creeper or liana, and slid a little way down it.

When he returned to our modest camp, the insides of his hands were full of tiny splinters or thorns.

Next day they were red and swollen.

On the day after, they were covered with little suppurating festering boils.

By the evening of the fourth day, they were in a horrible mess, each hand really one big sore; and, apart from the acute agony of attempting to do so, he could not use them at all; could not move the fingers; could not close them.

He was thus rendered helpless, and completely useless in the boat. Poor Miguel had become a passenger; a burden; white cargo.

And on the next day we had a fright.

We had scarcely seen signs of human beings or human habitation since we left Maroni; but, on this day, a big flat-bottomed clumsy sort of craft was pulled out from the river banks as we turned a bend, a sort of punt or scow, crowded with Indians armed with spears, bows and arrows, and the long blow-pipes through which they puff their deadly poisoned darts.

The moment they saw us they started a hullabaloo and came in our direction. Fortunately they soon got into water too deep for poling and had to take to their paddles. Of these there appeared to be a deficiency, and I imagine that this crude flat-bottomed boat was merely a sort of fishing-raft and means of progression close along the bank in shallow water.

Anyhow, by working as I had scarcely ever worked in my life before—and that, for a man who has been a hard-labour convict, is saying something—I kept the canoe out of range of their darts and arrows, and, having got past, contrived to increase the distance between us, and to draw away.

Had they possessed fire-arms we should have stood no chance.

That night we did not go ashore, and, though I could scarcely keep awake, I contrived to carry on, occasionally paddling, but, for the main part, too tired to do more than keep the boat toward the middle of the river. In the morning, there being no sign of our pursuers, I decided to go ashore, and eat, before continuing our journey.

Miguel seemed to be ill. His arms were swollen to double their size, and a rash of boils had broken out upon his body. He could do nothing, not even feed himself, much less catch fish, cook, or paddle the canoe.

When I decided that I had better push on, I found he was in a heavy slumber, a sleep so deep that it was more like a sort of coma. When I called to him he did not wake, and though I shook him by the shoulder, he made no response, not so much as opening his eyes. He had been very short of sleep ever since leaving Maroni, and was now making up for it.

This would not do. The Indians we had seen the previous day might well be following us, by water or by land. They might have returned to their village and embarked in swift canoes.

Or again, as we were getting nearer to the coast, the river banks might be more populated by these hostile savages.

I must get to civilization and Paramaribo as quickly as possible. I could not afford to escape the French, only to fall into the hands of Indians, after all I had been through. It was a case of *chacun pour soi* and *sauve qui peut*. I was ill myself, suffering from dysentery, malaria, starvation, exhaustion and exposure.

I am a person of logical mind and sound common-sense—and I am no sentimentalist. I am glad to remember that I left Miguel what I could spare; fish, fruit, a hook and line, and a few matches.

Money being quite useless to him in the jungle of Surinam, I took the packet of hundred-franc notes. In their wrapping of thin india-rubber they were intact, dry, clean and beautiful. That wad, over half an inch in thickness, contained one hundred and twenty-six notes, each of a hundred francs—five hundred pounds—twelve thousand five hundred *pesetas*.

It would take me to Aïn Mendit in comfort, however round-about the journey.

Pushing off, I paddled all day; drifted all night; rested on a sand-pit next morning; paddled on again all day; drifted all night; and, to my surprise, at sunrise the following morning, found that I was passing a village, a settlement that showed that I had reached civilization.

The next day I arrived at Paramaribo.

Money talks. In this case it said that I was a man of substance and position; a traveller; an explorer; a mad Englishman who had made his way—for the sake of doing something uncomfortable, different, difficult and dangerous—from the hinterland of British Guiana down through Dutch Guiana to the sea.

I bought clothes, a complete outfit; had my hair cut and my face clean-shaven; moved into the best hotel in the place, and engaged a berth on the first ship leaving Paramaribo.

This I discovered was going, not to Holland as I had hoped, and as would have suited me very nicely, but to Buenos Ayres. However, Buenos Ayres was safe, and any place that was safe would suit me well; and from Buenos Ayres I could get a first-class liner to England or Spain, any day in the week.

Having been interviewed by the representatives of the local Press and been delivered of a wonderful story, I felt that, although there was no terrific urgency, the sooner I got away the better. As I spoke perfect English and was obviously a gentleman, I do not suppose that a single soul for one moment entertained the absurd idea that I might be a fugitive from French Guiana. Why should they? English gentlemen of birth and breeding must be rare in that delectable spot; and even had I at all looked the part, how should a run-away convict be a wealthy man, as obviously I was?

Of course, I did not profess a word of French; only English, and, as it happened, just a little Spanish and German. And with English, Spanish and German, I got along very nicely with the officials of Paramaribo.

Never shall I forget the sensations with which I walked on board the *Andalusia*—miserable tub though she was—watched her cast off, and saw the coast of Guiana recede and sink from my sight —for the first and last time, please God.

What a part chance plays in our fives! Almost one is driven to believe in Predestination when one sees how little there really is of Free will, how feebly our own free will operates in determining our destinies.

Chance, Fate, Providence; what are our puny efforts against them? There *is* a Providence that shapes our ends, rough-hew them how we will.

Providence intended me to go to the Argentine.

My hope and intention had been to go to Europe.

Fate took me to Buenos Ayres.

Well, I knew that wonderful city from La Boca to the Pampas; and I knew some of its citizens who might prove very useful to me now, and give me a good time while I was waiting for my ship.

In Buenos Ayres I should be in no such hurry as I had been in Paramaribo. In the Guianas I was in great danger. In the Argentine I was in none whatsoever; absolutely safe. There, it would not be a case of the first ship out. I could take my time, and wait for the ship that was going to the country I chose.

I could take a boat to Vigo and thence to Cadiz; or I could go by British mail-steamer to Southampton, and thence by Royal Oriental to Gibraltar and by train to Cadiz; I could travel under the English, Spanish, or German flag; choose my time, my boat, and my company; and, after all those years of indescribable suffering, I was ready for a taste of the flesh-pots—and in few places on this earth are the flesh-pots better served than in Buenos Ayres.

On the other hand, five hundred pounds does not, believe me, go very far, or last very long, in that most delightful and most expensive of cities. I must leave myself enough to get me to where my heart was, Aïn Mendit; for where a man's treasure is there is his heart also.

I must have my bust, but I must keep enough for travelling expenses; and those of first-class travelling to Europe, thence to Africa, and the fitting-out of an adequate caravan would not be light. I must be careful not to over-do it in Buenos Ayres; and it might be advisable for me to keep away from the Jockey Club and the race-course, for I am a born gambler, ever ready to stake all on the turn of a card, a throw of the dice, the spin of a wheel, the speed of a horse.

No; I must be careful.

I need not have worried.

Fate had sent me to Buenos Ayres, and almost the first man I met in the bar of the *Hotel du Monde*, probably the finest and costliest hotel in the world, was an old acquaintance—a man of whom I knew a few of those useful facts that can sometimes be turned into money.

Yes. There are certain places in the world where, it is said, if you wait long enough, you will inevitably meet someone whom you know. I have heard this said of Charing Cross Station; of the Rue de la Paix, in Paris; La Cannabière in Marseilles; the Great Eastern in Port Said; Raffles Hotel in Singapore; the Galle Face in Colombo; St. Mark's Square, Venice; and Broadway, New York.

Well, you might have to wait a damn long time in some of them, but here in the *Hotel du Monde*, I met this man whom I had known in the French Foreign Legion, and had come across again in a Penal Battalion.

And who and what do you think he was—beside being an old comrade of mine. He was the famous Zigzig Guilmés, supreme head of the South American Branch of *Le Milieu*. Zigzig Guilmés escaped convict from Île Royale in French Guiana. None other.

Fact!

Think of that. One is apt to be a little contemptuous of the platitude to the effect that the world's a small place—but think of that!

Zigzig Guilmés, *alias* Pierre Boncœur, the Belgian crook, had been in the French Foreign Legion and deserted; had done two years in the Penal Battalions and been returned to the Legion; had deserted again; had been arrested in France after trouble with the police while about *Le Milieu's* business; and had been given ten year's penal servitude and transportation. He had been sent to Île Royale, done two years, and escaped by sea; his good friends of *Le Milieu* having fitted out a schooner at Macapa in Brazil, sailed to Île Royale, stood off and on, and picked him up one night in a little boat.

Here he was, safe in Buenos Ayres, at the very top of the tree; from captivity, destitution, and misery—to wealth, position, and every luxury, at a bound.

"*De pobre á rico, dos palmos; de rico á pobre, dos dedos.*"[22]

Le Milieu had made him rich.

What is *Le Milieu?* The Middle? The Centre?

It is one of the most powerful, wealthy, and wide-spread organizations in the world; the great Confraternity of White Slave Traffickers; also running an incredibly profitable side-line in drugs —cocaine, morphia, heroin, opium, hashish, veronal, chloral and such.

Risky, of course, but with profits in proportion. Immeasurable profits.

I knew him at once; for Zigzig Guilmés has the misfortune to be not only a marked man so far as the Police of every country in Europe are concerned, but also marked by Nature and—shall we say—Art.

For he is badly disfigured by small-pox and has a noble scar that extends his right eye well in the direction of his ear and another that almost connects his left ear with his mouth—an Arab sword having given him the one and a friend's knife the other. A lady preferred Zigzig to the friend; the latter swore to spoil Zigzig's beauty, and he made a job of it.

No, there was no mistaking the man.

What I should find interesting would be—to discover whether he would mistake me.

---

[22] From poverty to wealth, the breadth of two hands; from wealth to poverty, the breadth of two fingers.

He had known me when I was heavily bearded and moustached. I was now clean-shaven, and looking twenty years older than I had done five years ago. In point of fact, I scarcely knew myself, the first time I looked in a mirror, after the barber at Paramaribo had done with me.

"*Bon jour, Monsieur Guilmés. Bon jour, mon cher Zigzig,*" said I, walking up to him where he leant against the bar, talking with a trio of short stout swarthy friends, obviously Argentines.

Zigzig's right hand went to his hip-pocket and instantly the four froze into immobility and silence.

And as their cold eyes watched me from their expressionless faces, I was reminded of the snakes of the Surinam jungle.

After a long searching stare from Zigzig's brilliant eyes, that almost made me lower my own,

"A little mistake," he whispered silkily in French. "I'm afraid I have not the pleasure of Monsieur's acquaintance."

"No?" I asked in feigned astonishment.

"No. Nor the faintest desire to indulge in that pleasure."

"No? . . . And yet I myself both have and enjoy that pleasure; the inestimable pleasure, the incalculable honour, of the acquaintance of Monsieur Zigzig Guilmés," said I, and smiled sweetly.

"Ah, a *flic*[23] perhaps?" murmured Zigzig.

"Neither a *flic* nor a dick," I replied.

"Come, come, take another look and don't hurry," I added. "You remember my face, surely, *mon cher* Zigzig?"

"I have not, to my knowledge, ever seen your face before; and I do not, to my certain knowledge, desire to see it again," was the cold reply.

Undeniably Guilmés had a way with him. Very deterrent indeed. By no means a gentleman with whom to trifle. I'd as soon pat a *fer de lance*, a rattle-snake, or a king cobra, as be up against Monsieur Zigzig Guilmés.

"And yet I know yours well; oh, very well, Monsieur *le Légionnaire* Boncœur, *Numéro* 4687, Third Company, First Battalion, Second Regiment. Eh? I think I saw it first in Saida in Algérie. Eh? And didn't I get an occasional sight of it at Dar bel Hamrit? . . . And a glimpse at Bougie? Was not Monsieur Zigzig, in the name of Boncœur, an ornament of La Légion Étrangère and of a Penal Battalion?"

---

[23] Detective.

Guilmés' pink tongue nicked across his lips just as does the black forked tongue of the *fer de lance*, the rattle-snake, and the king cobra. Almost it seemed strange that his tongue also was not black and forked.

His Argentine friends remained motionless and silent as statues —until the hand of the one nearest to me moved slowly, very slowly, behind him.

"No, no, my friend," I said in Spanish. "It's all right," and smiled with all my teeth. "I am not a policeman."

"What are you, then?" whispered Zigzig.

"*Ex-légionnaire* of the *Deuxième Étranger*, like yourself. *Ex-pénitencier* of Biribi, like yourself. *Ex-convict of French Guiana, like yourself.*"

"My God!" exclaimed Guilmés." Here,—answer me three questions! Who was Captain of the Third Company of the First Battalion, Second Regiment, in your time? . . . What was the name of the husband of La Bella Lison of Casba-Tadla? . . . And who at this moment is Commandant of Maroni?"

I answered the three questions in a breath, and promptly Zigzig asked me three more; questions that no-one could possibly have answered who had not served in the Third Company of the First Battalion, Second Regiment, at Saida; had not been a military convict at Dar bel Hamrit; and had not been a *détenu* in the penal settlement of Maroni.

He then accepted me for what I was; but, although we had served together in the Legion, he had not recognized me, could in no wise remember me or my name—both of which facts pleased me mightily. For if an old comrade failed to recognize me, I was pretty safe; and if Zigzig Guilmés became my friend, I had the freedom of Buenos Ayres, and no fear as to my financial future until I should regain my treasure.

He did become my friend; I did have the freedom of Buenos Ayres; and I was relieved of all anxiety as to ways and means of getting to Aïn Mendit and my buried treasure. In me, Zigzig Guilmés discovered what he was looking for; exactly what he needed; a *cher collègue* with absolutely and identically the qualifications that were required; the ideal *Caftane*.

Good men, ready, willing and able to do exactly as they were told, jostling, begging, yearning for the job, he had in hundreds; but though tough, courageous, merciless, and of satisfactorily blemished record, they were not gentlemen; persons of quality;

men of such address, appearance, bearing, manner, and manners as he needed.

What he was looking for, and had found in me, was a man who could speak French, Spanish, German and English; who could move with equal grace and ease in Society, in the best Clubs, the finest Hotels and Liners, as well as in that of the underworld, the *caveau*, *casita*, the night-club, the thieves' kitchen and the brothel.

What he was looking for was a man of the assured, easy, well-to-do type, of whom no-one would have the slightest suspicion, whether young girl or experienced police-agent; a man of the world; man about town; sportsman; club-man. But at the same time, tough as steel; hard as nails; and, when necessary, ugly as the ugliest situation that could arise: a man, moreover, who, so far as the law was concerned, had burnt his own boats behind him and was now in the same boat as his employers and superiors of *Le Milieu*.

And of course, as it happened, I filled the bill exactly.

Guilmés could not possibly have found a better man for the job; and he was the first to admit it, to acclaim it.

He had round pegs for round holes, square pegs for square holes; and in me had found, as it were, a rare octagonal peg for the octagonal hole.

For it was in eight countries that Guilmés operated—Spain, France, Germany, Belgium, England, America, Austria and Algeria; the four languages of which countries I spoke, and in all of which I could move as a visitor or resident of position and standing.

Another chief of Le *Milieu* in Buenos Ayres dealt specially and separately with Poland (a great reservoir), Russia, and Turkey; a third with Italy, Greece and the Mediterranean Islands; a fourth with Syria, Palestine and Egypt; and a fifth with the Far East, China, and Japan, a very rich source of supply.

From the moment when I first addressed Zigzig Guilmés in the bar of the *Hotel du Monde*, I was scarcely out of his company for an hour, until I took the ferry-boat down to Monte Video to catch the *Rey del Pacifico* for Vigo.

Dismissing his four Argentine satellites with a curt word, he bade me accompany him up to his suite, the finest in the *Hotel du Monde*. He then proceeded to question me further as to my record; and when he had it all, or as much as I chose to give him, from the day of my duel in Cadiz to that of my landing from the *Andalusia*, he smote his thigh heavily, smote me more heavily on the back—a man of crude and demonstrative habit—declared that he saw the hand of *le bon Dieu* in this guiding of me to his very feet, and made me a dazzling proposition of employment under him, the Supreme Chief of the South American Branch of *Le Milieu*.

I was to be European representative for the eight countries with which he dealt. I was to be forwarding agent, secretary, treasurer, and overseas manager!

Excellent! I could take an advance from Guilmés; go to Spain, Algeria, and the Sahara at his expense; secure my buried treasure; and then retire from business of every kind; especially such risky, if profitable, business as that of *Le Milieu*.

I had had all the prison I wanted, and did not intend to run my head into the noose again. With my fortune of three-quarters of a million *pesetas* I should never have need to live dangerously again —dangerously so far as the Law is concerned, *bien entendu*.

Of course, I did not explain this to Zigzig Guilmés as we sat sipping champagne and smoking dollar cigars in his truly beautiful *appartement*.

I permitted him to assume that I was only too willing to go in on the ground floor and rise to the top one, by virtue of his patronage and help; only too thankful to shine in the light of his countenance for the rest of my life—instead of informing him that I merely wanted a good time in Buenos Ayres, a good sum on account, funds for working-expenses, and a free trip to Europe.

I was on velvet. Merrily I chuckled to myself as I lay on a *chaise-longue* and listened acquiescent while he rhapsodized.

He was a real enthusiast, a fanatic, an amateur—of profitable ladies—a virtuoso.

His heart was in his job and his work was his hobby.

"What is it, *le Milieu?*" he babbled. "It is a Corporation, a Syndicate, a Company, a Society, an International Body—of brilliant men who deal, not in oil nor steel nor coal nor land nor shipping-lines nor armaments nor wheat nor timber nor wines nor currency—but in women. They buy in the cheapest market and sell in the dearest; and, in addition to the colossally profitable merchandizing and marketing of the goods, the Corporation also employs them itself, in thousands, in tens of thousands, in hundreds of thousands, paying a low wage and receiving a most princely revenue from their earnings.

"The Corporation is so great, so powerful, so widely spread, that it is almost a State as well as a Power; a State with its own

Army, for it is perpetually at war—a successful victorious war—with the Police, the Police of the World. It operates on a truly enormous scale; its overhead charges are tremendous; its revenue almost immeasurable; its profits almost incalculable.

"All this is due to the fact that it meets one of the world's greatest demands with an almost equally great supply; and because its chiefs are the cleverest specialists, the finest students of mankind, the greatest masters of psychology, in the world; for they have made a life-study, attained a complete understanding, of the psychology of those who express the demand, as well as of those who are the material of its supply and satisfaction."

Oh, a real enthusiast, a devotee, *ce cher* Monsieur Zigzig Guilmés.

"Yes, a Power," he went on, "with Ambassadors to all other Powers, especially to the Police, a perpetually inimical Foreign Power. And, though *Le Milieu* is a Power without a country, it is nevertheless one of tremendous strength and influence, a beneficent force, an agency for good, an upholder of the freedom, dignity and rights of man, especially his rights over the inferior sex—the sex created in the Garden of Eden as an afterthought, for his comfort and pleasure."

Here I smiled; for, though I take a broad and tolerant view of the things that are labelled right and wrong, moral and immoral, I am no casuist, no hypocrite, and no confused thinker.

"And of course the work of the Great Corporation is equally beneficent for women?" I commented ironically.

"Quite so! Quite so!" agreed Guilmés, seriously. "Why, I should think that, at this moment, there are upwards of a quarter of a million socially superfluous women in full and regular employment, thanks to the business acumen and organizing powers of the Great Syndicate."

"In fact, it is fundamentally a genuine philanthropic society," I remarked; and the somewhat humourless Monsieur Zigzig entirely agreed.

And thus I took office, high office, under *Le Milieu*, the great philanthropic society, that was in need of a gentleman—of birth, breeding and education; who spoke French, Spanish, German and English; and who knew both the Continent and North Africa—to inspect, stimulate, and develop their local agencies, organizations and offices at Barcelona, Marseilles, Berlin, London and Algiers; to recruit the largest possible number of young ladies of charm, who should earn the Company, one way and another, a million *pesetas* for every thousand they cost it; appoint more sub-agents for this work; increase and improve the "contacts" who did the receiving and despatching of the ladies; work up and extend the special class, ranging from foreign pursers and head-stewards, to stokers (who looked after them on board ship and guarded them from temptation on the voyage) and all such as were willing to turn an honest penny while increasing the sphere of their usefulness and benevolence.

Of course, a good accommodating French or Spanish purser was worth almost anything, and willing deck-hands and stokers very valuable, in their humble way, at concealment of unlisted lady-passengers desirous of avoiding Port Authorities at both ends, as they came on board ship in the guise of local well-laden laundresses, and left it in that of stewardesses or relatives of the personnel.

After an extremely pleasant month in Buenos Ayres; full initiation into the local phenomena of South American supply and demand; of special local requirements, both in the city and the *campo;* of the technique, methods, difficulties, dangers and problems of recruitment; of the business aspect of the different sides of the business; I took a fond farewell of my Chief—whom I hoped and intended never to see again—a considerable capital sum of money by way of working expenses, an instalment of salary, and the good ship *Rey del Pacifico* for Vigo in Spain.

After a visit to Cadiz I went on to Algiers, and thence to the place I considered most suitable for the start of my desert journey to Aïn Mendit.

This was the town of Bouzen, a last outpost of real civilization; an excellent spot for my purpose, inasmuch as it was near the part of the desert I wished to penetrate; was a good place for the fitting-out of my caravan; and, being a tourist-resort and garrison-town, a likely and suitable place for the type of individual I was impersonating.

In Bouzen I would be a tourist, a tripper, a sort of amateur explorer, intending to see something of the genuine desert, wishing to get away from civilization, and dallying with the idea of actually crossing the Sahara.

I took a house that was vacant and ready against the tourist-season—a sort of Arab-European place with a tiled patio, huge verandahs and flat roof—that just suited me finely, the very place for a gay bachelor.

I had no fear of discovery.

There was no detachment of the Legion at Bouzen, and no

Penal Battalion or *travaux publics* gang, within a hundred miles. It was utterly improbable that I should encounter anybody who had ever set eyes on me; and almost impossible that, in the event of my doing so, I should be recognized.

The clean-shaven wealthy American tourist, Elmer J. Harrison, was as different from the heavily-bearded Spaniard, Manöel Maine, as he was from the English boy, William Jackson, who had deserted from the Legion so many years ago.

No; the danger of recognition was absolutely negligible.

But there was another danger in Bouzen, great, imminent, and terrible; the danger that had pursued me from boyhood; overtaken me; and dealt me all-but-fatal blows on three occasions. Women.

Women!

"De la mar la sal, y de la mujer mucho mal."[24]

Had I but known it, *The Fourth Woman* was in Bouzen; and she proved the whirlpool, the vortex, that drew to itself, sucked down, and submerged, the ship of my fortunes.

I say *Fourth Woman*—though she may have been the four-hundredth for all I know—because she was the fourth who had brought me to ruin, almost to destruction, thus avenging the other three hundred and ninety-six, perhaps? *Ha, ha!*

When I think of her, I almost wish I had really joined *Le Milieu* and devoted my life, under the aegis of the great Philanthropic Corporation, to sending women to Buenos Ayres, sending them by the hundred, avenging myself on the whole sex for the sake of these four, and most especially for the sake of this one, the Houri of Bouzen.

I could shoot myself when I think of how I let myself be fooled; how I played moth to her candle; let myself be singed, burnt, all but destroyed, in the heat of her flame, blinded by the light of her brilliance.

Carramba! Manöel Maine of the Foreign Legion, the Penal Battalions, the Convict Settlement of Maroni—a butterfly to be broken on her wheel! Had I not seen enough beautiful and poisonous flowers that I must sip at this one?

Sangre de Cristo! A wheel did I say? Broken on her wheel. Yes, but what about Fortune's Wheel?

Nombre de Dios! It has come round full circle. He laughs best who laughs last—and so does she, if she can laugh at all.

The Houri of Bouzen—famous throughout Algeria.

---

[24] From the sea comes salt; from women, evil.

Throughout Algeria do I say? Famous from Tangier to Cairo, as one of the loveliest things God ever made and the Devil ever marred.

What a prize if I could have got her for *Le Milieu*—by force or fraud, if she were too costly for purchase. Though even at her own figure there would have been a thousand per cent profit on her.

For she was no common Ouled Naïl dancing-wench, fat and coarse, with the ordinary repertoire of *danse du ventre*, nude *can-can*, and oriental nautch-stuff debauched with occidental variations.

Nothing of the sort. Although she had started at ten, and had sat in the Street of Bouzen, for a while, at fifteen, she was Youth and Beauty incarnate, fresh as a rosebud, sweet and pure as a lily—to look at.

She'd have been worth her weight in gold to *Le Milieu*. In point of fact, but for my treasure I'd have played *Le Milieu* myself. No need for any Syndicate, Corporation or Society. It would have been a syndicate of one—and I'd have been the one.

Yes, had it not been for my three quarters of a million *pesetas*, I'd have played Providence—and she should have played Provider —without troubling *Le Milieu* in the matter at all. She should have kept me in comfort for life.

As it was, I thought I'd just be kind to myself for a while, before embarking for the last time on the hardships, rigours, and deprivations of a long desert journey.

Madre de Dios! I almost fell in love with the woman; and that, perhaps, is the very highest tribute that could be paid to her beauty and fascination.

I certainly lost my head for a time.

And that's how I lost my money.

I trusted her. Believe it or not, I, Manöel Maine, trusted a woman; and that woman a professional beauty, called by a variety of nicknames, pet names, *noms d'amour*, and known throughout Northern Africa—such was her popularity—as The Houri of Bouzen.

Yes, I fell all right, whether I fell in love or not.

I admit it—with shame. But, as I say, she really was unique. She was half European, I believe. And besides being beautiful beyond description, she was really accomplished, clever, witty, charming, fascinating and . . . *je ne sais quoi* . . . dainty, sweet.

Good God, I had nearly said "innocent!"

Anyhow, she looked it. And she had travelled and moved in good society, for she'd risen to the very top of her profession, and been taken up by distinguished men—Generals, Governors, High Officials of the Colonial Service of France. She had been taken to Paris, and there she had met wealthy men who had taken her to Berlin, Rome, Athens, Madrid, Vienna.

Yes, she knew her world; and at times she had, well camouflaged, been of the *grand monde* as well as a queen of the *demi monde*.

You'd wonder she hadn't left Bouzen and Algeria for good.

You'd wonder, indeed, that she had not married—married a Title if not a Crown—but none of these *liasons* lasted long.

And why? Simply because she entertained an ineradicable hatred for Europeans, and particularly for Anglo-Saxons. Bitterly she hated all white men, beginning with the French, but she had an especial loathing for English-speaking people.

There again, you'd wonder that she had so much to do with all these officers and officials, these subalterns, captains, generals, governors, these European millionaires and aristocrats. You'd wonder why, since she hated them so. Well, it was *because* she hated them so; and it was because her profession and position enabled her to rob them, fool them, dupe them, skin them alive, ruin them.

Half her *affaires* ended in tragedy, and her path was strewn with the bodies of suicides, some of whom had shot themselves for love of her, others for hate of themselves, such wrecks had she made of them and their finances.

Well, I am not of those who shoot themselves. I prefer shooting other people. But she certainly left me among the wreckage in her wake, and not wholly financially-speaking, either.

I did not shoot myself, but for two pins I'd have shot her—if I could have got at her—and I swore, then and there, that I'd get even with her, some day.

Three women had done me down and got away with it; and I decided three would be enough. Quite enough.

I promised myself I'd settle with Number Four somewhere, some day, somehow.

Time's whirligig! *Ha, ha, ha!*

Yes, one bright morning I woke to find that she'd gone.

And all my money had gone with her; the last of it, that is to say; the sum I'd set aside as sufficient to enable me to go and get my treasure, take it to Europe, and dispose of it. Of course, I'd spent a great deal on her, one way and another, but with the satisfying comforting thought that it belonged to *Le Milieu;* and, like a fool, I'd told her that I was soon going off with a caravan into the desert.

For some reason, this seemed to annoy her and upset her tremendously. I hoped and thought for the moment that it was jealousy, until she said in her queer pretty English-French,

"*Alors? Mais, oui?* Oah, yess? Out into ze desairt? Just like *he* did with my mother. . . . An' you t'ink you take me too? Make me lof you and then leave me?"

And when I assured her that I must go alone, as I really had business, secret business, Secret Service business in fact, away out hundreds of miles into the desert, and could not possibly take her, she turned a little nasty, said I needn't apologize, and informed me that she'd no greater desire to go out into the desert with me than she had to go to Hell.

That night she could not spend the evening with me as usual, because she must—or said she must—go to dance at the house of a friend and patron of hers, a well-known very wealthy Arab of Bouzen, Abu Sheik Ahmed, who was giving a great *tamasha* for the French Commandant.

In point of fact, as I discovered afterwards, it was to meet her Arab boy-friend, Selim ben Yussuf, son of a big Sheik upon whom she had designs.

Although the old man was *persona grata* with the French, a friendly, and a loyal ally, the son and future Sheik, this Selim ben Yussuf, was not; and he was at this party incognito, to get a word with the girl.

He got his word with her, all right.

She came on, to my house, from Abu Sheik Ahmed's house; and when I awoke in the morning, she had vanished. So had my wad of hundred-franc notes.

Think of it! Can you imagine it? A thing like that to happen to me, Manöel Maine!

I really believe that, in spite of all I had been through, I touched the lowest depths of suffering at that moment. Of all the blows of Fortune that I had received, I think I felt this the most keenly. It was worse, somehow far worse, than when Lola went off with my diamond, my twenty-five thousand pounds.

I had not been in the least in love with Lola. I had been fooling her, playing a trick on her, and had given her the diamond myself, fully believing it to be glass.

Yes, in that *affaire* I had really fooled myself; but now, for the first time in my life, I had been fooled.

Yes, I had a *mauvais quart d'heure* when I found that she and my money had gone; that she and her faithful incorruptible servant, Abd'allah ibn Moussa, her bodyguard, watch-dog, devoted slave, had gone off with a few followers on fast riding-camels.

I learned later that she had met Selim ben Yussuf at the famous Mosque of the Marabout and ridden with him to the camp of his father, Yussuf ben Amir, the big Sheik whose guest she was supposed to be.

To this day I don't know how much of the rage, shame, suffering and agony of mind, with which I was almost beside myself, was due to loss of the girl with whom I, like everybody else, was in love; to the loss of my money; to humiliation at being duped; or to the fact that the cup of happiness had been dashed from my hand just as I had raised it to my lips, my buried treasure snatched away just as my fingers were extended to grasp it.

Was it possible, I asked myself, that this girl was the real treasure? Of course not. She was but the *ignis fatuus* that danced— was she ought but a dancing-girl—over the deadly swamp; the will o' the wisp, in the mirage of the desert where my *real* treasure lay.

Fool that I had almost been, to think of a woman as treasure! Fool that I had been, to let a woman fool me.

Consider my predicament.

There was I in Bouzen, known to the French authorities—and there is not much they don't know about most visitors to garrison towns on the fringe of the *zone dissidente*—as a wealthy American tourist, hospitable, agreeable, sporting, who had come there for the very purpose of a long expedition right out into the real Sahara.

And there I was penniless, with scarcely my fare back to Algiers.

How was I to get away without arousing suspicion as to my *bona fides*, and starting that last thing in the world that I desired, a searching inquiry as to my origin and record?

That was bad enough, but it was nothing to my position with regard to my treasure.

I only wonder I did not go mad.

Owing to that she-devil, there I was with it almost in my grasp —and yet it was as far from me as when I was in Maroni. I could no more get to it from Bouzen, without money, than I could fly.

Well, there's no use in crying over spilt blood—or over unspilt blood—and the only thing to do was to get some more money. But how? Thanks to this fiend in human form, my prospects with *Le Milieu* were ruined. There again, without money, I couldn't make money.

I could not present my credentials to the local agency of *Le Milieu* at Algiers. If I could plausibly explain away the loss of time, I couldn't explain the loss of the money. They are not fools, the gentlemen of *Le Milieu*.

As a matter of fact, far from going to them, it might, before long, be a case of their coming to me, and their representative would not come bringing gold either. It would be a different metal —either lead or steel.

Not only was I ruined, penniless, cut off from the buried treasure that should make me rich for life, but I was in the gravest danger. I was a traitor to, a defaulter from, an enemy of, a Secret Society more powerful than any Camorra, any Black Hand Society, any Vehmgericht, any Ku Klux Klan; an organization richer, better-managed, better equipped, more powerful, than any of them.

Thanks to this woman, my rich beneficent employers and protectors would now turn into a most relentless and powerful enemy, more dangerous than the Police themselves.

Yes, there I was in Bouzen, between the devil and the deep sea, with a few roaring lions on the cliff edge—between the French police who would return me to Maroni and certain death from redoubled hardship, on the one hand; and *Le Milieu*, who would see to it that I, who had been admitted to their innermost arcana, their most important secrets, died quickly, on the other.

And in addition to these imminent and terrible perils were the blunt facts of destitution. Food, shelter, clothing, and transport would soon become problems. There were creditors too. I was not, of course, in debt, so to speak; but there was a number of unsettled bills which I should have paid up before starting into the desert— rent, wine, food, clothes, service—bills representing a sum of money of no great importance until this calamitous catastrophe occurred, but which was now a very serious matter.

Imagine it, if you can. Most men would have succumbed, committed suicide, in fear, rage and chagrin.

Yesterday, on the top of the wave; a lover, rich, successful, socially established; a gentleman of means and position, and with a brilliant future.

To-day, penniless, ruined, deserted, a woman's laughing-stock, beggared, in imminent danger of exposure, in fear of creditors and of secret deadly enemies. There was nothing for it but flight—and no means of fleeing.

What a position! I was powerless, impotent. I could not go to the French Police to complain of the robbery. The less I saw of the French Police, and the less they saw of me, the better. I had had all the contact with the French Police that I wanted; quite enough to last the rest of my life-time.

How could I attempt to pursue the woman? Camel hire costs money and, even supposing I could get to the Sheik Yussuf Ben Amir's camp, I should merely have my throat cut for my pains. Young Selim ben Yussuf would see to that.

I was simply driven to fraud to get the wherewithal for my escape, my fare to Algiers, and the means of subsisting there until something turned up.

I made a swift round of my friends, beginning with Colonel Levasseur, the Commandant, a bluff soldier with whom I had made quite a hit.

Toujours l'audace! Rather amusing, to walk into a lion's den to borrow a piece of meat. Cursing the carelessness or stupidity of my rascally bankers, I half-laughingly, half-apologetically, begged him to accommodate me with a couple of hundred francs until I got an answer, from Paris, to my indignant expostulatory telegram. He insisted on doubling the amount.

I could, of course, have put the blame where it lay, and told the Commandant how I had been robbed by his admired Houri of Bouzen, but he would have insisted on calling in the Police, which would not have suited my book at all. And, to tell the truth, I was, moreover, ashamed to admit that I had been fooled like that, by a girl.

From him I hurried to every friend I had made in Bouzen; and from the last of them, straight to the railway-station.

At Algiers I had an idea.

L'audace, l'audace, et toujours l'audace. I would go to the Local Agent of the Subsidiary Company, of *Le Milieu*, the one concerned with the drug-traffic. Although I knew about him from Zigzig Guilmés, he would know nothing about me. Guilmés would not have communicated with him concerning me, as, until my fall in Bouzen, I had been far too important a person to be concerned with the drug-traffic agents. Any slinking hole-and-corner fly-by-night was good enough for the dope-peddling trade.

No, he would not know my name or anything about me; and, in any case he had never seen my face. I would go to him as a French-speaking German, give him proof that I was an initiate, and go into business with him as I had done with Zigzig Guilmés. Of course, it would be on a very much lower plane altogether, a terrible drop, and entirely unworthy of my abilities and qualifications; my gifts, birth and breeding. It would be like a Colonel of Hussars turning Sergeant in a native Foot Regiment.

But beggars cannot be choosers. I had to live and, moreover, I had to make money. I must, once again, painfully get together enough money for my caravan expedition to Aïn Mendit. It would be worse than useless for me to make the attempt single-handed. I should be no better off than I was when I left the stuff there. No, I could not get there alone, much less get into and out of that bottle-shaped well. And fancy arriving there alone and finding that there was ten feet of water in it.

The job had got to be done quickly too, a regular tip-and-run raid. I could not afford to have information reaching Fort Bugeaud, and a French patrol coming out to see who I was and what I was up to. It would be all very well telling my camel-men that I was an official going to examine the well in a hurry, but that yarn would not do for the French.

No. I must be careful to do the thing properly, and surely I could afford to exercise a little patience after all these years?

And, on second thoughts, I had probably exaggerated the immediate danger from *Le Milieu* a little, provided I did not go near them in Algiers and the drug-merchant did not discover my name. Although Zigzig Guilmés would have written to the *Le Milieu* office at Algiers to expect his representative, Señor Manöel Maine, he would not have sent a photograph, as there was not one to send; and whatever description he might have given would not tally with the appearance I should present in Algiers.

Hitherto, I had always been bearded or clean-shaven. I would now wear a moustache, as well as the largest sun-glasses I could procure. Nor would the Franco-German accent of the moustached goggle-wearer exactly suggest a Spanish *caballero* to these good people.

The head of the subsidiary company, the drug-importing-and-distributing agency in Algiers, was a fat Turk, as rascally a scoundrel as ever I encountered, but extremely clever. He lived in very good style up at Mustapha Supérieur, had an expensive open-and-above-board business in an antique-and-curio shop on a busy boulevard near the quay, and a very private and recondite rendezvous in an old rabbit-warren of an Arab house in the Kasbah.

I was very quickly able to prove to Djemal Bey that I was an initiate; an accredited member of the fraternity; of orthodox antecedents; a business gentleman of unimpeachable integrity; and in good standing with the great South American branch, as well as the German, French, Spanish, English and American branches.

What he also grasped (as he thought) with a leer, a wink, and a chuckle, was the, to him, welcome fact that I was out to make a trifle on the side; that, while going about my legitimate and far more important business for the Great Confraternity, as European Representative and Agent for South America, I wished surreptitiously to handle his own line of goods, on the side, as well.

Such a man as myself who could, without incurring the faintest suspicion, travel by *wagon-lit* on Blue Trains and in the luxury suites of the greatest liners and occupy the finest rooms in the grandest hotels, was admirably situated and equipped for the highest branches of the distribution side of the business—as being one of the last people on whom any suspicion of drug-smuggling would fall. My baggage would never be subject to more than the usual casual Customs search. In many countries where the *douaniers* were venal, it would not be searched at all.

But—and this the worthy Turk fully understood—the heads of *Le Milieu* must not know that I was doing a little drug-running on the side. That was a business secret between me and Djemel Bey, a secret that he would be only too willing to keep, since he was financially interested in guarding it. My help would considerably increase his turn-over, and incidentally his rake-off.

No—he must know absolutely nothing about my (purely imaginary) operations for *Le Milieu*, and never never make any reference to me whatsoever, when dealing (in drugs) with their Local Agency.

Fortunately I had borrowed enough money in Bouzen to set me up as a traveller in my new business until the profits began to accrue—to me as well as to the Algiers ring; sufficient to enable me to live, and more particularly, to travel, in style and in the role of a wealthy man, a gentleman of position, a position situated high above the miasma of suspicion.

No Police agent, Customs official, detective, or person of that sort would ever dream that I was connected with the dope-traffic. As I went to and fro, my baggage received but little attention, and my special arrangements for concealment received none whatever. I have carried extremely valuable cargoes of cocaine, for example, in my hat, in my overcoat pockets, in the dummy novel under my arm, in my tooth-powder box, my thermos-flask, my walking-stick, all sorts of places that would have been searched, had I looked a suspicious character and behaved otherwise than I did.

But it was dangerous. Far more dangerous than the other traffic. There was always risk of an accident, though little of discovery through deliberate search.

And my personal profits were small, for that damned Turk took seventy-five per cent of them, knowing perfectly well that I could not squeal. Moreover, my regular visits to Algiers were risky; and I had to go there frequently. I decided to use the experience that I had gained of the business, to transfer from Algiers to Spain.

Settled in business there, my only risks would be those normally attaching to the profession. Unless I were caught red-handed with a consignment of dope, the Spanish police had nothing against me; the old trouble on account of which I fled from Cadiz having blown over long ago.

So I severed connection with Djemel Bey, the Turk—alleging that I was being noticed and suspected by the French authorities in Algiers and giving him a great fright—and I'd have given him good cause for fear too, if I could have done it safely, the oily rogue, and settled down to a much safer and rather more profitable business between Barcelona and Rio de Janeiro, taking in Panama, Colon, Havana, Kingston and Bermuda on the return journey.

An agent of the United States branch always met me at Bermuda, taking a big consignment for New York, where he distributed it to the Chicago and other sub-agents. He is a clever chap, by the way, quite a well-known yachtsman, and, if possible, even further removed from suspicion than myself.

His smart yacht could tell some tales.

Of course I travelled by different lines as much as possible, never using the same ship more often than I could help, and never making the entire journey in the same one. Any purser or ship's-officer who remembered having seen me before, had no idea as to where I really began my whole journey, or where I ended it. Naturally I never sailed from Barcelona or returned to it by sea.

As a rule I took small inter-island ships between Colon, Jamaica, Cuba and Bermuda to Havana or Kingston to pick up a liner for Europe.

But on this last occasion, Fate intervened and, as I took my ease at Bermuda in the house of my yachtsman friend and colleague, in to port came the liner *Amazon*—and saved me the trouble of going down to Colon or up to Kingston or Havana to pick up a ship for home.

Most convenient and *à propos*. An unsuspicious English liner that would drop me at Vigo or Southampton—and big English liners, homeward bound, are neither regular nor frequent visitors to the Bermudas.

And—especially good and unusual—she had come to pick up the personnel of the Battery, and was going to drop them at Plymouth. At Plymouth where the Customs authorities are a little, what shall we say—rustic, bucolic, unsuspicious, amateur; and where, moreover, I was a complete stranger.

This happened to suit me most admirably, for I had a little consignment of my own—to peddle personally—and that would be an admirable place at which to get it ashore, and from which to run it up to London. There I could sell it myself and pocket the proceeds—to add to my none-too-sufficient salary and commission.

Yes! Well might I see the finger of Fate in this, the hand of Destiny out-stretched—for whom did I find on board the liner *Amazon*, a ship on which I had never expected to travel, a ship of which I had never heard?

The Fourth Woman!

The woman who had fooled me, robbed me, ruined me—brought me down from my assured position of wealth, safety, and prosperity, to dope-peddling for a living, drug-smuggling to make the money with which to go and get my buried treasure!

The Hand of Fate, eh? Did it lead me on to this ship? Bring me face-to-face with The Woman—the one person in the world whom I wanted to meet, to find to catch?

Did it?

The woman who ruined me—and through whom I have to live in danger of the law, in danger of anything from ten years to a life sentence, according to which country's Police catch me!

And instead of that, I have caught *her*.

Caught her! Got her under my thumb—*so*.

Got her between my hands—*so*. Got her by the throat—*so*.

And do you think I am going to let her go? Let her escape? Shed a few tears, stroke her hand, kiss her finger-tips and set her free?

I'd tear her heart out rather.

No. She's going to make reparation. She's going to pay back seven-fold.

And then?

Seventy times seven, then. She's going to keep me in ease and comfort for the rest of my life. She's going to pay down a cash sum that's going to waft me in luxury to Aïn Mendit. And if my treasure is not still there—she's going to make it good. Yes, if it takes the last penny she can raise.

And if that's not enough she's going to earn it . . . for *me*, and in the way I shall direct.

That's what she's going to do—this "sister" of yours, Mr. Otis Vanbrugh.

I think it was your humour to say "sister" wasn't it?

IV

Otis Vanbrugh took his cigarette-case from his pocket, tapped a cigarette, lit it, and blew a long cloud of smoke.

"I did say 'sister,' " he admitted mildly, "but to tell you the truth . . ."

"*Ha!*" laughed Spanish Maine—a jeering, jarring sound.

". . . I should have said 'half-sister,' " continued Otis Vanbrugh. "Yes. To be exact she is my half-sister."

"Hedging, eh?" sneered Spanish Maine.

"Yes, to that extent. Miss Consuela Vanbrugh is my half-sister."

"*Miss Consuela Vanbrugh!*" mocked Spanish Maine in bitter ridicule. "Sure it isn't quarter-sister or one-eighth—or is it a case of they are *all* your 'sisters under their skins'?"

"Well," mused Otis Vanbrugh, " 'a touch of nature makes the whole world kin.' I believe in the brotherhood of man and the sisterhood of women—to men. But, apart from that, Miss Consuela Vanbrugh is my half-sister."

Spanish Maine laughed.

"Have it your own way—but she's *my Fourth Woman*, anyway. What she's going to get out of being your—what is it now, half-sister?—I don't know. But I know what she's going to get out of being my Fourth Woman! Or rather, I know what *I'm* going to get out of it. Perhaps, since she's your—is it still half-sister?—you will take over her liabilities, eh?"

"Yes. I'm going to take over her liabilities," was the reply.

"Now then, I have listened to your very interesting story, with considerable patience and without interruption," continued Otis Vanbrugh. "And I may say I believe—a good deal of it."

Spanish Maine bowed.

"You are now going to hear a story from me. One good comic 'turn' deserves another, eh?"

Spanish Maine looked at his jewelled wrist-watch.

"Yes, I know it's late," observed Vanbrugh. "You have told me you are a gentleman, so I claim the favour of your courtesy."

"Oh, I think we've said it all, haven't we?" asked Spanish Maine.

"*You* have. I haven't," was the reply. "You are going to listen to me as I have listened to you. And I hope that by the time I have finished, you will have—changed your mind."

"Can the leopard change his spots?" smiled Spanish Maine.

"They say not. But one has heard of a black leopard. All black. And I suppose one could white-wash a leopard. And, since we are talking of leopards, one can shoot them. And one can catch them in traps."

Spanish Maine laughed merrily.

"You won't catch this one in a trap," he said.

"Nor shoot it?"

"I don't think so."

"I don't know," mused Otis Vanbrugh. "I don't know. I have never shot a black leopard.

"It's a sort of beast I don't like," he continued. "Black leopard. . . . Black brute. . . . Black heart. . . . Blackmail. . . ."

Spanish Maine yawned.

"You know, it's a very dangerous game—blackmail," said Vanbrugh, blowing a long cloud of smoke and eyeing the other man through half-closed eyes.

"So are drug-smuggling, dope-peddling and the White Slave Trade," was the reply.

"Very."

"And doesn't a person who admits to playing those games render himself liable to—er—blackmail? Is that what you are hinting at?" jeered Spanish Maine, in his turn blowing a long cloud of cigar smoke and eyeing the other through half-closed eyes. "But blackmail is so base a crime, isn't it? Not the sort of thing that a high-toned, high-souled, perfect little gentleman would care to do, especially one who was brother, or half-brother, or quarter-brother, to a fine lady of such high birth, perfect breeding, noble ideals, and unblemished antecedents as those of—the Houri of Bouzen. Her own half, or quarter, brother! He'd never stoop to blackmail, surely? Especially when he hadn't got a shadow of proof. So dishonourable. He couldn't do it."

"No," agreed Vanbrugh. "I suppose he couldn't. But he might simply call in the Police and make specific charges. Nothing dishonourable about that. And it might be dreadfully awkward if the accused person's effects were thoroughly searched, and, whatever the result, he came quite definitely under the suspicion of the Police."

"Yes," agreed Spanish Maine, "and it might be dreadfully awkward for the little gentleman and his sister—or half-sister or quarter-sister—if the accused man drew the attention of the Police, the Magistrate, the Judge, the Press, the Public, to the fact that the accusation had been brought *simply to get the poor fellow put away*. Put away because he was obnoxious to the said sister—or mistress. Obnoxious because he knew her for a common harlot as well as a thief. Obnoxious because she had lived with him; lived on him, *and* robbed him, before becoming the sister, half-sister, quarter-sister—or mistress—of the virtuous perfect little gentleman.

"No; I don't think we are going to trouble the Police," added Spanish Maine, stretching and yawning cavernously.

"Well, let's hope there will be no necessity," replied Vanbrugh. "As I said, I am going to tell you my side of the story now. Perhaps when you've heard it, there will be no need for blackmail, police, or any unpleasantness at all, and . . ."

"Will you have a drink, Mr. Vanbrugh," interrupted Spanish Maine smothering another yawn.

"No, thank you."

"You'll excuse me if I do, won't you?"

"Certainly. . . . Right? . . . Listen. . . ." And Otis Vanbrugh, in turn, told his story to Manöel Maine.

As follows:—

V

Would it surprise you, Señor Manöel Maine, to learn that I have the honour to claim some measure of, shall we say . . . similarity of record, comradeship, professional alliance, with your noble self?

Would it surprise you to learn that *et ego in Arcadia vixi*? That I, too, have served not only in the French Foreign Legion but in a Penal Battalion?

It does surprise you, I perceive.

But, meek and mild, silly and simple, as you see me, I too, have sinned and suffered with the tough ones of the earth. Of the earth, earthy.

I cannot claim to equal your record in the matter of transportation to a Penal Settlement; but I can, and will, give you ample proof of the truth of what I say with regard to the Foreign Legion and the Zephyrs.

No doubt you will conclude that I am given to romancing when I tell you that I can check-up on part of your Bouzen story because —I have been to Bouzen myself.

I knew Colonel Levasseur.

I have had the honour of being a fellow-guest, with him, of the excellent Abu Sheik Ahmed; have had speech with the old Sheik Yussuf ben Amir; and somewhat unpleasant intimate dealings with his son Selim ben Yussuf.

I was never at Saida, so cannot verify your story of the enterprising Zigzig Guilmés; though I don't doubt it for a moment.

And, to help you verify my story, do you remember Badineff of the Legion and the Zephyrs? He was pretty well known. Did you ever come across, or hear of, Smolensky, Rien, Ramon Gonzales or Jacopi Judescu, that lot who were wiped out when the Bedoui raided the road-gangs between Zaguig and the Great Oasis? Did you know the famous Rastignac the Mutineer, who killed the sentry, put on his uniform, broke into the store-shed, pinched a pot of paint and a brush, and escaped by marching from milestone to milestone touching up the kilometre figures as he went? He did it all the way to Oran, went on leave to France with the dead sentry's *livret* and leave papers, and omitted to return. Did you ever hear of Tou-Tou-Boil-the-Cat whom the other convicts killed and buried under their tent for squealing to a Sergeant? Did you know, or ever hear of, Dubitsch and Barre who tried to set the place on fire, so that they could escape in the confusion, were caught in the act and handed over by the Sergeant-Major to their fellow-convicts whom they would have burnt to death to save themselves?

Oh, yes; I have been through the mill, beginning with the Seventh Company of the Third Battalion of the First Regiment of the Foreign Legion and ending with Biribi—whence, like yourself, I escaped, or rather, was (quite unintentionally) liberated by the said Bedoui who raided the Zaguig road where we were working.

So you see I have been a companion in misfortune. But that is all, for I cannot claim to have been a companion in crime.

And how did I come to be a soldier in the Foreign Legion and a convict in a Penal Battalion?

I am going to tell you.

Also how I come to be upon this ship with my half-sister, Miss Consuela Vanbrugh. I'm going to tell you fully and freely and truthfully—and you're going to listen.

I will begin with my late father as, but for him, you would not be sitting in that chair; the lady whom you wish to blackmail would not be on this ship; and this unpleasant situation would never have arisen.

My father was a very remarkable man, of a type by no means unfamiliar to psychologists and other students of human nature, and always extremely interesting to them. He was a man of tremendous strength of character, personality, force, vitality, and vigour; a man of great ability, power of organization and command; considerable knowledge and great piety; deeply religious—a fundamentalist, believing that every word in the Bible is not only literally true and inspired by God, but actually dictated by Him. He did not merely believe in the truths of his religion, he simply knew that they were facts.

And, from knowing that what he believed was true, he gradually but inevitably grew into knowing that any statement that he made was true.

On this excellent state of affairs he yet further improved, and, by the time I was old enough to understand him, he had arrived at the even more blessed state, in which everything that he did was right—because he did it.

A man like that, while a beacon set upon a hill for all men to see, a shining light to lighten the neighbours, a model for all men to admire and to copy, can be something less than a comfort in the home.

While I do not deny that he was a model citizen, an admirable elder, a pattern to the community; I do not affirm that he was a model father. My mother broke down and died under the weight of his goodness, his piety, and his guidance. My elder brother, under the same influence, ran away from home, and stayed away. My younger sister became little better than a half-wit, if that much; while my other sister and I, concealing even from ourselves the fact that we hated him, took a trip to Europe together, when I inherited a comfortable fortune from my uncle.

I had been to Europe before, as a boy of seventeen, on a visit to my mother's home in England, at a place called Brandon Regis where my grandmother still lived. While there, I came to know the folk at Brandon Abbas close by, a mansion of considerable age, belonging to Sir Hector Brandon. The family consisted of Lady Brandon, her daughter Claudia, her niece Isobel, and three brothers of the name of Geste, also relations.

Although very young, I was old enough to fall in love with the niece.

I may here mention that my father, that pillar of piety, that rock of integrity, that model of propriety, had never visited Brandon Regis since marrying my mother. But he had crossed to Europe on business—cattle business—for he was a beef-baron and a cattle-king, as well as a noted breeder of blood horses.

With the view to experimenting with an Arab strain, he had crossed to Algeria, attended the Arab race-meetings at Biskra and elsewhere, purchased some of the finest pure-bred Arab horses that money could buy—and he was a wonderful judge of a horse—and, still in search of even finer horse-flesh, visited Bouzen near which place roamed the noted Sheik Yussuf ben Amir, the fame of whose horses was known throughout Algeria.

And, at Bouzen, this righteous man, whose life had been hitherto as straight and open as a railway-track—along which he had thundered almost as gently, quietly, delicately, perceptively, and sensitively as an express train—went clean off the rails.

Absolutely off the rails he went, taking with him one Zaza Blanchfleur, a very famous Ouled Naïl dancing-girl from the Street of Bouzen, the Street of a Thousand Delights.

I suppose the overstrained cord of virtue snapped at last; a phenomenon, as I say, not unknown, and extremely interesting to, the psychologist.

I don't for a moment suggest that my father was a whited

sepulchre, a humbug, a fraud. He wasn't. He was not self-indulgent nor vicious. His faults were those of self-righteousness, arrogance and tyranny. He merely crushed and broke the spirit of those who were dependant upon him, subordinate to him, or in his power; merely played the interfering superior person and hectoring bully to others.

I firmly believe that this was his first such lapse from grace.

It was some lapse. He had been so good for so long in public that he now had to be "bad" in private. The swing of the pendulum.

It was some swing.

Being the man he was, he did the thing thoroughly and properly. He fitted out a luxurious *kafilah*, a most generous caravan, and took the girl, Zaza Blanchfleur away out into the desert, to a distant oasis; and there lived his idyll. I imagine that, while it lasted, he must have been perfectly happy, must have really relaxed; given fullest rein to every impulse; become himself, natural, an ordinary fallen human-being, at last and for once; admittedly a sinner and glorying in his sin; revelling in his freedom, his return to nature and naturalness.

I am not for a moment judging him. I am neither praising nor condemning what he did. I am not commenting at all—merely recording. Recording the fact that this proclaimedly austere, professedly pious, publicly virtuous, openly religious man, put off his armour and relaxed.

The armour of righteousness? Of self-righteousness? Of unrighteousness? Anyway, he put off his armour. He donned soft silk; unbent; stooped; fell; and lay, relaxed and restful—on soft cushions; in a tent, by an oasis; with a woman.

I imagine that, until the hour of his awakening, this was the happiest period of his life; and I imagine that the hour of his awakening coincided with that of his satiety.

The pendulum swung back and he came to himself—his former self.

The idyll was over, finished, and must be forgotten.

Forgotten. The sooner the better. All memory of it put aside, put away, disregarded, denied, ignored; and thrust deep down into the unconscious mind.

I don't know, but I shouldn't be surprised, if he agonized; wrestled with the Devil; called upon God; smote his breast; and indulged in an orgy of repentance.

I don't know, but I shouldn't be surprised, if he turned upon the dancing-girl, Zaza Blanchfleur, companion of his sin, and called her the cause of his sin; turned and rent her, metaphorically speaking; and, without any metaphor at all, abandoned her.

But wasn't she already an abandoned woman—one who neither deserved, expected, nor hoped for, anything better than to be abandoned—by her lover?

Wasn't she probably thinking that it was high time the idyll ended, when his ready cash ended?

Was she anything more than a common courtesan, a hireling whose period of hire had expired?

Yes, she was something more than a common courtesan. She was a most uncommon one—for although Homer A. Vanbrugh was neither her first nor her twenty-first employer, admirer, lover, protector, he was her first *amant de cœur*.

She had fallen completely, absolutely, desperately in love with him.

Probably he was something quite novel, Nordic, enormous, blue-eyed, pink-cheeked, fair-haired—something wholly different from the Arabs and the Latins with whom she had come in contact as a dancing-girl of Bouzen; completely non-vicious; chivalrous—for he was an American and therefore accustomed to treating women as they are not treated in Africa. Serious, sober and solid, he would interest, intrigue, amaze the Ouled Naïl dancing-girl, Zaza Blanchfleur. This would be a love affair with an entirely new technique.

It speaks well for him that this experienced professional lover fell in *love* with him.

It speaks well for her that, in spite of the life to which she had been brought up as an Ouled Naïl dancing-girl, the life she had lived, as such, in the Street of Bouzen, she could love—really *love*.

You cannot call her an abandoned woman, if you remember that. Perfect love casteth out, not only fear, but a great many other things. We know of a woman who was "forgiven much because she loved much."

And how do I know this?

Because his desertion of her broke her heart; broke her life; broke her reason. She mourned and pined for him; and, in time, went melancholy mad and died, because of him.

What postponed her insanity and death was the birth of her daughter—who was his daughter.

What we call madness is a queer thing. From the day that Homer A. Vanbrugh left her, she changed her way of life absolutely. He was her first real lover. He was her last "lover" of any sort or kind.

From the day of her daughter's birth, she lived more as a nun than a dancing-girl. A fanciful person might say that this man who came out of the blue into her life so suddenly, remained in it for a few months, and left it as suddenly, saved her—and destroyed her.

Saved her soul—and killed her body, and her reason.

And yet the queer thing is that, although she became as virtuous as St. Cecilia, chaste as Diana, cold and inaccessible as the moon whose beauty her own equalled—her daughter grew up in her profession.

That is difficult to understand, unless one realizes that she was insane; and unless one knows something of the strength of caste and custom, in the East. The son invariably follows the father's profession; and, in the one "profession" open to women, the daughter follows in her mother's footsteps automatically.

Perhaps in this case *kismet, dastur,* the iron laws of custom, might have been broken had Zaza Blanchfleur retained her sanity. Probably she would have put Homer A. Vanbrugh's daughter with the Sisters of the Sacred Heart, or have found some means of communicating with the child's father.

Possibly she would have offered to send her to him.

But this dark-eyed Ophelia was mad.

She kept the child with her and, as the girl grew up, talked to her incessantly of love, of lovers, and of—her father.

Well, we are the product of our heredity and our environment; and the girl grew up—her mother's daughter and the daughter of the Street of a Thousand Delights; grew up, not only to rival, but to outshine the wondrous beauty, grace and fascination of her mother; to outshine even her mother's natural and acquired accomplishments.

The child adored her mother.

And as the girl grew to years of (how can one say discretion?) of wisdom, knowledge and understanding—and these things come young to the Daughters of the Street, poor souls—she understood what had happened to her mother.

But, for her mother's sake, she hated the man who had wrecked the poor woman's happiness, her reason, her life; and, for his sake, hated *all* men.

To her, men were lovers; lovers were swine; swine were animals from whose jewelled snouts she should snatch the precious stones as their filthy feet trampled the common stone that was her heart.

Willingly she would dance for men's pleasure, and for their money.

Unwillingly she would give herself for men's delight and for their money.

She adored her mother and she hated men; and she made no secret of the fact of her wish that they had but one universal throat that she might cut it. To no man was she kind save by contract, a contract that ended with his money.

Her frank attitude was,

"I hate you. I loathe you. You make me sick, and I'll punish you for pursuing me, if I can. You call me 'dear,' and I will be dear indeed. . . . A man robbed my mother of her heart and her soul and her life, robbed her and ruined her. For her sake I will rob you and ruin you if I can. For her sake, and my own; for I hate you all."

And then her mother, Zaza Blanchfleur, died.

Dying, she became sane; saw her daughter with the eyes of sanity and love; saw what she was, this daughter of her great lover; saw what she had made of her, and went mad again.

Mad she died; and, for a time, her daughter also was mad— with hatred of her father and of all men.

Mad with hatred, a living, growing, active hate.

And then, as her mother had done, she fell in love.

This ineffably lovely girl, whose heart was full of loathing of men, who was a seething cauldron of bitterness, hatred and vengeful feeling, fell in love.

I will tell you.

It is a remarkable story. Utterly amazing.

You have spoken of the Hand of Fate, the Finger of Destiny. What of this?

My father having returned home to the happy bosom of his delighted family and his great Wyoming ranch, I left it as quickly as possible, this time for France, the American Ambassador to which country, was a distant relative, a one-time neighbour, and a very old friend of my father's.

At least, that is what I told myself I was doing, when I sailed eastward from New York. In point of fact I did not disembark at Cherbourg at all, but went on to Southampton; and thence, instead of going to London, went to Brandon Regis. At Brandon Abbas I fell in love, afresh, with Lady Brandon's niece, Isobel.

Redintegratio amoris? No, I had never been out of love with her for a minute. Only, this time, she was bigger, older, more grown up, and, if possible, more beautiful, charming and *dear*. As she grew bigger and older, every beauty of her mind, body, and soul seemed to increase and intensify.

And, without any shadow of doubt, Isobel was delighted to see me. On catching sight of me, she gave me both her hands and welcomed me so warmly, so kindly, so sweetly, that I could not doubt that she was glad.

I decided that I would not let so long a time elapse again, before visiting Europe.

Returning home, I waited till the end of her seventeenth year, and then, for the third time, visited Brandon Regis, determined to ask her to marry me.

Isobel, at eighteen, it seemed to me, had again achieved the impossible and grown even more attractive in every way; lovelier; more charming; even dearer.

But she and the youngest of the three Geste brothers had fallen into complete and perfect love. How should it be otherwise? Who could live in the same house with Isobel and not love her? To me the wonder was that all the brothers had not fallen in love with her; that she had not been a disintegrating influence upon their wonderful affection for each other.

But the oldest brother, Michael, was in love with Claudia, Lady Brandon's daughter, and the second brother, Digby stood aside. It was typical of him.

I will say nothing of the effects upon me of this blow, save that, heavy as it was, it was made worse by the fact that Isobel was unhappy; was in great grief and distress. The three brothers had left their home, under a cloud, in disgrace. First the oldest; then the second brother; and John, even though Isobel's declared and accepted lover, had soon followed them.

There was nothing to be done except to assure Isobel that I would do anything, go anywhere in the whole wide world for her; and to stay at Brandon Regis as long as my company gave her any pleasure—that of having someone to whom she could talk about the absent John; to comfort her in any way I could.

I suffered rather badly, I who had come daring to hope that my love was returned and that she would many me; and it was not easy to be helpful and comforting and to talk to her of her lover, John, fond of him as I was.

Then she left Brandon Abbas for a time and I left Brandon Regis for Paris in a wild vain effort to forget; to drown sorrow in pleasure; to recover from a shattering stunning blow; to take up the threads of life again.

When *La Ville Lumière* seemed to me the dullest dreariest hole on earth, its pleasures and gaieties but dust and ashes in the mouth, I returned home to seek sympathy and comfort from my sister Mary to whom I was greatly attached.

My father was worse than ever. More overbearing, more tyrannical, more violent, more publicly and noisily pious, religious and self-righteous. I think he was devil-ridden. I should say conscience-stricken, save for my firm belief that his conscience troubled him not at all, simply because, by this time, he had, as I have remarked, reached the point where not only what he said was true because he said it, but what he did was right because he did it.

He had developed an absolute vice-complex; was for ever fulminating against Vice; and, whenever he mentioned Vice, he meant sexual vice; whenever he spoke of Sin, he meant sexual sin, and no other.

He even went the length of prohibiting the visit—*qua* visitor— of any man, to the ranch, unless he were an octogenarian or a saint, of virtue and piety equal almost to his own.

It was during this phase that, as I have said, my older brother left home for good; my younger sister Janey broke down; and Mary and I went off together, deeply regretting our inability to persuade Janey to come with us.

I was now financially able to go, and to take Mary with me, because, as I told you, I inherited my uncle's fortune.

Mary and I went to Europe, made the grand tour, London, Paris, Naples, Rome, Venice, Athens, the Riviera, and, the weather having turned cold and wet, thence across to Algiers for the winter. At Algiers, Mary, a most attractive, fascinating, delightful girl, as pretty as she was clever, was quickly popular, and had a great success, particularly among army officers stationed, or holiday-making, in that pleasant place.

Very prominent among her admirers was a Colonel Levasseur whom she had met in Paris. Going on from Algiers to see the races, and Arab oasis-life near the popular garrison town of Bouzen, we again encountered Colonel Levasseur, now on his native heath and going about his real business—the furtherance of France's peaceful penetration of the Sahara.

Hearing Mary express her desire to see "the real desert and an unspoilt native city," Colonel Levasseur warmly invited us to visit him at Zaguig as soon as he should be established there with the French Military Mission. It would be perfectly safe and precisely what she wanted, a real untouched Arab town in the heart of the very real desert.

Perhaps with the view of enlisting my sympathy and assistance in the matter—for he was desperately keen on getting Mary to come where he was monarch of all he surveyed and would have no rival for her interest, time, and attention—the good Colonel cultivated me as assiduously as his exacting duties in Bouzen allowed. These were numerous and manifold, for he was organizing the said Military Mission to Zaguig on a scale and in a manner that, to a prejudiced observer, made it look rather more like an invasion.

Just before his departure for Zaguig, Colonel Levasseur, desiring to give me a treat, took me to a party, a *nautch*, a *tamasha*, at the Bouzen house of one Abu Sheikh Ahmed, a well-known Arab patron of the arts—and of the artistes. Here Levasseur promised me I should see something quite out of the common, something rather wonderful, not only in the way of dancing, but of grace and beauty. I was to see the loveliest thing in Africa, if not in the world; a dancing-girl famous throughout Algeria; nay, famous from Morocco to Egypt; a girl known to Europeans as the Angel of Bouzen, the Houri of Bouzen; and, to Arabs, as the Angel of Death.

So little am I attracted by "night-life" and that sort of thing, that I should not have gone at all, but for my wish to avoid hurting the good Colonel's feelings. But so kindly, so warmly enthusiastic was he, so certain that he was able to give me real delight, that I had not the heart to decline. Or perhaps the fact was that I should have refused but, on the whole, found it less trouble to go than to persuade Colonel Levasseur that I did not wish to do so.

Anyhow, I went, and, half-heartedly as I did so, it proved to be one of the most momentous actions of my life.

After I had wearily watched some of the usual turns one sees at these entertainments, and was thinking of suggesting to Levasseur that we slip away from the garden—it was a moon-light *al fresco* show—the girl came from the house and danced on a large carpet spread in the centre of the square formed by Abu Sheikh Ahmed's guests.

It was not many seconds before I realized that neither rumour nor Colonel Levasseur had exaggerated.

The girl was amazing, wonderful, indescribably lovely, astonishingly graceful, fascinating.

What made her own beauty so arresting was the fact that she possessed that of both worlds, Eastern and Western. All the professional loveliness of an Arabian Nights princess as well as that of a Nordic fairy-tale princess. I was reminded of Snow White and Rose Red as well as of Balroubadin, Nurmahal and Scheherazade, for she had the white skin and rose-pink cheeks and red lips of the one type, the eyes, eye-lashes, eye-brows and hair of the other.

Dancing, or, rather, floating like thistledown, she came straight toward us, her toes scarcely seeming to touch the ground, stopped in front of me, looked, stared, gazed into my eyes as though she and I were there alone, and quickly gave me the sensation of being hypnotized. Although she said not a word, it seemed that she was speaking to me. I seemed to hear her voice speaking in broken French and broken English.

So strong was the hypnotic sensation that I, apparently with the greatest difficulty, withdrew my gaze from hers as with a physical wrench.

With a contemptuous glance she danced away, and, when she halted again, it was before a young Arab at the opposite corner of the square of seated on-lookers. To him she spoke, and then again floating, as it were, round the carpet, stopped before me.

This time she did speak.

Kneeling before me with her arms out-stretched, and bringing her face close to mine, she made love to me, bade me kiss her.

I felt as big a fool as I looked. I was in no humour for kissing dancing-girls, and doubtless behaved in a pompous priggish manner.

While the girl, her face growing angry, her eyes blazing, remained in a posture of insistent invitation, Colonel Levasseur suddenly sprang to his feet and shouted in Arabic.

I heard a blow and, as I turned, I felt one. The girl, drawing a little dagger from her sash struck me over the heart. I thought she had stabbed me; but, in punishment for my graceless stupidity and churlishness, she had made me look more foolish still, merely having drawn her dagger and given me a sharp tap on the shirt-front with her knuckles.

What had happened behind me was more serious. Just in time, Colonel Levasseur had prevented the young Arab, to whom she had spoken, from stabbing me in earnest. The girl had said something to make him more jealous than he already was, and, mad with his foolish hate, he had crept round behind me, a big curved dagger in his hand.

Colonel Levasseur flew into a tremendous rage, called him a black hound, and bade him slink away out of the garden before he kicked him out. Old Abu Sheikh Ahmed was dreadfully upset, apparently petrified with shame and horror, and loud with protestations and apologies.

"Very well," said Colonel Levasseur at last, "I will hold you responsible for watching the seditious dog and letting me know where he is and what he is doing; and if he goes to Zaguig without my knowing it, I will have you arrested at once."

The young Arab was Selim ben Yussuf, declared bitter enemy of the French, and son and heir of Yussuf ben Amir, a gentleman of the old school, friend, partisan, and ally of France.

We at once left Abu Sheikh Ahmed's garden and, on the way back to the European quarter, the Colonel took me through the Street of a Thousand Delights, and pointed out the house in which Zaza Blanchfleur, the mother of the Angel of Death, had lived and flourished; the house whence she had gone out into the desert with her lover, the man who was this dancing-girl's father; the house to which she returned when he left her; the house in which this dancing-girl was born; the house in which she grew to womanhood without ever having had a girlhood.

"He must have been a great lover, that one," said the Colonel. "Fancy winning and breaking the heart of an Ouled Naïl dancing-girl. Breaking it so thoroughly that she pined, went mad, and died."

"Who was he—a French officer?" I asked.

"No, a visitor; said to be an Englishman. But Zaza Blanchfleur always referred to him as Omar. Omar the Englishman."

"Well, Englishman or not, he was certainly European, judging by this girl's colouring," I observed, "and Northern European, too."

It was soon after this incident that Mary and I went to Zaguig as Colonel Levasseur's guests, he having again assured me that it would be perfectly safe for me to bring Mary.

At Zaguig, I discovered that the Chief Intelligence Officer, a Major de Beaujolais, was very far from sharing Colonel Levasseur's opinion on this point. On the contrary, he viewed the place rather as a smouldering volcano that might erupt at any moment.

He proved to be right.

There was a sudden rising, rioting, *jehad*, and attack upon the head-quarters of the Military Mission. So comparatively few were the troops guarding the Mission that the revolt became a massacre —a massacre of which I was almost the sole European survivor.

My sister Mary was saved by Major de Beaujolais, who took her with his caravan when he escaped from Zaguig.

She being safely out of the place, I contrived to join Colonel Levasseur, and was left for dead when the fanatical populace stormed and burnt the Residency.

Found, just breathing, by the relief force, I was patched up and sent to Algiers when convalescent, and there Mary rejoined me and announced her engagement to Major de Beaujolais.

Still feeling the effects of a sword-cut on the head, I attended their wedding, and later accompanied them to Paris, whence they continued their honeymoon, and I went to London to consult a specialist about my damaged skull, which was causing me terrible pain and insomnia. There I had the good luck to fall into the hands of Hanley Blythe, the great brain specialist and neurologist— double good luck because, when he sent me to his Nursing Home, I found that Isobel, now Isobel Geste, wife of John Geste, had also gone to him, and was an inmate of his Nursing Home.

I will say nothing about that meeting except that she told me tragic news of the boys and girls whom I had known so long and liked so much.

When the three boys disappeared from home, they joined the French Foreign Legion because the eldest, Michael, had "stolen" a model of Lady Brandon's famous sapphire, The Blue Water.

She had secretly sold the original without her husband's knowledge, and, as he was returning to Brandon Abbas after years of absence, Michael had stolen the dummy in the hope that Sir Hector Brandon would think he had stolen the real sapphire, and Lady Brandon would allow him to think it.

What the foolish boy hoped was that Lady Brandon would suppose he really was a thief, and was under the impression that he was stealing the genuine article; and that she would see no reason to tell her husband the truth—since the boy apparently was, both in act and intention, a criminal.

They had joined the Foreign Legion, and the two older ones had been killed. John had been saved by the courage and altruism of two Americans. Of these, one had gone off to die in the desert because their water-supply was clearly insufficient to keep life in all three of them; the other had seen John into safety and gone back to find his friend. Of this last fact John had known nothing, as he was, at the time, insensible and delirious in the worst stage of typhoid fever.

He had come back, married Isobel, and settled down at Brandon Regis.

Claudia, beloved of Michael, had married a millionaire, and

been killed in a motor-smash, blinded and burnt.

Her mother, Lady Brandon, had died, apparently of shock and grief at the very terrible death of her daughter.

Sir Hector Brandon had died abroad.

It was rather an overshadowed and tragic wedding at best, and, soon after it, John had fallen ill in mind and body; had been unable to sleep, eat, or do anything but worry about the two American comrades who had saved him, and whom, unwittingly, he had left, after one had offered his life for him, and the other had returned to probable death and certain danger of death, on the merest chance of finding and saving his friend.

With John it soon became such an obsession—this feeling of having deserted his comrades who had saved him; this reproach of living in luxury while they, if alive, were probably suffering the greatest hardship, possibly captives in the hands of the Arabs, or prisoners in those of the French military authorities—that he was in grave danger of a complete break-down, mental and physical. He had never really recovered from what he had been through in the Legion and in the desert afterwards.

At last things got so bad that Isobel felt the only possible thing was for him to do what she knew he wanted to do—to leave her and go back; to go back to Africa and stay there until he knew what had become of the two Americans, to find out where they were, and to do what he could for them.

He went, and, near the scene of his rescue, he was captured by the French military authorities, tried as a military criminal and deserter, and sentenced to eight years *travaux forcés* in a Penal Battalion. The undeniable truth was that he had killed a French *sous-officier*, in sheer self-defence, after the man, a sadistic maniac, had shot John's brother with his own hand.

What were my troubles beside all this?

What could I, who loved Isobel, do, but devote my life to helping him, dedicate myself to her service?

What better lot could I desire?

Of course, everything had been done, by official representation, wire-pulling and appeal, to get John Geste's case revised, and get him released. But without the slightest avail. Officially, nothing whatsoever could be done. Since there was neither help nor hope from above and in the light of day, any attempt must be made from below, in darkness and secrecy. Failing release, the alternative was escape. John must be rescued.

As a first step toward getting into touch with him, I joined the

French Foreign Legion with a view to being in a position to commit a military offence and be transferred to the Penal Battalion.

After that, I must be guided by circumstance, and depend on luck, skill, perseverance and money. The last-named for getting away and out of the country, once the escape had been effected. It would be of little use for any other purpose.

The commission of a military crime was unnecessary. Out on patrol, we were lost in a sand-storm, smothered, nearly buried alive, and a *cafard*-stricken Russian shot the Sergeant in charge of the patrol. A fight started, the wounded Sergeant shot two of the mutineers and called on me to carry on. Just then, a troop of Spahis, who had been sheltering in a *wadi* under the lee of a cliff some miles away, rode down on us, headed by their officer, who had heard the firing. As he rode up, the dying Sergeant pointed to me, said,

"This man . . . This man is . . .", and never spoke again.

The Spahi officer arrested the lot of us, and we were all, the mutineers and the one or two who had tried to defend the Sergeant, court-martialled and condemned to the severest punishment short of death. Some of us would have got the death-sentence but for the fact that three had been killed, and might be assumed to be the ring-leaders and murderers.

After serving, for a longer time than I care to remember, on *travaux publics*, I happened to be sent to work near Zaguig in the same road-gang as John Geste, though it was not until we were imprisoned together in a *silo* that I knew it.

While we were in the *silo*, the rest of the road-gang, guards and all, were wiped out in an Arab raid, and, a day or so later, we fell into the hands of the raiders, a section of Sheikh Yussuf ben Amir's tribe, led by his son Selim ben Yussuf who, unknown to the old man, were harrying small outposts, convoys and construction-work parties, for profit and amusement.

On holiday from Bouzen, the famous dancing-girl was staying in Sheikh Yussuf ben Amir's camp, and not getting on particularly well with her lover, Selim ben Yussuf, the old man's son.

When we, in our convict rags, were brought before the Sheikh, she recognized me. Selim did not; but was all for serving us, forthwith, as he considered French soldiers should be served.

I appealed to Sheikh Yussuf ben Amir, a gentleman of the old school, as I have said, for at least the three days' hospitality prescribed for the "guest of Allah," the traveller who is in need of it.

Selim promptly pointed out that a dog of a convict, however much hunted about by gaolers, was not exactly a traveller.

The old man, however, took the view that, convicts or travellers, we were undeniably unfortunate and fitting objects for the exercise of that mercy and compassion enjoined by Allah the Merciful, the Compassionate.

Ragged, ill, half-dead from hunger, thirst and confinement in darkness and great heat, we were certainly that, and unspeakably grateful that we were to be treated as guests, and thereafter allowed to go in peace.

And treated as honoured guests we were; fed, and clothed in Arab dress.

It was wonderful what complete rest, unlimited good food, baths, and the attentions of the Sheikh's barber and *hakim* did for us; and when the dancing-girl paid us a visit, we were presentable objects, clothed and in our right minds, and very different from the filthy ragged convicts whom she had seen a day or two before. So much so, that Selim ben Yussuf, visiting our guest-tent, recognized me at once, flew into a rage, and told me exactly what would happen when my three days as the tribe's guest had passed, and I was no longer under his father's protection.

I don't know whether my first meal was too much for me, or whether I was poisoned by the hakim's "medicine," or on Yussuf ben Selim's orders, but I was suddenly taken terribly ill.

The attack was so violent that, for a time, I was unconscious, probably delirious, with a very high temperature.

When I returned to consciousness, and a complete realization of my situation, I found that John Geste was no longer with me. The girl was, however; and I learned, to my utter amazement, that she had fallen in love with me—love at first sight—when she saw me at Bouzen; and that she intended to make practical demonstration of it by saving my life now.

Selim ben Yussuf should not kill or torture me, she promised. I was not to be afraid, for she would save me. As a matter of fact, she had done so already, for Selim thought I had been handed over to a French patrol who visited the camp while I lay ill.

Hidden in the *haremlik*, the women's side of the tent, she had heard Yussuf tell the French *sous-officier* that he had caught an escaped convict, doubtless one of the men of whom the Frenchman was in search. He had then gone out of the tent and sent a man to tell the guards in charge of the guest-tent to bring the *Roumi* who wore the blue burnous, when the French *peloton méhariste* called for their camels, to depart.

Swiftly she had hurried to the guest tent, sent for Abd'allah ben Moussa, her own incorruptible servant and body-guard, and bidden him change the prisoners' burnouses, and to see that when Selim's men came for one of the prisoners, it was to be the *other* one who was handed over.

Thus it was that, when the French *sous-officier* and his Arab *goumiers* rode away, one of them led a camel on which was a manacled prisoner, and that prisoner was John Geste.

Selim ben Yussuf thought it was I who was handed over to the French—his little jealous revenge.

I took it badly. All I had done and suffered, brought to nought at the last moment, through a dancing-girl's whim and a passing fancy for me because I had blue eyes, probably the first she'd seen; the cup dashed from my hand as I raised it to my lips; success snatched from my grasp as my fingers closed upon it.

I felt murderous towards the girl; and this was the moment she chose for making love to me. You can imagine my response, and also her re-action to being scorned, rejected, insulted, for the first time in her life.

She gave me an ultimatum, and it was perfectly obvious that she was absolutely in earnest. There was no possible shadow of doubt that if I did not become her lover I should become her victim —the victim of her very vengeful anger.

I had a choice between "love" and death or worse than death— blindness and mutilation.

I gave in. Apart from a definite distaste for being, murdered, I should not be of much further use to John Geste if I were killed, blinded, or otherwise completely incapacitated. And directly I gave in, the girl was all remorse, repentance, regret.

It was really rather pathetic; rather touching. She was undoubtedly and genuinely in love; and, as invariably and inevitably happens in a case of real love, it brought out all the best that was in her. Love gave her, whose life had been non-moral, aspirations for a different way of life; gave her, who had lived for self and "pleasure," the idea and ideal of unselfishness; made her, who had always demanded service from others, now wish to give service.

One has to remember that what she was, she had been made; that, into the life she lived, she had been born; and that she had known nothing else. Yet, suddenly, she seemed to see herself with new vision; to realize herself for what she was; and to loathe, detest and abhor what she was, and the life that she had led.

The proof of this was that she begged me to rescue her from herself, from her life, from Bouzen, and from Africa. She wanted to escape, to renounce and repudiate all that there was in her of her Arab blood; to develop, cling to, and cultivate, all that there was in her of her European father, Omar the Englishman, as she called him.

It was an amazing psychological drama, an astonishing spectacle, this re-creation, development, emancipation so to speak, of a soul. One was irresistibly reminded of the grub and the butterfly; of something free, lovely, beautiful, emerging from a cramping and confining darkness. Love had wrought the age-old miracle.

Emancipation . . . loathsome crawling grub . . . chrysalis . . . beautiful and glorious butterfly. It is difficult to express. It was more difficult to believe. But there it was, plain to see.

Well, this girl, this Houri of Bouzen, this Angel of Death, being what she was, I may be acquitted of smug complacency and conceit when I say that her love for me was so overwhelming that she was prepared to do anything to gratify it.

No, let me amend that and say—was prepared to do anything to win my love, to give expression to hers, to be happy with me. And this I turned to my own account in the furtherance of my life's purpose. I had found John Geste. I had got away with him. Thanks to this girl, I had lost him again; and I would use her in any possible way for his salvation.

We had need of each other.

She loved me, and everything else in her world was swallowed up in that one great obsession.

I needed her; for, without her help, I could hardly hope to escape from Selim ben Yussuf's clutches; as, although he thought that I—his rival and enemy—had suffered the worst of fates in being handed back to penal servitude with the road-gang, he would certainly not let his remaining *Roumi* prisoner go free; and the best I could hope for, so far as he was concerned, was slavery, with or without mutilation.

To find John Geste again, I must escape; and, to escape, I must have this girl's help. It was a curious position. The last thing in the world that she wanted was to see me go free; and the one condition on which I would give her my promise to marry her—for her love-obsession had taken that particular form—was that she should help me to escape.

Marriage, permanence, life with me until death should separate us, was her object. And with this was inextricably woven a yearning for what one must term respectability; escape from The Street and all that it connoted; utter renunciation of her way of life. She would have given her soul to have been *jeune fille*, "good," established, normal; and having, all her life, loathed Europeans for her father's sake, she now desired beyond all things to be a European, to wear European clothing, to talk only English and French, to live in Europe, for my sake.

It was pitiful.

Well, I made a bargain with her.

I gave her my word, my simple promise, without oath or protestation, that if she helped me to escape, helped me in every possible way to find out whither they had taken John Geste, and to rescue him—I would return to her as soon as he was out of the country.

She promised her fullest help, and I promised to return to her if we were successful. In any case, it was that or nothing, for I was most completely in her power. While she loved me I should come to no harm—but I should come to nothing else. I certainly should not come to the help of John Geste, for she would never let me go without my promise to come back to her.

And I thought it a remarkable proof of her love (and that it was true and genuine love) that she should be willing to accept my word, and that she, who had been the "lover" of so many men, should wish to change, to reform, to marry.

She helped me to the utmost of her power. Through her help, I escaped, and, very largely through her help, discovered that John Geste was again in the Zaguig road-gang, and was able to rescue him.

Having accompanied him to safety, I returned—to keep my promise to the girl.

She was still living in the tents of the Sheikh Yussuf ben Amir, near Bouzen. Selim ben Yussuf, his son, was a prisoner in the hands of the French.

We were to ride to Bouzen, and there be married, according to the Christian dispensation, on the next day. She was almost insane with joy at my return, which she took to be at once a proof of love and of my wonderful honour—though to the male mind this might seem a little inconsistent.

I found that an amazing change had taken place in her since I had seen her last. Gone was the arrogance, insolence, brazenness;

the flaunting impudence, the deliberate allure, the provocative challenge; all that had made her the Houri of Bouzen, the Angel of Death.

She was quiet, gentle, modest; so changed in spirit and demeanour as to be almost unrecognizable, to be recognizable only by her wonderful beauty.

Again I found her utterly pathetic; her new ambition, intention, hope, and desire, touching in the extreme.

If anything could have ameliorated, in the slightest degree, the misery and agony, the shame and the fear, that I suffered, it would have been this change.

Had I not myself been in love with another woman as truly and desperately as this girl was in love with me, the thought of marriage with her would have been rendered almost bearable, so different was she, so humble, gentle, repentant; so anxious to alter, amend, reform herself.

Had it been possible with sharp-edged knife or white-hot iron to cut from herself all defilement of the past, she would have hesitated at no self-mutilating agony.

And, as I asked myself, who was to blame but the man, the European, who had made her the child of a prostitute, and abandoned her to the life inevitable to her circumstances?

On the night before the bridal cavalcade was to ride from Sheikh Yussuf ben Amir's tents to Bouzen, she gave me her most cherished possession, her priceless amulet, her invaluable talisman, a thing curiously symbolic of herself, her soul, her dual origin and nature—a piece of the True Cross and a hair of the Beard of the Prophet Mahommet!

How she had come by the fragment of the "True" Cross, I do not know, but the Sultan of Morocco himself had given the other immeasurably sacred talisman to her mother.

Protected, on the one hand, by the holiest of Christian relics, and on the other by the holiest of Mussulman talismans, how could any harm befall her?

And now, nothing would please her but that I must come under their beneficent influence and protection.

Accordingly, she hung about my neck the tiny gold case, shaped like a book, which contained these priceless treasures as well as portraits of her mother and her father. She bade me wear it for ever. When out of her presence, it would remind me of her; and whether far from her or near, it would be my sure shield against any and every danger. Not that, as she explained, she would ever again invoke the aid of the Prophet and pray to Allah, but still—well, there could be no harm, could there, in keeping and wearing the most sacred thing that ever came out of Mecca? Of course, she was a true Christian now, and it was really only the fragment of the Cross that was the true invaluable talisman, she said. This was to be her wedding-gift to me, and perhaps I would value it because, all her life, she had worn it next her heart?

That night in my tent, wakeful, distraught, more wretchedly miserable than ever before in all my life; weary beyond words, though unable to sleep, I idly examined the trinket, and, playing with it, opened it. What I saw was a pair of miniatures, portraits of a woman and a man, the former presumably covering the hair of the Beard of the Prophet, the latter the splinter of the True Cross.

The woman was Zaza Blanchfleur.

The man, beyond the shadow of a doubt, was my father.

The Houri of Bouzen, the Angel of Death, the dancing-girl of The Street of a Thousand Delights, was my half-sister.

I was literally stunned.

For a time my mind ceased to function, and I could only stare, open-mouthed, at this amazing incredible conjunction; the Ouled Naïl dancing-girl, the Mussulman woman with her sacred relic, the hair of the Beard of the Prophet; and my father, the Christian, the loudly professing Christian, with the equally ineffably-sacred Christian relic, a splinter of the True Cross!

As my mind began to work, I realized that there was no possibility of mistake, no room for doubt.

Here was the dancing-girl's "Omar the Englishman"—in other words her " 'Omer" who spoke English—who was in very deed Homer the American, Homer A. Vanbrugh, my father.

Yes. He had been in Bouzen, buying Arab horses; and the Death Angel's age corresponded with the year in which he had been in Bouzen; and the months during which my unhappy mother had heard no word of him, corresponded with the months he had spent in the desert with the Ouled Naïl dancing-girl, the Mussulman woman whom the French officers of the garrison called Zaza Blanchfleur.

Anxious as I was, determined as I was, to find some loophole, some flaw, some possibility of a mistake, I was nevertheless convinced. Argue with myself as I might, I knew that "Omar the Englishman" was Homer my father, and that this girl, was flesh of my flesh, bone of my bone, blood of my blood, my father's daughter, my half-sister.

I would make sure, though; or rather, I would give him opportunity to deny, and if he could do it, to disprove, this dreadful thing, contradict this mute accusation of circumstantial evidence.

But I must go. I must escape. I must break my word.

No, it was my father who had done that. It was he who had rendered it impossible for me to keep my word.

On a scrap of paper I scribbled, in French, the words. "*I am Omar's son,*" folded it, addressed it to the girl, and put it on my pillow.

Then, like a thief in the night, I crept to where my camel was tethered beside that of Abdullah ibn Moussa. Making the camel-man, who was in charge of them, accompany me on Abd'allah ibn Moussa's camel, I fled, escaped, rode through the night, to Bouzen. There I gave the camel-man money and a letter for the girl, telling her the truth and begging her to believe that nothing but this absolute final insurmountable obstacle would have prevented me from keeping my word and doing what, as she knew, I had returned to do.

I also bade the camel-man wait three days in Bouzen, and then return to Sheikh ben Amir's camp and give the letter to the Angel of Death.

I took train for Algiers, still dressed as an Arab. There I obtained European clothes and, after waiting for some days, in hiding, sailed by the first ship that was going to America.

I went straight home by train, stage, and hired horse. I reached my father's ranch-house in time to witness a typical piece of blustering tyranny on his part, his loud-voiced violent and unwarrantable prohibition of my young sister's engagement to the man she loved.

Me, he received with angry and cold contempt.

As soon as he was alone with me, and had finished a tirade which ended with the words,

"Who are you to attempt to interfere, you insolent half-baked young hound?" I produced and opened the little gold book-shaped box that had hung upon its chain about the neck of Zaza Blanchfleur and that of her daughter.

The result was as though he had had a stroke.

In point of fact he had.

He literally staggered. He actually smote his forehead with his clenched fist. He dropped back into his chair. His face went white, and his great body shook and trembled.

It was one of the bad moments of my life.

"*Oh, God!*" he groaned. "*Oh, God!*" and to me,
"Where is she?"

And then of course I knew. I knew that my intuition had been right, and that the circumstantial evidence had not been false.

The Angel of Death was his daughter, my half-sister.

"Where is she?" he whispered.

"Dead," I replied.

"Thank God!" he breathed.

"How did you get it?" he asked, his face white and dreadful.

"I got it from your daughter," I said, "from my sister."

"*Oh, God! . . . Oh, God!*" he murmured again and collapsed, his hands covering his face.

"Where is she?" he asked again, removing his hands and gazing at me with frightened eyes.

"In Bouzen," I said. "In the Street of a Thousand Delights."

"Does she know who I am; where I am?"

"No," I said.

"Have you told anybody? Does anybody know?"

"No," I said.

From that hour he was a changed man; and, soon afterwards, he died. He died, I believe, of fear and shame; fear that he should be found out; and that he, the castigator of sin and sinner, should be castigated; of shame that I, his miserable worthless and contemptible son, should know of his shame.

Yes, I think it was the fall from the lofty pedestal upon which he had placed himself that killed him. I think it broke every bone in the body of his self-esteem.

He died—and I felt dreadful, terrible, haunted; a parricide. I could scarcely have felt worse if I had shot, him dead.

And when I began to recover, began to listen to the voice of my own common-sense—and tell myself that I was guiltless in fact because I was guiltless in intention—this horror, this terrible obsession, was gradually driven out by another; driven out by a worse one.

As, gradually and imperceptibly, I began to think less and less about my father's death and the manner of his dying—which had begun in the very moment that his eyes fell upon the portraits of himself and the woman with whom he had "sinned"—so, gradually and imperceptibly, I began to think more and more of his unfortunate daughter, of my poor unhappy wronged sister, dwelling in The Street of a Thousand Delights in Bouzen, living to give pleasure to the men she loathed, the brutes she hated and despised.

411

In time, the one obsession drove out the other, and, before long, I could think of nothing but of her, her dreadful life and inevitable fate.

Why should two of my father's daughters, Mary and Janey, be leading normal human lives, honoured and honourable, happy as the day was long, with devoted husbands; destined to lead full hopeful helpful lives, mothers of fine children; flowers of American womanhood, blooming in the light of day, the sunshine of all human joy—while his third daughter, as much his daughter as were Mary and Janey, was what she was?

Mary Vanbrugh . . . Mary de Beaujolais.

Janey Vanbrugh . . . Janey Lincoln.

Zaza 'Vanbrugh' . . . The Houri of Bouzen.

Life's an amazing thing. Life. Fate. Destiny. The Providence that shapes our ends. God's will. Whatever you choose to call it.

This growing obsession, this *idée fixe* concerning my sister, although it made me not only unhappy, miserable, in fact sick in mind and body, nevertheless saved me. Two things cannot occupy the same space at once. One cannot have two *idées fixes* at the same time.

My preoccupation with my sister saved me, helped me, tided me over the bad time that followed upon my again seeing the woman I loved, had always loved, the woman whose husband I had brought back to her, John Geste's wife, Isobel.

But perhaps I contrived to conquer that suffering and even, in time, to rejoice that I had been the instrument of bringing back joy into her life. Be that as it may, I thought less and less of Isobel, and more and more of my sister; thought of her by day; dreamed of her by night; until I ceased to dream because I could not sleep.

It seemed so cruel, so pitiful, that the child of an American father should be born in a house of ill-fame in a bazaar at Bouzen, without possibility of escaping her fate; should be brought up almost from the cradle, and actually from childhood, to be—what she was; so cruel, so pitiful, that, having for years lived the life to which she had been doomed and damned, she should have retained the power to love, really to love, without thought of self or gain; so cruel, so pitiful, that, in the light of this love, she should see her dreadful life in its true colours and should yearn to abandon it; so cruel, so pitiful that, on her wedding-eve such a blow should fall, her happiness should be crushed, her adored bridegroom prove to be but a brother.

Had I not a responsibility to this girl? Was it not my duty to assume my father's responsibility—as I should have assumed my father's debts?

Am I my brother's keeper? My sister's keeper?

Of course I am—and most especially when that term is literal.

In the Street of Bouzen dwelt my sister . . . my sister . . . my sister.

My father could hide behind the fact that he did not know—ignoring the fact that he had never tried to find out.

I could not so hide.

I had found out. I knew. In the Street of a Thousand Delights in Bouzen dwelt my sister.

And had not I played a coward's part in creeping away like a thief in the night, without a word of farewell, and with only written words of explanation?

I could plead shock, horror, instinctive recoil from the ghastly abyss that opened at my feet; I could plead all sorts of things, and still leave the true reason unnamed—cowardice.

I was a coward, a shirker of responsibility; and selfish; selfish to the depths of my nature.

What had I not done and dared, risked and suffered, for a woman who had no claim upon me, a woman happily married to my friend? I had renounced my life of ease, and undertaken one of great hardship. I had been prepared to proceed from that to one of incredible, intolerable hardship, branded as a criminal, a convict.

Actually this had come to pass; and through my own quixotic folly, I had become a convict; and, having been mercifully delivered from that dreadful state, had risked return to it.

I could do that for the woman I loved. I could do it because it gave me pleasure to run risks for her sake; to suffer for her; to stake my right to life, liberty, and the pursuit of happiness, on a chance of ending her sorrow and suffering, bringing joy into her life.

And what could I do for my own sister, flesh of my flesh, bone of my bone, blood of my blood, daughter of my father? I could run away, leaving her to bear alone a blow almost too heavy to be borne, a disappointment almost too great to be supported.

What was my former "suffering" but purest selfishness; that indulgence of the joy of the flagellant; that wallowing in the pain that was pleasure because it was borne for a beloved woman?

And what was it but its complement and counterpart, this sitting in comfortable idleness, this renunciation of responsibility?

For Isobel I could selfishly risk suffering. For Zaza I could selfishly avoid it.

I wrestled with myself until worn out; until I fell ill.

For long I resisted, for words could not express my fear and hatred of Africa, my terror of being recognized, re-captured and returned to the chain-gang with an added sentence; my dread, scarcely less, of meeting Zaza again.

In the end I had to go. To save my life I had to go.

There was nothing altruistic or noble about it, for it was simply that I *had* to go.

When I started for Bouzen I could not make sufficient haste; nor could I understand how it had been possible for me to lose the time that I had wasted since my father's death.

And, when I was able to start, I could not travel fast enough, as though haste now would atone for previous dilatoriness, indecision, and neglect.

Yet all the time, as my ship drew nearer and nearer to Algiers, my realization of difficulties and dangers increased; and on the last stage of my journey, in the train to Bouzen, apprehension and anxiety had me so strongly in their grip that I felt physically ill.

Perhaps it was the result upon my body of the loathing that filled my sub-conscious mind at this return to the scene of so much suffering. Not that my conscious mind was by any means unaware of the risks I ran. In the first place, suppose I were recognized, arrested, and returned to penal servitude, or shot? A fine end to my schemes and hopes of saving Zaza.

In the second place, suppose Zaza nursed a savage anger against me for deserting her on the eve of our marriage. Suppose she had refused to believe my story, and regarded me merely as a lying rascally deceiver who had jilted her, for some reason, at the last moment. Hell hath no fury like a woman scorned, and I could not imagine Hell producing a more terrible fury than the Angel of Death. I had had some experience of her ferocious cruelty when I was in Selim ben Yussuf's power.

Suppose, again, she had accepted my statement that I was her father's son; might it not well happen that she should transfer her life-long contempt, anger, and vengeful feeling, from him to me— or at least include me therein?

By the time the train actually reached Bouzen, I was in a miserable state of nervous anxiety and fear. Try as I might to reassure myself on the subject of my safety from arrest, I could not succeed, in spite of my realization of the fact that I had never been in Bouzen either as a *légionnaire* or a Zephyr; and that the last time I was here I was, as now, a wealthy American tourist. Anyone recognizing me would remember me as that. Why, had poor Colonel Levasseur been still alive I could have met him without risk or fear. Of course I was safe enough in my present role—reduplicating my former one in Bouzen. Of course I was safe enough. I should not be recognized except, possibly, at my hotel, which would be all to the good.

And as to Zaza, had it not been perfectly obvious, however stupid or modest I might have been, that she was genuinely and desperately in love? Might she not, then, give me credit for honesty and truthfulness; believe what I said and realize that I had acted rightly?

And having argued myself into a brief state of re-assurance and sense of security; fear, misery, and despair would quickly supervene. I would feel certain that one or other of the two catastrophes would overtake me, and that by the morrow I should either be a prisoner of the French or a victim of Zaza's vengeful wrath.

But as has been well said, our greatest anxiety generally arises from troubles that never happen. So in this case: no-one in Bouzen recognized me—even as the former American tourist. No-one recognized me as the escaped *légionnaire* and Zephyr.

And Zaza? Many good women of unimpeachable heredity and irreproachable environment might learn a lesson from this girl whom they would have called a fallen woman; a despicable unmentionable creature; from the contamination of whose touch they would have withdrawn the hem of their garments.

She behaved perfectly; and no good woman, however saintly a model of propriety and compendium of virtue, could have behaved better. She still loved me; but I verily believe that, from sheer decency—and I particularly beg that you will not laugh nor even smile—from sheer purity and innate goodness and rightness of mind, she had so controlled, guided, directed her love, that she had changed it . . . purged it . . . sublimated it.

Her love was partly filial, partly sisterly; it was based on gratitude—for God knows what.

Well, well! Laugh if you must—and, laughing, show yourself unable to comprehend, unable to rise to the higher level, her level.

It is not your fault.

But, once grasp the great eternal truth that there is good in everyone, and you have a starting-point toward understanding her.

We have it on high authority that it is a poor pastime to gild refined gold. Has it ever occurred to you that it is equally futile to paint it black? Does not the gold remain pure gold beneath?

And, in any case, if a wrong environment can influence a soul in the wrong direction, surely the reversal of the influence through the diametric change of environment, can also change the direction? And if the bad in the best of us can be developed and increased, so can the good in the worst of us.

Do you know, I, personally, cherish a theory, possibly foolish, that, like suffering, wickedness and sin are not a matter of doing but of *being;* and that a person can do wrong but *be* fundamentally right; can do evil and *be* fundamentally good.

However, I won't theorize.

I went straight from Bouzen railway-station to my former hotel; and, having arranged about accommodation and baggage, went at once to her house in the Street.

She was there and she was alone.

Following her man, Abd'allah ibn Moussa, who did not recognize me (he had only seen me disguised and in Arab dress) up the stair that led from that formerly ever-open outer door to her *salon*, I found her.

With a little cry, she sprang up from the divan on which she was seated beside a low Moorish coffee-table, the amber mouth-piece of a *narghile* between her lips, rushed to me, and flung her arms about my neck.

"I knew you would come,," she said. "I knew you would come. I prayed to God and to Jesus Christ and to the Virgin Miriam, and I knew you would come."

"You got my letter, Zaza?"

"Yes, I got your letter. The note you left in your tent broke my heart. I should have died as my mother died, but your letter came in time. It saved my life. I knew that you were telling me the truth; and slowly, slowly, it somehow made me almost happy. It was terrible at times; and often I took my sharp little knife from its sheath; but always when I did so I saw your face, and I knew you would come back to me. I knew you would take me away from here. I knew you would help me to escape from this life and to be different. You see, I knew you were truthful. I knew you were honest and good and fine. I was sure that, although you could never be my husband, you would be my friend. Real friend. Almost as though you were my real brother, my whole brother; not only my half-brother. When first I looked into your eyes, I knew that they were good eyes, true eyes, honest eyes. The people of the Ouled Naïl can read faces, can look through eyes into souls. They are never wrong. And at that time I was an Ouled Naïl dancing-girl. So I knew you would keep your promise, somehow. In some way. You had given me your word that if I saved your friend, you would come back to me, be my lover, be my husband. And I knew that when you found that to be impossible, you would keep your promise in some other way—would come back to me in some other way."

She clapped her hands twice and Abd'allah ibn Moussa stepped through the curtains into the room.

"Shut the outer door, Abd'allah," she ordered. "And do not open it again for anyone."

As the curtains fell together behind the man, she took my face between her hands and gazed into my eyes.

"My dear," she said, "keep your promise. Take me away from here. Help me to be all white, a European woman. Help me to be your sister, like your other sisters."

"That's what I have come for, Zaza," said I.

And she kissed me softly, gently, sweetly—entirely the kiss that a devoted sister might give to her brother.

"Oh, how glad I am," she said. "How thankful I am to God and to Jesus Christ and to the Virgin Miriam. You see, I could not go alone. I should not know exactly where to go; nor exactly what to do. I should make such mistakes and be so laughed at; get into such trouble, once I went alone beyond Bouzen and Algiers. And if I stay much longer in this Africa I shall die. I hate it so. I hate my life so. I hate myself so. I must get away from the desert, from these places, from Africa—to breathe. I will not give you any trouble; not wilfully, intentionally. I will try to be exactly like your real sisters; your whole sisters; like the women of your family; the women who are your friends. Do you know whom I will try to be specially like? Like that woman whom you love.

"Yes, yes. I have thought it all out. You didn't do what you did *only* for a friend. You did it for the woman who loved that friend. Whoever she is, I will try to be like her."

"Zaza," I said, "you will be the . . ."

"And I want you never again to call me Zaza," she interrupted. "What was your mother's name?"

"Consuela," I told her.

"May I take her name? Zaza was my name and my mother's name, but I don't want to be Zaza any more. A heathen name. A name fit for this Street. Would your mother hate it, and hate me, if I took her name?"

"I think my mother would love you if she knew you, Consuela," I said.

And that is how it comes about, Señor Manöel Maine, that this lady is my half-sister and is known as Miss Consuela Vanbrugh.

VI

Spanish Maine yawned prodigiously, stretched mightily, and consulted his wrist-watch openly.

"A very interesting story, Mr. Vanbrugh," he observed, pouring himself another drink. "What's the point of it?"

Otis Vanbrugh, with level gaze, eyed him straitly.

"The point is," he replied, "that I don't intend to have my sister made unhappy. She has had quite enough unhappiness. I don't intend to let her chance be destroyed; her chance of complete social re-establishment; her chance of winning to security, safety, peace. I don't intend to see my work undone. Since the day I went back to her, I have devoted my life to saving her from what seemed to be her fate. So far, I have succeeded; and with an ever-increasing success. Final success is near. Do you think I am going to be defeated now—and by *you?* Do you, for one moment, think I'm going to see my sister's happiness destroyed, her life ruined? . . . That is the 'point.' "

Spanish Maine smiled.

"And my story?" he said. "That had a point too. Did you see it? Did you notice it? Did you feel it? It was fairly sharp. You've been good enough to ask me what I think. Do I think this and think that? Let me ask you in return—do you think that, Fate having given me this literally golden opportunity, I'm going to reject it? Reject it for a woman whose fault it is that I am poor; whose fault it is that I am peddling drugs to make a stake big enough to enable me to undo the harm she did? You talk of this prost . . . this dancing-girl's . . . chance and opportunity. What of mine? Am I not as deserving of rehabilitation as she is? Isn't my return to my proper social sphere and status as important as her achieving a social position she never knew? I'm a gentleman . . ."

Otis Vanbrugh coughed somewhat artificially.

". . . a gentleman of birth and breeding; and it is my right and due that I should regain my proper station. This girl was born in the gutter, in the bazaar, and that is her proper place—and she can return there for all I care."

Otis Vanbrugh's face hardened, as his eyes narrowed and his lips pressed yet more firmly together.

"Besides," continued Spanish Maine. "It is not merely a case of

419

what you call blackmail. It is not merely a matter of my having learnt a valuable secret and intending to use it for all it is worth. It's not that at all. It's a case of, I won't say vengeance, but punishment; proper and fitting punishment; poetic justice, in fact. She's the cause of my not having recovered my buried treasure; and now I am going to make her the means of my doing so."

"You are not," said Otis Vanbrugh.

"Oh? We'll see. '*En los nidos de antaño, no hay pajaros hogaño.*'[25] . . . Haven't you been telling me how immeasurably precious to you is your half-sister's happiness, peace of mind, and social security?"

"I have."

"Well, then. What's the trouble? What are you boggling at? The matter is in your hands; not mine. You can secure her happiness, all right. I'm not the obstacle—it's you. You are refusing to pay for what you want. All good things have their price in this world, you know."

"Including yourself, eh?" observed Otis Vanbrugh.

"Well, I don't actually profess to be good. No; on the whole, I don't claim to be one of the good things of this world, but I certainly have my price—in this connection. Oh, yes, I have my price, or rather, my silence has. '*Al buen callar llaman Santo.*'[26] And this is going to be a real exemplification of the proverb that silence is golden. Yes, I'm afraid she has got to pay all right, Mr. Vanbrugh. She or you. I don't care which."

"And suppose I refuse?"

"Well, if we are going to waste our time supposing anything so silly, I'll tell you. If I don't have the satisfaction of endorsing a cheque, I shall have the pleasure of inditing a letter. I'm a bad man to cross, Mr. Vanbrugh. I have my pride, and I don't forgive quickly, easily, and foolishly. My family motto is *Nemo me impune lacessit*. Your 'sister' did me a very great wrong. She not only robbed and swindled me; but she cheated, insulted, and fooled me. Well, she pays me—or I pay her. She pays me back or I pay her out."

"As a matter of purely academic interest, what are your terms?" asked Vanbrugh.

"Ah! Now you're talking sense," approved Spanish Maine.

---

[25] (In last year's nests there are no birds of this year.) "Gather ye roses while ye may."

[26] (To wise silence men give the name of Saint.) "Speech is silvern, silence is golden."

"Oh, I don't know about 'sense.' Merely a matter of idle curiosity, amusement. Simply of passing interest to the psychologist."

"It will be of interest, all right," Spanish Maine asserted. "My terms? Well, let's see. First of all, there's damages. Damages for what she did to me in Bouzen, leaving me stranded, penniless, and in the greatest danger; leaving me without any option but to go into this drug-smuggling, dope-peddling business; causing me to embark upon this extremely risky and unsuitable way of life. I think for material, mental, and moral damages there, we will say— let's see . . . I want to be reasonable and just; just before I am generous perhaps, but at any rate, just."

It was Otis Vanbrugh's turn to yawn and consult his watch.

"For damages, I think we'll say a hundred and twenty-five thousand *pesetas*—say five thousand pounds. Then, for my silence for the remainder of my life—er—what shall we say?"

"Say anything you like," murmured Otis Vanbrugh.

"Thank you. Yes. Quite so," agreed Spanish Maine. "Your sister must have made a lot of money, oh, a lot ef money, one way and another—especially another. Her jewels alone must have been worth a fortune. I think perhaps . . ."

"Interrupting you for a moment," observed Vanbrugh, "though the fact is in no way relevant to our present conversation, I might mention that my sister sold the jewels to which you refer, capitalized all her property in fact, and gave everything to the Convent of the Sisters of the Sacred Heart."

Spanish Maine laughed.

"I'm sure she did," he said, and laughed again.

"I'm glad you are sure," said Vanbrugh. "It helps you to understand how utterly my sister renounced her way of life. She cut herself off from her past completely, and dissociated herself from everything connected with it. Everything and everybody."

"Except me," smiled Spanish Maine.

"No; particularly you, and people of your type," was the reply. "So in making these interesting and amusing calculations, you must bear in mind that my sister is penniless. She has nothing at all of her own, and is dependent entirely on me. The jewellery she now wears, I gave to her. She can, and will, pay you nothing."

"And you propose to transfer the burden to the wealthy milord, eh? To Sir Harry Vane?"

"Have you any Spanish proverbs that warn one against judging others by oneself, Señor Maine?"

"Oh, yes."

"You have mentioned once or twice that you are a gentleman of birth and breeding. Personally I make no such claim, but would nevertheless like to state that my sister is not a burden to me; and that, if she were, I should not be concerned to transfer the burden to Sir Harry Vane or anyone else."

"No?" smiled Spanish Maine. "No? But perhaps you might like to transfer the burden of Señor Manöel Maine's just debts and righteous claims to the wealthy Sir Harry Vane, eh?"

"I am not ashamed to say that I don't quite follow you."

"No? You surprise me. Is it not obvious that if our little Zaza marries Sir Harry Vane, it will be he who does the paying?"

Otis Vanbrugh moistened his lips.

"Why should Sir Harry Vane pay you anything in the event of my sister marrying him?" he asked.

"Oh come, come, Mr. Vanbrugh. You are trifling with me; sporting with my simplicity. You are not as dense as all that. The gold would be Sir Harry Vane's, but the giving hand would be that of our little Zaza. She'd do the actual disbursing—if she wanted peace, that security and safety of which you speak; and untroubled nuptial bliss."

"I see."

"I'm sure you do, Mr. Vanbrugh. You will also see that if the dear child were so foolish as to thwart me, and Sir Harry Vane learnt the ghastly truth about her, my income would be unaffected. Unless, of course, it were increased. Do you know, I fancy Sir Harry Vane—title conferred by James the First, I believe; name and estates conferred by God at the Creation, no doubt—I fancy Sir Harry Vane would pay quite a lot to keep Society and the general public from knowing that his wife Lady Vane had been a common . . ."

"That's enough. Hold your filthy tongue, you damned . . ."

"My dear Sir! My dear Sir! Why this heat? Facts are facts."

"Yes, and there are certain facts concerning you that I shall . . ."

"Come, come! Don't let's descend to personalities. It is vulgar. Do let's remember we are gentlemen. As I was saying—I fancy that Sir Harry Vane would pay quite a lot to keep certain facts concerning his wife from becoming public property. Well now, we were making calculations weren't we? Let's leave idle speculation and return to facts—and fictions—concerning your sister and the *status quo*. We were considering the question of the annual income, weren't we? I think perhaps we might put it at, what shall we say? The same as the damages? A hundred and twenty-five thousand *pesetas*, say five thousand pounds a year?"

"Say anything you like," repeated Vanbrugh patiently.

"Well then, five thousand pounds damages; and five thousand pounds a year for my silence. Now about recovering my buried treasure. Inasmuch as our little Zaza prevented my getting that, and deprived me of its usufruct all this time, we will say . . . what? Twenty-five thousand *pesetas* for expenses? One thousand pounds. That's a very reasonable estimate."

"Most reasonable," murmured Vanbrugh, unsmiling. "Do go on. There's more, surely."

"Well, yes. Naturally. You refer to the possibility of the treasure being stolen. Of course, as you realize, your sister's action has gravely jeopardized the situation. Suppose it has been stolen while I've been collecting the money that she . . . stole. As a reasonable man you will be the first to admit that if, through her, I have lost it, she must replace it. That would be, say, three-quarters of a million *pesetas*. Call it thirty thousand pounds."

"Yes, do call it that," said Otis Vanbrugh.

"So we have a total of nine hundred thousand *pesetas*. Say thirty-six thousand pounds lump sum, and an annual hundred and twenty-five thousand *pesetas*—say five thousand pounds. You will notice, Mr. Vanbrugh, that I am honest, careful, precise, meticulous. I don't airily make it a million *pesetas* lump sum, but just the exact nine hundred thousand."

"I marvel at your moderation," said Otis Vanbrugh.

"Thank you. That's settled then. Cash down—five thousand pounds damages, and one thousand pounds expenses, and one thousand two hundred and fifty pounds as first quarter's salary. Total seven thousand two hundred and fifty pounds. The question of the other thirty thousand pounds is, of course, in abeyance until I find out whether my buried treasure is still there and intact."

"Seven thousand five hundred pounds now, and thirty thousand pounds later, when you choose to declare that your buried treasure has vanished, eh?"

"Say 'if,' my dear Mr. Vanbrugh. Not 'when.' I don't know that it *has* been stolen; but, as I said before, your sister's theft of my money may well have been the cause of my losing the treasure."

"Another point of purely academic interest, Señor Maine. Should I be permitted to have a representative present at the time of your visit to the dried-up well—someone to hold a watching brief for me?"

"Someone to watch me, you mean? Come, come, Mr. Vanbrugh. Between gentlemen! If the treasure is there, I shall not approach you for its equivalent, the indemnity."

"Then why not let my representative go with you?"

Before Spanish Maine could reply, Vanbrugh laughed with genuine amusement.

Spanish Maine raised eyebrows of surprise.

"You find the situation—funny?" he inquired.

"No. Neither will you. It was an imaginary situation that made me laugh. I fancied myself hurrying ahead, getting in first, myself securing the treasure, and using it to pay your blackmail!"

And Otis Vanbrugh laughed again.

"Very funny. Very funny indeed," agreed Spanish Maine. "Funnier still, if you knew where the treasure is, or were able to get there first."

"Oh, I could get there first, by handing you over to the Police."

"But surely that would be mutual, my dear Mr. Vanbrugh. By your own confession, you are an escaped convict too."

"Oh, that wouldn't interest the English police. They've no concern with the French Foreign Legion and its military convicts. What would interest them is your drug-smuggling; dope-peddling; and the fact that you have a consignment of prohibited deadly drugs in your possession, here on a British ship."

"And supposing for one moment that you'd been so very unkind to your beloved half-sister as to antagonize me to that extent, and to get me put away, how do you suppose you'd find the treasure? You don't for one moment imagine that I have given you any true indication of where it really is, do you?"

"No, I'm afraid I don't credit you with having given me much in the way of true indications on any subject, Señor Maine. As I told you, it was merely a joke. It appealed to my wayward sense of humour as being really rather funny."

"Well, now let's talk business, shall we?" proposed Spanish Maine.

"Oh, no. Why talk business? Business would be so dull after these airy imaginings and fairy tales and pipe-dreams about hundreds of thousands of *pesetas*."

"Still, business is business, isn't it? Dull, I grant you, but there are duller things, Mr. Vanbrugh. You must ponder that fact, since you are so fond of your—what is it, half-sister? Besides, business, however dull, may lay the foundations of pleasure, happiness, success. And you want to succeed, don't you, Mr. Vanbrugh? You want your 'sister' to succeed too. So let's talk sense, if not business. I made my modest and moderate suggestions as to damages, compensation, and purchase of my silence. What do you propose?"

Otis Vanbrugh, studying the toe of his shoe, thought a while, sitting silent and still, with pursed lips, judgmatic.

Spanish Maine eyed him watchfully.

"Well," said Vanbrugh, suddenly looking up, "I think at the moment the best offer I can make is the business end of my heaviest boot for damages—plenty of them; a riding-whip for compensation—lots of it; and payment in kind, as purchase of silence—ten or fifteen years' free board-and-lodging. I believe they go in for silence a lot, in British gaols."

"Ah!" smiled Spanish Maine. "You may think differently to-morrow or a little later on, perhaps."

"Oh, quite possibly; especially as to purchase of silence. I'd hate to talk dramatically or threateningly, but a silly old tag occurs to me—I don't know why. A little *à propos* perhaps? I daresay you've heard it, both in English and Spanish, not to mention French, German and Arabic."

"Yes, what is it?"

" 'Dead men tell no tales.' Good-night."

And to the accompaniment of Spanish Maine's soft laughter, Otis Vanbrugh left the cabin.

VII

Lady Drusilla Vane, only daughter of the fourteenth Earl of Dorset, had been lovely and was still handsome. Had she graced an earlier age, she would have been "the toast of the County"; at a later period, "a reigning belle"; and yet later, "an Edwardian beauty." As it was, in a less flamboyant age, when the day of the professional Society Beauty was over, she was famous, and her doings chronicled by the Press, her portrait something of a *pièce de résistance* in the magazines, her gowns described in detail, and her movements duly and widely noted.

Persona grata at Court, from her coming out, although the subject of endless newspaper and social gossip, not the vilest rag nor the meanest scandal-monger had ever had any evil to say of Lady Drusilla Vane.

On the death of her husband, Sir Harry Vane, she retired from Society almost entirely, and devoted herself to her only son, successfully doing her utmost to be no more to him than a wise devoted mother should be; her favourite and most frequent admonition being,

"Think for yourself, my son. Make up your own mind as to what you really want to do—and do it."

When the boy came of age, she re-opened the Vane town-house, returned to Society, found life very good, and that, to her own surprise, she had accepted a proposal of marriage *en secondes noces* from that young, ambitious, and already famous Cabinet Minister, Lord Athelney.

At the age of forty-five, Lord Athelney, feeling equal to fulfilling any office whatsoever under the Crown, made no secret, to her at any rate, of his firm intention of becoming Viceroy of India, and later, Prime Minister of England.

At the age of forty-four, Lady Drusilla Vane, feeling as young as she had ever felt in her life, made no secret of the fact, to him at any rate, that she would greatly enjoy being Vicereine of India and, later, at Downing Street, the chief political hostess of the Empire.

It would be lovely. Athelney was a dear. She had been fond of him all her life, and if he had proposed before Harry Vane did, in her first season—who knows—she'd probably have married him then. Yes, he was a dear, and they'd get on splendidly. And they could have Harry out as aide-de-camp later on.

They had talked of his leaving the Guards and settling down at home, but that could be postponed. He'd look so nice in his Guards uniform at the *levées*. Her brother Eustace and his wife would be only too glad to look after Vane Court for just as long as Harry was in India with them—five years, presumably.

And, for a few weeks, she and Athelney were keeping their engagement almost a secret; and this lovely voyage was making a new woman of her.

Not that there was anything wrong, of course; but, after all, the Season is the Season, and when one is rising forty-five, one realizes it.

§2

Sir Harry Vane tapped at the door of his mother's cabin.

"Who's there?"

"Harry. Are you in bed yet, Mother? Can I come in?"

"Come along."

Closing and locking the door, Harry Vane pushed an arm-chair across to his mother's bed, seated himself, drew up the knees of his trousers, straightened his waistcoat and his dress tie, pulled his white silk handkerchief well into view, smoothed his hair with one hand, and

"The back of your coat-collar is all turned up," observed his mother.

"What a little liar you are, darling."

"Yes. I thought you wanted help to cover your confusion and all that. What is it, Harry? Looks bad to me."

"Darling, you look good to me. You look positively lovely."

"Thank you, dear. Now it looks *very* bad."

"Darling, you look positively very lovely."

"Harry dear, it's worse than I feared. What is it? Money? Cards? Debts? Horses—big or little? Wine, women, song?"

"Yes, Mother. I'm singing . . . singing inside like . . . like a damned great kettle. You know, bubbling and singing and . . ."

"Letting off steam," observed Lady Drusilla, who was well accustomed to confessions from her son, who had no secrets from her. "H'm. You'd hardly be singing and bubbling about *petits chevaux*, debts, duns or cards. Apart from the fact that there are none in your fair young life. You've got all the money you want. You're not singing under the influence of wine, and . . ."

"That leaves woman, eh? Clever lass."

"Yes, and at a guess her name's Consuela, what? Kiss me straight on the brow and part with the confession."

Sir Harry Vane kissed his mother, stroked her hair lovingly, and kissed her again.

"Serious, son?" she asked. "Honest to God, and first, last, and only? Rings; wedding-bells?"

"Wedding-bell rings," nodded Harry Vane, taking his mother's hand. "You like her, don't you, Drusilla?"

"Very much, dear. Her brother too. American gentleman in the grand manner. Said anything to her yet?"

"Well, gave her a hint that I rather liked her, you know."

"Signified in the usual manner?"

"Yes. Hugged her hard to harder—heart to hearter, I mean. Kissed her fair to moderate—immoderate perhaps."

"Harry, you're nervous. All girlish and blushful."

"So were you the other day, mother. About young Athelney."

"H'm. . . . Said anything to her brother yet?"

"No. Thought I'd come and . . . er . . . rehearse it, like . . . with you."

"Dear boy."

"Practise, you know. Get it by heart. Speech . . ."

"We don't know much about them, do we, Harry?"

"I know all I want to know about Consuela."

"You don't, my boy."

"No, you're right, Mother. I don't. There's lots more I want to know about her. That's why I'm going to marry her if she'll have me."

"Don't you think, Harry . . .?"

"No; I never think, Mother."

"No; it's an old complaint of mine against you, isn't it? Still, there's a good deal to think of, isn't there, darling. There's the Thirteenth Baronet and Vane Court, among other things."

"Yes, among other little things, there's the Thirteenth Baronet," agreed Harry Vane. "Unlucky number. Don't you think she'd be a lovely mother for little Number Thirteen?"

"Lovely, certainly."

"Well? . . . Anything against her, Drusilla Grundy?"

"Absolutely nothing, my dear. It's only *that*—the knowing nothing whatever about her, really—that's postponing my bursting into weak tears of joy, going all goosey, and slobbering over you. She's lovely, witty, charming and delightful. Most *piquante*, with that pretty little accent. What is it, by the way?"

"Oh, Taal-Yiddish-Esperanto. You know, Mother, one of those Patagonian Basuto dialects spoken in the Aleutian Islands."

"Yes, darling, I thought it was something like that. I suppose there is some good reason why she has it—and her brother hasn't."

"He's her half-brother; and the other half picked up the accent at school somewhere. . . . Shows you you can't be too careful. . . . Mother, I shall burst in a moment . . ."

"Not in here, darling."

"Simply blow up; burst; dance; sing. . .

"No; not that, darling. Don't sing."

"Well, old lady, what about it?"

"Nothing about it to-night, darling—except that I hope she'll turn out to be a Fairy Princess, and make you as happy . . . as happy . . . as I would have you be."

Harry Vane kissed his mother's hand. She stroked his sleek and handsome head.

"Don't do anything—sudden—will you, son? . . . And I'll have a long chat with her brother by and bye. Don't do anything drastic and final yet. . . . Not engaged. . . ."

"You won't wave flags and drink three bottles of champagne with me to-night then, Mother?"

"No, darling. I've said my prayers and done my face up, or I would. Good-night, sweetheart. I wouldn't talk solemn for worlds, when you are all bubbling and singing—but there's the Torch, old man. Got to hand it on, nicely. We want all the possible best for Number Twelve, but we've got to *do* all the possible best for Number Thirteen, haven't we?"

"Yes, the jolly old Torch," agreed Harry Vane. "Got to hand on the Vane torch. But you know what is the best fire and flame and fuel and all that, for Torches, don't you, Mother?"

"Yes, darling, I do. And it's the only one thing needful really."

"Well, Mother, this is the real thing. It's *love!* I'm on fire; *blazing.* . . ."

VIII

Among the good moments of earth, or rather sea, are those when one, gay, eupeptic, at peace with the world, comes up the broad companion from the dining-saloon and emerges upon the deck of a ship at nine o'clock on a perfect morning, inhales the pure ozonic air, and gazes around upon a lovely sea of deepest sapphire, diamond-studded.

Thus did Sir Harry Vane, rejoicing to be alive, to be in love, to be on the same earth, the same ocean, the same ship, with the girl who had changed the meaning of life for him; changed everything, including himself.

Oh, glorious World! Oh, lovely Life! Oh, great and beneficent Creator who had provided them, and then adorned and enriched them with Consuela!

What had he done to deserve her love? Nothing. How utterly undeserving was he of her love. But it was something, perhaps, that he could realize the fact; and at least he could try henceforth to deserve it, to be worthy of it. And he'd tell her so. He would lay his unworthiness before her to the last fault, misdeed, weakness and vice that he could remember.

There should be no false pretences. She should know the worst; and, by God, thereafter she should know the best, the best that was in him, the best that he could be and do.

His record wasn't too bad, but his "crime sheet," such as it was, should be produced and displayed. No finding out about Gina Grandison—who was probably Sally Higgins—afterwards; or being told by some kind friend about Gertie the Game-keeper's Grandchild, the cunning little beast. No, he'd start fair, and, by Jove, he'd play fair; and they'd be pals; and do everything together; and he'd never again look at another woman, save in the way of friendship.

No. No more nonsense. He'd sown his wild oats—and no more agriculture for Sir Harry Vane.

Ah, here she came, making the glorious bright day brighter and more glorious.

"Darling, you look like the morning."

"Darling, you look like the mourning of the dismal undertaker. *Vous avez l'air triste, comme lui qui mène le deuil.* What were you thinking about?"

"You."

"And that makes you so mournful?"

"Yes. When I think of how unworthy I am. Let's walk. No, we'll sit down. We'll find a quiet spot up on the boat-deck, and I'll try to tell you what a mistake you've made."

"I—make the mistake?"

"Yes. In liking me a little bit. I'm going to tell you what a bad hat I've . . ."

"You have a bad hat?"

"Been, I said."

"Bean? Old bean. Bad hat on the old bean? Yes, you tell me all the bad things you have done, and make me laugh. I'll be your mother confessor, daughter confessor, sister confessor."

"You know, Consuela darling, or rather you don't know, I've led a pretty rotten worthless sort of life up to now. . . . But we're going to change all that. . . . I've just lived to have a good time, and, by Jove, I've had one."

Both young people laughed merrily.

"You have gambled? Pulled horses? Thrown dice—all over the shop? You have drunk the wine, kissed the girl, sung the song? Been as wicked as wicked? I think I like wicked boys. Have you been so wicked that when the husband comes in at the door you fly out at the window?"

"Darling! I'm a respectable young man."

"Oh-h-h. I thought you said you are a wicked one? I am disappointed in you."

Harry Vane laughed, caught the girl's hand and kissed her mocking lips.

"Yes . . . I don't profess to know much about women; but I've a sort of a kind of an idea that they rather prefer possibly knaves to certainly fools, and haven't very much use for pimply prigs and mouldy mollycoddles."

"Ah, some of them like bad men of the best sort more than good men of the worst sort," observed Consuela, with an air of wisdom.

"Yes, that's the idea, darling. Well, I don't say anything about the best sort, but I've been a Bad Man. Very bad. Twice."

"Oh, darling, how interesting. You must write a book of your life; your confessions; and call it '*Twice wicked.*' What bit you?"

"Yes, '*Once Bit Twice Wicked,*' eh? . . . But, joking apart, darling, I want to make a clean breast of everything."

"That's right. Clean up the nice little chest. No, the old oak chest. I'll be your Ginevra. Yes, I'll creep into the chest when you have cleaned it up. Tell me all about your two wickeds."

"Well, when I was a youngster . . ."

"Can you remember as far back as that?"

"Yes, I can. I want you to be serious. This isn't easy for me, you know, darling; but I want you to know the worst about me."

"Go on, Blue-Beard, about your seven wives. Or weren't they? Yes, once upon a time, long long ago, when you were young and passionate. . . . Go on, Harry."

"Thank you, dearest. You are making it easier for me. . . . Well, when I was young and passionate, at the mature age of eighteen or so, there used to be an awfully pretty girl at one of the lodges at Vane Court. She was a game-keeper's wife's daughter but, according to rumour, not the game-keeper's daughter; so to keep her in the family like, all nice and respectable, we called her Gertie the Game-keeper's Grand-daughter."

"Wicked little Harry. Poor little Gertie. Harry made love to Gertie, and Gertie lapped it up like a kitten with cream, or a cat with a mouse?"

"Well, it was my first *affaire*. I thought I was a great lad. Even thought I was in love. Talked big; quite wildly; when they found out all about it. Going to marry her. Made Mother laugh like anything. So they sent poor Gertie away."

"I hope it was snowing, Harry."

"Why?"

"Oh, I hope she wandered out into the snow with her cheek-bones sticking through her shawl and the baby going '*yowl, yowl*' . . ."

"Baby? . . . Whose baby?"

"Her baby . . . I did not suppose it was your baby."

"*Consuela!*"

How girls did talk nowadays!

"Oh, but it was sad; *triste, triste!* And she left her footprints in the snow like the other Lucy, eh?"

"Lucy?"

"Lucy Grey. She was a little cottage girl too. She was seventeen years old, she *said*. I read about it in poetry books my brother gave to me. Yes, and I heard a sailor sing about her too. He sang that she was poor but she was honest. She crossed the moor and then, underneath the gas-lamps standing, victim of a rich man's whim. Her old parents in the Village, lived their lives out just the same, drank the champagne wine she sent them, but they never speak her name. Poor Gertie. Poor Harry. Poor baby."

"Consuela, my child, you shock me. You really do. Such knowledge and depravity."

"And now you shock me, Harry. Having Gerties and babies all over the shop and turning them out into the snow—with no shawl, did you say? Now what was the other Sin?"

"Well, darling, when I joined the Guards, I got into rather a fast set. We used to go to the Frivolity a lot, and drive some of the girls down to Maidenhead and take them on the river on Sunday. We used to take 'em out to supper after the show on week-days."

"*Ma foi!* Harry. How you worked! On duty all day, drilling and marching and shooting and sticking your chest right out in front; and then on duty again to dance at night, hugging them to the chest you have stuck out all day; and still you get no rest on Sunday and take them in the river like the Lorelei. My, what a life. And then you find time to sin. . . . Tell me all about her."

"Well, as a matter of fact she was—naturally—a Grandison, but she was a jolly good sort. Yes, called herself Gina Grandison. Well, I got very thick with her."

"Thick?"

"I mean—well—you know what I mean."

"You fell in love with her? She was your mistress?"

"I was terribly fond of her. I was not in love with her. I don't call *that* 'love.' I know what Love is now. Yes, she was my mistress. I'm sorry, Consuela."

"And is that all, Harry?"

"*All?* Isn't it enough?"

"Really all?"

"Yes, really. I've kissed a girl or two, of course, under misletoe, you know—that sort of thing."

"What is misletoe? Why do you get under it? Like an umbrella, yes? Or an eiderdown, no?"

"Oh, it's just a custom at Christmas time."

"I see. Sort of *Mardigras?* All run wild, eh? *Fiesta* day when nothing matters, eh? Oh, la-la! *Alors, les Anglais ne sont pas* toujours *si . . . correct . . . sévère . . . comme-il-faut . . . eh?*"

"Oh, just—a custom. Just a kiss. Means nothing. Girls don't have to go out in the snow afterwards, though it *is* Christmas. No, those were the only two; and I can't even begin to tell you how sorry I am. Can you ever forgive me, darling?"

"Could you forgive me Harry?"

"What do you mean?"

"Just what I say. Suppose there had been . . . two men . . . in my life, would you forgive me?"

"Don't talk nonsense, darling."

"I'm not. I'm asking you, Harry. You said, would I forgive you. I am asking you if you would forgive me."

"Darling, don't say anything so horrible. Don't talk like that."

"Why?"

"Because that would be absolutely different. You don't know what you're talking about. . . . That would be altogether different. . . . Dreadful. . . . Horrible. . . . Unthinkable."

"How?"

"In every way. Absolutely different. It's not the same thing at all. Oh, for God's sake, don't let's talk like this, darling. It's silly. Or do you mean that you find what I have told you . . . rather terrible? You mean that you can't forgive me—any more than I could forgive you?"

"You couldn't forgive me, then?"

"Oh, darling, *please*. . . . Consuela! . . . It all happened before I knew you; before I knew there was such a person; before I ever dreamed that there could be anything like you. I do most solemnly swear that I'd sooner die than do anything of that sort ever again, now that I have met you. Now that I love you and you love me. Can you forgive me, Consuela?"

"There's nothing to forgive, Harry. Nothing for me to 'forgive' you. Who am *I* to forgive *you*? Who is any woman to 'forgive' a man what he did with regard to other women, before ever he knew her? I don't think it is her business. If a man falls in love with a woman and then makes love to other women, he is a beast; and she can forgive him or not, as she likes. She has the right then to forgive him, and the right not to forgive him."

"Darling, thank God you look at it like that. Then you do forgive me; and it doesn't make any difference? You won't love me the less?"

"I tell you I don't forgive you, Harry. I might as well say I forgive the Sultan of Morocco for executing a man before I was born. I can't forgive—or blame—you for what you did not do to *me*. I'm not your Judge. If you do anything cruel to me now, I can blame you or I can forgive you. . . . I should forgive you, Harry, but don't do anything cruel to me. . . . I have had so much of . . . No . . . now listen, darling. Of course I don't love you any the less for something you did before ever I met you; and I love you, if possible, all the more for wanting to tell me—so as to, what you call, start fair and make a clean breast. I love you to-day, Harry, more than it is possible for any woman to love a man; and every day of my life, I will love you more than I did the day before. Do you understand, Harry? I will love you more than it is possible every day, and I will love you more than that every other day."

Their lips met in a long long fervent kiss. The girl threw her arms about the man's neck.

"Oh, Harry, I should die, I should *kill* myself, if you didn't love me any more."

"There, there, Harry darling. . . . There now . . . I must get my breath. Now I've told you truly and truly—as though I spoke to God—what I think and feel about forgiving. There is *no* 'forgiving,' Harry, between people who love each other, for the things each did before love came to them."

"No, darling, no! Thank God you do think and feel like that."

"And you, Harry? Do you think and feel like that?"

"Why, yes . . . Yes. Of course I do. As you say, what earthly right should I have to dare to 'forgive' you for anything you had done before I met you."

The girl took his face between her hands and kissed him again.

"You mean it, Harry? You truly mean it? You *really* think and feel and believe that?"

"Of course I do, darling. Good God! Who am *I* to forgive *you?* Not but what I imagine the biggest sin you've ever committed was to poke out your tongue at somebody, or to eat sweets in church, or stick a pin in your governess, or disobey your mother . . ."

"*Oh, God! . . . Oh, God! . . . Oh, Mother of God! . . .*" whispered Consuela.

"What? Why? Did you ever disobey your mother?

"No, Harry, I never disobeyed my mother. . . . Here comes that foul Spaniard. Let's go for a walk."

The young people arose, patrolled the boat-deck and then descended the companion to the promenade-deck below, where, in the most favoured spot, Lady Drusilla held court.

"Ah, there you are, darlings! Harry, bring a chair for Consuela here beside me. You can perch on my foot-rest. Have you met Mrs. Tunnicliffe? I find we have lots of friends in common. Do you know, she was at school with Athelney's young sister, Phoebe.

"And Sir Arthur and Lady Fieldinge. Sir Arthur met your father

435

in India. Put him up, when he was tiger-shooting in the CP."

And, as the small babel of rapid conversation which follows such introductions subsided, into the circle, dapper and debonair, smiling and smart, shining and assured, stepped Señor Manöel Maine.

"Good morning," he smiled with flashing teeth. "May I recall myself to Mr. Otis Vanbrugh and his charming sister? . . . I wonder if you remember me, Vanbrugh? We met in—was it Algiers or Tangier? . . . One runs about so much . . . I was staying in the same hotel. Yes, that was it. The St. George at Mustapha Supérieur; and we met at dinner at the Spanish Consul's, do you remember; and then at the Governor-General's *levée*, where I had the honour and pleasure of dancing with Miss Vanbrugh."

And with an eye as hard cold and compelling as his smile was bright, Spanish Maine extended the hand of friendship to Otis Vanbrugh.

"Or do I pay you a greater compliment than you pay me, Mr. Vanbrugh; and have you forgotten me completely?"

"How do you do?" replied Otis Vanbrugh after a perceptible pause, his voice cold, his manner non-committal.

"And Miss Vanbrugh?" Spanish Maine bowed low from the hips.

"Good morning," said Consuela, ignoring the extended hand.

"Might I beg that you be so good as to introduce me to Lady Drusilla Vane whom I have known so long, but never met, my dear Vanbrugh."

"My dear man! Known so long, and never met? Here's mysteries," laughed Lady Drusilla.

"Known by repute. Known by sight. Known by constant study of your admirable and delightful society-magazines, Lady Drusilla. I knew you the moment I set eyes upon you, and I offered myself my best felicitations."

"Well, after that, Mr. Vanbrugh. . . ."

"Señor Manöel Maine," said Vanbrugh, "of Cadiz, I believe and—er—elsewhere."

"And now I may say 'How do you do, Lady Drusilla,' may I not?"

"Now, and just as often as we meet, Mr. Maine," laughed the lady. "Have you met my son?"

"Señor, your very humble servant. May I offer my deepest sincerest felicitations?" and he glanced from Vane to Consuela.

"Er—no thanks. Bit premature. Untimely. Unlucky, I mean . . .

and all that. . . . Walking again, Consuela?"

"Yes, Harry. How small a ship seems, sometimes, doesn't it?"

"When one wants to go for a walk, eh?"

And as they strolled away, he added audibly,

"And when one wants to get away from people."

Upon the better-mannered of the group, with one exception, Señor Maine made a most favourable impression; and, at the end of half an hour when, with bright smiles and graceful bows, he withdrew,

"Charming man! Charming man!" observed Lady Drusilla. "Most agreeable. And how handsome—in the Spanish style. Brilliant conversationalist too—most thoroughly interesting . . . Thanks so much for bringing him along, Mr. Vanbrugh,"

And,

"My God!" observed Mr. Vanbrugh to himself, behind the impenetrability of his poker face.

IX

"D'you know, Mother, my lass," observed Harry Vane to the Lady Drusilla, a few days later, "I've either read somewhere, or heard, that it's a fact, a very remarkable fact, that even the nicest, most experienced and otherwise discriminating women, very often find great difficulty in distinguishing between a greasy bounder and a person of quality."

"Is that so, dear? How interesting. And do you think Consuela shares that failing with the other nice experienced and discriminating women, in 'taking up,' as they say, with Sir Harry Vane?"

"No, Mother, I don't. And if you can't help being feeble you can try not to be flippant, fatuous, futile. I was alluding to this Eye-talian ice-cream merchant or organ-grinder or whatever he is; this Spanish Maine fellow."

"Oh, is Señor Spanish Maine an Eye-talian? Well, well, how deceitful! Going under false pretences like that."

"What do you see in him, Mother?"

"Haven't looked far, my child. I find him a most amusing naughty man. He makes me laugh. I like him."

"Like him when he combs his hair?"

"Well, darling, we haven't got so intimate yet as to sit and watch each other combing our hair. I like him, but we don't visit. Though I told him I hope he will come and see us at Vane Court."

"Good Lord, Mother! What did you want to do that for?"

"Why not, my dear? He's a gentleman and . . ."

"He's *what?*"

"Oh, don't be so insular, Harry. What if he does carry a comb in his pocket? He's a foreigner. *Autre pays autre mœurs.* Most foreigners think we are the most mannerless barbarians in Europe."

"Well, good form and good manners are. . . ."

"My dear boy, one of the most delightful kings in Europe, a truly great, noble and chivalrous gentleman, always wipes his fingers on his trousers after he has eaten anything juicy or sticky. Never varies. Yes, he does vary, though. Sometimes he wipes them on the front and sometimes on the back; but always on his trousers. And his family have provided kings in Europe since B.C."

"Well, Consuela doesn't like this Spanish Maine, anyhow."

"Then she can leave him to me, can't she, darling, and there'll be no jealousy. Present company always excepted, there is nobody on the ship I'd sooner talk to. He knows my beloved Spain, of course, like the back of his hand; Germany, France, Algiers—all the places I know. I'm quite sure he is no saint, but he knows the world. He has lived, and he has done things."

"Well, go your own foolish way, Drusilla. Don't say I didn't warn you. If you want to know what *I* think . . ."

"Of course I do, darling. Who doesn't?"

"Well, I think it's a jolly good job you got your girlish self engaged to Athelney before you met this Dago."

"Perhaps you're right, darling. A wayward woman's heart is a wild and wanton thing; but as it is, you can regard me as safe, and let me play with The Bright Bermuda Boy. Why don't you like him?"

"Partly because Consuela loathes the sight of him."

"Why should she?"

"My dear Drusilla, I don't wish to be pointed, but the answer is because he's a shocking bounder; and no sensible decent woman would be seen dead in the same street with him."

"Oh well, that lets me out, Harry. I can truthfully say I'd hate to be seen dead in the street with him—or anybody else. I wonder why Consuela takes the trouble to loathe him."

"I wonder why you take the trouble to be civil to him."

"Does Mr. Vanbrugh share Consuela's repugnance and hatred of Señor Maine?"

"He certainly doesn't like him. Always refers to him as that 'dirty Dago.' "

"Not always, darling. I've heard him refer to him as a 'goddam Wop.' . . . Curious."

"Jolly sight more curious that you should chum up with him, Drue."

"Oh, darling, we're not positively chummy. He amuses me."

"And you've invited him to Vane Court."

"Yes. I hope he'll invite us to his place in Spain, afterwards."

"His 'Castle in Spain'?"

"No, darling. I believe he called it a *ganderia*. He's a land-owner, you know, with a few miles of vineyards and, as a hobby, a ranch for breeding fighting bulls for the bull-ring. He's got a place at Santander, a lovely little spot; a villa at San Sebastian; a hot-weather *pied à terre* at Ronda; and a house in Madrid. As he has a yacht in Arosa Bay, one ought to have rather a jolly holiday visiting him. Perhaps on our honeymoon . . ."

"Our? Yours and mine, Mother, with Athelney and Consuela in their respective parts?"

"Oh no, darling. I don't think we'll have a *char-à-banc* honeymoon all together, do you? I meant Athelney and I might have a European trip before the India business materializes. Why don't you and Consuela be nice to Señor Maine? You might go to Spain for your honeymoon too. If we reported favourably. Did I tell you I heard from Athelney at Hamilton? And he'd had it straight from the P.M. that he will be offered the Vice-royalty when Lord Ulster finishes his term next year. There was only Lancaster in the running, and his wife is so enormously fat. Colossal."

"But I fancy Orientals rather admire fat women. Buy and sell them by the pound, don't they, Drue?"

"I believe so, darling, but it was the heat I meant. The poor dear would have got so hot and bothered; all red and drippy. . . . Chair all damp. . . . Sopping. . . . So awkward at a big function . . . So mopping . . ."

"It's settled then, is it, Mother? I'm so glad. You'll love it, won't you? And I'll stand behind your chair at Viceregal Lodge, Calcutta, on the King's birthday, and tickle the back of your neck with a feather."

"No, darling, you'd stand behind Athelney's chair, and you simply must not dream of tickling the back of his neck with a feather when he's being all stately and receiving Maharajahs and things. Such an explosive man, if tickled. He'd say something that wasn't in the Book of the Words at all. But if this Consuela business comes to anything, Harry, I'm afraid you won't be coming with us, will you? I don't think aides-de-camp are allowed to marry. The women at Simla and Calcutta wouldn't think it fair and right of Athelney to bring a married aide-de-camp to Government House. So difficult all round. No; aides-de-camp have to be like monks and Bishops and Caesar's wife—celibate, and eligible, and all things to all women, and not above suspicion, and all that."

"Well, anyhow, darling, we could come out and have a cold weather with you, couldn't we? Or a hot weather up at Simla?"

"Yes, that would be lovely, Harry."

"You haven't invited Señor Manöel Maine to Viceregal Lodge yet, have you, Drusilla?"

"Yes, darling. Promised to get him some big-game shooting. He wants to take home some prize humped oxen."

"Prize humped oxen!" growled Harry Vane. "Gives one a prize

hump to listen to you, Mother. What on earth do you see in the man?"

"A charming Spanish *hidalgo*, my dear. Brings back my youth. Reminds me of my giddy girlhood. Moonlight, guitars, balconies, cloaks, swords, serenades and . . . oh . . ."

"Ice-cream and organ-grinders," supplied Harry Vane.

X

"Hullo! Who's that casualty?" inquired Captain Alexander Angus Browne of Surgeon MacDonald, as a man on crutches made his careful laborious way from the *Amazon* to the tender that was to take the passengers ashore at Plymouth.

"Damned if I know, Sir," replied the ship's doctor. "Nothing to do with me. I've had no foot or leg case. Queer."

Fortunately, the angle of the broad gangway, stretching between the open sally-port in the side of the *Amazon* and that of the tender, was slight, and the cripple had but little difficulty in crossing from the ship to the boat.

"There's been nobody about the ship on crutches either," continued the Surgeon. "Must have been very sudden."

"He'd come prepared for it, all right," observed Captain Browne.

"How d'you mean, Sir?"

"Well, look. Pretty obvious, isn't it? He's got his foot bound up to the size of a Christmas pudding, and a pair of crutches big and strong enough to take him round the world. He was anticipating that accident, wasn't he?"

"Oh, I see what you mean, Sir. Of course it may not have been an accident."

"No, indeed it may not," agreed Captain Browne.

"I mean, he may be subject to sudden attacks of gout or rheumatism, and has to be prepared; or he may have some sort of wound or sore that breaks out from time to time."

"Aye?" observed Captain Browne non-committally.

But Otis Vanbrugh, even more sceptical than Captain Browne, took out his pocket-knife as he followed Señor Manöel Maine across the gangway to the tender.

Watching him until he had ensconced himself in a quiet place on the lower deck at the stern of the boat, Vanbrugh, depositing his dispatch-case at the feet of Consuela, made his way to where Spanish Maine sat, his crutches and bandaged foot extended before him.

Opening his knife, he came up to the cripple and, with the back of the blade, rapped the stout leg of one of the crutches smartly. It was, as he had expected, of steel.

"And might one ask what the devil you think you're doing?" inquired Spanish Maine softly.

"Very bright idea that," replied Vanbrugh. "Very bright. I wonder how many pounds of cocaine those crutches hold, and how many tons of it you'd got wrapped round your foot. I call that a really brainy notion. You know, I've half a mind to let you get away with it."

"I'm sure you have," replied Spanish Maine. "More than half. In case you haven't, I'll mention that that bag of golf-clubs contains about as much. You notice the large proportion of drivers and brassies. All dummies; all hollow. So are the balls in the pouch and at the bottom of the bag. They won't fall out because, as you see, the bag's lashed nice and tight round the top."

"Another bright and brainy notion," observed Vanbrugh.

"Yes. That cylindrical case carelessly attached contains a thermos flask. That's full, too."

"And you've nothing to declare, I suppose."

"Oh, yes, I have. I'm always scrupulously honest, careful and precise. Meticulous even. I've got a couple of tablespoonfuls of brandy in this silver flask and a broken box of cigars in that suit-case. They will weigh the cigars, allow me the brandy, and charge me seven and six. Come and watch."

"I'm going to. I'm going to do more than that. I'm going to take a hand. I'm going to give you away, my friend. See you handed over to the police."

"Not you!" laughed Spanish Maine. "Not you!"

"Suppose I don't. And suppose they catch you themselves, without my help? Are you still going to spin your yarn about Miss Consuela Vanbrugh?"

"Er—no. Look here, Vanbrugh, I'm a sportsman. Come and watch me through the Customs. I'll bet you a hundred to one, in pounds sterling, they don't touch me; and, what's more, if they do, I'll undertake never to say a word about our little Zaza. Word of honour."

"Done," replied Vanbrugh. "If you are pinched you don't say a word about Miss Vanbrugh, and if you get through, I pay you one hundred pounds. That's it. I believe I'm fool enough to trust you."

"Señor Vanbrugh! Between gentlemen! I have given you my word of honour."

Vanbrugh laughed.

"It's a bet," he said.

In the waiting-room into which the passengers were herded

before being allowed, in batches, into the somewhat restricted space of the examination-room, Señor Manöel Maine was the recipient of much and genuine condolence from his friends, especially Lady Drusilla.

"Oh, poor dear Señor Maine! What *is* this? The sins of the port-drinking fathers visited upon the nice abstemious children unto the third and fourth generation? How very odd are the ways of God, if one may say so with all respect. They enjoy the port and we get the gout. Most unfair. So that is why we did not see you yesterday? I looked out for you; quite missed you."

"Lady Drusilla, really! It's worth any pain, any inconvenience, to hear you say that. It's nothing, nothing."

"I'm sure it is," observed Otis Vanbrugh.

"What d'you mean, Mr. Vanbrugh?" asked Lady Drusilla.

"Why, Ma'am, that it *is* nothing—er—to so brave a hero as Señor Maine."

"Pass along please!" boomed an enormous policeman. "About a dozen please. That's right, Sir. Mind the gentleman's foot."

And with a grim smile upon his face, Otis Vanbrugh watched the passage of Spanish Maine through the British Customs.

At this unfrequented port, where liners rarely berthed, the definitely easy-going Customs official, who appeared to combine his occasional work of Customs Officer with that of railway porter, producing a printed card, read out a long list of dutiable articles.

"Anything to declare Sir?"

"Er—yes; as a matter of fact, I have," replied Spanish Maine. "I've got a few cigars in a box in that suit-case . . . That one. Broken box, originally fifty. I suppose I've taken a dozen out. You don't make any charge for a broken box, do you?"

"Well yes, as a matter of fact we do, Sir. Cigars is cigars, and as such is dutiable."

"Oh, well, yes, but damn it all, I'm not importing cigars. They are only a few I've been smoking on the journey, just to last me from Jamaica to London. They're Jamaicans, you know. I don't suppose the duty on them is as heavy as on Havanas, is it?"

"All goes by weight, Sir. Yes, I'll have to weigh 'em and charge according. Will you open the suit-case."

"Would you mind doing it? It's unlocked. Everything's unlocked. That one."

"Very good, Sir."

And opening the suit-case, the official disclosed, nestling by the side of silk pyjamas and other gentleman-like impedimenta, a fifty box of Jamaican cigars.

"This all, Sir?"

"That's it. Well . . ."

Spanish Maine patted his right breast.

"I believe I've got one in my cigar-case here. Watt a minute."

"Oh, that'll be all-right, Sir," conceded the man. "You wait a moment. I'll take these and weigh 'em."

"Oh, here, hold on. Half a minute. Sorry—I've got a drop of brandy in this flask."

"How much Sir?"

"About a quarter full. It's just—er—medical comforts, you know. Always carry it about with me."

"That'll be all right, Sir."

"Well, be as quick as you can, like a good chap. I can't stand about for long, you know. This leg . . ."

"Quick as I can, Sir."

And five minutes later, hieroglyphics scrawled in chalk upon each of his suit-cases, trunks, his golf bag and dispatch-case, Spanish Maine passed through the little Customs House to the railway platform where the boat-train awaited him.

Seated at the window of a first-class carriage, he bowed and smiled pleasantly to his fellow-passengers as they hurried by.

Otis Vanbrugh approached.

"That will be a hundred pounds, Mr. Vanbrugh," smiled Spanish Maine.

"It will," was the reply. "But I doubt if you'll live to spend it. However, I will post you my cheque. What address?"

Spanish Maine showed his white teeth in the brightest of smiles.

"Send it to Vane Court, my dear chap, will you? To await arrival."

"*To Vane Court?*"

"Yes, to Vane Court. Paying Lady Drusilla a visit. Shall I have the pleasure of meeting you and our little Zaza there?"

"Miss Vanbrugh and I will be going to Vane Court, but I doubt whether our visit will coincide with yours, Señor Maine."

"Oh, I daresay we can arrange it. I'll have a chat with Lady Drusilla; and, meanwhile, where can I find you?"

"There will be no need to find me. I shan't be lost."

"My dear Mr. Vanbrugh, how literal! How very literal. I meant, where can I find you with a letter—to acknowledge the safe receipt of the cheque; or in case, by chance, it should go astray?"

"Don't worry."

"I won't. Why should I? It's you who have to worry, you know. I want an address at which I can find you—and our little Zaza."

"By God, if ever a man went looking for trouble!" growled Vanbrugh.

"No, no, wrong again. It's you who are looking for trouble. Don't forget that I shall be staying at Vane Court. I have an invitation—casual perhaps and hardly serious—but I'm going, and *I'm* going to be serious. Now then, if you don't want me to be—er —indiscreet, and to gossip, shall we say, at Vane Court, let me have an address at which I can find you if I want you."

And the piercing black eyes bored into the hard grey ones.

"A letter will always be forwarded to me from Brandon Abbas, Devonshire."

"You are going there shortly?"

"Yes."

Spanish Maine produced a note-book and detached from it a pencil.

"Brandon Abbas, Devonshire," he wrote. "Is that near Exeter?"

"Not far."

"Mind you, it will be the worse for you and our Zaza if there's any hanky-panky. Address you there, care of whom?"

"Care of John Geste, Esq."

"Right. I'll probably look you up."

"I shouldn't."

"No? . . . Ah! Here comes her ladyship."

"Safe through, Lady Drusilla? Did they find anything?"

"Not a thing, Señor Maine. Got the whole consignment through safely. Did you?"

"Most of it, dear lady. Most of it. But they stuck me ten bob for cigars. Too bad . . . Mr. Vanbrugh was just saying he'd kept this compartment, for us all. Come along."

And in the six-seated compartment, there travelled to London a somewhat ill-assorted party consisting of Lady Drusilla Vane, Consuela Vanbrugh, Sir Harry Vane, Mr. Otis Vanbrugh and Señor Manöel Maine, the last-named the merriest of them all, with Lady Drusilla a close second.

XI

Otis Vanbrugh paced the floor of the sitting-room that he shared with Consuela at the Imperial Hotel, Mayfair.

Up and down, up and down, to and fro, to and fro, he marched, as if on sentry-go, his brow heavy, his face expressive of the worry, anxiety, and trouble that oppressed his mind.

Consuela, sunk in a deep armchair, watched him uneasily.

"I don't know, my dear; I *don't* know. I don't know what to say. I don't see how you *can* go on."

"Otis, can't we *do* something? I could kill him. I *would* kill him if I had a chance. I'd kill him with my own hands. *Mais, oui, je ferais son affaire!* If only for making me feel like this, driving me back to what I was. I was forgetting how to hate, forgetting that ever I had hated—and now I'm talking about *killing*. He's driving me back to what I was; making me bad again. Oh, if he were here in this room."

"Forget it, Consuela. Cut it right out. Don't talk like that. I'll fix him, don't you worry. Whatever happens and whatever the result is, I'll fix him. But we've got to remember this is not the Sahara and it's not Wyoming. Look here, we'll go down to Vane Court with Harry to-morrow, and from there I'll go on to Brandon Abbas, and I will talk it over with John Geste. I'll come back to Vane Court and fetch you to Brandon Abbas. John's not only about the whitest man that ever lived, but he's wise, he's sound. We'll see what he advises You won't mind if I tell him everything, will you?"

"Oh, Otis . . . but . . . Well, you know best. I'll leave it entirely to you. If you think it's going to help."

"I do, my dear. Telling John Geste will be like telling a tombstone. He'd be just as likely to repeat it. He wouldn't even tell his wife, unless we asked him to.

"In point of fact, Consuela, I should have had to tell John something, even if we'd never met the Vanes and Spanish Maine. I wrote and told him we were coming to England and that I was bringing my half-sister; and when he was at the ranch in Wyoming there wasn't any half-sister! He knows Mary and Janey, and as he was going to take us around in British Society, I should have had to tell him something to explain your accent, and your being such a

447

brunette, so different from Mary and Janey.

"Now I want to tell him the whole story, and get his advice and help as to how to handle this Spanish Maine without coming up against the British law. Most law-abiding country in the world this, Consuela, and the British cop is your big brother so long as you are a good boy; but if you aren't, he gets you, and there's no escape. And once you are inside, there's no pull in the world can help you. No graft.

"You see, if we were back in the Wild and Woolly West of the U.S.A.—especially if we were on the ranch in Wyoming, this Spanish Maine would not arise. No, he surely would not. Six feet of earth would keep him down, if he tried to. But it is different over here, and we mustn't make any mistake. I want Spanish Maine to make the mistake; and the next thing I want is another man to talk to. To talk things over with. To put me wise.

"No. If you find you are sitting pretty at Vane Court, all comfortable and enjoying yourself, I'll get a car and run over and see John, first; talk it over with him, and then, according to how things go and what we decide, I can come and fetch you there, or not.

"But perhaps you wouldn't like to visit them after I'd spilt the beans, and he knew everything? . . . I wish Grandmother was still alive. You know I told you I used to come to Brandon Regis to visit her when I was a boy.

"But mind you, my dear, John Geste is not only one of the best, he's *the* best, and his wife, well . . ."

"She's the woman you loved so, isn't she?" said Consuela. "Yes, and but for her I should never have known you, Otis, and never have known Harry. I should still be in Bouzen. It was because you loved her that you came to Africa to look for her husband, wasn't it? Yes. Tell them, if you like. I don't care. They'd never never tell anybody else, would they?"

"They'd sooner die, Consuela. They'd sooner cut their tongues out."

"Well, tell them, then, and see if they can help. Yes, tell them. I don't care. I feel everything is slipping, slipping. . . . Oh, Otis, Otis, I shall die."

And the girl burst into a flood of passionate tears.

"There, there, there . . ."

"Oh, Virgin Mary," she wept, "help me. I do love him so. And, oh God, do help me to kill Spanish Maine. I do hate him so."

"There, there, Consuela. Don't carry on. I'll fix him. I'll fix him."

The girl rose to her feet.

"Otis! Don't you do anything to bring trouble on you! I won't have it! I've given you trouble enough. Promise me, Otis. I'll deal with El Señor Manöel Maine."

"Now, none of that, Consuela! Stop it! Cut it out, I tell you. Never mind about fixing Spanish Maine. Go and fix yourself. They'll be here to lunch in half an hour. Look, you'll have the whole afternoon and evening on the river with Harry."

"While I palaver with Drusilly," he added, a little ruefully.

And as the girl went from the room, Otis Vanbrugh seated himself in her chair, resting his chin upon his clenched fists.

"I don't know," he said. "I *don't* know. What a mess! What a God Almighty mess. She can't get away with it. We *can't*—with or without Mr. Spanish Maine.

"Mr. Spanish Maine! . . . Why, *hombre*, I begin to think you are the one bright spot in it; for I do surely promise myself a real shining moment with you—when the time comes."

XII

John Geste led the way into the room that had been his favourite from childhood, and was now known as his study, sanctum, and den. A big deep arm-chair on either side of a log-fire; a low table, on which stood a decanter, siphons and cigar-box; a general atmosphere of luxury, peace and quiet, invited rest and relaxation.

Switching on the lights and locking the door, he turned to his guest.

"Well, old chap, here we are. Sit down. The night's but young and we have got the rest of it. What's the trouble? Prefer anything to a whisky?"

"No thanks, John. I'd like a high-ball," replied Otis Vanbrugh. "Helps me to talk as well as anything, when I have to. And I have to now, John. And the tale of the trouble is a long one. I'm going to tell you everything and ask your opinion . . . your advice. I'm going to do more than that. I'm going to ask you to tell me—so far as you can—exactly what you'd do, in my place."

"I'll try, Otis. Of course I will give you my opinion and I'll give you my advice, for what it's worth. As to telling you what I'd do in your place—that's more difficult. Does one ever really know what one would do in another person's place? Anyhow, I will have a shot at it. What's the trouble?"

"Blackmail."

"Good Lord! That's a nasty thing. Nearly as bad as murder."

"Worse, sometimes," agreed Vanbrugh. "I'd make it a capital offence. Murder of happiness. Sometimes murder of mind and soul. Much worse than killing the body."

"Yes, I quite agree. There are lots of people who ought to be put to death, but nobody ought to be blackmailed. Yes, I've often wanted to commit murder, but I can't say I have ever contemplated the other crime. Which does rather suggest it's worse than murder, I suppose."

"Who's being blackmailed? Not you?" added John Geste, incredulous.

"Yes, indirectly."

"For a large amount?"

"Oh, six thousand pounds cash down, and five thousand a year;

450

with a contingent thirty thousand pounds—a contingency which I've no doubt will be made to arise."

John Geste whistled on a note of consternation and amazement.

"Who is it?" he asked.

"Our friend Señor Manöel Maine, approved and admired of Lady Drusilla Vane."

"Good Lord above us! A blackmailer?"

"Very black."

"Well, as I'm going to tell you exactly what I think and feel, give my opinion and advice, my immediate reaction to that, is—Police. What about the Police?"

"Yes," smiled Vanbrugh. "I supposed so. There is a different attitude, relationship, between the Public and the Police in Britain, though, isn't there? Aren't they a sort of universal uncles?"

"Well, in a case of blackmail, our Police and Law Courts are particularly sound and helpful. If you run a man in, for blackmail, your name is suppressed if you wish it to be."

"What? A conspiracy of silence between Police, Press and Judiciary?" asked Vanbrugh.

"The plaintiff is referred to as Mr. X, and the real name is not mentioned in Court at all. I'm not sure whether it is a penal offence for a newspaper to publish it, or whether the Law Court reporter never hears it; but, anyhow, if you prefer to be Mr. X, the public never knows you as anything but Mr. X."

"Amazing," observed Vanbrugh. "Excellent and admirable, and should go far to putting an end to blackmail. But what you say only refers to the general newspaper-reading public. The blackmailer always has the postal facilities at his disposal. You can prosecute and punish him for blackmail without public exposure, but you can't prevent private exposure; you can't stop his tongue and his pen until he goes to prison—if he does go."

"No, I suppose not," mused John Geste.

"Of course not," continued Vanbrugh. "It's bound to be known in one's own circle; and one's own circle is really a sphere. It is one's world. The world we move in *is* our world, and the real agony, misery, injury and ruin accrues through our own people knowing the secret—not the general public.

"This Mr. X business, in the papers, is all very well; but, of course, one's household, family, friends, circle of acquaintances, know that one is Mr. X if the general public doesn't. You yourself, for example, John, couldn't possibly have dealings with the police, with your solicitors, journeys to the local police-court in the first place, and then to your Sessions Court or Court of Assize, or whatever it is, without Isobel knowing, could you?

"And what about such relatives, friends, acquaintances, servants, tradespeople and such, who are called as witnesses, whether for the prosecution or defence? Your own circle must simply buzz with it; and they are the people who matter. And of course the circle is ever widening, like those cast by the throwing of a stone into a pond. No, there is no need for newspaper reporters to tell your friends all about it. They are bound to know, anyway, once you come to prosecute."

John Geste smoked in thoughtful silence.

"Yes; I suppose it is so," he said at length. "I suppose you are right. It would have to be known to lots of people."

"Of course it would, even if the case never appeared in the papers at all; with you as Mr. X or otherwise. Your household, your friends, your relations, your servants, your local acquaintances, must know, as I have said. Both sides must call witnesses too, and aren't the witnesses going to talk about it? They'd have nothing else to talk about for days."

"Yes, but look here—what does that matter, after all? Your household, family, relations, friends, know it's a damned lie. So do the people who are called as witnesses."

A brief silence.

"Suppose it isn't a lie?" asked Vanbrugh with a deep sigh.

"Oh! Well . . . you mean—something one wouldn't want one's people to know."

"Yes," said Otis Vanbrugh.

"But surely that would be preferable to blackmail, wouldn't it? I should imagine anything would be better than that. What's to limit it? Where's it to stop?" asked John Geste.

"The limit would be the utmost you could pay. It would stop when you died," replied Vanbrugh.

"Or when the blackmailer died," he added grimly.

"Well then, surely anything is better than that."

"You'd think so, wouldn't you? And generally speaking, you'd be right, I should say; but you can't generalize. You can't lay down a universal rule. Circumstances alter cases. Take this one, for example.

"Suppose someone, a girl, let's say, were, through no fault of her own, put into a horrible position, a terrible situation . . . apparently permanent. She escapes from it, and the ghastly awful past is behind her. Later, she finds herself in precisely the opposite sort of position, as desirable as the other was undesirable.

"And she is happy and safe.

"Then suddenly, like a bolt from the blue—her new beautiful calm clear blue sky—comes a blackmailer, the man who had known her in the former horrible position, situation, circumstances. He's got her absolutely; for she is about to be married. It's as good as death to the girl if he tells *her fiancé*—as bad as death—for it is the death of her happiness. It's social ruin, too; the inevitable end of the friendship of every friend she has. It's disgrace, downfall, dishonour, a terrible scandal. It means flight, hiding, the end of all things . . . ruin, downfall, destruction, probable suicide."

John Geste rose to his feet.

"The vile devil!" he said. "The unutterable swine! I'd like to thrash him within an inch of his life . . . break every bone in his body. Poor girl! Who is she?"

"My sister."

"*What?* What did you say?"

"My sister."

"Your *sister?* Being blackmailed?"

"Yes."

"Good God! By whom?"

"This fellow Maine. Señor Manöel Maine. Spanish Maine."

"But . . . but . . . What can he . . .?"

"I'll tell you."

Otis Vanbrugh filled his glass, lit a cigar, and settled down to tell John Geste the story of the metamorphosis of Zaza the Death Angel, daughter of Zaza Blanchfleur, into Consuela Vanbrugh.

Dimly, very vaguely indeed, John Geste had a faint elusive memory of a girl in the camp of Sheikh Yussuf ben Amir. He had been practically unconscious when he and Vanbrugh had been brought before Sheikh Yussuf ben Amir, his son Selim ben Yussuf, and the Angel of Death, as they sat in front of the old Sheikh's tent. But until Vanbrugh now spoke of her, he had entirely forgotten the incident, and, in any case, had no memory of her face.

The story finished, John Geste sat silent, almost incredulous, too astonished to speak, as he marvelled at the conduct respectively of the father and the son; that of the one whose lapse from grace, from loud-mouthed piety and profession of religion, had brought about this tragic and terrible situation; that of the other, whose fine sense of duty, self-respect, honour, altruism, had driven him to the work of mitigating, so far as was humanly possible, the harm that had been done.

The evil that men do lives after them. . . . What opinion could he express beyond condemnation of the righteous father and the rascally blackmailer? What advice could he give to this honourable upright man, placed in so false and difficult a position? How could he say what he would do in similar circumstances?

Suppose someone blackmailed Isobel? His first impulse would be to kill the man who was hounding her, threatening her, terrifying her; kill him with his bare hands. But he must not talk like that to Otis Vanbrugh. The wonder was that Otis had not done so already. It was a marvel that he had kept control of himself so completely and for so long.

"Now, John," said Vanbrugh breaking a lengthy silence. "There's the whole story; and I've told it as fully and as truthfully as I know how. I believe you are in possession of absolutely all the facts. Would you like to sleep on it, and tell me to-morrow what you think, what you advise, and what you yourself would do in my place?"

"I shouldn't sleep," replied John Geste. "Let's thrash it out between us now. Then we can sleep on it—perhaps."

"Good. I was hoping you'd say that, John, for I'm about at the end of my tether. I've bottled it up too long, and I've got to do something. Now take your time, old chap, and tell me what you think. Think out loud if you'd rather. It might be a help—to both of us."

"That's a good idea, Otis," replied John Geste, "Think out loud, and fumble toward a conclusion. Best way to find out what one really does think. Thought, I mean, apart from feeling. What I suppose the learned would call ratiocination unvitiated by emotion. It isn't easy, though. My blood boils when I think of this poisonous swine, Maine—the cold-blooded scoundrel. And then again, words fail me when I think of you and your . . ."

"Well, don't think of me at all, John. Let's think about Consuela, and the best thing to do for her."

"Yes," agreed John Geste, "that's the point. Well, she was—what she was—through no fault of her own, let's say; and now she is not what she was. She left that life behind from the day you went back to her at Bouzen. From that day to this, she has lived the ordinary life of a normal young woman, travelling with her favourite brother to whom she is greatly attached, and who is equally fond of her. . . . You are fond of her aren't you, Otis, or are you still acting purely from pity and a sense of duty?"

"I'm extremely fond of her, John. I don't think it's any exaggeration at all to say that I love her very much indeed, in a brotherly sort of way. It's a good love, too, because it has grown out of strong dislike, if not hatred. As you know, there is no friendship between men to equal the friendship that begins with enmity, a squabble, a little fighting, physical or otherwise; and turns first to toleration, then to understanding, and finally to mutual respect, admiration, and friendship. That's much better than those friendships that are based on accidental contact, the casual contiguity in work or pleasure or neighbourhood. Consuela began by terrifying me, and then she bored and bothered me, almost disgusted me, by developing an unrequited passion. Then I pitied her and sympathized with her.

"Before long I began to like her, and could not help admiring certain traits in her character. As I came to understand her, I liked and admired her very much, realizing that she was a thousand times more sinned against than sinning. The more I saw of her, the fonder I got of her; and any early indignation that I had had against her was now indignation *for* her, indignation against whose who'd made her what she was; those whose fault it was that she was born and bred to . . . to . . . to the Street of Bouzen. You know, John, once she'd got away from it all, and was leading a normal life, she changed, as it were, before one's eyes.

"Have you ever cleaned a dirty picture, or seen one cleaned? Imagine a dirty grimy smudge, that may or may not be the picture of a woman, and imagine it turning from a *croûte*, a daub, a dark filthy blotch with a frame round it, into a beautiful girl, young, fresh, engaging, attractive, yes and innocent-looking, I tell you. Innocent. Imagine it. The miracle of it. And what does it show— what does it indicate? I say it shows a genuine fundamental innocence, innocence of soul. And another thing; don't they always tell you that these . . . these . . . women are inevitably degenerates; born so; doomed from the cradle? Don't all the good people—as well as the prurient-minded sniffing hypocritical muck-rakers who 'study' the subject and do 'rescue' work—all say that it is impossible to rescue these women; that they cannot be reclaimed; that they inevitably return to that way of life because they prefer it; that they have a flaw, a kink, a predisposition to vice, a poison in the blood; and that these things cannot be eradicated? That you can no more change them than you can the colour of their eyes?

"Well, suppose it's true, that inevitably they relapse, return to vice because they are inherently vicious. Doesn't that go to prove my point—that she is fundamentally (excuse the word) pure? That in her heart and soul and mind, she is innocent? Why, Consuela would die—really, truly, and literally she would be burnt alive at the stake—rather than go back to the Street of Bouzen, or any other Street, for an hour, for a minute, for a second. I'm not talking rashly, John, and I am not talking figuratively, when I say that Consuela would rather die than lapse once, let alone lapse altogether.

"Well now, I had given her my solemn promise that I would go back to her, before I knew that she was my sister. When I did know, I determined to make it my life's work to get hold of her, get her away from Bouzen, save her, reclaim her, give her a chance in life—decent life. Having nothing else to do, I might well do that, and what better thing *could* I do than that? Until this fiend from Hell came on the scene, I hadn't told a soul, not even my brother, about her past. I wanted no-one in the wide world but myself to know. And no-one ever would have known, if the most devilish ill-luck had not brought this hound Maine across our path. She'd never have gone near Algeria or France again, and this man would never have come to England except to smuggle dope into some port, hand it over to the consignee, and clear out again. She'd have married Vane and settled down in peace and security in Devonshire."

Silence.

"Damn it, John, it's I who am doing the thinking out loud. Forgive me."

"Not at all," was the reply. "Think out loud all night long if it'll help, or give you any relief. It will certainly help me to make up my mind. At present I'm all emotion, all feeling, and incapable of detached thought. I don't know what to say, and God knows I want to say something useful, helpful.

"Look here, Otis, let's try to think about it calmly and with detachment and, so far as possible, from the points of view of the three other people beside ourselves. I don't say beside *yourself* because I want you to feel that I am as concerned in this as you are. But for you, I should not be alive, and I doubt if Isobel would be. I'm as much in this with you as your own brother would be, if he were over here.

"Let's look at it from the point of view of Consuela, Maine and . . . Sir Harry Vane.

"Now, as for Consuela.

"You've sprung this on me so suddenly that I've not had time to think about it, but I'm absolutely against the idea of her submitting to blackmail; and if I think about it for a month or a year, I'm quite sure I shall be of the same opinion still.

"She simply must not do it, nor let you do it for her.

"Don't you see, she puts herself completely into the hands of this blackguard; she admits the validity of his accusation by paying him not to utter it; and she enters on a life of anxiety, fear, and distress.

"Once she has admitted his power, and submitted to it, he'll put the screw on—and with increasing pressure.

"How does she know that he'll stop?

"What is to prevent him raising his price to what he considers the utmost limit of what she can pay or raise?

"And suppose she tried to compound with him for a lump sum —bought him out, paid him off—is it likely he won't return?

"It isn't as though he'd got letters that she could buy and destroy. Why, God help us, if the fellow died he could bequeath the secret to some other devil as bad as himself.

"That's my opinion, old chap, and I can't see myself changing it in any circumstances whatsoever. Consuela mustn't pay a farthing of blackmail nor allow you or anybody else to do so.

"Now about Maine. Couldn't we frighten him off?"

"No," replied Vanbrugh. "We couldn't. To give the skunk his due, he has the pluck of the Devil as well as the wickedness. I don't think the man is alive who could frighten Spanish Maine. He simply isn't afraid of man, beast, devil or God. I should say he doesn't know what fear is."

"Well, you know him better than I do," was the reply, "but I think you are wrong. I think a man who's done years of penal servitude in Africa and French Guiana does know what fear is—the fear of prison. And that was what I meant when I said 'Couldn't we frighten him.' I wasn't thinking of physical violence, for a moment. If we cannot put the fear of God in him, we might put the fear of the English police, mightn't we?"

"He knows we couldn't, and wouldn't, invoke the police," said Otis Vanbrugh. "He knows I am very badly wanted by the French, and he must know that I am not sure whether my offence qualifies me for extradition. I am not a British subject, you know. Then, of course, he knows that we should be afraid of his accusing Consuela. He'd certainly get Counsel, for his defence, to discredit me and my witnesses—by asking whether our motive in denouncing him was love of abstract justice or hatred of the accused, whom we wished to put away because he knew too much.

I mean, if we frighten him with the terrors of the Law, on the subject of drug-smuggling.

"He knows perfectly well we should never dream of invoking the law on the matter of blackmail, as the truth would inevitably come out. He knows, as well as we do, that Sir Harry Vane and his whole circle, the whole County, in fact, would know who Mr. X is —or, in this case, Miss X, which is far worse—and how the opportunity for blackmail arose. No, we can't frighten him, either with the Law or with violence.

"And apart from his being a courageous devil, he's a vindictive one. Having messed up his life by his own folly and villainy, he blames Fate, the world, life, people, especially people, anything and anybody but himself. He is particularly vindictive against any woman whom he has pursued and through whom he has come a cropper."

"Well, that's two of the three people most concerned," replied John Geste, "Consuela and Spanish Maine. I've given you my opinion as to Consuela and blackmail. She shouldn't dream of paying a farthing. From that I shan't budge. Then as to Spanish Maine, I say he shan't be bought off, you say he can't be frightened off, and yet if neither of these things is done, he'll wreck her chance in life. And you say that the Miss X business is absolutely beside the point, inasmuch as Vane—and everybody else who matters—is bound to know that she is the Miss X.

"Now as to the third person most concerned, Sir Harry Vane . . . It's difficult to say . . ." John Geste paused.

"Look here, Otis," he continued, "I know you would never, in any circumstances, take any sort or kind of offence at anything I might say, because you'd know how impossible it would be for me to wish to be offensive."

"Say on, John. Say what you think plainly. Say anything that occurs to yon, for you'll never say anything that will offend me."

"Well, what I'm driving at is this. Is it quite the clean potato, as far as Vane is concerned?"

"What d'you mean? Letting him in for being blackmailed himself, later on, by Maine?" asked Vanbrugh.

"Well, I hadn't got quite as far as that, though of course that does arise—later. What I meant is . . . well, is it right—apart from any question as to whether it is wise and—er—decent?"

"You were always great on what's 'decent,' weren't you, John?" interrupted Vanbrugh with the faintest shadow of bitterness in his voice.

"Yes, like yourself, Otis. I hope so. One's got to be—decent—of course, at any cost; at any price."

"To anybody," murmured Vanbrugh.

"Is it right," continued John Geste, "to let Vane marry Consuela in absolute ignorance of her . . . past?"

"Isn't he in love with her?" answered Vanbrugh hotly. "Desperately, madly, in love with her? And isn't he a gentleman? Would he want to back out? Doesn't he love the girl as she is to-day—Consuela as he sees her and knows her? What does anything else matter? What's it matter what may or may not have happened before he set eyes on her? Doesn't he love Consuela as he sees her and knows her, I say?"

"No," was the quiet sad reply. "No, he doesn't, Otis. He loves Consuela as he imagines her to be. A girl of his own sort and class and kind, with background, heredity, environment and experiences similar to his own; probably by no means ignorant, but certainly innocent."

"Environment and experiences similar to his own?" sneered Vanbrugh. "Wealthy young Guardee in a fast set—not ignorant but innocent! A man of the world—a man about town—a London club-man? D'you suppose his gardenia is the white flower of a blameless life? D'you suppose that Sir Harry Vane of the King's Guards is a pure-souled lily? *Experiences!* Good God!"

John Geste slowly shook his head.

"It won't do, old chap; and you know it won't. Rightly or wrongly, that's a different thing altogether. And I've no reason for supposing that Harry Vane isn't just what you said, a noble-souled Galahad, pure and unspotted from the world."

Otis Vanbrugh laughed unpleasantly.

"But, as I say, that's neither here nor there. Damnably unfair I admit, that the man should demand absolute innocence and purity of the woman, while the woman scarcely expects it of the man. It's vile. But the fact remains. And it's not as though Sir Harry Vane, twelfth Baronet, a figure in London Society, and in that of this County, were just a mere nobody."

"By Hell! You make me . . ." exploded Vanbrugh.

"Not a bit as though he were an ordinary nobody," continued John Geste. "And I'm not, as you think, talking mere snobbism. It's a big position that he has got to fill, with big duties and responsibilities; and he's got to marry the right woman. Just as, to compare small things with great, a king has got to marry the right woman."

"To Hell with kings," growled Vanbrugh.

"Now, answer the question honestly, truthfully, and with detachment, if you can. Is a girl born out of wedlock—and the English law unfortunately is cast-iron and cruel on that subject—brought up in a brothel by a courtesan, a girl who practised the profession of courtesan for years . . ."

"It was no fault of hers!" burst out Otis Vanbrugh. "She was . . ."

"I know; I know; Otis. But the facts remain. Now then—I hate saying it, as much as you hate hearing it—is that girl a fit and proper wife for a man in Vane's prominent position; a fit and proper daughter-in-law for Lord and Lady Athelney, future Viceroy and Vicereine of India?"

"Well, I'll answer your question, John. As God's my Judge, I believe Consuela is a good-enough wife for any man on this earth. What she was, she was by no fault of her own; and what she is, she is by virtue of her own innocent goodness and desire to be good, her own fundamental innocence of soul. *Innocence*, I say, man—of mind and soul and character. What does the body matter? She's as well-behaved as your Lady Athelney. Better perhaps. She's clever, wise, witty, kind, brave. . . . Damn it, man, tell me anything she's not, or rather that she hasn't, in the way of accomplishments, endowments and virtues.

"I don't play the Professing and Practising Christian trump on other folks' aces much—but *are* we Christians or not? *Is* this a Christian country or not? Damn it all, man, if they can't forgive a woman for sinning—can't they forgive a woman for being sinned against?

"Consuela not a fit wife for Sir Harry Vane? To Hell with Sir Harry Vane and all the rest of your stiff-necked high-hat aristocrats. She's fit to be wife of the President of the United States, I tell you; and would be an ornament to the White House."

"You've answered my question, Otis. You *do* honestly and truly consider her to be a fit wife for Sir Harry Vane and a fit daughter-in-law for Lord and Lady Athelney."

"I do."

"Right. Well, now then; do you consider it right that he should become the wife of Sir Harry Vane *without his knowing anything whatsoever of her past?*"

"Yes, I do."

"You don't."

"I do, I tell you, John."

"You don't, I tell you, Otis. You don't think anything of the sort. You think, and I honour you for it, that Consuela has had the cruellest, unfairest fate and luck and existence that a woman could possibly have—but you feel that it is no fault of hers, and that she deserves every compensation that the world can possibly give to her. You feel that Man has made her what she is—what she was, I mean—and that Man should make her what she wants to be.

"To come from the general to the particular, you feel that your father made her what she—was; and that Sir Harry Vane, or any other man, is good enough to make her—his wife. You think, or you feel, that the act of Homer A. Vanbrugh made her a half-caste, a bastard, a prostitute—and that the act of Sir Harry Vane should make her an honoured and honourable wife, a lady of rank and title, Lady Vane in short.

"That's what you feel, Otis. But you don't feel—you don't think, either—that it is *right*. That it's right it should be done at Harry Vane's expense, without telling him a word of the truth. It can't be right. You know it isn't—and, as you are about to tell me, you 'don't give a good-goddamn' whether it is right or not."

"You've said it."

"Very well, Otis. I've said it—and you agree. It isn't right. Well, old chap . . . Lord! How I hate talking like this . . . if it isn't right, don't do it—for no good will come of it."

"To Sir Harry Vane you mean."

"To Consuela, I mean; and to Sir Harry Vane; and to all their circle; and to you."

"Well, what's the alternative?"

"Tell him the truth, the whole truth, and nothing but the truth."

"*What?*"

"Let Consuela tell Harry Vane everything—and abide the consequences."

"Well, we know perfectly well what they will be, don't we?"

"No, we don't. And in any case they won't be worse than the consequences of her marrying him dishonestly, deceitfully . . . criminally."

"Strong language, John."

"Yes. I'm sorry, old chap, but I want it to be."

"And is she to address the family circle at Vane Court, with the great and good Lord Athelney in the Chair, by special request?"

"Certainly not. As I see it, the matter is entirely between Consuela and Harry Vane. If, having heard the truth, he chooses to marry her, that is his business and the concern of nobody else."

"Not Lady Drusilla Vane's?"

"No. It's not she who's marrying Consuela. It's Vane; and it's Vane's affair. Let Consuela tell him; and there is no earthly need for her—or for him—to tell a living soul. Quite a case of 'where ignorance is bliss,' so far as Lady Drusilla is concerned. If Vane finds that love is stronger than convention, prejudice, caste and all that; and if the facts of her past make no difference to that love, I see no reason whatsoever why he should tell his mother. In fact, I think it would be a damned silly thing to do."

"Do you imagine for one moment, John, that Sir Harry Vane is big enough, is man enough, is gentleman enough, to hear her story and say,

" 'What does all that matter to me, Consuela? It's you I love. *You*, the girl you are, the girl I know. I met you, and love you, as Consuela Vanbrugh. I never knew you, never heard of you, as the Houri of Bouzen. She doesn't interest me. She exists no longer. There is no such person . . .'

"Is he man enough for that, John?"

"I don't know. It would be a terrible test—of love. You say, 'Would he be man enough?' I don't think it's a question of that, so much as of whether he'd be lover enough . . . I don't know, I'm sure . . . And there's one thing, Otis. You can't quite realize what a tremendous deed it would be, if a man in Vane's position could say, and did say, '*I don't care.*' "

"You think a hell of a lot of 'position,' John."

"Do I? I don't think so. But Vane's name . . ."

"Oh, damn Vane's name. Look here, John. You've been telling me to answer questions as honestly and truthfully as I can. Answer me this one. Suppose it were yourself. Suppose you'd been in Vane's place on that ship, had met Consuela, seen her, danced with her, talked with her, gone around with her for weeks on end, and fallen head over ears in love with her; had proposed to her, and been accepted. Just suppose that the poor girl in a moment of madness, the madness of love, had accepted you, and then I'd come to you with this story. Would you have turned her down?"

"I don't know. Truly, honestly, Otis, I don't know."

"Well, I do," replied Vanbrugh. "I do. You wouldn't have been capable of anything so damned cruel—so damned *wicked*—as to have turned her down."

"Very well," replied John Geste, "give Harry Vane the chance of doing as you think I'd have done."

"And suppose he's not such a man as you, John? Suppose he

does talk it over with Mother. And 'has the honour to regret, but unfortunately . . .' "

"Well, once again, far better that, a thousand times, than let him find it out after marriage. . . . My dear chap, think of the state of mind in which she'd live, day after day, night after night, day *and* night; the state of anxiety and fear in which she'd spend the rest of her life. Why—can't you see, that if this Spanish Maine had never come into it, she'd still have lived a life of fear and anxiety that something should crop up to betray her?

"But as it is, with this remorseless implacable merciless blood-hound—no, a bloodhound's a decent animal—this hell-hound, on her track, absolutely at the door, actually threatening the very fate that she must anyhow spend her life in fearing . . . Why man, the thing's absurd. Honestly, I marvel that you could ever have contemplated such a thing as letting Vane marry her in ignorance of her past."

"That's your last word, is it, John?"

"Absolutely."

"Well . . . *I quite agree with you,*" said Otis Vanbrugh, sadly. "I've felt it that way in my bones—the whole time. Besides, if Vane, knowing the whole truth, had married her, that wouldn't affect the position as to Spanish Maine. He'd merely blackmail Vane instead. And though Vane would be willing to play Mr. X on his own account, he wouldn't dare risk his wife's name. As we agreed, all their world would know about her, if the general public never did. He'd have to leave the Guards, and drop out of Society altogether. . . . Ruin. . . . And yet I don't know what to do. You see it's her life, John, I verily believe; and I've made her my life, so to speak. Made it my life's work to see that she gets a fair deal at last."

"Well, this would not be a fair deal—for Vane or for her."

"No, I'm admitting it, John. I've known it all the time. I knew it from the first—and I ought to have interfered at the start. But when she told me, although my heart sank into my boots, I couldn't bring myself to do it—to interfere. I somehow felt that things might come right. I could no more dash that cup from her lips than . . . Well, damn it, John, if a little child ran laughing to you, ran across that great lovely lawn in the glorious sunlight, to-morrow, ran laughing to you with its arms outstretched—you couldn't kick it in the stomach, could you, John?

"Of course you couldn't. And no more could I—when Consuela told me—say,

" 'Stop it! Drop it! Come off it, d'you hear. You know what you *are!*' . . . I couldn't, John. And I've let it drift on till now, hoping. And God knows what I hoped for—or rather how I could possibly hope."

"Probably you hoped that you or Consuela would decide to tell Vane, and that Vane would—truthfully—say that he didn't care, that love was the beginning and the end and the all of it. Love—everything; the rest—nothing."

"Something like that, probably," sighed Vanbrugh. "Something like that; but without any real intention, any real hope, because there's another aspect of it, as I've recognized from the first. We don't want him to marry her out of pity; marry her with a smile that hides a shrinking horror and disgust.

"And another thing, too," he went on. "We don't want him to marry her in the heat of passion and the folly of infatuation; and then, gradually, as the glow and the glamour, the romance and the rosiness fade, to awake to facts. . . . For when the stark facts began to obtrude, to stand out, to grow clearer and clearer, one day the skeleton would walk out of the cupboard—and, during a tiff or a sudden fit of anger, Vane, suddenly, before he knew what he'd done, might call her what she . . . I mean, say something unforgivable, unforgettable."

"He's not that sort of man, Otis."

"Perhaps not, to-day, John. What sort of a man will he be five or ten or twenty years hence? He's not that sort of man, as you say, when he's in love. What sort of man will he be when he's out of love—when he's in love with somebody else, perhaps?"

"Don't you think we're going too fast and far? Nobody knows how any marriage is going to turn out; and if Consuela told him, and it made no difference, and they were married, that sort of thing might never arise."

"But you haven't much hope, John, much faith, if the wedding did take place?"

"Frankly, no," replied John Geste. "I haven't. I don't think—I can't think—that a marriage could happily and successfully survive a start like that, a handicap like that. It isn't the easiest relationship in the world. It isn't the easiest conceivable thing for two people to live their lives out together quite happily—never getting on each other's nerves, and that sort of thing—when the conditions are ideally favourable. But in such conditions as those . . ."

"You don't think that the very unusualness, the very difficulty, might work favourably; might make for greater consideration on his part, greater forbearance and . . ."

"My dear chap, that's not happy successful marriage! Forbearance, good God! Suppose Sir Harry Vane were a stone saint out of a niche in a cathedral wall, come to life. Is he to stand oozing forbearance at every pore, for the whole of their married career? Radiating forgiveness for the poor fallen woman whom he has raised up to her feet; raised up to his noble level? Ask yourself, Otis."

"I'll ask you something, John, instead. You have asked me not to take offence and I'll ask you not to take offence. Suppose it had been—Isobel."

"Don't. I . . ."

"But I do. I ask you."

"Well, I can't answer you."

"You mean you refuse to imagine such a thing, refuse to talk about it."

"No. Sorry, Otis; I don't. I did for a moment; but I don't. I mean I simply cannot answer you. I don't know. It doesn't bear contemplation."

"Well, my little job does," replied Vanbrugh. "It has to. I've got to contemplate it, all day and most of the night, and if it worries *me* up to the Gates of Hell and half-way through them, what must it be for Consuela? And she's in love, mind you, John, in a way in which neither you nor I can comprehend. I thought I knew something of love, and you think that you know something of love. But you and I, my dear chap, beside her, are green smouldering wood compared with dynamite. We don't know what love is."

"Say passion, Otis."

"Well, say what you like."

A long silence.

"Well, John, are we any for'arder?"

"Yes, this much, Otis. Not a farthing of blackmail to be paid to Spanish Maine; and Harry Vane is not to marry Consuela in ignorance. We've got that far, haven't we? You do agree?"

"I don't know, John. I don't know. That may take us so far along the path of noble virtue. The path I want is the road to happiness for Consuela; and I don't know that either of these is going to lead to it."

"Well, the other way won't, Otis; believe me. You'll buy no happiness by paying Spanish Maine; and you'll get none by deceiving, cheating, and swindling Harry Vane."

"Suppose she tells him, John, and he turns her down."

"Well; that'll be that. I'd hate to be, or even to sound, unsympathetic—but that'll be that. Poor Consuela will have to grin and bear it. And I verily believe it would in the long-run be worse if Vane married her—especially while Spanish Maine is alive—unless Vane is superhuman and his love supernatural, so mighty and everlasting that he could chuck *everything*, and really and permanently consider the 'world well lost for love.' But he isn't superhuman and his love isn't supernatural. No. I'm afraid Consuela has got to grin and bear it."

"I'll tell you who won't grin, and who's going to 'bear it' some day—and that's that damned Dago," growled Vanbrugh. "John, I'm going to *get* him—and see how far that clears the situation. Will you help me?"

"No."

"John, you don't understand Consuela. I do. She's been my constant companion for so long now, that I know her inside out; and the one thing that'll give her an interest in life, if Vane turns her down, will be telling this black hound, Maine, where he gets off. And I tell you this. If things come to eternal smash for her, Consuela is going to see that Spanish Maine gets his. Now, here in England, this mightily law-abiding country, that might cause a lot of trouble."

John Geste agreed that it might indeed cause a lot of trouble.

"Yes; in France they understand the *crime passionel* better than you do here in England; and in America, well, say, we haven't very much use for skunks or any insuperable objection to anyone who exterminates one. There are ways and means over there. Sometimes we get more Justice than Law that kind of way, John; and I think that here sometimes you get more Law than Justice. Now Consuela mustn't have that sort of trouble on top of the other."

"No. Indeed she must not, Otis," agreed John Geste.

"Though mind you, there's only one way of preventing it," continued Vanbrugh. "She's not a Britisher like you, John. She's not an American like me. She's got some very wild blood and some very wild instincts; very quick on the trigger, metaphorically speaking; and I should say uncommon quick on the knife, literally speaking. Well, dead men not only tell no tales, but—they cannot be killed by impulsive girls looking for trouble. That's why *I'm*. going to get Spanish Maine—partly. Before she does. Will you help me, John?"

"No."

"John Geste, I hate to say it. It makes me sick at my stomach to hint at it. But—did I, or did I not, do my damnedest to give my life for yours? Did I save you, John? Did I send you back? Did I send you straight to Isobel whom I . . . ?"

"You did, Otis. You did one of the finest and bravest, one of the noblest, most unselfish, things of which I ever heard. You did save my life at the risk of your own, and almost at the cost of your own."

"And you are indebted to me, John?"

"I am, eternally; as much as ever one man was indebted to another."

"Will you pay that debt?"

"If I can. I'd give my right hand to do . . ."

"Once again, will you help me get this Spanish Maine?"

"No."

"Why not?"

"Lots of reasons."

"Give us a few.

"First of all, I don't wish to see you hanged in a British gaol This is not America, as you've already pointed out. Nor do I wish to see myself sentenced to ten years penal servitude in the same British gaol, as an accessory before and after the fact of murder. What becomes of Consuela if you hang, and what becomes of Isobel if I go to Dartmoor or Portland for a decade or so? And apart from those considerations, I don't like murder. I don't believe in it. We've a terrible respect for human life here, and really put 'Thou shalt not kill' as Number One in the Decalogue. And, all other things apart, what would be the good of it?"

"Well, I should have thought that would have been obvious, John. In the first place, as I've said, dead men tell no tales; and there's an end to poor little Consuela's immediate troubles. And, in the second place, he deserves it. You yourself admit that blackmail's a fouler crime than murder, and that there are lots of people who deserve to be killed and who ought to be killed— whereas nobody ought to be blackmailed. A pity that that same Decalogue that you're so fond of, doesn't mention 'Thou shalt not blackmail.' "

"I think it does," replied John Geste. "What about 'Thou shalt not bear false witness'?"

"Oh, shucks! Who's talking about bearing false witness? I'm talking about blackmail, which is asking for money under *threat* of bearing false witness—or it may be true witness. No; I think your Decalogue is a bit faulty. If there had been less about the Sabbath

and the Lord's name and graven images and honouring your father
—and something about the worst crime in the world instead. Or
perhaps Old Man Moses never even visualized such human
rattlesnakes as Spanish Maine, even among the assorted bunch of
stiffs for whom he legislated. . . . However, that's beside the point.
. . . You absolutely refuse to help me cut the Gordian knot that
way?"

"Of course I do, Otis. Don't you see, you'd make bad infinitely
worse. Surely we are in trouble enough, without having a murder
on our hands as well? In this old-fashioned country you can't
simply shoot a man up because he deserves it, and then forget all
about it until the Sheriff meets you one day and remarks that you
sure done a good job on that low-lifer and saved the trouble of
corralling him. There's absolutely no such thing in England as
lynch-law, and even less is there anything like condonation of
private punishment, taking the law into your own hands. My dear
chap, if you killed Spanish Maine, you'd hang as surely as the sun
will rise to-morrow."

"What, if we decoyed him here into Brandon Abbas, tried him,
condemned him, shot him, and buried him in one of those vaults
waiting all ready there, in the ruins of the old Abbey? Don't you
see that, except for our circle, the man's absolutely without
acquaintances, friends, connections, here in England? He'd simply
disappear, and it would be supposed that he'd gone back to Spain.
In point of fact, who'd know he'd disappeared, or take any interest
in the fact if he had? It isn't as though he were an ordinary human
being, with relations and friends who'd want to know what had
become of him. He's a lone wolf. He's an escaped criminal. (Like
us, John!) If he disappeared, Lady Drusilla would say,

" 'What's become of that nice man, Señor Maine?' and that
would be that. Who'd ever dream that that nice man, Señor Maine,
was doubling-up with a late Abbot of Brandon Abbas in the ruins
back of the park?"

John Geste smiled wearily.

"You and I would, Otis. . . . Murderers."

"And wouldn't we occasionally smile and catch each other's
eye and rub our hands, boy, when we thought of how and where
that snake fetched up, and what he got out of hounding Consuela?"

"My dear Otis, I'll have nothing to do with murder, nor, for
your own sake, will I let you. And besides, suppose the man were
struck by lightning to-morrow, blasted and killed—as I wish he
might be—that doesn't mean that you'd then be free to carry out

the cheating, deceiving, swindling of Sir Harry Vane, does it? Nor that it would really be a kind thing, in the long run, to let Consuela marry him after telling him the truth. Anyhow, no killing—even of a blackmailer."

"So that's all your gratitude's worth, eh, John? You won't help me?"

"Don't say 'won't,' Otis, say 'can't.' God knows I'd do anything on earth that I could do. But I won't help you to be hanged for murder; and I won't advise you to submit to being blackmailed by Spanish Maine."

"Nor," continued John Geste, "will I agree to Harry Vane's being deceived about Consuela."

"And that's all your friendship and gratitude are worth, eh?"

John Geste rested his elbows on his knees, his head on his hands, and sat in silence, his face concealed, the while Otis Vanbrugh watched him closely, eyed him thoughtfully.

"What can I do? . . . What can I do?" groaned John Geste.

Otis Vanbrugh rose to his feet, crossed to his friend, and laid his hand upon his shoulder.

"Do? You've done it, John! You've given me true advice. The only sound advice. You are right. . . . Once again—I thank you John. Good-night."

And leaving John Geste staring into the fire Otis Vanbrugh went from the room.

XIII

Next day, Otis Vanbrugh bade a temporary farewell to his host and hostess at Brandon Abbas, to pay his promised visit to Lady Drusilla and Sir Harry Vane at Vane Court, where, for the previous few days, Consuela had been their guest.

One of the show places of England, though far from being as ancient and historical a seat as Brandon Abbas, it interested the American greatly; its magnificent Jacobean house with its Inigo Jones, Grinling Gibbons, and Adams work; its wonderful old English, Italian, Dutch and Japanese gardens; its vast velvet peacock-haunted lawns, cared for by hand for three hundred years; its park, dotted with spreading trees that had been trees when Normans held their sway, and wherein the deer themselves seemed conscious of their duties as decorative pieces.

He saw it without prejudice, for what it was; admired it whole-heartedly, and returned thanks that it was not his lot to live out his life in its ruled, regulated, and ordered precincts.

The interior life of the house interested him no less; its silent, smooth-working domestic organization; its reduction of the *ars vivendi* to a fine art indeed; its picture-gallery with the portraits of Vane men and women, in unbroken line, from the days when oil-painting portraiture began in England; Vanes by Holbein, Vandyke, Godfrey Kneller; the glorious furniture of drawing-room, banqueting-room, library, flagged hall, corridor and landing, each a museum piece, a gem of its period.

How different from the great sprawling Wyoming ranch-house in which he had grown up. How truly beautiful—and inevitably suffocating. On the whole, he decided he'd rather live on the ranch and visit Vane Court than live at Vane Court and visit the ranch.

Other things apart, could Consuela stand it?

Could she bear this ordered, muted life of social ritual and routine; one's risings-up and lyings-down, one's comings-in and goings-out, one's meals, one's indoor amusements, regulated, arranged, decreed—a religion of which the butler was the High Priest? Yes, of course, that's what Manton was—a High Priest. No wonder he looked like a Bishop. Yes—and the valets and footmen and under-footmen were the vicars and curates committed to his charge.

How would Consuela take to a life like this—other things apart, once again?

What about *amor omnia vincit*, or words to that effect?

"Well, my dear? How have you made out?" he asked, as Consuela and he walked alone in the Italian garden.

"Oh, it's been *lovely*, Otis. *Perfect*. I've never been so happy in all my life.

"And I never shall be again," she added sadly. "I couldn't be. I don't think we are meant to be as happy as I've been this last week. Not but what I've been happy for years—ever since you came back to me, Otis. But this has been . . . Oh, I can't explain . . . Ecstasy . . . Madness . . ."

"Yes, my dear. That's what it has been, I'm afraid. Madness."

"And Lady Drusilla has been so kind, such a dear. Of course she's pumped me a lot . . . and I've told her a lot."

"Any of it true?"

"Oh, *yes*, Otis. I told her the exact truth whenever it was . . ."

"Convenient?"

"Possible. Whenever it was possible, Otis, I told the exact truth. Exactly how old I am; exactly what a wonderful huge big ranch we have in Wyoming; and such millions and millions of cattle; and what a wonderful man you are, dear; and how you've travelled and been a soldier; and how you are the great friend of Mr. Geste at Brandon Abbas; and that you were staying there; and that we should go on there from here."

"And that seemed to hearten the dame, some, eh?"

"Yes, Otis, Lady Drusilla seemed quite glad to know we were old friends of the Gestes of Brandon Abbas; and that you'd known the present Mr. Geste for years and years and years, and had travelled and been shooting with him abroad. You did go shooting with him, didn't you, Otis?"

"Yes, honey. . . . Arabs. . . . Quite a shooting party."

"And after that she wanted to know if the Gestes of Brandon Abbas knew our people."

"Which they certainly do," smiled Vanbrugh.

"And so I told her,

" 'Oh, yes; my other brother has known the Gestes of Brandon Abbas even longer than Otis has. He was an old friend of Michael Geste and Digby Geste as well as of John,' and I said that our brother went shooting a lot with them, too."

"Hank certainly did," agreed Vanbrugh. "Quite a lot of Arabs."

"And I told her you used to visit at the house and play with them when they were all children; and that Isobel Geste was a very dear old friend of yours; and that you knew Claudia, of course; and their Aunt Patricia; and that no doubt you must have met Harry over there, because when you were in England, as a boy, you used to be one of Michael Geste's band, and Harry used to stay there too. And he said he quite remembered being admitted to it as what Michael called one of the squeakers, and was allowed to be a Thief when they were playing Robbers and Thieves, and an Ancient Briton when they were being Romans, and riding them down in chariots. They used to do that with a pony and trap, Harry said. And Harry says he thinks he remembers your teaching them to be Red Indians, and how he was tied to a stake, and he really thought that they were going to set him on fire. He said the name Vanbrugh was familiar directly he heard it; but he thought he must have been connecting it with Sir John Vanbrugh who lives at Vanbrugh Castle. And then, when I began to tell them—in the drawing-room last night when Lady Drusilla was pumping me again—all about your visiting at Brandon Abbas as a boy, he began to remember."

"I'm sure he did," agreed Vanbrugh. "He must be ten years younger than I. Oh, well; he might, I suppose. I was sixteen then. He might have been a kid of six. There was a bunch of them."

"And then Lady Drusilla said,

" 'Oh, yes; are you related to Sir John Vanbrugh?' and I said he was a distant relation."

"He certainly is," agreed Vanbrugh again. "Distant."

"And that our father went to America from Brandon Regis; and it was to visit his mother, our grandmother, that you came to Brandon Regis when you were a boy; and that was how you came to know the Gestes. Lady Drusilla seemed quite glad about Sir John Vanbrugh."

"You certainly put it over on them, Consuela."

"Yes; and although she'd been kindness itself all the time, she seemed to like me even better when I talked about our being friends of the Gestes of Brandon Abbas and descended from a relation of Sir John Vanbrugh of Brandon Regis. She said,

" 'Why, you are practically English.' "

"Gee!" ejaculated Vanbrugh. "What did you say to that?"

"I said,

" 'Well, I don't know about that, Lady Drusilla; but I do feel that if I stay in England much longer, I shall become little better than an Englishwoman.' "

"Good. . . . And you've had no trouble from—him?"

"Only a letter."

"Demanding money?"

"Yes."

"Did you keep the letter?"

"*Mon Dieu!* Yes, I'll make him eat it some day, *le sale mauvais bougre!*"

"We may be able to do better with it than that; though I don't know. He hasn't been here, of course?"

"No, he comes the day after to-morrow."

"Does he? Well, we'll go the day before to-morrow then. . . . You'll love the Gestes, both of them, and of course, Harry can come over and see you there."

"Have you heard anything from—that man, Otis?"

"No. But he's heard something from me. I sent him a cheque for one hundred pounds."

"Did you? Why?"

"Because he won it from me—a bet. And because it may be worth it—worth it, to be able to prove that he's had a hundred pounds out of me already. . . . He may be the wise guy he thinks he is—and possibly I may be the wise guy he doesn't think I am."

"*Espèce de cafouilleux qu'il est!* Where did you address it?"

"Here. To Vane Court. *This is* his address. Can you beat it?"

"It will be Brandon Abbas next!"

"I shouldn't be surprised."

XIV

As her brother prophesied, and as he phrased it, Consuela fell for John and Isobel Geste at first sight. Here was genuine kindness. Kindliness incarnate, without criticism, reserve, or *arrière pensée*.

Obviously they both loved Otis, and that fact alone opened the road to her heart; and again obviously they were prepared, ready, willing and anxious to love her for her brother's sake. Also, and evidently before long, for her own sake.

"My dear," said Isobel Geste to her husband, "I think she's fascinating; absolutely delightful and charming. So utterly different from anyone I have ever met."

"Yes," agreed John, "an intriguing fascinating girl, if ever there was one."

And studying her, he thought back, and wondered if it were possible that she could be the girl who, to save Otis from Selim ben Yussuf, had handed himself over to the French patrol. Vaguely and faintly he remembered the girl in Arab dress at Yussuf ben Amir's camp.

Could this English-speaking, Paris-dressed, and obviously European girl, chic, poised, *soignée*, cool, balanced and sophisticated, be the termagant of whom Otis had at that time spoken, the girl who had danced before Sergeant Lebaudy and his men as Salome danced before Herod?

Well, Otis had done a wonderful work there. But then, of course, blood will tell, and if she had Arab blood, she also shared the blood that ran in the veins of the wonderful brothers Hank and Otis Vanbrugh.

But as Lady Vane? No, he couldn't see her as Lady Vane.

And he wouldn't, if it could be prevented.

Neither for her own sake, nor for that of Harry Vane, must such a thing be permitted.

But how could he prevent it unless, indeed, what he had said to Otis should bear fruit in strengthening Otis's conviction that it could not be done; that it must not be done.

Otis could prevent it by telling the whole truth to Harry Vane.

But could he? Suppose Harry Vane turned stubborn—and he was a lad with a chin, a lad whose ancestors had been noted fighting-men and fine fellows for hundreds of years—and merely said, with the beautiful ardour and candour of young love, that he didn't care; it didn't interest him; he didn't give a damn.

One couldn't forbid the banns; one couldn't literally and actually prevent their marrying.

And supposing Otis, finding Harry Vane undeterred by the truth, went with the story to Lady Drusilla?

How much would her wish, her objection, her prohibition, her horror, weigh with her son?

There could be no possible doubt as to what her attitude would be.

She'd be shocked and horrified to the depths of her being.

Naturally. Very naturally and very rightly. It made one "go hot and cold all over," to think of it. In fact, it was unthinkable.

The next Sir Harry Vane's mother a bastard half-caste prostitute. . . .

Lord! How awful it sounded like that!

And how was she to be described in the announcement of the wedding?

A marriage has been arranged and will take place between Sir Harry Vane, twelfth Baronet (son of the late Sir Harry Vane of Vane Court and Lady Drusilla Vane only daughter of the fourteenth Earl of Dorset) and Consuela, daughter of the late Homer A. Vanbrugh of Wyoming, U.S.A. and . . .

Yes, and when they got to the "*and*" what was to follow?

Either an absolute abominable lie or the absolute abominable truth. One of the two.

And as they couldn't put the truth, they'd have to start their engagement with a public lie, marry in the ugly grinning presence of the lie which would be repeated in the register, and spend the rest of their lives under its shadow.

Yes, grinning, like a skull, the skeleton in the cupboard, the skeleton at the feast, when they were alone: the skeleton at the feast of life.

But couldn't all reference to her origin be omitted from the announcement?

No, that would at once start everybody talking, inquiring and ferreting.

Nothing could seem more suspicious, in the eyes of the County, than complete suppression of such information. How could ten thousand tea parties possibly progress without the information? As well attempt to have a tea-party without tea.

What was the commonest remark one heard at that sort of

function?

" 'Who was Lady Blank?' Why, my dear, she was a De Vere."
"Of course she was. I was thinking, for the moment, she was a
FitzUrse. . . ."

Well, why have any banns or press announcements of the
engagement at all? Why not a Registrar's-office wedding? A
wedding without public pomp and ceremony, fanfare of trumpets
and the usual rather horrible show-business?

Well, that would be just as bad from the point of view of
gossip.

Why should Sir Harry Vane and Consuela Vanbrugh slink into
a side-street Municipal Office and be married by a Registrar?

Something queer about that. Very fishy. An absolute scandal.

Rather hard on Lady Drusilla, who'd simply love a St.
Margaret's or a Guards' Chapel wedding.

And why not?

It would, of course, be proof positive to her that there was
something wrong. Something very wrong. Something ghastly, if
Harry came to her and said that they wanted a wedding of that sort.
Disappointment for the whole family, family circle, the vast circle
of relations, friends and acquaintants, as well as for the tenantry.

The Vanes did not do things in that sort of fashion, and it
wasn't as though Harry had ever been eccentric, a crank, a person
with views on the subject of weddings and other social functions.

He was a perfectly normal young man of the world, who
enjoyed life and had always acted according to the fashion of his
kind, the manner of his kin, and the customs of the caste, class, and
circle in which he had grown up.

Still, he might triumph over all that; or, rather, love might. If
one were to call it a triumph—to insist on his own way in spite of
the wishes of those who loved him and all who knew him.

But after all, wasn't this perhaps rather petty, and hadn't Harry
a perfect right to go his own road, do what seemed best to him in
the matter of so private and intimate an affair as his wedding? Go
his own way and live his own life?

No, not with a girl who'd been what Consuela had been . . . a
. . . It really was unthinkable. And yet look at her.

Look at her there.

A picture. A picture of beauty, grace, culture and refinement.
Horrible words, but quite agreeable realities—culture and
refinement.

And—when all was said and done—she was now an absolutely

good girl.

Probably no woman in England less likely ever to go off the rails than Consuela Vanbrugh.

Why, it was, on the whole, probably more likely that some hand-picked ornament of County Society, chosen by Lady Drusilla herself, would err, throw her cap over the windmill, than that this girl would.

By Jove, that would be an extraordinary thing, an interesting though deplorable thing, if young Harry Vane, in the mellow light of reason, on the promptings of his own common sense, and by the advice of his admirable mother, backed out of this engagement, turned Consuela down, married the desirable girl of his later—or his mother's later—choice, and the said girl made a mess of her life and his, caused a horrible scandal in Society, and bolted with another man, a brother officer of Vane's or, perchance worse, a riding-master, her child's music-master, or a footman. . . .

Heavens! Whither were his thoughts tending?

Still, it was the sort of fantastic little irony of which Fate was not only capable, but rather fond.

However, that got one no-where.

The point was that Harry Vane was engaged to Consuela Vanbrugh—and it wouldn't do. Not even if Harry knew absolutely all there was to know and accepted it, or, rather, counted it as nothing beside his love.

Truly, "Love is a madness." A man in love is a madman, and may be expected to do mad things.

It was quite possible that he'd take the wrong line.

But *was* it wrong? Who was to say so? After all, what are titles, lands, worldly possessions?

If a man truly and wholly loves a woman, *loves* a woman; and the woman truly and wholly loves the man, *loves* the man; does anything else matter much? Is not this love, this holy sacred God-given love, this colossal thing (that more than all else distinguishes Man from the beasts) greater, immeasurably, infinitely greater, than titles, estates, position?

Yes, of course it is.

No, of course it is not.

There is a greater thing than love. Duty.

A man has his duty, not only to himself, but to his ancestors and his descendants, to his position, his relations, his people.

Selfless love. . . .

But isn't all love selfish?

No, there had been nothing selfish about Otis Vanbrugh's love.

Heavens above, it was a problem!

But, however involved and insoluble, there was one thing clear. Crystal clear. No deception.

Harry Vane must know.

And once he knew, was one to pray that he saw wisdom and put an end to it all, while there was yet time; or that he saw a higher wisdom and said,

"I am a man and this is my woman. To the devil with my title and estates and everything else."

And which was the higher and which was the lower wisdom?

What would Isobel think about it?

Of all people in this world, he looked to Isobel when he needed advice, counsel; someone with whom to talk things over.

He did not pretend that she was a female Solomon, and was very glad she wasn't one. It might be extremely trying and difficult, to live with a female Solomon.

But she was broad-minded, sane, sensible, poised and wise. She was not, like so many women, ruled entirely by her emotions. She could think as well as feel. And she was so infinitely kind, understanding, sympathetic. Her outlook was always so reasonable and unbiassed.

He would thrash it all out with her, and then she'd talk it all over with Consuela—provided Consuela asked for her opinion and advice—and try to be to her what a really wise, good, and loving mother would have been. Not that Isobel was old enough to be Consuela's mother, but she was old enough to be her great-great-grandmother so far as knowledge, wisdom, and understanding of English County life and the ways of English Society were concerned.

Other things apart, married life together might be well enough for Harry Vane and Consuela if they proposed to live in tents in an Algerian or Moroccan oasis; to wander about with a caravan, lead an *al fresco* desert life.

Or again, if they were going to live as the wealthy Vanbrughs did, on the great cattle-ranch in the Far West, where it was a day's ride across their own estate; where their neighbours were few and far between, and very far away; where there was no public to form and cherish an adverse public opinion; where there were no such things as gossip, scandal and ostracism as there was none to gossip, scandal-monger, or ostracize.

But Harry Vane was anchored, rooted; as much rooted in the

soil of his estates and his county as were his historic trees. The life that he and his ancestors had led was his life, the only life for him, and in any other he'd be like a fish out of water.

God knew that he, John Geste, was the last man in the world to think or speak cynically of love, but could it possibly be, in such a case as this, an instance of "the world well lost for love?"

Would not Harry Vane—if he lost Consuela—find sooner or later (and probably a great deal sooner) another girl as beautiful, attractive, intriguing and fascinating as Consuela?

Of course he would.

By all accounts, he'd found one or two already. And what a truly dreadful terrible thing, if he wrecked and ruined his career and his life over this girl; and, by the time the ruin was well and truly effected and complete, he found that some Miss Fine Flower of English Girlhood and Society was his real soul-mate, the woman for whom his heart had been waiting.

Of course there had been English earls, lords, viscounts, baronets and what-not who had either risen or sunk to be seamen, cow-boys, miners, lumber-jacks and so forth; men of title gone out into the wide open spaces (or the "wide-open" towns) of the United States and the Colonies, and who had returned from ranch, mine, plantation, ship or jungle to civilization, full of honours—or complaints.

But what earthly reason was there why young Harry Vane, at the very outset of his career—a career that might, and probably would, be one of great usefulness to his county and his country—throw in his hand, break everything off, abandon the life to which he was born, and for which he was fitted? It was absurd.

It wasn't right or fair—to himself or to his family, his friends, his estates, his dependants and employees or anybody else.

Well, somehow or other, he'd been thinking wholly and solely about Sir Harry Vane—looking at the matter entirely from the point of view of a neighbour and brother land-owner.

But what about the girl?

Hadn't she a right to life, liberty and the pursuit of happiness?

Wasn't she as much to be considered as Harry Vane?

In point of fact, was there not a very great deal in what Otis contended, that, as Fate had given her such a raw deal, Life had been so cruel to her, she had a right to far greater consideration than Harry Vane, whose lot had been cast in such pleasant places; Harry Vane who had been born in the purple, had grown up on velvet, and always would be on velvet?

In the sight of God, Consuela Vanbrugh was as good as Sir Harry Vane, as important as Sir Harry Vane, in every way as deserving of happiness as Sir Harry Vane.

And a great deal more so, one might imagine, if there were more rejoicing in Heaven over a lost sheep that was found than over the ninety and nine that had never strayed out into the wilderness.

And this poor lamb had not strayed out into the wilderness at all—it had been born there!

Of course Consuela Vanbrugh had as much right to happiness as Harry Vane had; as much right to salvation; and it was fairly arguable that this would be her salvation.

As much right to happiness? But had anybody any right to happiness at the cost of that of someone else? No, definitely not. And yet, what a terrible amount of happiness, pleasure, joy, success was built on other people's misery, pain, grief, failure.

Oh, well! . . . What would the dear old Chaplain have said? An interesting speculation, that. Doubtless it would have been,

"We are in the hands of God, my dear John. Leave it to God."

Yes, but Heaven helps those who help themselves; and it doesn't do, as a matter of actual practice, to sit idly by, with folded hands, and leave things to God. One wouldn't apply that doctrine to the case of a child wandering along the edge of a cliff, or to that of a friend in danger.

If one were going to drag the Almighty into the matter, one might begin by thinking back and realizing that the Almighty didn't interfere to prevent the poor girl from being born into the Street of Bouzen, and from thereafter inevitably growing up to be what her mother taught her to be.

Nor did Providence interfere to prevent her travelling by the *Amazon* and meeting not only Harry Vane but Spanish Maine as well.

No, things happened, things were what they were, either by the will of God, ordained in His infinite though unfathomable wisdom; or else things were just the mess that men made of them.

Anyhow, this wasn't the time for speculating on what the Chaplain would have said, though it might very well be the time for realizing that, being a man incapable of wrong-doing, he would have begged one to do the thing one believed to be right.

He would never, for one moment, have counselled doing the slightest wrong in the hope that right might come of it; would never agree to do a little evil that good might follow.

But then again what could one do, wise or otherwise, right or wrong, except give what one believed to be the best possible advice if it were asked for?

He believed he had done that in the case of Otis; but would he be given the opportunity of doing it in the case of Harry Vane? And if not, should he make an opportunity?

No, he couldn't.

What Otis had told him had been told in absolute confidence, after he had given his word. He must never repeat it to a living soul.

Of course he couldn't warn Harry Vane.

Could he presume to offer his alleged wise counsel to Consuela?

No, not unless she invited it.

But he hoped and prayed she'd talk to Isobel.

Suppose Isobel—perhaps strongly aided and abetted by Otis—could induce Consuela to go to Harry Vane and herself tell him the whole truth; and suppose Harry played the noble foolish gentlemanly and quixotic hero; one might then be able to butt in, perhaps; try to show the boy that he had no right, in his position, to marry Consuela, and that it could not possibly lead to his happiness.

And one might possibly be able to persuade Consuela that she had no right to marry Vane, and that her doing so could not possibly lead to *her* happiness.

But that would be Isobel's job, if the affair developed in that direction and reached that stage.

God! What a business! What an *impasse!* What a tragedy!

Anyway, first things first. He'd got his duty as host to perform, and he must do something. She didn't play cards or billiards.

By Jove, an idea! That would take her mind off things for a while, and genuinely interest her. He could show her something she'd never seen before, in spite of her experience and travels.

Yes, as he and Isobel were now the only two people alive who knew the trick of it, he might very well disclose it to Consuela and Otis.

"Consuela," said John Geste as she and Vanbrugh, strolling up and down the terrace, passed one of the open french-windows of the drawing-room, "How would you like to see the Priests' Hole?"

"And who's made a hole in the poor priest?" asked Consuela, smiling at her admired host.

"No, it isn't a hole in a priest. It's a hole for a priest."

"And why do you put the poor priest in a hole and make him say,

" '*Mon Dieu!* I am in a hole! I'm in a frightful hole.' "

"For safety, when people were hunting him."

"Oh, and you have priest-hunting—like fox-hunting and otter-hunting—in England?"

"Not—er—to any extent, nowadays. It's not a popular sport. It used to be, though. When the King or Queen was Roman Catholic, it was close season then for Catholic priests; and Protestant priests were hunted. But when that King or Queen went—to Heaven, perhaps, who knows?—and a Protestant King or Queen followed, then all those priests came out of their holes, said 'feign-its,' and it was the turn of the Roman Catholic priests to go into the holes."

"Would you really show us the Priests' Hole, John?" cried Vanbrugh eagerly. "That intrigued me a lot when I was a boy. Michael used to tell wonderful tales about it."

"Spent half his young life trying to find the secret of it, too," smiled John sadly. "Yes, he was always drawing plans and sketches, and trying to find what he called an unaccounted-for space. Always thumping panels and tapping on floors, and saying he was on the trail. Poor old Michael."

"He never found the secret, did he?" asked Vanbrugh.

"Nor anyone else. I believe the secret has never been discovered. It is passed on from father to son, or from owner to owner; and only one other person is supposed to know it, so that if the father never told the son, or they both died together, or something of that sort, the secret would not be lost. . . . Of course, in the old days it was a jolly useful thing to have a hiding-place in the house, whether for yourself, one of the household, a friend, or for valuables. There have been both Catholic and Protestant priests hidden in this one; as well as at least one Royalist during the Great Rebellion. There's a legend, of course, that Charles the Second hid in it. We've documentary evidence that Father Campion was concealed there in Queen Elizabeth's time. The wonder is that she never slept there."

"Perhaps she did," observed Consuela. "Could I sleep in it to-night?"

"Well, you could, my dear, but I wouldn't advise it. A bit stuffy and uncomfortable, not to mention dusty. It has not been opened for years and years and donkey's years."

"Oh, you don't use it nowadays for valuables?" asked

Vanbrugh. "The famous Blue Water Sapphire used to live there, didn't it?"

"It did. The Chaplain used to go and get it and fetch it downstairs, when Aunt Patricia would let us have it out to handle and look at. But since it disappeared—and Michael and Digby . . . disappeared—we have never used the place at all. Never shall. In point of fact, I hate it. Reminds me of the others too much."

"Don't bother about showing it to us, then," protested Vanbrugh.

"Oh, yes; rather. I'd love to. I'm sure it would interest you both enormously. We'll open it up this once; and then I don't suppose I'll ever touch it again. Come along."

And John Geste led the way to the panelled room he called his den.

"Well, we start here," said he, "first of all finding the key. There's a marvellous lock, of which the works are something like the works of a clock, and rather over a foot square. Sort of Benvenuto Cellini kind of thing. They used to put them in a great many of their money-chests, five hundred years ago; and the lock used to cover the whole of the lid, sometimes.

"With frills too, such as a long poisoned blade that shot out if you put the key into the lock without pressing a spring first. Any unauthorized person who got the key and didn't know the trick, stooping down to look at the box and inserting the key, would get the point well into his throat or chest or eye, or something like that.

"You see the two oak figures there, one each side of the mantelpiece and forming part of it. See if you can move the right-hand one, Consuela."

Consuela did her best to move the figure of a knight in armour, broad, thick, strong, and heavy, and some two feet in height.

"But it's part of the wood," she declared, abandoning the attempt.

"No, the other one is; but that isn't. Take him by the hips and turn him round—the wrong way, so to speak, the opposite way to a screw. Twist hard. Go on. . . . There you are."

And with a final effort, Consuela turned the figure round so that his back was towards her.

"Now again, and again. That's right. Now, you see, you can screw him right out and lift him down on to the floor. Shall I do it for you?"

"No, no. Please let me do it. . . . There. . . . Now, what do I do?"

"Stand up on tiptoe, put your hand down into the little well that you've uncovered, and you'll find a key."

"Yes, yes! I have it. What a strange old key. And how big!"

"Yes. We'll leave Uncle Archibald on the floor until we come back, and then screw him in over the key again. The next thing is a door. Can you see any door in this room, beside the one we came in by?"

"No, I can't," replied Consuela. "Is there one?"

Crossing to an old *armoire*, a tall oak press or cupboard richly carved, some seven feet in height, four in width, and one in depth, John Geste opened its heavy doors and pointed to a row of strong thick pegs which ran along the back of it at some five feet above the ground, pegs apparently intended for the hanging up of cloaks, swords or plumed hats.

"Here we are," said John Geste. "That's the door."

"But it's a cupboard!"

"Yes. Unscrew the second peg at each end. Shall I do it?"

"No, no, let me. Do," replied Consuela, and her strong little hands were soon at work, trying to unscrew the peg at each end.

"No, not that way. Do it the wrong way, again."

And with a sturdy wrench, Consuela turned the peg to the right and unscrewed it.

The iron screw portion, hitherto concealed in the wood, proved remarkably long.

Similarly with the other one.

"There we are. Now put them on the table so that we shan't mislay them, and shut the doors. Now, can you reach up, put both hands on top of the cupboard, and pull towards you? It won't come down on top of you. . . . Half a moment, I'll move the rug that lives against the foot of it."

Following the directions, Consuela placed her hands on the top of the cupboard and pulled hard.

"Stand back and let it go. It won't fall," said John Geste.

To the amazement of Consuela and her brother, neither of whom had ever seen or heard of this device, the ancient heavy cupboard came slowly forward and, having been started on its downward way, continued without haste or audible impact until it lay flat on the floor before them. Two long iron arms, semi-circular, extended from the back of the cupboard through iron loops, and ended in large heavy balls of metal.

And, while watching its slow descent, they realized that it was uncovering and disclosing the entrance to a flagged passage, some three feet in width, that led between rough stone walls to the foot of a flight of narrow steep steps.

"There we are," said John. "The way to the Priests' Hole. And don't be afraid to walk on to the back of the cupboard. It's of solid oak, two inches thick. The iron-lined hole at each, side of the entrance is where the screws of the pegs go in and hold the cupboard in place. The wing we are going into now, is part of the original Monastery, and must be seven or eight hundred years old. It is rather interesting to notice how little worn the flags of the passage and the stone steps are. Obviously it wasn't a frequented thoroughfare, or very much used. I should think that in the pre-Reformation days when there was no Catholic-Protestant strife and no need for what was later called a Priests' Hole, it was a sort of *oubliette*."

"What is that?" asked Consuela.

"Well, as you know, '*oublier*' is 'to forget'; and I imagine that an *oubliette* was a place where people were—conveniently—forgotten; sealed-up, so to speak; thrown into the secret cell and never heard of again. There are several traditions and legends about desiccated corpses, in a dress of bygone years, having been found here, in each of the centuries that have passed since the place was built. There used to be a very quaint old hat knocking around when we were children, a hat that had been found in the Priests' Hole by Sir Hector Brandon's great-grandfather, and which must have been left in there about the time of James the First.

"It was a wicked shame that it wasn't taken care of. Ought to have been put in a museum. And there's a sword I'll show you by and by—still hanging up in one of the corridors downstairs—that was found in the Priests' Hole too. Probably left there by one of the Royalists who hid here during the Great Rebellion. This part of the world and Cornwall were very loyal to the King, you know. Now then, let's go upstairs."

And the party trooped, in single file, along the narrow passage and up the stone stairs, at the top of which was a very narrow old door.

"Hullo, the key's in the lock! Whoever was up here last, should have locked that door and brought the key down. Of course it ought to have been in the mantelpiece under Uncle Archibald. It used to turn very easily."

Consuela turned the key, lifted the heavy loop handle with both hands, reversed it, and leaning against the door, pushed it open, disclosing a high oblong room, panelled from the floor to within a foot of the ceiling, in ancient black oak.

Above the panelling on the left-hand side, one or two arrow-slits and apertures in the thick wall admitted sufficient light.

"Is this it?" asked Consuela.

"By no means," smiled John Geste, "More to do yet."

"How many panels do you imagine there are in the room?" he asked.

"Oh, hundreds."

"Yes, as a matter of fact, there are. A good many hundreds. Forty short of a thousand. Nine hundred and sixty. And of those nine hundred and sixty panels—each of which, as you see, has a small boss or knob in the middle—one does the trick.

"Anybody, not knowing the secret, and getting as far as this, has got to pick out the one, from nine hundred and sixty, and then find out how it works. Take the bottom right-hand corner of the right-hand wall (looking from the door) and count up along the centre diagonal line of knobs to the ninth one. Then, along the line in which that ninth knob is, count five knobs. Then go up two and that is the knob we want."

"Why not take it direct from the right or left-hand side, or up from the bottom?" asked Vanbrugh.

"Because you wouldn't get it. The panels are, as you see, of different sizes, and you can't count straight along from left or right or straight up from the bottom. Nine, five, and two, is the direct way of it.

"Now, Consuela, both hands on it and press hard."

The girl obeyed, pressed heavily with the base of the thumb of the right hand, which the left hand covered.

Suddenly there was a loud click, as though a powerful spring had been released, and the panel, about twelve inches by nine in size, tilted outward into her hands as she withdrew them, disclosing as it did so, a smaller aperture in the stone, and a strong steel chain that hung inside it.

"There we are. Now take the chain, pull hard downwards, and don't be surprised at what happens."

Seizing the chain, Consuela pulled.

There was a faint rumble and a section of the panelling, some five feet high by three feet wide, on the immediately opposite side of the room, rose upward and outward from the wall—and out of the room. The base of this section of panelling was now five feet from the ground, level with its hinged top, and opening out of the room toward yet another door. It was really a flap which now rested on a level with its own doorway and was held in place at the inner end by its horizontal hinges, and, at the outer end, by the chain to which it was attached, and which had pulled it up.

"What makes it stay up there?" inquired Consuela.

"There's a heavy weight on the other end of the chain," was the reply. "The chain, of course, runs across, up in the roof, hidden by a beam at the ends of which are pulley-wheels, and comes down inside this little ante-room between the panelling and the Priests' Hole. Directly you pulled the chain, you disturbed the balance in favour of the heavy weight that slides up and down inside the panelling over there on the other side of the room. When we pull this flap down again behind us, the leaden weight will come up into its place. . . . Now for the key, my dear, and we are in the Priests' Hole. Pretty ingenious, isn't it?"

And with the key that she had brought up from John Geste's den, Consuela unlocked the door of the Priests' Hole, pushed it open, and entered a small bare stone room, containing nothing but a heavy table and chair, both obviously of ancient make.

"You keep nothing at all hidden up here nowadays then, John?" asked Vanbrugh.

"Absolutely nothing. It's quite empty, as you see. For some reason I dislike the place too much to use it. The Blue Water sapphire used to live here, in a casket kept in a small safe that Sir Hector Brandon had brought up to the room. Rather unnecessary, as, presumably, anyone ingenious enough to find his way here could tackle an ordinary safe easily enough. . . . It's in my dressing-room nowadays."

"What, the Blue Water sapphire that Otis was telling me about?" asked Consuela.

"No, my dear. The safe, I meant. Isobel's pearls and things live in it now. The Blue Water went back to India, you know—to a descendant of its original owner. It was a family jewel, belonging to the Sultans of Mysore, or one of the other great ruling houses, and the seventh Sir Hector Brandon pinched it during the conquest of the Deccan, and brought it here. No, there's nothing in this room but that furniture—and a curse, I should think."

"Air isn't too bad," observed Vanbrugh.

"No, it's amazing, isn't it?" agreed John Geste. "A shaft must run from that hole in the stone roof there, to the outer air somewhere; though probably not in a straight line. And another remarkable thing about the place is that no noise made inside it is audible anywhere in the house or outside it. You could shout; a

woman could scream; or you could fire a gun in here, and you
wouldn't hear a sound of it, even in my den, or out in the grounds.
There used to be a window, I believe, or rather a light-shaft; but it
has been walled up at some time."

"Well, no, I suppose no sound would be heard," replied
Vanbrugh, "seeing how thick the walls and doors are; and what a
long way it is from the inhabited part of the house. Do you know
exactly where we are?"

"Yes, roughly. Somewhere near where the sixteenth-century
house was built on to the ruins of the ancient Monastery. Fairly
high up. I imagine that there's a walled-up passage, somewhere
about here, that once led from that outer room into the Monastery,
probably to the Abbot's Parlour. . . . Anyhow, it's marvellously
concealed, isn't it? No wonder nobody ever discovered the secret
of it. No, and if they did, they'd still need two very special keys, if
both the doors were locked."

"And we three are the only people in the world who know the
secret of the Priests' Hole at Brandon Abbas!" smiled Vanbrugh.

"Four," corrected John. "Isobel knows it. But you and
Consuela are the only two people in the world who know it, except
Isobel and me."

"Mighty interesting! Mighty interesting!" mused Vanbrugh.
"Well, we thank you very much indeed, John, for the pleasure and
for the honour."

"We do indeed, Mr. Geste," agreed Consuela.

"John, please."

"Thank you, *John*—then—if I may. It's kind of you. I've
enjoyed it so. It's such an honour, as Otis says."

"And you won't tell anybody."

Consuela laughed.

"Hardly! It would be a bit difficult, if one wanted to, wouldn't
it? May I put it all straight again?"

"Yes. You've only got to pull this door shut and it locks itself.
. . . That's it. Now, Otis and I will go into the panelled room, then
you reach up to the foot of the panel flap-door, give it a good pull,
and step out as it comes down. It will come quite slowly."

Consuela obeyed, and the heavy hinged flap quietly came
down into its place, while the chain was seen, through the aperture
of the panelling at the other side of the room, to be travelling
slowly upward.

"Wonderful how it fits," said Vanbrugh, "and of course every
other section of panelling of the same size and shape is made to

look exactly like it."

"Yes. And it all stands an inch or two away from the stone wall behind it, so that wherever you tap, you get the same sound. Now, to put the panel back into the hole."

This Consuela raised from the floor, inserted into its frame, and pressed.

A sharp click announced that the panel was once more secure as well as obscure, among its nine hundred and fifty-nine counterparts.

"Now we'll go out of this room, and if you will pull the door to, behind us, it will lock itself. We'll bring the key-away this time, and put it along with the other, under Uncle Archibald. . . . Now, down the stairs, along the corridor, into my den. . . . Stoop and put your fingers under the edge of the cupboard here, and you'll find it will go back into place quite easily. Very little strength is needed as the weights counterbalance it. There we are. Now put the two keys in the hole and put Uncle Archibald back in his place. Better let me do that."

"No, no, please let me do it. I should love to be able to boast— inside myself, of course—that I alone had done it all; all the things to get into the Priests' Hole and then—undone them."

And without difficulty Consuela dropped the keys into the well in the woodwork, replaced the wooden figure and screwed it back into position.

"Now, I consider that the most interesting thing I've ever seen, John. I certainly am grateful," said Vanbrugh.

"I too, John. You're a dear. I could kiss you."

"You could, you can, and you shall," smiled John, and 'made it so.'

"That's that then," he said, as they seated themselves in the den, "and I'll never go up into that place again as long as I live. . . . It's haunted. . . ."

Consuela shivered slightly.

XV

At Vane Court, Señor Manöel Maine scored a distinct success. With the Lady Drusilla he made it, and perhaps the more completely by reason of the fact that Sir Harry Vane was not present.

"All-right darling, I will make your apologies," she had said to her departing son.

"Pray don't, my child," he had replied.

"I'll tell him that you've gone over to Brandon Abbas where your Consuela and her brother are staying. He'll quite understand and will excuse you."

"I'm sure he will," was the reply. "And I don't care a tuppenny damn whether he does or not. Don't forget to tell Manton to be specially careful about locking up the silver at night; and you put all your jewellery in the safe when you go to bed, Mother."

"Yes, darling. Shall I put myself in the safe too?"

"Wouldn't be half a bad idea," was the reply. "Honestly, though, Mother, what on earth did you want to go and invite the man here for?"

"Well, I've told you, darling. Partly because I didn't, for a moment, suppose he'd come; and partly because I should like him to invite Athelney and me to Spain, before we go to India."

And so it came to pass that there was no fly in the ointment of Señor Manöel Maine's happiness as he sojourned at Vane Court and wallowed in its luxuries.

This was the life for el Señor Manöel Maine! After all he'd been through as Spanish Maine, *légionnaire*, convict, *déporté*, this was the sort of life for him, the man who had suffered so long and so much, had been used so ill by Fate; had been doomed to poverty, misery, cruel suffering, penal servitude and transportation for life. He could enjoy this sort of thing after—that sort of thing. Yes, thanks to the little devil Zaza Blanchfleur who called herself Consuela Vanbrugh, and thanks to the buried treasure, this was the sort of life he'd live in Spain.

He had suffered shamefully at the hands of women, and bitterly he had railed against them; but, after all, when he came to think of it, but for the Dolores Floramar girl in Cadiz, he'd never have gone to Heidelberg; and but for the Gretchen Kellner girl there, he'd never have gone to the Foreign Legion; and but for the Estella Margarita girl there, he'd never have got the treasure out of old Mendoza; and now but for this girl, he'd never have had the magnificent income that he was about to enjoy, and the lump sum that he would apply to the recovery of the original treasure.

Really, if you looked at it that way, the women had been a blessing rather than a curse—but no thanks to them, the devils. Not one of them had had the intention of doing him any good in that direction—especially the last and most valuable of them all. And incidentally it was about time he put the screw on, and got the first instalment out of her or her brother.

And if they did not choose to cough up promptly and satisfactorily, well then, all-right; he could wait.

He could lie low until she was married; and *then* what about it?

Perhaps, on the whole, it might be better not to put the screw on too hard, until then.

Mustn't do anything that would in any way interfere with the marriage.

There'd be three fine fish in his net then, each one of which would be only too glad to get its freedom.

But especially the husband, if they forced him to tackle the fellow at once. And of course they'd never do that. Naturally she'd pay—to the uttermost farthing she could raise—rather than have him expose her to her husband.

No; the thing would be to squeeze her absolutely dry, and then tell the brother that he must save her, at Spanish Maine's own price, or he'd have to tap Vane.

Then, when Vanbrugh was squeezed as dry as his sister, he'd go on to Vane; and what wouldn't Vane pay to keep it dark!

And once he'd started on Vane, and increased his demand every time, *what* a colossal fortune he'd make!

Why, it would make the buried treasure hunt a side-show, a pleasant little holiday trip.

He'd go out to Aïn Mendit, not only in absolute luxury, but without worry or anxiety as to the result.

He'd scarcely care whether the treasure were there or not.

Why, by the time he'd done with the excellent Sir Harry Vane —if he ever were done with him—thirty thousand pounds would be neither here nor there. In point of fact, it would be there—*ha! ha!* —until he went and fetched it. A nice little nest-egg for a rainy day.

Not that there were ever going to be any more rainy days among those to be enjoyed by Manöel Maine.

Not one.

Nevertheless, it might perhaps be worth while going and gathering-in that buried thirty thousand pounds, and banking it. He'd know it was all right then, and it might just as well be earning interest. One could never be too rich.

Well, well, happy days! And even happier nights.

And having enjoyed himself, spied out the land, learned a good deal, and come to certain conclusions and decisions, Spanish Maine then took his reluctant departure from the perfectly delightful Vane Court and its truly charming hostess.

His *adieux* were rendered the more pleasant by her faithful promise to visit him, toward the end of her honeymoon, for a long stay on his estates and in his various houses, in one of which she'd be interested to find a rather fine oil-painting of that Captain Charles Maine, brother officer of Sir Harry Smith, through whom he himself had the British blood of which he was so proud.

Yes, it was a pity to have to leave Vane Court, but—business before pleasure; and there was a most useful piece of business to be done, over the private consignment of cocaine that he had brought ashore at Plymouth.

Very valuable indeed. And funds were running low. This living in first-class hotels and travelling in the cabins-de-luxe of the best liners might be necessary to the maintenance of one's prestige and position far above suspicion; but it was very expensive.

However, that would not matter, once he had started tapping the new and inexhaustible source of supply.

When was that wedding to take place? It wasn't likely that ardent young people in their position would go in for a long engagement.

Anyhow, he must go up to London and get into touch with One Lung as they called Li Wun Lung, and with Rimiski and Almonte. They'd give him top prices.

Yes, and then the devils would sell it for ten times what they paid him, in spite of their whining about how they had to compete with Bulgar Berkovica who got it, or brought it himself, direct from the factory at home in Bulgaria.

Yes, he'd have a few days in London and enjoy himself thoroughly.

Then he'd demand a straight answer from the girl, as to when the wedding was to take place; and if it were not for some time, there'd have to be a bit on account—and a good bit, too.

And perhaps something else, as well, from the provocative, desirable young devil.

XVI

There seems to be a *morale manquée* somewhere, in the undeniable fact that misfortune should have overtaken Spanish Maine as a direct consequence of his attending Divine Service.

Being, as has been said, a very religious man, he attended Mass with such regularity as his somewhat irregular way of life permitted.

When in London, it was his habit and his pleasure to attend a certain rather beautiful little church which ministers to the spiritual needs of the population of the Spanish quarter of Soho.

The congregation of this Roman Catholic church is by no means confined, however, to Spanish restaurateurs, *criadoes*, barbers, waiters, shop-assistants, shop-keepers and the workmen who are their lodgers. From all parts of London, including the Embassy itself, come *caballeros* and their *señoras* and *señoritas* to attend High Mass at this famous Church of the Immaculate Conception.

And there, on the following Sunday morning, came Spanish Maine from the fashionable and expensive West End hotel that he patronized by reason of the fact that its proprietors, staff, and much of its *clientèle*, were Spanish.

Though of preternaturally acute senses, Spanish Maine, not possessing eyes in the back of his head, was unaware of the fact that his presence in the Church was causing considerable and painful excitement in a pew situated at some distance behind his own.

A white-haired, sallow, leather-faced, upright man, observing his entrance, had suddenly become rigid as a rod, motionless as a rock; as, with starting eyes and open mouth, he caught sight of him, recognized him, and stared incredulous.

"*Carramba!*" he whispered. "It is he! . . . Oh, kind and merciful Mother of God, it is he!"

A fellow-Spaniard beside him nudged him sharply.

"What is it? What's the matter?" he whispered in Spanish.

"It is he!" replied the other. "Note him well. Mark him. Stare at him; and if you lose sight of him before I have him where I want him, I'll pith you. Yea, were you twice my brother, I would strike you dead."

"Who is it? Who is it?" asked the brother.

"It is *he*, I tell you. It is *he*," was the reply.

And turning to the younger man on his left he repeated his instructions.

"Watch him! Mark him! So that you would know him among a thousand, a million. And let him not out of your sight until I give the word, or go you from my sight for ever."

"Who is he?" asked the young man.

"It is *he!*" was the unilluminating reply.

And so it came to pass that when, erect, jaunty, smiling, Spanish Maine walked from the church, he was followed, at different distances, by three men, one of whom, on the opposite side of the road, kept almost abreast of him, another close behind him, and a third where he could see all three, save when they turned a corner.

And when he had entered his fashionable hotel, the three held conference.

"Look you, Ramon, and you, Carlos. One of you must be with me always. You, Ramon, first; and you, Carlos, relieve Ramon when you can. I cannot speak English well enough. I don't know how to take the ticket properly at the railway-station. I shall lose him if I watch and follow him alone. I would kill him, here in the street, next time he comes out of this fine hotel, but that I don't wish to die. Life is sweet, and will be doubly sweet when I have killed that dog."

The others nodded with completest agreement and understanding.

"If I cannot kill him without being caught and garrotted myself —then I must die. But there is no need to bungle it like that. I am a man of skill and of finesse."

The younger man took the speaker's hand and squeezed it warmly, while the older patted him reassuringly upon the shoulder.

And thus it came about that when, a few days later, the Señor Manöel Maine, dressed in the height of fashion, smiling, spruce and debonair, seated himself in a first-class compartment of the Western Express at Waterloo, three inconspicuous quietly-dressed Spaniards stood outside a third-class compartment at the opposite end of the train.

"Adios, my good Ramon; and all the thanks of my grateful heart. Young Carlos and I will return to you when my work is done. And with you I will hide for a while. There will be no

495

danger."

Ramon made an airy gesture with his cigarette.

"Danger?" he scoffed. "Gladly would I accompany you now."

"No, no. The two of us are one too many, and I would go alone did I not fear to make a misunderstanding, make a mistake. If only I spoke the English language as you and Carlos do, I should not be troubling you."

"Trouble?" Again Ramon waved the hand that held his cigarette. "It is an honour, a pleasure, and more than a pleasure. It is business. Our business. The business of the whole family. And when it is done, we will all return to Spain."

"And live happy ever after," smiled Carlos, "with clear consciences and the sense of duty done."

"So. Indeed so," smiled the white-haired Spaniard. "*Adios*, good Ramon. We will write no letters."

And when, at Exeter, Spanish Maine alighted and changed trains, he was quite unaware of two quietly-dressed inconspicuous men who, from their third-class carriage, watched him cross the platform, ere leaving their own compartment and making quickly for another in the waiting train.

That night the two, well-provisioned, camped in a thicket in the wood that rose above that pleasant spot in the Brandon Abbas grounds, known as the Bower, lacking nothing but a glowing camp-fire thoroughly to enjoy such an evening as so often they had spent before in other lands.

"A murderer," mused the older man, "what is he? We know nothing of a murderer save that he has killed his man—a thing that any honest, honourable, self-respecting *caballero* may have to do. *Pues*, one kills one's enemy. There is no disgrace in that, I trust?"

"No," agreed the other, "though there may be black disgrace in the failing to kill one's enemy, in certain cases. One's wife: one's daughter: one's honour. It may become a man's first and chief duty to kill."

"*Si, si!* Without a shadow of a doubt. Such a case as this, for example. To slay a man who has done you no wrong, is not good. It is bad. To rob a man of all he has, is not good. It is bad. But to slay and to rob a man who has not only done you no harm but has saved your life, who has offered his life for yours, a man who is your friend, your benefactor, your saviour: to slay *him*—that is . . ."

"Abominable. Incredible. Unthinkable," interrupted Carlos. "It is to do that which dooms you to a million years of purgatory. It is that which leaves you undeserving of the last offices of the Church as you lie upon your death-bed."

"What does such a man deserve?" asked the older of the two.

"Death here, and damnation hereafter," was the reply.

"He does. He does. And, whatever God may do to him in the Hereafter, I will kill him here. Here and now. He is undeserving of mercy, pity, or forgiveness. He is unforgivable. I will tell you.

"When I was over there—for life, as They intended—and my one hope, one chance, lay in the money that Ramon and you (God bless you both, and grant you long life and happiness here, and eternal bliss hereafter), the money that you and Ramon sent me so cleverly, so generously—I met this man.

"And because he was, as I thought, a real *caballero*, a *hidalgo* of Castille, a gentleman, a nobleman, I helped him, befriended him, served him.

"I, Miguel Braganza el Torero, first Matador of Spain—hero of the arena, idol of the populace of Seville, Barcelona, Madrid, Valencia, Malaga, and every bull-ring of repute in Spain—made myself his servant.

"He would have died but for me. Ten times over, he would have died.

"He would have been killed by the *picaros*, the *ladrons* of our gang; or have died of dysentery, malaria, disease, starvation.

"I saved him. I put hope in his heart and food in his stomach. He is a brave man, mind. I grant him that. Oh, he's brave enough. But he would have died.

"Courage would not have saved him against the gang, nor against the fevers of the swamp.

"I saved his life.

"I softened his bed and smoothed his path, and when I decided that I had enough money to warrant an attempt at escape—though I doubled my risk, I took him with me.

"It was my money, the money you had sent me, and which I shall return ten-fold, that did what bribing was necessary and possible, procured food, and enabled us to get away successfully.

"And when we were clear of Maroni, safe into the jungle of French Guiana, it was I who kept him alive.

"Time after time I carried him for miles, though *my* strength was no greater than his, my food the same as his, save when I had given him the bigger share.

"By my help alone, we got afloat when we could walk no farther. At the risk of my life, I got a canoe, venturing into a camp of sleeping Indians who would have filled me with arrows and spears till I should have looked like a pincushion, had they awakened; and twice swimming the river, alive with alligators and filled with the *pirana* fish that will turn a live man into a clean-picked skeleton in five minutes.

"Down the Surinam River I paddled him, keeping him alive with the fish, iguana, fruit, berries, fungus and such things that I procured.

"And one day, as we were nearing Paramaribo and safety, I was bending over our fire, grilling fish that I had caught, when suddenly the world went black, and I knew no more.

"When I came to my senses, I was alone; my head was bashed in; my chest burnt, where I had fallen on to the embers and heated stones of our fire; and when I moved to sit up, I coughed blood, for I had been stabbed in the back.

"Ere I collapsed again, I looked about for the body of my poor comrade. When I came round again, and could get to my hands and knees that I might help him if possible, I found the foot-prints of my 'poor comrade' leading to where our canoe had been hauled up on to the sand.

"Yes, there were the foot-prints of us both, coming from the canoe to the fire; and there were his foot-prints alone, leading back to the boat, a deep foot-print showing where he had used his weight and strength to push the canoe off, and had jumped into it.

"No other foot-mark! No sign of Indians! He had slain, robbed, and deserted me—his friend and benefactor! I refused to believe it.

"And when I found that my money had gone, I nearly died of grief. For grief came before anger, rage, the passion for vengeance.

"This man for whom I had offered my life, had clubbed me from behind, doubtless with a paddle, and stabbed me as I lay across the fire, pulled me off it that he might get at my money, found it next to my skin, taken it, and left me for dead—fully believing me to be dead.

"Doubtless what had saved my life, so far, was the fact that his tools had not been as good as his intentions. The paddle had proved an unsatisfactory club—perhaps breaking in his hand. The knife with which he had stabbed me had been but of soft iron—a knife that I myself had made for him from a cook-house spoon. Doubtless again, the point had been turned as it struck a rib or shoulder-blade.

"A poor effort at murder. I could have killed a regiment of men, one by one, with that knife.

"But I was in a bad way, for I had fed him better than I had fed myself, for weeks and weeks; and one does not start out from the Penal Settlement of Maroni—after years of life there—in the best of health.

"However, I am tough; and, after lying like a dying dog for two or three days, moving only to crawl to the water and drink like a dog, I began to feel less like death. A few days later, I could stagger into the jungle for the bananas which grew in profusion close by; and I could fish, for, by the mercy and grace of God, the fishing-line had been left down while I was cooking our supper, the night that he tried to murder me.

"That was not the end of the mercy and grace of God, for I was saved. Miraculously saved.

"Not that the actual saving was any miracle, for I was within a day or two of Paramaribo—that was why the murder and robbery had been postponed until then—and the river was not used solely by savage Indians.

"Down-stream, one evening, came a small flotilla of canoes. In the leading one was a white man. Nor was he, as I feared and expected, a Dutch official, the sort of man who'd have been suspicious of me, arrested me on the chance that I was an escaper from French Guiana.

"He was a scientist, one of those peculiar people who devote the good life that a merciful God has given them, to inquisitive interference with the lives of harmless bugs and such things; or to discovering flowers that happen to be different from the flowers in their own back-garden; or to catching butterflies.

"Oh, yes, there are grown men that catch butterflies.

"But let me not speak slightingly of this good man, whether he were mad or not; for, beside being a bold insect-hunter and butterfly-slayer, he was a doctor. And what is more he was an Englishman, on his way to England. That was the miracle. That is where I see the hand of God; and that is how Señor Manöel Maine is about to feel the weight of the hand of Miguel Braganza.

"Yes, this Señor was a good man, kind, friendly and unsuspicious.

"He had a headman, an interpreter, a Venezuelan, who of course knew Spanish, and could speak English. Through him I told the Señor that I was a poor unfortunate, but honest, half-caste Brazilian, a Portuguese Indian, who knew a little Spanish as he had lived in Venezuela. I had been trying to make a living in the jungle, hunting balata, looking for gold, gathering rubber, and trying to scratch a living from the soil round the shack which I had built.

That, having been inundated, I was making my way to Paramaribo when I was attacked by Indians who had left me for dead and gone off with my canoe and few poor possessions.

"He was a good man—a Good Samaritan in fact. He could not have doctored me better had I been a rich patient from whom he could extract a fat fee. He could not have treated me more kindly had I been his brother. And I rejoice to say I was able, in some measure, to repay him for his merciful goodness, help, and kindness.

"His half-caste headman and interpreter was, like most of his kind, a rogue and scoundrel—who had no intention whatsoever of reaching Paramaribo with his employer. His idea was to serve him pretty much as Señor Manöel Maine had served me; that is to say, to abandon him in the night, with or without adding murder to the crime.

"The Venezuelan cook and the Indian paddlers were his creatures, and only too willing to share in the valuable loot of guns, ammunition, apparatus, kit, clothes, medicines, stores and canoes, not to mention whatever sum of money might be found in the white man's possession.

"Supposing me to be asleep, and imagining that I knew but little Spanish, the headman and the cook muttered together over a dying camp-fire, quite freely.

"Now, apart from this villainy, which angered me, I had every intention of being taken to Paramaribo by the Englishman, and no desire whatsoever to be left stranded there again, or taken back up the Surinam by the headman and his Indians.

"So, that night, the headman was gathered to his fathers. Yes, he died, and went to his own place. Nor was his body ever found, unless it were by an alligator.

"And then I talked to the cook, and when I had finished talking to the cook—well—he cooked worse than ever, owing to the shaking of his hands and the trembling of his body.

"But he spoke to the Indians, and there was trouble. They were truculent. They said they would go no farther down the river; they said they were afraid to go to Paramaribo; they said anything that came into their heads or that the cook put there.

"And then I waded into them.

"Mother of God! I showed them some of the things I'd learned in Maroni. And if I could not put the fear of God into their godless hearts I put that of Miguel Braganza. *Sangre de Cristo*, I did!

"The English doctor thought I was a little unconstitutional in my procedure, a little drastic in my methods; but, as I pointed out to him, I would rather be unconstitutional than dead. And by the time I'd hurried those dogs into the canoes at the muzzle of a gun, and had got myself and the doctor into the last one, bringing up the rear, and had told him what I'd heard the missing headman saying to the cook, he was more reasonable—and extremely grateful.

"And by refusing to let them land again, and by sending an occasional bullet pretty close over their heads, I got them and us safe to Paramaribo. And when the English *caballero*, who had picked up comic odds and ends of South American Spanish, thanked me and wished to reward me, I said all I asked was that he'd tell the Dutch authorities that I belonged to his party—which by that time I did, God knows—and take me with him to England, since he wasn't going to Spain.

"England suited me well enough. I should be safe there from the French. I could find Ramon and you in Soho; and from there—to make some money for my quest—I would go back to Seville and find out whether they still remembered Miguel Braganza el Torero, Miguel the Matador, to whom the King himself had awarded both ears, the tail and the heart of the bravest and fiercest bull that ever he had seen killed by the Perfect Toreador.

"And then to think that I should go to church to make my soul —and there meet my enemy, the man to the pursuit of whom I had dedicated my life.

"The Hand of God, I say, Carlos! And the Hand of Fate—pointed straight at his heart."

"No. At his neck," corrected the younger man with a chuckle. "At the back of his neck where the skull rests upon the top of the back-bone."

Miguel smiled.

"Yes. He shall have it there because he was once my friend; he shall have the honour of being killed as though he were a noble bull instead of a pariah dog, a rat, a snake. A death too good for him.

"Yes, the hand of God; not only that I should have been guided there to meet him, but that he should have come so soon to this quiet country-side where things can be done peacefully and safely —he and I alone together.

"No-one to see; no witness of the deed. For, though willingly I would go to the scaffold for Manöel Maine, how much more willingly, how much more happily, with what delight and joy and satisfaction in my heart, will I go back to Spain, knowing that I have had my vengeance, paid my debt.

"Either at his Inn, or on the road, or at this house, I will get him."

"He and I, *alone*.

"Here, I think. One night, as he goes from the big house back to his Inn. In the Inn it is difficult—and difficult to escape. And right from the Inn door he walks in sight of the lodge. And from the lodge at the gate where he enters, who knows what eyes are watching?

"I must get him in the shadow as he leaves the house. In the drive, where it is pitch dark under the big trees. Somewhere. Somehow.

"But I will have patience. I will not bungle it. I will get him; and they shall not get me, these so clever English detectives and police.

"No I will not be foolish. He has been here by daylight and I doubt not he will come here by night, the thief, the *ladron*. He will come by night—and *then* I will get him.

"He and I alone in the darkness—if only for a second—and I will do his business, and I will escape. . . ."

XVII

Señor Manöel Maine was in doubt. *Solvitur ambulando*. With soft and cat-like tread, he paced the floor of his sitting-room in the famous old *Bluff King Hal* that has stood for upwards of four hundred years on the road to Brandon Regis, not far from the main entrance-gate of Brandon Abbas.

Should he write, should he telephone, or should he call?

The girl and her half-brother *(sous ce nom la!)*, were both at Brandon Abbas. Whom should he tackle first?

The girl, undoubtedly, and for several reasons.

Should he write, should he telephone, or should he call?

His natural hardihood and instinctive impulse to take the bull by the horns, or the cow by the tail, led him to prefer the bold course. It would be splendid fun to drive up the avenue, haul on the great bell-chain that he had seen when he reconnoitred the place, send in his card, and march into the house unbidden, with as much assurance as he had walked into Vane Court, on Lady Drusilla's invitation.

That was an idea too. Make the girl invite him there. Insist on it. That'd be a situation—to settle down there in Brandon Abbas and twist the tails of the men, and the woman, with the threat of twisting that of the youth, if they didn't jump to his word of command.

Let the man Vanbrugh know that the time had come for him to cough-up a little on account; have a long talk with the girl when the rest had gone to bed; find out about the date of the wedding, and let her know that, quite independently of her brother's little account, it was time she started contributing too.

On the other hand, once inside that ancient dwelling-place, part modem house, part medieval monastery, part ancient castle, he certainly would be well inside the lion's den, his head in the lion's jaws. And Vanbrugh looked as though he might be a bit of a lion too, when roused. And one had to remember that the fellow had not only served in the French Foreign Legion but in a Penal Battalion too. Something of a tough guy undoubtedly. No ordinary law-abiding English country-gentleman.

And the girl, a devil incarnate, once really roused. She'd shoot you or stick a knife in you as soon as look at you.

No; it wouldn't be the line of a really sensible man, actually to go and stay in the place.

He might go to bed in great peace and comfort one night and wake up in Heaven, where, on the best authority, earthly treasure is without value.

Save for that, it would be great fun. Really and truly amusing.

But it would be a beastly experience to have one's throat cut, just when one's ship came home, and one had arrived safely in port with a real treasure-galleon.

Besides, apart from any question of plain murder—and in an English country house, even Vanbrugh and his woman might stop short of that—there was always the risk of an argument, or a little homily from Spanish Maine, flaring up into a row, and of a sudden quick shooting putting an end to all his hopes, nay, certainties, of happiness and success.

So one had to be careful. One had to walk warily.

Never given to wavering, mind-changing, indecision, he nevertheless looked ahead and thought out the strategy and tactics of his campaigns and, like a good chess-player, considered all the implications, connotations and *sequelæ* of his next move.

Well he knew, none better, that the victim of blackmail must not be driven to desperation; must never be driven to that point where fear and detestation of the blackmailer and his extortion equals or exceeds fear of the publication of his shameful or dangerous secret.

Well he knew, none better, that a blackmailer defied is a blackmailer impotent; that directly the victim of blackmail says,

"Go and do your damnedest; shout it from the housetops; put it in the newspapers," the game is up; and the utmost that is left to the blackmailer is the poor comfort and pleasure of the petty revenge of doing as his victim says.

And that's no good at all; cuts no ice whatever.

What he has got to do, and what he does do, if he knows his business, is to lead the victim on; to show how much better a small payment is than the great horror of exposure; and gradually to increase his demands, once the fly is in his spider-web.

And this case must be handled with the utmost care and with all his great skill.

It was a splendid case. He'd never heard of a better. For he was in a position literally and completely to blast and destroy the happiness, the social security, the fair name, and the whole future, of one of the most prominent, widely-known and admired young men of that part of the world; in a position to drive him from the eclectic society of which he was an ornament, and from the very famous Regiment to which he belonged.

Now, if anything at all was certain in this uncertain world, it was that this extremely wealthy youth would part with a very considerable portion of his riches before he would suffer social death and extinction; and when you add to that the fact that he was desperately in love, and that the same blow that destroyed his life would shatter his love-romance, well, the position was a pretty strong one.

And the beauty of it was that all this was in reserve; yes, was what *Le Milieu* and all the other great Financial Trusts call the Reserve Fund. And that need not be tapped, in fact must not be tapped, for many a long day. Not until the last sovereign, dollar, peseta, franc, had been squeezed from the other two.

They'd pay and pay and pay—and then some—before they'd lose their new-won position in English society; before she would lose her lover; lose her established position—solid as a rock, so long as she was amenable to the desires of Manöel Maine.

Yes, desires. A good word in this connection. A very desirable *houri*, as she had always been.

Oho, Sir Harry Vane! What a tale we could tell you, eh?

"Yes," chuckled Spanish Maine aloud, "I look forward to the day when I have a private and heart-to-heart talk with my Fourth Woman."

But meanwhile the girl would need, not exactly careful handling—he wasn't going to be careful with the little devil—but reasonable handling. The screw must not be put on too violently. She must not be terrified. He mustn't let her get anywhere near the mental situation, the frame of mind, in which she should begin to scream and tear her hair and say,

"Oh! *Go and tell him.* I'll see you in Hell before I'll give you another farthing. *Go and tell him!* I'll tell him myself, before you get there, and I hope he'll put a bullet through your heart."

No, there must be no rough-stuff of that sort.

But at the same time, she must clearly understand that he'd got her; that it was no good to wriggle or squeal; that she'd got to pay; and that she might as well look pleasant and be pleasant, kind, complaisant. Yes, pleasant and complaisant.

And anyway, what was the good of the girl trying to pull this high-falutin' stuff. She knew that he knew what she'd been—and what she was.

She knew that he knew that she'd hooked a couple of mugs, first Vanbrugh and now Vane. So what was the good of acting the *doncella* to him?

Silly! And what was more, he wouldn't stand it. Why couldn't the girl come off it? Act sensibly and come in with him?

After all, how was she better than any common gun-moll? If he had no objection to her calling him a gangster, a gun-man, and a crook, what objection could she have to his calling her a gun-moll and bidding her behave as such?

Besides, he wasn't a gangster. He was a lone wolf, which was a very much superior thing. A gangster, forsooth!

He, Manöel Maine of Cadiz University, and a hidalgo of Spain! Though, as to "gangster," what's in a name? He could use, and he had used, a little gun as well as anybody. But that didn't make him a gun-man in the common use of the phrase. And as for crook, well, Zaza Blanchfleur should talk! What had been her last dealings with him? A fly-by-night theft and jilting.

And, *por Dios*, that jilting should be the very first thing that she made good, before any question arose of what she and her brother should pay by way of what they'd call blackmail. She should pay him the kisses and so forth that she owed him.

She should keep her love-bargain.

According to their agreement—for which he had paid hand-somely—she'd had no right to leave him until his caravan was ready, and he himself left Bouzen.

He had paid for her company, and he was of the sort that gets what it pays for.

Yes, *por Dios*, before anything else she should pay what she had stolen. Repay what she had cheated him of, both in money and in—kisses.

Laughing softly to himself Spanish Maine took up the telephone that stood in the corner of his sitting-room.

"Brandon Abbas?"

"Yes, Sir."

"Who's speaking?"

"The butler at Brandon Abbas, Sir."

"Oh, will you say that Mr. Manöel Maine would like to speak to Miss Vanbrugh."

"I beg your pardon, Sir?"

"Mr. Maine would like to speak to Miss Vanbrugh."

"I beg your pardon, Sir, but Mr. Vanbrugh is out in the coverts with Mr. Geste."

"*Miss* Vanbrugh, I said. Miss Consuela Vanbrugh."

"Oh, I beg pardon, Sir. Miss Vanbrugh is out driving with Mrs. Geste, Sir. Gone to Exeter, I believe, Sir."

"Oh—ah—quite certain?"

"Yes, Sir, quite certain. Miss Vanbrugh and Mrs. Geste will be returning to lunch, Sir."

"Oh well, when Miss Vanbrugh comes in, will you tell her that Mr. Maine rang up, and that he will be glad if she'll ring him up at the *Bluff King Hal*, where he is staying?"

"Yes, Sir."

"Got it right?"

"Yes, Sir. Mr. Maine rang up Miss Vanbrugh and will she give him a ring at the *King Hal*."

"Thank you."

"Thank you, Sir. Good-morning, Sir."

But, through some oversight or misunderstanding, or possibly by reason of too painfully clear sight and understanding, Miss Vanbrugh failed to ring-up Mr. Maine that morning or afternoon.

§2

"He's here, John," said Otis Vanbrugh to John Geste, as they sat over coffee and cigars in John's den, after lunch, that afternoon.

"He's here, putting up at the *Bluff King Hal*, and had the nerve to ring up Consuela and to leave a message with Burdon to ask her to give him a ring when she came in. She hasn't done it, of course. What would be the best line, do you think? Ignore him?"

John Geste considered a while.

"No, I don't think so, Otis," he said. "I'm all for getting down to brass tacks. I think that, in a case like this, the sooner cards are on the table and both sides understand each other, the better. What about calling his bluff?"

"Well, I shouldn't altogether care to do that, John. In the first place, Spanish Maine is the wrong sort of man. In the second place, we mustn't do anything without Consuela's consent; and I am perfectly certain she'd sooner die than run the risk of Sir Harry Vane knowing—everything."

"Unless of course she'd screwed herself up to the point of telling him herself," he added.

"Ah, that'd be the real solution," said John Geste. "Tell Harry Vane absolutely everything, tell Spanish Maine to go to the Devil —and abide the result."

"Well, you know what I think, John. I think the result would be next thing to fatal for Consuela, and I am quite sure it would be fatal for Spanish Maine. And mighty quick. Whether he spilt the beans or Consuela were forced to spill them—through his action—it would be 'Good-morning Peter' for Spanish Maine, *pronto*."

"Peter?" inquired John Geste.

"Sure—*Saint* Peter. About the very next morning after that happened, Spanish Maine'd be knocking on Heaven's gate."

"Consuela'd kill him, you mean?"

"No. *I* would. To save Consuela the trouble, or rather the danger. If we were in the Sahara or even the open-hearted West, I wouldn't rob her of the pleasure."

"I wish you wouldn't talk like that, Otis. As I've said before, all question of the justifiability of—murder—apart, it can't be done, here in England."

"Can't it, John? You watch me."

"I mean it can't be done with impunity. You can't do it and get away with it. I've no doubt you could get him all-right, but the Police'd get you. We've had all that out before. Come off it."

John Geste rose to his feet and walked uneasily, thoughtfully, broodingly, about the room.

Once again, what a ghastly business. An utter *impasse*. If this girl, fundamentally wild, lawless, dangerous, were rendered desperate by this blackmailer, then, to save her from becoming a murderess, her brother, John Geste's truest noblest friend, would almost certainly become a murderer—to forestall her.

If, on the other hand, she made confession to her lover, to thwart and defeat the blackmailer; and, equally, if she made confession simply at the promptings of her higher and better nature, which was undoubtedly awakened; her attitude to Spanish Maine would be the same. Vengeful. Ferocious.

What could he, John Geste, do? How could he help his friend —his friend who had offered his life to save him? How could he help him and this poor girl? What would Michael have done in like case? Undoubtedly he'd have made some *beau geste* or other, sufficient and successful. And if Beau could have done it, could not he himself think of something?

Could he buy the man off?

No; that was the devilish part of this hellish business of blackmail. There's no buying off. The more you pay, the more is demanded. Supposing ten thousand pounds would satisfy this man, and send him away; how soon would he come back? Just as soon as the end of the ten thousand was in sight.

And then again, supposing, for one moment, that ten thousand pounds was enough; suppose it would satisfy him and shut his mouth for ever; that was only one half of the trouble. Sir Harry Vane had got to be told—even if, with permission of Otis, he had to tell him himself.

And that would be a nice task for John Geste, the brother in spirit of Otis Vanbrugh, actually to butt in and make it his business to tell tales against this poor girl who had never done him any harm.

Still, there it was. He had known Lady Drusilla and young Harry all his life, and he simply could not, he must not, stand aside and let Harry marry Consuela in ignorance of her past.

Or could he? Was he his brother's keeper—to that extent, once again?

Nice problem—very pretty conscience-case for casuists.

Anyway, one's instinct and promptings were clear and direct—in favour of warning the Vanes. But at the same time, one's very soul recoiled from such treachery to Consuela Vanbrugh.

Anyhow, one thing really was plain. The accusation against Consuela Vanbrugh must not come from this Spanish Maine—if it did not come from Consuela herself.

What could one do to help these unfortunate people? Really, if it were only a case of Spanish Maine and what he could do, he'd be inclined to go and kill him himself. But, as a matter of simple and sober fact, if Spanish Maine died to-morrow, the situation between Consuela and Harry Vane would remain the same—and so would his own duty in the matter.

Still, Spanish Maine must be eliminated.

What an unfortunate expression! Sounded rather as though Otis were talking. "Eliminated." What did they call it nowadays—being "taken for a ride"; "bumped off?" That wasn't what he had meant at all. Maine must somehow be eliminated from this case, and the issue left plain and clear between Consuela and Harry.

And how could he be eliminated? Could any possible good ensue from a talk between himself and Spanish Maine? No, only money talks—to a creature like that. Still, no harm could be done surely, by a sort of Round Table Conference, especially if all cards were laid on the said table.

He turned to where his friend sat, tense, concentrated, frowning, angrily chewing the end of the cigar that he was smoking.

"I say, John," said Vanbrugh, "since the gentleman has come into the immediate neighbourhood, doesn't it seem inhospitable not to invite him here? Since he's rung up Brandon Abbas, let's ring up the old *King Hal*—and invite him to dinner."

"What?"

"Invite him to dinner; treat him as an ordinary guest; say nothing at all of this matter over the port; join the ladies in the ordinary way; then bring him up to this den and have it out.

"Have it out, so that when the man goes out of this house we know exactly where we stand—absolutely exactly what his real genuine demands are, and what are the very lowest terms to which he will agree."

John Geste thought for a while.

"It's an idea," he said, "though I can't say dinner appeals to me. Get the fellow here, put a bold face on it, talk to him for his good, and see if we can bluff him. You say he is not the sort of man who can be bluffed."

"No. I'll say he's not. But you never know, John. I've played Poker some, myself. And if he considers himself a tough guy, we can remind him of the fact that, like himself, we have both been in the Legion—and in the road-gangs too. We *might*. You never know. We can try, anyway."

"He is not a man who can be frightened," said John Geste.

"No, I'll say he's not. I doubt if the Devil himself could frighten Spanish Maine. Whatever his faults—and he's a foul poisonous piece of work—he's no coward. No, we couldn't hope to frighten him, John, whatever we did. But there again, you never know. We might think up something that. . . ."

"But he'll be our guest, Otis. We've got to remember that. One can't very well invite a man to dinner, and . . ."

"And then pull a gun on him?" interrupted Vanbrugh. "No, I suppose we can't. You can't, anyway. You might leave him here alone with me, though."

"No. Absolutely not. Nothing of the sort. If we invited him to dinner, he'd come under—not exactly a flag of truce and its protection—but under a sort of safe-conduct, of course. If Isobel consented to write him a nice little invitation to dinner, that invitation would be his passport in—and out again—safe and sound."

"Yes. I suppose so. I suppose you're right, John, even in the case of a snake like that. No. We couldn't ask him to dinner and then do him in."

"Of course not. You couldn't ask a man to break bread and eat salt and drink wine with you, and stab him in the back."

"Or shoot him in the front," amended Otis Vanbrugh.

"Of course not. Do you know that picture *A Glass of Wine with the Borgias*—a fellow sitting at table and Lucretia Borgia pouring him a glass of poisoned wine, while her father, Pope Alexander VI, looks on and smiles? I should always remember that if we invited him here, and any harm came to him. No. There's no point in inviting him here, like that, Otis. And if there were, I doubt if I could go through with dinner. Or let Isobel. And what about Consuela?"

"Oh, she'd enjoy it: though to tell you the truth, I think she'd be sorely tempted."

"What, to put something unwholesome in his coffee?"

"You've said it, John. I suppose she wouldn't play any tricks if she promised not to, but it would be an awful temptation. Seeing what he's trying to do to her, she'd be quite equal to trying to do something to him. No; it was a silly idea of mine, John. Cut it out. Not but what he'd have come. He'd have been tickled to death to come, just as Consuela would to have him come—and to see that he didn't go."

"Well, what about asking him here for a formal business conference at eleven o'clock in the morning, with no hospitality about it? Simply ask him to come and see us. Don't you think that might be a good plan?"

"Yes. I doubt if it would do any good, but I don't see how it could do any harm."

"Do you think he'd come, just as he would have come to dinner?"

"Yes, I'll say he'd come running. In the first place, he'd think it was a sure sign of a climb-down on our part, and that we were getting nervous and willing to talk turkey; and secondly that we were probably going to try to put one over on him, soften his hard heart, and ask him to let us down lightly. And anyhow, he'd see we wanted to get together and do business, all pleasant, agreeable and satisfactory, and no hard feelings.

"But mind you, John," continued Otis Vanbrugh, "I've nothing more to say to him, and I shall be hard put to it to keep my hands— or my gun—off him. You say, 'Don't pay him a farthing,' and I think you're right, if only we can get him to keep his mouth shut until Consuela has either decided that she'll risk it and tell Sir Harry Vane everything—or else has decided that she'll risk it the other way, and tell him nothing at all."

"Well, it would be something, wouldn't it, if we got a promise from him—to give us time; a promise not to say anything at all to anybody until we either agree to comply with his terms, or absolutely refuse to give him a farthing. . . . By the way, would he keep a promise, do you think?"

"Well; he would if he thought he would; and he wouldn't if he thought he wouldn't; if you know what I mean. If he talked high-falutin' stuff about being a man of honour (my God, a man of honour!) he'd probably stand to what he said, unless there was some new and extra reason for breaking his word."

"Otis, I wish you'd let me have him arrested, and be done with it. Let him get the ten years he rightly deserves for blackmail, not to mention drug-running and dope-peddling."

"No, no, that'd be premature, John. He'd squeal at once. At the top of his voice. His defence would be that we were frightened because he knew all about Consuela whom we were trying to marry to Sir Harry Vane; and this was a put-up job to get him out of the way. In point of fact, have we got any Court-of-Law evidence, at the present moment, as to blackmail, or as to drug-smuggling? We have only his word for the latter; and as to the blackmail, there's nothing in writing, and he has never used threats of it before witnesses.

"No, that won't do, John. If the time comes that we decide that we don't care, and we are really going to get him, we could lay a trap for him. We'd agree to submit to blackmail, and pay him off by cheque or marked notes, and demand a written receipt and a promise not to use his information against us.

"Then prosecute—and get him that way. I suppose all that would be good enough evidence; and if he wouldn't take a cheque or give us anything in writing, we might work it here—have a meeting with him, hand over marked banknotes, and arrange for detectives to hear everything that was said.

"And I suppose we could catch him on the drug business by paying someone to go and buy a consignment from him? But all that will come later—I hope."

"How much later, I wonder?" mused John.

"Well, poor little Consuela's thinking mighty hard; and I want to leave her to it. I don't want to try to influence her, any more. I've said it all. She'll make up her mind if we give her time; and that will be that. I'll know better what to do, and what to ask you to help me to do, John, when she's made her decision. If she says she's going to confess to Harry Vane, then let her do it in her own way and time. . . . And then Mr. Spanish Maine will get his, the Lord helping.

"If, on the other hand, she decides that she cannot, and that she will not, tell Harry Vane everything, then we'll lay information against Spanish Maine, get him, arrested for blackmail, and for dope-peddling too, and let him squeal, if he must. Let it go to Sir Harry Vane that way. We can make the rattle-snake serve us to that extent, and save both you and me from the filthy job of telling on Consuela."

"No," objected John Geste. "If it worked out that way, and there were a scandal, and Harry Vane asked Consuela if it were true, what then?"

"Then it's up to Consuela and Harry Vane. But at any rate, it'll clear the air, settle the business, and Spanish Maine will be where he ought to be. And I guess he won't escape from a British gaol in a hurry."

"Suppose we told Consuela that that is the programme?" suggested John Geste.

"I don't want to, John. I'd rather not. As I've just said, I want her to make up her mind herself—come to her own decision. You know, if a woman does that, there is some hope of her remaining satisfied with the result. If you rush her into making up her mind, she'll blame you for the rest of her life, if the result isn't satisfactory. I don't mean she'll necessarily say so, but she'll feel that way. What I am hoping, nowadays, is that she'll come to me—and mighty soon too—and say,

" 'It's all right, Otis. I'm going to tell Harry, and leave it to him.' "

"And then, if they marry, we can only hope it will turn out well," said John Geste. "Personally, I say again, it's impossible. Still . . ."

"Well, we haven't decided what we are going to do about this man Maine," he continued. "Shall we get him over and talk to him? Or look here, suppose I see him alone. I haven't had the honour of a chat with him yet. Wonder if it's possible that I could scare him off? A few winged words about the majesty of the English Law."

"Do no harm, John. Do no harm, and might very possibly do some good. Anyway, you'd be able to form your own opinion as to exactly how dangerous he is, and what are the cheapest terms on which we could escape if it really came to cash and a show-down."

"Show-down if you like, but I'm not going to talk cash to him," replied John. "Absolutely not. But if you see no objection, I'd certainly like to have an interview with him. Since he calls himself a gentleman, it is just possible that one might appeal—I won't say to his better nature because he hasn't got one—but to his conceit of himself, and so get under his skin."

"We shall do that, John, when we can get under the hide of a rhinoceros with a tooth-pick. But see him, by all means. I wish you would. You'll know what we are up against, and you might possibly modify your views on paying him off."

"*No!*"

"I mean—for a little while. Just until Consuela is quite clear and certain in her mind: decides exactly what she is going to do. You see him, anyhow."

"Right," said John. "I'll ring him up."

Spanish Maine, rolling a cigarette as he sat in his room, next morning, chuckled when the telephone-bell rang. There could be but one person who would be calling him.

So she was coming to heel, was she? Well, she'd better. She'd better. For if she did drive him to be nasty, well he'd be very nasty indeed. He'd make her life a hell upon earth. But trust the little devil to know on which side her bread was buttered

"*Hullo?*"

A man's voice.

What was this? Treachery?

By God, if she . . .

The police?

Oh! Mr. Geste of Brandon Abbas! Oh yes, with pleasure. What could be more delightful; unless Mr. Geste would come down here? Sitting-room very comfortable; complete privacy. No? Very well. Yes.

Mr. Maine would give himself the pleasure, then, of calling at three o'clock this afternoon. Three o'clock sharp. Good-bye.

§2

At the conclusion of the interview with Spanish Maine, although it had lasted for over an hour, John Geste was unable to feel that he had made any head-way or done any good. Save for this, the tone of the conversation had been pleasant enough. He had found Señor Manöel Maine of easy address, agreeable manner and conversation, and, in all externals, a gentleman.

But he had come reluctantly to the conclusion that the man had indeed no higher nature to which to appeal; was devoid of bowels of compassion; and knew no mercy. What he wanted and what he intended to have, and to have quickly, was money. Money in such quantity as the resources of his victims could provide.

Nor had John Geste obtained any satisfaction through pointing out that the blackmailer's secret was of value only so long as it was a secret, and that as soon as it was told, the blackmailer's power was ended.

"Quite so," Spanish Maine had agreed. "You are absolutely

right, Mr. Geste. If you have a horse to sell, you can sell it only while it is of value to somebody else, and no longer. Should it go permanently lame, or die, well—you can't sell it. You can only give it away, gratis. The same applies to a secret, or rather to silence concerning a secret. If my silence is of value, I can sell it; and I am willing to do so. If it is not of value, I cannot sell it, and there's an end of the matter. I can then only give it away, gratis. Am I to understand that it is a matter of indifference to your—ah— principals, friends, whether I tell my secret to Sir Harry Vane or not? If so, say so; and I shall give myself the pleasure of telling him —and go my way."

"I doubt it," replied John Geste.

"But why not? Why not? Who's to hinder me? I've done no harm, no wrong. I have not broken your law, surely? I have merely mentioned that I have something for sale—my silence concerning a secret—and you can buy it or not, as you like."

"But suppose you did clearly grasp, completely realize and thoroughly understand, beyond shadow of a doubt, that neither Miss Vanbrugh nor her brother would, in any circumstances whatsoever, pay you one solitary farthing?" asked John Geste.

"Well? Let's suppose it. Suppose that, under no circumstances whatsoever, was one farthing forthcoming. Well?"

"What would you gain by going to Sir Harry Vane with this tale?"

"Satisfaction."

"And you call yourself a gentleman, a *caballero*, a *hidalgo?*"

"Never mind what I call myself, Mr. Geste. I can tell you what I call Zaza Blanchfleur, *alias* Consuela Vanbrugh. I can tell you what she did to me. And, in absolutely final answer to your question, I can tell you once again what I should gain by denouncing her to Sir Harry Vane. I should gain the gratification of knowing that I had got even with her—at last. And moreover, although I don't pretend for one moment that it is my primary motive, I should have the further satisfaction of knowing that I had done my duty."

"Your *duty!*" shrugged John Geste.

"Yes. We all get a certain feeling of pleasure from knowing that we have done our duty, however painful, don't we? I have conceived a considerable liking and admiration for Sir Harry Vane; and I don't think it right that he should be allowed to marry this . . . this . . . ."

"That will do," said John Geste quietly.

"This lady, I was going to say . . . without knowing rather more than she will have told him, about her origin. I think he ought to know that I, for example, am an erstwhile lover of hers, a lover left disconsolate, jilted, for—an Arab! For a native; a black man, as Sir Harry Vane would call him . . . And if I learned that I were not, of course, her first lover—but her hundred-and-first—I should not be surprised. On second thoughts, I should be surprised. A thousand-and-one would be nearer the mark—of her Arabian Nights Tale of . . ."

"Let's stick to *your* tale, please," interrupted John Geste. "I gather that you'd feel compelled to inform Sir Harry Vane, so that you might be avenged upon a girl for something she either has or has not done to you; and also in obedience to the dictates of your tender conscience."

"Exactly. My compliments, Mr. Geste, on the accuracy both of your understanding and your expression."

"Well, Mr. Maine, if that is your last word . . ."

"Absolutely."

"If that is your last word, I was going to say—I can only point out that you have not a monopoly of conscience. Think *that* over."

"Agreed, Mr. Geste. And, in return, you think over what I have said; and please understand—I don't abate one farthing of my reasonable demand."

"And how long a period do you give me, in which to think it over? For I believe that Mr. and Miss Vanbrugh will take my advice and act as I suggest."

"Well, I am a busy man. . . . What shall we say? A week?"

"Yes. A week. And you do faithfully promise that you will make no move, take no step, do nothing whatsoever in this matter, for a week?"

"Yes. I agree. But after that—no shilly-shallying. I'll give you a week in which to make up your minds, and then I—act."

"And I can trust you?"

"Word of a *caballero*. You can trust me. I give you my word of honour that I will neither say nor write anything whatsoever, for a week. At the end of that time I shall consider myself free to repeat my demand for the *last* time, and to act in accordance with the reply I get. A week. And there's my hand on it, Mr. Geste."

John Geste regarded the hand and, concealing his feelings, reluctantly took it.

"Very well, I'll tell my friends what you say. I'll give them the advice I think best; and you can ask them for their decision in a week's time."

"*De acuerdo*. It is understood. Between gentlemen, Mr. Geste. . . . So pleasant to deal with people of one's own kind. We understand each other. . . . Agreed."

"Incidentally, that being so, Mr. Maine, there is no need for you to remain any longer at the Inn, is there? I don't wish to be rude, but we should all prefer it, if you went away. Particularly Miss Vanbrugh."

"I am sure she would," smiled Spanish Maine pleasantly, showing bright teeth beneath his curling moustache. "I'm sure she would. Yes, I will go this evening."

"It would be wiser, I think," observed John Geste gravely, and rang the bell.

XIX

By accident, by chance, by luck, by the ordination of Fate or the direct intention and intervention of Providence, Spanish Maine, striding jauntily down the avenue that leads from Brandon Abbas house to the main-entrance gates, encountered Consuela as, with Isobel Geste, she returned from a ride.

Riding was Consuela's present passion, and only when on the back of a big powerful and difficult horse did she seem happy and at ease. Only then did she cease to frown, cease to show signs of anxiety, worry, and strain.

All the morning she had ridden with her brother, and that afternoon Isobel, of her kindness, had offered to accompany her.

With debonair and graceful salutation, Spanish Maine greeted the ladies, made to pass them, then, suddenly turning, raised a hand as though to pat the neck of Consuela's horse, and said,

"Might I trouble you just for one moment, Miss Vanbrugh? If Mrs. Geste would be so very good as to excuse me for a second . . ."

Isobel glanced at Consuela who, answering her with a brief nod of acquiescence, asked coldly,

"What do you want?" as she brought her horse to a halt, and Isobel walked her horse slowly up the drive.

"Listen," said Spanish Maine as Isobel drew out of earshot. "The big drawing-room into which I was shown just now; the end door; opening out on to the terrace; nearest to here. I shall be there to-night when the lights go out, downstairs. Let me in. I want a long talk with you."

"Well, I haven't the faintest desire for the shortest talk with you," replied Consuela.

"Would you rather I had the talk with Harry Vane, then? Now look here. No nonsense. I'm leaving to-morrow, and if you won't meet me to-night, I shall go by way of Vane Court. I've had enough of this shilly-shallying. If I get nothing—you get what's coming to you, *pronto*. And if I get what I want, you get Sir Harry Vane—and no trouble or interference from me whatsoever."

"And what do you want? I've got no money to give you, even if I were fool enough to do it."

"I'll tell you what I want, all-right. You come down and open the end french-window, as soon as everybody's gone to bed, and the house is quiet. As early as is safe. I shall be watching from under the trees, and don't you keep me waiting or—you know what will happen. I've had enough of this, and I'm going to put an end to it, one way or the other. You can decide for yourself which way it is to be."

Isobel had turned her horse and was walking it slowly back in their direction.

"Well?" snarled Spanish Maine.

Consuela looked him in the eyes, a long, searching, and thoughtful look.

The expression of her face changed. A look not so much of hope as of intention replaced that of despairing misery. Her mouth hardened.

"I shall be there," she said.

And as, with a flourish and a bow, Spanish Maine again raised his hat, she rode on to join Isobel.

"I didn't know whether to go away or to stay with you, my dear, so I did both and neither," smiled Isobel.

"Yes, thank you so much. I wanted to hear what the creature had to say."

"Anything new?"

"No; just another turn of the screw," said Consuela. "Oh, how I wish we could *do* something."

"Yes," agreed Isobel. "It is absolutely incredible that one should be so helpless. Actually be in the hands of a loathsome blackmailer like that. It's absurd, you know. It's impossible. It doesn't happen in England, nowadays. And it isn't like John or Otis to let a reptile of that sort hold them up—and get away with it."

"No, it's my fault. I wish to God I'd never brought this trouble on you."

"Trouble! My dear! Where's the trouble? It's no *trouble* to us. It's an agony of sympathy. I was thinking about you. It seems so extraordinary that John and Otis can't *do* something—set you free, save you, once and for all, from this rascally swindling. . . ."

"It's my fault, as I say," interrupted Consuela. "I've only got to give Harry up."

"Tell him, my dear. Tell him."

"Well, that would be giving him up, wouldn't it? No, Isobel, I can't . . . I *can't*. . . . Could you give John up?"

"Look here, my dear, you love Harry?"

"Desperately. More than life. Far far more than life. I . . ."

"Then you want him to be happy?"

"Happy? I'd die to make him happy. That's partly what keeps me from telling him. It's partly shame, I know. I should burn up and die of shame, cowardice, and fear—the fear of losing him. That keeps me from telling him.

"But it's also partly the knowledge that it would kill his happiness. It is more than partly that, it is largely that. I honestly believe that my strongest reason for not telling him is the fact that it would be such a blow to him. It would kill his happiness dead: and he is so happy with me, Isobel.

"Why can't people leave us alone, leave us to be happy together? What does the past matter? What does it matter to Society, or to Lady Drusilla or to anybody else, what happened before ever I met Harry? What does it matter? If he truly loves me and I absolutely worship him, what does the rest matter to anybody in the world? I can't tell him. I *won't* tell him."

She stopped, dashed tears from her eyes, bit her lips and regained control.

"And this man will," she continued, "unless I give him whatever he asks. That's why John and Otis are powerless to do anything. I tie their hands. My love, my cowardice, my shame, my fear, tie their hands; and I and Otis and Harry are at the mercy of this . . . this convict."

"It's dreadful," agreed Isobel, "but I'm perfectly certain that something can be done, something will be done. After all, this is England, and that sort of thing doesn't go on, here."

"No, except when a woman's weak and wicked and cowardly —and loving—as I am," said Consuela. "Oh, I'd kill him. I'd *kill* him if . . ."

"Don't talk like that, darling," soothed Isobel. "You trust John and Otis. And you just live a little longer with the idea of making the fullest confession to Harry.

"Or at any rate," she added, being a woman, "a full enough confession to take the wind out of the sails of this Maine man. Then you are free from him for ever, and we can put him in prison."

"And Harry?" said Consuela wearily.

"I was going to say," replied Isobel. "Don't you think that if Harry loves you as you love him, he'll take exactly the view that you were taking just now—that it matters to nobody in the whole world."

"Yes, but it *will* matter to them, Isobel. It'll matter to every scandal-monger in England, and to every mean-souled dirty little scribbler that can earn a shilling by getting a paragraph into the gutter-press.

"And suppose Harry did take that view," she continued. "Suppose he did insist on our marrying, do you really think that I could compensate him for—everything; all that makes up his life and has made up his life until now; the whole of his circle; his home; his position; his Regiment? Suppose he thought, in the first flush of love, that I could; and we went away, went to the South Sea Islands or somewhere—how long would it last? How long would it be before he opened his eyes one day, stared at me, and said,

" '*I have lost everything, everything that made life worth living, for this woman! . . . Why? . . . There are a million more like her—and unlike her in the fact that they are irreproachable*, pure, *chaste* . . .*' Oh, God!"

Silence. . . .

"Tell him, Consuela," urged Isobel. "It is absolutely the only possible thing to do—the only conceivable hope of a ghost of a chance of happiness for either of you."

XX

Consuela sat in her room that evening, thinking, pondering, scheming, wondering.

Should she go down late to-night and see this man, hear what he had to say?

Should she let him spend the night standing there, hiding under the trees, waiting?

No. Why stir up and irritate the poisonous snake that you are not in a position to kill? Why spur and strike the bad and dangerous horse that may bolt with you to your death, when you cannot control it because a rein is broken?

Was the rein broken? Was she really helpless, she, Consuela Vanbrugh who had been Zaza Blanchfleur, the daughter of Zaza Blanchfleur?

She who had dealt with violent and wicked men, European and African, on equal terms; she who had often defied and defeated those who had over-stepped the limit, broken the rules of the game?

Was it possible that she, with her experience—oh, God, her "experience!"—could not cope with, and defeat, a thing like Spanish Maine?

Rising from the arm-chair in which she had been seated, Consuela walked about her room, glancing at pictures without seeing them, picking up and replacing bric-a-brac and ornaments without being aware that she had touched them; went to the window, pushed it open wide and stared out, unseeing, into the brightly moon-lit evening.

How utterly lovely, how perfectly quiet, how restful, friendly . . . *peaceful* . . .

And suddenly the girl did what she had not done for many a long year, did what she had but very rarely done before in all her life—burst into a flood of tears.

Turning from the window and throwing herself upon her bed, she sobbed and sobbed and sobbed until she could cry no more.

Then, rising from the bed and drying her eyes, she went to the Sheraton writing-table that stood beneath the window on the opposite side of the room.

Taking a sheet of paper of the largest size from one of the pigeon-holes at the back of the writing-table, she picked up a large, coloured quill-pen and began to write.

From the first words,

"My own Beloved, my most adored darling Harry" to the signature, "Your worshipping Consuela-whom-you-love" she did not pause or falter.

Page after page, for upwards of an hour, she wrote, exalted as a martyr at the stake, rejoicing in an agony of pain, burning in an agony of shame . . . wrote the naked truth without gloss; without reticence; without palliation, justification, or word of excuse; the bald and naked truth; the truth, the whole truth and nothing but the truth. Wrote herself to a stand-still.

Wrote from burning fever heat of love and sorrow and shame —to an empty coldness, numbness, death of all feeling and emotion.

And as she put the unread letter into an envelope and addressed it, she felt that love was dead, shame was dead, grief was dead, pain was dead.

Dead . . . dead . . . dead. . . .

And rising from the desk, she stood for minutes, motionless as a statue, undecided. Then slowly she withdrew the letter from its envelope and unfolded it; and, seating herself again at the desk, added at the foot beneath her signature,

"*Come to me, if you can forgive me, and love me still. Write to me if you cannot.*"

Having sealed the letter she sat, numbed with misery and despair.

Suddenly she came to life, and rang the bell.

Jennie would answer it. Jennie liked her; probably because she liked Jennie. Yes, she'd manage it.

The girl knocked and entered.

"Did you ring, Miss?"

"Yes, Jennie. Look here. I want you to do something for me, will you?"

"Why, yes, Miss. Of course I will."

"See! Can you take this note yourself to George, the groom in charge of the horse I ride? And could you ask him if he would go over to Vane Court with it? I want it to get there to-night."

Jennie was thrilled. A love-letter, in haste, from this nice foreign young lady to Sir Harry, at Vane Court. A love-letter. Must get there to-night.

Why, it was like the films.

"Oh, yes, Miss. He'd go on his motor-bike."

"Oh, has he a motor-bicycle? Splendid. He'd get there in an hour or less."

"Yes, Miss. A hower less a quarter, it takes him, he told me. His young lady's there, Miss."

"Well, look here, Jennie, if you'd give him this—and this *pourboire*—and ask him if he'll take it to Vane Court and bring back the answer. . . . He's to wait for an answer. You understand, he's to wait for an answer."

And Consuela handed the precious letter to the girl.

"Oh, thank you, Miss."

"George is here, I suppose."

"Yes, Miss. I know he's here and'll be only too pleased of the excuse to go over. He'll be back by the time you come out from dinner, Miss."

"Splendid. And look here, Jennie. Secret, see? I don't want anyone to know. Only you and I and George—and Sir Harry Vane. See?"

And Consuela forced a smile.

Jennie twinkled and dimpled. Lovely.

"Why, yes, Miss. I'll give it to George on the quiet, and he won't say a word."

"Good. It will really be all-right then?"

"Why, yes, Miss. Never fear. That'll be all-right—and George will be back with the answer long before you go to bed."

George was; but without an answer to the letter. According to Jennie, the butler had took the letter and told George he would put it on the hall table for Sir Harry to see when he come in, he having gone to London with her Ladyship, out to dinner, and not expected back till pretty late.

*   *   *   *   *   *   *

So there the letter lay, on the post-box table in the big hall at Vane Court. Lay there where Harry might see it, or might not see it. The letter that told him everything.

Told him also that he was free; that, even could he forgive her, even could he still love her, it was ended.

That she would know it was ended for ever—unless he came himself and told her it was not.

Would he come . . . and save her?

525

XXI

Consuela opened the french-window at the end of the big drawing-room, stepped back into the room, and seated herself upon a huge settee, cushioned, deep, and broad, that, in a patch of moonlight, faced toward the terrace.

A minute later she saw a man come softly up the steps, cross the terrace and enter the room, throwing, as he did so, a broad-brimmed felt hat and a cloak on to the long white seat that stood outside, against the wall, beside the door.

She knew that somewhat foreign-looking hat, almost a sombrero, and the cape. She had seen them, on the *Amazon*, adorning the soldierly figure of El Señor Manöel Maine.

It was amazing with what cat-like silence and swiftness so big a man could move.

She rose to her feet, ghost-like in the moonlight.

"Ah!" whispered Maine. "You have done wisely, my dear. Is that other door locked?"

"No."

"Then go and lock it, you fool. The key is this side. I took note of that this afternoon. . . . Yes, with that door locked and this one open, I shall have my line of retreat safe, if anyone comes. First principles of tactics. The old soldier, my love, eh? All right; sit still. I think I'll lock it myself."

"And suppose someone came to this terrace-door?" asked Consuela.

"H'm. That would be awkward. For him. Look here; have you a little game on? Is this a trap? Because if so, you are in it too—for I'd wring your neck as soon as look at you."

"And your money, then?"

"Don't you worry about my money. I'll look after that. And there are other things besides money, too. . . . Anyhow, if your alleged brother, or the excellent Mr. Geste, comes to that french-window, it will be the last window he'll ever come to, for I'll shoot him like a dog. And you too. So if that is the game you'd better say so, and make some other arrangement."

"There's no game and there's no trap," replied Consuela. "Don't be frightened."

Frightened! Spanish Maine drew a sharp breath audibly.

"You said you wanted to speak to me," continued the girl. "Well?"

"Ah, that's better. It is all-right, eh? And we can talk business? Got the whole night to ourselves, have we?"

"I've come to hear what you've got to say," replied Consuela. "If by 'business' you mean blackmail, haven't you said it all, and had your answer? Or is there anything new? Have you anything fresh to propose, or is it the same old blackmail story?"

"Well, that stands, of course, but it isn't what I came to talk about to-night. Let's forget all about that for the moment, shall we, my dear?"

"*Forget!*" whispered Consuela.

"Yes. We'll forget about that for the moment, for something else. The matter of whether the wedding-day is fixed—and also of a little debt. Yes, of a little debt, Zaza. Do you remember? Do you remember that night in Bouzen when you deserted me? That night when you took two things away with you—my money and my heart."

"Your money? I no more took your money than I took the heart that you haven't got, the heart without which you were born. What do you mean—'I took your money'?"

"Anyhow, when I woke up that morning and went to my dispatch-case which was in my trunk which was in my dressing-room, my wallet was gone. My wallet, with practically every franc I had in the world."

"And because I had gone away, does that prove that I had taken your money? Because suddenly I could bear Bouzen no longer and had to get out into the clean desert or go mad—does that prove that I took your money? Are there no professional thieves in Bouzen? Are temporary, hired, Arab servants always honest? I have never stolen money, or anything else, in all my life."

"Come, come, my love! I wasn't born yesterday. Hired servants! What about hired *filles de joie*? When one instals a light-o'-love for the week-end, and she vanishes in the middle of the night, and so does one's money, well—I ask you! What view would my friend the Chief of Police have taken, do you think? Anyhow, I want that money back."

"I didn't take your money."

"Don't let's waste time, my dear. I want to get on to—other matters. Whether you took it or not—and of course you took it—I want it back. As I mentioned before, and as you may have noticed, I am not a man who is easily diddled, swindled, bilked. I made an arrangement with you, and I kept my side of it—and you are going to keep yours. I want payment in cash or kind . . . and in kindness."

"What do you mean?"

"What I say. I want the money you took. We'll call it five hundred pounds, at the present rate of exchange. I wish to be fair. Or I want its equivalent in . . . What have you got? Pearls, diamonds, rings? If you can't lay your hands on the cash, the junk would do. And I want the kindness as well."

"The kindness?"

"Yes, Little Innocent! The kindness, the kisses, the love, the ardour. . . ."

Consuela rose to her feet and the man, seizing her arm, pulled her down again beside him.

"That's what I've come for to-night, Zaza—to tell you to hurry up the wedding. And to collect a debt. A double debt. And I want payment in full. I ought, as a business man, to demand interest, of course. I will waive that, however. But I don't go until I have got five hundred pounds in my pocket—and had you in my arms."

The girl struggled to her feet.

The man rose, seized her, thrust her back upon the settee and held her there.

"What's the idea? What's the game? What are you struggling for? What are you kicking at? What are you boggling over—the cash or the kisses? What *are* you? Have I strayed into a Nunnery, by any chance? Keep still, damn you. . . . What? Business first? . . . Now you're talking, my little dove."

Spanish Maine released the girl and sat up.

"Business first, then. Have you five hundred in the house?"

"Of course I haven't."

"Has Vanbrugh? Or Geste?"

"Is it likely my brother would have five hundred pounds lying about in cash? Or Mr. Geste either. And suppose he had?"

"Well, if we knew that he had, and we knew where he kept it— there might be a burglary, mightn't there? That's an idea, Zaza, isn't it? Suppose I left this house, by and by, with five hundred pounds in my pocket—not necessarily in cash—and you personally were none the poorer. Suppose Mrs. Geste's pearls or . . ."

"*You* . . . *you* . . . !" The girl sprang to her feet again. "I'll . . ."

"Oh, no, you won't! Sit down!" and once more she was dragged back on to the settee. "You've let me into this house in the middle of the night—and it would take some explaining away, wouldn't it? You're my accomplice. That's what you are, my dear.

You've let me in here, and it looks ugly, doesn't it? And you can't say you were playing decoy—trapping me for Vanbrugh and Geste, can you? Couldn't tell them or the Police that, if there were a rumpus here, and it came to a show-down. But as I said, if it is a trap, I will shoot your precious Vanbrugh dead as a door-nail, and Geste as well. See this?"

And on his hand lay, dully glinting in the moonlight, the neat efficient automatic, moon-beams glinting on the gold inlay of its gun-metal handle, on the polished glaze of its blued barrel.

A pass of the long-fingered hand and it was gone.

"So, as I said before, my good wench, if you think you're going to put me on the spot—it will be a damned hot spot for your boy friends."

"There's no trap," said the girl, "and I'm not your accomplice. You are a blackmailer. A low foul sewer-rat. A swindler of women, and . . ."

"And you are sitting nice and cosy beside me on the sofa, eh?"

And flinging his right arm about the girl, imprisoning her right hand and crushing her to him, he forced her head back with his other hand and fixed his mouth upon hers.

"There!" he said at last, releasing her and drawing breath. *"There! W*hat about *that?"*

"I think it was what they call—yes—the last straw," said the girl quietly.

"Not it. Not the last—by hundreds," laughed Spanish Maine softly. "Now, like all women, you chatter too much . . . Business first. . . . How much money can you lay hands on, now?"

"Of my own? Scarcely any."

"Well then, you can go and write a cheque. And you'll just make it out as an open bearer cheque. We'll see about that in a minute, and I'll go with you."

"Come with me?"

"Yes. Where is your cheque-book? In your bedroom, isn't it?"

"Yes."

"Are your pearls there too? Those three very nice strings— might almost call them ropes—that you were wearing on board the *Amazon*. Are they in your bedroom too?"

"No."

"Don't you tell me they are at the Bank, because you are only staying here a few days."

As he spoke, Spanish Maine suddenly snatched at the girl's left hand.

"Hullo, where's the engagement-ring? Now then, which is it to be? A cheque for five hundred pounds—and God have mercy on you, if there's any hanky panky about it, for I'll have none—or shall we say the pearls and the engagement-ring instead? You can tell the young man that the ring fell off your finger while you were trailing your hand in the water when you were out in a boat on the lake. Say I was rowing you!" and again Spanish Maine laughed softly.

"Are they in your jewel-case in your bedroom?"

"No."

"Where are they, then?"

"Mrs. Geste was rather nervous about my jewellery, in case there were a burglary while I was in the house."

"Knew I was in the neighbourhood, you mean?" laughed Spanish Maine.

"Certainly she knew; and certainly she said she didn't want me to leave valuables in my bedroom."

"*So?* In the safe, eh, along with hers?"

"Well, not exactly a safe."

"What then?"

"Oh, it's a panel in the . . ."

"*So?* A panel? You slide it on one side and uncover a little iron door. You open that, and there's the little *cache* for the family jewels? And is that sapphire they call The Blue Water there? I have been hearing all the Brandon Abbas tales and legends from mine host of the *King Hal.* . . . The jewels are in a room with a secret panel, eh? Well, well! Now I call that interesting."

The girl made no reply.

Turning her head she contemplated the face of Spanish Maine which shone white, with heavy black shadows, in the bright moonlight; studied it, considering, thoughtful.

The face of a huge, deadly, merciless, cruel rat. The Human Rat.

Scarcely she seemed to be listening to what he was saying; rather to be weighing pros and cons, considering, deciding, passing judgment.

"Do you hear? Where's the room in which the secret panel is?"

"Upstairs."

"Difficult to get at?"

"No."

"Near your bedroom?"

"Yes."

"Then I foresee, my love, that I am about to make a personally-conducted tour of the premises—or of this part of them. You are going to be my guiding star—but not shining, for the moment—and you are going to lead me to it. You are going to take me by the hand and lead me to it. But first of all, what about the key, the key of the little iron door behind the panel?"

"How do you know there's an iron door behind the panel?"

"There always is. There's one here, isn't there?"

"No."

"Well, that's a good thing—for you. For you'd have had to go and get it. Just a panel, is it?"

"Yes."

"And the only trick is to know which panel, and how to work it."

"Yes."

"And you know?"

"Yes."

"Well then, the old slogan once more—Business before Pleasure. We'll visit the room with the panel in it, first. And once again, you Lump of Hypocrisy, if there's trouble, you will share it —with your 'brother' and the other guy. And I'll tell you another thing, my love, and don't you forget it. I was at some pains to let mine host of the *Bluff King Hal* know where I was going. Get me? If I'm not there at breakfast, bright and early to-morrow, it'll be here that I shall be inquired for.

" '*Mr. Maine. Missing from his hotel, the Bluff King Hal, since last night. According to the evidence of the landlord, strolled out after dinner, mentioning that he might be back late, as he was going to drop in at Brandon Abbas for a chat with his old friend Mr. Vanbrugh, staying with Mr. Geste. Bed not slept in, luggage and effects untouched. Nothing missing. Breakfast waiting*' and what had they got to say about it at Brandon Abbas? . . . The old soldier again, eh, my love? Tactics for ever!"

"And if I take you to the hiding-place, what are you going to do?" asked Consuela.

"I'm going to see that you pay your debt; the cash debt. That first. The other debt afterwards. You are going to pay the cash debt of five hundred pounds—and you can do it with your own stuff or with anybody else's. That's up to you, but I'm going to have it— first."

"You don't believe me when I say that I owe you no debt, that I stole nothing whatever from you?"

"Of course I don't. You vanished, and my money vanished at the same time. And it was not only the loss of the money. It was far worse than that. It was ruin; or would have been if I hadn't some brains in my head. You not only did me out of that five hundred pounds, but you did me out of thirty thousand pounds besides. However, you are going to pay it all back, you and your 'brother'— or Harry Vane. It doesn't matter to me. Yes, I'm going to teach you to rob and swindle and bilk the man who trusted you, you she-devil."

Still eyeing him, studying him as though a concrete problem for her solution, or a creature for classification, a case for her judgment, she spoke in a voice of quiet detachment.

"You know nothing of mercy, I imagine? You have no mercy at all? Supposing I had robbed you of this money, you couldn't forgive me, you who are yourself a robber? You'd take absolutely everything that you could get, without any thought whatsoever of what it cost your victim? You'd never forgive anyone? You'd never spare anybody?"

"What do *you* think?"

"I think you would not. Rats have no knowledge of mercy. I think you would not."

"You are right. I would not. Especially you. Do you know who you are? You are my 'Fourth Woman.' I came a cropper over three, and they got away with it. You won't.

"The burnt child . . . Burnt three times, and then hadn't learnt his lesson. But the fourth one—-well, you're the fourth and you shall see. . . . Once bit, twice shy, eh? What about four times bit? . . . Yes, you're my Fourth Woman—and you are going to pay for the other three. Messed up my life with women. Now a woman's going to make it all delightful, all rosy and golden, eh?

"Mercy! '*The quality of mercy is not strained,*' eh? No, it isn't going to be. Not the slightest strain. . . . Well, we must have been chattering here the best part of a quarter of an hour. What's the time? . . . Ah . . . I should think everybody has been in bed and asleep these two hours. We shan't be likely to run into anybody, I suppose? No sleep-walkers? No night-watchmen?"

"They don't have watchmen in English houses, Rat. We shall not meet anyone."

"Well, all the better for them—and for you. One more long long kiss."

The girl sprang to her feet.

"*No! . . . No! . . . No! . . .*" she cried in a hoarse whisper.

"Business first, eh?" grinned Spanish Maine. "Perhaps you're right. Lead on. And for your own sake be careful. Don't make a noise."

"You go too fast, Rat. I must go and get a key. The room with the panel is kept locked, naturally."

"I'll go with you and get it."

"You won't. It's much too dangerous. If by any chance I were seen taking the key, I could say I wasn't sure whether I'd put my jewels away or not, and I was just going to make sure, as the jewel-case wasn't in my bedroom. I'd suddenly wakened, and wondered whether I'd put them away or not. Something like that. It would sound perfectly natural, whereas if you were seen with me . . ." and Consuela shrugged her shoulders expressively.

Spanish Maine considered for a minute.

"Very well. Get the key—and be quick. And if you *are* playing me a trick . . ."

"Oh, you make me tired. Tricks and traps. If you are frightened, say so, and . . ."

"Get the key," smiled Spanish Maine, and re-seated himself upon the sofa.

Consuela crept from the room.

A few minutes later the girl returned.

"Ah!" whispered Spanish Maine as she came noiselessly into the room. "I began to think you'd done something foolish. *Here!* What's that, a gun?"

"No. Don't be alarmed, Rat. It's an electric torch and a key. Come along. It's across the hall, up a flight of stairs, through a room, along a little passage, up a flight of steps into another room, and in that is the door of the room that has the secret panel. We mustn't switch lights on, or knock anything over, and make a lot of noise. You are not afraid?"

"In turn, you make *me* tired, my love. I am not frightened and I hope you won't be, by the time I go."

"Come along, then, Rat. Where there's no moonlight, I'll switch on the torch, if necessary."

The lofty stone-flagged hall was faintly illuminated by moonbeams that passed through stained-glass windows. Nor were the stairs in darkness.

Pausing at a door, Consuela gently opened it, switched on the torch and kept its rays directed upon the floor before her feet.

Crossing the thickly carpeted room, she stepped up on to what appeared to be a dais, halting and showing the light for a moment, that the man might not stumble.

Along a stone passage and up a flight of stairs she crept, lighting the way before her as she went.

Through a half-open door she passed into a lofty room, the windows of which, placed high up in the wall, admitted the moonlight.

Across this room she tip-toed, switched off her torch and led on through a doorway, to where another door stood half-open.

"*Through* this room," she whispered, took a few steps into the darkness of the Priest's Hole, dropped the torch on the stone floor, shrieked—in a whisper,

"*Oh, God! . . . What's that! . . .*" sprang aside in the inky blackness, and dashed from the Hole—shutting the self-locking door behind her as she did so.

The Rat was trapped.

XXII

Consuela staggered against the wall of the entry leading to the door of the Priests' Hole and leant against it, panting as though she had run a race; shaking as though with an ague; almost in a state of collapse; so great had been the strain of the interview, the mental conflict, the accomplishment of her purpose.

Summoning her strength and courage, she threw off the weakness that assailed her, the faintness that threatened to overwhelm her, and, for a minute, stood facing the closed door, the door whose ancient oak and iron were so heavy, so thick and close-fitting, that no sound could be heard from within.

"Well, Rat," she whispered, "who wins? . . . You'd kiss me, would you? . . . Me, whom Harry Vane has kissed. . . . You'd come to my bedroom, would you—for the payment of a debt? . . . A debt . . . *you!*

"Now lie there, you dog. Lie there in the dark . . . until I choose to let you out again! . . . And that won't be till I've had his answer. . . . And when I let you out, it will be on terms; unless I make you step out of there into the arms of the English Police.

"I have told him! . . . I have told him! . . . Thank God, I have told him the truth before you could tell him your lies. And if I have lost him and he is free—it is I who have set him free . . . You'd hurt my lover, would you; you'd blackmail him for the rest of his life, would you? First me, and then my brother, the best of men—and then Harry.

"*Oh, Harry! Harry!*" and she burst into tears.

Ere stepping forth into the outer room, Consuela pulled down the heavy panelled door from where it hung raised above her head on its horizontal hinges.

"Nothing frightens you, eh? Then lie there in that stifling darkness and think you are there for ever and for ever. See if that'll frighten you. Perhaps it will teach you a lesson. I'd keep you there a week if I thought you'd be alive at the end of it—alive to go to prison for the rest of your foul life, you drug-seller, you blackmailer, you murderer. Three days and nights you shall he there, though you won't know night from day. Three days and nights—at least.

"I'll tell Otis to-morrow and he shall decide."

535

Creeping from the high panelled room, after replacing the wall-panel, she closed the heavy door behind her, locked it, took the key, and descended the stairs to the room known as John Geste's den.

Raising the weight-balanced cupboard from the floor, she let it swing gently up into its place and then, replacing both keys in the receptacle below the right-hand figure of the old carved oak mantelpiece, she screwed it back into place.

Softly closing the door of the room behind her, she descended the stairs and re-entered the drawing-room.

That was done. Neatly done.

And now to remove all traces of the man.

The Gestes must not know, until Harry had answered, and Otis had decided what should be done with the Rat.

Decided whether he should be released from the trap and allowed to slink away, harmless, his poisonous teeth drawn; or whether he should be handed over to the Police on charges of blackmail, menace and assault, drug-smuggling, and being an escaped convict.

On the blackmail and drug-smuggling alone, he'd get best part of a life-sentence, and for long years the world would be rid of a danger and a pest.

And to-morrow she'd hear from Harry.

He would not write.

He'd telegraph; he'd telephone; or he'd come himself—early.

He'd ride over; he'd get on to that beautiful big hunter, the best horse in his stables, and gallop like a Spahi.

No, he wouldn't; he'd get into the fastest car in the Vane Court garages and burn the road, to come and comfort her; to tell her that nothing mattered—but love; to tell her that he loved her; that love was the very greatest thing of all; that it was life, joy, salvation, Heaven on earth—and to ask her what, in comparison with Love, were the wretched trifles of malicious gossip, scandal, the opinion of "Society."

Bon Dieu! What *was* this so wonderful County Society of England?

And why stay in England?

There were a hundred and twenty million people in the United States. What would any of them know of the scandal—or care—if she and Harry went and lived on a glorious great ranch in the West?

Who'd know or care about the scandal, supposing he preferred to stay under the British flag, and they ranched in Canada?

They could live in lovely places there, where they'd never see another white person from month's end to month's end—and those they did see, wouldn't know; and those who did know, wouldn't care.

This wretched little "County" stuff!

The place was an old woman's whispering gallery. Surely they needn't live in it?

Look how vast a country Australia is. A continent in itself. She had been there with Otis on her travels. Who'd know or care anything about what had happened to her before ever she met Harry? There too, they could live right away from towns and gossip and scandal and all human filth and foulness.

Or the desert, the glorious clean sun-drenched illimitable desert.

They could have their own oasis with a beautiful Moorish house beneath the trees. Make the place one vast garden. They could have their flocks and herds and breed horses and camels.

They could go about with their own caravan; travel from end to end of Morocco and Algeria; stay in lovely places.

As Harry was so fond of sport, they could go big-game shooting in East Africa, and instead of a caravan have a *safari* and live a glorious open-air life of freedom.

And all the time they would have—love and each other. Of course Harry would come in the morning. . . .

And when he came—and told her that she was a little fool, and that he had nothing but pity for her girlhood and love for her womanhood—she would let that Rat go free.

In the joy of her heart, she would say to him,

"Get out, poor Rat. I've told my husband everything. Go, before he and my brother and John Geste horse-whip you, break every bone in your body, lash the soul out of you . . . Go, Sewer-Rat. I forgive you."

Wasn't she a Christian now, and wasn't the very first principle of that religion, love, forgiveness?

Had she not read a hundred times, a thousand times, in that Book that Otis had given her, words such as,

"Let him who is without sin among you cast the first stone?"

And had not Harry himself told her that he was not without "sin?" And thank God for that.

And was not the whole teaching (the whole religion itself) Mercy and Forgiveness and Understanding—the refusal to sit in judgment?

"*Go, sin no more . . . Thy sins are forgiven thee . . .*"

God knew that she would sin no more.

And surely Harry would forgive her.

Otis loved her—knowing what she had been.

If brother-love could be so great and kind and understanding and forgiving, surely lover-love could be greater still?

If Otis could be so kind and generous, so noble and loving and forgiving, surely Harry could—and would—do all that Otis had done, and far more?

Of course he'd forgive her.

Why, if he'd lived the life of a—*the life of a Spanish Maine*—up to the day that they had met, wouldn't she have forgiven him for everything he had done, when he'd told her all about it, after they'd fallen in love?

It would be nothing. She wouldn't forgive him really, though, because she'd have nothing to forgive.

What does a woman care about the faults, the sins, the crimes, of her man, provided they are not faults and sins and crimes against love, against her?

And Harry knew that if he'd been kidnapped when he was a baby and brought up as a small boy in a den of robbers, a thieves' kitchen, and taught and trained and made to steal, he'd be a criminal. . . . And if he had escaped from that slum, that criminal environment—some place like the *Vieux Port* at that awful Marseilles—escaped from it, been saved from it, had thrown it off, and now hated it, and then had met her, fallen in love with her, and told her all about it, wouldn't she have loved him the more because she pitied him as well?

Wouldn't she have taken him in her arms, taken his poor head to her breast, and mothered him and loved him, and loved him, more and more, and evermore?

Of course she would.

And so would he love her even more, when he knew that she had been born into such surroundings, bred in them, brought up in them, been taught and trained and *made* to be what she had been—and had escaped, been saved, before ever he met her?

He would feel to her exactly as she would have felt toward him, in similar circumstances.

He would.

Would he?

Men are different from women. They have not the same power of forgiveness.

But Harry was different. Harry wasn't an ordinary heartless kind of man; and theirs was no arranged *mariage de convenance*. It was *love*. They had chosen each other from the whole wide world.

Of course Harry would come and take her in his arms; would put her before his mother, his family, his position, his friends, his circle.

But would he?

Could he?

Could a man love like that? A cold man of the North—an Englishman?

But Harry wasn't cold. Of course he wasn't. His love was a burning fire. Not like hers, naturally, but he was on fire with love for her.

Of course it would make no difference. Had not he himself had —experiences?

But men looked at those things so differently where women— their own women, *c'est à dire*—were concerned. With a man it was a peccadillo. With a woman it was mortal sin, defilement, the ultimate horror.

So it would be if, loving Harry; if, having married Harry; she did such a thing.

She'd deserve to be tortured by Arabs. By Arab women.

Worse still, she'd deserve to lose his love, if ever she committed such a sin as that. That would be the sin against the Holy Ghost that the Bible spoke of. The sin, the unforgivable sin against the Holy Spirit, the spirit of Love, the Holiest Spirit of all.

But as to what had happened before she was saved from Africa, from Bouzen, from that life, from that terrible Street—that was different. It was those who had put her there who had sinned. She had been more sinned against than sinning. Surely?

But this wouldn't do. She must get to bed—to look her best for when Harry came to-morrow . . . if he came.

If only he would.

If only he'd come and—save her.

What had she come down here for?

To shut and lock the door leading on to the terrace.

Oh, and of course, to get the Rat's hat and cloak. She had seen him throw them on to the long white settee, outside the french-window.

What could she do with them?

Well—take them upstairs and hide them in her room until she

let the Rat out. Or better still, give them to Otis, to-morrow.

He'd know what to do with them. He'd lock them in a wardrobe in his room, no doubt, until the creature was either kicked out into the road or handed over to the police.

How dark it was, now that the moon had gone down behind the trees. . . . She'd be able to put her hand on the hat and cloak quite easily though.

Opening the french-window, Consuela stepped out on to the terrace and, bending toward the seat, groped with outstretched hands, for the clothing. . . .

And Miguel Braganza struck.

Had he not stood so long in the darkness against the wall . . . waiting . . . waiting . . . waiting . . . while his blood boiled as he remembered his wrongs and the foul treachery of the man who had been his friend; and had there been more light; he would have spoken first.

And, as a craftsman, he would have done himself more justice. A neat sufficient puncture at the base of the skull.

But he was too insane with anger, for coolness and finesse; and the light was not good enough for choice and artistry.

In fact, there was almost no light at all.

In the darkness, he saw the darker blur of a figure come between him and the white seat whereon lay the garments—the bait as it were, the bait for that foul rat.

The bait—and he himself, Miguel Braganza, the human trap to slay that rat.

And so, in the darkness, he *struck*, with all his strength, at the shapeless form—and felt the stiletto sink to the hilt in its back.

"*Ugh!*" he grunted as he stabbed, and

"Take that—from Miguel Braganza," he growled in Spanish, and turned and fled, literally for his life.

XXIII

It was Harry Vane who found her when he arrived at dawn.

EPILOGUE

Miguel Braganza sits and laughs to himself, outside his favourite *posada* in sunny Spain.

He smiles grimly whenever he thinks of how he closed the account between himself and El Señor Manöel Maine.

The Police of four countries and two continents still seek for Spanish Maine, the murderer. . . . Was not his cloak found in the dead hands of his victim, Consuela Vanbrugh?

The Priests' Hole of Brandon Abbas maintains its long silence.

Available P. C. Wren Titles
from
Riner Publishing Company

The Collected Short Stories

Volume One: ISBN 9780985032609
Volume Two: ISBN 9780985032616
Volume Three: ISBN 9780985032623
Volume Four: ISBN 9780985032630
Volume Five: ISBN 9780985032647

The Collected Novels

Volume One: *The Geste Novels*
   Part A: ISBN 9780985032678
   Part B: ISBN 9780985032685
Volume Two: *The Sinbad Novels*
   Part A: ISBN 9780692639382
   Part B: ISBN 9780692639429
Volume Three: *The Foreign Legion Novels*
   Part A: ISBN 9780999074909
   Part B: ISBN 9780999074916
Volume Four: *The Earlier India Novels*
   Part A: ISBN 9780999074923
   Part B: ISBN 9780999074930
Volume Five: *The Later India Novels*
   Part A: ISBN 9780999074947
   Part B: ISBN 9780999074954

Further information can be found at
rinerpublishing.wordpress.com

14 June 2019

CPSIA information can be obtained
at www.ICGtesting.com
Printed in the USA
BVHW080716290919
559704BV00001B/8/P